ARSÈNE LU
COLLECTION
VOL 1:

ARSÈNE LUPIN, GENTLEMAN BURGLAR,
ARSÈNE LUPIN VS. HERLOCK SHOLMES,
ARSÈNE LUPIN.
(3x1)

MAURICE LEBLANC

TRANSLATED BY ALEXANDER TEXEIRA DA MATOS

CONTENTS

CONTENTS 3

BOOK ONE.   THE EXTRAORDINARY ADVENTURES OF ARSÈNE LUPIN, GENTLEMAN-BURGLAR 1

   I. THE ARREST OF ARSÈNE LUPIN 3

   II. ARSÈNE LUPIN IN PRISON 13

   III. THE ESCAPE OF ARSÈNE LUPIN 30

   IV. THE MYSTERIOUS TRAVELLER 47

   V. THE QUEEN'S NECKLACE 59

   VI. THE SEVEN OF HEARTS 73

   VII. MADAME IMBERT'S SAFE 101

   VIII. THE BLACK PEARL 110

   IX. HERLOCK SHOLMES ARRIVES TOO LATE 121

BOOK TWO. ARSÈNE LUPIN   VERSUS HERLOCK SHOLMES 142

   I. LOTTERY TICKET NO. 514. 144

   II. THE BLUE DIAMOND. 165

   III. HERLOCK SHOLMES OPENS HOSTILITIES. 185

   IV. LIGHT IN THE DARKNESS. 204

   V. AN ABDUCTION. 222

   VI. SECOND ARREST OF ARSÈNE LUPIN. 242

   VII. THE SHIPWRECK. 285

BOOK THREE. ARSENE LUPIN 309

   I. THE MILLIONAIRE'S DAUGHTER 311

   II. THE COMING OF THE CHAROLAIS 319

   III. LUPIN'S WAY 325

   IV. THE DUKE INTERVENES 334

   V. A LETTER FROM LUPIN 340

VI. AGAIN THE CHAROLAIS.. 348

VII. THE THEFT OF THE MOTOR-CARS................................. 353

VIII. THE DUKE ARRIVES.. 361

IX. M. FORMERY OPENS THE INQUIRY................................. 368

X. GUERCHARD ASSISTS... 377

XI. THE FAMILY ARRIVES 386

XII. THE THEFT OF THE PENDANT... 392

XIII. LUPIN WIRES 401

XIV. GUERCHARD PICKS UP THE TRUE SCENT 406

XV. THE EXAMINATION OF SONIA 413

XVI. VICTOIRE'S SLIP 418

XVII. SONIA'S ESCAPE.. 425

XVIII. THE DUKE STAYS... 434

XIX. THE DUKE GOES.. 444

XX. LUPIN COMES HOME 454

XXI. THE CUTTING OF THE TELEPHONE WIRES 461

XXII. THE BARGAIN 470

XXIII. THE END OF THE DUEL.. 480

BOOK ONE.
THE EXTRAORDINARY
ADVENTURES OF ARSÈNE LUPIN,
GENTLEMAN-BURGLAR

I. THE ARREST OF ARSÈNE LUPIN

It was a strange ending to a voyage that had commenced in a most auspicious manner. The transatlantic steamship 'La Provence' was a swift and comfortable vessel, under the command of a most affable man. The passengers constituted a select and delightful society. The charm of new acquaintances and improvised amusements served to make the time pass agreeably. We enjoyed the pleasant sensation of being separated from the world, living, as it were, upon an unknown island, and consequently obliged to be sociable with each other.

Have you ever stopped to consider how much originality and spontaneity emanate from these various individuals who, on the preceding evening, did not even know each other, and who are now, for several days, condemned to lead a life of extreme intimacy, jointly defying the anger of the ocean, the terrible onslaught of the waves, the violence of the tempest and the agonizing monotony of the calm and sleepy water? Such a life becomes a sort of tragic existence, with its storms and its grandeurs, its monotony and its diversity; and that is why, perhaps, we embark upon that short voyage with mingled feelings of pleasure and fear.

But, during the past few years, a new sensation had been added to the life of the transatlantic traveler. The little floating island is now attached to the world from which it was once quite free. A bond united them, even in the very heart of the watery wastes of the Atlantic. That bond is the wireless telegraph, by means of which we receive news in the most mysterious manner. We know full well that the message is not transported by the medium of a hollow wire. No, the mystery is even more inexplicable, more romantic, and we must have recourse to the wings of the air in order to explain this new miracle. During the first day of the voyage, we felt that we were being followed, escorted, preceded even, by that distant voice, which, from time to time, whispered to one of us a few words from the receding world. Two friends spoke to me. Ten, twenty others sent gay or somber words of parting to other passengers.

On the second day, at a distance of five hundred miles from the French coast, in the midst of a violent storm, we received the following message by means of the wireless telegraph:

"Arsène Lupin is on your vessel, first cabin, blonde hair, wound right forearm, traveling alone under name of R........"

At that moment, a terrible flash of lightning rent the stormy skies. The electric waves were interrupted. The remainder of the dispatch never reached us. Of the name under which Arsène Lupin was concealing himself, we knew only the initial.

If the news had been of some other character, I have no doubt that the secret would have been carefully guarded by the telegraphic operator as well as by the officers of the vessel. But it was one of those events calculated to escape from the most rigorous discretion. The same day, no one knew how, the incident became a matter of current gossip and every passenger was aware that the famous Arsène Lupin was hiding in our midst.

Arsène Lupin in our midst! the irresponsible burglar whose exploits had been narrated in all the newspapers during the past few months! the mysterious individual with whom Ganimard, our shrewdest detective, had been engaged in an implacable conflict amidst interesting and picturesque surroundings. Arsène Lupin, the eccentric gentleman who operates only in the chateaux and salons, and who, one night, entered the residence of Baron Schormann, but emerged empty-handed, leaving, however, his card on which he had scribbled these words: "Arsène Lupin, gentleman-burglar, will return when the furniture is genuine." Arsène Lupin, the man of a thousand disguises: in turn a chauffer, detective, bookmaker, Russian physician, Spanish bull-fighter, commercial traveler, robust youth, or decrepit old man.

Then consider this startling situation: Arsène Lupin was wandering about within the limited bounds of a transatlantic steamer; in that very small corner of the world, in that dining saloon, in that smoking room, in that music room! Arsène Lupin was, perhaps, this gentleman.... or that one.... my neighbor at the table.... the sharer of my stateroom....

"And this condition of affairs will last for five days!" exclaimed Miss Nelly Underdown, next morning. "It is unbearable! I hope he will be arrested."

Then, addressing me, she added:

"And you, Monsieur d'Andrézy, you are on intimate terms with the captain; surely you know something?"

I should have been delighted had I possessed any information that would interest Miss Nelly. She was one of those magnificent creatures who inevitably attract attention in every assembly. Wealth and beauty form an irresistible combination, and Nelly possessed both.

Educated in Paris under the care of a French mother, she was now going to visit her father, the millionaire Underdown of Chicago. She was accompanied by one of her friends, Lady Jerland.

At first, I had decided to open a flirtation with her; but, in the rapidly growing intimacy of the voyage, I was soon impressed by her charming manner and my feelings became too deep and reverential for a mere flirtation. Moreover, she accepted my attentions with a certain degree of favor. She condescended to laugh at my witticisms and display an interest in my stories. Yet I felt that I had a rival in the person of a young man with quiet and refined tastes; and it struck me, at times, that she preferred his taciturn humor to my Parisian frivolity. He formed one in the circle of admirers that surrounded Miss Nelly at the time she addressed to me the foregoing question. We were all comfortably seated in our deck-chairs. The storm of the preceding evening had cleared the sky. The weather was now delightful.

"I have no definite knowledge, mademoiselle," I replied, "but can not we, ourselves, investigate the mystery quite as well as the detective Ganimard, the personal enemy of Arsène Lupin?"

"Oh! oh! you are progressing very fast, monsieur."

"Not at all, mademoiselle. In the first place, let me ask, do you find the problem a complicated one?"

"Very complicated."

"Have you forgotten the key we hold for the solution to the problem?"

"What key?"

"In the first place, Lupin calls himself Monsieur R————."

"Rather vague information," she replied.

"Secondly, he is traveling alone."

"Does that help you?" she asked.

"Thirdly, he is blonde."

"Well?"

"Then we have only to peruse the passenger-list, and proceed by process of elimination."

I had that list in my pocket. I took it out and glanced through it. Then I remarked:

"I find that there are only thirteen men on the passenger-list whose names begin with the letter R."

"Only thirteen?"

"Yes, in the first cabin. And of those thirteen, I find that nine of them are accompanied by women, children or servants. That leaves only four who are traveling alone. First, the Marquis de Raverdan————"

"Secretary to the American Ambassador," interrupted Miss Nelly. "I know him."

"Major Rawson," I continued.

"He is my uncle," some one said.

"Mon. Rivolta."

"Here!" exclaimed an Italian, whose face was concealed beneath a heavy black beard.

Miss Nelly burst into laughter, and exclaimed: "That gentleman can scarcely be called a blonde."

"Very well, then," I said, "we are forced to the conclusion that the guilty party is the last one on the list."

"What is his name?"

"Mon. Rozaine. Does anyone know him?"

No one answered. But Miss Nelly turned to the taciturn young man, whose attentions to her had annoyed me, and said:

"Well, Monsieur Rozaine, why do you not answer?"

All eyes were now turned upon him. He was a blonde. I must confess that I myself felt a shock of surprise, and the profound silence that followed her question indicated that the others present also viewed the situation with a feeling of sudden alarm. However, the idea was an absurd one, because the gentleman in question presented an air of the most perfect innocence.

"Why do I not answer?" he said. "Because, considering my name, my position as a solitary traveler and the color of my hair, I have already reached the same conclusion, and now think that I should be arrested."

He presented a strange appearance as he uttered these words. His thin lips were drawn closer than usual and his face was ghastly pale, whilst his eyes were streaked with blood. Of course, he was joking, yet his appearance and attitude impressed us strangely.

"But you have not the wound?" said Miss Nelly, naively.

"That is true," he replied, "I lack the wound."

Then he pulled up his sleeve, removing his cuff, and showed us his arm. But that action did not deceive me. He had shown us his left arm, and I was on the point of calling his attention to the fact, when another incident diverted our attention. Lady Jerland, Miss Nelly's friend, came running towards us in a state of great excitement, exclaiming:

"My jewels, my pearls! Some one has stolen them all!"

No, they were not all gone, as we soon found out. The thief had taken only part of them; a very curious thing. Of the diamond sunbursts, jeweled pendants, bracelets and necklaces, the thief had taken, not the largest but the finest and most valuable stones. The mountings were lying upon the table. I saw them there, despoiled of their jewels, like flowers from which the beautiful colored petals had been ruthlessly plucked. And this theft must have been committed at the time Lady Jerland was taking her tea; in broad daylight, in a stateroom opening on a much frequented corridor; moreover, the thief had been obliged to force open the door of the stateroom, search for the jewel-case, which was hidden at the bottom of a hat-box, open it, select his booty and remove it from the mountings.

Of course, all the passengers instantly reached the same conclusion; it was the work of Arsène Lupin.

That day, at the dinner table, the seats to the right and left of Rozaine remained vacant; and, during the evening, it was rumored that the captain had placed him under arrest, which information produced a feeling of safety and relief. We breathed once more. That evening, we resumed our games and dances. Miss Nelly, especially, displayed a spirit of thoughtless gayety which convinced me that if Rozaine's attentions had been agreeable to her in the beginning, she had already forgotten them. Her charm and good-humor completed my conquest. At midnight, under a bright moon, I declared my devotion with an ardor that did not seem to displease her.

But, next day, to our general amazement, Rozaine was at liberty. We learned that the evidence against him was not sufficient. He had produced documents that were perfectly regular, which showed that he was the son of a wealthy merchant of Bordeaux. Besides, his arms did not bear the slightest trace of a wound.

"Documents! Certificates of birth!" exclaimed the enemies of Rozaine, "of course, Arsène Lupin will furnish you as many as you desire. And as to the wound, he never had it, or he has removed it."

Then it was proven that, at the time of the theft, Rozaine was promenading on the deck. To which fact, his enemies replied that a man like Arsène Lupin could commit a crime without being actually present. And then, apart from all other circumstances, there remained one point which even the most skeptical could not answer: Who except Rozaine, was traveling alone, was a blonde, and bore a name beginning with R? To whom did the telegram point, if it were not Rozaine?

And when Rozaine, a few minutes before breakfast, came boldly toward our group, Miss Nelly and Lady Jerland arose and walked away.

An hour later, a manuscript circular was passed from hand to hand amongst the sailors, the stewards, and the passengers of all classes. It announced that Mon. Louis Rozaine offered a reward of ten thousand francs for the discovery of Arsène Lupin or other person in possession of the stolen jewels.

"And if no one assists me, I will unmask the scoundrel myself," declared Rozaine.

Rozaine against Arsène Lupin, or rather, according to current opinion, Arsène Lupin himself against Arsène Lupin; the contest promised to be interesting.

Nothing developed during the next two days. We saw Rozaine wandering about, day and night, searching, questioning, investigating. The captain, also, displayed commendable activity. He caused the vessel to be searched from stern to stern; ransacked every stateroom under the plausible theory that the jewels might be concealed anywhere, except in the thief's own room.

"I suppose they will find out something soon," remarked Miss Nelly to me. "He may be a wizard, but he cannot make diamonds and pearls become invisible."

"Certainly not," I replied, "but he should examine the lining of our hats and vests and everything we carry with us."

Then, exhibiting my Kodak, a 9x12 with which I had been photographing her in various poses, I added: "In an apparatus no larger than that, a person could hide all of Lady Jerland's jewels. He could pretend to take pictures and no one would suspect the game."

"But I have heard it said that every thief leaves some clue behind him."

"That may be generally true," I replied, "but there is one exception: Arsène Lupin."

"Why?"

"Because he concentrates his thoughts not only on the theft, but on all the circumstances connected with it that could serve as a clue to his identity."

"A few days ago, you were more confident."

"Yes, but since I have seen him at work."

"And what do you think about it now?" she asked.

"Well, in my opinion, we are wasting our time."

And, as a matter of fact, the investigation had produced no result. But, in the meantime, the captain's watch had been stolen. He was furious. He quickened his efforts and watched Rozaine more closely than before. But, on the following day, the watch was found in the second officer's collar box.

This incident caused considerable astonishment, and displayed the humorous side of Arsène Lupin, burglar though he was, but dilettante as well.

He combined business with pleasure. He reminded us of the author who almost died in a fit of laughter provoked by his own play. Certainly, he was an artist in his particular line of work, and whenever I saw Rozaine, gloomy and reserved, and thought of the double role that he was playing, I accorded him a certain measure of admiration.

On the following evening, the officer on deck duty heard groans emanating from the darkest corner of the ship. He approached and found a man lying there, his head enveloped in a thick gray scarf and his hands tied together with a heavy cord. It was Rozaine. He had been assaulted, thrown down and robbed. A card, pinned to his coat, bore these words: "Arsène Lupin accepts with pleasure the ten thousand francs offered by Mon. Rozaine." As a matter of fact, the stolen pocket-book contained twenty thousand francs.

Of course, some accused the unfortunate man of having simulated this attack on himself. But, apart from the fact that he could not have bound himself in that manner, it was established that the writing on the card was entirely different from that of Rozaine, but, on the contrary, resembled the handwriting of Arsène Lupin as it was reproduced in an old newspaper found on board.

Thus it appeared that Rozaine was not Arsène Lupin; but was Rozaine, the son of a Bordeaux merchant. And the presence of Arsène Lupin was once more affirmed, and that in a most alarming manner.

Such was the state of terror amongst the passengers that none would remain alone in a stateroom or wander singly in unfrequented parts of the vessel. We clung together as a matter of safety. And yet the most intimate acquaintances were estranged by a mutual feeling of distrust. Arsène Lupin was, now, anybody and everybody. Our excited imaginations attributed to him miraculous and unlimited power. We supposed him capable of assuming the most unexpected disguises; of being, by turns, the highly respectable Major Rawson or the noble Marquis de Raverdan, or even—for we no longer stopped with the accusing letter of R—or even such or such a person well known to all of us, and having wife, children and servants.

The first wireless dispatches from America brought no news; at least, the captain did not communicate any to us. The silence was not reassuring.

Our last day on the steamer seemed interminable. We lived in constant fear of some disaster. This time, it would not be a simple theft or a comparatively harmless assault; it would be a crime, a murder. No one imagined that Arsène Lupin would confine himself to those two trifling offenses. Absolute master of the ship, the authorities powerless, he could do whatever he pleased; our property and lives were at his mercy.

Yet those were delightful hours for me, since they secured to me the confidence of Miss Nelly. Deeply moved by those startling events and being of a highly nervous nature, she spontaneously sought at my side a protection and security that I was pleased to give her. Inwardly, I blessed Arsène Lupin. Had he not been the means of bringing me and Miss Nelly closer to each other? Thanks to him, I could now indulge in delicious dreams of love and happiness—dreams that, I felt, were not unwelcome to Miss Nelly. Her smiling eyes authorized me to make them; the softness of her voice bade me hope.

As we approached the American shore, the active search for the thief was apparently abandoned, and we were anxiously awaiting the supreme moment in which the mysterious enigma would be explained. Who was Arsène Lupin? Under what name, under what disguise was the famous Arsène Lupin concealing himself? And, at last, that supreme moment arrived. If I live one hundred years, I shall not forget the slightest details of it.

"How pale you are, Miss Nelly," I said to my companion, as she leaned upon my arm, almost fainting.

"And you!" she replied, "ah! you are so changed."

"Just think! this is a most exciting moment, and I am delighted to spend it with you, Miss Nelly. I hope that your memory will sometimes revert——"

But she was not listening. She was nervous and excited. The gangway was placed in position, but, before we could use it, the uniformed customs officers came on board. Miss Nelly murmured:

"I shouldn't be surprised to hear that Arsène Lupin escaped from the vessel during the voyage."

"Perhaps he preferred death to dishonor, and plunged into the Atlantic rather than be arrested."

"Oh, do not laugh," she said.

Suddenly I started, and, in answer to her question, I said:

"Do you see that little old man standing at the bottom of the gangway?"

"With an umbrella and an olive-green coat?"

"It is Ganimard."

"Ganimard?"

"Yes, the celebrated detective who has sworn to capture Arsène Lupin. Ah! I can understand now why we did not receive any news from this side of the Atlantic. Ganimard was here! and he always keeps his business secret."

"Then you think he will arrest Arsène Lupin?"

"Who can tell? The unexpected always happens when Arsène Lupin is concerned in the affair."

"Oh!" she exclaimed, with that morbid curiosity peculiar to women, "I should like to see him arrested."

"You will have to be patient. No doubt, Arsène Lupin has already seen his enemy and will not be in a hurry to leave the steamer."

The passengers were now leaving the steamer. Leaning on his umbrella, with an air of careless indifference, Ganimard appeared to be paying no attention to the crowd that was hurrying down the gangway. The Marquis de Raverdan, Major Rawson, the Italian Rivolta, and many others had already left the vessel before Rozaine appeared. Poor Rozaine!

"Perhaps it is he, after all," said Miss Nelly to me. "What do you think?"

"I think it would be very interesting to have Ganimard and Rozaine in the same picture. You take the camera. I am loaded down."

I gave her the camera, but too late for her to use it. Rozaine was already passing the detective. An American officer, standing behind Ganimard, leaned forward and whispered in his ear. The French detective shrugged his shoulders and Rozaine passed on. Then, my God, who was Arsène Lupin?

"Yes," said Miss Nelly, aloud, "who can it be?"

Not more than twenty people now remained on board. She scrutinized them one by one, fearful that Arsène Lupin was not amongst them.

"We cannot wait much longer," I said to her.

She started toward the gangway. I followed. But we had not taken ten steps when Ganimard barred our passage.

"Well, what is it?" I exclaimed.

"One moment, monsieur. What's your hurry?"

"I am escorting mademoiselle."

"One moment," he repeated, in a tone of authority. Then, gazing into my eyes, he said:

"Arsène Lupin, is it not?"

I laughed, and replied: "No, simply Bernard d'Andrézy."

"Bernard d'Andrézy died in Macedonia three years ago."

"If Bernard d'Andrézy were dead, I should not be here. But you are mistaken. Here are my papers."

"They are his; and I can tell you exactly how they came into your possession."

"You are a fool!" I exclaimed. "Arsène Lupin sailed under the name of R——"

"Yes, another of your tricks; a false scent that deceived them at Havre. You play a good game, my boy, but this time luck is against you."

I hesitated a moment. Then he hit me a sharp blow on the right arm, which caused me to utter a cry of pain. He had struck the wound, yet unhealed, referred to in the telegram.

I was obliged to surrender. There was no alternative. I turned to Miss Nelly, who had heard everything. Our eyes met; then she glanced at the Kodak I had placed in her hands, and made a gesture that conveyed to me the impression that she understood everything. Yes, there, between the narrow folds of black leather, in the hollow centre of the small object that I had taken the precaution to place in her hands before Ganimard arrested me, it was there I had deposited Rozaine's twenty thousand francs and Lady Jerland's pearls and diamonds.

Oh! I pledge my oath that, at that solemn moment, when I was in the grasp of Ganimard and his two assistants, I was perfectly indifferent to everything, to my arrest, the hostility of the people, everything except this one question: what will Miss Nelly do with the things I had confided to her?

In the absence of that material and conclusive proof, I had nothing to fear; but would Miss Nelly decide to furnish that proof? Would she betray me? Would she act the part of an enemy who cannot forgive, or that of a woman whose scorn is softened by feelings of indulgence and involuntary sympathy?

She passed in front of me. I said nothing, but bowed very low. Mingled with the other passengers, she advanced to the gangway with my Kodak in her hand. It occurred to me that she would not dare to expose me publicly, but she might do so when she reached a more private place. However, when she had passed only a few feet down the gangway, with a movement of simulated awkwardness, she let the camera fall into the water between the vessel and the pier. Then she walked down the gangway, and was quickly lost to sight in the crowd. She had passed out of my life forever.

For a moment, I stood motionless. Then, to Ganimard's great astonishment, I muttered:

"What a pity that I am not an honest man!"

Such was the story of his arrest as narrated to me by Arsène Lupin himself. The various incidents, which I shall record in writing at a later day, have established between us certain ties.... shall I say of friendship? Yes, I venture to believe that Arsène Lupin honors me with his friendship, and that it is through friendship that he occasionally calls on me, and brings, into the silence of my library, his youthful exuberance of spirits, the contagion of his enthusiasm, and the mirth of a man for whom destiny has naught but favors and smiles.

His portrait? How can I describe him? I have seen him twenty times and each time he was a different person; even he himself said to me on one occasion: "I no longer know who I am. I cannot recognize myself in the mirror." Certainly, he was a great actor, and possessed a marvelous faculty for disguising himself. Without the slightest effort, he could adopt the voice, gestures and mannerisms of another person.

"Why," said he, "why should I retain a definite form and feature? Why not avoid the danger of a personality that is ever the same? My actions will serve to identify me."

Then he added, with a touch of pride:

"So much the better if no one can ever say with absolute certainty: There is Arsène Lupin! The essential point is that the public may be able to refer to my work and say, without fear of mistake: Arsène Lupin did that!"

II. ARSÈNE LUPIN IN PRISON

There is no tourist worthy of the name who does not know the banks of the Seine, and has not noticed, in passing, the little feudal castle of the Malaquis, built upon a rock in the centre of the river. An arched bridge connects it with the shore. All around it, the calm waters of the great river play peacefully amongst the reeds, and the wagtails flutter over the moist crests of the stones.

The history of the Malaquis castle is stormy like its name, harsh like its outlines. It has passed through a long series of combats, sieges, assaults, rapines and massacres. A recital of the crimes that have been committed there would cause the stoutest heart to tremble. There are many mysterious legends connected with the castle, and they tell us of a famous subterranean tunnel that formerly led to the abbey of Jumieges and to the manor of Agnes Sorel, mistress of Charles VII.

In that ancient habitation of heroes and brigands, the Baron Nathan Cahorn now lived; or Baron Satan as he was formerly called on the Bourse, where he had acquired a fortune with incredible rapidity. The lords of Malaquis, absolutely ruined, had been obliged to sell the ancient castle at a great sacrifice. It contained an admirable collection of furniture, pictures, wood carvings, and faience. The Baron lived there alone, attended by three old servants. No one ever enters the place. No one had ever beheld the three Rubens that he possessed, his two Watteau, his Jean Goujon pulpit, and the many other treasures that he had acquired by a vast expenditure of money at public sales.

Baron Satan lived in constant fear, not for himself, but for the treasures that he had accumulated with such an earnest devotion and with so much perspicacity that the shrewdest merchant could not say that the Baron had ever erred in his taste or judgment. He loved them—his bibelots. He loved them intensely, like a miser; jealously, like a lover. Every day, at sunset, the iron gates at either end of the bridge and at the entrance to the court of honor are closed and barred. At the least touch on these gates, electric bells will ring throughout the castle.

One Thursday in September, a letter-carrier presented himself at the gate at the head of the bridge, and, as usual, it was the Baron himself who partially opened the heavy portal. He scrutinized the man as minutely as if he were a stranger, although the honest face and twinkling eyes of the postman had been familiar to the Baron for many years. The man laughed, as he said:

"It is only I, Monsieur le Baron. It is not another man wearing my cap and blouse."

"One can never tell," muttered the Baron.

The man handed him a number of newspapers, and then said:

"And now, Monsieur le Baron, here is something new."

"Something new?"

"Yes, a letter. A registered letter."

Living as a recluse, without friends or business relations, the baron never received any letters, and the one now presented to him immediately aroused within him a feeling of suspicion and distrust. It was like an evil omen. Who was this mysterious correspondent that dared to disturb the tranquility of his retreat?

"You must sign for it, Monsieur le Baron."

He signed; then took the letter, waited until the postman had disappeared beyond the bend in the road, and, after walking nervously to and fro for a few minutes, he leaned against the parapet of the bridge and opened the envelope. It contained a sheet of paper, bearing this heading: Prison de la Santé, Paris. He looked at the signature: Arsène Lupin. Then he read:

"Monsieur le Baron: "There is, in the gallery in your castle, a picture of Philippe de Champaigne, of exquisite finish, which pleases me beyond measure.

Your Rubens are also to my taste, as well as your smallest Watteau.

In the salon to the right, I have noticed the Louis XIII cadence-table, the tapestries of Beauvais, the Empire gueridon signed 'Jacob,' and the Renaissance chest. In the salon to the left, all the cabinet full of jewels and miniatures.

"For the present, I will content myself with those articles that can be conveniently removed. I will therefore ask you to pack them carefully and ship them to me, charges prepaid, to the station at Batignolles, within eight days, otherwise I shall be obliged to remove them myself during the night of 27 September; but, under those circumstances, I shall not content myself with the articles above mentioned. "Accept my apologies for any inconvenience I may cause you, and believe me to be your humble servant, "Arsène Lupin." "

P. S.—Please do not send the largest Watteau. Although you paid thirty thousand francs for it, it is only a copy, the original having been burned, under the Directoire by Barras, during a night of debauchery. Consult the memoirs of Garat. "I do not care for the Louis XV chatelaine, as I doubt its authenticity."

That letter completely upset the baron. Had it borne any other signature, he would have been greatly alarmed—but signed by Arsène Lupin!

As an habitual reader of the newspapers, he was versed in the history of recent crimes, and was therefore well acquainted with the exploits of the mysterious burglar. Of course, he knew that Lupin had been arrested in America by his enemy Ganimard and was at present incarcerated in the Prison de la Santé. But he knew also that any miracle might be expected from Arsène Lupin. Moreover, that exact knowledge of the castle, the location of the pictures and furniture, gave the affair an alarming aspect. How could he have acquired that information concerning things that no one had ever seen?

The baron raised his eyes and contemplated the stern outlines of the castle, its steep rocky pedestal, the depth of the surrounding water, and shrugged his shoulders. Certainly, there was no danger. No one in the world could force an entrance to the sanctuary that contained his priceless treasures.

No one, perhaps, but Arsène Lupin! For him, gates, walls and drawbridges did not exist. What use were the most formidable obstacles or the most careful precautions, if Arsène Lupin had decided to effect an entrance?

That evening, he wrote to the Procurer of the Republique at Rouen. He enclosed the threatening letter and solicited aid and protection.

The reply came at once to the effect that Arsène Lupin was in custody in the Prison de la Santé, under close surveillance, with no opportunity to write such a letter, which was, no doubt, the work of some imposter. But, as an act of precaution, the Procurer had submitted the letter to an expert in handwriting, who declared that, in spite of certain resemblances, the writing was not that of the prisoner.

But the words "in spite of certain resemblances" caught the attention of the baron; in them, he read the possibility of a doubt which appeared to him quite sufficient to warrant the intervention of the law. His fears increased. He read Lupin's letter over and over again. "I shall be obliged to remove them myself." And then there was the fixed date: the night of 27 September.

To confide in his servants was a proceeding repugnant to his nature; but now, for the first time in many years, he experienced the necessity of seeking counsel with some one. Abandoned by the legal official of his own district, and feeling unable to defend himself with his own resources, he was on the point of going to Paris to engage the services of a detective.

Two days passed; on the third day, he was filled with hope and joy as he read the following item in the `Reveil de Caudebec', a newspaper published in a neighboring town:

"We have the pleasure of entertaining in our city, at the present time, the veteran detective Mon. Ganimard who acquired a world-wide reputation by his clever capture of Arsène Lupin. He has come here for rest and recreation, and, being an enthusiastic fisherman, he threatens to capture all the fish in our river."

Ganimard! Ah, here is the assistance desired by Baron Cahorn! Who could baffle the schemes of Arsène Lupin better than Ganimard, the patient and astute detective? He was the man for the place.

The baron did not hesitate. The town of Caudebec was only six kilometers from the castle, a short distance to a man whose step was accelerated by the hope of safety.

After several fruitless attempts to ascertain the detective's address, the baron visited the office of the `Reveil,' situated on the quai. There he found the writer of the article who, approaching the window, exclaimed:

"Ganimard? Why, you are sure to see him somewhere on the quai with his fishing-pole. I met him there and chanced to read his name engraved on his rod. Ah, there he is now, under the trees."

"That little man, wearing a straw hat?"

"Exactly. He is a gruff fellow, with little to say."

Five minutes later, the baron approached the celebrated Ganimard, introduced himself, and sought to commence a conversation, but that was a failure. Then he broached the real object of his interview, and briefly stated his case. The other listened, motionless, with his attention riveted on his fishing-rod. When the baron had finished his story, the fisherman turned, with an air of profound pity, and said:

"Monsieur, it is not customary for thieves to warn people they are about to rob. Arsène Lupin, especially, would not commit such a folly."

"But——"

"Monsieur, if I had the least doubt, believe me, the pleasure of again capturing Arsène Lupin would place me at your disposal. But, unfortunately, that young man is already under lock and key."

"He may have escaped."

"No one ever escaped from the Santé."

"But, he——"

"He, no more than any other."

"Yet——"

"Well, if he escapes, so much the better. I will catch him again. Meanwhile, you go home and sleep soundly. That will do for the present. You frighten the fish."

The conversation was ended. The baron returned to the castle, reassured to some extent by Ganimard's indifference. He examined the bolts, watched the servants, and, during the next forty-eight hours, he became almost persuaded that his fears were groundless. Certainly, as Ganimard had said, thieves do not warn people they are about to rob.

The fateful day was close at hand. It was now the twenty-sixth of September and nothing had happened. But at three o'clock the bell rang. A boy brought this telegram:

"No goods at Batignolles station. Prepare everything for tomorrow night. Arsène."

This telegram threw the baron into such a state of excitement that he even considered the advisability of yielding to Lupin's demands.

However, he hastened to Caudebec. Ganimard was fishing at the same place, seated on a campstool. Without a word, he handed him the telegram.

"Well, what of it?" said the detective.

"What of it? But it is tomorrow."

"What is tomorrow?"

"The robbery! The pillage of my collections!"

Ganimard laid down his fishing-rod, turned to the baron, and exclaimed, in a tone of impatience:

"Ah! Do you think I am going to bother myself about such a silly story as that!"

"How much do you ask to pass tomorrow night in the castle?"

"Not a sou. Now, leave me alone."

"Name your own price. I am rich and can pay it."

This offer disconcerted Ganimard, who replied, calmly:

"I am here on a vacation. I have no right to undertake such work."

"No one will know. I promise to keep it secret."

"Oh! nothing will happen."

"Come! three thousand francs. Will that be enough?"

The detective, after a moment's reflection, said:

"Very well. But I must warn you that you are throwing your money out of the window."

"I do not care."

"In that case... but, after all, what do we know about this devil Lupin! He may have quite a numerous band of robbers with him. Are you sure of your servants?"

"My faith——"

"Better not count on them. I will telegraph for two of my men to help me. And now, go! It is better for us not to be seen together. Tomorrow evening about nine o'clock."

The following day—the date fixed by Arsène Lupin—Baron Cahorn arranged all his panoply of war, furbished his weapons, and, like a sentinel, paced to and fro in front of the castle. He saw nothing, heard nothing. At half-past eight o'clock in the evening, he dismissed his servants. They occupied rooms in a wing of the building, in a retired spot, well removed from the main portion of the castle. Shortly thereafter, the baron heard the sound of approaching footsteps. It was Ganimard and his two assistants— great, powerful fellows with immense hands, and necks like bulls. After asking a few questions relating to the location of the various entrances and rooms, Ganimard carefully closed and barricaded all the doors and windows through which one could gain access to the threatened rooms. He inspected the walls, raised the tapestries, and finally installed his assistants in the central gallery which was located between the two salons.

"No nonsense! We are not here to sleep. At the slightest sound, open the windows of the court and call me. Pay attention also to the water-side. Ten metres of perpendicular rock is no obstacle to those devils."

Ganimard locked his assistants in the gallery, carried away the keys, and said to the baron:

"And now, to our post."

He had chosen for himself a small room located in the thick outer wall, between the two principal doors, and which, in former years, had been the watchman's quarters. A peep-hole opened upon the bridge; another on the court. In one corner, there was an opening to a tunnel.

"I believe you told me, Monsieur le Baron, that this tunnel is the only subterranean entrance to the castle and that it has been closed up for time immemorial?"

"Yes."

"Then, unless there is some other entrance, known only to Arsène Lupin, we are quite safe."

He placed three chairs together, stretched himself upon them, lighted his pipe and sighed:

"Really, Monsieur le Baron, I feel ashamed to accept your money for such a sinecure as this. I will tell the story to my friend Lupin. He will enjoy it immensely."

The baron did not laugh. He was anxiously listening, but heard nothing save the beating of his own heart. From time to time, he leaned over the tunnel and cast a fearful eye into its depths. He heard the clock strike eleven, twelve, one.

Suddenly, he seized Ganimard's arm. The latter leaped up, awakened from his sleep.

"Do you hear?" asked the baron, in a whisper.

"Yes."

"What is it?"

"I was snoring, I suppose."

"No, no, listen."

"Ah! yes, it is the horn of an automobile."

"Well?"

"Well! it is very improbable that Lupin would use an automobile like a battering-ram to demolish your castle. Come, Monsieur le Baron, return to your post. I am going to sleep. Good-night."

That was the only alarm. Ganimard resumed his interrupted slumbers, and the baron heard nothing except the regular snoring of his companion. At break of day, they left the room. The castle was enveloped in a profound calm; it was a peaceful dawn on the bosom of a tranquil river. They mounted the stairs, Cahorn radiant with joy, Ganimard calm as usual. They heard no sound; they saw nothing to arouse suspicion.

"What did I tell you, Monsieur le Baron? Really, I should not have accepted your offer. I am ashamed."

He unlocked the door and entered the gallery. Upon two chairs, with drooping heads and pendent arms, the detective's two assistants were asleep.

"Tonnerre de nom d'un chien!" exclaimed Ganimard. At the same moment, the baron cried out:

"The pictures! The credence!"

He stammered, choked, with arms outstretched toward the empty places, toward the denuded walls where naught remained but the useless nails and cords. The Watteau, disappeared! The Rubens, carried away! The tapestries taken down! The cabinets, despoiled of their jewels!

"And my Louis XVI candelabra! And the Regent chandelier!...And my twelfth-century Virgin!"

He ran from one spot to another in wildest despair. He recalled the purchase price of each article, added up the figures, counted his losses, pell-mell, in confused words and unfinished phrases. He stamped with rage; he groaned with grief. He acted like a ruined man whose only hope is suicide.

If anything could have consoled him, it would have been the stupefaction displayed by Ganimard. The famous detective did not move. He appeared to be petrified; he examined the room in a listless manner. The windows?.... closed. The locks on the doors?.... intact. Not a break in the ceiling; not a hole in the floor. Everything was in perfect order. The theft had been carried out methodically, according to a logical and inexorable plan.

"Arsène Lupin....Arsène Lupin," he muttered.

Suddenly, as if moved by anger, he rushed upon his two assistants and shook them violently. They did not awaken.

"The devil!" he cried. "Can it be possible?"

He leaned over them and, in turn, examined them closely. They were asleep; but their response was unnatural.

"They have been drugged," he said to the baron.

"By whom?"

"By him, of course, or his men under his discretion. That work bears his stamp."

"In that case, I am lost—nothing can be done."

"Nothing," assented Ganimard.

"It is dreadful; it is monstrous."

"Lodge a complaint."

"What good will that do?"

"Oh; it is well to try it. The law has some resources."

"The law! Bah! it is useless. You represent the law, and, at this moment, when you should be looking for a clue and trying to discover something, you do not even stir."

"Discover something with Arsène Lupin! Why, my dear monsieur, Arsène Lupin never leaves any clue behind him. He leaves nothing to chance. Sometimes I think he put himself in my way and simply allowed me to arrest him in America."

"Then, I must renounce my pictures! He has taken the gems of my collection. I would give a fortune to recover them. If there is no other way, let him name his own price."

Ganimard regarded the baron attentively, as he said:

"Now, that is sensible. Will you stick to it?"

"Yes, yes. But why?"

"An idea that I have."

"What is it?"

"We will discuss it later—if the official examination does not succeed. But, not one word about me, if you wish my assistance."

He added, between his teeth:

"It is true I have nothing to boast of in this affair."

The assistants were gradually regaining consciousness with the bewildered air of people who come out of an hypnotic sleep. They opened their eyes and looked about them in astonishment. Ganimard questioned them; they remembered nothing.

"But you must have seen some one?"

"No."

"Can't you remember?"

"No, no."

"Did you drink anything?"

They considered a moment, and then one of them replied:

"Yes, I drank a little water."

"Out of that carafe?"

"Yes."

"So did I," declared the other.

Ganimard smelled and tasted it. It had no particular taste and no odor.

"Come," he said, "we are wasting our time here. One can't decide an Arsène Lupin problem in five minutes. But, morbleau! I swear I will catch him again."

The same day, a charge of burglary was duly performed by Baron Cahorn against Arsène Lupin, a prisoner in the Prison de la Santé.

The baron afterwards regretted making the charge against Lupin when he saw his castle delivered over to the gendarmes, the procureur, the judge d'instruction, the newspaper reporters and photographers, and a throng of idle curiosity-seekers.

The affair soon became a topic of general discussion, and the name of Arsène Lupin excited the public imagination to such an extent that the newspapers filled their columns with the most fantastic stories of his exploits which found ready credence amongst their readers.

But the letter of Arsène Lupin that was published in the `Echo de France' (no one ever knew how the newspaper obtained it), that letter in which Baron Cahorn was impudently warned of the coming theft, caused considerable excitement. The most fabulous theories were advanced. Some recalled the existence of the famous subterranean tunnels, and that was the line of research pursued by the officers of the law, who searched the house from top to bottom, questioned every stone, studied the wainscoting and the chimneys, the window-frames and the girders in the ceilings. By the light of torches, they examined the immense cellars where the lords of Malaquis were wont to store their munitions and provisions. They sounded the rocky foundation to its very centre. But it was all in vain. They discovered no trace of a subterranean tunnel. No secret passage existed.

But the eager public declared that the pictures and furniture could not vanish like so many ghosts. They are substantial, material things and require doors and windows for their exits and their entrances, and so do the people that remove them. Who were those people? How did they gain access to the castle? And how did they leave it?

The police officers of Rouen, convinced of their own impotence, solicited the assistance of the Parisian detective force. Mon. Dudouis, chief of the Sûreté, sent the best sleuths of the iron brigade. He himself spent forty-eight hours at the castle, but met with no success. Then he sent for Ganimard, whose past services had proved so useful when all else failed.

Ganimard listened, in silence, to the instructions of his superior; then, shaking his head, he said:

"In my opinion, it is useless to ransack the castle. The solution of the problem lies elsewhere."

"Where, then?"

"With Arsène Lupin."

"With Arsène Lupin! To support that theory, we must admit his intervention."

"I do admit it. In fact, I consider it quite certain."

"Come, Ganimard, that is absurd. Arsène Lupin is in prison."

"I grant you that Arsène Lupin is in prison, closely guarded; but he must have fetters on his feet, manacles on his wrists, and gag in his mouth before I change my opinion."

"Why so obstinate, Ganimard?"

"Because Arsène Lupin is the only man in France of sufficient calibre to invent and carry out a scheme of that magnitude."

"Mere words, Ganimard."

"But true ones. Look! What are they doing? Searching for subterranean passages, stones swinging on pivots, and other nonsense of that kind. But Lupin doesn't employ such old-fashioned methods. He is a modern cracksman, right up to date."

"And how would you proceed?"

"I should ask your permission to spend an hour with him."

"In his cell?"

"Yes. During the return trip from America we became very friendly, and I venture to say that if he can give me any information without compromising himself he will not hesitate to save me from incurring useless trouble."

It was shortly after noon when Ganimard entered the cell of Arsène Lupin. The latter, who was lying on his bed, raised his head and uttered a cry of apparent joy.

"Ah! This is a real surprise. My dear Ganimard, here!"

"Ganimard himself."

"In my chosen retreat, I have felt a desire for many things, but my fondest wish was to receive you here."

"Very kind of you, I am sure."

"Not at all. You know I hold you in the highest regard."

"I am proud of it."

"I have always said: Ganimard is our best detective. He is almost,—you see how candid I am!—he is almost as clever as Herlock Sholmes. But I am sorry that I cannot offer you anything better than this hard stool. And no refreshments! Not even a glass of beer! Of course, you will excuse me, as I am here only temporarily."

Ganimard smiled, and accepted the proffered seat. Then the prisoner continued:

"Mon Dieu, how pleased I am to see the face of an honest man. I am so tired of those devils of spies who come here ten times a day to ransack my pockets and my cell to satisfy themselves that I am not preparing to escape. The government is very solicitous on my account."

"It is quite right."

"Why so? I should be quite contented if they would allow me to live in my own quiet way."

"On other people's money."

"Quite so. That would be so simple. But here, I am joking, and you are, no doubt, in a hurry. So let us come to business, Ganimard. To what do I owe the honor of this visit?

"The Cahorn affair," declared Ganimard, frankly.

"Ah! Wait, one moment. You see I have had so many affairs! First, let me fix in my mind the circumstances of this particular case....Ah! yes, now I have it. The Cahorn affair, Malaquis castle, Seine-Inférieure....Two Rubens, a Watteau, and a few trifling articles."

"Trifling!"

"Oh! ma foi, all that is of slight importance. But it suffices to know that the affair interests you. How can I serve you, Ganimard?"

"Must I explain to you what steps the authorities have taken in the matter?"

"Not at all. I have read the newspapers and I will frankly state that you have made very little progress."

"And that is the reason I have come to see you."

"I am entirely at your service."

"In the first place, the Cahorn affair was managed by you?"

"From A to Z."

"The letter of warning? the telegram?"

"All mine. I ought to have the receipts somewhere."

Arsène opened the drawer of a small table of plain white wood which, with the bed and stool, constituted all the furniture in his cell, and took therefrom two scraps of paper which he handed to Ganimard.

"Ah!" exclaimed the detective, in surprise, "I though you were closely guarded and searched, and I find that you read the newspapers and collect postal receipts."

"Bah! these people are so stupid! They open the lining of my vest, they examine the soles of my shoes, they sound the walls of my cell, but they never imagine that Arsène Lupin would be foolish enough to choose such a simple hiding place."

Ganimard laughed, as he said:

"What a droll fellow you are! Really, you bewilder me. But, come now, tell me about the Cahorn affair."

"Oh! oh! not quite so fast! You would rob me of all my secrets; expose all my little tricks. That is a very serious matter."

"Was I wrong to count on your complaisance?"

"No, Ganimard, and since you insist——-"

Arsène Lupin paced his cell two or three times, then, stopping before Ganimard, he asked:

"What do you think of my letter to the baron?"

"I think you were amusing yourself by playing to the gallery."

"Ah! playing to the gallery! Come, Ganimard, I thought you knew me better. Do I, Arsène Lupin, ever waste my time on such puerilities? Would I have written that letter if I could have robbed the baron without writing to him? I want you to understand that the letter was indispensable; it was the motor that set the whole machine in motion. Now, let us discuss together a scheme for the robbery of the Malaquis castle. Are you willing?"

"Yes, proceed."

"Well, let us suppose a castle carefully closed and barricaded like that of the Baron Cahorn. Am I to abandon my scheme and renounce the treasures that I covet, upon the pretext that the castle which holds them is inaccessible?"

"Evidently not."

"Should I make an assault upon the castle at the head of a band of adventurers as they did in ancient times?"

"That would be foolish."

"Can I gain admittance by stealth or cunning?"

"Impossible."

"Then there is only one way open to me. I must have the owner of the castle invite me to it."

"That is surely an original method."

"And how easy! Let us suppose that one day the owner receives a letter warning him that a notorious burglar known as Arsène Lupin is plotting to rob him. What will he do?"

"Send a letter to the Procureur."

"Who will laugh at him, *because the said Arsène Lupin is actually in prison.* Then, in his anxiety and fear, the simple man will ask the assistance of the first-comer, will he not?"

"Very likely."

"And if he happens to read in a country newspaper that a celebrated detective is spending his vacation in a neighboring town——"

"He will seek that detective."

"Of course. But, on the other hand, let us presume that, having foreseen that state of affairs, the said Arsène Lupin has requested one of his friends to visit Caudebec, make the acquaintance of the editor of the `Réveil,' a newspaper to which the baron is a subscriber, and let said editor understand that such person is the celebrated detective—then, what will happen?"

"The editor will announce in the `Réveil' the presence in Caudebec of said detective."

"Exactly; and one of two things will happen: either the fish—I mean Cahorn—will not bite, and nothing will happen; or, what is more likely, he will run and greedily swallow the bait. Thus, behold my Baron Cahorn imploring the assistance of one of my friends against me."

"Original, indeed!"

"Of course, the pseudo-detective at first refuses to give any assistance. On top of that comes the telegram from Arsène Lupin. The frightened baron rushes once more to my friend and offers him a definite sum of money for his services. My friend accepts and summons two members of our band, who, during the night, whilst Cahorn is under the watchful eye of his protector, removes certain articles by way of the window and lowers them with ropes into a nice little launch chartered for the occasion. Simple, isn't it?"

"Marvelous! Marvelous!" exclaimed Ganimard. "The boldness of the scheme and the ingenuity of all its details are beyond criticism. But who is the detective whose name and fame served as a magnet to attract the baron and draw him into your net?"

"There is only one name could do it—only one."

"And that is?"

"Arsène Lupin's personal enemy—the most illustrious Ganimard."

"I?"

"Yourself, Ganimard. And, really, it is very funny. If you go there, and the baron decides to talk, you will find that it will be your duty to arrest yourself, just as you arrested me in America. Hein! the revenge is really amusing: I cause Ganimard to arrest Ganimard."

Arsène Lupin laughed heartily. The detective, greatly vexed, bit his lips; to him the joke was quite devoid of humor. The arrival of a prison guard gave Ganimard an opportunity to recover himself. The man brought Arsène Lupin's luncheon, furnished by a neighboring restaurant. After depositing the tray upon the table, the guard retired. Lupin broke his bread, ate a few morsels, and continued:

"But, rest easy, my dear Ganimard, you will not go to Malaquis. I can tell you something that will astonish you: the Cahorn affair is on the point of being settled."

"Excuse me; I have just seen the Chief of the Sureté."

"What of that? Does Mon. Dudouis know my business better than I do myself? You will learn that Ganimard—excuse me—that the pseudo-Ganimard still remains on very good terms with the baron. The latter has authorized him to negotiate a very delicate transaction with me, and, at the present moment, in consideration of a certain sum, it is probable that the baron has recovered possession of his pictures and other treasures. And on their return, he will withdraw his complaint. Thus, there is no longer any theft, and the law must abandon the case."

Ganimard regarded the prisoner with a bewildered air.

"And how do you know all that?"

"I have just received the telegram I was expecting."

"You have just received a telegram?"

"This very moment, my dear friend. Out of politeness, I did not wish to read it in your presence. But if you will permit me——"

"You are joking, Lupin."

"My dear friend, if you will be so kind as to break that egg, you will learn for yourself that I am not joking."

Mechanically, Ganimard obeyed, and cracked the egg-shell with the blade of a knife. He uttered a cry of surprise. The shell contained nothing but a small piece of blue paper. At the request of Arsène he unfolded it. It was a telegram, or rather a portion of a telegram from which the post-marks had been removed. It read as follows:

"Contract closed. Hundred thousand balls delivered. All well."

"One hundred thousand balls?" said Ganimard.

"Yes, one hundred thousand francs. Very little, but then, you know, these are hard times....And I have some heavy bills to meet. If you only knew my budget.... living in the city comes very high."

Ganimard arose. His ill humor had disappeared. He reflected for a moment, glancing over the whole affair in an effort to discover a weak point; then, in a tone and manner that betrayed his admiration of the prisoner, he said:

"Fortunately, we do not have a dozen such as you to deal with; if we did, we would have to close up shop."

Arsène Lupin assumed a modest air, as he replied:

"Bah! a person must have some diversion to occupy his leisure hours, especially when he is in prison."

"What!" exclaimed Ganimard, "your trial, your defense, the examination—isn't that sufficient to occupy your mind?"

"No, because I have decided not to be present at my trial."

"Oh! oh!"

Arsène Lupin repeated, positively:

"I shall not be present at my trial."

"Really!"

"Ah! my dear monsieur, do you suppose I am going to rot upon the wet straw? You insult me. Arsène Lupin remains in prison just as long as it pleases him, and not one minute more."

"Perhaps it would have been more prudent if you had avoided getting there," said the detective, ironically.

"Ah! monsieur jests? Monsieur must remember that he had the honor to effect my arrest. Know then, my worthy friend, that no one, not even you, could have placed a hand upon me if a much more important event had not occupied my attention at that critical moment."

"You astonish me."

"A woman was looking at me, Ganimard, and I loved her. Do you fully understand what that means: to be under the eyes of a woman that one loves? I cared for nothing in the world but that. And that is why I am here."

"Permit me to say: you have been here a long time."

"In the first place, I wished to forget. Do not laugh; it was a delightful adventure and it is still a tender memory. Besides, I have been suffering from neurasthenia. Life is so feverish these days that it is necessary to take the `rest cure' occasionally, and I find this spot a sovereign remedy for my tired nerves."

"Arsène Lupin, you are not a bad fellow, after all."

"Thank you," said Lupin. "Ganimard, this is Friday. On Wednesday next, at four o'clock in the afternoon, I will smoke my cigar at your house in the rue Pergolese."

"Arsène Lupin, I will expect you."

They shook hands like two old friends who valued each other at their true worth; then the detective stepped to the door.

"Ganimard!"

"What is it?" asked Ganimard, as he turned back.

"You have forgotten your watch."

"My watch?"

"Yes, it strayed into my pocket."

He returned the watch, excusing himself.

"Pardon me.... a bad habit. Because they have taken mine is no reason why I should take yours. Besides, I have a chronometer here that satisfies me fairly well."

He took from the drawer a large gold watch and heavy chain.

"From whose pocket did that come?" asked Ganimard.

Arsène Lupin gave a hasty glance at the initials engraved on the watch.

"J.B.....Who the devil can that be?....Ah! yes, I remember. Jules Bouvier, the judge who conducted my examination. A charming fellow!...."

III. THE ESCAPE OF ARSÈNE LUPIN

Arsène Lupin had just finished his repast and taken from his pocket an excellent cigar, with a gold band, which he was examining with unusual care, when the door of his cell was opened. He had barely time to throw the cigar into the drawer and move away from the table. The guard entered. It was the hour for exercise.

"I was waiting for you, my dear boy," exclaimed Lupin, in his accustomed good humor.

They went out together. As soon as they had disappeared at a turn in the corridor, two men entered the cell and commenced a minute examination of it. One was Inspector Dieuzy; the other was Inspector Folenfant. They wished to verify their suspicion that Arsène Lupin was in communication with his accomplices outside of the prison. On the preceding evening, the `Grand Journal' had published these lines addressed to its court reporter:

"Monsieur:

"In a recent article you referred to me in most unjustifiable terms. Some days before the opening of my trial I will call you to account. Arsène Lupin."

The handwriting was certainly that of Arsène Lupin. Consequently, he sent letters; and, no doubt, received letters. It was certain that he was preparing for that escape thus arrogantly announced by him.

The situation had become intolerable. Acting in conjunction with the examining judge, the chief of the Sûreté, Mon. Dudouis, had visited the prison and instructed the gaoler in regard to the precautions necessary to insure Lupin's safety. At the same time, he sent the two men to examine the prisoner's cell. They raised every stone, ransacked the bed, did everything customary in such a case, but they discovered nothing, and were about to abandon their investigation when the guard entered hastily and said:

"The drawer.... look in the table-drawer. When I entered just now he was closing it."

They opened the drawer, and Dieuzy exclaimed:

"Ah! we have him this time."

Folenfant stopped him.

"Wait a moment. The chief will want to make an inventory."

"This is a very choice cigar."

"Leave it there, and notify the chief."

Two minutes later Mon. Dudouis examined the contents of the drawer. First he discovered a bundle of newspaper clippings relating to Arsène Lupin taken from the `Argus de la Presse,' then a tobacco-box, a pipe, some paper called "onion-peel," and two books. He read the titles of the books. One was an English edition of Carlyle's "Hero-worship"; the other was a charming elzevir, in modern binding, the "Manual of Epictetus," a German translation published at Leyden in 1634. On examining the books, he found that all the pages were underlined and annotated. Were they prepared as a code for correspondence, or did they simply express the studious character of the reader? Then he examined the tobacco-box and the pipe. Finally, he took up the famous cigar with its gold band.

"Fichtre!" he exclaimed. "Our friend smokes a good cigar. It's a Henry Clay."

With the mechanical action of an habitual smoker, he placed the cigar close to his ear and squeezed it to make it crack. Immediately he uttered a cry of surprise. The cigar had yielded under the pressure of his fingers. He examined it more closely, and quickly discovered something white between the leaves of tobacco. Delicately, with the aid of a pin, he withdrew a roll of very thin paper, scarcely larger than a toothpick. It was a letter. He unrolled it, and found these words, written in a feminine handwriting:

"The basket has taken the place of the others. Eight out of ten are ready. On pressing the outer foot the plate goes downward. From twelve to sixteen every day, H-P will wait. But where? Reply at once. Rest easy; your friend is watching over you."

Mon. Dudouis reflected a moment, then said:

"It is quite clear.... the basket.... the eight compartments.... From twelve to sixteen means from twelve to four o'clock."

"But this H-P, that will wait?"

"H-P must mean automobile. H-P, horsepower, is the way they indicate strength of the motor. A twenty-four H-P is an automobile of twenty-four horsepower."

Then he rose, and asked:

"Had the prisoner finished his breakfast?"

"Yes."

"And as he has not yet read the message, which is proved by the condition of the cigar, it is probable that he had just received it."

"How?"

"In his food. Concealed in his bread or in a potato, perhaps."

"Impossible. His food was allowed to be brought in simply to trap him, but we have never found anything in it."

"We will look for Lupin's reply this evening. Detain him outside for a few minutes. I shall take this to the examining judge, and, if he agrees with me, we will have the letter photographed at once, and in an hour you can replace the letter in the drawer in a cigar similar to this. The prisoner must have no cause for suspicion."

It was not without a certain curiosity that Mon. Dudouis returned to the prison in the evening, accompanied by Inspector Dieuzy. Three empty plates were sitting on the stove in the corner.

"He has eaten?"

"Yes," replied the guard.

"Dieuzy, please cut that macaroni into very small pieces, and open that bread-roll....Nothing?"

"No, chief."

Mon. Dudouis examined the plates, the fork, the spoon, and the knife—an ordinary knife with a rounded blade. He turned the handle to the left; then to the right. It yielded and unscrewed. The knife was hollow, and served as a hiding-place for a sheet of paper.

"Peuh!" he said, "that is not very clever for a man like Arsène. But we mustn't lose any time. You, Dieuzy, go and search the restaurant."

Then he read the note:

"I trust to you, H-P will follow at a distance every day. I will go ahead. Au revoir, dear friend."

"At last," cried Mon. Dudouis, rubbing his hands gleefully, "I think we have the affair in our own hands. A little strategy on our part, and the escape will be a success in so far as the arrest of his confederates are concerned."

"But if Arsène Lupin slips through your fingers?" suggested the guard.

"We will have a sufficient number of men to prevent that. If, however, he displays too much cleverness, ma foi, so much the worse for him! As to his band of robbers, since the chief refuses to speak, the others must."

And, as a matter of fact, Arsène Lupin had very little to say. For several months, Mon. Jules Bouvier, the examining judge, had exerted himself in vain. The investigation had been reduced to a few uninteresting arguments between the judge and the advocate, Maître Danval, one of the leaders of the bar. From time to time, through courtesy, Arsène Lupin would speak. One day he said:

"Yes, monsieur, le judge, I quite agree with you: the robbery of the Crédit Lyonnais, the theft in the rue de Babylone, the issue of the counterfeit bank-notes, the burglaries at the various châteaux, Armesnil, Gouret, Imblevain, Groseillers, Malaquis, all my work, monsieur, I did it all."

"Then will you explain to me——"

"It is useless. I confess everything in a lump, everything and even ten times more than you know nothing about."

Wearied by his fruitless task, the judge had suspended his examinations, but he resumed them after the two intercepted messages were brought to his attention; and regularly, at mid-day, Arsène Lupin was taken from the prison to the Dépôt in the prison-van with a certain number of other prisoners. They returned about three or four o'clock.

Now, one afternoon, this return trip was made under unusual conditions. The other prisoners not having been examined, it was decided to take back Arsène Lupin first, thus he found himself alone in the vehicle.

These prison-vans, vulgarly called "panniers à salade"—or salad-baskets—are divided lengthwise by a central corridor from which open ten compartments, five on either side. Each compartment is so arranged that the occupant must assume and retain a sitting posture, and, consequently, the five prisoners are seated one upon the other, and yet separated one from the other by partitions. A municipal guard, standing at one end, watches over the corridor.

Arsène was placed in the third cell on the right, and the heavy vehicle started. He carefully calculated when they left the quai de l'Horloge, and when they passed the Palais de Justice. Then, about the centre of the bridge Saint Michel, with his outer foot, that is to say, his right foot, he pressed upon the metal plate that closed his cell. Immediately something clicked, and the metal plate moved. He was able to ascertain that he was located between the two wheels.

He waited, keeping a sharp look-out. The vehicle was proceeding slowly along the boulevard Saint Michel. At the corner of Saint Germain it stopped. A truck horse had fallen. The traffic having been interrupted, a vast throng of fiacres and omnibuses had gathered there. Arsène Lupin looked out. Another prison-van had stopped close to the one he occupied. He moved the plate still farther, put his foot on one of the spokes of the wheel and leaped to the ground. A coachman saw him, roared with laughter, then tried to raise an outcry, but his voice was lost in the noise of the traffic that had commenced to move again. Moreover, Arsène Lupin was already far away.

He had run for a few steps; but, once upon the sidewalk, he turned and looked around; he seemed to scent the wind like a person who is uncertain which direction to take. Then, having decided, he put his hands in his pockets, and, with the careless air of an idle stroller, he proceeded up the boulevard. It was a warm, bright autumn day, and the cafés were full. He took a seat on the terrace of one of them. He ordered a bock and a package of cigarettes. He emptied his glass slowly, smoked one cigarette and lighted a second. Then he asked the waiter to send the proprietor to him. When the proprietor came, Arsène spoke to him in a voice loud enough to be heard by everyone:

"I regret to say, monsieur, I have forgotten my pocketbook. Perhaps, on the strength of my name, you will be pleased to give me credit for a few days. I am Arsène Lupin."

The proprietor looked at him, thinking he was joking. But Arsène repeated:

"Lupin, prisoner at the Santé, but now a fugitive. I venture to assume that the name inspires you with perfect confidence in me."

And he walked away, amidst shouts of laughter, whilst the proprietor stood amazed.

Lupin strolled along the rue Soufflot, and turned into the rue Saint Jacques. He pursued his way slowly, smoking his cigarettes and looking into the shop-windows. At the Boulevard de Port Royal he took his bearings, discovered where he was, and then walked in the direction of the rue de la Santé. The high forbidding walls of the prison were now before him. He pulled his hat forward to shade his face; then, approaching the sentinel, he asked:

"It this the prison de la Santé?"

"Yes."

"I wish to regain my cell. The van left me on the way, and I would not abuse—"

"Now, young man, move along—quick!" growled the sentinel.

"Pardon me, but I must pass through that gate. And if you prevent Arsène Lupin from entering the prison it will cost you dear, my friend."

"Arsène Lupin! What are you talking about!"

"I am sorry I haven't a card with me," said Arsène, fumbling in his pockets.

The sentinel eyed him from head to foot, in astonishment. Then, without a word, he rang a bell. The iron gate was partly opened, and Arsène stepped inside. Almost immediately he encountered the keeper of the prison, gesticulating and feigning a violent anger. Arsène smiled and said:

"Come, monsieur, don't play that game with me. What! they take the precaution to carry me alone in the van, prepare a nice little obstruction, and imagine I am going to take to my heels and rejoin my friends. Well, and what about the twenty agents of the Sûreté who accompanied us on foot, in fiacres and on bicycles? No, the arrangement did not please me. I should not have got away alive. Tell me, monsieur, did they count on that?"

He shrugged his shoulders, and added:

"I beg of you, monsieur, not to worry about me. When I wish to escape I shall not require any assistance."

On the second day thereafter, the `Echo de France,' which had apparently become the official reporter of the exploits of Arsène Lupin,—it was said that he was one of its principal shareholders—published a most complete account of this attempted escape. The exact wording of the messages exchanged between the prisoner and his mysterious friend, the means by which correspondence was constructed, the complicity of the police, the promenade on the Boulevard Saint Michel, the incident at the café Soufflot, everything was disclosed. It was known that the search of the restaurant and its waiters by Inspector Dieuzy had been fruitless. And the public also learned an extraordinary thing which demonstrated the infinite variety of resources that Lupin possessed: the prison-van, in which he was being carried, was prepared for the occasion and substituted by his accomplices for one of the six vans which did service at the prison.

The next escape of Arsène Lupin was not doubted by anyone. He announced it himself, in categorical terms, in a reply to Mon. Bouvier on the day following his attempted escape. The judge having made a jest about the affair, Arsène was annoyed, and, firmly eyeing the judge, he said, emphatically:

"Listen to me, monsieur! I give you my word of honor that this attempted flight was simply preliminary to my general plan of escape."

"I do not understand," said the judge.

"It is not necessary that you should understand."

And when the judge, in the course of that examination which was reported at length in the columns of the `Echo de France,' when the judge sought to resume his investigation, Arsène Lupin exclaimed, with an assumed air of lassitude:

"Mon Dieu, Mon Dieu, what's the use! All these questions are of no importance!"

"What! No importance?" cried the judge.

"No; because I shall not be present at the trial."

"You will not be present?"

"No; I have fully decided on that, and nothing will change my mind."

Such assurance combined with the inexplicable indiscretions that Arsène committed every day served to annoy and mystify the officers of the law. There were secrets known only to Arsène Lupin; secrets that he alone could divulge. But for what purpose did he reveal them? And how?

Arsène Lupin was changed to another cell. The judge closed his preliminary investigation. No further proceedings were taken in his case for a period of two months, during which time Arsène was seen almost constantly lying on his bed with his face turned toward the wall. The changing of his cell seemed to discourage him. He refused to see his advocate. He exchanged only a few necessary words with his keepers.

During the fortnight preceding his trial, he resumed his vigorous life. He complained of want of air. Consequently, early every morning he was allowed to exercise in the courtyard, guarded by two men.

Public curiosity had not died out; every day it expected to be regaled with news of his escape; and, it is true, he had gained a considerable amount of public sympathy by reason of his verve, his gayety, his diversity, his inventive genius and the mystery of his life. Arsène Lupin must escape. It was his inevitable fate. The public expected it, and was surprised that the event had been delayed so long. Every morning the Préfect of Police asked his secretary:

"Well, has he escaped yet?"

"No, Monsieur le Préfect."

"To-morrow, probably."

And, on the day before the trial, a gentleman called at the office of the `Grand Journal,' asked to see the court reporter, threw his card in the reporter's face, and walked rapidly away. These words were written on the card: "Arsène Lupin always keeps his promises."

It was under these conditions that the trial commenced. An enormous crowd gathered at the court. Everybody wished to see the famous Arsène

Lupin. They had a gleeful anticipation that the prisoner would play some audacious pranks upon the judge. Advocates and magistrates, reporters and men of the world, actresses and society women were crowded together on the benches provided for the public.

It was a dark, sombre day, with a steady downpour of rain. Only a dim light pervaded the courtroom, and the spectators caught a very indistinct view of the prisoner when the guards brought him in. But his heavy, shambling walk, the manner in which he dropped into his seat, and his passive, stupid appearance were not at all prepossessing. Several times his advocate—one of Mon. Danval's assistants—spoke to him, but he simply shook his head and said nothing.

The clerk read the indictment, then the judge spoke:

"Prisoner at the bar, stand up. Your name, age, and occupation?"

Not receiving any reply, the judge repeated:

"Your name? I ask you your name?"

A thick, slow voice muttered:

"Baudru, Désiré."

A murmur of surprise pervaded the courtroom. But the judge proceeded:

"Baudru, Désiré? Ah! a new alias! Well, as you have already assumed a dozen different names and this one is, no doubt, as imaginary as the others, we will adhere to the name of Arsène Lupin, by which you are more generally known."

The judge referred to his notes, and continued:

"For, despite the most diligent search, your past history remains unknown. Your case is unique in the annals of crime. We know not whom you are, whence you came, your birth and breeding—all is a mystery to us. Three years ago you appeared in our midst as Arsène Lupin, presenting to us a strange combination of intelligence and perversion, immorality and generosity. Our knowledge of your life prior to that date is vague and problematical. It may be that the man called Rostat who, eight years ago, worked with Dickson, the prestidigitator, was none other than Arsène Lupin. It is probable that the Russian student who, six years ago, attended the laboratory of Doctor Altier at the Saint Louis Hospital, and who often astonished the doctor by the ingenuity of his hypotheses on subjects of bacteriology and the boldness of his experiments in diseases of the skin, was none other than Arsène Lupin. It is probable, also, that Arsène Lupin was the professor who introduced the Japanese art of jiu-jitsu to the Parisian public. We have some reason to believe that Arsène Lupin was the bicyclist who won the Grand Prix de l'Exposition, received his ten thousand francs, and was never heard of again. Arsène Lupin may have been, also, the person who saved so many lives through the little dormer-window at the Charity Bazaar; and, at the same time, picked their pockets."

The judge paused for a moment, then continued:

"Such is that epoch which seems to have been utilized by you in a thorough preparation for the warfare you have since waged against society; a methodical apprenticeship in which you developed your strength, energy and skill to the highest point possible. Do you acknowledge the accuracy of these facts?"

During this discourse the prisoner had stood balancing himself, first on one foot, then on the other, with shoulders stooped and arms inert. Under the strongest light one could observe his extreme thinness, his hollow cheeks, his projecting cheek-bones, his earthen-colored face dotted with small red spots and framed in a rough, straggling beard. Prison life had caused him to age and wither. He had lost the youthful face and elegant figure we had seen portrayed so often in the newspapers.

It appeared as if he had not heard the question propounded by the judge. Twice it was repeated to him. Then he raised his eyes, seemed to reflect, then, making a desperate effort, he murmured:

"Baudru, Désiré."

The judge smiled, as he said:

"I do not understand the theory of your defense, Arsène Lupin. If you are seeking to avoid responsibility for your crimes on the ground of imbecility, such a line of defense is open to you. But I shall proceed with the trial and pay no heed to your vagaries."

He then narrated at length the various thefts, swindles and forgeries charged against Lupin. Sometimes he questioned the prisoner, but the latter simply grunted or remained silent. The examination of witnesses commenced. Some of the evidence given was immaterial; other portions of it seemed more important, but through all of it there ran a vein of contradictions and inconsistencies. A wearisome obscurity enveloped the proceedings, until Detective Ganimard was called as a witness; then interest was revived.

From the beginning the actions of the veteran detective appeared strange and unaccountable. He was nervous and ill at ease. Several times he looked at the prisoner, with obvious doubt and anxiety. Then, with his hands resting on the rail in front of him, he recounted the events in which he had participated, including his pursuit of the prisoner across Europe and his arrival in America. He was listened to with great avidity, as his capture of Arsène Lupin was well known to everyone through the medium of the press. Toward the close of his testimony, after referring to his conversations with Arsène Lupin, he stopped, twice, embarrassed and undecided. It was apparent that he was possessed of some thought which he feared to utter. The judge said to him, sympathetically:

"If you are ill, you may retire for the present."

"No, no, but——"

He stopped, looked sharply at the prisoner, and said:

"I ask permission to scrutinize the prisoner at closer range. There is some mystery about him that I must solve."

He approached the accused man, examined him attentively for several minutes, then returned to the witness-stand, and, in an almost solemn voice, he said:

"I declare, on oath, that the prisoner now before me is not Arsène Lupin."

A profound silence followed the statement. The judge, nonplused for a moment, exclaimed:

"Ah! What do you mean? That is absurd!"

The detective continued:

"At first sight there is a certain resemblance, but if you carefully consider the nose, the mouth, the hair, the color of skin, you will see that it is not Arsène Lupin. And the eyes! Did he ever have those alcoholic eyes!"

"Come, come, witness! What do you mean? Do you pretend to say that we are trying the wrong man?"

"In my opinion, yes. Arsène Lupin has, in some manner, contrived to put this poor devil in his place, unless this man is a willing accomplice."

This dramatic dénouement caused much laughter and excitement amongst the spectators. The judge adjourned the trial, and sent for Mon. Bouvier, the gaoler, and guards employed in the prison.

When the trial was resumed, Mon. Bouvier and the gaoler examined the accused and declared that there was only a very slight resemblance between the prisoner and Arsène Lupin.

"Well, then!" exclaimed the judge, "who is this man? Where does he come from? What is he in prison for?"

Two of the prison-guards were called and both of them declared that the prisoner was Arsène Lupin. The judged breathed once more.

But one of the guards then said:

"Yes, yes, I think it is he."

"What!" cried the judge, impatiently, "you *think* it is he! What do you mean by that?"

"Well, I saw very little of the prisoner. He was placed in my charge in the evening and, for two months, he seldom stirred, but laid on his bed with his face to the wall."

"What about the time prior to those two months?"

"Before that he occupied a cell in another part of the prison. He was not in cell 24."

Here the head gaoler interrupted, and said:

"We changed him to another cell after his attempted escape."

"But you, monsieur, you have seen him during those two months?"

"I had no occasion to see him. He was always quiet and orderly."

"And this prisoner is not Arsène Lupin?"

"No."

"Then who is he?" demanded the judge.

"I do not know."

"Then we have before us a man who was substituted for Arsène Lupin, two months ago. How do you explain that?"

"I cannot."

In absolute despair, the judge turned to the accused and addressed him in a conciliatory tone:

"Prisoner, can you tell me how, and since when, you became an inmate of the Prison de la Santé?"

The engaging manner of the judge was calculated to disarm the mistrust and awaken the understanding of the accused man. He tried to reply. Finally, under clever and gentle questioning, he succeeded in framing a few phrases from which the following story was gleaned: Two months ago he had been taken to the Dépôt, examined and released. As he was leaving the building, a free man, he was seized by two guards and placed in the prison-van. Since then he had occupied cell 24. He was contented there, plenty to eat, and he slept well—so he did not complain.

All that seemed probable; and, amidst the mirth and excitement of the spectators, the judge adjourned the trial until the story could be investigated and verified.

The following facts were at once established by an examination of the prison records: Eight weeks before a man named Baudru Désiré had slept at the Dépôt. He was released the next day, and left the Dépôt at two o'clock in the afternoon. On the same day at two o'clock, having been examined for the last time, Arsène Lupin left the Dépôt in a prison-van.

Had the guards made a mistake? Had they been deceived by the resemblance and carelessly substituted this man for their prisoner?

Another question suggested itself: Had the substitution been arranged in advance? In that event Baudru must have been an accomplice and must have caused his own arrest for the express purpose of taking Lupin's place. But then, by what miracle had such a plan, based on a series of improbable chances, been carried to success?

Baudru Désiré was turned over to the anthropological service; they had never seen anything like him. However, they easily traced his past history. He was known at Courbevois, at Asnières and at Levallois. He lived on alms and slept in one of those rag-picker's huts near the barrier de Ternes. He had disappeared from there a year ago.

Had he been enticed away by Arsène Lupin? There was no evidence to that effect. And even if that was so, it did not explain the flight of the prisoner. That still remained a mystery. Amongst twenty theories which sought to explain it, not one was satisfactory. Of the escape itself, there was no doubt; an escape that was incomprehensible, sensational, in which the public, as well as the officers of the law, could detect a carefully prepared plan, a combination of circumstances marvelously dove-tailed, whereof the dénouement fully justified the confident prediction of Arsène Lupin: "I shall not be present at my trial."

After a month of patient investigation, the problem remained unsolved. The poor devil of a Baudru could not be kept in prison indefinitely, and to place him on trial would be ridiculous. There was no charge against him. Consequently, he was released; but the chief of the Sûreté resolved to keep him under surveillance. This idea originated with Ganimard. From his point of view there was neither complicity nor chance. Baudru was an instrument upon which Arsène Lupin had played with his extraordinary skill. Baudru, when set at liberty, would lead them to Arsène Lupin or, at least, to some of his accomplices. The two inspectors, Folenfant and Dieuzy, were assigned to assist Ganimard.

One foggy morning in January the prison gates opened and Baudru Désiré stepped forth—a free man. At first he appeared to be quite embarrassed, and walked like a person who has no precise idea whither he is going. He followed the rue de la Santé and the rue Saint Jacques. He stopped in front of an old-clothes shop, removed his jacket and his vest, sold his vest on which he realized a few sous; then, replacing his jacket, he proceeded on his way. He crossed the Seine. At the Châtelet an omnibus passed him. He wished to enter it, but there was no place. The controller advised him to secure a number, so he entered the waiting-room.

Ganimard called to his two assistants, and, without removing his eyes from the waiting room, he said to them:

"Stop a carriage.... no, two. That will be better. I will go with one of you, and we will follow him."

The men obeyed. Yet Baudru did not appear. Ganimard entered the waiting-room. It was empty.

"Idiot that I am!" he muttered, "I forgot there was another exit."

There was an interior corridor extending from the waiting-room to the rue Saint Martin. Ganimard rushed through it and arrived just in time to observe Baudru upon the top of the Batignolles-Jardin de Plates omnibus as it was turning the corner of the rue de Rivoli. He ran and caught the omnibus. But he had lost his two assistants. He must continue the pursuit alone. In his anger he was inclined to seize the man by the collar without ceremony. Was it not with premeditation and by means of an ingenious ruse that his pretended imbecile had separated him from his assistants?

He looked at Baudru. The latter was asleep on the bench, his head rolling from side to side, his mouth half-opened, and an incredible expression of stupidity on his blotched face. No, such an adversary was incapable of deceiving old Ganimard. It was a stroke of luck—nothing more.

At the Galleries-Lafayette, the man leaped from the omnibus and took the La Muette tramway, following the boulevard Haussmann and the avenue Victor Hugo. Baudru alighted at La Muette station; and, with a nonchalant air, strolled into the Bois de Boulogne.

He wandered through one path after another, and sometimes retraced his steps. What was he seeking? Had he any definite object? At the end of an hour, he appeared to be faint from fatigue, and, noticing a bench, he sat down. The spot, not far from Auteuil, on the edge of a pond hidden amongst the trees, was absolutely deserted. After the lapse of another half-hour, Ganimard became impatient and resolved to speak to the man. He approached and took a seat beside Baudru, lighted a cigarette, traced some figures in the sand with the end of his cane, and said:

"It's a pleasant day."

No response. But, suddenly the man burst into laughter, a happy, mirthful laugh, spontaneous and irresistible. Ganimard felt his hair stand on end in horror and surprise. It was that laugh, that infernal laugh he knew so well!

With a sudden movement, he seized the man by the collar and looked at him with a keen, penetrating gaze; and found that he no longer saw the man Baudru. To be sure, he saw Baudru; but, at the same time, he saw the other, the real man, Lupin. He discovered the intense life in the eyes, he filled up the shrunken features, he perceived the real flesh beneath the flabby skin, the real mouth through the grimaces that deformed it. Those were the eyes and mouth of the other, and especially his keen, alert, mocking expression, so clear and youthful!

"Arsène Lupin, Arsène Lupin," he stammered.

Then, in a sudden fit of rage, he seized Lupin by the throat and tried to hold him down. In spite of his fifty years, he still possessed unusual strength, whilst his adversary was apparently in a weak condition. But the struggle was a brief one. Arsène Lupin made only a slight movement, and, as suddenly as he had made the attack, Ganimard released his hold. His right arm fell inert, useless.

"If you had taken lessons in jiu-jitsu at the quai des Orfèvres," said Lupin, "you would know that that blow is called udi-shi-ghi in Japanese. A second more, and I would have broken your arm and that would have been just what you deserve. I am surprised that you, an old friend whom I respect and before whom I voluntarily expose my incognito, should abuse my confidence in that violent manner. It is unworthy—Ah! What's the matter?"

Ganimard did not reply. That escape for which he deemed himself responsible—was it not he, Ganimard, who, by his sensational evidence, had led the court into serious error? That escape appeared to him like a dark cloud on his professional career. A tear rolled down his cheek to his gray moustache.

"Oh! mon Dieu, Ganimard, don't take it to heart. If you had not spoken, I would have arranged for some one else to do it. I couldn't allow poor Baudru Désiré to be convicted."

"Then," murmured Ganimard, "it was you that was there? And now you are here?"

"It is I, always I, only I."

"Can it be possible?"

"Oh, it is not the work of a sorcerer. Simply, as the judge remarked at the trial, the apprenticeship of a dozen years that equips a man to cope successfully with all the obstacles in life."

"But your face? Your eyes?"

"You can understand that if I worked eighteen months with Doctor Altier at the Saint-Louis hospital, it was not out of love for the work. I considered that he, who would one day have the honor of calling himself Arsène Lupin, ought to be exempt from the ordinary laws governing appearance and identity. Appearance? That can be modified at will. For instance, a hypodermic injection of paraffine will puff up the skin at the desired spot. Pyrogallic acid will change your skin to that of an Indian. The juice of the greater celandine will adorn you with the most beautiful eruptions and tumors. Another chemical affects the growth of your beard and hair; another changes the tone of your voice. Add to that two months of dieting in cell 24; exercises repeated a thousand times to enable me to hold my features in a certain grimace, to carry my head at a certain inclination, and adapt my back and shoulders to a stooping posture. Then five drops of atropine in the eyes to make them haggard and wild, and the trick is done."

"I do not understand how you deceived the guards."

"The change was progressive. The evolution was so gradual that they failed to notice it."

"But Baudru Désiré?" "Baudru exists. He is a poor, harmless fellow whom I met last year; and, really, he bears a certain resemblance to me. Considering my arrest as a possible event, I took charge of Baudru and studied the points wherein we differed in appearance with a view to correct them in my own person. My friends caused him to remain at the Dépôt overnight, and to leave there next day about the same hour as I did—a coincidence easily arranged. Of course, it was necessary to have a record of his detention at the Dépôt in order to establish the fact that such a person was a reality; otherwise, the police would have sought elsewhere to find out my identity. But, in offering to them this excellent Baudru, it was inevitable, you understand, inevitable that they would seize upon him, and, despite the insurmountable difficulties of a substitution, they would prefer to believe in a substitution than confess their ignorance."

"Yes, yes, of course," said Ganimard.

"And then," exclaimed Arsène Lupin, "I held in my hands a trump-card: an anxious public watching and waiting for my escape. And that is the fatal error into which you fell, you and the others, in the course of that fascinating game pending between me and the officers of the law wherein the stake was my liberty. And you supposed that I was playing to the gallery; that I was intoxicated with my success. I, Arsène Lupin, guilty of such weakness! Oh, no! And, no longer ago than the Cahorn affair, you said: "When Arsène Lupin cries from the housetops that he will escape, he has some object in view." But, sapristi, you must understand that in order to escape I must create, in advance, a public belief in that escape, a belief amounting to an article of faith, an absolute conviction, a reality as glittering as the sun. And I did create that belief that Arsène Lupin would escape, that Arsène Lupin would not be present at his trial. And when you gave your evidence and said: "That man is not Arsène Lupin," everybody was prepared to believe you. Had one person doubted it, had any one uttered this simple restriction: Suppose it is Arsène Lupin?—from that moment, I was lost. If anyone had scrutinized my face, not imbued with the idea that I was not Arsène Lupin, as you and the others did at my trial, but with the idea that I might be Arsène Lupin; then, despite all my precautions, I should have been recognized. But I had no fear. Logically, psychologically, no once could entertain the idea that I was Arsène Lupin."

He grasped Ganimard's hand.

"Come, Ganimard, confess that on the Wednesday after our conversation in the prison de la Santé, you expected me at your house at four o'clock, exactly as I said I would go."

"And your prison-van?" said Ganimard, evading the question.

"A bluff! Some of my friends secured that old unused van and wished to make the attempt. But I considered it impractical without the concurrence of a number of unusual circumstances. However, I found it useful to carry out that attempted escape and give it the widest publicity. An audaciously planned escape, though not completed, gave to the succeeding one the character of reality simply by anticipation."

"So that the cigar...."

"Hollowed by myself, as well as the knife."

"And the letters?"

"Written by me."

"And the mysterious correspondent?"

"Did not exist."

Ganimard reflected a moment, then said:

"When the anthropological service had Baudru's case under consideration, why did they not perceive that his measurements coincided with those of Arsène Lupin?"

"My measurements are not in existence."

"Indeed!"

"At least, they are false. I have given considerable attention to that question. In the first place, the Bertillon system of records the visible marks of identification—and you have seen that they are not infallible—and, after that, the measurements of the head, the fingers, the ears, etc. Of course, such measurements are more or less infallible."

"Absolutely."

"No; but it costs money to get around them. Before we left America, one of the employees of the service there accepted so much money to insert false figures in my measurements. Consequently, Baudru's measurements should not agree with those of Arsène Lupin."

After a short silence, Ganimard asked:

"What are you going to do now?"

"Now," replied Lupin, "I am going to take a rest, enjoy the best of food and drink and gradually recover my former healthy condition. It is all very well to become Baudru or some other person, on occasion, and to change your personality as you do your shirt, but you soon grow weary of the change. I feel exactly as I imagine the man who lost his shadow must have felt, and I shall be glad to be Arsène Lupin once more."

He walked to and fro for a few minutes, then, stopping in front of Ganimard, he said:

"You have nothing more to say, I suppose?"

"Yes. I should like to know if you intend to reveal the true state of facts connected with your escape. The mistake that I made——"

"Oh! no one will ever know that it was Arsène Lupin who was discharged. It is to my own interest to surround myself with mystery, and therefore I shall permit my escape to retain its almost miraculous character. So, have no fear on that score, my dear friend. I shall say nothing. And now, good-bye. I am going out to dinner this evening, and have only sufficient time to dress."

"I though you wanted a rest."

"Ah! there are duties to society that one cannot avoid. To-morrow, I shall rest."

"Where do you dine to-night?"

IV. THE MYSTERIOUS TRAVELLER

The evening before, I had sent my automobile to Rouen by the highway. I was to travel to Rouen by rail, on my way to visit some friends that live on the banks of the Seine.

At Paris, a few minutes before the train started, seven gentlemen entered my compartment; five of them were smoking. No matter that the journey was a short one, the thought of traveling with such a company was not agreeable to me, especially as the car was built on the old model, without a corridor. I picked up my overcoat, my newspapers and my time-table, and sought refuge in a neighboring compartment.

It was occupied by a lady, who, at sight of me, made a gesture of annoyance that did not escape my notice, and she leaned toward a gentleman who was standing on the step and was, no doubt, her husband. The gentleman scrutinized me closely, and, apparently, my appearance did not displease him, for he smiled as he spoke to his wife with the air of one who reassures a frightened child. She smiled also, and gave me a friendly glance as if she now understood that I was one of those gallant men with whom a woman can remain shut up for two hours in a little box, six feet square, and have nothing to fear.

Her husband said to her:

"I have an important appointment, my dear, and cannot wait any longer. Adieu."

He kissed her affectionately and went away. His wife threw him a few kisses and waved her handkerchief. The whistle sounded, and the train started.

At that precise moment, and despite the protests of the guards, the door was opened, and a man rushed into our compartment. My companion, who was standing and arranging her luggage, uttered a cry of terror and fell upon the seat. I am not a coward—far from it—but I confess that such intrusions at the last minute are always disconcerting. They have a suspicious, unnatural aspect.

However, the appearance of the new arrival greatly modified the unfavorable impression produced by his precipitant action. He was correctly and elegantly dressed, wore a tasteful cravat, correct gloves, and his face was refined and intelligent. But, where the devil had I seen that face before?

Because, beyond all possible doubt, I had seen it. And yet the memory of it was so vague and indistinct that I felt it would be useless to try to recall it at that time.

Then, directing my attention to the lady, I was amazed at the pallor and anxiety I saw in her face. She was looking at her neighbor—they occupied seats on the same side of the compartment—with an expression of intense alarm, and I perceived that one of her trembling hands was slowly gliding toward a little traveling bag that was lying on the seat about twenty inches from her. She finished by seizing it and nervously drawing it to her. Our eyes met, and I read in hers so much anxiety and fear that I could not refrain from speaking to her:

"Are you ill, madame? Shall I open the window?"

Her only reply was a gesture indicating that she was afraid of our companion. I smiled, as her husband had done, shrugged my shoulders, and explained to her, in pantomime, that she had nothing to fear, that I was there, and, besides, the gentleman appeared to be a very harmless individual. At that moment, he turned toward us, scrutinized both of us from head to foot, then settled down in his corner and paid us no more attention.

After a short silence, the lady, as if she had mustered all her energy to perform a desperate act, said to me, in an almost inaudible voice:

"Do you know who is on our train?"

"Who?"

"He.... he....I assure you...."

"Who is he?"

"Arsène Lupin!"

She had not taken her eyes off our companion, and it was to him rather than to me that she uttered the syllables of that disquieting name. He drew his hat over his face. Was that to conceal his agitation or, simply, to arrange himself for sleep? Then I said to her:

"Yesterday, through contumacy, Arsène Lupin was sentenced to twenty years' imprisonment at hard labor. Therefore it is improbable that he would be so imprudent, to-day, as to show himself in public. Moreover, the newspapers have announced his appearance in Turkey since his escape from the Santé."

"But he is on this train at the present moment," the lady proclaimed, with the obvious intention of being heard by our companion; "my husband is one of the directors in the penitentiary service, and it was the stationmaster himself who told us that a search was being made for Arsène Lupin."

"They may have been mistaken——"

"No; he was seen in the waiting-room. He bought a first-class ticket for Rouen."

"He has disappeared. The guard at the waiting-room door did not see him pass, and it is supposed that he had got into the express that leaves ten minutes after us."

"In that case, they will be sure to catch him."

"Unless, at the last moment, he leaped from that train to come here, into our train.... which is quite probable.... which is almost certain."

"If so, he will be arrested just the same; for the employees and guards would no doubt observe his passage from one train to the other, and, when we arrive at Rouen, they will arrest him there."

"Him—never! He will find some means of escape."

"In that case, I wish him 'bon voyage.'"

"But, in the meantime, think what he may do!"

"What?"

"I don't know. He may do anything."

She was greatly agitated, and, truly, the situation justified, to some extent, her nervous excitement. I was impelled to say to her:

"Of course, there are many strange coincidences, but you need have no fear. Admitting that Arsène Lupin is on this train, he will not commit any indiscretion; he will be only too happy to escape the peril that already threatens him."

My words did not reassure her, but she remained silent for a time. I unfolded my newspapers and read reports of Arsène Lupin's trial, but, as they contained nothing that was new to me, I was not greatly interested. Moreover, I was tired and sleepy. I felt my eyelids close and my head drop.

"But, monsieur, you are not going to sleep!"

She seized my newspaper, and looked at me with indignation.

"Certainly not," I said.

"That would be very imprudent."

"Of course," I assented.

I struggled to keep awake. I looked through the window at the landscape and the fleeting clouds, but in a short time all that became confused and indistinct; the image of the nervous lady and the drowsy gentleman were effaced from my memory, and I was buried in the soothing depths of a profound sleep. The tranquility of my response was soon disturbed by disquieting dreams, wherein a creature that had played the part and bore the name of Arsène Lupin held an important place. He appeared to me with his back laden with articles of value; he leaped over walls, and plundered castles. But the outlines of that creature, who was no longer Arsène Lupin, assumed a more definite form. He came toward me, growing larger and larger, leaped into the compartment with incredible agility, and landed squarely on my chest. With a cry of fright and pain, I awoke. The man, the traveller, our companion, with his knee on my breast, held me by the throat.

My sight was very indistinct, for my eyes were suffused with blood. I could see the lady, in a corner of the compartment, convulsed with fright. I tried even not to resist. Besides, I did not have the strength. My temples throbbed; I was almost strangled. One minute more, and I would have breathed my last. The man must have realized it, for he relaxed his grip, but did not remove his hand. Then he took a cord, in which he had prepared a slip-knot, and tied my wrists together. In an instant, I was bound, gagged, and helpless.

Certainly, he accomplished the trick with an ease and skill that revealed the hand of a master; he was, no doubt, a professional thief. Not a word, not a nervous movement; only coolness and audacity. And I was there, lying on the bench, bound like a mummy, I—Arsène Lupin!

It was anything but a laughing matter, and yet, despite the gravity of the situation, I keenly appreciated the humor and irony that it involved. Arsène Lupin seized and bound like a novice! robbed as if I were an unsophisticated rustic—for, you must understand, the scoundrel had deprived me of my purse and wallet! Arsène Lupin, a victim, duped, vanquished....What an adventure!

The lady did not move. He did not even notice her. He contented himself with picking up her traveling-bag that had fallen to the floor and taking from it the jewels, purse, and gold and silver trinkets that it contained. The lady opened her eyes, trembled with fear, drew the rings from her fingers and handed them to the man as if she wished to spare him unnecessary trouble. He took the rings and looked at her. She swooned.

Then, quite unruffled, he resumed his seat, lighted a cigarette, and proceeded to examine the treasure that he had acquired. The examination appeared to give him perfect satisfaction.

But I was not so well satisfied. I do not speak of the twelve thousand francs of which I had been unduly deprived: that was only a temporary loss, because I was certain that I would recover possession of that money after a very brief delay, together with the important papers contained in my wallet: plans, specifications, addresses, lists of correspondents, and compromising letters. But, for the moment, a more immediate and more serious question troubled me: How would this affair end? What would be the outcome of this adventure?

As you can imagine, the disturbance created by my passage through the Saint-Lazare station has not escaped my notice. Going to visit friends who knew me under the name of Guillaume Berlat, and amongst whom my resemblance to Arsène Lupin was a subject of many innocent jests, I could not assume a disguise, and my presence had been remarked. So, beyond question, the commissary of police at Rouen, notified by telegraph, and assisted by numerous agents, would be awaiting the train, would question all suspicious passengers, and proceed to search the cars.

Of course, I had foreseen all that, but it had not disturbed me, as I was certain that the police of Rouen would not be any shrewder than the police of Paris and that I could escape recognition; would it not be sufficient for me to carelessly display my card as "député," thanks to which I had inspired complete confidence in the gate-keeper at Saint-Lazare?—But the situation was greatly changed. I was no longer free. It was impossible to attempt one of my usual tricks. In one of the compartments, the commissary of police would find Mon. Arsène Lupin, bound hand and foot, as docile as a lamb, packed up, all ready to be dumped into a prison-van. He would have simply to accept delivery of the parcel, the same as if it were so much merchandise or a basket of fruit and vegetables. Yet, to avoid that shameful dénouement, what could I do?—bound and gagged, as I was? And the train was rushing on toward Rouen, the next and only station.

Another problem was presented, in which I was less interested, but the solution of which aroused my professional curiosity. What were the intentions of my rascally companion? Of course, if I had been alone, he could, on our arrival at Rouen, leave the car slowly and fearlessly. But the lady? As soon as the door of the compartment should be opened, the lady, now so quiet and humble, would scream and call for help. That was the dilemma that perplexed me! Why had he not reduced her to a helpless condition similar to mine? That would have given him ample time to disappear before his double crime was discovered.

He was still smoking, with his eyes fixed upon the window that was now being streaked with drops of rain. Once he turned, picked up my time-table, and consulted it.

The lady had to feign a continued lack of consciousness in order to deceive the enemy. But fits of coughing, provoked by the smoke, exposed her true condition. As to me, I was very uncomfortable, and very tired. And I meditated; I plotted.

The train was rushing on, joyously, intoxicated with its own speed.

Saint Etienne!....At that moment, the man arose and took two steps toward us, which caused the lady to utter a cry of alarm and fall into a genuine swoon. What was the man about to do? He lowered the window on our side. A heavy rain was now falling, and, by a gesture, the man expressed his annoyance at his not having an umbrella or an overcoat. He glanced at the rack. The lady's umbrella was there. He took it. He also took my overcoat and put it on.

We were now crossing the Seine. He turned up the bottoms of his trousers, then leaned over and raised the exterior latch of the door. Was he going to throw himself upon the track? At that speed, it would have been instant death. We now entered a tunnel. The man opened the door half-way and stood on the upper step. What folly! The darkness, the smoke, the noise, all gave a fantastic appearance to his actions. But suddenly, the train diminished its speed. A moment later it increased its speed, then slowed up again. Probably, some repairs were being made in that part of the tunnel which obliged the trains to diminish their speed, and the man was aware of the fact. He immediately stepped down to the lower step, closed the door behind him, and leaped to the ground. He was gone.

The lady immediately recovered her wits, and her first act was to lament the loss of her jewels. I gave her an imploring look. She understood, and quickly removed the gag that stifled me. She wished to untie the cords that bound me, but I prevented her.

"No, no, the police must see everything exactly as it stands. I want them to see what the rascal did to us."

"Suppose I pull the alarm-bell?"

"Too late. You should have done that when he made the attack on me."

"But he would have killed me. Ah! monsieur, didn't I tell you that he was on this train. I recognized him from his portrait. And now he has gone off with my jewels."

"Don't worry. The police will catch him."

"Catch Arsène Lupin! Never."

"That depends on you, madame. Listen. When we arrive at Rouen, be at the door and call. Make a noise. The police and the railway employees will come. Tell what you have seen: the assault made on me and the flight of

Arsène Lupin. Give a description of him—soft hat, umbrella—yours—gray overcoat...."

"Yours," said she.

"What! mine? Not at all. It was his. I didn't have any."

"It seems to me he didn't have one when he came in."

"Yes, yes.... unless the coat was one that some one had forgotten and left in the rack. At all events, he had it when he went away, and that is the essential point. A gray overcoat—remember!....Ah! I forgot. You must tell your name, first thing you do. Your husband's official position will stimulate the zeal of the police."

We arrived at the station. I gave her some further instructions in a rather imperious tone:

"Tell them my name—Guillaume Berlat. If necessary, say that you know me. That will save time. We must expedite the preliminary investigation. The important thing is the pursuit of Arsène Lupin. Your jewels, remember! Let there be no mistake. Guillaume Berlat, a friend of your husband."

"I understand....Guillaume Berlat."

She was already calling and gesticulating. As soon as the train stopped, several men entered the compartment. The critical moment had come.

Panting for breath, the lady exclaimed:

"Arsène Lupin.... he attacked us.... he stole my jewels....I am Madame Renaud.... my husband is a director of the penitentiary service....Ah! here is my brother, Georges Ardelle, director of the Crédit Rouennais.... you must know...."

She embraced a young man who had just joined us, and whom the commissary saluted. Then she continued, weeping:

"Yes, Arsène Lupin.... while monsieur was sleeping, he seized him by the throat....Mon. Berlat, a friend of my husband."

The commissary asked:

"But where is Arsène Lupin?"

"He leaped from the train, when passing through the tunnel."

"Are you sure that it was he?"

"Am I sure! I recognized him perfectly. Besides, he was seen at the Saint-Lazare station. He wore a soft hat——"

"No, a hard felt, like that," said the commissary, pointing to my hat.

"He had a soft hat, I am sure," repeated Madame Renaud, "and a gray overcoat."

"Yes, that is right," replied the commissary, "the telegram says he wore a gray overcoat with a black velvet collar."

"Exactly, a black velvet collar," exclaimed Madame Renaud, triumphantly.

I breathed freely. Ah! the excellent friend I had in that little woman.

The police agents had now released me. I bit my lips until they ran blood. Stooping over, with my handkerchief over my mouth, an attitude quite natural in a person who has remained for a long time in an uncomfortable position, and whose mouth shows the bloody marks of the gag, I addressed the commissary, in a weak voice:

"Monsieur, it was Arsène Lupin. There is no doubt about that. If we make haste, he can be caught yet. I think I may be of some service to you."

The railway car, in which the crime occurred, was detached from the train to serve as a mute witness at the official investigation. The train continued on its way to Havre. We were then conducted to the station-master's office through a crowd of curious spectators.

Then, I had a sudden access of doubt and discretion. Under some pretext or other, I must gain my automobile, and escape. To remain there was dangerous. Something might happen; for instance, a telegram from Paris, and I would be lost.

Yes, but what about my thief? Abandoned to my own resources, in an unfamiliar country, I could not hope to catch him.

"Bah! I must make the attempt," I said to myself. "It may be a difficult game, but an amusing one, and the stake is well worth the trouble."

And when the commissary asked us to repeat the story of the robbery, I exclaimed:

"Monsieur, really, Arsène Lupin is getting the start of us. My automobile is waiting in the courtyard. If you will be so kind as to use it, we can try...."

The commissary smiled, and replied:

"The idea is a good one; so good, indeed, that it is already being carried out. Two of my men have set out on bicycles. They have been gone for some time."

"Where did they go?"

"To the entrance of the tunnel. There, they will gather evidence, secure witnesses, and follow on the track of Arsène Lupin."

I could not refrain from shrugging my shoulders, as I replied:

"Your men will not secure any evidence or any witnesses."

"Really!"

"Arsène Lupin will not allow anyone to see him emerge from the tunnel. He will take the first road——"

"To Rouen, where we will arrest him."

"He will not go to Rouen."

"Then he will remain in the vicinity, where his capture will be even more certain."

"He will not remain in the vicinity."

"Oh! oh! And where will he hide?"

I looked at my watch, and said:

"At the present moment, Arsène Lupin is prowling around the station at Darnétal. At ten fifty, that is, in twenty-two minutes from now, he will take the train that goes from Rouen to Amiens."

"Do you think so? How do you know it?"

"Oh! it is quite simple. While we were in the car, Arsène Lupin consulted my railway guide. Why did he do it? Was there, not far from the spot where he disappeared, another line of railway, a station upon that line, and a train stopping at that station? On consulting my railway guide, I found such to be the case."

"Really, monsieur," said the commissary, "that is a marvelous deduction. I congratulate you on your skill."

I was now convinced that I had made a mistake in displaying so much cleverness. The commissary regarded me with astonishment, and I thought a slight suspicion entered his official mind....Oh! scarcely that, for the photographs distributed broadcast by the police department were too imperfect; they presented an Arsène Lupin so different from the one he had before him, that he could not possibly recognize me by it. But, all the same, he was troubled, confused and ill-at-ease.

"Mon Dieu! nothing stimulates the comprehension so much as the loss of a pocketbook and the desire to recover it. And it seems to me that if you will give me two of your men, we may be able...."

"Oh! I beg of you, monsieur le commissaire," cried Madame Renaud, "listen to Mon. Berlat."

The intervention of my excellent friend was decisive. Pronounced by her, the wife of an influential official, the name of Berlat became really my own, and gave me an identity that no mere suspicion could affect. The commissary arose, and said:

"Believe me, Monsieur Berlat, I shall be delighted to see you succeed. I am as much interested as you are in the arrest of Arsène Lupin."

He accompanied me to the automobile, and introduced two of his men, Honoré Massol and Gaston Delivet, who were assigned to assist me. My chauffer cranked up the car and I took my place at the wheel. A few seconds later, we left the station. I was saved.

Ah! I must confess that in rolling over the boulevards that surrounded the old Norman city, in my swift thirty-five horse-power Moreau-Lepton, I experienced a deep feeling of pride, and the motor responded, sympathetically to my desires. At right and left, the trees flew past us with startling rapidity, and I, free, out of danger, had simply to arrange my little personal affairs with the two honest representatives of the Rouen police who were sitting behind me. Arsène Lupin was going in search of Arsène Lupin!

Modest guardians of social order—Gaston Delivet and Honoré Massol— how valuable was your assistance! What would I have done without you? Without you, many times, at the cross-roads, I might have taken the wrong route! Without you, Arsène Lupin would have made a mistake, and the other would have escaped!

But the end was not yet. Far from it. I had yet to capture the thief and recover the stolen papers. Under no circumstances must my two acolytes be permitted to see those papers, much less to seize them. That was a point that might give me some difficulty.

We arrived at Darnétal three minutes after the departure of the train. True, I had the consolation of learning that a man wearing a gray overcoat with a black velvet collar had taken the train at the station. He had bought a second-class ticket for Amiens. Certainly, my début as detective was a promising one.

Delivet said to me:

"The train is express, and the next stop is Montérolier-Buchy in nineteen minutes. If we do not reach there before Arsène Lupin, he can proceed to Amiens, or change for the train going to Clères, and, from that point, reach Dieppe or Paris."

"How far to Montérolier?"

"Twenty-three kilometres."

"Twenty-three kilometres in nineteen minutes....We will be there ahead of him."

We were off again! Never had my faithful Moreau-Repton responded to my impatience with such ardor and regularity. It participated in my anxiety.

It indorsed my determination. It comprehended my animosity against that rascally Arsène Lupin. The knave! The traitor!

"Turn to the right," cried Delivet, "then to the left."

We fairly flew, scarcely touching the ground. The mile-stones looked like little timid beasts that vanished at our approach. Suddenly, at a turn of the road, we saw a vortex of smoke. It was the Northern Express. For a kilometre, it was a struggle, side by side, but an unequal struggle in which the issue was certain. We won the race by twenty lengths.

In three seconds we were on the platform standing before the second-class carriages. The doors were opened, and some passengers alighted, but not my thief. We made a search through the compartments. No sign of Arsène Lupin.

"Sapristi!" I cried, "he must have recognized me in the automobile as we were racing, side by side, and he leaped from the train."

"Ah! there he is now! crossing the track."

I started in pursuit of the man, followed by my two acolytes, or rather followed by one of them, for the other, Massol, proved himself to be a runner of exceptional speed and endurance. In a few moments, he had made an appreciable gain upon the fugitive. The man noticed it, leaped over a hedge, scampered across a meadow, and entered a thick grove. When we reached this grove, Massol was waiting for us. He went no farther, for fear of losing us.

"Quite right, my dear friend," I said. "After such a run, our victim must be out of wind. We will catch him now."

I examined the surroundings with the idea of proceeding alone in the arrest of the fugitive, in order to recover my papers, concerning which the authorities would doubtless ask many disagreeable questions. Then I returned to my companions, and said:

"It is all quite easy. You, Massol, take your place at the left; you, Delivet, at the right. From there, you can observe the entire posterior line of the bush, and he cannot escape without you seeing him, except by that ravine, and I shall watch it. If he does not come out voluntarily, I will enter and drive him out toward one or the other of you. You have simply to wait. Ah! I forgot: in case I need you, a pistol shot."

Massol and Delivet walked away to their respective posts. As soon as they had disappeared, I entered the grove with the greatest precaution so as to be neither seen nor heard. I encountered dense thickets, through which narrow paths had been cut, but the overhanging boughs compelled me to adopt a stooping posture. One of these paths led to a clearing in which I found footsteps upon the wet grass. I followed them; they led me to the foot of a mound which was surmounted by a deserted, dilapidated hovel.

"He must be there," I said to myself. "It is a well-chosen retreat."

I crept cautiously to the side of the building. A slight noise informed me that he was there; and, then, through an opening, I saw him. His back was turned toward me. In two bounds, I was upon him. He tried to fire a revolver that he held in his hand. But he had no time. I threw him to the ground, in such a manner that his arms were beneath him, twisted and helpless, whilst I held him down with my knee on his breast.

"Listen, my boy," I whispered in his ear. "I am Arsène Lupin. You are to deliver over to me, immediately and gracefully, my pocketbook and the lady's jewels, and, in return therefore, I will save you from the police and enroll you amongst my friends. One word: yes or no?"

"Yes," he murmured.

"Very good. Your escape, this morning, was well planned. I congratulate you."

I arose. He fumbled in his pocket, drew out a large knife and tried to strike me with it.

"Imbecile!" I exclaimed.

With one hand, I parried the attack; with the other, I gave him a sharp blow on the carotid artery. He fell—stunned!

In my pocketbook, I recovered my papers and bank-notes. Out of curiosity, I took his. Upon an envelope, addressed to him, I read his name: Pierre Onfrey. It startled me. Pierre Onfrey, the assassin of the rue Lafontaine at Auteuil! Pierre Onfrey, he who had cut the throats of Madame Delbois and her two daughters. I leaned over him. Yes, those were the features which, in the compartment, had evoked in me the memory of a face I could not then recall.

But time was passing. I placed in an envelope two bank-notes of one hundred francs each, with a card bearing these words: "Arsène Lupin to his worthy colleagues Honoré Massol and Gaston Delivet, as a slight token of his gratitude." I placed it in a prominent spot in the room, where they would be sure to find it. Beside it, I placed Madame Renaud's handbag. Why could I not return it to the lady who had befriended me? I must confess that I had taken from it everything that possessed any interest or value, leaving there only a shell comb, a stick of rouge Dorin for the lips, and an empty purse.

But, you know, business is business. And then, really, her husband is engaged in such a dishonorable vocation!

The man was becoming conscious. What was I to do? I was unable to save him or condemn him. So I took his revolver and fired a shot in the air.

"My two acolytes will come and attend to his case," I said to myself, as I hastened away by the road through the ravine. Twenty minutes later, I was seated in my automobile.

At four o'clock, I telegraphed to my friends at Rouen that an unexpected event would prevent me from making my promised visit. Between ourselves, considering what my friends must now know, my visit is postponed indefinitely. A cruel disillusion for them!

At six o'clock I was in Paris. The evening newspapers informed me that Pierre Onfrey had been captured at last.

Next day,—let us not despise the advantages of judicious advertising,— the `Echo de France' published this sensational item:

"Yesterday, near Buchy, after numerous exciting incidents, Arsène Lupin effected the arrest of Pierre Onfrey. The assassin of the rue Lafontaine had robbed Madame Renaud, wife of the director in the penitentiary service, in a railway carriage on the Paris-Havre line. Arsène Lupin restored to Madame Renaud the hand-bag that contained her jewels, and gave a generous recompense to the two detectives who had assisted him in making that dramatic arrest."

V. THE QUEEN'S NECKLACE

Two or three times each year, on occasions of unusual importance, such as the balls at the Austrian Embassy or the soirées of Lady Billingstone, the Countess de Dreux-Soubise wore upon her white shoulders "The Queen's Necklace."

It was, indeed, the famous necklace, the legendary necklace that Bohmer and Bassenge, court jewelers, had made for Madame Du Barry; the veritable necklace that the Cardinal de Rohan-Soubise intended to give to Marie-Antoinette, Queen of France; and the same that the adventuress Jeanne de Valois, Countess de la Motte, had pulled to pieces one evening in February, 1785, with the aid of her husband and their accomplice, Rétaux de Villette.

To tell the truth, the mounting alone was genuine. Rétaux de Villette had kept it, whilst the Count de la Motte and his wife scattered to the four winds of heaven the beautiful stones so carefully chosen by Bohmer. Later, he sold the mounting to Gaston de Dreux-Soubise, nephew and heir of the Cardinal, who re-purchased the few diamonds that remained in the possession of the English jeweler, Jeffreys; supplemented them with other stones of the same size but of much inferior quality, and thus restored the marvelous necklace to the form in which it had come from the hands of Bohmer and Bassenge.

For nearly a century, the house of Dreux-Soubise had prided itself upon the possession of this historic jewel. Although adverse circumstances had greatly reduced their fortune, they preferred to curtail their household expenses rather than part with this relic of royalty. More particularly, the present count clung to it as a man clings to the home of his ancestors. As a matter of prudence, he had rented a safety-deposit box at the Crédit Lyonnais in which to keep it. He went for it himself on the afternoon of the day on which his wife wished to wear it, and he, himself, carried it back next morning.

On this particular evening, at the reception given at the Palais de Castille, the Countess achieved a remarkable success; and King Christian, in whose honor the fête was given, commented on her grace and beauty. The thousand facets of the diamond sparkled and shone like flames of fire about her shapely neck and shoulders, and it is safe to say that none but she could have borne the weight of such an ornament with so much ease and grace.

This was a double triumph, and the Count de Dreux was highly elated when they returned to their chamber in the old house of the faubourg Saint-Germain. He was proud of his wife, and quite as proud, perhaps, of the necklace that had conferred added luster to his noble house for generations. His wife, also, regarded the necklace with an almost childish vanity, and it was not without regret that she removed it from her shoulders and handed it to her husband who admired it as passionately as if he had never seen it before. Then, having placed it in its case of red leather, stamped with the Cardinal's arms, he passed into an adjoining room which was simply an alcove or cabinet that had been cut off from their chamber, and which could be entered only by means of a door at the foot of their bed. As he had done on previous occasions, he hid it on a high shelf amongst hat-boxes and piles of linen. He closed the door, and retired.

Next morning, he arose about nine o'clock, intending to go to the Crédit Lyonnais before breakfast. He dressed, drank a cup of coffee, and went to the stables to give his orders. The condition of one of the horses worried him. He caused it to be exercised in his presence. Then he returned to his wife, who had not yet left the chamber. Her maid was dressing her hair. When her husband entered, she asked:

"Are you going out?"

"Yes, as far as the bank."

"Of course. That is wise."

He entered the cabinet; but, after a few seconds, and without any sign of astonishment, he asked:

"Did you take it, my dear?"

"What?....No, I have not taken anything."

"You must have moved it."

"Not at all. I have not even opened that door."

He appeared at the door, disconcerted, and stammered, in a scarcely intelligible voice:

"You haven't....It wasn't you?....Then...."

She hastened to his assistance, and, together, they made a thorough search, throwing the boxes to the floor and overturning the piles of linen. Then the count said, quite discouraged:

"It is useless to look any more. I put it here, on this shelf."

"You must be mistaken."

"No, no, it was on this shelf—nowhere else."

They lighted a candle, as the room was quite dark, and then carried out all the linen and other articles that the room contained. And, when the room was emptied, they confessed, in despair, that the famous necklace had disappeared. Without losing time in vain lamentations, the countess notified the commissary of police, Mon. Valorbe, who came at once, and, after hearing their story, inquired of the count:

"Are you sure that no one passed through your chamber during the night?"

"Absolutely sure, as I am a very light sleeper. Besides, the chamber door was bolted, and I remember unbolting it this morning when my wife rang for her maid."

"And there is no other entrance to the cabinet?"

"None."

"No windows?"

"Yes, but it is closed up."

"I will look at it."

Candles were lighted, and Mon. Valorbe observed at once that the lower half of the window was covered by a large press which was, however, so narrow that it did not touch the casement on either side.

"On what does this window open?"

"A small inner court."

"And you have a floor above this?"

"Two; but, on a level with the servant's floor, there is a close grating over the court. That is why this room is so dark."

When the press was moved, they found that the window was fastened, which would not have been the case if anyone had entered that way.

"Unless," said the count, "they went out through our chamber."

"In that case, you would have found the door unbolted."

The commissary considered the situation for a moment, then asked the countess:

"Did any of your servants know that you wore the necklace last evening?"

"Certainly; I didn't conceal the fact. But nobody knew that it was hidden in that cabinet."

"No one?"

"No one.... unless...."

"Be quite sure, madam, as it is a very important point."

She turned to her husband, and said:

"I was thinking of Henriette."

"Henriette? She didn't know where we kept it."

"Are you sure?"

"Who is this woman Henriette?" asked Mon. Valorbe.

"A school-mate, who was disowned by her family for marrying beneath her. After her husband's death, I furnished an apartment in this house for her and her son. She is clever with her needle and has done some work for me."

"What floor is she on?"

"Same as ours.... at the end of the corridor.... and I think.... the window of her kitchen...."

"Opens on this little court, does it not?"

"Yes, just opposite ours."

Mon. Valorbe then asked to see Henriette. They went to her apartment; she was sewing, whilst her son Raoul, about six years old, was sitting beside her, reading. The commissary was surprised to see the wretched apartment that had been provided for the woman. It consisted of one room without a fireplace, and a very small room that served as a kitchen. The commissary proceeded to question her. She appeared to be overwhelmed on learning of the theft. Last evening she had herself dressed the countess and placed the necklace upon her shoulders.

"Good God!" she exclaimed, "it can't be possible!"

"And you have no idea? Not the least suspicion? Is it possible that the thief may have passed through your room?"

She laughed heartily, never supposing that she could be an object of suspicion.

"But I have not left my room. I never go out. And, perhaps, you have not seen?"

She opened the kitchen window, and said:

"See, it is at least three metres to the ledge of the opposite window."

"Who told you that we supposed the theft might have been committed in that way?"

"But.... the necklace was in the cabinet, wasn't it?"

"How do you know that?"

"Why, I have always known that it was kept there at night. It had been mentioned in my presence."

Her face, though still young, bore unmistakable traces of sorrow and resignation. And it now assumed an expression of anxiety as if some danger threatened her. She drew her son toward her. The child took her hand, and kissed it affectionately.

When they were alone again, the count said to the commissary:

"I do not suppose you suspect Henriette. I can answer for her. She is honesty itself."

"I quite agree with you," replied Mon. Valorbe. "At most, I thought there might have been an unconscious complicity. But I confess that even that theory must be abandoned, as it does not help solve the problem now before us."

The commissary of police abandoned the investigation, which was now taken up and completed by the examining judge. He questioned the servants, examined the condition of the bolt, experimented with the opening and closing of the cabinet window, and explored the little court from top to bottom. All was in vain. The bolt was intact. The window could not be opened or closed from the outside.

The inquiries especially concerned Henriette, for, in spite of everything, they always turned in her direction. They made a thorough investigation of her past life, and ascertained that, during the last three years, she had left the house only four times, and her business, on those occasions, was satisfactorily explained. As a matter of fact, she acted as chambermaid and seamstress to the countess, who treated her with great strictness and even severity.

At the end of a week, the examining judge had secured no more definite information than the commissary of police. The judge said:

"Admitting that we know the guilty party, which we do not, we are confronted by the fact that we do not know how the theft was committed. We are brought face to face with two obstacles: a door and a window—both closed and fastened. It is thus a double mystery. How could anyone enter, and, moreover, how could any one escape, leaving behind him a bolted door and a fastened window?"

At the end of four months, the secret opinion of the judge was that the count and countess, being hard pressed for money, which was their normal condition, had sold the Queen's Necklace. He closed the investigation.

The loss of the famous jewel was a severe blow to the Dreux-Soubise. Their credit being no longer propped up by the reserve fund that such a treasure constituted, they found themselves confronted by more exacting creditors and money-lenders. They were obliged to cut down to the quick, to sell or mortgage every article that possessed any commercial value. In brief, it would have been their ruin, if two large legacies from some distant relatives had not saved them.

Their pride also suffered a downfall, as if they had lost a quartering from their escutcheon. And, strange to relate, it was upon her former schoolmate, Henriette, that the countess vented her spleen. Toward her, the countess displayed the most spiteful feelings, and even openly accused her. First, Henriette was relegated to the servants' quarters, and, next day, discharged.

For some time, the count and countess passed an uneventful life. They traveled a great deal. Only one incident of record occurred during that period. Some months after the departure of Henriette, the countess was surprised when she received and read the following letter, signed by Henriette:

"Madame," "I do not know how to thank you; for it was you, was it not, who sent me that? It could not have been anyone else. No one but you knows where I live. If I am wrong, excuse me, and accept my sincere thanks for your past favors...."

What did the letter mean? The present or past favors of the countess consisted principally of injustice and neglect. Why, then, this letter of thanks?

When asked for an explanation, Henriette replied that she had received a letter, through the mails, enclosing two bank-notes of one thousand francs each. The envelope, which she enclosed with her reply, bore the Paris post-mark, and was addressed in a handwriting that was obviously disguised. Now, whence came those two thousand francs? Who had sent them? And why had they sent them?

Henriette received a similar letter and a like sum of money twelve months later. And a third time; and a fourth; and each year for a period of six years, with this difference, that in the fifth and sixth years the sum was doubled. There was another difference: the post-office authorities having seized one of the letters under the pretext that it was not registered, the last two letters were duly sent according to the postal regulations, the first dated from Saint-Germain, the other from Suresnes. The writer signed the first one, "Anquety"; and the other, "Péchard." The addresses that he gave were false.

At the end of six years, Henriette died, and the mystery remained unsolved.

All these events are known to the public. The case was one of those which excite public interest, and it was a strange coincidence that this necklace, which had caused such a great commotion in France at the close of the eighteenth century, should create a similar commotion a century later. But what I am about to relate is known only to the parties directly interested and a few others from whom the count exacted a promise of secrecy. As it is probable that some day or other that promise will be broken, I have no hesitation in rending the veil and thus disclosing the key to the mystery, the explanation of the letter published in the morning papers two days ago; an extraordinary letter which increased, if possible, the mists and shadows that envelope this inscrutable drama.

Five days ago, a number of guests were dining with the Count de Dreux-Soubise. There were several ladies present, including his two nieces and his cousin, and the following gentlemen: the president of Essaville, the deputy Bochas, the chevalier Floriani, whom the count had known in Sicily, and General Marquis de Rouzières, and old club friend.

After the repast, coffee was served by the ladies, who gave the gentlemen permission to smoke their cigarettes, provided they would not desert the salon. The conversation was general, and finally one of the guests chanced to speak of celebrated crimes. And that gave the Marquis de Rouzières, who delighted to tease the count, an opportunity to mention the affair of the Queen's Necklace, a subject that the count detested.

Each one expressed his own opinion of the affair; and, of course, their various theories were not only contradictory but impossible.

"And you, monsieur," said the countess to the chevalier Floriani, "what is your opinion?"

"Oh! I—I have no opinion, madame."

All the guests protested; for the chevalier had just related in an entertaining manner various adventures in which he had participated with his father, a magistrate at Palermo, and which established his judgment and taste in such manners.

"I confess," said he, "I have sometimes succeeded in unraveling mysteries that the cleverest detectives have renounced; yet I do not claim to be Herlock Sholmes. Moreover, I know very little about the affair of the Queen's Necklace."

Everybody now turned to the count, who was thus obliged, quite unwillingly, to narrate all the circumstances connected with the theft. The chevalier listened, reflected, asked a few questions, and said:

"It is very strange.... at first sight, the problem appears to be a very simple one."

The count shrugged his shoulders. The others drew closer to the chevalier, who continued, in a dogmatic tone:

"As a general rule, in order to find the author of a crime or a theft, it is necessary to determine how that crime or theft was committed, or, at least, how it could have been committed. In the present case, nothing is more simple, because we are face to face, not with several theories, but with one positive fact, that is to say: the thief could only enter by the chamber door or the window of the cabinet. Now, a person cannot open a bolted door from the outside. Therefore, he must have entered through the window."

"But it was closed and fastened, and we found it fastened afterward," declared the count.

"In order to do that," continued Floriani, without heeding the interruption, "he had simply to construct a bridge, a plank or a ladder, between the balcony of the kitchen and the ledge of the window, and as the jewel-case——"

"But I repeat that the window was fastened," exclaimed the count, impatiently.

This time, Floriani was obliged to reply. He did so with the greatest tranquility, as if the objection was the most insignificant affair in the world.

"I will admit that it was; but is there not a transom in the upper part of the window?"

"How do you know that?"

"In the first place, that was customary in houses of that date; and, in the second place, without such a transom, the theft cannot be explained."

"Yes, there is one, but it was closed, the same as the window. Consequently, we did not pay attention to it."

"That was a mistake; for, if you had examined it, you would have found that it had been opened."

"But how?"

"I presume that, like all others, it opens by means of a wire with a ring on the lower end."

"Yes, but I do not see——-"

"Now, through a hole in the window, a person could, by the aid of some instrument, let us say a poker with a hook at the end, grip the ring, pull down, and open the transom."

The count laughed and said:

"Excellent! excellent! Your scheme is very cleverly constructed, but you overlook one thing, monsieur, there is no hole in the window."

"There was a hole."

"Nonsense, we would have seen it."

"In order to see it, you must look for it, and no one has looked. The hole is there; it must be there, at the side of the window, in the putty. In a vertical direction, of course."

The count arose. He was greatly excited. He paced up and down the room, two or three times, in a nervous manner; then, approaching Floriani, said:

"Nobody has been in that room since; nothing has been changed."

"Very well, monsieur, you can easily satisfy yourself that my explanation is correct."

"It does not agree with the facts established by the examining judge. You have seen nothing, and yet you contradict all that we have seen and all that we know."

Floriani paid no attention to the count's petulance. He simply smiled and said:

"Mon Dieu, monsieur, I submit my theory; that is all. If I am mistaken, you can easily prove it."

"I will do so at once....I confess that your assurance——"

The count muttered a few more words; then suddenly rushed to the door and passed out. Not a word was uttered in his absence; and this profound silence gave the situation an air of almost tragic importance. Finally, the count returned. He was pale and nervous. He said to his friends, in a trembling voice:

"I beg your pardon.... the revelations of the chevalier were so unexpected....I should never have thought...."

His wife questioned him, eagerly:

"Speak.... what is it?"

He stammered: "The hole is there, at the very spot, at the side of the window——"

He seized the chevalier's arm, and said to him in an imperious tone:

"Now, monsieur, proceed. I admit that you are right so far, but now.... that is not all.... go on.... tell us the rest of it."

Floriani disengaged his arm gently, and, after a moment, continued:

"Well, in my opinion, this is what happened. The thief, knowing that the countess was going to wear the necklace that evening, had prepared his gangway or bridge during your absence. He watched you through the window and saw you hide the necklace. Afterward, he cut the glass and pulled the ring."

"Ah! but the distance was so great that it would be impossible for him to reach the window-fastening through the transom."

"Well, then, if he could not open the window by reaching through the transom, he must have crawled through the transom."

"Impossible; it is too small. No man could crawl through it."

"Then it was not a man," declared Floriani.

"What!"

"If the transom is too small to admit a man, it must have been a child."

"A child!"

"Did you not say that your friend Henriette had a son?"

"Yes; a son named Raoul."

"Then, in all probability, it was Raoul who committed the theft."

"What proof have you of that?"

"What proof! Plenty of it....For instance——"

He stopped, and reflected for a moment, then continued:

"For instance, that gangway or bridge. It is improbable that the child could have brought it in from outside the house and carried it away again without being observed. He must have used something close at hand. In the little room used by Henriette as a kitchen, were there not some shelves against the wall on which she placed her pans and dishes?"

"Two shelves, to the best of my memory."

"Are you sure that those shelves are really fastened to the wooden brackets that support them? For, if they are not, we could be justified in presuming that the child removed them, fastened them together, and thus formed his bridge. Perhaps, also, since there was a stove, we might find the bent poker that he used to open the transom."

Without saying a word, the count left the room; and, this time, those present did not feel the nervous anxiety they had experienced the first time. They were confident that Floriani was right, and no one was surprised when the count returned and declared:

"It was the child. Everything proves it."

"You have seen the shelves and the poker?"

"Yes. The shelves have been unnailed, and the poker is there yet."

But the countess exclaimed:

"You had better say it was his mother. Henriette is the guilty party. She must have compelled her son——"

"No," declared the chevalier, "the mother had nothing to do with it."

"Nonsense! they occupied the same room. The child could not have done it without the mother's knowledge."

"True, they lived in the same room, but all this happened in the adjoining room, during the night, while the mother was asleep."

"And the necklace?" said the count. "It would have been found amongst the child's things."

"Pardon me! He had been out. That morning, on which you found him reading, he had just come from school, and perhaps the commissary of police, instead of wasting his time on the innocent mother, would have been better employed in searching the child's desk amongst his school-books."

"But how do you explain those two thousand francs that Henriette received each year? Are they not evidence of her complicity?"

"If she had been an accomplice, would she have thanked you for that money? And then, was she not closely watched? But the child, being free, could easily go to a neighboring city, negotiate with some dealer and sell him one diamond or two diamonds, as he might wish, upon condition that the money should be sent from Paris, and that proceeding could be repeated from year to year."

An indescribable anxiety oppressed the Dreux-Soubise and their guests. There was something in the tone and attitude of Floriani—something more than the chevalier's assurance which, from the beginning, had so annoyed the count. There was a touch of irony, that seemed rather hostile than sympathetic. But the count affected to laugh, as he said:

"All that is very ingenious and interesting, and I congratulate you upon your vivid imagination."

"No, not at all," replied Floriani, with the utmost gravity, "I imagine nothing. I simply describe the events as they must have occurred."

"But what do you know about them?"

"What you yourself have told me. I picture to myself the life of the mother and child down there in the country; the illness of the mother, the schemes of and inventions of the child sell the precious stones in order to save his mother's life, or, at least, soothe her dying moments. Her illness overcomes her. She dies. Years roll on. The child becomes a man; and then—and now I will give my imagination a free rein—let us suppose that the man feels a desire to return to the home of his childhood, that he does so, and that he meets there certain people who suspect and accuse his mother.... do you realize the sorrow and anguish of such an interview in the very house wherein the original drama was played?"

His words seemed to echo for a few seconds in the ensuing silence, and one could read upon the faces of the Count and Countess de Dreux a bewildered effort to comprehend his meaning and, at the same time, the fear and anguish of such a comprehension. The count spoke at last, and said:

"Who are you, monsieur?"

"I? The chevalier Floriani, whom you met at Palermo, and whom you have been gracious enough to invite to your house on several occasions."

"Then what does this story mean?"

"Oh! nothing at all! It is simply a pastime, so far as I am concerned. I endeavor to depict the pleasure that Henriette's son, if he still lives, would have in telling you that he was the guilty party, and that he did it because his mother was unhappy, as she was on the point of losing the place of a....

servant, by which she lived, and because the child suffered at sight of his mother's sorrow."

He spoke with suppressed emotion, rose partially and inclined toward the countess. There could be no doubt that the chevalier Floriani was Henriette's son. His attitude and words proclaimed it. Besides, was it not his obvious intention and desire to be recognized as such?

The count hesitated. What action would he take against the audacious guest? Ring? Provoke a scandal? Unmask the man who had once robbed him? But that was a long time ago! And who would believe that absurd story about the guilty child? No; better far to accept the situation, and pretend not to comprehend the true meaning of it. So the count, turning to Floriani, exclaimed:

"Your story is very curious, very entertaining; I enjoyed it much. But what do you think has become of this young man, this model son? I hope he has not abandoned the career in which he made such a brilliant début."

"Oh! certainly not."

"After such a début! To steal the Queen's Necklace at six years of age; the celebrated necklace that was coveted by Marie-Antoinette!"

"And to steal it," remarked Floriani, falling in with the count's mood, "without costing him the slightest trouble, without anyone thinking to examine the condition of the window, or to observe that the window-sill was too clean—that window-sill which he had wiped in order to efface the marks he had made in the thick dust. We must admit that it was sufficient to turn the head of a boy at that age. It was all so easy. He had simply to desire the thing, and reach out his hand to get it."

"And he reached out his hand."

"Both hands," replied the chevalier, laughing.

His companions received a shock. What mystery surrounded the life of the so-called Floriani? How wonderful must have been the life of that adventurer, a thief at six years of age, and who, to-day, in search of excitement or, at most, to gratify a feeling of resentment, had come to brave his victim in her own house, audaciously, foolishly, and yet with all the grace and delicacy of a courteous guest!

He arose and approached the countess to bid her adieu. She recoiled, unconsciously. He smiled.

"Oh! Madame, you are afraid of me! Did I pursue my role of parlor-magician a step too far?"

She controlled herself, and replied, with her accustomed ease:

"Not at all, monsieur. The legend of that dutiful son interested me very much, and I am pleased to know that my necklace had such a brilliant destiny. But do you not think that the son of that woman, that Henriette, was the victim of hereditary influence in the choice of his vocation?"

He shuddered, feeling the point, and replied:

"I am sure of it; and, moreover, his natural tendency to crime must have been very strong or he would have been discouraged."

"Why so?"

"Because, as you must know, the majority of the diamonds were false. The only genuine stones were the few purchased from the English jeweler, the others having been sold, one by one, to meet the cruel necessities of life."

"It was still the Queen's Necklace, monsieur," replied the countess, haughtily, "and that is something that he, Henriette's son, could not appreciate."

"He was able to appreciate, madame, that, whether true or false, the necklace was nothing more that an object of parade, an emblem of senseless pride."

The count made a threatening gesture, but his wife stopped him.

"Monsieur," she said, "if the man to whom you allude has the slightest sense of honor——"

She stopped, intimidated by Floriani's cool manner.

"If that man has the slightest sense of honor," he repeated.

She felt that she would not gain anything by speaking to him in that manner, and in spite of her anger and indignation, trembling as she was from humiliated pride, she said to him, almost politely:

"Monsieur, the legend says that Rétaux de Villette, when in possession of the Queen's Necklace, did not disfigure the mounting. He understood that the diamonds were simply the ornament, the accessory, and that the mounting was the essential work, the creation of the artist, and he respected it accordingly. Do you think that this man had the same feeling?"

"I have no doubt that the mounting still exists. The child respected it."

"Well, monsieur, if you should happen to meet him, will you tell him that he unjustly keeps possession of a relic that is the property and pride of a certain family, and that, although the stones have been removed, the Queen's necklace still belongs to the house of Dreux-Soubise. It belongs to us as much as our name or our honor."

The chevalier replied, simply:

"I shall tell him, madame."

He bowed to her, saluted the count and the other guests, and departed.

Four days later, the countess de Dreux found upon the table in her chamber a red leather case bearing the cardinal's arms. She opened it, and found the Queen's Necklace.

But as all things must, in the life of a man who strives for unity and logic, converge toward the same goal—and as a little advertising never does any harm—on the following day, the `Echo de France' published these sensational lines:

"The Queen's Necklace, the famous historical jewelry stolen from the family of Dreux-Soubise, has been recovered by Arsène Lupin, who hastened to restore it to its rightful owner. We cannot too highly commend such a delicate and chivalrous act."

VI. THE SEVEN OF HEARTS

I am frequently asked this question: "How did you make the acquaintance of Arsène Lupin?"

My connection with Arsène Lupin was well known. The details that I gather concerning that mysterious man, the irrefutable facts that I present, the new evidence that I produce, the interpretation that I place on certain acts of which the public has seen only the exterior manifestations without being able to discover the secret reasons or the invisible mechanism, all establish, if not an intimacy, at least amicable relations and regular confidences.

But how did I make his acquaintance? Why was I selected to be his historiographer? Why I, and not some one else?

The answer is simple: chance alone presided over my choice; my merit was not considered. It was chance that put me in his way. It was by chance that I was participant in one of his strangest and most mysterious adventures; and by chance that I was an actor in a drama of which he was the marvelous stage director; an obscure and intricate drama, bristling with such thrilling events that I feel a certain embarrassment in undertaking to describe it.

The first act takes place during that memorable night of 22 June, of which so much has already been said. And, for my part, I attribute the anomalous conduct of which I was guilty on that occasion to the unusual frame of mind in which I found myself on my return home. I had dined with some friends at the Cascade restaurant, and, the entire evening, whilst we smoked and the orchestra played melancholy waltzes, we talked only of crimes and thefts, and dark and frightful intrigues. That is always a poor overture to a night's sleep.

The Saint-Martins went away in an automobile. Jean Daspry—that delightful, heedless Daspry who, six months later, was killed in such a tragic manner on the frontier of Morocco—Jean Daspry and I returned on foot through the dark, warm night. When we arrived in front of the little house in which I had lived for a year at Neuilly, on the boulevard Maillot, he said to me:

"Are you afraid?"

"What an idea!"

"But this house is so isolated.... no neighbors.... vacant lots....Really, I am not a coward, and yet——"

"Well, you are very cheering, I must say."

"Oh! I say that as I would say anything else. The Saint-Martins have impressed me with their stories of brigands and thieves."

We shook hands and said good-night. I took out my key and opened the door.

"Well, that is good," I murmured, "Antoine has forgotten to light a candle."

Then I recalled the fact that Antoine was away; I had given him a short leave of absence. Forthwith, I was disagreeably oppressed by the darkness and silence of the night. I ascended the stairs on tiptoe, and reached my room as quickly as possible; then, contrary to my usual habit, I turned the key and pushed the bolt.

The light of my candle restored my courage. Yet I was careful to take my revolver from its case—a large, powerful weapon—and place it beside my bed. That precaution completed my reassurance. I laid down and, as usual, took a book from my night-table to read myself to sleep. Then I received a great surprise. Instead of the paper-knife with which I had marked my place on the preceding, I found an envelope, closed with five seals of red wax. I seized it eagerly. It was addressed to me, and marked: "Urgent."

A letter! A letter addressed to me! Who could have put it in that place? Nervously, I tore open the envelope, and read:

"From the moment you open this letter, whatever happens, whatever you may hear, do not move, do not utter one cry. Otherwise you are doomed."

I am not a coward, and, quite as well as another, I can face real danger, or smile at the visionary perils of imagination. But, let me repeat, I was in an anomalous condition of mind, with my nerves set on edge by the events of the evening. Besides, was there not, in my present situation, somet startling and mysterious, calculated to disturb the most courageous spirit?

My feverish fingers clutched the sheet of paper, and I read and re-read those threatening words: "Do not move, do not utter one cry. Otherwise, you are doomed."

"Nonsense!" I thought. "It is a joke; the work of some cheerful idiot."

I was about to laugh—a good loud laugh. Who prevented me? What haunting fear compressed my throat?

At least, I would blow out the candle. No, I could not do it. "Do not move, or you are doomed," were the words he had written.

These auto-suggestions are frequently more imperious than the most positive realities; but why should I struggle against them? I had simply to close my eyes. I did so.

At that moment, I heard a slight noise, followed by crackling sounds, proceeding from a large room used by me as a library. A small room or antechamber was situated between the library and my bedchamber.

The approach of an actual danger greatly excited me, and I felt a desire to get up, seize my revolver, and rush into the library. I did not rise; I saw one of the curtains of the left window move. There was no doubt about it: the curtain had moved. It was still moving. And I saw—oh! I saw quite distinctly—in the narrow space between the curtains and the window, a human form; a bulky mass that prevented the curtains from hanging straight. And it is equally certain that the man saw me through the large meshes of the curtain. Then, I understood the situation. His mission was to guard me while the others carried away their booty. Should I rise and seize my revolver? Impossible! He was there! At the least movement, at the least cry, I was doomed.

Then came a terrific noise that shook the house; this was followed by lighter sounds, two or three together, like those of a hammer that rebounded. At least, that was the impression formed in my confused brain. These were mingled with other sounds, thus creating a veritable uproar which proved that the intruders were not only bold, but felt themselves secure from interruption.

They were right. I did not move. Was it cowardice? No, rather weakness, a total inability to move any portion of my body, combined with discretion; for why should I struggle? Behind that man, there were ten others who would come to his assistance. Should I risk my life to save a few tapestries and bibelots?

...out the night, my torture endured. Insufferable torture, terrible ... ... noises had stopped, but I was in constant fear of their renewal. ... ...! The man who was guarding me, weapon in hand. My fearful ... ...d cast in his direction. And my heart beat! And a profuse perspiration oozed from every pore of my body!

Suddenly, I experienced an immense relief; a milk-wagon, whose sound was familiar to me, passed along the boulevard; and, at the same time, I had an impression that the light of a new day was trying to steal through the closed window-blinds.

At last, daylight penetrated the room; other vehicles passed along the boulevard; and all the phantoms of the night vanished. Then I put one arm out of the bed, slowly and cautiously. My eyes were fixed upon the curtain, locating the exact spot at which I must fire; I made an exact calculation of the movements I must make; then, quickly, I seized my revolver and fired.

I leaped from my bed with a cry of deliverance, and rushed to the window. The bullet had passed through the curtain and the window-glass, but it had not touched the man—for the very good reason that there was none there. Nobody! Thus, during the entire night, I had been hypnotized by a fold of the curtain. And, during that time, the malefactors....Furiously, with an enthusiasm that nothing could have stopped, I turned the key, opened the door, crossed the antechamber, opened another door, and rushed into the library. But amazement stopped me on the threshold, panting, astounded, more astonished than I had been by the absence of the man. All the things that I supposed had been stolen, furniture, books, pictures, old tapestries, everything was in its proper place.

It was incredible. I could not believe my eyes. Notwithstanding that uproar, those noises of removal....I made a tour, I inspected the walls, I made a mental inventory of all the familiar objects. Nothing was missing. And, what was more disconcerting, there was no clue to the intruders, not a sign, not a chair disturbed, not the trace of a footstep.

"Well! Well!" I said to myself, pressing my hands on my bewildered head, "surely I am not crazy! I hear something!"

Inch by inch, I made a careful examination of the room. It was in vain. Unless I could consider this as a discovery: Under a small Persian rug, I found a card—an ordinary playing card. It was the seven of hearts; it was like any other seven of hearts in French playing-cards, with this slight but curious exception: The extreme point of each of the seven red spots or hearts was pierced by a hole, round and regular as if made with the point of an awl.

Nothing more. A card and a letter found in a book. But was not that sufficient to affirm that I had not been the plaything of a dream?

Throughout the day, I continued my searches in the library. It was a large room, much too large for the requirements of such a house, and the decoration of which attested the bizarre taste of its founder. The floor was a mosaic of multicolored stones, formed into large symmetrical designs. The walls were covered with a similar mosaic, arranged in panels, Pompeiian allegories, Byzantine compositions, frescoes of the Middle Ages. A Bacchus bestriding a cask. An emperor wearing a gold crown, a flowing beard, and holding a sword in his right hand.

Quite high, after the style of an artist's studio, there was a large window—the only one in the room. That window being always open at night, it was probable that the men had entered through it, by the aid of a ladder. But, again, there was no evidence. The bottom of the ladder would have left some marks in the soft earth beneath the window; but there were none. Nor were there any traces of footsteps in any part of the yard.

I had no idea of informing the police, because the facts I had before me were so absurd and inconsistent. They would laugh at me. However, as I was then a reporter on the staff of the `Gil Blas,' I wrote a lengthy account of my adventure and it was published in the paper on the second day thereafter. The article attracted some attention, but no one took it seriously. They regarded it as a work of fiction rather than a story of real life. The Saint-Martins rallied me. But Daspry, who took an interest in such matters, came to see me, made a study of the affair, but reached no conclusion.

A few mornings later, the door-bell rang, and Antoine came to inform me that a gentleman desired to see me. He would not give his name. I directed Antoine to show him up. He was a man of about forty years of age with a very dark complexion, lively features, and whose correct dress, slightly frayed, proclaimed a taste that contrasted strangely with his rather vulgar manners. Without any preamble, he said to me—in a rough voice that confirmed my suspicion as to his social position:

"Monsieur, whilst in a café, I picked up a copy of the `Gil Blas,' and read your article. It interested me very much.

"Thank you."

"And here I am."

"Ah!"

"Yes, to talk to you. Are all the facts related by you quite correct?"

"Absolutely so."

"Well, in that case, I can, perhaps, give you some information."

"Very well; proceed."

"No, not yet. First, I must be sure that the facts are exactly as you have related them."

"I have given you my word. What further proof do you want?"

"I must remain alone in this room."

"I do not understand," I said, with surprise.

"It's an idea that occurred to me when reading your article. Certain details established an extraordinary coincidence with another case that came under my notice. If I am mistaken, I shall say nothing more. And the only means of ascertaining the truth is by my remaining in the room alone."

What was at the bottom of this proposition? Later, I recalled that the man was exceedingly nervous; but, at the same time, although somewhat astonished, I found nothing particularly abnormal about the man or the request he had made. Moreover, my curiosity was aroused; so I replied:

"Very well. How much time do you require?"

"Oh! three minutes—not longer. Three minutes from now, I will rejoin you."

I left the room, and went downstairs. I took out my watch. One minute passed. Two minutes. Why did I feel so depressed? Why did those moments seem so solemn and weird? Two minutes and a half....Two minutes and three quarters. Then I heard a pistol shot.

I bounded up the stairs and entered the room. A cry of horror escaped me. In the middle of the room, the man was lying on his left side, motionless. Blood was flowing from a wound in his forehead. Near his hand was a revolver, still smoking.

But, in addition to this frightful spectacle, my attention was attracted by another object. At two feet from the body, upon the floor, I saw a playing-card. It was the seven of hearts. I picked it up. The lower extremity of each of the seven spots was pierced with a small round hole.

A half-hour later, the commissary of police arrived, then the coroner and the chief of the Sûreté, Mon. Dudouis. I had been careful not to touch the corpse. The preliminary inquiry was very brief, and disclosed nothing. There were no papers in the pockets of the deceased; no name upon his clothes; no initial upon his linen; nothing to give any clue to his identity. The room was in the same perfect order as before. The furniture had not been disturbed. Yet this man had not come to my house solely for the purpose of killing himself, or because he considered my place the most convenient one for his suicide! There must have been a motive for his act of despair, and that motive was, no doubt, the result of some new fact ascertained by him during the three minutes he was alone.

What was that fact? What had he seen? What frightful secret had been revealed to him? There was no answer to these questions. But, at the last moment, an incident occurred that appeared to us of considerable importance. As two policemen were raising the body to place it on a stretcher, the left hand thus being disturbed, a crumpled card fell from it. The card bore these words: "Georges Andermatt, 37 Rue de Berry."

What did that mean? Georges Andermatt was a rich banker in Paris, the founder and president of the Metal Exchange which had given such an impulse to the metallic industries in France. He lived in princely style; was the possessor of numerous automobiles, coaches, and an expensive racing-stable. His social affairs were very select, and Madame Andermatt was noted for her grace and beauty.

"Can that be the man's name?" I asked. ————————————-

The chief of the Sûreté leaned over him.

"It is not he. Mon. Andermatt is a thin man, and slightly grey."

"But why this card?"

"Have you a telephone, monsieur?"

"Yes, in the vestibule. Come with me."

He looked in the directory, and then asked for number 415.21.

"Is Mon. Andermatt at home?....Please tell him that Mon. Dudouis wished him to come at once to 102 Boulevard Maillot. Very important."

Twenty minutes later, Mon. Andermatt arrived in his automobile. After the circumstances had been explained to him, he was taken in to see the corpse. He displayed considerable emotion, and spoke, in a low tone, and apparently unwillingly:

"Etienne Varin," he said.

"You know him?"

"No.... or, at least, yes.... by sight only. His brother...."

"Ah! he has a brother?"

"Yes, Alfred Varin. He came to see me once on some matter of business....I forget what it was."

"Where does he live?"

"The two brothers live together—rue de Provence, I think."

"Do you know any reason why he should commit suicide?"

"None."

"He held a card in his hand. It was your card with your address."

"I do not understand that. It must have been there by some chance that will be disclosed by the investigation."

A very strange chance, I thought; and I felt that the others entertained the same impression.

I discovered the same impression in the papers next day, and amongst all my friends with whom I discussed the affair. Amid the mysteries that enveloped it, after the double discovery of the seven of hearts pierced with seven holes, after the two inscrutable events that had happened in my house, that visiting card promised to throw some light on the affair. Through it, the truth may be revealed. But, contrary to our expectations, Mon. Andermatt furnished no explanation. He said:

"I have told you all I know. What more can I do? I am greatly surprised that my card should be found in such a place, and I sincerely hope the point will be cleared up."

It was not. The official investigation established that the Varin brothers were of Swiss origin, had led a shifting life under various names, frequenting gambling resorts, associating with a band of foreigners who had been dispersed by the police after a series of robberies in which their participation was established only by their flight. At number 24 rue de Provence, where the Varin brothers had lived six years before, no one knew what had become of them.

I confess that, for my part, the case seemed to me so complicated and so mysterious that I did not think the problem would ever be solved, so I concluded to waste no more time upon it. But Jean Daspry, whom I frequently met at that period, became more and more interested in it each day. It was he who pointed out to me that item from a foreign newspaper which was reproduced and commented upon by the entire press. It was as follows:

"The first trial of a new model of submarine boat, which is expected to revolutionize naval warfare, will be given in presence of the former Emperor at a place that will be kept secret until the last minute. An indiscretion has revealed its name; it is called 'The Seven-of-Hearts.'"

The Seven-of-Hearts! That presented a new problem. Could a connection be established between the name of the sub-marine and the incidents which we have related? But a connection of what nature? What had happened here could have no possible relation with the sub-marine.

"What do you know about it?" said Daspry to me. "The most diverse effects often proceed from the same cause."

Two days later, the following foreign news item was received and published:

"It is said that the plans of the new sub-marine `Seven-of-Hearts' were prepared by French engineers, who, having sought, in vain, the support of their compatriots, subsequently entered into negotiations with the British Admiralty, without success."

I do not wish to give undue publicity to certain delicate matters which once provoked considerable excitement. Yet, since all danger of injury therefrom has now come to an end, I must speak of the article that appeared in the `Echo de France,' which aroused so much comment at that time, and which threw considerable light upon the mystery of the Seven-of-Hearts. This is the article as it was published over the signature of Salvator:

"THE AFFAIR OF THE SEVEN-OF-HEARTS. "A CORNER OF THE VEIL RAISED.

"We will be brief. Ten years ago, a young mining engineer, Louis Lacombe, wishing to devote his time and fortune to certain studies, resigned his position he then held, and rented number 102 boulevard Maillot, a small house that had been recently built and decorated for an Italian count. Through the agency of the Varin brothers of Lausanne, one of whom assisted in the preliminary experiments and the other acted as financial agent, the young engineer was introduced to Georges Andermatt, the founder of the Metal Exchange.

"After several interviews, he succeeded in interesting the banker in a sub-marine boat on which he was working, and it was agreed that as soon as the invention was perfected, Mon. Andermatt would use his influence with the Minister of Marine to obtain a series of trials under the direction of the government. For two years, Louis Lacombe was a frequent visitor at Andermatt's house, and he submitted to the banker the various improvements he made upon his original plans, until one day, being satisfied with the perfection of his work, he asked Mon. Andermatt to communicate with the Minister of Marine.

That day, Louis Lacombe dined at Mon. Andermatt's house. He left there about half-past eleven at night. He has not been seen since. "A perusal of the newspapers of that date will show that the young man's family caused every possible inquiry to be made, but without success; and it was the general opinion that Louis Lacombe— who was known as an original and visionary youth—had quietly left for parts unknown. "Let us accept that theory—improbable, though it be,—and let us consider another question, which is a most important one for our country: What has become of the plans of the sub-marine? Did Louis Lacombe carry them away? Are they destroyed? "After making a thorough investigation, we are able to assert, positively, that the plans are in existence, and are now in the possession of the two brothers Varin.

How did they acquire such a possession? That is a question not yet determined; nor do we know why they have not tried to sell them at an earlier date. Did they fear that their title to them would be called in question? If so, they have lost that fear, and we can announce definitely, that the plans of Louis Lacombe are now the property of foreign power, and we are in a position to publish the correspondence that passed between the Varin brothers and the representative of that power. The `Seven-of-Hearts' invented by Louis Lacombe has been actually constructed by our neighbor. "Will the invention fulfill the optimistic expectations of those who were concerned in that treacherous act?"

And a post-script adds:

"Later.—Our special correspondent informs us that the preliminary trial of the `Seven-of-Hearts' has not been satisfactory. It is quite likely that the plans sold and delivered by the Varin brothers did not include the final document carried by Louis Lacombe to Mon. Andermatt on the day of his disappearance, a document that was indispensable to a thorough understanding of the invention. It contained a summary of the final conclusions of the inventor, and estimates and figures not contained in the other papers.

Without this document, the plans are incomplete; on the other hand, without the plans, the document is worthless. "Now is the time to act and recover what belongs to us. It may be a difficult matter, but we rely upon the assistance of Mon. Andermatt.

It will be to his interest to explain his conduct which has hitherto been so strange and inscrutable. He will explain not only why he concealed these facts at the time of the suicide of Etienne Varin, but also why he has never revealed the disappearance of the paper—a fact well known to him.

He will tell why, during the last six years, he paid spies to watch the movements of the Varin brothers. We expect from him, not only words, but acts. And at once. Otherwise—-"

The threat was plainly expressed. But of what did it consist? What whip was Salvator, the anonymous writer of the article, holding over the head of Mon. Andermatt?

An army of reporters attacked the banker, and ten interviewers announced the scornful manner in which they were treated. Thereupon, the `Echo de France' announced its position in these words:

"Whether Mon. Andermatt is willing or not, he will be, henceforth, our collaborator in the work we have undertaken."

Daspry and I were dining together on the day on which that announcement appeared. That evening, with the newspapers spread over my table, we discussed the affair and examined it from every point of view with that exasperation that a person feels when walking in the dark and finding himself constantly falling over the same obstacles. Suddenly, without any warning whatsoever, the door opened and a lady entered. Her face was hidden behind a thick veil. I rose at once and approached her.

"Is it you, monsieur, who lives here?" she asked.

"Yes, madame, but I do not understand——"

"The gate was not locked," she explained.

"But the vestibule door?"

She did not reply, and it occurred to me that she had used the servants' entrance. How did she know the way? Then there was a silence that was quite embarrassing. She looked at Daspry, and I was obliged to introduce him. I asked her to be seated and explain the object of her visit. She raised her veil, and I saw that she was a brunette with regular features and, though not handsome, she was attractive—principally, on account of her sad, dark eyes.

"I am Madame Andermatt," she said.

"Madame Andermatt!" I repeated, with astonishment.

After a brief pause, she continued with a voice and manner that were quite easy and natural:

"I have come to see you about that affair—you know. I thought I might be able to obtain some information——"

"Mon Dieu, madame, I know nothing but what has already appeared in the papers. But if you will point out in what way I can help you...."

"I do not know....I do not know."

Not until then did I suspect that her calm demeanor was assumed, and that some poignant grief was concealed beneath that air of tranquility. For a moment, we were silent and embarrassed. Then Daspry stepped forward, and said:

"Will you permit me to ask you a few questions?"

"Yes, yes," she cried. "I will answer."

"You will answer.... whatever those questions may be?"

"Yes."

"Did you know Louis Lacombe?" he asked.

"Yes, through my husband."

"When did you see him for the last time?"

"The evening he dined with us."

"At that time, was there anything to lead you to believe that you would never see him again?"

"No. But he had spoken of a trip to Russia—in a vague way."

"Then you expected to see him again?"

"Yes. He was to dine with us, two days later."

"How do you explain his disappearance?"

"I cannot explain it."

"And Mon. Andermatt?"

"I do not know."

"Yet the article published in the `Echo de France' indicates——"

"Yes, that the Varin brothers had something to do with his disappearance."

"Is that your opinion?"

"Yes."

"On what do you base your opinion?"

"When he left our house, Louis Lacombe carried a satchel containing all the papers relating to his invention. Two days later, my husband, in a conversation with one of the Varin brothers, learned that the papers were in their possession."

"And he did not denounce them?"

"No."

"Why not?"

"Because there was something else in the satchel—something besides the papers of Louis Lacombe."

"What was it?"

She hesitated; was on the point of speaking, but, finally, remained silent. Daspry continued:

"I presume that is why your husband has kept a close watch over their movements instead of informing the police. He hoped to recover the papers and, at the same time, that compromising article which has enabled the two brothers to hold over him threats of exposure and blackmail."

"Over him, and over me."

"Ah! over you, also?"

"Over me, in particular."

She uttered the last words in a hollow voice. Daspry observed it; he paced to and fro for a moment, then, turning to her, asked:

"Had you written to Louis Lacombe?"

"Of course. My husband had business with him—"

"Apart from those business letters, had you written to Louis Lacombe.... other letters? Excuse my insistence, but it is absolutely necessary that I should know the truth. Did you write other letters?"

"Yes," she replied, blushing.

"And those letters came into the possession of the Varin brothers?"

"Yes."

"Does Mon. Andermatt know it?"

"He has not seen them, but Alfred Varin has told him of their existence and threatened to publish them if my husband should take any steps against him. My husband was afraid.... of a scandal."

"But he has tried to recover the letters?"

"I think so; but I do not know. You see, after that last interview with Alfred Varin, and after some harsh words between me and my husband in which he called me to account—we live as strangers."

"In that case, as you have nothing to lose, what do you fear?"

"I may be indifferent to him now, but I am the woman that he has loved, the one he would still love—oh! I am quite sure of that," she murmured, in a fervent voice, "he would still love me if he had not got hold of those cursed letters——"

"What! Did he succeed?....But the two brothers still defied him?"

"Yes, and they boasted of having a secure hiding-place."

"Well?"

"I believe my husband discovered that hiding-place."

"Well?"

"I believe my husband has discovered that hiding-place."

"Ah! where was it?"

"Here."

"Here!" I cried in alarm.

"Yes. I always had that suspicion. Louis Lacombe was very ingenious and amused himself in his leisure hours, by making safes and locks. No doubt, the Varin brothers were aware of that fact and utilized one of Lacombe's safes in which to conceal the letters.... and other things, perhaps."

"But they did not live here," I said.

"Before you came, four months ago, the house had been vacant for some time. And they may have thought that your presence here would not interfere with them when they wanted to get the papers. But they did not count on my husband, who came here on the night of 22 June, forced the safe, took what he was seeking, and left his card to inform the two brothers that he feared them no more, and that their positions were now reversed. Two days later, after reading the article in the `Gil Blas,' Etienne Varin came here, remained alone in this room, found the safe empty, and.... killed himself."

After a moment, Daspry said:

"A very simple theory....Has Mon. Andermatt spoken to you since then?"

"No."

"Has his attitude toward you changed in any way? Does he appear more gloomy, more anxious?"

"No, I haven't noticed any change."

"And yet you think he has secured the letters. Now, in my opinion, he has not got those letters, and it was not he who came here on the night of 22 June."

"Who was it, then?"

"The mysterious individual who is managing this affair, who holds all the threads in his hands, and whose invisible but far-reaching power we have felt from the beginning. It was he and his friends who entered this house on 22 June; it was he who discovered the hiding-place of the papers; it was he who left Mon. Andermatt's card; it is he who now holds the correspondence and the evidence of the treachery of the Varin brothers."

"Who is he?" I asked, impatiently.

"The man who writes letters to the `Echo de France'.... Salvator! Have we not convincing evidence of that fact? Does he not mention in his letters certain details that no one could know, except the man who had thus discovered the secrets of the two brothers?"

"Well, then," stammered Madame Andermatt, in great alarm, "he has my letters also, and it is he who now threatens my husband. Mon Dieu! What am I to do?"

"Write to him," declared Daspry. "Confide in him without reserve. Tell him all you know and all you may hereafter learn. Your interest and his interest are the same. He is not working against Mon. Andermatt, but against Alfred Varin. Help him."

"How?"

"Has your husband the document that completes the plans of Louis Lacombe?"

"Yes."

"Tell that to Salvator, and, if possible, procure the document for him. Write to him at once. You risk nothing."

The advice was bold, dangerous even at first sight, but Madame Andermatt had no choice. Besides, as Daspry had said, she ran no risk. If the unknown writer were an enemy, that step would not aggravate the situation. If he were a stranger seeking to accomplish a particular purpose, he would attach to those letters only a secondary importance. Whatever might happen, it was the only solution offered to her, and she, in her anxiety, was only too glad to act on it. She thanked us effusively, and promised to keep us informed.

In fact, two days later, she sent us the following letter that she had received from Salvator:

"Have not found the letters, but I will get them. Rest easy. I am watching everything. S."

I looked at the letter. It was in the same handwriting as the note I found in my book on the night of 22 June.

Daspry was right. Salvator was, indeed, the originator of that affair.

We were beginning to see a little light coming out of the darkness that surrounded us, and an unexpected light was thrown on certain points; but other points yet remained obscure—for instance, the finding of the two seven-of-hearts. Perhaps I was unnecessarily concerned about those two cards whose seven punctured spots had appeared to me under such startling circumstances! Yet I could not refrain from asking myself: What role will they play in the drama? What importance do they bear? What conclusion must be drawn from the fact that the submarine constructed from the plans of Louis Lacombe bore the name of `Seven-of-Hearts'?

Daspry gave little thought to the other two cards; he devoted all his attention to another problem which he considered more urgent; he was seeking the famous hiding-place.

"And who knows," said he, "I may find the letters that Salvator did not find—by inadvertence, perhaps. It is improbable that the Varin brothers would have removed from a spot, which they deemed inaccessible, the weapon which was so valuable to them."

And he continued to search. In a short time, the large room held no more secrets for him, so he extended his investigations to the other rooms. He examined the interior and the exterior, the stones of the foundation, the bricks in the walls; he raised the slates of the roof.

One day, he came with a pickaxe and a spade, gave me the spade, kept the pickaxe, pointed to the adjacent vacant lots, and said: "Come."

I followed him, but I lacked his enthusiasm. He divided the vacant land into several sections which he examined in turn. At last, in a corner, at the angle formed by the walls of two neighboring proprietors, a small pile of earth and gravel, covered with briers and grass, attracted his attention. He attacked it. I was obliged to help him. For an hour, under a hot sun, we labored without success. I was discouraged, but Daspry urged me on. His ardor was as strong as ever.

At last, Daspry's pickaxe unearthed some bones—the remains of a skeleton to which some scraps of clothing still hung. Suddenly, I turned pale. I had discovered, sticking in the earth, a small piece of iron cut in the form of a rectangle, on which I thought I could see red spots. I stooped and picked it up. That little iron plate was the exact size of a playing-card, and the red spots, made with red lead, were arranged upon it in a manner similar to the seven-of-hearts, and each spot was pierced with a round hole similar to the perforations in the two playing cards.

"Listen, Daspry, I have had enough of this. You can stay if it interests you. But I am going."

Was that simply the expression of my excited nerves? Or was it the result of a laborious task executed under a burning sun? I know that I trembled as I walked away, and that I went to bed, where I remained forty-eight hours, restless and feverish, haunted by skeletons that danced around me and threw their bleeding hearts at my head.

Daspry was faithful to me. He came to my house every day, and remained three or four hours, which he spent in the large room, ferreting, thumping, tapping.

"The letters are here, in this room," he said, from time to time, "they are here. I will stake my life on it."

On the morning of the third day I arose—feeble yet, but cured. A substantial breakfast cheered me up. But a letter that I received that afternoon contributed, more than anything else, to my complete recovery, and aroused in me a lively curiosity. This was the letter:

"Monsieur,

"The drama, the first act of which transpired on the night of 22 June, is now drawing to a close.

Force of circumstances compel me to bring the two principal actors in that drama face to face, and I wish that meeting to take place in your house, if you will be so kind as to give me the use of it for this evening from nine o'clock to eleven. It will be advisable to give your servant leave of absence for the evening, and, perhaps, you will be so kind as to leave the field open to the two adversaries.

You will remember that when I visited your house on the night of 22 June, I took excellent care of your property. I feel that I would do you an injustice if I should doubt, for one moment, your absolute discretion in this affair.

Your devoted,

"SALVATOR."

I was amused at the facetious tone of his letter and also at the whimsical nature of his request. There was a charming display of confidence and candor in his language, and nothing in the world could have induced me to deceive him or repay his confidence with ingratitude.

I gave my servant a theatre ticket, and he left the house at eight o'clock. A few minutes later, Daspry arrived. I showed him the letter.

"Well?" said he.

"Well, I have left the garden gate unlocked, so anyone can enter."

"And you—are you going away?"

"Not at all. I intend to stay right here."

"But he asks you to go——"

"But I am not going. I will be discreet, but I am resolved to see what takes place."

"Ma foi!" exclaimed Daspry, laughing, "you are right, and I shall stay with you. I shouldn't like to miss it."

We were interrupted by the sound of the door-bell.

"Here already?" said Daspry, "twenty minutes ahead of time! Incredible!"

I went to the door and ushered in the visitor. It was Madame Andermatt. She was faint and nervous, and in a stammering voice, she ejaculated:

"My husband.... is coming.... he has an appointment.... they intend to give him the letters...."

"How do you know?" I asked.

"By chance. A message came for my husband while we were at dinner. The servant gave it to me by mistake. My husband grabbed it quickly, but he was too late. I had read it."

"You read it?"

"Yes. It was something like this: `At nine o'clock this evening, be at Boulevard Maillot with the papers connected with the affair. In exchange, the letters.' So, after dinner, I hastened here."

"Unknown to your husband?"

"Yes."

"What do you think about it?" asked Daspry, turning to me.

"I think as you do, that Mon. Andermatt is one of the invited guests."

"Yes, but for what purpose?"

"That is what we are going to find out."

I led the men to a large room. The three of us could hide comfortably behind the velvet chimney-mantle, and observe all that should happen in the room. We seated ourselves there, with Madame Andermatt in the centre.

The clock struck nine. A few minutes later, the garden gate creaked upon its hinges. I confess that I was greatly agitated. I was about to learn the key to the mystery. The startling events of the last few weeks were about to be explained, and, under my eyes, the last battle was going to be fought. Daspry seized the hand of Madame Andermatt, and said to her:

"Not a word, not a movement! Whatever you may see or hear, keep quiet!"

Some one entered. It was Alfred Varin. I recognized him at once, owing to the close resemblance he bore to his brother Etienne. There was the same slouching gait; the same cadaverous face covered with a black beard.

He entered with the nervous air of a man who is accustomed to fear the presence of traps and ambushes; who scents and avoids them. He glanced about the room, and I had the impression that the chimney, masked with a velvet portiere, did not please him. He took three steps in our direction, when something caused him to turn and walk toward the old mosaic king, with the flowing beard and flamboyant sword, which he examined minutely, mounting on a chair and following with his fingers the outlines of the shoulders and head and feeling certain parts of the face. Suddenly, he leaped from the chair and walked away from it. He had heard the sound of approaching footsteps. Mon. Andermatt appeared at the door.

"You! You!" exclaimed the banker. "Was it you who brought me here?"

"I? By no means," protested Varin, in a rough, jerky voice that reminded me of his brother, "on the contrary, it was your letter that brought me here."

"My letter?"

"A letter signed by you, in which you offered——-"

"I never wrote to you," declared Mon. Andermatt.

"You did not write to me!"

Instinctively, Varin was put on his guard, not against the banker, but against the unknown enemy who had drawn him into this trap. A second time, he looked in our direction, then walked toward the door. But Mon. Andermatt barred his passage.

"Well, where are you going, Varin?"

"There is something about this affair I don't like. I am going home. Good evening."

"One moment!"

"No need of that, Mon. Andermatt. I have nothing to say to you."

"But I have something to say to you, and this is a good time to say it."

"Let me pass."

"No, you will not pass."

Varin recoiled before the resolute attitude of the banker, as he muttered:

"Well, then, be quick about it."

One thing astonished me; and I have no doubt my two companions experienced a similar feeling. Why was Salvator not there? Was he not a necessary party at this conference? Or was he satisfied to let these two adversaries fight it out between themselves? At all events, his absence was a great disappointment, although it did not detract from the dramatic strength of the situation.

After a moment, Mon. Andermatt approached Varin and, face to face, eye to eye, said:

"Now, after all these years and when you have nothing more to fear, you can answer me candidly: What have you done with Louis Lacombe?"

"What a question! As if I knew anything about him!"

"You do know! You and your brother were his constant companions, almost lived with him in this very house. You knew all about his plans and his work. And the last night I ever saw Louis Lacombe, when I parted with him at my door, I saw two men slinking away in the shadows of the trees. That, I am ready to swear to."

"Well, what has that to do with me?"

"The two men were you and your brother."

"Prove it."

"The best proof is that, two days later, you yourself showed me the papers and the plans that belonged to Lacombe and offered to sell them. How did these papers come into your possession?"

"I have already told you, Mon. Andermatt, that we found them on Louis Lacombe's table, the morning after his disappearance."

"That is a lie!"

"Prove it."

"The law will prove it."

"Why did you not appeal to the law?"

"Why? Ah! Why——," stammered the banker, with a slight display of emotion.

"You know very well, Mon. Andermatt, if you had the least certainty of our guilt, our little threat would not have stopped you."

"What threat? Those letters? Do you suppose I ever gave those letters a moment's thought?"

"If you did not care for the letters, why did you offer me thousands of francs for their return? And why did you have my brother and me tracked like wild beasts?"

"To recover the plans."

"Nonsense! You wanted the letters. You knew that as soon as you had the letters in your possession, you could denounce us. Oh! no, I couldn't part with them!"

He laughed heartily, but stopped suddenly, and said:

"But, enough of this! We are merely going over old ground. We make no headway. We had better let things stand as they are."

"We will not let them stand as they are," said the banker, "and since you have referred to the letters, let me tell you that you will not leave this house until you deliver up those letters."

"I shall go when I please."

"You will not."

"Be careful, Mon. Andermatt. I warn you——"

"I say, you shall not go."

"We will see about that," cried Varin, in such a rage that Madame Andermatt could not suppress a cry of fear. Varin must have heard it, for he now tried to force his way out. Mon. Andermatt pushed him back. Then I saw him put his hand into his coat pocket.

"For the last time, let me pass," he cried.

"The letters, first!"

Varin drew a revolver and, pointing it at Mon. Andermatt, said:

"Yes or no?"

The banker stooped quickly. There was the sound of a pistol-shot. The weapon fell from Varin's hand. I was amazed. The shot was fired close to me. It was Daspry who had fired it at Varin, causing him to drop the revolver. In a moment, Daspry was standing between the two men, facing Varin; he said to him, with a sneer:

"You were lucky, my friend, very lucky. I fired at your hand and struck only the revolver."

Both of them looked at him, surprised. Then he turned to the banker, and said:

"I beg your pardon, monsieur, for meddling in your business; but, really, you play a very poor game. Let me hold the cards."

Turning again to Varin, Daspry said:

"It's between us two, comrade, and play fair, if you please. Hearts are trumps, and I play the seven."

Then Daspry held up, before Varin's bewildered eyes, the little iron plate, marked with the seven red spots. It was a terrible shock to Varin. With livid features, staring eyes, and an air of intense agony, the man seemed to be hypnotized at the sight of it.

"Who are you?" he gasped.

"One who meddles in other people's business, down to the very bottom."

"What do you want?"

"What you brought here tonight."

"I brought nothing."

"Yes, you did, or you wouldn't have come. This morning, you received an invitation to come here at nine o'clock, and bring with you all the papers held by you. You are here. Where are the papers?"

There was in Daspry's voice and manner a tone of authority that I did not understand; his manner was usually quite mild and conciliatory. Absolutely conquered, Varin placed his hand on one of his pockets, and said:

"The papers are here."

"All of them?"

"Yes."

"All that you took from Louis Lacombe and afterwards sold to Major von Lieben?"

"Yes."

"Are these the copies or the originals?"

"I have the originals."

"How much do you want for them?"

"One hundred thousand francs."

"You are crazy," said Daspry. "Why, the major gave you only twenty thousand, and that was like money thrown into the sea, as the boat was a failure at the preliminary trials."

"They didn't understand the plans."

"The plans are not complete."

"Then, why do you ask me for them?"

"Because I want them. I offer you five thousand francs—not a sou more."

"Ten thousand. Not a sou less."

"Agreed," said Daspry, who now turned to Mon. Andermatt, and said:

"Monsieur will kindly sign a check for the amount."

"But....I haven't got——"

"Your check-book? Here it is."

Astounded, Mon. Andermatt examined the check-book that Daspry handed to him.

"It is mine," he gasped. "How does that happen?"

"No idle words, monsieur, if you please. You have merely to sign."

The banker took out his fountain pen, filled out the check and signed it. Varin held out his hand for it.

"Put down your hand," said Daspry, "there is something more." Then, to the banker, he said: "You asked for some letters, did you not?"

"Yes, a package of letters."

"Where are they, Varin?"

"I haven't got them."

"Where are they, Varin?"

"I don't know. My brother had charge of them."

"They are hidden in this room."

"In that case, you know where they are."

"How should I know?"

"Was it not you who found the hiding-place? You appear to be as well informed.... as Salvator."

"The letters are not in the hiding-place."

"They are."

"Open it."

Varin looked at him, defiantly. Were not Daspry and Salvator the same person? Everything pointed to that conclusion. If so, Varin risked nothing in disclosing a hiding-place already known.

"Open it," repeated Daspry.

"I have not got the seven of hearts."

"Yes, here it is," said Daspry, handing him the iron plate. Varin recoiled in terror, and cried:

"No, no, I will not."

"Never mind," replied Daspry, as he walked toward the bearded king, climbed on a chair and applied the seven of hearts to the lower part of the sword in such a manner that the edges of the iron plate coincided exactly with the two edges of the sword. Then, with the assistance of an awl which he introduced alternately into each of the seven holes, he pressed upon seven of the little mosaic stones. As he pressed upon the seventh one, a clicking sound was heard, and the entire bust of the King turned upon a pivot, disclosing a large opening lined with steel. It was really a fire-proof safe.

"You can see, Varin, the safe is empty."

"So I see. Then, my brother has taken out the letters."

Daspry stepped down from the chair, approached Varin, and said:

"Now, no more nonsense with me. There is another hiding-place. Where is it?"

"There is none."

"Is it money you want? How much?"

"Ten thousand."

"Monsieur Andermatt, are those letters worth then thousand francs to you?"

"Yes," said the banker, firmly.

Varin closed the safe, took the seven of hearts and placed it again on the sword at the same spot. He thrust the awl into each of the seven holes. There was the same clicking sound, but this time, strange to relate, it was only a portion of the safe that revolved on the pivot, disclosing quite a small safe that was built within the door of the larger one. The packet of letters was here, tied with a tape, and sealed. Varin handed the packet to Daspry. The latter turned to the banker, and asked:

"Is the check ready, Monsieur Andermatt?"

"Yes."

"And you have also the last document that you received from Louis Lacombe—the one that completes the plans of the sub-marine?"

"Yes."

The exchange was made. Daspry pocketed the document and the checks, and offered the packet of letters to Mon. Andermatt.

"This is what you wanted, Monsieur."

The banker hesitated a moment, as if he were afraid to touch those cursed letters that he had sought so eagerly. Then, with a nervous movement, he took them. Close to me, I heard a moan. I grasped Madame Andermatt's hand. It was cold.

"I believe, monsieur," said Daspry to the banker, "that our business is ended. Oh! no thanks. It was only by a mere chance that I have been able to do you a good turn. Good-night."

Mon. Andermatt retired. He carried with him the letters written by his wife to Louis Lacombe.

"Marvelous!" exclaimed Daspry, delighted. "Everything is coming our way. Now, we have only to close our little affair, comrade. You have the papers?"

"Here they are—all of them."

Daspry examined them carefully, and then placed them in his pocket.

"Quite right. You have kept your word," he said.

"But——"

"But what?"

"The two checks? The money?" said Varin, eagerly.

"Well, you have a great deal of assurance, my man. How dare you ask such a thing?"

"I ask only what is due to me."

"Can you ask pay for returning papers that you stole? Well, I think not!"

Varin was beside himself. He trembled with rage; his eyes were bloodshot.

"The money.... the twenty thousand...." he stammered.

"Impossible! I need it myself."

"The money!"

"Come, be reasonable, and don't get excited. It won't do you any good."

Daspry seized his arm so forcibly, that Varin uttered a cry of pain. Daspry continued:

"Now, you can go. The air will do you good. Perhaps you want me to show you the way. Ah! yes, we will go together to the vacant lot near here, and I will show you a little mound of earth and stones and under it——"

"That is false! That is false!"

"Oh! no, it is true. That little iron plate with the seven spots on it came from there. Louis Lacombe always carried it, and you buried it with the body—and with some other things that will prove very interesting to a judge and jury."

Varin covered his face with his hands, and muttered:

"All right, I am beaten. Say no more. But I want to ask you one question. I should like to know——"

"What is it?"

"Was there a little casket in the large safe?"

"Yes."

"Was it there on the night of 22 June?"

"Yes."

"What did it contain?"

"Everything that the Varin brothers had put in it—a very pretty collection of diamonds and pearls picked up here and there by the said brothers."

"And did you take it?"

"Of course I did. Do you blame me?"

"I understand.... it was the disappearance of that casket that caused my brother to kill himself."

"Probably. The disappearance of your correspondence was not a sufficient motive. But the disappearance of the casket....Is that all you wish to ask me?"

"One thing more: your name?"

"You ask that with an idea of seeking revenge."

"Parbleu! The tables may be turned. Today, you are on top. To-morrow——"

"It will be you."

"I hope so. Your name?"

"Arsène Lupin."

"Arsène Lupin!"

The man staggered, as though stunned by a heavy blow. Those two words had deprived him of all hope.

Daspry laughed, and said:

"Ah! did you imagine that a Monsieur Durand or Dupont could manage an affair like this? No, it required the skill and cunning of Arsène Lupin. And now that you have my name, go and prepare your revenge. Arsène Lupin will wait for you."

Then he pushed the bewildered Varin through the door.

"Daspry! Daspry!" I cried, pushing aside the curtain. He ran to me.

"What? What's the matter?"

"Madame Andermatt is ill."

He hastened to her, caused her to inhale some salts, and, while caring for her, questioned me:

"Well, what did it?"

"The letters of Louis Lacombe that you gave to her husband."

He struck his forehead and said:

"Did she think that I could do such a thing!...But, of course she would. Imbecile that I am!"

Madame Andermatt was now revived. Daspry took from his pocket a small package exactly similar to the one that Mon. Andermatt had carried away.

"Here are your letters, Madame. These are the genuine letters."

"But.... the others?"

"The others are the same, rewritten by me and carefully worded. Your husband will not find anything objectionable in them, and will never suspect the substitution since they were taken from the safe in his presence."

"But the handwriting——"

"There is no handwriting that cannot be imitated."

She thanked him in the same words she might have used to a man in her own social circle, so I concluded that she had not witnessed the final scene between Varin and Arsène Lupin. But the surprising revelation caused me considerable embarrassment. Lupin! My club companion was none other than Arsène Lupin. I could not realize it. But he said, quite at his ease:

"You can say farewell to Jean Daspry."

"Ah!"

"Yes, Jean Daspry is going on a long journey. I shall send him to Morocco. There, he may find a death worthy of him. I may say that that is his expectation."

"But Arsène Lupin will remain?"

"Oh! Decidedly. Arsène Lupin is simply at the threshold of his career, and he expects——"

I was impelled by curiosity to interrupt him, and, leading him away from the hearing of Madame Andermatt, I asked:

"Did you discover the smaller safe yourself—the one that held the letters?"

"Yes, after a great deal of trouble. I found it yesterday afternoon while you were asleep. And yet, God knows it was simple enough! But the simplest things are the ones that usually escape our notice." Then, showing me the seven-of-hearts, he added: "Of course I had guessed that, in order to open the larger safe, this card must be placed on the sword of the mosaic king."

"How did you guess that?"

"Quite easily. Through private information, I knew that fact when I came here on the evening of 22 June——"

"After you left me——"

"Yes, after turning the subject of our conversation to stories of crime and robbery which were sure to reduce you to such a nervous condition that you would not leave your bed, but would allow me to complete my search uninterrupted."

"The scheme worked perfectly."

"Well, I knew when I came here that there was a casket concealed in a safe with a secret lock, and that the seven-of-hearts was the key to that lock. I had merely to place the card upon the spot that was obviously intended for it. An hour's examination showed me where the spot was."

"One hour!"

"Observe the fellow in mosaic."

"The old emperor?"

"That old emperor is an exact representation of the king of hearts on all playing cards."

"That's right. But how does the seven of hearts open the larger safe at one time and the smaller safe at another time? And why did you open only the larger safe in the first instance? I mean on the night of 22 June."

"Why? Because I always placed the seven of hearts in the same way. I never changed the position. But, yesterday, I observed that by reversing the card, by turning it upside down, the arrangement of the seven spots on the mosaic was changed."

"Parbleu!"

"Of course, parbleu! But a person has to think of those things."

"There is something else: you did not know the history of those letters until Madame Andermatt——"

"Spoke of them before me? No. Because I found in the safe, besides the casket, nothing but the correspondence of the two brothers which disclosed their treachery in regard to the plans."

"Then it was by chance that you were led, first, to investigate the history of the two brothers, and then to search for the plans and documents relating to the sub-marine?"

"Simply by chance."

"For what purpose did you make the search?"

"Mon Dieu!" exclaimed Daspry, laughing, "how deeply interested you are!"

"The subject fascinates me."

"Very well, presently, after I have escorted Madame Andermatt to a carriage, and dispatched a short story to the `Echo de France,' I will return and tell you all about it."

He sat down and wrote one of those short, clear-cut articles which served to amuse and mystify the public. Who does not recall the sensation that followed that article produced throughout the entire world?

"Arsène Lupin has solved the problem recently submitted by Salvator. Having acquired possession of all the documents and original plans of the engineer Louis Lacombe, he has placed them in the hands of the Minister of Marine, and he has headed a subscription list for the purpose of presenting to the nation the first submarine constructed from those plans. His subscription is twenty thousand francs."

"Twenty thousand francs! The checks of Mon. Andermatt?" I exclaimed, when he had given me the paper to read.

"Exactly. It was quite right that Varin should redeem his treachery."

And that is how I made the acquaintance of Arsène Lupin. That is how I learned that Jean Daspry, a member of my club, was none other than Arsène

Lupin, gentleman-thief. That is how I formed very agreeable ties of friendship with that famous man, and, thanks to the confidence with which he honored me, how I became his very humble and faithful historiographer.

VII. MADAME IMBERT'S SAFE

At three o'clock in the morning, there were still half a dozen carriages in front of one of those small houses which form only the side of the boulevard Berthier. The door of that house opened, and a number of guests, male and female, emerged. The majority of them entered their carriages and were quickly driven away, leaving behind only two men who walked down Courcelles, where they parted, as one of them lived in that street. The other decided to return on foot as far as the Porte-Maillot. It was a beautiful winter's night, clear and cold; a night on which a brisk walk is agreeable and refreshing.

But, at the end of a few minutes, he had the disagreeable impression that he was being followed. Turning around, he saw a man sulking amongst the trees. He was not a coward; yet he felt it advisable to increase his speed. Then his pursuer commenced to run; and he deemed it prudent to draw his revolver and face him. But he had no time. The man rushed at him and attacked him violently. Immediately, they were engaged in a desperate struggle, wherein he felt that his unknown assailant had the advantage. He called for help, struggled, and was thrown down on a pile of gravel, seized by the throat, and gagged with a handkerchief that his assailant forced into his mouth. His eyes closed, and the man who was smothering him with his weight arose to defend himself against an unexpected attack. A blow from a cane and a kick from a boot; the man uttered two cries of pain, and fled, limping and cursing. Without deigning to pursue the fugitive, the new arrival stooped over the prostrate man and inquired:

"Are you hurt, monsieur?"

He was not injured, but he was dazed and unable to stand. His rescuer procured a carriage, placed him in it, and accompanied him to his house on the avenue de la Grande-Armée. On his arrival there, quite recovered, he overwhelmed his saviour with thanks.

"I owe you my life, monsieur, and I shall not forget it. I do not wish to alarm my wife at this time of night, but, to-morrow, she will be pleased to thank you personally. Come and breakfast with us. My name is Ludovic Imbert. May I ask yours?"

"Certainly, monsieur."

And he handed Mon. Imbert a card bearing the name: "Arsène Lupin."

At that time, Arsène Lupin did not enjoy the celebrity which the Cahorn affair, his escape from the Prison de la Santé, and other brilliant exploits, afterwards gained for him. He had not even used the name of Arsène Lupin. The name was specially invented to designate the rescuer of Mon. Imbert; that is to say, it was in that affair that Arsène Lupin was baptized. Fully armed and ready for the fray, it is true, but lacking the resources and authority which command success, Arsène Lupin was then merely an apprentice in a profession wherein he soon became a master.

With what a thrill of joy he recalled the invitation he received that night! At last, he had reached his goal! At last, he had undertaken a task worthy of his strength and skill! The Imbert millions! What a magnificent feast for an appetite like his!

He prepared a special toilet for the occasion; a shabby frock-coat, baggy trousers, a frayed silk hat, well-worn collar and cuffs, all quite correct in form, but bearing the unmistakable stamp of poverty. His cravat was a black ribbon pinned with a false diamond. Thus accoutred, he descended the stairs of the house in which he lived at Montmartre. At the third floor, without stopping, he rapped on a closed door with the head of his cane. He walked to the exterior boulevards. A tram-car was passing. He boarded it, and some one who had been following him took a seat beside him. It was the lodger who occupied the room on the third floor. A moment later, this man said to Lupin:

"Well, governor?"

"Well, it is all fixed."

"How?"

"I am going there to breakfast."

"You breakfast—there!"

"Certainly. Why not? I rescued Mon. Ludovic Imbert from certain death at your hands. Mon. Imbert is not devoid of gratitude. He invited me to breakfast."

There was a brief silence. Then the other said:

"But you are not going to throw up the scheme?"

"My dear boy," said Lupin, "When I arranged that little case of assault and battery, when I took the trouble at three o'clock in the morning, to rap you with my cane and tap you with my boot at the risk of injuring my only friend, it was not my intention to forego the advantages to be gained from a rescue so well arranged and executed. Oh! no, not at all."

"But the strange rumors we hear about their fortune?"

"Never mind about that. For six months, I have worked on this affair, investigated it, studied it, questioned the servants, the money-lenders and men of straw; for six months, I have shadowed the husband and wife. Consequently, I know what I am talking about. Whether the fortune came to them from old Brawford, as they pretend, or from some other source, I do not care. I know that it is a reality; that it exists. And some day it will be mine."

"Bigre! One hundred millions!"

"Let us say ten, or even five—that is enough! They have a safe full of bonds, and there will be the devil to pay if I can't get my hands on them."

The tram-car stopped at the Place de l'Etoile. The man whispered to Lupin:

"What am I to do now?"

"Nothing, at present. You will hear from me. There is no hurry."

Five minutes later, Arsène Lupin was ascending the magnificent flight of stairs in the Imbert mansion, and Mon. Imbert introduced him to his wife. Madame Gervaise Imbert was a short plump woman, and very talkative. She gave Lupin a cordial welcome.

"I desired that we should be alone to entertain our saviour," she said.

From the outset, they treated "our saviour" as an old and valued friend. By the time dessert was served, their friendship was well cemented, and private confidences were being exchanged. Arsène related the story of his life, the life of his father as a magistrate, the sorrows of his childhood, and his present difficulties. Gervaise, in turn, spoke of her youth, her marriage, the kindness of the aged Brawford, the hundred millions that she had inherited, the obstacles that prevented her from obtaining the enjoyment of her inheritance, the moneys she had been obliged to borrow at an exorbitant rate of interest, her endless contentions with Brawford's nephews, and the litigation! the injunctions! in fact, everything!

"Just think of it, Monsieur Lupin, the bonds are there, in my husband's office, and if we detach a single coupon, we lose everything! They are there, in our safe, and we dare not touch them."

Monsieur Lupin shivered at the bare idea of his proximity to so much wealth. Yet he felt quite certain that Monsieur Lupin would never suffer from the same difficulty as his fair hostess who declared she dare not touch the money.

"Ah! they are there!" he repeated, to himself; "they are there!"

A friendship formed under such circumstances soon led to closer relations. When discreetly questioned, Arsène Lupin confessed his poverty and distress. Immediately, the unfortunate young man was appointed private secretary to the Imberts, husband and wife, at a salary of one hundred francs a month. He was to come to the house every day and receive orders for his work, and a room on the second floor was set apart as his office. This room was directly over Mon. Imbert's office.

Arsène soon realized that his position as secretary was essentially a sinecure. During the first two months, he had only four important letters to recopy, and was called only once to Mon. Imbert's office; consequently, he had only one opportunity to contemplate, officially, the Imbert safe. Moreover, he noticed that the secretary was not invited to the social functions of the employer. But he did not complain, as he preferred to remain, modestly, in the shade and maintain his peace and freedom.

However, he was not wasting any time. From the beginning, he made clandestine visits to Mon. Imbert's office, and paid his respects to the safe, which was hermetically closed. It was an immense block of iron and steel, cold and stern in appearance, which could not be forced open by the ordinary tools of the burglar's trade. But Arsène Lupin was not discouraged.

"Where force fails, cunning prevails," he said to himself. "The essential thing is to be on the spot when the opportunity occurs. In the meantime, I must watch and wait."

He made immediately some preliminary preparations. After careful soundings made upon the floor of his room, he introduced a lead pipe which penetrated the ceiling of Mon. Imbert's office at a point between the two screeds of the cornice. By means of this pipe, he hoped to see and hear what transpired in the room below.

Henceforth, he passed his days stretched at full length upon the floor. He frequently saw the Imberts holding a consultation in front of the safe, investigating books and papers. When they turned the combination lock, he tried to learn the figures and the number of turns they made to the right and left. He watched their movements; he sought to catch their words. There was also a key necessary to complete the opening of the safe. What did they do with it? Did they hide it?

One day, he saw them leave the room without locking the safe. He descended the stairs quickly, and boldly entered the room. But they had returned.

"Oh! excuse me," said, "I made a mistake in the door."

"Come in, Monsieur Lupin, come in," cried Madame Imbert, "are you not at home here? We want your advice. What bonds should we sell? The foreign securities or the government annuities?"

"But the injunction?" said Lupin, with surprise.

"Oh! it doesn't cover all the bonds."

She opened the door of the safe and withdrew a package of bonds. But her husband protested.

"No, no, Gervaise, it would be foolish to sell the foreign bonds. They are going up, whilst the annuities are as high as they ever will be. What do you think, my dear friend?"

The dear friend had no opinion; yet he advised the sacrifice of the annuities. Then she withdrew another package and, from it, she took a paper at random. It proved to be a three-per-cent annuity worth two thousand francs. Ludovic placed the package of bonds in his pocket. That afternoon, accompanied by his secretary, he sold the annuities to a stock-broker and realized forty-six thousand francs.

Whatever Madame Imbert might have said about it, Arsène Lupin did not feel at home in the Imbert house. On the contrary, his position there was a peculiar one. He learned that the servants did not even know his name. They called him "monsieur." Ludovic always spoke of him in the same way: "You will tell monsieur. Has monsieur arrived?" Why that mysterious appellation?

Moreover, after their first outburst of enthusiasm, the Imberts seldom spoke to him, and, although treating him with the consideration due to a benefactor, they gave him little or no attention. They appeared to regard him as an eccentric character who did not like to be disturbed, and they respected his isolation as if it were a stringent rule on his part. On one occasion, while passing through the vestibule, he heard Madame Imbert say to the two gentlemen:

"He is such a barbarian!"

"Very well," he said to himself, "I am a barbarian."

And, without seeking to solve the question of their strange conduct, he proceeded with the execution of his own plans. He had decided that he could not depend on chance, nor on the negligence of Madame Imbert, who carried the key of the safe, and who, on locking the safe, invariably scattered the letters forming the combination of the lock. Consequently, he must act for himself.

Finally, an incident precipitated matters; it was the vehement campaign instituted against the Imberts by certain newspapers that accused the Imberts of swindling. Arsène Lupin was present at certain family conferences when this new vicissitude was discussed. He decided that if he waited much longer, he would lose everything. During the next five days, instead of leaving the house about six o'clock, according to his usual habit, he locked himself in his room. It was supposed that he had gone out. But he was lying on the floor surveying the office of Mon. Imbert. During those five evenings, the favorable opportunity that he awaited did not take place. He left the house about midnight by a side door to which he held the key.

But on the sixth day, he learned that the Imberts, actuated by the malevolent insinuations of their enemies, proposed to make an inventory of the contents of the safe.

"They will do it to-night," thought Lupin.

And truly, after dinner, Imbert and his wife retired to the office and commenced to examine the books of account and the securities contained in the safe. Thus, one hour after another passed away. He heard the servants go upstairs to their rooms. No one now remained on the first floor. Midnight! The Imberts were still at work.

"I must get to work," murmured Lupin.

He opened his window. It opened on a court. Outside, everything was dark and quiet. He took from his desk a knotted rope, fastened it to the balcony in front of his window, and quietly descended as far as the window below, which was that of the of Imbert's office. He stood upon the balcony for a moment, motionless, with attentive ear and watchful eye, but the heavy curtains effectually concealed the interior of the room. He cautiously pushed on the double window. If no one had examined it, it ought to yield to the slightest pressure, for, during the afternoon, he had so fixed the bolt that it would not enter the staple.

The window yielded to his touch. Then, with infinite care, he pushed it open sufficiently to admit his head. He parted the curtains a few inches, looked in, and saw Mon. Imbert and his wife sitting in front of the safe, deeply absorbed in their work and speaking softly to each other at rare intervals.

He calculated the distance between him and them, considered the exact movements he would require to make in order to overcome them, one after the other, before they could call for help, and he was about to rush upon them, when Madame Imbert said:

"Ah! the room is getting quite cold. I am going to bed. And you, my dear?"

"I shall stay and finish."

"Finish! Why, that will take you all night."

"Not at all. An hour, at the most."

She retired. Twenty minutes, thirty minutes passed. Arsène pushed the window a little farther open. The curtains shook. He pushed once more. Mon. Imbert turned, and, seeing the curtains blown by the wind, he rose to close the window.

There was not a cry, not the trace of struggle. With a few precise moments, and without causing him the least injury, Arsène stunned him, wrapped the curtain about his head, bound him hand and foot, and did it all in such a manner that Mon. Imbert had no opportunity to recognize his assailant.

Quickly, he approached the safe, seized two packages that he placed under his arm, left the office, and opened the servants' gate. A carriage was stationed in the street.

"Take that, first—and follow me," he said to the coachman. He returned to the office, and, in two trips, they emptied the safe. Then Arsène went to his own room, removed the rope, and all other traces of his clandestine work.

A few hours later, Arsène Lupin and his assistant examined the stolen goods. Lupin was not disappointed, as he had foreseen that the wealth of the Imberts had been greatly exaggerated. It did not consist of hundreds of millions, nor even tens of millions. Yet it amounted to a very respectable sum, and Lupin expressed his satisfaction.

"Of course," he said, "there will be a considerable loss when we come to sell the bonds, as we will have to dispose of them surreptitiously at reduced prices. In the meantime, they will rest quietly in my desk awaiting a propitious moment."

Arsène saw no reason why he should not go to the Imbert house the next day. But a perusal of the morning papers revealed this startling fact: Ludovic and Gervaise Imbert had disappeared.

When the officers of the law seized the safe and opened it, they found there what Arsène Lupin had left—nothing.

Such are the facts; and I learned the sequel to them, one day, when Arsène Lupin was in a confidential mood. He was pacing to and fro in my room, with a nervous step and a feverish eye that were unusual to him.

"After all," I said to him, "it was your most successful venture."

Without making a direct reply, he said:

"There are some impenetrable secrets connected with that affair; some obscure points that escape my comprehension. For instance: What caused their flight? Why did they not take advantage of the help I unconsciously gave them? It would have been so simple to say: 'The hundred millions were in the safe. They are no longer there, because they have been stolen.'"

"They lost their nerve."

"Yes, that is it—they lost their nerve...On the other hand, it is true—-"

"What is true?"

"Oh! nothing."

What was the meaning of Lupin's reticence? It was quite obvious that he had not told me everything; there was something he was loath to tell. His conduct puzzled me. It must indeed be a very serious matter to cause such a man as Arsène Lupin even a momentary hesitation. I threw out a few questions at random.

"Have you seen them since?"

"No."

"And have you never experienced the slightest degree of pity for those unfortunate people?"

"I!" he exclaimed, with a start.

His sudden excitement astonished me. Had I touched him on a sore spot? I continued:

"Of course. If you had not left them alone, they might have been able to face the danger, or, at least, made their escape with full pockets."

"What do you mean?" he said, indignantly. "I suppose you have an idea that my soul should be filled with remorse?"

"Call it remorse or regrets—anything you like—-"

"They are not worth it."

"Have you no regrets or remorse for having stolen their fortune?"

"What fortune?"

"The packages of bonds you took from their safe."

"Oh! I stole their bonds, did I? I deprived them of a portion of their wealth? Is that my crime? Ah! my dear boy, you do not know the truth. You never imagined that those bonds were not worth the paper they were written on. Those bonds were false—they were counterfeit—every one of them—do you understand? THEY WERE COUNTERFEIT!"

I looked at him, astounded.

"Counterfeit! The four or five millions?"

"Yes, counterfeit!" he exclaimed, in a fit of rage. "Only so many scraps of paper! I couldn't raise a sou on the whole of them! And you ask me if I have any remorse. THEY are the ones who should have remorse and pity. They played me for a simpleton; and I fell into their trap. I was their latest victim, their most stupid gull!"

He was affected by genuine anger—the result of malice and wounded pride. He continued:

"From start to finish, I got the worst of it. Do you know the part I played in that affair, or rather the part they made me play? That of André Brawford! Yes, my boy, that is the truth, and I never suspected it. It was not until afterwards, on reading the newspapers, that the light finally dawned in my stupid brain. Whilst I was posing as his "saviour," as the gentleman who had risked his life to rescue Mon. Imbert from the clutches of an assassin, they were passing me off as Brawford. Wasn't that splendid? That eccentric individual who had a room on the second floor, that barbarian that was exhibited only at a distance, was Brawford, and Brawford was I! Thanks to me, and to the confidence that I inspired under the name of Brawford, they were enabled to borrow money from the bankers and other money-lenders. Ha! what an experience for a novice! And I swear to you that I shall profit by the lesson!"

He stopped, seized my arm, and said to me, in a tone of exasperation:

"My dear fellow, at this very moment, Gervaise Imbert owes me fifteen hundred francs."

I could not refrain from laughter, his rage was so grotesque. He was making a mountain out of a molehill. In a moment, he laughed himself, and said:

"Yes, my boy, fifteen hundred francs. You must know that I had not received one sou of my promised salary, and, more than that, she had borrowed from me the sum of fifteen hundred francs. All my youthful savings! And do you know why? To devote the money to charity! I am giving you a straight story. She wanted it for some poor people she was assisting— unknown to her husband. And my hard-earned money was wormed out of me by that silly pretense! Isn't it amusing, hein? Arsène Lupin done out of fifteen hundred francs by the fair lady from whom he stole four millions in counterfeit bonds! And what a vast amount of time and patience and cunning I expended to achieve that result! It was the first time in my life that I was played for a fool, and I frankly confess that I was fooled that time to the queen's taste!"

VIII. THE BLACK PEARL

A violent ringing of the bell awakened the concierge of number nine, avenue Hoche. She pulled the doorstring, grumbling:

"I thought everybody was in. It must be three o'clock!"

"Perhaps it is some one for the doctor," muttered her husband.

"Third floor, left. But the doctor won't go out at night."

"He must go to-night."

The visitor entered the vestibule, ascended to the first floor, the second, the third, and, without stopping at the doctor's door, he continued to the fifth floor. There, he tried two keys. One of them fitted the lock.

"Ah! good!" he murmured, "that simplifies the business wonderfully. But before I commence work I had better arrange for my retreat. Let me see.... have I had sufficient time to rouse the doctor and be dismissed by him? Not yet.... a few minutes more."

At the end of ten minutes, he descended the stairs, grumbling noisily about the doctor. The concierge opened the door for him and heard it click behind him. But the door did not lock, as the man had quickly inserted a piece of iron in the lock in such a manner that the bolt could not enter. Then, quietly, he entered the house again, unknown to the concierge. In case of alarm, his retreat was assured. Noiselessly, he ascended to the fifth floor once more. In the antechamber, by the light of his electric lantern, he placed his hat and overcoat on one of the chairs, took a seat on another, and covered his heavy shoes with felt slippers.

"Ouf! Here I am—and how simple it was! I wonder why more people do not adopt the profitable and pleasant occupation of burglar. With a little care and reflection, it becomes a most delightful profession. Not too quiet and monotonous, of course, as it would then become wearisome."

He unfolded a detailed plan of the apartment.

"Let me commence by locating myself. Here, I see the vestibule in which I am sitting. On the street front, the drawing-room, the boudoir and dining-room. Useless to waste any time there, as it appears that the countess has a deplorable taste.... not a bibelot of any value!...Now, let's get down to business!... Ah! here is a corridor; it must lead to the bed chambers. At a distance of three metres, I should come to the door of the wardrobe-closet which connects with the chamber of the countess." He folded his plan, extinguished his lantern, and proceeded down the corridor, counting his distance, thus:

"One metre.... two metres.... three metres....Here is the door....Mon Dieu, how easy it is! Only a small, simple bolt now separates me from the chamber, and I know that the bolt is located exactly one metre, forty-three centimeters, from the floor. So that, thanks to a small incision I am about to make, I can soon get rid of the bolt."

He drew from his pocket the necessary instruments. Then the following idea occurred to him:

"Suppose, by chance, the door is not bolted. I will try it first."

He turned the knob, and the door opened.

"My brave Lupin, surely fortune favors you....What's to be done now? You know the situation of the rooms; you know the place in which the countess hides the black pearl. Therefore, in order to secure the black pearl, you have simply to be more silent than silence, more invisible than darkness itself."

Arsène Lupin was employed fully a half-hour in opening the second door—a glass door that led to the countess' bedchamber. But he accomplished it with so much skill and precaution, that even had had the countess been awake, she would not have heard the slightest sound. According to the plan of the rooms, that he holds, he has merely to pass around a reclining chair and, beyond that, a small table close to the bed. On the table, there was a box of letter-paper, and the black pearl was concealed in that box. He stooped and crept cautiously over the carpet, following the outlines of the reclining-chair. When he reached the extremity of it, he stopped in order to repress the throbbing of his heart. Although he was not moved by any sense of fear, he found it impossible to overcome the nervous anxiety that one usually feels in the midst of profound silence. That circumstance astonished him, because he had passed through many more solemn moments without the slightest trace of emotion. No danger threatened him. Then why did his heart throb like an alarm-bell? Was it that sleeping woman who affected him? Was it the proximity of another pulsating heart?

He listened, and thought he could discern the rhythmical breathing of a person asleep. It gave him confidence, like the presence of a friend. He sought and found the armchair; then, by slow, cautious movements, advanced toward the table, feeling ahead of him with outstretched arm. His right had touched one of the feet of the table. Ah! now, he had simply to rise, take the pearl, and escape. That was fortunate, as his heart was leaping in his breast like a wild beast, and made so much noise that he feared it would waken the countess. By a powerful effort of the will, he subdued the wild throbbing of his heart, and was about to rise from the floor when his left hand encountered, lying on the floor, an object which he recognized as a candlestick—an overturned candlestick. A moment later, his hand encountered another object: a clock—one of those small traveling clocks, covered with leather. —————

Well! What had happened? He could not understand. That candlestick, that clock; why were those articles not in their accustomed places? Ah! what had happened in the dread silence of the night?

Suddenly a cry escaped him. He had touched—oh! some strange, unutterable thing! "No! no!" he thought, "it cannot be. It is some fantasy of my excited brain." For twenty seconds, thirty seconds, he remained motionless, terrified, his forehead bathed with perspiration, and his fingers still retained the sensation of that dreadful contact.

Making a desperate effort, he ventured to extend his arm again. Once more, his hand encountered that strange, unutterable thing. He felt it. He must feel it and find out what it is. He found that it was hair, human hair, and a human face; and that face was cold, almost icy.

However frightful the circumstances may be, a man like Arsène Lupin controls himself and commands the situation as soon as he learns what it is. So, Arsène Lupin quickly brought his lantern into use. A woman was lying before him, covered with blood. Her neck and shoulders were covered with gaping wounds. He leaned over her and made a closer examination. She was dead.

"Dead! Dead!" he repeated, with a bewildered air.

He stared at those fixed eyes, that grim mouth, that livid flesh, and that blood—all that blood which had flowed over the carpet and congealed there in thick, black spots. He arose and turned on the electric lights. Then he beheld all the marks of a desperate struggle. The bed was in a state of great disorder. On the floor, the candlestick, and the clock, with the hands pointing to twenty minutes after eleven; then, further away, an overturned chair; and, everywhere, there was blood, spots of blood and pools of blood.

"And the black pearl?" he murmured.

The box of letter-paper was in its place. He opened it, eagerly. The jewel-case was there, but it was empty.

"Fichtre!" he muttered. "You boasted of your good fortune much too soon, my friend Lupin. With the countess lying cold and dead, and the black pearl vanished, the situation is anything but pleasant. Get out of here as soon as you can, or you may get into serious trouble."

Yet, he did not move.

"Get out of here? Yes, of course. Any person would, except Arsène Lupin. He has something better to do. Now, to proceed in an orderly way. At all events, you have a clear conscience. Let us suppose that you are the commissary of police and that you are proceeding to make an inquiry concerning this affair——Yes, but in order to do that, I require a clearer brain. Mine is muddled like a ragout."

He tumbled into an armchair, with his clenched hands pressed against his burning forehead.

The murder of the avenue Hoche is one of those which have recently surprised and puzzled the Parisian public, and, certainly, I should never have mentioned the affair if the veil of mystery had not been removed by Arsène Lupin himself. No one knew the exact truth of the case.

Who did not know—from having met her in the Bois—the fair Léotine Zalti, the once-famous cantatrice, wife and widow of the Count d'Andillot; the Zalti, whose luxury dazzled all Paris some twenty years ago; the Zalti who acquired an European reputation for the magnificence of her diamonds and pearls? It was said that she wore upon her shoulders the capital of several banking houses and the gold mines of numerous Australian companies. Skilful jewelers worked for Zalti as they had formerly wrought for kings and queens. And who does not remember the catastrophe in which all that wealth was swallowed up? Of all that marvelous collection, nothing remained except the famous black pearl. The black pearl! That is to say a fortune, if she had wished to part with it.

But she preferred to keep it, to live in a commonplace apartment with her companion, her cook, and a man-servant, rather than sell that inestimable jewel. There was a reason for it; a reason she was not afraid to disclose: the black pearl was the gift of an emperor! Almost ruined, and reduced to the most mediocre existence, she remained faithful to the companion of her happy and brilliant youth. The black pearl never left her possession. She wore it during the day, and, at night, concealed it in a place known to her alone.

All these facts, being republished in the columns of the public press, served to stimulate curiosity; and, strange to say, but quite obvious to those who have the key to the mystery, the arrest of the presumed assassin only complicated the question and prolonged the excitement. Two days later, the newspapers published the following item:

"Information has reached us of the arrest of Victor Danègre, the servant of the Countess d'Andillot. The evidence against him is clear and convincing. On the silken sleeve of his liveried waistcoat, which chief detective Dudouis found in his garret between the mattresses of his bed, several spots of blood were discovered. In addition, a cloth-covered button was missing from that garment, and this button was found beneath the bed of the victim.

"It is supposed that, after dinner, in place of going to his own room, Danègre slipped into the wardrobe-closet, and, through the glass door, had seen the countess hide the precious black pearl. This is simply a theory, as yet unverified by any evidence. There is, also, another obscure point. At seven o'clock in the morning, Danègre went to the tobacco-shop on the Boulevard de Courcelles; the concierge and the shop-keeper both affirm this fact. On the other hand, the countess' companion and cook, who sleep at the end of the hall, both declare that, when they arose at eight o'clock, the door of the antechamber and the door of the kitchen were locked. These two persons have been in the service of the countess for twenty years, and are above suspicion. The question is: How did Danègre leave the apartment? Did he have another key? These are matters that the police will investigate."

As a matter of fact, the police investigation threw no light on the mystery. It was learned that Victor Danègre was a dangerous criminal, a drunkard and a debauchee. But, as they proceeded with the investigation, the mystery deepened and new complications arose. In the first place, a young woman, Mlle. De Sinclèves, the cousin and sole heiress of the countess, declared that the countess, a month before her death, had written a letter to her and in it described the manner in which the black pearl was concealed. The letter disappeared the day after she received it. Who had stolen it?

Again, the concierge related how she had opened the door for a person who had inquired for Doctor Harel. On being questioned, the doctor testified that no one had rung his bell. Then who was that person? An accomplice?

The theory of an accomplice was thereupon adopted by the press and public, and also by Ganimard, the famous detective.

"Lupin is at the bottom of this affair," he said to the judge.

"Bah!" exclaimed the judge, "you have Lupin on the brain. You see him everywhere."

"I see him everywhere, because he is everywhere."

"Say rather that you see him every time you encounter something you cannot explain. Besides, you overlook the fact that the crime was committed at twenty minutes past eleven in the evening, as is shown by the clock, while the nocturnal visit, mentioned by the concierge, occurred at three o'clock in the morning."

Officers of the law frequently form a hasty conviction as to the guilt of a suspected person, and then distort all subsequent discoveries to conform to their established theory. The deplorable antecedents of Victor Danègre, habitual criminal, drunkard and rake, influenced the judge, and despite the fact that nothing new was discovered in corroboration of the early clues, his official opinion remained firm and unshaken. He closed his investigation, and, a few weeks later, the trial commenced. It proved to be slow and tedious. The judge was listless, and the public prosecutor presented the case in a careless manner. Under those circumstances, Danègre's counsel had an easy task. He pointed out the defects and inconsistencies of the case for the prosecution, and argued that the evidence was quite insufficient to convict the accused. Who had made the key, the indispensable key without which Danègre, on leaving the apartment, could not have locked the door behind him? Who had ever seen such a key, and what had become of it? Who had seen the assassin's knife, and where is it now?

"In any event," argued the prisoner's counsel, "the prosecution must prove, beyond any reasonable doubt, that the prisoner committed the murder. The prosecution must show that the mysterious individual who entered the house at three o'clock in the morning is not the guilty party. To be sure, the clock indicated eleven o'clock. But what of that? I contend, that proves nothing. The assassin could turn the hands of the clock to any hour he pleased, and thus deceive us in regard to the exact hour of the crime."

Victor Danègre was acquitted.

He left the prison on Friday about dusk in the evening, weak and depressed by his six months' imprisonment. The inquisition, the solitude, the trial, the deliberations of the jury, combined to fill him with a nervous fear. At night, he had been afflicted with terrible nightmares and haunted by weird visions of the scaffold. He was a mental and physical wreck.

Under the assumed name of Anatole Dufour, he rented a small room on the heights of Montmartre, and lived by doing odd jobs wherever he could find them. He led a pitiful existence. Three times, he obtained regular employment, only to be recognized and then discharged. Sometimes, he had an idea that men were following him—detectives, no doubt, who were seeking to trap and denounce him. He could almost feel the strong hand of the law clutching him by the collar.

One evening, as he was eating his dinner at a neighboring restaurant, a man entered and took a seat at the same table. He was a person about forty years of age, and wore a frock-coat of doubtful cleanliness. He ordered soup, vegetables, and a bottle of wine. After he had finished his soup, he turned his eyes on Danègre, and gazed at him intently. Danègre winced. He was certain that this was one of the men who had been following him for several weeks. What did he want? Danègre tried to rise, but failed. His limbs refused to support him. The man poured himself a glass of wine, and then filled Danègre's glass. The man raised his glass, and said:

"To your health, Victor Danègre."

Victor started in alarm, and stammered:

"I!....I!.... no, no....I swear to you...."

"You will swear what? That you are not yourself? The servant of the countess?"

"What servant? My name is Dufour. Ask the proprietor."

"Yes, Anatole Dufour to the proprietor of this restaurant, but Victor Danègre to the officers of the law."

"That's not true! Some one has lied to you."

The new-comer took a card from his pocket and handed it to Victor, who read on it: "Grimaudan, ex-inspector of the detective force. Private business transacted." Victor shuddered as he said:

"You are connected with the police?"

"No, not now, but I have a liking for the business and I continue to work at it in a manner more—profitable. From time to time I strike upon a golden opportunity—such as your case presents."

"My case?"

"Yes, yours. I assure you it is a most promising affair, provided you are inclined to be reasonable."

"But if I am not reasonable?"

"Oh! my good fellow, you are not in a position to refuse me anything I may ask."

"What is it.... you want?" stammered Victor, fearfully.

"Well, I will inform you in a few words. I am sent by Mademoiselle de Sinclèves, the heiress of the Countess d'Andillot."

"What for?"

"To recover the black pearl."

"Black pearl?"

"That you stole."

"But I haven't got it."

116

"You have it."

"If I had, then I would be the assassin."

"You are the assassin."

Danègre showed a forced smile.

"Fortunately for me, monsieur, the Assizecourt was not of your opinion. The jury returned an unanimous verdict of acquittal. And when a man has a clear conscience and twelve good men in his favor——"

The ex-inspector seized him by the arm and said:

"No fine phrases, my boy. Now, listen to me and weigh my words carefully. You will find they are worthy of your consideration. Now, Danègre, three weeks before the murder, you abstracted the cook's key to the servants' door, and had a duplicate key made by a locksmith named Outard, 244 rue Oberkampf."

"It's a lie—it's a lie!" growled Victor. "No person has seen that key. There is no such key."

"Here it is."

After a silence, Grimaudan continued:

"You killed the countess with a knife purchased by you at the Bazar de la Republique on the same day as you ordered the duplicate key. It has a triangular blade with a groove running from end to end."

"That is all nonsense. You are simply guessing at something you don't know. No one ever saw the knife."

"Here it is."

Victor Danègre recoiled. The ex-inspector continued:

"There are some spots of rust upon it. Shall I tell you how they came there?"

"Well!.... you have a key and a knife. Who can prove that they belong to me?"

"The locksmith, and the clerk from whom you bought the knife. I have already refreshed their memories, and, when you confront them, they cannot fail to recognize you."

His speech was dry and hard, with a tone of firmness and precision. Danègre was trembling with fear, and yet he struggled desperately to maintain an air of indifference.

"Is that all the evidence you have?"

"Oh! no, not at all. I have plenty more. For instance, after the crime, you went out the same way you had entered. But, in the centre of the wardrobe-room, being seized by some sudden fear, you leaned against the wall for support."

"How do you know that? No one could know such a thing," argued the desperate man.

"The police know nothing about it, of course. They never think of lighting a candle and examining the walls. But if they had done so, they would have found on the white plaster a faint red spot, quite distinct, however, to trace in it the imprint of your thumb which you had pressed against the wall while it was wet with blood. Now, as you are well aware, under the Bertillon system, thumb-marks are one of the principal means of identification."

Victor Danègre was livid; great drops of perspiration rolled down his face and fell upon the table. He gazed, with a wild look, at the strange man who had narrated the story of his crime as faithfully as if he had been an invisible witness to it. Overcome and powerless, Victor bowed his head. He felt that it was useless to struggle against this marvelous man. So he said:

"How much will you give me, if I give you the pearl?"

"Nothing."

"Oh! you are joking! Or do you mean that I should give you an article worth thousands and hundreds of thousands and get nothing in return?"

"You will get your life. Is that nothing?"

The unfortunate man shuddered. Then Grimaudan added, in a milder tone:

"Come, Danègre, that pearl has no value in your hands. It is quite impossible for you to sell it; so what is the use of your keeping it?"

"There are pawnbrokers.... and, some day, I will be able to get something for it."

"But that day may be too late."

"Why?"

"Because by that time you may be in the hands of the police, and, with the evidence that I can furnish—the knife, the key, the thumb-mark—what will become of you?"

Victor rested his head on his hands and reflected. He felt that he was lost, irremediably lost, and, at the same time, a sense of weariness and depression overcame him. He murmured, faintly:

"When must I give it to you?"

"To-night——within an hour."

"If I refuse?"

"If you refuse, I shall post this letter to the Procureur of the Republic; in which letter Mademoiselle de Sinclèves denounces you as the assassin."

Danègre poured out two glasses of wine which he drank in rapid succession, then, rising, said:

"Pay the bill, and let us go. I have had enough of the cursed affair."

Night had fallen. The two men walked down the rue Lepic and followed the exterior boulevards in the direction of the Place de l'Etoile. They pursued their way in silence; Victor had a stooping carriage and a dejected face. When they reached the Parc Monceau, he said:

"We are near the house."

"Parbleu! You only left the house once, before your arrest, and that was to go to the tobacco-shop."

"Here it is," said Danègre, in a dull voice.

They passed along the garden wall of the countess' house, and crossed a street on a corner of which stood the tobacco-shop. A few steps further on, Danègre stopped; his limbs shook beneath him, and he sank to a bench.

"Well! what now?" demanded his companion.

"It is there."

"Where? Come, now, no nonsense!"

"There—in front of us."

"Where?"

"Between two paving-stones."

"Which?"

"Look for it."

"Which stones?"

Victor made no reply.

"Ah; I see!" exclaimed Grimaudan, "you want me to pay for the information."

"No.... but....I am afraid I will starve to death."

"So! that is why you hesitate. Well, I'll not be hard on you. How much do you want?"

"Enough to buy a steerage pass to America."

"All right."

"And a hundred francs to keep me until I get work there."

"You shall have two hundred. Now, speak."

"Count the paving-stones to the right from the sewer-hole. The pearl is between the twelfth and thirteenth."

"In the gutter?"

"Yes, close to the sidewalk."

Grimaudan glanced around to see if anyone were looking. Some tram-cars and pedestrians were passing. But, bah, they will not suspect anything. He opened his pocketknife and thrust it between the twelfth and thirteenth stones.

"And if it is not there?" he said to Victor.

"It must be there, unless someone saw me stoop down and hide it."

Could it be possible that the back pearl had been cast into the mud and filth of the gutter to be picked up by the first comer? The black pearl—a fortune!

"How far down?" he asked.

"About ten centimetres."

He dug up the wet earth. The point of his knife struck something. He enlarged the hole with his finger. Then he abstracted the black pearl from its filthy hiding-place.

"Good! Here are your two hundred francs. I will send you the ticket for America."

On the following day, this article was published in the `Echo de France,' and was copied by the leading newspapers throughout the world:

"Yesterday, the famous black pearl came into the possession of Arsène Lupin, who recovered it from the murderer of the Countess d'Andillot. In a short time, fac-similes of that precious jewel will be exhibited in London, St. Petersburg, Calcutta, Buenos Ayres and New York.

"Arsène Lupin will be pleased to consider all propositions submitted to him through his agents."

"And that is how crime is always punished and virtue rewarded," said Arsène Lupin, after he had told me the foregoing history of the black pearl.

"And that is how you, under the assumed name of Grimaudan, ex-inspector of detectives, were chosen by fate to deprive the criminal of the benefit of his crime."

"Exactly. And I confess that the affair gives me infinite satisfaction and pride. The forty minutes that I passed in the apartment of the Countess d'Andillot, after learning of her death, were the most thrilling and absorbing moments of my life. In those forty minutes, involved as I was in a most dangerous plight, I calmly studied the scene of the murder and reached the conclusion that the crime must have been committed by one of the house servants. I also decided that, in order to get the pearl, that servant must be arrested, and so I left the wainscoat button; it was necessary, also, for me to hold some convincing evidence of his guilt, so I carried away the knife which I found upon the floor, and the key which I found in the lock. I closed and locked the door, and erased the finger-marks from the plaster in the wardrobe-closet. In my opinion, that was one of those flashes—"

"Of genius," I said, interrupting.

"Of genius, if you wish. But, I flatter myself, it would not have occurred to the average mortal. To frame, instantly, the two elements of the problem— an arrest and an acquittal; to make use of the formidable machinery of the law to crush and humble my victim, and reduce him to a condition in which, when free, he would be certain to fall into the trap I was laying for him!"

"Poor devil—"

"Poor devil, do you say? Victor Danègre, the assassin! He might have descended to the lowest depths of vice and crime, if he had retained the black pearl. Now, he lives! Think of that: Victor Danègre is alive!"

"And you have the black pearl."

He took it out of one of the secret pockets of his wallet, examined it, gazed at it tenderly, and caressed it with loving fingers, and sighed, as he said:

"What cold Russian prince, what vain and foolish rajah may some day possess this priceless treasure! Or, perhaps, some American millionaire is destined to become the owner of this morsel of exquisite beauty that once adorned the fair bosom of Leontine Zalti, the Countess d'Andillot."

IX. HERLOCK SHOLMES ARRIVES TOO LATE

"It is really remarkable, Velmont, what a close resemblance you bear to Arsène Lupin!"

"How do you know?"

"Oh! like everyone else, from photographs, no two of which are alike, but each of them leaves the impression of a face.... something like yours."

Horace Velmont displayed some vexation.

"Quite so, my dear Devanne. And, believe me, you are not the first one who has noticed it."

"It is so striking," persisted Devanne, "that if you had not been recommended to me by my cousin d'Estevan, and if you were not the celebrated artist whose beautiful marine views I so admire, I have no doubt I should have warned the police of your presence in Dieppe."

This sally was greeted with an outburst of laughter. The large dining-hall of the Château de Thibermesnil contained on this occasion, besides Velmont, the following guests: Father Gélis, the parish priest, and a dozen officers whose regiments were quartered in the vicinity and who had accepted the invitation of the banker Georges Devanne and his mother. One of the officers then remarked:

"I understand that an exact description of Arsène Lupin has been furnished to all the police along this coast since his daring exploit on the Paris-Havre express."

"I suppose so," said Devanne. "That was three months ago; and a week later, I made the acquaintance of our friend Velmont at the casino, and, since then, he has honored me with several visits—an agreeable preamble to a more serious visit that he will pay me one of these days—or, rather, one of these nights."

This speech evoked another round of laughter, and the guests then passed into the ancient "Hall of the Guards," a vast room with a high ceiling, which occupied the entire lower part of the Tour Guillaume—William's Tower—and wherein Georges Devanne had collected the incomparable treasures which the lords of Thibermesnil had accumulated through many centuries. It contained ancient chests, credences, andirons and chandeliers. The stone walls were overhung with magnificent tapestries. The deep embrasures of the four windows were furnished with benches, and the Gothic windows were composed of small panes of colored glass set in a leaden frame. Between the door and the window to the left stood an immense bookcase of Renaissance style, on the pediment of which, in letters of gold, was the world "Thibermesnil," and, below it, the proud family device: "Fais ce que veulx" (Do what thou wishest). When the guests had lighted their cigars, Devanne resumed the conversation.

"And remember, Velmont, you have no time to lose; in fact, to-night is the last chance you will have."

"How so?" asked the painter, who appeared to regard the affair as a joke. Devanne was about to reply, when his mother mentioned to him to keep silent, but the excitement of the occasion and a desire to interest his guests urged him to speak.

"Bah!" he murmured. "I can tell it now. It won't do any harm."

The guests drew closer, and he commenced to speak with the satisfied air of a man who has an important announcement to make.

"To-morrow afternoon at four o'clock, Herlock Sholmes, the famous English detective, for whom such a thing as mystery does not exist; Herlock Sholmes, the most remarkable solver of enigmas the world has ever known, that marvelous man who would seem to be the creation of a romantic novelist—Herlock Sholmes will be my guest!"

Immediately, Devanne was the target of numerous eager questions. "Is Herlock Sholmes really coming?" "Is it so serious as that?" "Is Arsène Lupin really in this neighborhood?"

"Arsène Lupin and his band are not far away. Besides the robbery of the Baron Cahorn, he is credited with the thefts at Montigny, Gruchet and Crasville."

"Has he sent you a warning, as he did to Baron Cahorn?"

"No," replied Devanne, "he can't work the same trick twice."

"What then?"

"I will show you."

He rose, and pointing to a small empty space between the two enormous folios on one of the shelves of the bookcase, he said:

"There used to be a book there—a book of the sixteenth century entitled `Chronique de Thibermesnil,' which contained the history of the castle since its construction by Duke Rollo on the site of a former feudal fortress. There were three engraved plates in the book; one of which was a general view of the whole estate; another, the plan of the buildings; and the third—I call your attention to it, particularly—the third was the sketch of a subterranean passage, an entrance to which is outside the first line of ramparts, while the other end of the passage is here, in this very room. Well, that book disappeared a month ago."

"The deuce!" said Velmont, "that looks bad. But it doesn't seem to be a sufficient reason for sending for Herlock Sholmes."

"Certainly, that was not sufficient in itself, but another incident happened that gives the disappearance of the book a special significance. There was another copy of this book in the National Library at Paris, and the two books differed in certain details relating to the subterranean passage; for instance, each of them contained drawings and annotations, not printed, but written in ink and more or less effaced. I knew those facts, and I knew that the exact location of the passage could be determined only by a comparison of the two books. Now, the day after my book disappeared, the book was called for in the National Library by a reader who carried it away, and no one knows how the theft was effected."

The guests uttered many exclamations of surprise.

"Certainly, the affair looks serious," said one.

"Well, the police investigated the matter, and, as usual, discovered no clue whatever."

"They never do, when Arsène Lupin is concerned in it."

"Exactly; and so I decided to ask the assistance of Herlock Sholmes, who replied that he was ready and anxious to enter the lists with Arsène Lupin."

"What glory for Arsène Lupin!" said Velmont. "But if our national thief, as they call him, has no evil designs on your castle, Herlock Sholmes will have his trip in vain."

"There are other things that will interest him, such as the discovery of the subterranean passage."

"But you told us that one end of the passage was outside the ramparts and the other was in this very room!"

"Yes, but in what part of the room? The line which represents the passage on the charts ends here, with a small circle marked with the letters `T.G.,' which no doubt stand for `Tour Guillaume.' But the tower is round, and who can tell the exact spot at which the passage touches the tower?"

Devanne lighted a second cigar and poured himself a glass of Benedictine. His guests pressed him with questions and he was pleased to observe the interest that his remarks had created. The he continued:

"The secret is lost. No one knows it. The legend is to the effect that the former lords of the castle transmitted the secret from father to son on their deathbeds, until Geoffroy, the last of the race, was beheaded during the Revolution in his nineteenth year."

"That is over a century ago. Surely, someone has looked for it since that time?"

"Yes, but they failed to find it. After I purchased the castle, I made a diligent search for it, but without success. You must remember that this tower is surrounded by water and connected with the castle only by a bridge; consequently, the passage must be underneath the old moat. The plan that was in the book in the National Library showed a series of stairs with a total of forty-eight steps, which indicates a depth of more than ten meters. You see, the mystery lies within the walls of this room, and yet I dislike to tear them down."

"Is there nothing to show where it is?"

"Nothing."

"Mon. Devanne, we should turn our attention to the two quotations," suggested Father Gélis.

"Oh!" exclaimed Mon. Devanne, laughing, "our worthy father is fond of reading memoirs and delving into the musty archives of the castle. Everything relating to Thibermesnil interests him greatly. But the quotations that he mentions only serve to complicate the mystery. He has read somewhere that two kings of France have known the key to the puzzle."

"Two kings of France! Who were they?"

"Henry the Fourth and Louis the Sixteenth. And the legend runs like this: On the eve of the battle of Arques, Henry the Fourth spent the night in this castle. At eleven o'clock in the evening, Louise de Tancarville, the prettiest woman in Normandy, was brought into the castle through the subterranean passage by Duke Edgard, who, at the same time, informed the king of the secret passage. Afterward, the king confided the secret to his minister Sully, who, in turn, relates the story in his book, "Royales Economies d'Etat," without making any comment upon it, but linking with it this incomprehensible sentence: `Turn one eye on the bee that shakes, the other eye will lead to God!'"

After a brief silence, Velmont laughed and said:

"Certainly, it doesn't throw a dazzling light upon the subject."

"No; but Father Gélis claims that Sully concealed the key to the mystery in this strange sentence in order to keep the secret from the secretaries to whom he dictated his memoirs."

"That is an ingenious theory," said Velmont.

"Yes, and it may be nothing more; I cannot see that it throws any light on the mysterious riddle."

"And was it also to receive the visit of a lady that Louis the Sixteenth caused the passage to be opened?"

"I don't know," said Mon. Devanne. "All I can say is that the king stopped here one night in 1784, and that the famous Iron Casket found in the Louvre contained a paper bearing these words in the king's own writing: `Thibermesnil 3-4-11.'"

Horace Velmont laughed heartily, and exclaimed:

"At last! And now that we have the magic key, where is the man who can fit it to the invisible lock?"

"Laugh as much as you please, monsieur," said Father Gèlis, "but I am confident the solution is contained in those two sentences, and some day we will find a man able to interpret them."

"Herlock Sholmes is the man," said Mon. Devanne, "unless Arsène Lupin gets ahead of him. What is your opinion, Velmont?"

Velmont arose, placed his hand on Devanne's shoulder, and declared:

"I think that the information furnished by your book and the book of the National Library was deficient in a very important detail which you have now supplied. I thank you for it."

"What is it?"

"The missing key. Now that I have it, I can go to work at once," said Velmont.

"Of course; without losing a minute," said Devanne, smiling.

"Not even a second!" replied Velmont. "To-night, before the arrival of Herlock Sholmes, I must plunder your castle."

"You have no time to lose. Oh! by the way, I can drive you over this evening."

"To Dieppe?"

"Yes. I am going to meet Monsieur and Madame d'Androl and a young lady of their acquaintance who are to arrive by the midnight train."

Then addressing the officers, Devanne added:

"Gentlemen, I shall expect to see all of you at breakfast to-morrow."

The invitation was accepted. The company dispersed, and a few moments later Devanne and Velmont were speeding toward Dieppe in an automobile. Devanne dropped the artist in front of the Casino, and proceeded to the railway station. At twelve o'clock his friends alighted from the train. A half hour later the automobile was at the entrance to the castle. At one o'clock, after a light supper, they retired. The lights were extinguished, and the castle was enveloped in the darkness and silence of the night.

The moon appeared through a rift in the clouds, and filled the drawing-room with its bright white light. But only for a moment. Then the moon again retired behind its ethereal draperies, and darkness and silence reigned supreme. No sound could be heard, save the monotonous ticking of the clock. It struck two, and then continued its endless repetitions of the seconds. Then, three o'clock.

Suddenly, something clicked, like the opening and closing of a signal-disc that warns the passing train. A thin stream of light flashed to every corner of the room, like an arrow that leaves behind it a trail of light. It shot forth from the central fluting of a column that supported the pediment of the bookcase. It rested for a moment on the panel opposite like a glittering circle of burnished silver, then flashed in all directions like a guilty eye that scrutinizes every shadow. It disappeared for a short time, but burst forth again as a whole section of the bookcase revolved on a picot and disclosed a large opening like a vault.

A man entered, carrying an electric lantern. He was followed by a second man, who carried a coil of rope and various tools. The leader inspected the room, listened a moment, and said:

"Call the others."

Then eight men, stout fellows with resolute faces, entered the room, and immediately commenced to remove the furnishings. Arsène Lupin passed quickly from one piece of furniture to another, examined each, and, according to its size or artistic value, he directed his men to take it or leave it. If ordered to be taken, it was carried to the gaping mouth of the tunnel, and ruthlessly thrust into the bowels of the earth. Such was the fate of six armchairs, six small Louis XV chairs, a quantity of Aubusson tapestries, some candelabra, paintings by Fragonard and Nattier, a bust by Houdon, and some statuettes. Sometimes, Lupin would linger before a beautiful chest or a superb picture, and sigh:

"That is too heavy.... too large.... what a pity!"

In forty minutes the room was dismantled; and it had been accomplished in such an orderly manner and with as little noise as if the various articles had been packed and wadded for the occasion.

Lupin said to the last man who departed by way of the tunnel:

"You need not come back. You understand, that as soon as the auto-van is loaded, you are to proceed to the grange at Roquefort."

"But you, patron?"

"Leave me the motor-cycle."

When the man had disappeared, Arsène Lupin pushed the section of the bookcase back into its place, carefully effaced the traces of the men's footsteps, raised a portiere, and entered a gallery, which was the only means of communication between the tower and the castle. In the center of this gallery there was a glass cabinet which had attracted Lupin's attentions. It contained a valuable collection of watches, snuff-boxes, rings, chatelaines and miniatures of rare and beautiful workmanship. He forced the lock with a small jimmy, and experienced a great pleasure in handling those gold and silver ornaments, those exquisite and delicate works of art.

He carried a large linen bag, specially prepared for the removal of such knick-knacks. He filled it. Then he filled the pockets of his coat, waistcoat and trousers. And he was just placing over his left arm a number of pearl reticules when he heard a slight sound. He listened. No, he was not deceived. The noise continued. Then he remembered that, at one end of the gallery, there was a stairway leading to an unoccupied apartment, but which was probably occupied that night by the young lady whom Mon. Devanne had brought from Dieppe with his other visitors.

Immediately he extinguished his lantern, and had scarcely gained the friendly shelter of a window-embrasure, when the door at the top of the stairway was opened and a feeble light illuminated the gallery. He could feel—for, concealed by a curtain, he could not see—that a woman was cautiously descending the upper steps of the stairs. He hoped she would come no closer. Yet, she continued to descend, and even advanced some distance into the room. Then she uttered a faint cry. No doubt she had discovered the broken and dismantled cabinet.

She advanced again. Now he could smell the perfume, and hear the throbbing of her heart as she drew closer to the window where he was concealed. She passed so close that her skirt brushed against the window-curtain, and Lupin felt that she suspected the presence of another, behind her, in the shadow, within reach of her hand. He thought: "She is afraid. She will go away." But she did not go. The candle, that she carried in her trembling hand, grew brighter. She turned, hesitated a moment, appeared to listen, then suddenly drew aside the curtain.

They stood face to face. Arsène was astounded. He murmured, involuntarily:

"You—you—mademoiselle."

It was Miss Nelly. Miss Nelly! his fellow passenger on the transatlantic steamer, who had been the subject of his dreams on that memorable voyage, who had been a witness to his arrest, and who, rather than betray him, had dropped into the water the Kodak in which he had concealed the bank-notes and diamonds. Miss Nelly! that charming creature, the memory of whose face had sometimes sheered, sometimes saddened the long hours of imprisonment.

It was such an unexpected encounter that brought them face to face in that castle at that hour of the night, that they could not move, nor utter a word; they were amazed, hypnotized, each at the sudden apparition of the other. Trembling with emotion, Miss Nelly staggered to a seat. He remained standing in front of her.

Gradually, he realized the situation and conceived the impression he must have produced at that moment with his arms laden with knick-knacks, and his pockets and a linen sack overflowing with plunder. He was overcome with confusion, and he actually blushed to find himself in the position of a thief caught in the act. To her, henceforth, he was a thief, a man who puts his hand in another's pocket, who steals into houses and robs people while they sleep.

A watch fell upon the floor; then another. These were followed by other articles which slipped from his grasp one by one. Then, actuated by a sudden decision, he dropped the other articles into an armchair, emptied his pockets and unpacked his sack. He felt very uncomfortable in Nelly's presence, and stepped toward her with the intention of speaking to her, but she shuddered, rose quickly and fled toward the salon. The portiere closed behind her. He followed her. She was standing trembling and amazed at the sight of the devastated room. He said to her, at once:

"To-morrow, at three o'clock, everything will be returned. The furniture will be brought back."

She made no reply, so he repeated:

"I promise it. To-morrow, at three o'clock. Nothing in the world could induce me to break that promise....To-morrow, at three o'clock."

Then followed a long silence that he dared not break, whilst the agitation of the young girl caused him a feeling of genuine regret. Quietly, without a word, he turned away, thinking: "I hope she will go away. I can't endure her presence." But the young girl suddenly spoke, and stammered:

"Listen.... footsteps....I hear someone...."

He looked at her with astonishment. She seemed to be overwhelmed by the thought of approaching peril.

"I don't hear anything," he said.

"But you must go—you must escape!"

"Why should I go?"

"Because—you must. Oh! do not remain here another minute. Go!"

She ran, quickly, to the door leading to the gallery and listened. No, there was no one there. Perhaps the noise was outside. She waited a moment, then returned reassured.

But Arsène Lupin had disappeared.

As soon as Mon. Devanne was informed of the pillage of his castle, he said to himself: It was Velmont who did it, and Velmont is Arsène Lupin. That theory explained everything, and there was no other plausible explanation. And yet the idea seemed preposterous. It was ridiculous to suppose that Velmont was anyone else than Velmont, the famous artist, and club-fellow of his cousin d'Estevan. So, when the captain of the gendarmes arrived to investigate the affair, Devanne did not even think of mentioning his absurd theory.

Throughout the forenoon there was a lively commotion at the castle. The gendarmes, the local police, the chief of police from Dieppe, the villagers, all circulated to and fro in the halls, examining every nook and corner that was open to their inspection. The approach of the maneuvering troops, the rattling fire of the musketry, added to the picturesque character of the scene.

The preliminary search furnished no clue. Neither the doors nor windows showed any signs of having been disturbed. Consequently, the removal of the goods must have been effected by means of the secret passage. Yet, there were no indications of footsteps on the floor, nor any unusual marks upon the walls.

Their investigations revealed, however, one curious fact that denoted the whimsical character of Arsène Lupin: the famous Chronique of the sixteenth century had been restored to its accustomed place in the library and, beside it, there was a similar book, which was none other than the volume stolen from the National Library.

At eleven o'clock the military officers arrived. Devanne welcomed them with his usual gayety; for, no matter how much chagrin he might suffer from the loss of his artistic treasures, his great wealth enabled him to bear his loss philosophically. His guests, Monsieur and Madame d'Androl and Miss Nelly, were introduced; and it was then noticed that one of the expected guests had not arrived. It was Horace Velmont. Would he come? His absence had awakened the suspicions of Mon. Devanne. But at twelve o'clock he arrived. Devanne exclaimed:

"Ah! here you are!"

"Why, am I not punctual?" asked Velmont.

"Yes, and I am surprised that you are.... after such a busy night! I suppose you know the news?"

"What news?"

"You have robbed the castle."

"Nonsense!" exclaimed Velmont, smiling.

"Exactly as I predicted. But, first escort Miss Underdown to the dining-room. Mademoiselle, allow me——"

He stopped, as he remarked the extreme agitation of the young girl. Then, recalling the incident, he said:

"Ah! of course, you met Arsène Lupin on the steamer, before his arrest, and you are astonished at the resemblance. Is that it?"

She did not reply. Velmont stood before her, smiling. He bowed. She took his proffered arm. He escorted her to her place, and took his seat opposite her. During the breakfast, the conversation related exclusively to Arsène Lupin, the stolen goods, the secret passage, and Herlock Sholmes. It was only at the close of the repast, when the conversation had drifted to other subjects, that Velmont took any part in it. Then he was, by turns, amusing and grave, talkative and pensive. And all his remarks seemed to be directed to the young girl. But she, quite absorbed, did not appear to hear them.

Coffee was served on the terrace overlooking the court of honor and the flower garden in front of the principal façade. The regimental band played on the lawn, and scores of soldiers and peasants wandered through the park.

Miss Nelly had not forgotten, for one moment, Lupin's solemn promise: "To-morrow, at three o'clock, everything will be returned."

At three o'clock! And the hands of the great clock in the right wing of the castle now marked twenty minutes to three. In spite of herself, her eyes wandered to the clock every minute. She also watched Velmont, who was calmly swinging to and fro in a comfortable rocking chair.

Ten minutes to three!....Five minutes to three!....Nelly was impatient and anxious. Was it possible that Arsène Lupin would carry out his promise at the appointed hour, when the castle, the courtyard, and the park were filled with people, and at the very moment when the officers of the law were pursuing their investigations? And yet....Arsène Lupin had given her his solemn promise. "It will be exactly as he said," thought she, so deeply was she impressed with the authority, energy and assurance of that remarkable man. To her, it no longer assumed the form of a miracle, but, on the contrary, a natural incident that must occur in the ordinary course of events. She blushed, and turned her head.

Three o'clock! The great clock struck slowly: one.... two.... three....Horace Velmont took out his watch, glanced at the clock, then returned the watch to his pocket. A few seconds passed in silence; and then the crowd in the courtyard parted to give passage to two wagons, that had just entered the park-gate, each drawn by two horses. They were army-wagons, such as are used for the transportation of provisions, tents, and other necessary military stores. They stopped in front of the main entrance, and a commissary-sergeant leaped from one of the wagons and inquired for Mon. Devanne. A moment later, that gentleman emerged from the house, descended the steps, and, under the canvas covers of the wagons, beheld his furniture, pictures and ornaments carefully packaged and arranged.

When questioned, the sergeant produced an order that he had received from the officer of the day. By that order, the second company of the fourth battalion were commanded to proceed to the crossroads of Halleux in the forest of Arques, gather up the furniture and other articles deposited there, and deliver same to Monsieur Georges Devanne, owner of the Thibermesnil castle, at three o'clock. Signed: Col. Beauvel.

"At the crossroads," explained the sergeant, "we found everything ready, lying on the grass, guarded by some passers-by. It seemed very strange, but the order was imperative."

One of the officers examined the signature. He declared it a forgery; but a clever imitation. The wagons were unloaded, and the goods restored to their proper places in the castle.

During this commotion, Nelly had remained alone at the extreme end of the terrace, absorbed by confused and distracted thoughts. Suddenly, she observed Velmont approaching her. She would have avoided him, but the balustrade that surrounded the terrace cut off her retreat. She was cornered. She could not move. A gleam of sunshine, passing through the scant foliage of a bamboo, lighted up her beautiful golden hair. Some one spoke to her in a low voice:

"Have I not kept my promise?"

Arsène Lupin stood close to her. No one else was near. He repeated, in a calm, soft voice:

"Have I not kept my promise?"

He expected a word of thanks, or at least some slight movement that would betray her interest in the fulfillment of his promise. But she remained silent.

Her scornful attitude annoyed Arsène Lupin; and he realized the vast distance that separated him from Miss Nelly, now that she had learned the truth. He would gladly have justified himself in her eyes, or at least pleaded extenuating circumstances, but he perceived the absurdity and futility of such an attempt. Finally, dominated by a surging flood of memories, he murmured:

"Ah! how long ago that was! You remember the long hours on the deck of the `Provence.' Then, you carried a rose in your hand, a white rose like the one you carry to-day. I asked you for it. You pretended you did not hear me. After you had gone away, I found the rose—forgotten, no doubt—and I kept it."

She made no reply. She seemed to be far away. He continued:

"In memory of those happy hours, forget what you have learned since. Separate the past from the present. Do not regard me as the man you saw last night, but look at me, if only for a moment, as you did in those far-off days when I was Bernard d'Andrezy, for a short time. Will you, please?"

She raised her eyes and looked at him as he had requested. Then, without saying a word, she pointed to a ring he was wearing on his forefinger. Only the ring was visible; but the setting, which was turned toward the palm of his hand, consisted of a magnificent ruby. Arsène Lupin blushed. The ring belonged to Georges Devanne. He smiled bitterly, and said:

"You are right. Nothing can be changed. Arsène Lupin is now and always will be Arsène Lupin. To you, he cannot be even so much as a memory. Pardon me....I should have known that any attention I may now offer you is simply an insult. Forgive me."

He stepped aside, hat in hand. Nelly passed before him. He was inclined to detain her and beseech her forgiveness. But his courage failed, and he contented himself by following her with his eyes, as he had done when she descended the gangway to the pier at New York. She mounted the steps leading to the door, and disappeared within the house. He saw her no more.

A cloud obscured the sun. Arsène Lupin stood watching the imprints of her tiny feet in the sand. Suddenly, he gave a start. Upon the box which contained the bamboo, beside which Nelly had been standing, he saw the rose, the white rose which he had desired but dared not ask for. Forgotten, no doubt—it, also! But how—designedly or through distraction? He seized it eagerly. Some of its petals fell to the ground. He picked them up, one by one, like precious relics.

"Come!" he said to himself, "I have nothing more to do here. I must think of my safety, before Herlock Sholmes arrives."

The park was deserted, but some gendarmes were stationed at the park-gate. He entered a grove of pine trees, leaped over the wall, and, as a short cut to the railroad station, followed a path across the fields. After walking about ten minutes, he arrived at a spot where the road grew narrower and ran between two steep banks. In this ravine, he met a man traveling in the opposite direction. It was a man about fifty years of age, tall, smooth-shaven, and wearing clothes of a foreign cut. He carried a heavy cane, and a small satchel was strapped across his shoulder. When they met, the stranger spoke, with a slight English accent:

"Excuse me, monsieur, is this the way to the castle?"

"Yes, monsieur, straight ahead, and turn to the left when you come to the wall. They are expecting you."

"Ah!"

"Yes, my friend Devanne told us last night that you were coming, and I am delighted to be the first to welcome you. Herlock Sholmes has no more ardent admirer than.... myself."

There was a touch of irony in his voice that he quickly regretted, for Herlock Sholmes scrutinized him from head to foot with such a keen, penetrating eye that Arsène Lupin experienced the sensation of being seized, imprisoned and registered by that look more thoroughly and precisely than he had ever been by a camera.

"My negative is taken now," he thought, "and it will be useless to use a disguise with that man. He would look right through it. But, I wonder, has he recognized me?"

They bowed to each other as if about to part. But, at that moment, they heard a sound of horses' feet, accompanied by a clinking of steel. It was the gendarmes. The two men were obliged to draw back against the embankment, amongst the brushes, to avoid the horses. The gendarmes passed by, but, as they followed each other at a considerable distance, they were several minutes in doing so. And Lupin was thinking:

"It all depends on that question: has he recognized me? If so, he will probably take advantage of the opportunity. It is a trying situation."

When the last horseman had passed, Herlock Sholmes stepped forth and brushed the dust from his clothes. Then, for a moment, he and Arsène Lupin gazed at each other; and, if a person could have seen them at that moment, it would have been an interesting sight, and memorable as the first meeting of two remarkable men, so strange, so powerfully equipped, both of superior quality, and destined by fate, through their peculiar attributes, to hurl themselves one at the other like two equal forces that nature opposes, one against the other, in the realms of space.

Then the Englishman said: "Thank you, monsieur."

They parted. Lupin went toward the railway station, and Herlock Sholmes continued on his way to the castle.

The local officers had given up the investigation after several hours of fruitless efforts, and the people at the castle were awaiting the arrival of the English detective with a lively curiosity. At first sight, they were a little disappointed on account of his commonplace appearance, which differed so greatly from the pictures they had formed of him in their own minds. He did not in any way resemble the romantic hero, the mysterious and diabolical personage that the name of Herlock Sholmes had evoked in their imaginations. However, Mon. Devanne exclaimed with much gusto:

"Ah! monsieur, you are here! I am delighted to see you. It is a long-deferred pleasure. Really, I scarcely regret what has happened, since it affords me the opportunity to meet you. But, how did you come?"

"By the train."

"But I sent my automobile to meet you at the station."

"An official reception, eh? with music and fireworks! Oh! no, not for me. That is not the way I do business," grumbled the Englishman.

This speech disconcerted Devanne, who replied, with a forced smile:

"Fortunately, the business has been greatly simplified since I wrote to you."

"In what way?"

"The robbery took place last night."

"If you had not announced my intended visit, it is probable the robbery would not have been committed last night."

"When, then?"

"To-morrow, or some other day."

"And in that case?"

"Lupin would have been trapped," said the detective.

"And my furniture?"

"Would not have been carried away."

"Ah! but my goods are here. They were brought back at three o'clock."

"By Lupin."

"By two army-wagons."

Herlock Sholmes put on his cap and adjusted his satchel. Devanne exclaimed, anxiously:

"But, monsieur, what are you going to do?"

"I am going home."

"Why?"

"Your goods have been returned; Arsène Lupin is far away—there is nothing for me to do."

"Yes, there is. I need your assistance. What happened yesterday, may happen again to-morrow, as we do not know how he entered, or how he escaped, or why, a few hours later, he returned the goods."

"Ah! you don't know—"

The idea of a problem to be solved quickened the interest of Herlock Sholmes.

"Very well, let us make a search—at once—and alone, if possible."

Devanne understood, and conducted the Englishman to the salon. In a dry, crisp voice, in sentences that seemed to have been prepared in advance, Holmes asked a number of questions about the events of the preceding evening, and enquired also concerning the guests and the members of the household. Then he examined the two volumes of the "Chronique," compared the plans of the subterranean passage, requested a repetition of the sentences discovered by Father Gélis, and then asked:

"Was yesterday the first time you have spoken hose two sentences to any one?"

"Yes."

"You had never communicated then to Horace Velmont?"

"No."

"Well, order the automobile. I must leave in an hour."

"In an hour?"

"Yes; within that time, Arsène Lupin solved the problem that you placed before him."

"I.... placed before him—"

"Yes, Arsène Lupin or Horace Velmont—same thing."

"I thought so. Ah! the scoundrel!"

"Now, let us see," said Holmes, "last night at ten o'clock, you furnished Lupin with the information that he lacked, and that he had been seeking for many weeks. During the night, he found time to solve the problem, collect his men, and rob the castle. I shall be quite as expeditious."

He walked from end to end of the room, in deep thought, then sat down, crossed his long legs and closed his eyes.

Devanne waited, quite embarrassed. Thought he: "Is the man asleep? Or is he only meditating?" However, he left the room to give some orders, and when he returned he found the detective on his knees scrutinizing the carpet at the foot of the stairs in the gallery.

"What is it?" he enquired.

"Look.... there.... spots from a candle."

"You are right—and quite fresh."

"And you will also find them at the top of the stairs, and around the cabinet that Arsène Lupin broke into, and from which he took the bibelots that he afterward placed in this armchair."

"What do you conclude from that?"

"Nothing. These facts would doubtless explain the cause for the restitution, but that is a side issue that I cannot wait to investigate. The main question is the secret passage. First, tell me, is there a chapel some two or three hundred metres from the castle?"

"Yes, a ruined chapel, containing the tomb of Duke Rollo."

"Tell your chauffer to wait for us near that chapel."

"My chauffer hasn't returned. If he had, they would have informed me. Do you think the secret passage runs to the chapel? What reason have—"

"I would ask you, monsieur," interrupted the detective, "to furnish me with a ladder and a lantern."

"What! do you require a ladder and a lantern?"

"Certainly, or I shouldn't have asked for them."

Devanne, somewhat disconcerted by this crude logic, rang the bell. The two articles were given with the sternness and precision of military commands.

"Place the ladder against the bookcase, to the left of the word Thibermesnil."

Devanne placed the ladder as directed, and the Englishman continued:

"More to the left.... to the right....There!....Now, climb up.... All the letters are in relief, aren't they?"

"Yes."

"First, turn the letter I one way or the other."

"Which one? There are two of them."

"The first one."

Devanne took hold of the letter, and exclaimed:

"Ah! yes, it turns toward the right. Who told you that?"

Herlock Sholmes did not reply to the question, but continued his directions:

"Now, take the letter B. Move it back and forth as you would a bolt."

Devanne did so, and, to his great surprise, it produced a clicking sound.

"Quite right," said Holmes. "Now, we will go to the other end of the word Thibermesnil, try the letter I, and see if it will open like a wicket."

With a certain degree of solemnity, Devanne seized the letter. It opened, but Devanne fell from the ladder, for the entire section of the bookcase, lying between the first and last letters of the words, turned on a picot and disclosed the subterranean passage.

Herlock Sholmes said, coolly:

"You are not hurt?"

"No, no," said Devanne, as he rose to his feet, "not hurt, only bewildered. I can't understand now.... those letters turn.... the secret passage opens...."

"Certainly. Doesn't that agree exactly with the formula given by Sully? Turn one eye on the bee that shakes, the other eye will lead to God."

"But Louis the sixteenth?" asked Devanne.

"Louis the sixteenth was a clever locksmith. I have read a book he wrote about combination locks. It was a good idea on the part of the owner of Thibermesnil to show His Majesty a clever bit of mechanism. As an aid to his memory, the king wrote: 3-4-11, that is to say, the third, fourth and eleventh letters of the word."

"Exactly. I understand that. It explains how Lupin got out of the room, but it does not explain how he entered. And it is certain he came from the outside."

Herlock Sholmes lighted his lantern, and stepped into the passage.

"Look! All the mechanism is exposed here, like the works of a clock, and the reverse side of the letters can be reached. Lupin worked the combination from this side—that is all."

"What proof is there of that?"

"Proof? Why, look at that puddle of oil. Lupin foresaw that the wheels would require oiling."

"Did he know about the other entrance?"

"As well as I know it," said Holmes. "Follow me."

"Into that dark passage?"

"Are you afraid?"

"No, but are you sure you can find the way out?"

"With my eyes closed."

At first, they descended twelve steps, then twelve more, and, farther on, two other flights of twelve steps each. Then they walked through a long passageway, the brick walls of which showed the marks of successive restorations, and, in spots, were dripping with water. The earth, also, was very damp.

"We are passing under the pond," said Devanne, somewhat nervously.

At last, they came to a stairway of twelve steps, followed by three others of twelve steps each, which they mounted with difficulty, and then found themselves in a small cavity cut in the rock. They could go no further.

"The deuce!" muttered Holmes, "nothing but bare walls. This is provoking."

"Let us go back," said Devanne. "I have seen enough to satisfy me."

But the Englishman raised his eye and uttered a sigh of relief. There, he saw the same mechanism and the same word as before. He had merely to work the three letters. He did so, and a block of granite swung out of place. On the other side, this granite block formed the tombstone of Duke Rollo, and the word "Thibermesnil" was engraved on it in relief. Now, they were in the little ruined chapel, and the detective said:

"The other eye leads to God; that means, to the chapel."

"It is marvelous!" exclaimed Devanne, amazed at the clairvoyance and vivacity of the Englishman. "Can it be possible that those few words were sufficient for you?"

"Bah!" declared Holmes, "they weren't even necessary. In the chart in the book of the National Library, the drawing terminates at the left, as you know, in a circle, and at the right, as you do not know, in a cross. Now, that cross must refer to the chapel in which we now stand."

Poor Devanne could not believe his ears. It was all so new, so novel to him. He exclaimed:

"It is incredible, miraculous, and yet of a childish simplicity! How is it that no one has ever solved the mystery?"

"Because no one has ever united the essential elements, that is to say, the two books and the two sentences. No one, but Arsène Lupin and myself."

"But, Father Gélis and I knew all about those things, and, likewise—"

Holmes smiled, and said:

"Monsieur Devanne, everybody cannot solve riddles."

"I have been trying for ten years to accomplish what you did in ten minutes."

"Bah! I am used to it."

They emerged from the chapel, and found an automobile.

"Ah! there's an auto waiting for us."

"Yes, it is mine," said Devanne.

"Yours? You said your chauffeur hadn't returned."

They approached the machine, and Mon. Devanne questioned the chauffer:

"Edouard, who gave you orders to come here?"

"Why, it was Monsieur Velmont."

"Mon. Velmont? Did you meet him?"

"Near the railway station, and he told me to come to the chapel."

"To come to the chapel! What for?"

"To wait for you, monsieur, and your friend."

Devanne and Holmes exchanged looks, and Mon. Devanne said:

"He knew the mystery would be a simple one for you. It is a delicate compliment."

A smile of satisfaction lighted up the detective's serious features for a moment. The compliment pleased him. He shook his head, as he said:

"A clever man! I knew that when I saw him."

"Have you seen him?"

"I met him a short time ago—on my way from the station."

"And you knew it was Horace Velmont—I mean, Arsène Lupin?"

"That is right. I wonder how it came—"

"No, but I supposed it was—from a certain ironical speech he made."

"And you allowed him to escape?"

"Of course I did. And yet I had everything on my side, such as five gendarmes who passed us."

"Sacrableu!" cried Devanne. "You should have taken advantage of the opportunity."

"Really, monsieur," said the Englishman, haughtily, "when I encounter an adversary like Arsène Lupin, I do not take advantage of chance opportunities, I create them."

But time pressed, and since Lupin had been so kind as to send the automobile, they resolved to profit by it. They seated themselves in the comfortable limousine; Edouard took his place at the wheel, and away they went toward the railway station. Suddenly, Devanne's eyes fell upon a small package in one of the pockets of the carriage.

"Ah! what is that? A package! Whose is it? Why, it is for you."

"For me?"

"Yes, it is addressed: Herlock Sholmes, from Arsène Lupin."

The Englishman took the package, opened it, and found that it contained a watch.

"Ah!" he exclaimed, with an angry gesture.

"A watch," said Devanne. "How did it come there?"

The detective did not reply.

"Oh! it is your watch! Arsène Lupin returns your watch! But, in order to return it, he must have taken it. Ah! I see! He took your watch! That is a good one! Herlock Sholmes' watch stolen by Arsène Lupin! Mon Dieu! that is funny! Really.... you must excuse me....I can't help it."

He roared with laughter, unable to control himself. After which, he said, in a tone of earnest conviction:

"A clever man, indeed!"

The Englishman never moved a muscle. On the way to Dieppe, he never spoke a word, but fixed his gaze on the flying landscape. His silence was terrible, unfathomable, more violent than the wildest rage. At the railway station, he spoke calmly, but in a voice that impressed one with the vast energy and will power of that famous man. He said:

"Yes, he is a clever man, but some day I shall have the pleasure of placing on his shoulder the hand I now offer to you, Monsieur Devanne. And I believe that Arsène Lupin and Herlock Sholmes will meet again some day. Yes, the world is too small—we will meet—we must meet—and then—"

THE END

BOOK TWO.
ARSÈNE LUPIN
VERSUS HERLOCK SHOLMES

I. LOTTERY TICKET NO. 514.

On the eighth day of last December, Mon. Gerbois, professor of mathematics at the College of Versailles, while rummaging in an old curiosity-shop, unearthed a small mahogany writing-desk which pleased him very much on account of the multiplicity of its drawers.

"Just the thing for Suzanne's birthday present," thought he. And as he always tried to furnish some simple pleasures for his daughter, consistent with his modest income, he enquired the price, and, after some keen bargaining, purchased it for sixty-five francs. As he was giving his address to the shopkeeper, a young man, dressed with elegance and taste, who had been exploring the stock of antiques, caught sight of the writing-desk, and immediately enquired its price.

"It is sold," replied the shopkeeper.

"Ah! to this gentleman, I presume?"

Monsieur Gerbois bowed, and left the store, quite proud to be the possessor of an article which had attracted the attention of a gentleman of quality. But he had not taken a dozen steps in the street, when he was overtaken by the young man who, hat in hand and in a tone of perfect courtesy, thus addressed him:

"I beg your pardon, monsieur; I am going to ask you a question that you may deem impertinent. It is this: Did you have any special object in view when you bought that writing-desk?"

"No, I came across it by chance and it struck my fancy."

"But you do not care for it particularly?"

"Oh! I shall keep it—that is all."

"Because it is an antique, perhaps?"

"No; because it is convenient," declared Mon. Gerbois.

"In that case, you would consent to exchange it for another desk that would be quite as convenient and in better condition?"

"Oh! this one is in good condition, and I see no object in making an exchange."

"But——"

Mon. Gerbois is a man of irritable disposition and hasty temper. So he replied, testily:

"I beg of you, monsieur, do not insist."

But the young man firmly held his ground.

"I don't know how much you paid for it, monsieur, but I offer you double."

"No."

"Three times the amount."

"Oh! that will do," exclaimed the professor, impatiently; "I don't wish to sell it."

The young man stared at him for a moment in a manner that Mon. Gerbois would not readily forget, then turned and walked rapidly away.

An hour later, the desk was delivered at the professor's house on the Viroflay road. He called his daughter, and said:

"Here is something for you, Suzanne, provided you like it."

Suzanne was a pretty girl, with a gay and affectionate nature. She threw her arms around her father's neck and kissed him rapturously. To her, the desk had all the semblance of a royal gift. That evening, assisted by Hortense, the servant, she placed the desk in her room; then she dusted it, cleaned the drawers and pigeon-holes, and carefully arranged within it her papers, writing material, correspondence, a collection of post-cards, and some souvenirs of her cousin Philippe that she kept in secret.

Next morning, at half past seven, Mon. Gerbois went to the college. At ten o'clock, in pursuance of her usual custom, Suzanne went to meet him, and it was a great pleasure for him to see her slender figure and childish smile waiting for him at the college gate. They returned home together.

"And your writing desk—how is it this morning!"

"Marvellous! Hortense and I have polished the brass mountings until they look like gold."

"So you are pleased with it?"

"Pleased with it! Why, I don't see how I managed to get on without it for such a long time."

As they were walking up the pathway to the house, Mon. Gerbois said:

"Shall we go and take a look at it before breakfast?"

"Oh! yes, that's a splendid idea!"

She ascended the stairs ahead of her father, but, on arriving at the door of her room, she uttered a cry of surprise and dismay.

"What's the matter?" stammered Mon. Gerbois.

"The writing-desk is gone!"

When the police were called in, they were astonished at the admirable simplicity of the means employed by the thief. During Suzanne's absence, the servant had gone to market, and while the house was thus left unguarded, a drayman, wearing a badge—some of the neighbors saw it—stopped his cart in front of the house and rang twice. Not knowing that Hortense was absent, the neighbors were not suspicious; consequently, the man carried on his work in peace and tranquility.

Apart from the desk, not a thing in the house had been disturbed. Even Suzanne's purse, which she had left upon the writing-desk, was found upon an adjacent table with its contents untouched. It was obvious that the thief had come with a set purpose, which rendered the crime even more mysterious; because, why did he assume so great a risk for such a trifling object?

The only clue the professor could furnish was the strange incident of the preceding evening. He declared:

"The young man was greatly provoked at my refusal, and I had an idea that he threatened me as he went away."

But the clue was a vague one. The shopkeeper could not throw any light on the affair. He did not know either of the gentlemen. As to the desk itself, he had purchased it for forty francs at an executor's sale at Chevreuse, and believed he had resold it at its fair value. The police investigation disclosed nothing more.

But Mon. Gerbois entertained the idea that he had suffered an enormous loss. There must have been a fortune concealed in a secret drawer, and that was the reason the young man had resorted to crime.

"My poor father, what would we have done with that fortune?" asked Suzanne.

"My child! with such a fortune, you could make a most advantageous marriage."

Suzanne sighed bitterly. Her aspirations soared no higher than her cousin Philippe, who was indeed a most deplorable object. And life, in the little house at Versailles, was not so happy and contented as of yore.

Two months passed away. Then came a succession of startling events, a strange blending of good luck and dire misfortune!

On the first day of February, at half-past five, Mon. Gerbois entered the house, carrying an evening paper, took a seat, put on his spectacles, and commenced to read. As politics did not interest him, he turned to the inside of the paper. Immediately his attention was attracted by an article entitled:

"Third Drawing of the Press Association Lottery.

"No. 514, series 23, draws a million."

The newspaper slipped from his fingers. The walls swam before his eyes, and his heart ceased to beat. He held No. 514, series 23. He had purchased it from a friend, to oblige him, without any thought of success, and behold, it was the lucky number!

Quickly, he took out his memorandum-book. Yes, he was quite right. The No. 514, series 23, was written there, on the inside of the cover. But the ticket?

He rushed to his desk to find the envelope-box in which he had placed the precious ticket; but the box was not there, and it suddenly occurred to him that it had not been there for several weeks. He heard footsteps on the gravel walk leading from the street.

He called:

"Suzanne! Suzanne!"

She was returning from a walk. She entered hastily. He stammered, in a choking voice:

"Suzanne ... the box ... the box of envelopes?"

"What box?"

"The one I bought at the Louvre ... one Saturday ... it was at the end of that table."

"Don't you remember, father, we put all those things away together."

"When?"

"The evening ... you know ... the same evening...."

"But where?... Tell me, quick!... Where?"

"Where? Why, in the writing-desk."

"In the writing-desk that was stolen?"

"Yes."

"Oh, mon Dieu!... In the stolen desk!"

He uttered the last sentence in a low voice, in a sort of stupor. Then he seized her hand, and in a still lower voice, he said:

"It contained a million, my child."

"Ah! father, why didn't you tell me?" she murmured, naively.

"A million!" he repeated. "It contained the ticket that drew the grand prize in the Press Lottery."

The colossal proportions of the disaster overwhelmed them, and for a long time they maintained a silence that they feared to break. At last, Suzanne said:

"But, father, they will pay you just the same."

"How? On what proof?"

"Must you have proof?"

"Of course."

"And you haven't any?"

"It was in the box."

"In the box that has disappeared."

"Yes; and now the thief will get the money."

"Oh! that would be terrible, father. You must prevent it."

For a moment he was silent; then, in an outburst of energy, he leaped up, stamped on the floor, and exclaimed:

"No, no, he shall not have that million; he shall not have it! Why should he have it? Ah! clever as he is, he can do nothing. If he goes to claim the money, they will arrest him. Ah! now, we will see, my fine fellow!"

"What will you do, father?"

"Defend our just rights, whatever happens! And we will succeed. The million francs belong to me, and I intend to have them."

A few minutes later, he sent this telegram:

"Governor Crédit Foncier

"rue Capucines, Paris.

"Am holder of No. 514, series 23. Oppose by all legal means any other claimant.

"GERBOIS."

Almost at the same moment, the Crédit Foncier received the following telegram:

"No. 514, series 23, is in my possession.

"ARSÈNE LUPIN."

Every time I undertake to relate one of the many extraordinary adventures that mark the life of Arsène Lupin, I experience a feeling of embarrassment, as it seems to me that the most commonplace of those adventures is already well known to my readers. In fact, there is not a movement of our "national thief," as he has been so aptly described, that has not been given the widest publicity, not an exploit that has not been studied in all its phases, not an action that has not been discussed with that particularity usually reserved for the recital of heroic deeds.

For instance, who does not know the strange history of "The Blonde Lady," with those curious episodes which were proclaimed by the newspapers with heavy black headlines, as follows: "Lottery Ticket No. 514!" ... "The Crime on the Avenue Henri-Martin!" ... "The Blue Diamond!" ... The interest created by the intervention of the celebrated English detective, Herlock Sholmes! The excitement aroused by the various vicissitudes which marked the struggle between those famous artists! And what a commotion on the boulevards, the day on which the newsboys announced: "Arrest of Arsène Lupin!"

My excuse for repeating these stories at this time is the fact that I produce the key to the enigma. Those adventures have always been enveloped in a certain degree of obscurity, which I now remove. I reproduce old newspaper articles, I relate old-time interviews, I present ancient letters; but I have arranged and classified all that material and reduced it to the exact truth. My collaborators in this work have been Arsène Lupin himself, and also the ineffable Wilson, the friend and confidant of Herlock Sholmes.

Every one will recall the tremendous burst of laughter which greeted the publication of those two telegrams. The name "Arsène Lupin" was in itself a stimulus to curiosity, a promise of amusement for the gallery. And, in this case, the gallery means the entire world.

An investigation was immediately commenced by the Crédit Foncier, which established these facts: That ticket No. 514, series 23, had been sold by the Versailles branch office of the Lottery to an artillery officer named Bessy, who was afterward killed by a fall from his horse. Some time before his death, he informed some of his comrades that he had transferred his ticket to a friend.

"And I am that friend," affirmed Mon. Gerbois.

"Prove it," replied the governor of the Crédit Foncier.

"Of course I can prove it. Twenty people can tell you that I was an intimate friend of Monsieur Bessy, and that we frequently met at the Café de la Place-d'Armes. It was there, one day, I purchased the ticket from him for twenty francs—simply as an accommodation to him.

"Have you any witnesses to that transaction?"

"No."

"Well, how do you expect to prove it?"

"By a letter he wrote to me."

"What letter?"

"A letter that was pinned to the ticket."

"Produce it."

"It was stolen at the same time as the ticket."

"Well, you must find it."

It was soon learned that Arsène Lupin had the letter. A short paragraph appeared in the *Echo de France*—which has the honor to be his official organ, and of which, it is said, he is one of the principal shareholders—the paragraph announced that Arsène Lupin had placed in the hands of Monsieur Detinan, his advocate and legal adviser, the letter that Monsieur Bessy had written to him—to him personally.

This announcement provoked an outburst of laughter. Arsène Lupin had engaged a lawyer! Arsène Lupin, conforming to the rules and customs of modern society, had appointed a legal representative in the person of a well-known member of the Parisian bar!

Mon. Detinan had never enjoyed the pleasure of meeting Arsène Lupin—a fact he deeply regretted—but he had actually been retained by that mysterious gentleman and felt greatly honored by the choice. He was prepared to defend the interests of his client to the best of his ability. He was pleased, even proud, to exhibit the letter of Mon. Bessy, but, although it proved the transfer of the ticket, it did not mention the name of the purchaser. It was simply addressed to "My Dear Friend."

"My Dear Friend! that is I," added Arsène Lupin, in a note attached to Mon. Bessy's letter. "And the best proof of that fact is that I hold the letter."

The swarm of reporters immediately rushed to see Mon. Gerbois, who could only repeat:

"My Dear Friend! that is I.... Arsène Lupin stole the letter with the lottery ticket."

"Let him prove it!" retorted Lupin to the reporters.

"He must have done it, because he stole the writing-desk!" exclaimed Mon. Gerbois before the same reporters.

"Let him prove it!" replied Lupin.

Such was the entertaining comedy enacted by the two claimants of ticket No. 514; and the calm demeanor of Arsène Lupin contrasted strangely with the nervous perturbation of poor Mon. Gerbois. The newspapers were filled with the lamentations of that unhappy man. He announced his misfortune with pathetic candor.

"Understand, gentlemen, it was Suzanne's dowry that the rascal stole! Personally, I don't care a straw for it,... but for Suzanne! Just think of it, a whole million! Ten times one hundred thousand francs! Ah! I knew very well that the desk contained a treasure!"

It was in vain to tell him that his adversary, when stealing the desk, was unaware that the lottery ticket was in it, and that, in any event, he could not foresee that the ticket would draw the grand prize. He would reply;

"Nonsense! of course, he knew it ... else why would he take the trouble to steal a poor, miserable desk?"

"For some unknown reason; but certainly not for a small scrap of paper which was then worth only twenty francs."

"A million francs! He knew it;... he knows everything! Ah! you do not know him—the scoundrel!... He hasn't robbed you of a million francs!"

The controversy would have lasted for a much longer time, but, on the twelfth day, Mon. Gerbois received from Arsène Lupin a letter, marked "confidential," which read as follows:

"Monsieur, the gallery is being amused at our expense. Do you not think it is time for us to be serious? The situation is this: I possess a ticket to which I have no legal right, and you have the legal right to a ticket you do not possess. Neither of us can do anything. You will not relinquish your rights to me; I will not deliver the ticket to you. Now, what is to be done?

"I see only one way out of the difficulty: Let us divide the spoils. A half-million for you; a half-million for me. Is not that a fair division? In my opinion, it is an equitable solution, and an immediate one. I will give you three days' time to consider the proposition. On Thursday morning I shall expect to read in the personal column of the Echo de France a discreet message addressed to *M. Ars. Lup*, expressing in veiled terms your consent to my offer. By so doing you will recover immediate possession of the ticket; then you can collect the money and send me half a million in a manner that I will describe to you later.

"In case of your refusal, I shall resort to other measures to accomplish the same result. But, apart from the very serious annoyances that such obstinacy on your part will cause you, it will cost you twenty-five thousand francs for supplementary expenses.

"Believe me, monsieur, I remain your devoted servant, ARSÈNE LUPIN."

In a fit of exasperation Mon. Gerbois committed the grave mistake of showing that letter and allowing a copy of it to be taken. His indignation overcame his discretion.

"Nothing! He shall have nothing!" he exclaimed, before a crowd of reporters. "To divide my property with him? Never! Let him tear up the ticket if he wishes!"

"Yet five hundred thousand francs is better than nothing."

"That is not the question. It is a question of my just right, and that right I will establish before the courts."

"What! attack Arsène Lupin? That would be amusing."

"No; but the Crédit Foncier. They must pay me the million francs."

"Without producing the ticket, or, at least, without proving that you bought it?"

"That proof exists, since Arsène Lupin admits that he stole the writing-desk."

"But would the word of Arsène Lupin carry any weight with the court?"

"No matter; I will fight it out."

The gallery shouted with glee; and wagers were freely made upon the result with the odds in favor of Lupin. On the following Thursday the personal column in the *Echo de France* was eagerly perused by the expectant public, but it contained nothing addressed to *M. Ars. Lup.* Mon. Gerbois had not replied to Arsène Lupin's letter. That was the declaration of war.

That evening the newspapers announced the abduction of Mlle. Suzanne Gerbois.

The most entertaining feature in what might be called the Arsène Lupin dramas is the comic attitude displayed by the Parisian police. Arsène Lupin talks, plans, writes, commands, threatens and executes as if the police did not exist. They never figure in his calculations.

And yet the police do their utmost. But what can they do against such a foe—a foe that scorns and ignores them?

Suzanne had left the house at twenty minutes to ten; such was the testimony of the servant. On leaving the college, at five minutes past ten, her father did not find her at the place she was accustomed to wait for him. Consequently, whatever had happened must have occurred during the course of Suzanne's walk from the house to the college. Two neighbors had met her about three hundred yards from the house. A lady had seen, on the avenue, a young girl corresponding to Suzanne's description. No one else had seen her.

Inquiries were made in all directions; the employees of the railways and street-car lines were questioned, but none of them had seen anything of the missing girl. However, at Ville-d'Avray, they found a shopkeeper who had furnished gasoline to an automobile that had come from Paris on the day of the abduction. It was occupied by a blonde woman—extremely blonde, said the witness. An hour later, the automobile again passed through Ville-d'Avray on its way from Versailles to Paris. The shopkeeper declared that the automobile now contained a second woman who was heavily veiled. No doubt, it was Suzanne Gerbois.

The abduction must have taken place in broad daylight, on a frequented street, in the very heart of the town. How? And at what spot? Not a cry was heard; not a suspicious action had been seen. The shopkeeper described the automobile as a royal-blue limousine of twenty-four horse-power made by the firm of Peugeon & Co. Inquiries were then made at the Grand-Garage, managed by Madame Bob-Walthour, who made a specialty of abductions by automobile. It was learned that she had rented a Peugeon limousine on that day to a blonde woman whom she had never seen before nor since.

"Who was the chauffeur?"

"A young man named Ernest, whom I had engaged only the day before. He came well recommended."

"Is he here now?"

"No. He brought back the machine, but I haven't seen him since," said Madame Bob-Walthour.

"Do you know where we can find him?"

"You might see the people who recommended him to me. Here are the names."

Upon inquiry, it was learned that none of these people knew the man called Ernest. The recommendations were forged.

Such was the fate of every clue followed by the police. It ended nowhere. The mystery remained unsolved.

Mon. Gerbois had not the strength or courage to wage such an unequal battle. The disappearance of his daughter crushed him;, he capitulated to the enemy. A short an announcement in the *Echo de France* proclaimed his unconditional surrender.

Two days later, Mon. Gerbois visited the office of the Crédit Foncier and handed lottery ticket number 514, series 23, to the governor, who exclaimed, with surprise:

"Ah! you have it! He has returned it to you!"

"It was mislaid. That was all," replied Mon. Gerbois.

"But you pretended that it had been stolen."

"At first, I thought it had ... but here it is."

"We will require some evidence to establish your right to the ticket."

"Will the letter of the purchaser, Monsieur Bessy, be sufficient!"

"Yes, that will do."

"Here it is," said Mon. Gerbois, producing the letter.

"Very well. Leave these papers with us. The rules of the lottery allow us fifteen days' time to investigate your claim. I will let you know when to call for your money. I presume you desire, as much as I do, that this affair should be closed without further publicity."

"Quite so."

Mon. Gerbois and the governor henceforth maintained a discreet silence. But the secret was revealed in some way, for it was soon commonly known that Arsène Lupin had returned the lottery ticket to Mon. Gerbois. The public received the news with astonishment and admiration. Certainly, he was a bold gamester who thus threw upon the table a trump card of such importance as the precious ticket. But, it was true, he still retained a trump card of equal importance. However, if the young girl should escape? If the hostage held by Arsène Lupin should be rescued?

The police thought they had discovered the weak spot of the enemy, and now redoubled their efforts. Arsène Lupin disarmed by his own act, crushed by the wheels of his own machination, deprived of every sou of the coveted million ... public interest now centered in the camp of his adversary.

But it was necessary to find Suzanne. And they did not find her, nor did she escape. Consequently, it must be admitted, Arsène Lupin had won the first hand. But the game was not yet decided. The most difficult point remained. Mlle. Gerbois is in his possession, and he will hold her until he receives five hundred thousand francs. But how and where will such an exchange be made? For that purpose, a meeting must be arranged, and then what will prevent Mon. Gerbois from warning the police and, in that way, effecting the rescue of his daughter and, at the same time, keeping his money? The professor was interviewed, but he was extremely reticent. His answer was:

"I have nothing to say."

"And Mlle. Gerbois?"

"The search is being continued."

"But Arsène Lupin has written to you?"

"No."

"Do you swear to that?"

"No."

"Then it is true. What are his instructions?"

"I have nothing to say."

Then the interviewers attacked Mon. Detinan, and found him equally discreet.

"Monsieur Lupin is my client, and I cannot discuss his affairs," he replied, with an affected air of gravity.

These mysteries served to irritate the gallery. Obviously, some secret negotiations were in progress. Arsène Lupin had arranged and tightened the meshes of his net, while the police maintained a close watch, day and night, over Mon. Gerbois. And the three and only possible dénouements—the arrest, the triumph, or the ridiculous and pitiful abortion—were freely discussed; but the curiosity of the public was only partially satisfied, and it was reserved for these pages to reveal the exact truth of the affair.

On Monday, March 12th, Mon. Gerbois received a notice from the Crédit Foncier. On Wednesday, he took the one o'clock train for Paris. At two o'clock, a thousand bank-notes of one thousand francs each were delivered to him. Whilst he was counting them, one by one, in a state of nervous agitation—that money, which represented Suzanne's ransom—a carriage containing two men stopped at the curb a short distance from the bank. One of the men had grey hair and an unusually shrewd expression which formed a striking contrast to his shabby make-up. It was Detective Ganimard, the relentless enemy of Arsène Lupin. Ganimard said to his companion, Folenfant:

"In five minutes, we will see our clever friend Lupin. Is everything ready?"

"Yes."

"How many men have we?"

"Eight—two of them on bicycles."

"Enough, but not too many. On no account, must Gerbois escape us; if he does, it is all up. He will meet Lupin at the appointed place, give half a million in exchange for the girl, and the game will be over."

"But why doesn't Gerbois work with us? That would be the better way, and he could keep all the money himself."

"Yes, but he is afraid that if he deceives the other, he will not get his daughter."

"What other?"

"Lupin."

Ganimard pronounced the word in a solemn tone, somewhat timidly, as if he were speaking of some supernatural creature whose claws he already felt.

"It is very strange," remarked Folenfant, judiciously, "that we are obliged to protect this gentleman contrary to his own wishes."

"Yes, but Lupin always turns the world upside down," said Ganimard, mournfully.

A moment later, Mon. Gerbois appeared, and started up the street. At the end of the rue des Capucines, he turned into the boulevards, walking slowly, and stopping frequently to gaze at the shop-windows.

"Much too calm, too self-possessed," said Ganimard. "A man with a million in his pocket would not have that air of tranquillity."

"What is he doing?"

"Oh! nothing, evidently.... But I have a suspicion that it is Lupin—yes, Lupin!"

At that moment, Mon. Gerbois stopped at a news-stand, purchased a paper, unfolded it and commenced to read it as he walked slowly away. A moment later, he gave a sudden bound into an automobile that was standing at the curb. Apparently, the machine had been waiting for him, as it started away rapidly, turned at the Madeleine and disappeared.

"Nom de nom!" cried Ganimard, "that's one of his old tricks!"

Ganimard hastened after the automobile around the Madeleine. Then, he burst into laughter. At the entrance to the Boulevard Malesherbes, the automobile had stopped and Mon. Gerbois had alighted.

"Quick, Folenfant, the chauffeur! It may be the man Ernest."

Folenfant interviewed the chauffeur. His name was Gaston; he was an employee of the automobile cab company; ten minutes ago, a gentleman had engaged him and told him to wait near the news-stand for another gentleman.

"And the second man—what address did he give?" asked Folenfant.

"No address. 'Boulevard Malesherbes ... avenue de Messine ... double pourboire.' That is all."

But, during this time, Mon. Gerbois had leaped into the first passing carriage.

"To the Concorde station, Metropolitan," he said to the driver.

He left the underground at the Place du Palais-Royal, ran to another carriage and ordered it to go to the Place de la Bourse. Then a second journey by the underground to the Avenue dc Villiers, followed by a third carriage drive to number 25 rue Clapeyron.

Number 25 rue Clapeyron is separated from the Boulevard des Batignolles by the house which occupies the angle formed by the two streets. He ascended to the first floor and rang. A gentleman opened the door.

"Does Monsieur Detinan live here?"

"Yes, that is my name. Are you Monsieur Gerbois?"

"Yes."

"I was expecting you. Step in."

As Mon. Gerbois entered the lawyer's office, the clock struck three. He said:

"I am prompt to the minute. Is he here?"

"Not yet."

Mon. Gerbois took a seat, wiped his forehead, looked at his watch as if he did not know the time, and inquired, anxiously:

"Will he come?"

"Well, monsieur," replied the lawyer, "that I do not know, but I am quite as anxious and impatient as you are to find out. If he comes, he will run a great risk, as this house has been closely watched for the last two weeks. They distrust me."

"They suspect me, too. I am not sure whether the detectives lost sight of me or not on my way here."

"But you were—"

"It wouldn't be my fault," cried the professor, quickly. "You cannot reproach me. I promised to obey his orders, and I followed them to the very letter. I drew the money at the time fixed by him, and I came here in the manner directed by him. I have faithfully performed my part of the agreement—let him do his!"

After a short silence, he asked, anxiously:

"He will bring my daughter, won't he?"

"I expect so."

"But ... you have seen him?"

"I? No, not yet. He made the appointment by letter, saying both of you would be here, and asking me to dismiss my servants before three o'clock and admit no one while you were here. If I would not consent to that arrangement, I was to notify him by a few words in *the Echo de France*. But I am only too happy to oblige Mon. Lupin, and so I consented."

"Ah! how will this end?" moaned Mon. Gerbois.

He took the bank-notes from his pocket, placed them on the table and divided them into two equal parts. Then the two men sat there in silence. From time to time, Mon. Gerbois would listen. Did someone ring?... His nervousness increased every minute, and Monsieur Detinan also displayed considerable anxiety. At last, the lawyer lost his patience. He rose abruptly, and said:

"He will not come.... We shouldn't expect it. It would be folly on his part. He would run too great a risk."

And Mon. Gerbois, despondent, his hands resting on the bank-notes, stammered:

"Oh! Mon Dieu! I hope he will come. I would give the whole of that money to see my daughter again."

The door opened.

"Half of it will be sufficient, Monsieur Gerbois."

These words were spoken by a well-dressed young man who now entered the room and was immediately recognized by Mon. Gerbois as the person who had wished to buy the desk from him at Versailles. He rushed toward him.

"Where is my daughter—my Suzanne?"

Arsène Lupin carefully closed the door, and, while slowly removing his gloves, said to the lawyer:

"My dear maître, I am indebted to you very much for your kindness in consenting to defend my interests. I shall not forget it."

Mon. Detinan murmured:

"But you did not ring. I did not hear the door—"

"Doors and bells are things that should work without being heard. I am here, and that is the important point."

"My daughter! Suzanne! Where is she!" repeated the professor.

"Mon Dieu, monsieur," said Lupin, "what's your hurry? Your daughter will be here in a moment."

Lupin walked to and fro for a minute, then, with the pompous air of an orator, he said:

"Monsieur Gerbois, I congratulate you on the clever way in which you made the journey to this place."

Then, perceiving the two piles of bank-notes, he exclaimed:

"Ah! I see! the million is here. We will not lose any time. Permit me."

"One moment," said the lawyer, placing himself before the table. "Mlle. Gerbois has not yet arrived."

"Well?"

"Is not her presence indispensable?"

"I understand! I understand! Arsène Lupin inspires only a limited confidence. He might pocket the half-million and not restore the hostage. Ah! monsieur, people do not understand me. Because I have been obliged, by force of circumstances, to commit certain actions a little ... out of the ordinary, my good faith is impugned ... I, who have always observed the utmost scrupulosity and delicacy in business affairs. Besides, my dear monsieur if you have any fear, open the window and call. There are at least a dozen detectives in the street."

"Do you think so?"

Arsène Lupin raised the curtain.

"I think that Monsieur Gerbois could not throw Ganimard off the scent.... What did I tell you? There he is now."

"Is it possible!" exclaimed the professor. "But I swear to you—"

"That you have not betrayed me?... I do not doubt you, but those fellows are clever—sometimes. Ah! I can see Folenfant, and Greaume, and Dieuzy— all good friends of mine!"

Mon. Detinan looked at Lupin in amazement. What assurance! He laughed as merrily as if engaged in some childish sport, as if no danger threatened him. This unconcern reassured the lawyer more than the presence of the detectives. He left the table on which the bank-notes were lying. Arsène Lupin picked up one pile of bills after the other, took from each of them twenty-five bank-notes which he offered to Mon. Detinan, saying:

"The reward of your services to Monsieur Gerbois and Arsène Lupin. You well deserve it."

"You owe me nothing," replied the lawyer.

"What! After all the trouble we have caused you!"

"And all the pleasure you have given me!"

"That means, my dear monsieur, that you do not wish to accept anything from Arsène Lupin. See what it is to have a bad reputation."

He then offered the fifty thousand francs to Mon. Gerbois, saying:

"Monsieur, in memory of our pleasant interview, permit me to return you this as a wedding-gift to Mlle. Gerbois."

Mon. Gerbois took the money, but said:

"My daughter will not marry."

"She will not marry if you refuse your consent; but she wishes to marry."

"What do you know about it!"

"I know that young girls often dream of such things unknown to their parents. Fortunately, there are sometimes good genii like Arsène Lupin who discover their little secrets in the drawers of their writing desks."

"Did you find anything else?" asked the lawyer. "I confess I am curious to know why you took so much trouble to get possession of that desk."

"On account of its historic interest, my friend. Although despite the opinion of Monsieur Gerbois, the desk contained no treasure except the lottery ticket—and that was unknown to me—I had been seeking it for a long time. That writing-desk of yew and mahogany was discovered in the little house in which Marie Walêwska once lived in Boulogne, and, on one of the drawers there is this inscription: '*Dedicated to Napoleon I, Emperor of the French, by his very faithful servant, Mancion.*' And above it, these words, engraved with the point of a knife: '*To you, Marie.*' Afterwards, Napoleon had a similar desk made for the Empress Josephine; so that the secretary that was so much admired at the Malmaison was only an imperfect copy of the one that will henceforth form part of my collection."

"Ah! if I had known, when in the shop, I would gladly have given it up to you," said the professor.

Arsène Lupin smiled, as he replied:

"And you would have had the advantage of keeping for your own use lottery ticket number 514."

"And you would not have found it necessary to abduct my daughter."

"Abduct your daughter?"

"Yes."

"My dear monsieur, you are mistaken. Mlle. Gerbois was not abducted."

"No?"

"Certainly not. Abduction means force or violence. And I assure you that she served as hostage of her own free will."

"Of her own free will!" repeated Mon. Gerbois, in amazement.

"In fact, she almost asked to be taken. Why, do you suppose that an intelligent young girl like Mlle. Gerbois, and who, moreover, nourishes an unacknowledged passion, would hesitate to do what was necessary to secure her dowry. Ah! I swear to you it was not difficult to make her understand that it was the only way to overcome your obstinacy."

Mon. Detinan was greatly amused. He replied to Lupin:

"But I should think it was more difficult to get her to listen to you. How did you approach her?"

"Oh! I didn't approach her myself. I have not the honor of her acquaintance. A friend of mine, a lady, carried on the negotiations."

"The blonde woman in the automobile, no doubt."

"Precisely. All arrangements were made at the first interview near the college. Since then, Mlle. Gerbois and her new friend have been travelling in Belgium and Holland in a manner that should prove most pleasing and instructive to a young girl. She will tell you all about it herself—"

The bell of the vestibule door rang, three rings in quick succession, followed by two isolated rings.

"It is she," said Lupin. "Monsieur Detinan, if you will be so kind—"

The lawyer hastened to the door.

Two young women entered. One of them threw herself into the arms of Mon. Gerbois. The other approached Lupin. The latter was a tall woman of a good figure, very pale complexion, and with blond hair, parted over her forehead in undulating waves, that glistened and shone like the setting sun. She was dressed in black, with no display of jewelled ornaments; but, on the contrary, her appearance indicated good taste and refined elegance. Arsène Lupin spoke a few words to her; then, bowing to Mlle. Gerbois, he said:

"I owe you an apology, mademoiselle, for all your troubles, but I hope you have not been too unhappy—"

"Unhappy! Why, I should have been very happy, indeed, if it hadn't been for leaving my poor father."

"Then all is for the best. Kiss him again, and take advantage of the opportunity—it is an excellent one—to speak to him about your cousin."

"My cousin! What do you mean? I don't understand."

"Of course, you understand. Your cousin Philippe. The young man whose letters you kept so carefully."

Suzanne blushed; but, following Lupin's advice, she again threw herself into her father's arms. Lupin gazed upon them with a tender look.

"Ah! Such is my reward for a virtuous act! What a touching picture! A happy father and a happy daughter! And to know that their joy is your work, Lupin! Hereafter these people will bless you, and reverently transmit your name unto their descendants, even unto the fourth generation. What a glorious reward, Lupin, for one act of kindness!"

He walked to the window.

"Is dear old Ganimard still waiting?... He would like very much to be present at this charming domestic scene!... Ah! he is not there.... Nor any of the others.... I don't see anyone. The deuce! The situation is becoming serious. I dare say they are already under the porte-cochere ... talking to the concierge, perhaps ... or, even, ascending the stairs!"

Mon. Gerbois made a sudden movement. Now, that his daughter had been restored to him, he saw the situation in a different light. To him, the arrest of his adversary meant half-a-million francs. Instinctively, he made a step forward. As if by chance, Lupin stood in his way.

"Where are you going, Monsieur Gerbois! To defend me against them! That is very kind of you, but I assure you it is not necessary. They are more worried than I."

Then he continued to speak, with calm deliberation:

"But, really, what do they know! That you are here, and, perhaps, that Mlle. Gerbois is here, for they may have seen her arrive with an unknown lady. But they do not imagine that I am here. How is it possible that I could be in a house that they ran-sacked from cellar to garret this morning! They suppose that the unknown lady was sent by me to make the exchange, and they will be ready to arrest her when she goes out—"

At that moment, the bell rang. With a brusque movement, Lupin seized Mon. Gerbois, and said to him, in an imperious tone:

"Do not move! Remember your daughter, and be prudent—otherwise— As to you, Monsieur Detinan, I have your promise."

Mon. Gerbois was rooted to the spot. The lawyer did not stir. Without the least sign of haste, Lupin picked up his hat and brushed the dust from off it with his sleeve.

"My dear Monsieur Detinan, if I can ever be of service to you.... My best wishes, Mademoiselle Suzanne, and my kind regards to Monsieur Philippe."

He drew a heavy gold watch from his pocket.

"Monsieur Gerbois, it is now forty-two minutes past three. At forty-six minutes past three, I give you permission to leave this room. Not one minute sooner than forty-six minutes past three."

"But they will force an entrance," suggested Mon. Detinan.

"You forget the law, my dear monsieur! Ganimard would never venture to violate the privacy of a French citizen. But, pardon me, time flies, and you are all slightly nervous."

He placed his watch on the table, opened the door of the room and addressing the blonde lady he said:

"Are you ready my dear?"

He drew back to let her pass, bowed respectfully to Mlle. Gerbois, and went out, closing the door behind him. Then they heard him in the vestibule, speaking, in a loud voice: "Good-day, Ganimard, how goes it? Remember me to Madame Ganimard. One of these days, I shall invite her to breakfast. Au revoir, Ganimard."

The bell rang violently, followed by repeated rings, and voices on the landing.

"Forty-five minutes," muttered Mon. Gerbois.

After a few seconds, he left the room and stepped into the vestibule. Arsène Lupin and the blonde lady had gone.

"Papa!... you mustn't! Wait!" cried Suzanne.

"Wait! you are foolish!... No quarter for that rascal!... And the half-million?"

He opened the outer door. Ganimard rushed in.

"That woman—where is she? And Lupin?"

"He was here ... he is here."

Ganimard uttered a cry of triumph.

"We have him. The house is surrounded."

"But the servant's stairway?" suggested Mon. Detinan.

"It leads to the court," said Ganimard. "There is only one exit—the street-door. Ten men are guarding it."

"But he didn't come in by the street-door, and he will not go out that way."

"What way, then?" asked Ganimard. "Through the air?"

He drew aside a curtain and exposed a long corridor leading to the kitchen. Ganimard ran along it and tried the door of the servants' stairway. It was locked. From the window he called to one of his assistants:

"Seen anyone?"

"No."

"Then they are still in the house!" he exclaimed. "They are hiding in one of the rooms! They cannot have escaped. Ah! Lupin, you fooled me before, but, this time, I get my revenge."

At seven o'clock in the evening, Mon. Dudonis, chief of the detective service, astonished at not receiving any news, visited the rue Clapeyron. He questioned the detectives who were guarding the house, then ascended to Mon. Detinan's apartment. The lawyer led him into his room. There, Mon. Dudonis beheld a man, or rather two legs kicking in the air, while the body to which they belonged was hidden in the depths of the chimney.

"Ohé!... Ohé!" gasped a stifled voice. And a more distant voice, from on high, replied:

"Ohé!... Ohé!"

Mon. Dudonis laughed, and exclaimed:

"Here! Ganimard, have you turned chimney-sweep?"

The detective crawled out of the chimney. With his blackened face, his sooty clothes, and his feverish eyes, he was quite unrecognizable.

"I am looking for *him*," he growled.

"Who?"

"Arsène Lupin ... and his friend."

"Well, do you suppose they are hiding in the chimney?"

Ganimard arose, laid his sooty hand on the sleeve of his superior officer's coat, and exclaimed, angrily:

"Where do you think they are, chief? They must be somewhere! They are flesh and blood like you and me, and can't fade away like smoke."

"No, but they have faded away just the same."

"But how? How? The house is surrounded by our men—even on the roof."

"What about the adjoining house?"

"There's no communication with it."

"And the apartments on the other floors?"

164

"I know all the tenants. They have not seen anyone."

"Are you sure you know all of them?"

"Yes. The concierge answers for them. Besides, as an extra precaution, I have placed a man in each apartment. They can't escape. If I don't get them to-night, I will get them to-morrow. I shall sleep here."

He slept there that night and the two following nights. Three days and nights passed away without the discovery of the irrepressible Lupin or his female companion; more than that, Ganimard did not unearth the slightest clue on which to base a theory to explain their escape. For that reason, he adhered to his first opinion.

"There is no trace of their escape; therefore, they are here."

It may be that, at the bottom of his heart, his conviction was less firmly established, but he would not confess it. No, a thousand times, no! A man and a woman could not vanish like the evil spirits in a fairy tale. And, without losing his courage, he continued his searches, as if he expected to find the fugitives concealed in some impenetrable retreat, or embodied in the stone walls of the house.

II. THE BLUE DIAMOND.

On the evening of March 27, at number 134 avenue Henri-Martin, in the house that he had inherited from his brother six months before, the old general Baron d'Hautrec, ambassador at Berlin under the second Empire, was asleep in a comfortable armchair, while his secretary was reading to him, and the Sister Auguste was warming his bed and preparing the night-lamp. At eleven o'clock, the Sister, who was obliged to return to the convent of her order at that hour, said to the secretary:

"Mademoiselle Antoinette, my work is finished; I am going."

"Very well, Sister."

"Do not forget that the cook is away, and that you are alone in the house with the servant."

"Have no fear for the Baron. I sleep in the adjoining room and always leave the door open."

The Sister left the house. A few moments later, Charles, the servant, came to receive his orders. The Baron was now awake, and spoke for himself.

"The usual orders, Charles: see that the electric bell rings in your room, and, at the first alarm, run for the doctor. Now, Mademoiselle Antoinette, how far did we get in our reading?"

"Is Monsieur not going to bed now?"

"No, no, I will go later. Besides, I don't need anyone."

Twenty minutes later, he was sleeping again, and Antoinette crept away on tiptoe. At that moment, Charles was closing the shutters on the lower floor. In the kitchen, he bolted the door leading to the garden, and, in the vestibule, he not only locked the door but hooked the chain as well. Then he ascended to his room on the third floor, went to bed, and was soon asleep.

Probably an hour had passed, when he leaped from his bed in alarm. The bell was ringing. It rang for some time, seven or eight seconds perhaps, without intermission.

"Well!" muttered Charles, recovering his wits, "another of the Baron's whims."

He dressed himself quickly, descended the stairs, stopped in front of the door, and rapped, according to his custom. He received no reply. He opened the door and entered.

"Ah! no light," he murmured. "What is that for?"

Then, in a low voice, he called:

"Mademoiselle?"

No reply.

"Are you there, mademoiselle? What's the matter? Is Monsieur le Baron ill?"

No reply. Nothing but a profound silence that soon became depressing. He took two steps forward; his foot struck a chair, and, having touched it, he noticed that it was overturned. Then, with his hand, he discovered other objects on the floor—a small table and a screen. Anxiously, he approached the wall, felt for the electric button, and turned on the light.

In the centre of the room, between the table and dressing-case, lay the body of his master, the Baron d'Hautrec.

"What!... It can't be possible!" he stammered.

He could not move. He stood there, with bulging eyes, gazing stupidly at the terrible disorder, the overturned chairs, a large crystal candelabra shattered in a thousand pieces, the clock lying on the marble hearthstone, all evidence of a fearful and desperate struggle. The handle of a stiletto glittered, not far from the corpse; the blade was stained with blood. A handkerchief, marked with red spots, was lying on the edge of the bed.

Charles recoiled with horror: the body lying at his feet extended itself for a moment, then shrunk up again; two or three tremors, and that was the end.

He stooped over the body. There was a clean-cut wound on the neck from which the blood was flowing and then congealing in a black pool on the carpet. The face retained an expression of extreme terror.

"Some one has killed him!" he muttered, "some one has killed him!"

Then he shuddered at the thought that there might be another dreadful crime. Did not the baron's secretary sleep in the adjoining room! Had not the assassin killed her also! He opened the door; the room was empty. He concluded that Antoinette had been abducted, or else she had gone away before the crime. He returned to the baron's chamber, his glance falling on the secretary, he noticed that that article of furniture remained intact. Then, he saw upon a table, beside a bunch of keys and a pocketbook that the baron placed there every night, a handful of golden louis. Charles seized the pocketbook, opened it, and found some bank-notes. He counted them; there were thirteen notes of one hundred francs each.

Instinctively, mechanically, he put the bank-notes in his pocket, rushed down the stairs, drew the bolt, unhooked the chain, closed the door behind him, and fled to the street.

Charles was an honest man. He had scarcely left the gate, when, cooled by the night air and the rain, he came to a sudden halt. Now, he saw his action in its true light, and it filled him with horror. He hailed a passing cab, and said to the driver:

"Go to the police-office, and bring the commissary. Hurry! There has been a murder in that house."

The cab-driver whipped his horse. Charles wished to return to the house, but found the gate locked. He had closed it himself when he came out, and it could not be opened from the outside. On the other hand, it was useless to ring, as there was no one in the house.

It was almost an hour before the arrival of the police. When they came, Charles told his story and handed the bank-notes to the commissary. A locksmith was summoned, and, after considerable difficulty, he succeeded in forcing open the garden gate and the vestibule door. The commissary of police entered the room first, but, immediately, turned to Charles and said:

"You told me that the room was in the greatest disorder."

Charles stood at the door, amazed, bewildered; all the furniture had been restored to its accustomed place. The small table was standing between the two windows, the chairs were upright, and the clock was on the centre of the mantel. The debris of the candelabra had been removed.

"Where is.... Monsieur le Baron?" stammered Charles.

"That's so!" exclaimed the officer, "where is the victim?"

He approached the bed, and drew aside a large sheet, under which reposed the Baron d'Hautrec, formerly French Ambassador at Berlin. Over him, lay his military coat, adorned with the Cross of Honor. His features were calm. His eyes were closed.

"Some one has been here," said Charles.

"How did they get in?"

"I don't know, but some one has been here during my absence. There was a stiletto on the floor—there! And a handkerchief, stained with blood, on the bed. They are not here now. They have been carried away. And some one has put the room in order."

"Who would do that?"

"The assassin."

"But we found all the doors locked."

"He must have remained in the house."

"Then he must be here yet, as you were in front of the house all the time."

Charles reflected a moment, then said, slowly:

"Yes ... of course.... I didn't go away from the gate."

"Who was the last person you saw with the baron?"

"Mademoiselle Antoinette, his secretary."

"What has become of her?"

"I don't know. Her bed wasn't occupied, so she must have gone out. I am not surprised at that, as she is young and pretty."

"But how could she leave the house?"

"By the door," said Charles.

"But you had bolted and chained it."

"Yes, but she must have left before that."

"And the crime was committed after her departure?"

"Of course," said the servant.

The house was searched from cellar to garret, but the assassin had fled. How? And when? Was it he or an accomplice who had returned to the scene of the crime and removed everything that might furnish a clue to his identity? Such were the questions the police were called upon to solve.

The coroner came at seven o'clock; and, at eight o'clock, Mon. Dudouis, the head of the detective service, arrived on the scene. They were followed by the Procureur of the Republic and the investigating magistrate. In addition to these officials, the house was overrun with policemen, detectives, newspaper reporters, photographers, and relatives and acquaintances of the murdered man.

A thorough search was made; they studied out the position of the corpse according to the information furnished by Charles; they questioned Sister Auguste when she arrived; but they discovered nothing new. Sister Auguste was astonished to learn of the disappearance of Antoinette Bréhat. She had engaged the young girl twelve days before, on excellent recommendations, and refused to believe that she would neglect her duty by leaving the house during the night.

"But, you see, she hasn't returned yet," said the magistrate, "and we are still confronted with the question: What has become of her?"

"I think she was abducted by the assassin," said Charles.

The theory was plausible, and was borne out by certain facts. Mon. Dudouis agreed with it. He said:

"Abducted? ma foi! that is not improbable."

"Not only improbable," said a voice, "but absolutely opposed to the facts. There is not a particle of evidence to support such a theory."

The voice was harsh, the accent sharp, and no one was surprised to learn that the speaker was Ganimard. In no one else, would they tolerate such a domineering tone.

"Ah! it is you, Ganimard!" exclaimed Mon. Dudouis. "I had not seen you before."

"I have been here since two o'clock."

"So you are interested in some things outside of lottery ticket number 514, the affair of the rue Clapeyron, the blonde lady and Arsène Lupin?"

"Ha-ha!" laughed the veteran detective. "I would not say that Lupin is a stranger to the present case. But let us forget the affair of the lottery ticket for a few moments, and try to unravel this new mystery."

Ganimard is not one of those celebrated detectives whose methods will create a school, or whose name will be immortalized in the criminal annals of his country. He is devoid of those flashes of genius which characterize the work of Dupin, Lecoq and Sherlock Holmes. Yet, it must be admitted, he possesses superior qualities of observation, sagacity, perseverance and even intuition. His merit lies in his absolute independence. Nothing troubles or influences him, except, perhaps, a sort of fascination that Arsène Lupin holds over him. However that may be, there is no doubt that his position on that morning, in the house of the late Baron d'Hautrec, was one of undoubted superiority, and his collaboration in the case was appreciated and desired by the investigating magistrate.

"In the first place," said Ganimard, "I will ask Monsieur Charles to be very particular on one point: He says that, on the occasion of his first visit to the room, various articles of furniture were overturned and strewn about the place; now, I ask him whether, on his second visit to the room, he found all those articles restored to their accustomed places—I mean, of course, correctly placed."

"Yes, all in their proper places," replied Charles.

"It is obvious, then, that the person who replaced them must have been familiar with the location of those articles."

The logic of this remark was apparent to his hearers. Ganimard continued:

"One more question, Monsieur Charles. You were awakened by the ringing of your bell. Now, who, do you think, rang it?"

"Monsieur le baron, of course."

"When could he ring it!"

"After the struggle ... when he was dying."

"Impossible; because you found him lying, unconscious, at a point more than four metres from the bell-button."

"Then he must have rung during the struggle."

"Impossible," declared Ganimard, "since the ringing, as you have said, was continuous and uninterrupted, and lasted seven or eight seconds. Do you think his antagonist would have permitted him to ring the bell in that leisurely manner?"

"Well, then, it was before the attack."

"Also, quite impossible, since you have told us that the lapse of time between the ringing of the bell and your entrance to the room was not more than three minutes. Therefore, if the baron rang before the attack, we are forced to the conclusion that the struggle, the murder and the flight of the assassin, all occurred within the short space of three minutes. I repeat: that is impossible."

"And yet," said the magistrate, "some one rang. If it were not the baron, who was it?"

"The murderer."

"For what purpose?"

"I do not know. But the fact that he did ring proves that he knew that the bell communicated with the servant's room. Now, who would know that, except an inmate of the house?"

Ganimard was drawing the meshes of his net closer and tighter. In a few clear and logical sentences, he had unfolded and defined his theory of the crime, so that it seemed quite natural when the magistrate said:

"As I understand it, Ganimard, you suspect the girl Antoinette Bréhat?"

"I do not suspect her; I accuse her."

"You accuse her of being an accomplice?"

"I accuse her of having killed Baron d'Hautrec."

"Nonsense! What proof have you?"

"The handful of hair I found in the right hand of the victim."

He produced the hair; it was of a beautiful blond color, and glittered like threads of gold. Charles looked at it, and said:

"That is Mademoiselle Antoinette's hair. There can be no doubt of it. And, then, there is another thing. I believe that the knife, which I saw on my first visit to the room, belonged to her. She used it to cut the leaves of books."

A long, dreadful silence followed, as if the crime had acquired an additional horror by reason of having been committed by a woman. At last, the magistrate said:

"Let us assume, until we are better informed, that the baron was killed by Antoinette Bréhat. We have yet to learn where she concealed herself after the crime, how she managed to return after Charles left the house, and how she made her escape after the arrival of the police. Have you formed any opinion on those points Ganimard?"

"None."

"Well, then, where do we stand?"

Ganimard was embarrassed. Finally, with a visible effort, he said:

"All I can say is that I find in this case the same method of procedure as we found in the affair of the lottery ticket number 514; the same phenomena, which might be termed the faculty of disappearing. Antoinette Bréhat has appeared and disappeared in this house as mysteriously as Arsène Lupin entered the house of Monsieur Detinan and escaped therefrom in the company of the blonde lady."

"Does that signify anything?"

"It does to me. I can see a probable connection between those two strange incidents. Antoinette Bréhat was hired by Sister Auguste twelve days ago, that is to say, on the day after the blonde Lady so cleverly slipped through my fingers. In the second place, the hair of the blonde Lady was exactly of the same brilliant golden hue as the hair found in this case."

"So that, in your opinion, Antoinette Bréhat—"

"Is the blonde Lady—precisely."

"And that Lupin had a hand in both cases!"

"Yes, that is my opinion."

This statement was greeted with an outburst of laughter. It came from Mon. Dudouis.

"Lupin! always Lupin! Lupin is into everything; Lupin is everywhere!"

"Yes, Lupin is into everything of any consequence," replied Ganimard, vexed at the ridicule of his superior.

"Well, so far as I see," observed Mon. Dudouis, "you have not discovered any motive for this crime. The secretary was not broken into, nor the pocketbook carried away. Even, a pile of gold was left upon the table."

"Yes, that is so," exclaimed Ganimard, "but the famous diamond?"

"What diamond?"

"The blue diamond! The celebrated diamond which formed part of the royal crown of France, and which was given by the Duke d'Aumale to Leonide Lebrun, and, at the death of Leonide Lebrun, was purchased by the Baron d'Hautrec as a souvenir of the charming comedienne that he had loved so well. That is one of those things that an old Parisian, like I, does not forget."

"It is obvious that if the blue diamond is not found, the motive for the crime is disclosed," said the magistrate. "But where should we search for it?"

"On the baron's finger," replied Charles. "He always wore the blue diamond on his left hand."

"I saw that hand, and there was only a plain gold ring on it," said Ganimard, as he approached the corpse.

"Look in the palm of the hand," replied the servant.

Ganimard opened the stiffened hand. The bezel was turned inward, and, in the centre of that bezel, the blue diamond shone with all its glorious splendor.

"The deuce!" muttered Ganimard, absolutely amazed, "I don't understand it."

"You will now apologize to Lupin for having suspected him, eh?" said Mon. Dudouis, laughing.

Ganimard paused for a moment's reflection, and then replied, sententiously:

"It is only when I do not understand things that I suspect Arsène Lupin."

Such were the facts established by the police on the day after the commission of that mysterious crime. Facts that were vague and incoherent in themselves, and which were not explained by any subsequent discoveries. The movements of Antoinette Bréhat remained as inexplicable as those of the blonde Lady, and the police discovered no trace of that mysterious creature with the golden hair who had killed Baron d'Hautrec and had failed to take from his finger the famous diamond that had once shone in the royal crown of France.

The heirs of the Baron d'Hautrec could not fail to benefit by such notoriety. They established in the house an exhibition of the furniture and other objects which were to be sold at the auction rooms of Drouot & Co. Modern furniture of indifferent taste, various objects of no artistic value ... but, in the centre of the room, in a case of purple velvet, protected by a glass globe, and guarded by two officers, was the famous blue diamond ring.

A large magnificent diamond of incomparable purity, and of that indefinite blue which the clear water receives from an unclouded sky, of that blue which can be detected in the whiteness of linen. Some admired, some enthused ... and some looked with horror on the chamber of the victim, on the spot where the corpse had lain, on the floor divested of its blood-stained carpet, and especially the walls, the unsurmountable walls over which the criminal must have passed. Some assured themselves that the marble mantel did not move, others imagined gaping holes, mouths of tunnels, secret connections with the sewers, and the catacombs—

The sale of the blue diamond took place at the salesroom of Drouot & Co. The place was crowded to suffocation, and the bidding was carried to the verge of folly. The sale was attended by all those who usually appear at similar events in Paris; those who buy, and those who make a pretense of being able to buy; bankers, brokers, artists, women of all classes, two cabinet ministers, an Italian tenor, an exiled king who, in order to maintain his credit, bid, with much ostentation, and in a loud voice, as high as one hundred thousand francs. One hundred thousand francs! He could offer that sum without any danger of his bid being accepted. The Italian tenor risked one hundred and fifty thousand, and a member of the Comédie-Française bid one hundred and seventy-five thousand francs.

When the bidding reached two hundred thousand francs, the smaller competitors fell out of the race. At two hundred and fifty thousand, only two bidders remained in the field: Herschmann, the well-known capitalist, the king of gold mines; and the Countess de Crozon, the wealthy American, whose collection of diamonds and precious stones is famed throughout the world.

"Two hundred and sixty thousand ... two hundred and seventy thousand ... seventy-five ... eighty...." exclaimed the auctioneer, as he glanced at the two competitors in succession. "Two hundred and eighty thousand for madame.... Do I hear any more?"

"Three hundred thousand," said Herschmann.

There was a short silence. The countess was standing, smiling, but pale from excitement. She was leaning against the back of the chair in front of her. She knew, and so did everyone present, that the issue of the duel was certain; logically, inevitably, it must terminate to the advantage of the capitalist, who had untold millions with which to indulge his caprices. However, the countess made another bid:

"Three hundred and five thousand."

Another silence. All eyes were now directed to the capitalist in the expectation that he would raise the bidding. But Herschmann was not paying any attention to the sale; his eyes were fixed on a sheet of paper which he held in his right hand, while the other hand held a torn envelope.

"Three hundred and five thousand," repeated the auctioneer. "Once!... Twice!... For the last time.... Do I hear any more?... Once!... Twice!... Am I offered any more? Last chance!..."

Herschmann did not move.

"Third and last time!... Sold!" exclaimed the auctioneer, as his hammer fell.

"Four hundred thousand," cried Herschman, starting up, as if the sound of the hammer had roused him from his stupor.

Too late; the auctioneer's decision was irrevocable. Some of Herschmann's acquaintances pressed around him. What was the matter? Why did he not speak sooner? He laughed, and said:

"Ma foi! I simply forgot—in a moment of abstraction."

"That is strange."

"You see, I just received a letter."

"And that letter was sufficient—"

"To distract my attention? Yes, for a moment."

Ganimard was there. He had come to witness the sale of the ring. He stopped one of the attendants of the auction room, and said:

"Was it you who carried the letter to Monsieur Herschmann?"

"Yes."

"Who gave it to you?"

"A lady."

"Where is she?"

"Where is she?... She was sitting down there ... the lady who wore a thick veil."

"She has gone?"

"Yes, just this moment."

Ganimard hastened to the door, and saw the lady descending the stairs. He ran after her. A crush of people delayed him at the entrance. When he reached the sidewalk, she had disappeared. He returned to the auction room, accosted Herschmann, introduced himself, and enquired about the letter. Herschmann handed it to him. It was carelessly scribbled in pencil, in a handwriting unknown to the capitalist, and contained these few words:

"The blue diamond brings misfortune. Remember the Baron d'Hautrec."

The vicissitudes of the blue diamond were not yet at an end. Although it had become well-known through the murder of the Baron d'Hautrec and the incidents at the auction-rooms, it was six months later that it attained even greater celebrity. During the following summer, the Countess de Crozon was robbed of the famous jewel she had taken so much trouble to acquire.

Let me recall that strange affair, of which the exciting and dramatic incidents sent a thrill through all of us, and over which I am now permitted to throw some light.

On the evening of August 10, the guests of the Count and Countess de Crozon were assembled in the drawing-room of the magnificent château which overlooks the Bay de Somme. To entertain her friends, the countess seated herself at the piano to play for them, after first placing her jewels on a small table near the piano, and, amongst them, was the ring of the Baron d'Hautrec.

An hour later, the count and the majority of the guests retired, including his two cousins and Madame de Réal, an intimate friend of the countess. The latter remained in the drawing-room with Herr Bleichen, the Austrian consul, and his wife.

They conversed for a time, and then the countess extinguished the large lamp that stood on a table in the centre of the room. At the same moment, Herr Bleichen extinguished the two piano lamps. There was a momentary darkness; then the consul lighted a candle, and the three of them retired to their rooms. But, as soon as she reached her apartment, the countess remembered her jewels and sent her maid to get them. When the maid returned with the jewels, she placed them on the mantel without the countess looking at them. Next day, Madame de Crozon found that one of her rings was missing; it was the blue diamond ring.

She informed her husband, and, after talking it over, they reached the conclusion that the maid was above suspicion, and that the guilty party must be Herr Bleichen.

The count notified the commissary of police at Amiens, who commenced an investigation and, discreetly, exercised a strict surveillance over the Austrian consul to prevent his disposing of the ring.

The château was surrounded by detectives day and night. Two weeks passed without incident. Then Herr Bleichen announced his intended departure. That day, a formal complaint was entered against him. The police made an official examination of his luggage. In a small satchel, the key to which was always carried by the consul himself, they found a bottle of dentifrice, and in that bottle they found the ring.

Madame Bleichen fainted. Her husband was placed under arrest.

Everyone will remember the line of defense adopted by the accused man. He declared that the ring must have been placed there by the Count de Crozen as an act of revenge. He said:

"The count is brutal and makes his wife very unhappy. She consulted me, and I advised her to get a divorce. The count heard of it in some way, and, to be revenged on me, he took the ring and placed it in my satchel."

The count and countess persisted in pressing the charge. Between the explanation which they gave and that of the consul, both equally possible and equally probable, the public had to choose. No new fact was discovered to turn the scale in either direction. A month of gossip, conjectures and investigations failed to produce a single ray of light.

Wearied of the excitement and notoriety, and incapable of securing the evidence necessary to sustain their charge against the consul, the count and countess at last sent to Paris for a detective competent to unravel the tangled threads of this mysterious skein. This brought Ganimard into the case.

For four days, the veteran detective searched the house from top to bottom, examined every foot of the ground, had long conferences with the maid, the chauffeur, the gardeners, the employees in the neighboring post-offices, visited the rooms that had been occupied by the various guests. Then, one morning, he disappeared without taking leave of his host or hostess. But a week later, they received this telegram:

"Please come to the Japanese Tea-room, rue Boissy d'Anglas, to-morrow, Friday, evening at five o'clock. Ganimard."

At five o'clock, Friday evening, their automobile stopped in front of number nine rue Boissy-d'Anglas. The old detective was standing on the sidewalk, waiting for them. Without a word, he conducted them to the first floor of the Japanese Tea-room. In one of the rooms, they met two men, whom Ganimard introduced in these words:

"Monsieur Gerbois, professor in the College of Versailles, from whom, you will remember, Arsène Lupin stole half a million; Monsieur Léonce d'Hautrec, nephew and sole legatee of the Baron d'Hautrec."

A few minutes later, another man arrived. It was Mon. Dudouis, head of the detective service, and he appeared to be in a particularly bad temper. He bowed, and then said:

"What's the trouble now, Ganimard! I received your telephone message asking me to come here. Is it anything of consequence?"

"Yes, chief, it is a very important matter. Within an hour, the last two cases to which I was assigned will have their dénouement here. It seemed to me that your presence was indispensable."

"And also the presence of Dieuzy and Folenfant, whom I noticed standing near the door as I came in?"

"Yes, chief."

"For what? Are you going to make an arrest, and you wish to do it with a flourish? Come, Ganimard, I am anxious to hear about it."

Ganimard hesitated a moment, then spoke with the obvious intention of making an impression on his hearers:

"In the first place, I wish to state that Herr Bleichen had nothing to do with the theft of the ring."

"Oh! oh!" exclaimed Mon. Dudouis, "that is a bold statement and a very serious one."

"And is that all you have discovered?" asked the Count de Crozon.

"Not at all. On the second day after the theft, three of your guests went on an automobile trip as far as Crécy. Two of them visited the famous battlefield; and, while they were there, the third party paid a hasty visit to the post-office, and mailed a small box, tied and sealed according to the regulations, and declared its value to be one hundred francs."

"I see nothing strange in that," said the count.

"Perhaps you will see something strange in it when I tell you that this person, in place of giving her true name, sent the box under the name of Rousseau, and the person to whom it was addressed, a certain Monsieur Beloux of Paris, moved his place of residence immediately after receiving the box, in other words, the ring."

"I presume you refer to one of my cousins d'Andelle?"

"No," replied Ganimard.

"Madame de Réal, then?"

"Yes."

"You accuse my friend, Madam de Réal?" cried the countess, shocked and amazed.

"I wish to ask you one question, madame," said Ganimard. "Was Madam de Réal present when you purchased the ring?"

"Yes, but we did not go there together."

"Did she advise you to buy the ring?"

The countess considered for a moment, then said:

"Yes, I think she mentioned it first—"

"Thank you, madame. Your answer establishes the fact that it was Madame de Réal who was the first to mention the ring, and it was she who advised you to buy it."

"But, I consider my friend is quite incapable—"

"Pardon me, countess, when I remind you that Madame de Réal is only a casual acquaintance and not your intimate friend, as the newspapers have announced. It was only last winter that you met her for the first time. Now, I can prove that everything she has told you about herself, her past life, and her relatives, is absolutely false; that Madame Blanche de Réal had no actual existence before she met you, and she has now ceased to exist."

"Well?"

"Well?" replied Ganimard.

"Your story is a very strange one," said the countess, "but it has no application to our case. If Madame de Réal had taken the ring, how do you explain the fact that it was found in Herr Bleichen's tooth-powder? Anyone who would take the risk and trouble of stealing the blue diamond would certainly keep it. What do you say to that?"

"I—nothing—but Madame de Réal will answer it."

"Oh! she does exist, then?"

"She does—and does not. I will explain in a few words. Three days ago, while reading a newspaper, I glanced over the list of hotel arrivals at Trouville, and there I read: 'Hôtel Beaurivage—Madame de Réal, etc.'

"I went to Trouville immediately, and interviewed the proprietor of the hotel. From the description and other information I received from him, I concluded that she was the very Madame de Réal that I was seeking; but she had left the hotel, giving her address in Paris as number three rue de Colisée. The day before yesterday I went to that address, and learned that there was no person there called Madame de Réal, but there was a Madame Réal, living on the second floor, who acted as a diamond broker and was frequently away from home. She had returned from a journey on the preceding evening. Yesterday, I called on her and, under an assumed name, I offered to act as an intermedium in the sale of some diamonds to certain wealthy friends of mine. She is to meet me here to-day to carry out that arrangement."

"What! You expect her to come here?"

"Yes, at half-past five."

"Are you sure it is she?"

"Madame de Réal of the Château de Crozon? Certainly. I have convincing evidence of that fact. But ... listen!... I hear Folenfant's signal."

It was a whistle. Ganimard arose quickly.

"There is no time to lose. Monsieur and Madame de Crozon, will you be kind enough to go into the next room. You also, Monsieur d'Hautrec, and you, Monsieur Gerbois. The door will remain open, and when I give the signal, you will come out. Of course, Chief, you will remain here."

"We may be disturbed by other people," said Mon. Dudouis.

"No. This is a new establishment, and the proprietor is one of my friends. He will not let anyone disturb us—except the blonde Lady."

"The blonde Lady! What do you mean?"

"Yes, the blonde Lady herself, chief; the friend and accomplice of Arsène Lupin, the mysterious blonde Lady against whom I hold convincing evidence; but, in addition to that, I wish to confront her with all the people she has robbed."

He looked through the window.

"I see her. She is coming in the door now. She can't escape: Folenfant and Dieuzy are guarding the door.... The blonde Lady is captured at last, Chief!"

A moment later a woman appeared at the door; she was tall and slender, with a very pale complexion and bright golden hair. Ganimard trembled with excitement; he could not move, nor utter a word. She was there, in front of him, at his mercy! What a victory over Arsène Lupin! And what a revenge! And, at the same time, the victory was such an easy one that he asked himself if the blonde Lady would not yet slip through his fingers by one of those miracles that usually terminated the exploits of Arsène Lupin. She remained standing near the door, surprised at the silence, and looked about her without any display of suspicion or fear.

"She will get away! She will disappear!" thought Ganimard.

Then he managed to get between her and the door. She turned to go out.

"No, no!" he said. "Why are you going away?"

"Really, monsieur, I do not understand what this means. Allow me—"

"There is no reason why you should go, madame, and very good reasons why you should remain."

"But—"

"It is useless, madame. You cannot go."

Trembling, she sat on a chair, and stammered:

"What is it you want?"

Ganimard had won the battle and captured the blonde Lady. He said to her:

"Allow me to present the friend I mentioned, who desires to purchase some diamonds. Have you procured the stones you promised to bring?"

"No—no—I don't know. I don't remember."

"Come! Jog your memory! A person of your acquaintance intended to send you a tinted stone.... 'Something like the blue diamond,' I said, laughing; and you replied: 'Exactly, I expect to have just what you want.' Do you remember!"

She made no reply. A small satchel fell from her hand. She picked it up quickly, and held it securely. Her hands trembled slightly.

"Come!" said Ganimard, "I see you have no confidence in us, Madame de Réal. I shall set you a good example by showing you what I have."

He took from his pocketbook a paper which he unfolded, and disclosed a lock of hair.

"These are a few hairs torn from the head of Antoinette Bréhat by the Baron d'Hautrec, which I found clasped in his dead hand. I have shown them to Mlle. Gerbois, who declares they are of the exact color of the hair of the blonde Lady. Besides, they are exactly the color of your hair—the identical color."

Madame Réal looked at him in bewilderment, as if she did not understand his meaning. He continued:

"And here are two perfume bottles, without labels, it is true, and empty, but still sufficiently impregnated with their odor to enable Mlle. Gerbois to recognize in them the perfume used by that blonde Lady who was her traveling companion for two weeks. Now, one of these bottles was found in the room that Madame de Réal occupied at the Château de Crozon, and the other in the room that you occupied at the Hôtel Beaurivage."

"What do you say?... The blonde Lady ... the Château de Crozon...."

The detective did not reply. He took from his pocket and placed on the table, side by side, four small sheets of paper. Then he said:

"I have, on these four pieces of paper, various specimens of handwriting; the first is the writing of Antoinette Bréhat; the second was written by the woman who sent the note to Baron Herschmann at the auction sale of the blue diamond; the third is that of Madame de Réal, written while she was stopping at the Château de Crozon; and the fourth is your handwriting, madame ... it is your name and address, which you gave to the porter of the Hôtel Beaurivage at Trouville. Now, compare the four handwritings. They are identical."

"What absurdity is this! really, monsieur, I do not understand. What does it mean?"

"It means, madame," exclaimed Ganimard, "that the blonde Lady, the friend and accomplice of Arsène Lupin, is none other than you, Madame Réal."

Ganimard went to the adjoining room and returned with Mon. Gerbois, whom he placed in front of Madame Réal, as he said:

"Monsieur Gerbois, is this the person who abducted your daughter, the woman you saw at the house of Monsieur Detinan?"

"No."

Ganimard was so surprised that he could not speak for a moment; finally, he said: "No?... You must be mistaken...."

"I am not mistaken. Madame is blonde, it is true, and in that respect resembles the blonde Lady; but, in all other respects, she is totally different."

"I can't believe it. You must be mistaken."

Ganimard called in his other witnesses.

"Monsieur d'Hautrec," he said, "do you recognize Antoinette Bréhat?"

"No, this is not the person I saw at my uncle's house."

"This woman is not Madame de Réal," declared the Count de Crozon.

That was the finishing touch. Ganimard was crushed. He was buried beneath the ruins of the structure he had erected with so much care and assurance. His pride was humbled, his spirit was broken, by the force of this unexpected blow.

Mon. Dudouis arose, and said:

"We owe you an apology, madame, for this unfortunate mistake. But, since your arrival here, I have noticed your nervous agitation. Something troubles you; may I ask what it is?"

"Mon Dieu, monsieur, I was afraid. My satchel contains diamonds to the value of a hundred thousand francs, and the conduct of your friend was rather suspicious."

"But you were frequently absent from Paris. How do you explain that?"

"I make frequent journeys to other cities in the course of my business. That is all."

Mon. Dudouis had nothing more to ask. He turned to his subordinate, and said:

"Your investigation has been very superficial, Ganimard, and your conduct toward this lady is really deplorable. You will come to my office to-morrow and explain it."

The interview was at an end, and Mon. Dudouis was about to leave the room when a most annoying incident occurred. Madame Réal turned to Ganimard, and said:

"I understand that you are Monsieur Ganimard. Am I right?"

"Yes."

"Then, this letter must be for you. I received it this morning. It was addressed to 'Mon. Justin Ganimard, care of Madame Réal.' I thought it was a joke, because I did not know you under that name, but it appears that your unknown correspondent knew of our rendezvous."

Ganimard was inclined to put the letter in his pocket unread, but he dared not do so in the presence of his superior, so he opened the envelope and read the letter aloud, in an almost inaudible tone:

"Once upon a time, there were a blonde Lady, a Lupin, and a Ganimard. Now, the wicked Ganimard had evil designs on the pretty blonde Lady, and the good Lupin was her friend and protector. When the good Lupin wished the blonde Lady to become the friend of the Countess de Crozon, he caused her to assume the name of Madame de Réal, which is a close resemblance to the name of a certain diamond broker, a woman with a pale complexion and golden hair. And the good Lupin said to himself: If ever the wicked Ganimard gets upon the track of the blonde Lady, how useful it will be to me if he should be diverted to the track of the honest diamond broker. A wise precaution that has borne good fruit. A little note sent to the newspaper read by the wicked Ganimard, a perfume bottle intentionally forgotten by the genuine blonde Lady at the Hôtel Beaurivage, the name and address of Madame Réal written on the hotel register by the genuine blonde Lady, and the trick is played. What do you think of it, Ganimard! I wished to tell you the true story of this affair, knowing that you would be the first to laugh over it. Really, it is quite amusing, and I have enjoyed it very much.

"Accept my best wishes, dear friend, and give my kind regards to the worthy Mon. Dudouis.

"ARSÈNE LUPIN."

"He knows everything," muttered Ganimard, but he did not see the humor of the situation as Lupin had predicted. "He knows some things I have never mentioned to any one. How could he find out that I was going to invite you here, chief? How could he know that I had found the first perfume bottle? How could he find out those things?"

He stamped his feet and tore his hair—a prey to the most tragic despair. Mon. Dudouis felt sorry for him, and said:

"Come, Ganimard, never mind; try to do better next time."

And Mon. Dudouis left the room, accompanied by Madame Réal.

During the next ten minutes, Ganimard read and re-read the letter of Arsène Lupin. Monsieur and Madame de Crozon, Monsieur d'Hautrec and Monsieur Gerbois were holding an animated discussion in a corner of the room. At last, the count approached the detective, and said:

"My dear monsieur, after your investigation, we are no nearer the truth than we were before."

"Pardon me, but my investigation has established these facts: that the blonde Lady is the mysterious heroine of these exploits, and that Arsène Lupin directed them."

"Those facts do not solve the mystery; in fact, they render it more obscure. The blonde Lady commits a murder in order to steal the blue diamond, and yet she does not steal it. Afterward she steals it and gets rid of it by secretly giving it to another person. How do you explain her strange conduct?"

"I cannot explain it."

"Of course; but, perhaps, someone else can."

"Who?"

The Count hesitated, so the Countess replied, frankly:

"There is only one man besides yourself who is competent to enter the arena with Arsène Lupin and overcome him. Have you any objection to our engaging the services of Herlock Sholmes in this case?"

Ganimard was vexed at the question, but stammered a reply:

"No ... but ... I do not understand what——"

"Let me explain. All this mystery annoys me. I wish to have it cleared up. Monsieur Gerbois and Monsieur d'Hautrec have the same desire, and we have agreed to send for the celebrated English detective."

"You are right, madame," replied the detective, with a loyalty that did him credit, "you are right. Old Ganimard is not able to overcome Arsène Lupin. But will Herlock Sholmes succeed? I hope so, as I have the greatest admiration for him. But ... it is improbable."

"Do you mean to say that he will not succeed?"

"That is my opinion. I can foresee the result of a duel between Herlock Sholmes and Arsène Lupin. The Englishman will be defeated."

"But, in any event, can we count on your assistance?"

"Quite so, madame. I shall be pleased to render Monsieur Sholmes all possible assistance."

"Do you know his address?"

"Yes; 219 Parker street."

That evening Monsieur and Madame de Crozon withdrew the charge they had made against Herr Bleichen, and a joint letter was addressed to Herlock Sholmes.

III. HERLOCK SHOLMES OPENS HOSTILITIES.

"What does monsieur wish?"

"Anything," replied Arsène Lupin, like a man who never worries over the details of a meal; "anything you like, but no meat or alcohol."

The waiter walked away, disdainfully.

"What! still a vegetarian?" I exclaimed.

"More so than ever," replied Lupin

"Through taste, faith, or habit?"

"Hygiene."

"And do you never fall from grace?"

"Oh! yes ... when I am dining out ... and wish to avoid being considered eccentric."

We were dining near the Northern Railway station, in a little restaurant to which Arsène Lupin had invited me. Frequently he would send me a telegram asking me to meet him in some obscure restaurant, where we could enjoy a quiet dinner, well served, and which was always made interesting to me by his recital of some startling adventure theretofore unknown to me.

On that particular evening he appeared to be in a more lively mood than usual. He laughed and joked with careless animation, and with that delicate sarcasm that was habitual with him—a light and spontaneous sarcasm that was quite free from any tinge of malice. It was a pleasure to find him in that jovial mood, and I could not resist the desire to tell him so.

"Ah! yes," he exclaimed, "there are days in which I find life as bright and gay as a spring morning; then life seems to be an infinite treasure which I can never exhaust. And yet God knows I lead a careless existence!"

"Too much so, perhaps."

"Ah! but I tell you, the treasure is infinite. I can spend it with a lavish hand. I can cast my youth and strength to the four winds of Heaven, and it is replaced by a still younger and greater force. Besides, my life is so pleasant!... If I wished to do so, I might become—what shall I say?... An orator, a manufacturer, a politician.... But, I assure you, I shall never have such a desire. Arsène Lupin, I am; Arsène Lupin, I shall remain. I have made a vain search in history to find a career comparable to mine; a life better filled or more intense.... Napoleon? Yes, perhaps.... But Napoleon, toward the close of his career, when all Europe was trying to crush him, asked himself on the eve of each battle if it would not be his last."

Was he serious? Or was he joking? He became more animated as he proceeded:

"That is everything, do you understand, the danger! The continuous feeling of danger! To breathe it as you breathe the air, to scent it in every breath of wind, to detect it in every unusual sound.... And, in the midst of the tempest, to remain calm ... and not to stumble! Otherwise, you are lost. There is only one sensation equal to it: that of the chauffeur in an automobile race. But that race lasts only a few hours; my race continues until death!"

"What fantasy!" I exclaimed. "And you wish me to believe that you have no particular motive for your adoption of that exciting life?"

"Come," he said, with a smile, "you are a clever psychologist. Work it out for yourself."

He poured himself a glass of water, drank it, and said:

"Did you read 'Le Temps' to-day?"

"No."

"Herlock Sholmes crossed the Channel this afternoon, and arrived in Paris about six o'clock."

"The deuce! What is he coming for?"

"A little journey he has undertaken at the request of the Count and Countess of Crozon, Monsieur Gerbois, and the nephew of Baron d'Hautrec. They met him at the Northern Railway station, took him to meet Ganimard, and, at this moment, the six of them are holding a consultation."

Despite a strong temptation to do so, I had never ventured to question Arsène Lupin concerning any action of his private life, unless he had first mentioned the subject to me. Up to that moment his name had not been mentioned, at least officially, in connection with the blue diamond. Consequently, I consumed my curiosity in patience. He continued:

"There is also in 'Le Temps' an interview with my old friend Ganimard, according to whom a certain blonde lady, who should be my friend, must have murdered the Baron d'Hautrec and tried to rob Madame de Crozon of her famous ring. And—what do you think?—he accuses me of being the instigator of those crimes."

I could not suppress a slight shudder. Was this true? Must I believe that his career of theft, his mode of existence, the logical result of such a life, had drawn that man into more serious crimes, including murder? I looked at him. He was so calm, and his eyes had such a frank expression! I observed his hands: they had been formed from a model of exceeding delicacy, long and slender; inoffensive, truly; and the hands of an artist....

"Ganimard has pipe-dreams," I said.

"No, no!" protested Lupin. "Ganimard has some cleverness; and, at times, almost inspiration."

"Inspiration!"

"Yes. For instance, that interview is a master-stroke. In the first place, he announces the coming of his English rival in order to put me on my guard, and make his task more difficult. In the second place, he indicates the exact point to which he has conducted the affair in order that Sholmes will not get credit for the work already done by Ganimard. That is good warfare."

"Whatever it may be, you have two adversaries to deal with, and such adversaries!"

"Oh! one of them doesn't count."

"And the other?"

"Sholmes? Oh! I confess he is a worthy foe; and that explains my present good humor. In the first place, it is a question of self-esteem; I am pleased to know that they consider me a subject worthy the attention of the celebrated English detective. In the next place, just imagine the pleasure a man, such as I, must experience in the thought of a duel with Herlock Sholmes. But I shall be obliged to strain every muscle; he is a clever fellow, and will contest every inch of the ground."

"Then you consider him a strong opponent?"

"I do. As a detective, I believe, he has never had an equal. But I have one advantage over him; he is making the attack and I am simply defending myself. My rôle is the easier one. Besides, I am familiar with his method of warfare, and he does not know mine. I am prepared to show him a few new tricks that will give him something to think about."

He tapped the table with his fingers as he uttered the following sentences, with an air of keen delight:

"Arsène Lupin against Herlock Sholmes.... France against England.... Trafalgar will be revenged at last.... Ah! the rascal ... he doesn't suspect that I am prepared ... and a Lupin warned—"

He stopped suddenly, seized with a fit of coughing, and hid his face in his napkin, as if something had stuck in his throat.

"A bit of bread?" I inquired. "Drink some water."

"No, it isn't that," he replied, in a stifled voice.

"Then, what is it?"

"The want of air."

"Do you wish a window opened?"

"No, I shall go out. Give me my hat and overcoat, quick! I must go."

"What's the matter?"

"The two gentlemen who came in just now.... Look at the taller one ... now, when we go out, keep to my left, so he will not see me."

"The one who is sitting behind you?"

"Yes. I will explain it to you, outside."

"Who is it?"

"Herlock Sholmes."

He made a desperate effort to control himself, as if he were ashamed of his emotion, replaced his napkin, drank a glass of water, and, quite recovered, said to me, smiling:

"It is strange, hein, that I should be affected so easily, but that unexpected sight—"

"What have you to fear, since no one can recognize you, on account of your many transformations? Every time I see you it seems to me your face is changed; it's not at all familiar. I don't know why."

"But *he* would recognize me," said Lupin. "He has seen me only once; but, at that time, he made a mental photograph of me—not of my external appearance but of my very soul—not what I appear to be but just what I am. Do you understand? And then ... and then.... I did not expect to meet him here.... Such a strange encounter!... in this little restaurant...."

"Well, shall we go out?"

"No, not now," said Lupin.

"What are you going to do?"

"The better way is to act frankly ... to have confidence in him—trust him...."

"You will not speak to him?"

"Why not! It will be to my advantage to do so, and find out what he knows, and, perhaps, what he thinks. At present I have the feeling that his gaze is on my neck and shoulders, and that he is trying to remember where he has seen them before."

He reflected a moment. I observed a malicious smile at the corner of his mouth; then, obedient, I think, to a whim of his impulsive nature, and not to the necessities of the situation, he arose, turned around, and, with a bow and a joyous air, he said:

"By what lucky chance? Ah! I am delighted to see you. Permit me to introduce a friend of mine."

For a moment the Englishman was disconcerted; then he made a movement as if he would seize Arsène Lupin. The latter shook his head, and said:

"That would not be fair; besides, the movement would be an awkward one and ... quite useless."

The Englishman looked about him, as if in search of assistance.

"No use," said Lupin. "Besides, are you quite sure you can place your hand on me? Come, now, show me that you are a real Englishman and, therefore, a good sport."

This advice seemed to commend itself to the detective, for he partially rose and said, very formally:

"Monsieur Wilson, my friend and assistant—Monsieur Arsène Lupin."

Wilson's amazement evoked a laugh. With bulging eyes and gaping mouth, he looked from one to the other, as if unable to comprehend the situation. Herlock Sholmes laughed and said:

"Wilson, you should conceal your astonishment at an incident which is one of the most natural in the world."

"Why do you not arrest him?" stammered Wilson.

"Have you not observed, Wilson, that the gentleman is between me and the door, and only a few steps from the door. By the time I could move my little finger he would be outside."

"Don't let that make any difference," said Lupin, who now walked around the table and seated himself so that the Englishman was between him and the door—thus placing himself at the mercy of the foreigner.

Wilson looked at Sholmes to find out if he had the right to admire this act of wanton courage. The Englishman's face was impenetrable; but, a moment later, he called:

"Waiter!"

When the waiter came he ordered soda, beer and whisky. The treaty of peace was signed—until further orders. In a few moments the four men were conversing in an apparently friendly manner.

Herlock Sholmes is a man such as you might meet every day in the business world. He is about fifty years of age, and looks as if he might have passed his life in an office, adding up columns of dull figures or writing out formal statements of business accounts. There was nothing to distinguish him from the average citizen of London, except the appearance of his eyes, his terribly keen and penetrating eyes.

But then he is Herlock Sholmes—which means that he is a wonderful combination of intuition, observation, clairvoyance and ingenuity. One could readily believe that nature had been pleased to take the two most extraordinary detectives that the imagination of man has hitherto conceived, the Dupin of Edgar Allen Poe and the Lecoq of Emile Gaboriau, and, out of that material, constructed a new detective, more extraordinary and supernatural than either of them. And when a person reads the history of his exploits, which have made him famous throughout the entire world, he asks himself whether Herlock Sholmes is not a mythical personage, a fictitious hero born in the brain of a great novelist—Conan Doyle, for instance.

When Arsène Lupin questioned him in regard to the length of his sojourn in France he turned the conversation into its proper channel by saying:

"That depends on you, monsieur."

"Oh!" exclaimed Lupin, laughing, "if it depends on me you can return to England to-night."

"That is a little too soon, but I expect to return in the course of eight or nine days—ten at the outside."

"Are you in such a hurry?"

"I have many cases to attend to; such as the robbery of the Anglo-Chinese Bank, the abduction of Lady Eccleston.... But, don't you think, Monsieur Lupin, that I can finish my business in Paris within a week?"

"Certainly, if you confine your efforts to the case of the blue diamond. It is, moreover, the length of time that I require to make preparations for my safety in case the solution of that affair should give you certain dangerous advantages over me."

"And yet," said the Englishman, "I expect to close the business in eight or ten days."

"And arrest me on the eleventh, perhaps?"

"No, the tenth is my limit."

Lupin shook his head thoughtfully, as he said:

"That will be difficult—very difficult."

"Difficult, perhaps, but possible, therefore certain—"

"Absolutely certain," said Wilson, as if he had clearly worked out the long series of operations which would conduct his collaborator to the desired result.

"Of course," said Herlock Sholmes, "I do not hold all the trump cards, as these cases are already several months old, and I lack certain information and clues upon which I am accustomed to base my investigations."

"Such as spots of mud and cigarette ashes," said Wilson, with an air of importance.

"In addition to the remarkable conclusions formed by Monsieur Ganimard, I have obtained all the articles written on the subject, and have formed a few deductions of my own."

"Some ideas which were suggested to us by analysis or hypothesis," added Wilson, sententiously.

"I wish to enquire," said Arsène Lupin, in that deferential tone which he employed in speaking to Sholmes, "would I be indiscreet if I were to ask you what opinion you have formed about the case?"

Really, it was a most exciting situation to see those two men facing each other across the table, engaged in an earnest discussion as if they were obliged to solve some abstruse problem or come to an agreement upon some controverted fact. Wilson was in the seventh heaven of delight. Herlock Sholmes filled his pipe slowly, lighted it, and said:

"This affair is much simpler than it appeared to be at first sight."

"Much simpler," said Wilson, as a faithful echo.

"I say 'this affair,' for, in my opinion, there is only one," said Sholmes. "The death of the Baron d'Hautrec, the story of the ring, and, let us not forget, the mystery of lottery ticket number 514, are only different phases of what one might call the mystery of the blonde Lady. Now, according to my view, it is simply a question of discovering the bond that unites those three episodes in the same story—the fact which proves the unity of the three events. Ganimard, whose judgment is rather superficial, finds that unity in the faculty of disappearance; that is, in the power of coming and going unseen and unheard. That theory does not satisfy me."

"Well, what is your idea?" asked Lupin.

"In my opinion," said Sholmes, "the characteristic feature of the three episodes is your design and purpose of leading the affair into a certain channel previously chosen by you. It is, on your part, more than a plan; it is a necessity, an indispensable condition of success."

"Can you furnish any details of your theory?"

"Certainly. For example, from the beginning of your conflict with Monsieur Gerbois, is it not evident that the apartment of Monsieur Detinan is the place selected by you, the inevitable spot where all the parties must meet? In your opinion, it was the only safe place, and you arranged a rendezvous there, publicly, one might say, for the blonde Lady and Mademoiselle Gerbois."

"The professor's daughter," added Wilson. "Now, let us consider the case of the blue diamond. Did you try to appropriate it while the Baron d'Hautrec possessed it! No. But the baron takes his brother's house. Six months later we have the intervention of Antoinette Bréhat and the first attempt. The diamond escapes you, and the sale is widely advertised to take place at the Drouot auction-rooms. Will it be a free and open sale? Is the richest amateur sure to carry off the jewel! No. Just as the banker Herschmann is on the point of buying the ring, a lady sends him a letter of warning, and it is the Countess de Crozon, prepared and influenced by the same lady, who becomes the purchaser of the diamond. Will the ring disappear at once? No; you lack the opportunity. Therefore, you must wait. At last the Countess goes to her château. That is what you were waiting for. The ring disappears."

"To reappear again in the tooth-powder of Herr Bleichen," remarked Lupin.

"Oh! such nonsense!" exclaimed Sholmes, striking the table with his fist, "don't tell me such a fairy tale. I am too old a fox to be led away by a false scent."

"What do you mean?"

"What do I mean?" said Sholmes, then paused a moment as if he wished to arrange his effect. At last he said:

"The blue diamond that was found in the tooth-powder was false. You kept the genuine stone."

Arsène Lupin remained silent for a moment; then, with his eyes fixed on the Englishman, he replied, calmly:

"You are impertinent, monsieur."

"Impertinent, indeed!" repeated Wilson, beaming with admiration.

"Yes," said Lupin, "and, yet, to do you credit, you have thrown a strong light on a very mysterious subject. Not a magistrate, not a special reporter, who has been engaged on this case, has come so near the truth. It is a marvellous display of intuition and logic."

"Oh! a person has simply to use his brains," said Herlock Sholmes, nattered at the homage of the expert criminal.

"And so few have any brains to use," replied Lupin. "And, now, that the field of conjectures has been narrowed down, and the rubbish cleared away——"

"Well, now, I have simply to discover why the three episodes were enacted at 25 rue Clapeyron, 134 avenue Henri-Martin, and within the walls of the Château de Crozon and my work will be finished. What remains will be child's play. Don't you think so?"

"Yes, I think you are right."

"In that case, Monsieur Lupin, am I wrong in saying that my business will be finished in ten days?"

"In ten days you will know the whole truth," said Lupin.

"And you will be arrested."

"No."

"No?"

"In order that I may be arrested there must occur such a series of improbable and unexpected misfortunes that I cannot admit the possibility of such an event."

"We have a saying in England that 'the unexpected always happens.'"

They looked at each other for a moment calmly and fearlessly, without any display of bravado or malice. They met as equals in a contest of wit and skill. And this meeting was the formal crossing of swords, preliminary to the duel.

"Ah!" exclaimed Lupin, "at last I shall have an adversary worthy of the name—one whose defeat will be the proudest achievement in my career."

"Are you not afraid!" asked Wilson.

"Almost, Monsieur Wilson," replied Lupin, rising from his chair, "and the proof is that I am about to make a hasty retreat. Then, we will say ten days, Monsieur Sholmes?"

"Yes, ten days. This is Sunday. A week from next Wednesday, at eight o'clock in the evening, it will be all over."

"And I shall be in prison?"

"No doubt of it."

"Ha! not a pleasant outlook for a man who gets so much enjoyment out of life as I do. No cares, a lively interest in the affairs of the world, a justifiable contempt for the police, and the consoling sympathy of numerous friends and admirers. And now, behold, all that is about to be changed! It is the reverse side of the medal. After sunshine comes the rain. It is no longer a laughing matter. Adieu!"

"Hurry up!" said Wilson, full of solicitude for a person in whom Herlock Sholmes had inspired so much respect, "do not lose a minute."

"Not a minute, Monsieur Wilson; but I wish to express my pleasure at having met you, and to tell you how much I envy the master in having such a valuable assistant as you seem to be."

Then, after they had courteously saluted each other, like adversaries in a duel who entertain no feeling of malice but are obliged to fight by force of circumstances, Lupin seized me by the arm and drew me outside.

"What do you think of it, dear boy? The strange events of this evening will form an interesting chapter in the memoirs you are now preparing for me."

He closed the door of the restaurant behind us, and, after taking a few steps, he stopped and said:

"Do you smoke?"

"No. Nor do you, it seems to me."

"You are right, I don't."

He lighted a cigarette with a wax-match, which he shook several times in an effort to extinguish it. But he threw away the cigarette immediately, ran across the street, and joined two men who emerged from the shadows as if called by a signal. He conversed with them for a few minutes on the opposite sidewalk, and then returned to me.

"I beg your pardon, but I fear that cursed Sholmes is going to give me trouble. But, I assure you, he is not yet through with Arsène Lupin. He will find out what kind of fuel I use to warm my blood. And now—au revoir! The genial Wilson is right; there is not a moment to lose."

He walked away rapidly.

Thus ended the events of that exciting evening, or, at least, that part of them in which I was a participant. Subsequently, during the course of the evening, other stirring incidents occurred which have come to my knowledge through the courtesy of other members of that unique dinner-party.

At the very moment in which Lupin left me, Herlock Sholmes rose from the table, and looked at his watch.

"Twenty minutes to nine. At nine o'clock I am to meet the Count and Countess at the railway station."

"Then, we must be off!" exclaimed Wilson, between two drinks of whisky. They left the restaurant.

"Wilson, don't look behind. We may be followed, and, in that case, let us act as if we did not care. Wilson, I want your opinion: why was Lupin in that restaurant?"

"To get something to eat," replied Wilson, quickly.

"Wilson, I must congratulate you on the accuracy of your deduction. I couldn't have done better myself."

Wilson blushed with pleasure, and Sholmes continued:

"To get something to eat. Very well, and, after that, probably, to assure himself whether I am going to the Château de Crozon, as announced by Ganimard in his interview. I must go in order not to disappoint him. But, in order to gain time on him, I shall not go."

"Ah!" said Wilson, nonplused.

"You, my friend, will walk down this street, take a carriage, two, three carriages. Return later and get the valises that we left at the station, and make for the Elysée-Palace at a galop."

"And when I reach the Elysée-Palace?"

"Engage a room, go to sleep, and await my orders."

Quite proud of the important rôle assigned to him, Wilson set out to perform his task. Herlock Sholmes proceeded to the railway station, bought a ticket, and repaired to the Amiens' express in which the Count and Countess de Crozon were already installed. He bowed to them, lighted his pipe, and had a quiet smoke in the corridor. The train started. Ten minutes later he took a seat beside the Countess, and said to her:

"Have you the ring here, madame?"

"Yes."

"Will you kindly let me see it?"

He took it, and examined it closely.

"Just as I suspected: it is a manufactured diamond."

"A manufactured diamond?"

"Yes; a new process which consists in submitting diamond dust to a tremendous heat until it melts and is then molded into a single stone."

"But my diamond is genuine."

"Yes, *your* diamond is; but this is not yours."

"Where is mine?"

"It is held by Arsène Lupin."

"And this stone?"

"Was substituted for yours, and slipped into Herr Bleichen's tooth-powder, where it was afterwards found."

"Then you think this is false?"

"Absolutely false."

The Countess was overwhelmed with surprise and grief, while her husband scrutinized the diamond with an incredulous air. Finally she stammered:

"Is it possible? And why did they not merely steal it and be done with it? And how did they steal it?"

"That is exactly what I am going to find out."

"At the Château de Crozon?"

"No. I shall leave the train at Creil and return to Paris. It is there the game between me and Arsène Lupin must be played. In fact, the game has commenced already, and Lupin thinks I am on my way to the château."

"But—"

"What does it matter to you, madame? The essential thing is your diamond, is it not?"

"Yes."

"Well, don't worry. I have just undertaken a much more difficult task than that. You have my promise that I will restore the true diamond to you within ten days."

The train slackened its speed. He put the false diamond in his pocket and opened the door. The Count cried out:

"That is the wrong side of the train. You are getting out on the tracks."

"That is my intention. If Lupin has anyone on my track, he will lose sight of me now. Adieu."

An employee protested in vain. After the departure of the train, the Englishman sought the station-master's office. Forty minutes later he leaped into a train that landed him in Paris shortly before midnight. He ran across the platform, entered the lunch-room, made his exit at another door, and jumped into a cab.

"Driver—rue Clapeyron."

Having reached the conclusion that he was not followed, he stopped the carriage at the end of the street, and proceeded to make a careful examination of Monsieur Detinan's house and the two adjoining houses. He made measurements of certain distances and entered the figures in his notebook.

"Driver—avenue Henri-Martin."

At the corner of the avenue and the rue de la Pompe, he dismissed the carriage, walked down the street to number 134, and performed the same operations in front of the house of the late Baron d'Hautrec and the two adjoining houses, measuring the width of the respective façades and calculating the depth of the little gardens that stood in front of them.

The avenue was deserted, and was very dark under its four rows of trees, between which, at considerable intervals, a few gas-lamps struggled in vain to light the deep shadows. One of them threw a dim light over a portion of the house, and Sholmes perceived the "To-let" sign posted on the gate, the neglected walks which encircled the small lawn, and the large bare windows of the vacant house.

"I suppose," he said to himself, "the house has been unoccupied since the death of the baron.... Ah! if I could only get in and view the scene of the murder!"

No sooner did the idea occur to him than he sought to put it in execution. But how could he manage it? He could not climb over the gate; it was too high. So he took from his pocket an electric lantern and a skeleton key which he always carried. Then, to his great surprise, he discovered that the gate was not locked; in fact, it was open about three or four inches. He entered the garden, and was careful to leave the gate as he had found it—partly open. But he had not taken many steps from the gate when he stopped. He had seen a light pass one of the windows on the second floor.

He saw the light pass a second window and a third, but he saw nothing else, except a silhouette outlined on the walls of the rooms. The light descended to the first floor, and, for a long time, wandered from room to room.

"Who the deuce is walking, at one o'clock in the morning, through the house in which the Baron d'Hautrec was killed?" Herlock Sholmes asked himself, deeply interested.

There was only one way to find out, and that was to enter the house himself. He did not hesitate, but started for the door of the house. However, at the moment when he crossed the streak of gaslight that came from the street-lamp, the man must have seen him, for the light in the house was suddenly extinguished and Herlock Sholmes did not see it again. Softly, he tried the door. It was open, also. Hearing no sound, he advanced through the hallway, encountered the foot of the stairs, and ascended to the first floor. Here there was the same silence, the same darkness.

He entered, one of the rooms and approached a window through which came a feeble light from the outside. On looking through the window he saw the man, who had no doubt descended by another stairway and escaped by another door. The man was threading his way through the shrubbery which bordered the wall that separated the two gardens.

"The deuce!" exclaimed Sholmes, "he is going to escape."

He hastened down the stairs and leaped over the steps in his eagerness to cut off the man's retreat. But he did not see anyone, and, owing to the darkness, it was several seconds before he was able to distinguish a bulky form moving through the shrubbery. This gave the Englishman food for reflection. Why had the man not made his escape, which he could have done so easily! Had he remained in order to watch the movements of the intruder who had disturbed him in his mysterious work!

"At all events," concluded Sholmes, "it is not Lupin; he would be more adroit. It may be one of his men."

For several minutes Herlock Sholmes remained motionless, with his gaze fixed on the adversary who, in his turn was watching the detective. But as that adversary had become passive, and as the Englishman was not one to consume his time in idle waiting, he examined his revolver to see if it was in good working order, remove his knife from its sheath, and walked toward the enemy with that cool effrontery and scorn of danger for which he had become famous.

He heard a clicking sound; it was his adversary preparing his revolver. Herlock Sholmes dashed boldly into the thicket, and grappled with his foe. There was a sharp, desperate struggle, in the course of which Sholmes suspected that the man was trying to draw a knife. But the Englishman, believing his antagonist to be an accomplice of Arsène Lupin and anxious to win the first trick in the game with that redoubtable foe, fought with unusual strength and determination. He hurled his adversary to the ground, held him there with the weight of his body, and, gripping him by the throat with one hand, he used his free hand to take out his electric lantern, press the button, and throw the light over the face of his prisoner.

"Wilson!" he exclaimed, in amazement.

"Herlock Sholmes!" stammered a weak, stifled voice.

For a long time they remained silent, astounded, foolish. The shriek of an automobile rent the air. A slight breeze stirred the leaves. Suddenly, Herlock Sholmes seized his friend by the shoulders and shook him violently, as he cried:

"What are you doing here? Tell me.... What?... Did I tell you to hide in the bushes and spy on me!"

"Spy on you!" muttered Wilson, "why, I didn't know it was you."

"But what are you doing here? You ought to be in bed."

"I was in bed."

"You ought to be asleep."

"I was asleep."

"Well, what brought you here?" asked Sholmes.

"Your letter."

"My letter? I don't understand."

"Yes, a messenger brought it to me at the hotel."

"From me? Are you crazy?"

"It is true—I swear it."

"Where is the letter?"

Wilson handed him a sheet of paper, which he read by the light of his lantern. It was as follows:

"Wilson, come at once to avenue Henri-Martin. The house is empty. Inspect the whole place and make an exact plan. Then return to hotel.—Herlock Sholmes."

"I was measuring the rooms," said Wilson, "when I saw a shadow in the garden. I had only one idea——"

"That was to seize the shadow.... The idea was excellent.... But remember this, Wilson, whenever you receive a letter from me, be sure it is my handwriting and not a forgery."

"Ah!" exclaimed Wilson, as the truth dawned on him, "then the letter wasn't from you?"

"No."

"Who sent it, then?"

"Arsène Lupin."

"Why? For what purpose?" asked Wilson.

"I don't know, and that's what worries me. I don't understand why he took the trouble to disturb you. Of course, if he had sent me on such a foolish errand I wouldn't be surprised; but what was his object in disturbing you?"

"I must hurry back to the hotel."

"So must I, Wilson."

They arrived at the gate. Wilson, who was ahead, took hold of it and pulled.

"Ah! you closed it?" he said.

"No, I left it partly open."

Sholmes tried the gate; then, alarmed, he examined the lock. An oath escaped him:

"Good God! it is locked! locked with a key!"

He shook the gate with all his strength; then, realizing the futility of his efforts, he dropped his arms, discouraged, and muttered, in a jerky manner:

"I can see it all now—it is Lupin. He fore-saw that I would leave the train at Creil, and he prepared this neat little trap for me in case I should commence my investigation this evening. Moreover, he was kind enough to send me a companion to share my captivity. All done to make me lose a day, and, perhaps, also, to teach me to mind my own business."

"Do you mean to say we are prisoners?"

"Exactly. Herlock Sholmes and Wilson are the prisoners of Arsène Lupin. It's a bad beginning; but he laughs best who laughs last."

Wilson seized Sholmes' arm, and exclaimed:

"Look!... Look up there!... A light...."

A light shone through one of the windows of the first floor. Both of them ran to the house, and each ascended by the stairs he had used on coming out a short time before, and they met again at the entrance to the lighted chamber. A small piece of a candle was burning in the center of the room. Beside it there was a basket containing a bottle, a roasted chicken, and a loaf of bread.

Sholmes was greatly amused, and laughed heartily.

"Wonderful! we are invited to supper. It is really an enchanted place, a genuine fairy-land. Come, Wilson, cheer up! this is not a funeral. It's all very funny."

"Are you quite sure it is so very funny?" asked Wilson, in a lugubrious tone.

"Am I sure?" exclaimed Sholmes, with a gaiety that was too boisterous to be natural, "why, to tell the truth, it's the funniest thing I ever saw. It's a jolly good comedy! What a master of sarcasm this Arsène Lupin is! He makes a fool of you with the utmost grace and delicacy. I wouldn't miss this feast for all the money in the Bank of England. Come, Wilson, you grieve me. You should display that nobility of character which rises superior to misfortune. I don't see that you have any cause for complaint, really, I don't."

After a time, by dint of good humor and sarcasm, he managed to restore Wilson to his normal mood, and make him swallow a morsel of chicken and a glass of wine. But when the candle went out and they prepared to spend the night there, with the bare floor for a mattress and the hard wall for a pillow, the harsh and ridiculous side of the situation was impressed upon them. That particular incident will not form a pleasant page in the memoirs of the famous detective.

Next morning Wilson awoke, stiff and cold. A slight noise attracted his attention: Herlock Sholmes was kneeling on the floor, critically examining some grains of sand and studying some chalk-marks, now almost effaced, which formed certain figures and numbers, which figures he entered in his notebook.

Accompanied by Wilson, who was deeply interested in the work, he examined each room, and found similar chalk-marks in two other apartments. He noticed, also, two circles on the oaken panels, an arrow on a wainscot, and four figures on four steps of the stairs. At the end of an hour Wilson said:

"The figures are correct, aren't they!"

"I don't know; but, at all events, they mean something," replied Sholmes, who had forgotten the discomforts of the night in the joy created by his new discoveries.

"It is quite obvious," said Wilson, "they represent the number of pieces in the floor."

"Ah!"

"Yes. And the two circles indicate that the panels are false, as you can readily ascertain, and the arrow points in the direction in which the panels move."

Herlock Sholmes looked at Wilson, in astonishment.

"Ah! my dear friend, how do you know all that? Your clairvoyance makes my poor ability in that direction look quite insignificant."

"Oh! it is very simple," said Wilson, inflated with pride; "I examined those marks last night, according to your instructions, or, rather, according to the instructions of Arsène Lupin, since he wrote the letter you sent to me."

At that moment Wilson faced a greater danger than he had during his struggle in the garden with Herlock Sholmes. The latter now felt a furious desire to strangle him. But, dominating his feelings, Sholmes made a grimace which was intended for a smile, and said:

"Quite so, Wilson, you have done well, and your work shows commendable progress. But, tell me, have you exercised your powers of observation and analysis on any other points? I might profit by your deductions."

"Oh! no, I went no farther."

"That's a pity. Your début was such a promising one. But, since that is all, we may as well go."

"Go! but how can we get out?"

"The way all honest people go out: through the gate."

"But it is locked."

"It will be opened."

"By whom?"

"Please call the two policemen who are strolling down the avenue."

"But——"

"But what?"

"It is very humiliating. What will be said when it becomes known that Herlock Sholmes and Wilson were the prisoners of Arsène Lupin?"

"Of course, I understand they will roar with laughter," replied Herlock Sholmes, in a dry voice and with frowning features, "but we can't set up housekeeping in this place."

"And you will not try to find another way out?"

"No."

"But the man who brought us the basket of provisions did not cross the garden, coming or going. There is some other way out. Let us look for it, and not bother with the police."

"Your argument is sound, but you forget that all the detectives in Paris have been trying to find it for the last six months, and that I searched the house from top to bottom while you were asleep. Ah! my dear Wilson, we have not been accustomed to pursue such game as Arsène Lupin. He leaves no trail behind him."

At eleven o'clock, Herlock Sholmes and Wilson were liberated, and conducted to the nearest police station, where the commissary, after subjecting them to a severe examination, released them with an affectation of good-will that was quite exasperating.

"I am very sorry, messieurs, that this unfortunate incident has occurred. You will have a very poor opinion of French hospitality. Mon Dieu! what a night you must have passed! Ah! that rascally Lupin is no respecter of persons."

They took a carriage to their hotel. At the office Wilson asked for the key of his room.

After some search the clerk replied, much astonished:

"But, monsieur, you have given up the room."

"I gave it up? When?"

"This morning, by the letter your friend brought here."

"What friend?"

"The gentleman who brought your letter.... Ah! your card is still attached to the letter. Here they are."

Wilson looked at them. Certainly, it was one of his cards, and the letter was in his handwriting.

"Good Lord!" he muttered, "this is another of his tricks," and he added, aloud: "Where is my luggage?"

"Your friend took it."

"Ah!... and you gave it to him?"

"Certainly; on the strength of your letter and card."

"Of course ... of course."

They left the hotel and walked, slowly and thoughtfully, through the Champs-Elysées. The avenue was bright and cheerful beneath a clear autumn sun; the air was mild and pleasant.

At Rond-Point, Herlock Sholmes lighted his pipe. Then Wilson spoke:

"I can't understand you, Sholmes. You are so calm and unruffled. They play with you as a cat plays with a mouse, and yet you do not say a word."

Sholmes stopped, as he replied:

"Wilson, I was thinking of your card."

"Well!"

"The point is this: here is a man who, in view of a possible struggle with us, procures specimens of our handwriting, and who holds, in his possession, one or more of your cards. Now, have you considered how much precaution and skill those facts represent?"

"Well!"

"Well, Wilson, to overcome an enemy so well prepared and so thoroughly equipped requires the infinite shrewdness of ... of a Herlock Sholmes. And yet, as you have seen, Wilson, I have lost the first round."

At six o 'clock the *Echo de France* published the following article in its evening edition:

"This morning Mon. Thenard, commissary of police in the sixteenth district, released Herlock Sholmes and his friend Wilson, both of whom had been locked in the house of the late Baron d'Hautrec, where they spent a very pleasant night—thanks to the thoughtful care and attention of Arsène Lupin."

"In addition to their other troubles, these gentlemen have been robbed of their valises, and, in consequence thereof, they have entered a formal complaint against Arsène Lupin."

"Arsène Lupin, satisfied that he has given them a mild reproof, hopes these gentlemen will not force him to resort to more stringent measures."

"Bah!" exclaimed Herlock Sholmes, crushing the paper in his hands, "that is only child's play! And that is the only criticism I have to make of Arsène Lupin: he plays to the gallery. There is that much of the fakir in him."

"Ah! Sholmes, you are a wonderful man! You have such a command over your temper. Nothing ever disturbs you."

"No, nothing disturbs me," replied Sholmes, in a voice that trembled from rage; "besides, what's the use of losing my temper?... I am quite confident of the final result; I shall have the last word."

IV. LIGHT IN THE DARKNESS.

However well-tempered a man's character may be—and Herlock Sholmes is one of those men over whom ill-fortune has little or no hold—there are circumstances wherein the most courageous combatant feels the necessity of marshaling his forces before risking the chances of a battle.

"I shall take a vacation to-day," said Sholmes.

"And what shall I do?" asked Wilson.

"You, Wilson—let me see! You can buy some underwear and linen to replenish our wardrobe, while I take a rest."

"Very well, Sholmes, I will watch while you sleep."

Wilson uttered these words with all the importance of a sentinel on guard at the outpost, and therefore exposed to the greatest danger. His chest was expanded; his muscles were tense. Assuming a shrewd look, he scrutinized, officially, the little room in which they had fixed their abode.

"Very well, Wilson, you can watch. I shall occupy myself in the preparation of a line of attack more appropriate to the methods of the enemy we are called upon to meet. Do you see, Wilson, we have been deceived in this fellow Lupin. My opinion is that we must commence at the very beginning of this affair."

"And even before that, if possible. But have we sufficient time?"

"Nine days, dear boy. That is five too many."

The Englishman spent the entire afternoon in smoking and sleeping. He did not enter upon his new plan of attack until the following day. Then he said:

"Wilson, I am ready. Let us attack the enemy."

"Lead on, Macduff!" exclaimed Wilson, full of martial ardor. "I wish to fight in the front rank. Oh! have no fear. I shall do credit to my King and country, for I am an Englishman."

In the first place, Sholmes had three long and important interviews: With Monsieur Detinan, whose rooms he examined with the greatest care and precision; with Suzanne Gerbois, whom he questioned in regard to the blonde Lady; and with Sister Auguste, who had retired to the convent of the Visitandines since the murder of Baron d'Hautrec.

At each of these interviews Wilson had remained outside; and each time he asked:

"Satisfactory?"

"Quite so."

"I was sure we were on the right track."

They paid a visit to the two houses adjoining that of the late Baron d'Hautrec in the avenue Henri-Martin; then they visited the rue Clapeyron, and, while he was examining the front of number 25, Sholmes said:

"All these houses must be connected by secret passages, but I can't find them."

For the first time in his life, Wilson doubted the omnipotence of his famous associate. Why did he now talk so much and accomplish so little?

"Why?" exclaimed Sholmes, in answer to Wilson's secret thought, "because, with this fellow Lupin, a person has to work in the dark, and, instead of deducting the truth from established facts, a man must extract it from his own brain, and afterward learn if it is supported by the facts in the case."

"But what about the secret passages?"

"They must exist. But even though I should discover them, and thus learn how Arsène Lupin made his entrance to the lawyer's house and how the blonde Lady escaped from the house of Baron d'Hautrec after the murder, what good would it do? How would it help me? Would it furnish me with a weapon of attack?"

"Let us attack him just the same," exclaimed Wilson, who had scarcely uttered these words when he jumped back with a cry of alarm. Something had fallen at their feet; it was a bag filled with sand which might have caused them serious injury if it had struck them.

Sholmes looked up. Some men were working on a scaffolding attached to the balcony at the fifth floor of the house. He said:

"We were lucky; one step more, and that heavy bag would have fallen on our heads. I wonder if—"

Moved by a sudden impulse, he rushed into the house, up the five flights of stairs, rang the bell, pushed his way into the apartment to the great surprise and alarm of the servant who came to the door, and made his way to the balcony in front of the house. But there was no one there.

"Where are the workmen who were here a moment ago?" he asked the servant.

"They have just gone."

"Which way did they go?"

"By the servants' stairs."

Sholmes leaned out of the window. He saw two men leaving the house, carrying bicycles. They mounted them and quickly disappeared around the corner.

"How long have they been working on this scaffolding!"

"Those men!... only since this morning. It's their first day."

Sholmes returned to the street, and joined Wilson. Together they returned to the hotel, and thus the second day ended in a mournful silence.

On the following day their programme was almost similar. They sat together on a bench in the avenue Henri-Martin, much to Wilson's disgust, who did not find it amusing to spend long hours watching the house in which the tragedy had occurred.

"What do you expect, Sholmes! That Arsène Lupin will walk out of the house!"

"No."

"That the blonde Lady will make her appearance!"

"No."

"What then!"

"I am looking for something to occur; some slight incident that will furnish me with a clue to work on."

"And if it does not occur!"

"Then I must, myself, create the spark that will set fire to the powder."

A solitary incident—and that of a disagreeable nature—broke the monotony of the forenoon.

A gentleman was riding along the avenue when his horse suddenly turned aside in such a manner that it ran against the bench on which they were sitting, and struck Sholmes a slight blow on the shoulder.

"Ha!" exclaimed Sholmes, "a little more and I would have had a broken shoulder."

The gentleman struggled with his horse. The Englishman drew his revolver and pointed it; but Wilson seized his arm, and said:

"Don't be foolish! What are you going to do! Kill the man!"

"Leave me alone, Wilson! Let go!"

During the brief struggle between Sholmes and Wilson the stranger rode away.

"Now, you can shoot," said Wilson, triumphantly, when the horseman was at some distance.

"Wilson, you're an idiot! Don't you understand that the man is an accomplice of Arsène Lupin?"

Sholmes was trembling from rage. Wilson stammered pitifully:

"What!... that man ... an accomplice?"

"Yes, the same as the workmen who tried to drop the bag of sand on us yesterday."

"It can't be possible!"

"Possible or not, there was only one way to prove it."

"By killing the man?"

"No—by killing the horse. If you hadn't grabbed my arm, I should have captured one of Lupin's accomplices. Now, do you understand the folly of your act?"

Throughout the afternoon both men were morose. They did not speak a word to each other. At five o'clock they visited the rue Clapeyron, but were careful to keep at a safe distance from the houses. However, three young men who were passing through the street, arm in arm, singing, ran against Sholmes and Wilson and refused to let them pass. Sholmes, who was in an ill humor, contested the right of way with them. After a brief struggle, Sholmes resorted to his fists. He struck one of the men a hard blow on the chest, another a blow in the face, and thus subdued two of his adversaries. Thereupon the three of them took to their heels and disappeared.

"Ah!" exclaimed Sholmes, "that does me good. I needed a little exercise."

But Wilson was leaning against the wall. Sholmes said:

"What's the matter, old chap? You're quite pale."

Wilson pointed to his left arm, which hung inert, and stammered:

"I don't know what it is. My arm pains me."

"Very much?... Is it serious?"

"Yes, I am afraid so."

He tried to raise his arm, but it was helpless. Sholmes felt it, gently at first, then in a rougher way, "to see how badly it was hurt," he said. He concluded that Wilson was really hurt, so he led him to a neighboring pharmacy, where a closer examination revealed the fact that the arm was broken and that Wilson was a candidate for the hospital. In the meantime they bared his arm and applied some remedies to ease his suffering.

"Come, come, old chap, cheer up!" said Sholmes, who was holding Wilson's arm, "in five or six weeks you will be all right again. But I will pay them back ... the rascals! Especially Lupin, for this is his work ... no doubt of that. I swear to you if ever——"

He stopped suddenly, dropped the arm—which caused Wilson such an access of pain that he almost fainted—and, striking his forehead, Sholmes said:

"Wilson, I have an idea. You know, I have one occasionally."

He stood for a moment, silent, with staring eyes, and then muttered, in short, sharp phrases:

"Yes, that's it ... that will explain all ... right at my feet ... and I didn't see it ... ah, parbleu! I should have thought of it before.... Wilson, I shall have good news for you."

Abruptly leaving his old friend, Sholmes ran into the street and went directly to the house known as number 25. On one of the stones, to the right of the door, he read this inscription: "Destange, architect, 1875."

There was a similar inscription on the house numbered 23.

Of course, there was nothing unusual in that. But what might be read on the houses in the avenue Henri-Martin?

A carriage was passing. He engaged it and directed the driver to take him to No. 134 avenue Henri-Martin. He was roused to a high pitch of excitement. He stood up in the carriage and urged the horse to greater speed. He offered extra pourboires to the driver. Quicker! Quicker!

How great was his anxiety as they turned from the rue de la Pompe! Had he caught a glimpse of the truth at last?

On one of the stones of the late Baron's house he read the words: "Destange, architect, 1874." And a similar inscription appeared on the two adjoining houses.

The reaction was such that he settled down in the seat of the carriage, trembling from joy. At last, a tiny ray of light had penetrated the dark shadows which encompassed these mysterious crimes! In the vast sombre forest wherein a thousand pathways crossed and re-crossed, he had discovered the first clue to the track followed by the enemy!

He entered a branch postoffice and obtained telephonic connection with the château de Crozon. The Countess answered the telephone call.

"Hello!... Is that you, madame?"

"Monsieur Sholmes, isn't it? Everything going all right?"

"Quite well, but I wish to ask you one question.... Hello!"

"Yes, I hear you."

"Tell me, when was the château de Crozon built?"

"It was destroyed by fire and rebuilt about thirty years ago."

"Who built it, and in what year?"

"There is an inscription on the front of the house which reads: 'Lucien Destange, architect, 1877.'"

"Thank you, madame, that is all. Good-bye."

He went away, murmuring: "Destange ... Lucien Destange ... that name has a familiar sound."

He noticed a public reading-room, entered, consulted a dictionary of modern biography, and copied the following information: "Lucien Destange, born 1840, Grand-Prix de Rome, officer of the Legion of Honor, author of several valuable books on architecture, etc...."

Then he returned to the pharmacy and found that Wilson had been taken to the hospital. There Sholmes found him with his arm in splints, and shivering with fever.

"Victory! Victory!" cried Sholmes. "I hold one end of the thread."

"Of what thread?"

"The one that leads to victory. I shall now be walking on solid ground, where there will be footprints, clues...."

"Cigarette ashes?" asked Wilson, whose curiosity had overcome his pain.

"And many other things! Just think, Wilson, I have found the mysterious link which unites the different adventures in which the blonde Lady played a part. Why did Lupin select those three houses for the scenes of his exploits?"

"Yes, why?"

"Because those three houses were built by the same architect. That was an easy problem, eh? Of course ... but who would have thought of it?"

"No one but you."

"And who, except I, knows that the same architect, by the use of analogous plans, has rendered it possible for a person to execute three distinct acts which, though miraculous in appearance, are, in reality, quite simple and easy?"

"That was a stroke of good luck."

"And it was time, dear boy, as I was becoming very impatient. You know, this is our fourth day."

"Out of ten."

"Oh! after this———"

Sholmes was excited, delighted, and gayer than usual.

"And when I think that these rascals might have attacked me in the street and broken my arm just as they did yours! Isn't that so, Wilson?"

Wilson simply shivered at the horrible thought. Sholmes continued:

"We must profit by the lesson. I can see, Wilson, that we were wrong to try and fight Lupin in the open, and leave ourselves exposed to his attacks."

"I can see it, and feel it, too, in my broken arm," said Wilson.

"You have one consolation, Wilson; that is, that I escaped. Now, I must be doubly cautious. In an open fight he will defeat me; but if I can work in the dark, unseen by him, I have the advantage, no matter how strong his forces may be."

"Ganimard might be of some assistance."

"Never! On the day that I can truly say: Arsène Lupin is there; I show you the quarry, and how to catch it; I shall go and see Ganimard at one of the two addresses that he gave me—his residence in the rue Pergolèse, or at the Suisse tavern in the Place du Châtelet. But, until that time, I shall work alone."

He approached the bed, placed his hand on Wilson's shoulder—on the sore one, of course—and said to him:

"Take care of yourself, old fellow. Henceforth your rôle will be to keep two or three of Arsène Lupin's men busy watching here in vain for my return to enquire about your health. It is a secret mission for you, eh!"

"Yes, and I shall do my best to fulfil it conscientiously. Then you do not expect to come here any more?"

"What for?" asked Sholmes.

"I don't know ... of course.... I am getting on as well as possible. But, Herlock, do me a last service: give me a drink."

"A drink?"

"Yes, I am dying of thirst; and with my fever——"

"To be sure—directly——"

He made a pretense of getting some water, perceived a package of tobacco, lighted his pipe, and then, as if he had not heard his friend's request, he went away, whilst Wilson uttered a mute prayer for the inaccessible water.

"Monsieur Destange!"

The servant eyed from head to foot the person to whom he had opened the door of the house—the magnificent house that stood at the corner of the Place Malesherbes and the rue Montchanin—and at the sight of the man with gray hairs, badly shaved, dressed in a shabby black coat, with a body as ill-formed and ungracious as his face, he replied with the disdain which he thought the occasion warranted:

"Monsieur Destange may or may not be at home. That depends. Has monsieur a card?"

Monsieur did not have a card, but he had a letter of introduction and, after the servant had taken the letter to Mon. Destange, he was conducted into the presence of that gentleman who was sitting in a large circular room or rotunda which occupied one of the wings of the house. It was a library, and contained a profusion of books and architectural drawings. When the stranger entered, the architect said to him:

"You are Monsieur Stickmann?"

"Yes, monsieur."

"My secretary tells me that he is ill, and has sent you to continue the general catalogue of the books which he commenced under my direction, and, more particularly, the catalogue of German books. Are you familiar with that kind of work?"

"Yes, monsieur, quite so," he replied, with a strong German accent.

Under those circumstances the bargain was soon concluded, and Mon. Destange commenced work with his new secretary.

Herlock Sholmes had gained access to the house.

In order to escape the vigilance of Arsène Lupin and gain admittance to the house occupied by Lucien Destange and his daughter Clotilde, the famous detective had been compelled to resort to a number of stratagems, and, under a variety of names, to ingratiate himself into the good graces and confidence of a number of persons—in short, to live, during forty-eight hours, a most complicated life. During that time he had acquired the following information: Mon. Destange, having retired from active business on account of his failing health, now lived amongst the many books he had accumulated on the subject of architecture. He derived infinite pleasure in viewing and handling those dusty old volumes.

His daughter Clotilde was considered eccentric. She passed her time in another part of the house, and never went out.

"Of course," Sholmes said to himself, as he wrote in a register the titles of the books which Mon. Destange dictated to him, "all that is vague and incomplete, but it is quite a long step in advance. I shall surely solve one of these absorbing problems: Is Mon. Destange associated with Arsène Lupin? Does he continue to see him? Are the papers relating to the construction of the three houses still in existence? Will those papers not furnish me with the location of other houses of similar construction which Arsène Lupin and his associates will plunder in the future?

"Monsieur Destange, an accomplice of Arsène Lupin! That venerable man, an officer of the Legion of Honor, working in league with a burglar—such an idea was absurd! Besides, if we concede that such a complicity exists, how could Mon. Destange, thirty years ago, have possibly foreseen the thefts of Arsène Lupin, who was then an infant?"

No matter! The Englishman was implacable. With his marvellous scent, and that instinct which never fails him, he felt that he was in the heart of some strange mystery. Ever since he first entered the house, he had been under the influence of that impression, and yet he could not define the grounds on which he based his suspicions.

Up to the morning of the second day he had not made any significant discovery. At two o'clock of that day he saw Clotilde Destange for the first time; she came to the library in search of a book. She was about thirty years of age, a brunette, slow and silent in her movements, with features imbued with that expression of indifference which is characteristic of people who live a secluded life. She exchanged a few words with her father, and then retired, without even looking at Sholmes.

The afternoon dragged along monotonously. At five o'clock Mon. Destange announced his intention to go out. Sholmes was alone on the circular gallery that was constructed about ten feet above the floor of the rotunda. It was almost dark. He was on the point of going out, when he heard a slight sound and, at the same time, experienced the feeling that there was someone in the room. Several minutes passed before he saw or heard anything more. Then he shuddered; a shadowy form emerged from the gloom, quite close to him, upon the balcony. It seemed incredible. How long had this mysterious visitor been there? Whence did he come?

The strange man descended the steps and went directly to a large oaken cupboard. Sholmes was a keen observer of the man's movements. He watched him searching amongst the papers with which the cupboard was filled. What was he looking for?

Then the door opened and Mlle. Destange entered, speaking to someone who was following her:

"So you have decided not to go out, father?... Then I will make a light ... one second ... do not move...."

The strange man closed the cupboard and hid in the embrasure of a large window, drawing the curtains together. Did Mlle. Destange not see him? Did she not hear him? Calmly she turned on the electric lights; she and her father sat down close to each other. She opened a book she had brought with her, and commenced to read. After the lapse of a few minutes she said:

"Your secretary has gone."

"Yes, I don't see him."

"Do you like him as well as you did at first?" she asked, as if she were not aware of the illness of the real secretary and his replacement by Stickmann.

"Oh! yes."

Monsieur Destange's head bobbed from one side to the other. He was asleep. The girl resumed her reading. A moment later one of the window curtains was pushed back, and the strange man emerged and glided along the wall toward the door, which obliged him to pass behind Mon. Destange but in front of Clotilde, and brought him into the light so that Herlock Sholmes obtained a good view of the man's face. It was Arsène Lupin.

The Englishman was delighted. His forecast was verified; he had penetrated to the very heart of the mystery, and found Arsène Lupin to be the moving spirit in it.

Clotilde had not yet displayed any knowledge of his presence, although it was quite improbable that any movement of the intruder had escaped her notice. Lupin had almost reached the door and, in fact, his hand was already seeking the door-knob, when his coat brushed against a small table and knocked something to the floor. Monsieur Destange awoke with a start. Arsène Lupin was already standing in front of him, hat in hand, smiling.

"Maxime Bermond," exclaimed Mon. Destange, joyfully. "My dear Maxime, what lucky chance brings you here?"

"The wish to see you and Mademoiselle Destange."

"When did you return from your journey?"

"Yesterday."

"You must stay to dinner."

"No, thank you, I am sorry, but I have an appointment to dine with some friends at a restaurant."

"Come, to-morrow, then, Clotilde, you must urge him to come to-morrow. Ah! my dear Maxime.... I thought of you many times during your absence."

"Really?"

"Yes, I went through all my old papers in that cupboard, and found our last statement of account."

"What account?"

"Relating to the avenue Henri-Martin."

"Ah! do you keep such papers? What for?"

Then the three of them left the room, and continued their conversation in a small parlor which adjoined the library.

"Is it Lupin?" Sholmes asked himself, in a sudden access of doubt. Certainly, from all appearances, it was he; and yet it was also someone else who resembled Arsène Lupin in certain respects, and who still maintained his own individuality, features, and color of hair. Sholmes could hear Lupin's voice in the adjoining room. He was relating some stories at which Mon. Destange laughed heartily, and which even brought a smile to the lips of the melancholy Clotilde. And each of those smiles appeared to be the reward which Arsène Lupin was seeking, and which he was delighted to have secured. His success caused him to redouble his efforts and, insensibly, at the sound of that clear and happy voice, Clotilde's face brightened and lost that cold and listless expression which usually pervaded it.

"They love each other," thought Sholmes, "but what the deuce can there be in common between Clotilde Destange and Maxime Bermond? Does she know that Maxime is none other than Arsène Lupin?"

Until seven o'clock Sholmes was an anxious listener, seeking to profit by the conversation. Then, with infinite precaution, he descended from the gallery, crept along the side of the room to the door in such a manner that the people in the adjoining room did not see him.

When he reached the street Sholmes satisfied himself that there was neither an automobile nor a cab waiting there; then he slowly limped along the boulevard Malesherbes. He turned into an adjacent street, donned the overcoat which he had carried on his arm, altered the shape of his hat, assumed an upright carriage, and, thus transformed, returned to a place whence he could watch the door of Mon. Destange's house.

In a few minutes Arsène Lupin came out, and proceeded to walk toward the center of Paris by way of the rues de Constantinople and London. Herlock Sholmes followed at a distance of a hundred paces.

Exciting moments for the Englishman! He sniffed the air, eagerly, like a hound following a fresh scent. It seemed to him a delightful thing thus to follow his adversary. It was no longer Herlock Sholmes who was being watched, but Arsène Lupin, the invisible Arsène Lupin. He held him, so to speak, within the grasp of his eye, by an imperceptible bond that nothing could break. And he was pleased to think that the quarry belonged to him.

But he soon observed a suspicious circumstance. In the intervening space between him and Arsène Lupin he noticed several people traveling in the same direction, particularly two husky fellows in slouch hats on the left side of the street, and two others on the right wearing caps and smoking cigarettes. Of course, their presence in that vicinity may have been the result of chance, but Sholmes was more astonished when he observed that the four men stopped when Lupin entered a tobacco shop; and still more surprised when the four men started again after Lupin emerged from the shop, each keeping to his own side of the street.

"Curse it!" muttered Sholmes; "he is being followed."

He was annoyed at the idea that others were on the trail of Arsène Lupin; that someone might deprive him, not of the glory—he cared little for that—but of the immense pleasure of capturing, single-handed, the most formidable enemy he had ever met. And he felt that he was not mistaken; the men presented to Sholmes' experienced eye the appearance and manner of those who, while regulating their gait to that of another, wish to present a careless and natural air.

"Is this some of Ganimard's work?" muttered Sholmes. "Is he playing me false?"

He felt inclined to speak to one of the men with a view of acting in concert with him; but as they were now approaching the boulevard the crowd was becoming denser, and he was afraid he might lose sight of Lupin. So he quickened his pace and turned into the boulevard just in time to see Lupin ascending the steps of the Hungarian restaurant at the corner of the rue du Helder. The door of the restaurant was open, so that Sholmes, while sitting on a bench on the other side of the boulevard, could see Lupin take a seat at a table, luxuriously appointed and decorated with flowers, at which three gentlemen and two ladies of elegant appearance were already seated and who extended to Lupin a hearty greeting.

Sholmes now looked about for the four men and perceived them amongst a crowd of people who were listening to a gipsy orchestra that was playing in a neighboring café. It was a curious thing that they were paying no attention to Arsène Lupin, but seemed to be friendly with the people around them. One of them took a cigarette from his pocket and approached a gentleman who wore a frock coat and silk hat. The gentleman offered the other his cigar for a light, and Sholmes had the impression that they talked to each other much longer than the occasion demanded. Finally the gentleman approached the Hungarian restaurant, entered and looked around. When he caught sight of Lupin he advanced and spoke to him for a moment, then took a seat at an adjoining table. Sholmes now recognized this gentleman as the horseman who had tried to run him down in the avenue Henri-Martin.

Then Sholmes understood that these men were not tracking Arsène Lupin; they were a part of his band. They were watching over his safety. They were his bodyguard, his satellites, his vigilant escort. Wherever danger threatened Lupin, these confederates were at hand to avert it, ready to defend him. The four men were accomplices. The gentleman in the frock coat was an accomplice. These facts furnished the Englishman with food for reflection. Would he ever succeed in capturing that inaccessible individual? What unlimited power was possessed by such an organization, directed by such a chief!

He tore a leaf from his notebook, wrote a few lines in pencil, which he placed in an envelope, and said to a boy about fifteen years of age who was sitting on the bench beside him:

"Here, my boy; take a carriage and deliver this letter to the cashier of the Suisse tavern, Place du Châtelet. Be quick!"

He gave him a five-franc piece. The boy disappeared.

A half hour passed away. The crowd had grown larger, and Sholmes perceived only at intervals the accomplices of Arsène Lupin. Then someone brushed against him and whispered in his ear:

"Well! what is it, Monsieur Sholmes?"

"Ah! it is you, Ganimard?"

"Yes; I received your note at the tavern. What's the matter?"

"He is there."

"What do you mean?"

"There ... in the restaurant. Lean to the right.... Do you see him now?"

"No."

"He is pouring a glass of champagne for the lady."

"That is not Lupin."

"Yes, it is."

"But I tell you.... Ah! yet, it may be. It looks a great deal like him," said Ganimard, naively. "And the others—accomplices?"

"No; the lady sitting beside him is Lady Cliveden; the other is the Duchess de Cleath. The gentleman sitting opposite Lupin is the Spanish Ambassador to London."

Ganimard took a step forward. Sholmes retained him.

"Be prudent. You are alone."

"So is he."

"No, he has a number of men on the boulevard mounting guard. And inside the restaurant that gentleman——"

"And I, when I take Arsène Lupin by the collar and announce his name, I shall have the entire room on my side and all the waiters."

"I should prefer to have a few policemen."

"But, Monsieur Sholmes, we have no choice. We must catch him when we can."

He was right; Sholmes knew it. It was better to take advantage of the opportunity and make the attempt. Sholmes simply gave this advice to Ganimard:

"Conceal your identity as long as possible."

Sholmes glided behind a newspaper kiosk, whence he could still watch Lupin, who was leaning toward Lady Cliveden, talking and smiling.

Ganimard crossed the street, hands in his pockets, as if he were going down the boulevard, but when he reached the opposite sidewalk he turned quickly and bounded up the steps of the restaurant. There was a shrill whistle. Ganimard ran against the head waiter, who had suddenly planted himself in the doorway and now pushed Ganimard back with a show of indignation, as if he were an intruder whose presence would bring disgrace upon the restaurant. Ganimard was surprised. At the same moment the gentleman in the frock coat came out. He took the part of the detective and entered into an exciting argument with the waiter; both of them hung on to Ganimard, one pushing him in, the other pushing him out in such a manner that, despite all his efforts and despite his furious protestations, the unfortunate detective soon found himself on the sidewalk.

The struggling men were surrounded by a crowd. Two policemen, attracted by the noise, tried to force their way through the crowd, but encountered a mysterious resistance and could make no headway through the opposing backs and pressing shoulders of the mob.

But suddenly, as if by magic, the crowd parted and the passage to the restaurant was clear. The head waiter, recognizing his mistake, was profuse in his apologies; the gentleman in the frock coat ceased his efforts on behalf of the detective, the crowd dispersed, the policemen passed on, and Ganimard hastened to the table at which the six guests were sitting. But now there were only five! He looked around.... The only exit was the door.

"The person who was sitting here!" he cried to the five astonished guests. "Where is he?"

"Monsieur Destro?"

"No; Arsène Lupin!"

A waiter approached and said:

"The gentleman went upstairs."

Ganimard rushed up in the hope of finding him. The upper floor of the restaurant contained private dining-rooms and had a private stairway leading to the boulevard.

"No use looking for him now," muttered Ganimard. "He is far away by this time."

He was not far away—two hundred yards at most—in the Madeleine-Bastille omnibus, which was rolling along very peacefully with its three horses across the Place de l'Opéra toward the Boulevard des Capucines. Two sturdy fellows were talking together on the platform. On the roof of the omnibus near the stairs an old fellow was sleeping; it was Herlock Sholmes.

With bobbing head, rocked by the movement of the vehicle, the Englishman said to himself:

"If Wilson could see me now, how proud he would be of his collaborator!... Bah! It was easy to foresee that the game was lost, as soon as the man whistled; nothing could be done but watch the exits and see that our man did not escape. Really, Lupin makes life exciting and interesting."

At the terminal point Herlock Sholmes, by leaning over, saw Arsène Lupin leaving the omnibus, and as he passed in front of the men who formed his bodyguard Sholmes heard him say: "A l'Etoile."

"A l'Etoile, exactly, a rendezvous. I shall be there," thought Sholmes. "I will follow the two men."

Lupin took an automobile; but the men walked the entire distance, followed by Sholmes. They stopped at a narrow house, No. 40 rue Chalgrin, and rang the bell. Sholmes took his position in the shadow of a doorway, whence he could watch the house in question. A man opened one of the windows of the ground floor and closed the shutters. But the shutters did not reach to the top of the window. The impost was clear.

At the end of ten minutes a gentleman rang at the same door and a few minutes later another man came. A short time afterward an automobile stopped in front of the house, bringing two passengers: Arsène Lupin and a lady concealed beneath a large cloak and a thick veil.

"The blonde Lady, no doubt," said Sholmes to himself, as the automobile drove away.

Herlock Sholmes now approached the house, climbed to the window-ledge and, by standing on tiptoe, he was able to see through the window above the shutters. What did he see?

Arsène Lupin, leaning against the mantel, was speaking with considerable animation. The others were grouped around him, listening to him attentively. Amongst them Sholmes easily recognized the gentleman in the frock coat and he thought one of the other men resembled the head-waiter of the restaurant. As to the blonde Lady, she was seated in an armchair with her back to the window.

"They are holding a consultation," thought Sholmes. "They are worried over the incident at the restaurant and are holding a council of war. Ah! what a master stroke it would be to capture all of them at one fell stroke!"

One of them, having moved toward the door, Sholmes leaped to the ground and concealed himself in the shadow. The gentleman in the frock coat and the head-waiter left the house. A moment later a light appeared at the windows of the first floor, but the shutters were closed immediately and the upper part of the house was dark as well as the lower.

"Lupin and the woman are on the ground floor; the two confederates live on the upper floor," said Sholmes.

Sholmes remained there the greater part of the night, fearing that if he went away Arsène Lupin might leave during his absence. At four o'clock, seeing two policemen at the end of the street, he approached them, explained the situation and left them to watch the house. He went to Ganimard's residence in the rue Pergolese and wakened him.

"I have him yet," said Sholmes.

"Arsène Lupin?"

"Yes."

"If you haven't got any better hold on him than you had a while ago, I might as well go back to bed. But we may as well go to the station-house."

They went to the police station in the rue Mesnil and from there to the residence of the commissary, Mon. Decointre. Then, accompanied by half a dozen policemen, they went to the rue Chalgrin.

"Anything new?" asked Sholmes, addressing the two policemen.

"Nothing."

It was just breaking day when, after taking necessary measures to prevent escape, the commissary rang the bell and commenced to question the concierge. The woman was greatly frightened at this early morning invasion, and she trembled as she replied that there were no tenants on the ground floor.

"What! not a tenant?" exclaimed Ganimard.

"No; but on the first floor there are two men named Leroux. They have furnished the apartment on the ground floor for some country relations."

"A gentleman and lady."

"Yes."

"Who came here last night."

"Perhaps ... but I don't know ... I was asleep. But I don't think so, for the key is here. They did not ask for it."

With that key the commissary opened the door of the ground-floor apartment. It comprised only two rooms and they were empty.

"Impossible!" exclaimed Sholmes. "I saw both of them in this room."

"I don't doubt your word," said the commissary; "but they are not here now."

"Let us go to the first floor. They must be there."

"The first floor is occupied by two men named Leroux."

"We will examine the Messieurs Leroux."

They all ascended the stairs and the commissary rang. At the second ring a man opened the door; he was in his shirt-sleeves. Sholmes recognized him as one of Lupin's bodyguard. The man assumed a furious air:

"What do you mean by making such a row at this hour of the morning ... waking people up...."

But he stopped suddenly, astounded.

"God forgive me!... really, gentlemen, I didn't notice who it was. Why, it is Monsieur Decointre!... and you, Monsieur Ganimard. What can I do for you!"

Ganimard burst into an uncontrollable fit of laughter, which caused him to bend double and turn black in the face.

"Ah! it is you, Leroux," he stammered. "Oh! this is too funny! Leroux, an accomplice of Arsène Lupin! Oh, I shall die! and your brother, Leroux, where is he?"

"Edmond!" called the man. "It is Ganimard, who has come to visit us."

Another man appeared and at sight of him Ganimard's mirth redoubled.

"Oh! oh! we had no idea of this! Ah! my friends, you are in a bad fix now. Who would have ever suspected it?"

Turning to Sholmes, Ganimard introduced the man:

"Victor Leroux, a detective from our office, one of the best men in the iron brigade ... Edmond Leroux, chief clerk in the anthropometric service."

V. AN ABDUCTION.

Herlock Sholmes said nothing. To protest? To accuse the two men? That would be useless. In the absence of evidence which he did not possess and had no time to seek, no one would believe him. Moreover, he was stifled with rage, but would not display his feelings before the triumphant Ganimard. So he bowed respectfully to the brothers Leroux, guardians of society, and retired.

In the vestibule he turned toward a low door which looked like the entrance to a cellar, and picked up a small red stone; it was a garnet. When he reached the street he turned and read on the front of the house this inscription: "Lucien Destange, architect, 1877."

The adjoining house, No. 42, bore the same inscription.

"Always the double passage—numbers 40 and 42 have a secret means of communication. Why didn't I think of that? I should have remained with the two policemen."

He met the policemen near the corner and said to them:

"Two people came out of house No. 42 during my absence, didn't they?"

"Yes; a gentleman and lady."

Ganimard approached. Sholmes took his arm, and as they walked down the street he said:

"Monsieur Ganimard, you have had a good laugh and will no doubt forgive me for the trouble I have caused you."

"Oh! there's no harm done; but it was a good joke."

"I admit that; but the best jokes have only a short life, and this one can't last much longer."

"I hope not."

"This is now the seventh day, and I can remain only three days more. Then I must return to London."

"Oh!"

"I wish to ask you to be in readiness, as I may call on you at any hour on Tuesday or Wednesday night."

"For an expedition of the same kind as we had to-night?"

"Yes, monsieur, the very same."

"With what result?"

"The capture of Arsène Lupin," replied Sholmes.

"Do you think so!"

"I swear it, on my honor, monsieur."

Sholmes bade Ganimard good-bye and went to the nearest hotel for a few hours' sleep; after which, refreshed and with renewed confidence in himself, he returned to the rue Chalgrin, slipped two louis into the hand of the concierge, assured himself that the brothers Leroux had gone out, learned that the house belonged to a Monsieur Harmingeat, and, provided with a candle, descended to the cellar through the low door near which he had found the garnet. At the bottom of the stairs he found another exactly like it.

"I am not mistaken," he thought; "this is the means of communication. Let me see if my skeleton-key will open the cellar reserved for the tenant of the ground floor. Yes; it will. Now, I will examine those cases of wine... oh! oh! here are some places where the dust has been cleared away ... and some footprints on the ground...."

A slight noise caused him to listen attentively. Quickly he pushed the door shut, blew out his candle and hid behind a pile of empty wine cases. After a few seconds he noticed that a portion of the wall swung on a pivot, the light of a lantern was thrown into the cellar, an arm appeared, then a man entered.

He was bent over, as if he were searching for something. He felt in the dust with his fingers and several times he threw something into a cardboard box that he carried in his left hand. Afterward he obliterated the traces of his footsteps, as well as the footprints left by Lupin and the blonde lady, and he was about to leave the cellar by the same way as he had entered, when he uttered a harsh cry and fell to the ground. Sholmes had leaped upon him. It was the work of a moment, and in the simplest manner in the world the man found himself stretched on the ground, bound and handcuffed. The Englishman leaned over him and said:

"Have you anything to say?... To tell what you know?"

The man replied by such an ironical smile that Sholmes realized the futility of questioning him. So he contented himself by exploring the pockets of his captive, but he found only a bunch of keys, a handkerchief and the small cardboard box which contained a dozen garnets similar to those which Sholmes had found.

Then what was he to do with the man? Wait until his friends came to his help and deliver all of them to the police? What good would that do? What advantage would that give him over Lupin?

He hesitated; but an examination of the box decided the question. The box bore this name and address: "Leonard, jeweler, rue de la Paix."

He resolved to abandon the man to his fate. He locked the cellar and left the house. At a branch postoffice he sent a telegram to Monsieur Destange, saying that he could not come that day. Then he went to see the jeweler and, handing him the garnets, said:

"Madame sent me with these stones. She wishes to have them reset."

Sholmes had struck the right key. The jeweler replied:

"Certainly; the lady telephoned to me. She said she would be here to-day."

Sholmes established himself on the sidewalk to wait for the lady, but it was five o'clock when he saw a heavily-veiled lady approach and enter the store. Through the window he saw her place on the counter a piece of antique jewelry set with garnets.

She went away almost immediately, walking quickly and passed through streets that were unknown to the Englishman. As it was now almost dark, he walked close behind her and followed her into a five-story house of double flats and, therefore, occupied by numerous tenants. At the second floor she stopped and entered. Two minutes later the Englishman commenced to try the keys on the bunch he had taken from the man in the rue Chalgrin. The fourth key fitted the lock.

Notwithstanding the darkness of the rooms, he perceived that they were absolutely empty, as if unoccupied, and the various doors were standing open so that he could see all the apartments. At the end of a corridor he perceived a ray of light and, by approaching on tiptoe and looking through the glass door, he saw the veiled lady who had removed her hat and dress and was now wearing a velvet dressing-gown. The discarded garments were lying on the only chair in the room and a lighted lamp stood on the mantel.

Then he saw her approach the fireplace and press what appeared to be the button of an electric bell. Immediately the panel to the right of the fireplace moved and slowly glided behind the adjoining panel, thus disclosing an opening large enough for a person to pass through. The lady disappeared through this opening, taking the lamp with her.

The operation was a very simple one. Sholmes adopted it and followed the lady. He found himself in total darkness and immediately he felt his face brushed by some soft articles. He lighted a match and found that he was in a very small room completely filled with cloaks and dresses suspended on hangers. He picked his way through until he reached a door that was draped with a portiere. He peeped through and, behold, the blonde lady was there, under his eyes, and almost within reach of his hand.

224

She extinguished the lamp and turned on the electric lights. Then for the first time Herlock Sholmes obtained a good look at her face. He was amazed. The woman, whom he had overtaken after so much trouble and after so many tricks and manoeuvres, was none other than Clotilde Destange.

Clotilde Destange, the assassin of the Baron d'Hautrec and the thief who stole the blue diamond! Clotilde Destange, the mysterious friend of Arsène Lupin! And the blonde lady!

"Yes, I am only a stupid ass," thought Herlock Sholmes at that moment. "Because Lupin's friend was a blonde and Clotilde is a brunette, I never dreamed that they were the same person. But how could the blonde lady remain a blonde after the murder of the baron and the theft of the diamond?"

Sholmes could see a portion of the room; it was a boudoir, furnished with the most delightful luxury and exquisite taste, and adorned with beautiful tapestries and costly ornaments. A mahogany couch, upholstered in silk, was located on the side of the room opposite the door at which Sholmes was standing. Clotilde was sitting on this couch, motionless, her face covered by her hands. Then he perceived that she was weeping. Great tears rolled down her pale cheeks and fell, drop by drop, on the velvet corsage. The tears came thick and fast, as if their source were inexhaustible.

A door silently opened behind her and Arsène Lupin entered. He looked at her for a long time without making his presence known; then he approached her, knelt at her feet, pressed her head to his breast, folded her in his arms, and his actions indicated an infinite measure of love and sympathy. For a time not a word was uttered, but her tears became less abundant.

"I was so anxious to make you happy," he murmured.

"I am happy."

"No; you are crying.... Your tears break my heart, Clotilde."

The caressing and sympathetic tone of his voice soothed her, and she listened to him with an eager desire for hope and happiness. Her features were softened by a smile, and yet how sad a smile! He continued to speak in a tone of tender entreaty:

"You should not be unhappy, Clotilde; you have no cause to be."

She displayed her delicate white hands and said, solemnly:

"Yes, Maxime; so long as I see those hands I shall be sad."

"Why?"

"They are stained with blood."

"Hush! Do not think of that!" exclaimed Lupin. "The dead is past and gone. Do not resurrect it."

And he kissed the long, delicate hand, while she regarded him with a brighter smile as if each kiss effaced a portion of that dreadful memory.

"You must love me, Maxime; you must—because no woman will ever love you as I do. For your sake, I have done many things, not at your order or request, but in obedience to your secret desires. I have done things at which my will and conscience revolted, but there was some unknown power that I could not resist. What I did I did involuntarily, mechanically, because it helped you, because you wished it ... and I am ready to do it again to-morrow ... and always."

"Ah, Clotilde," he said, bitterly, "why did I draw you into my adventurous life? I should have remained the Maxime Bermond that you loved five years ago, and not have let you know the ... other man that I am."

She replied in a low voice:

"I love the other man, also, and I have nothing to regret."

"Yes, you regret your past life—the free and happy life you once enjoyed."

"I have no regrets when you are here," she said, passionately. "All faults and crimes disappear when I see you. When you are away I may suffer, and weep, and be horrified at what I have done; but when you come it is all forgotten. Your love wipes it all away. And I am happy again.... But you must love me!"

"I do not love you on compulsion, Clotilde. I love you simply because ... I love you."

"Are you sure of it?"

"I am just as sure of my own love as I am of yours. Only my life is a very active and exciting one, and I cannot spend as much time with you as I would like—just now."

"What is it? Some new danger? Tell me!"

"Oh! nothing serious. Only...."

"Only what?" she asked.

"Well, he is on our track."

"Who? Herlock Sholmes?"

"Yes; it was he who dragged Ganimard into that affair at the Hungarian restaurant. It was he who instructed the two policemen to watch the house in the rue Chalgrin. I have proof of it. Ganimard searched the house this morning and Sholmes was with him. Besides——"

"Besides? What?"

"Well, there is another thing. One of our men is missing."

"Who?"

"Jeanniot."

"The concierge?"

"Yes."

"Why, I sent him to the rue Chalgrin this morning to pick up the garnets that fell out of my brooch."

"There is no doubt, then, that Sholmes caught him."

"No; the garnets were delivered to the jeweler in the rue de la Paix."

"Then, what has become of him!"

"Oh! Maxime, I am afraid."

"There is nothing to be afraid of, but I confess the situation is very serious. What does he know? Where does he hide himself? His isolation is his strong card. I cannot reach him."

"What are you going to do?"

"Act with extreme prudence, Clotilde. Some time ago I decided to change my residence to a safer place, and Sholmes' appearance on the scene has prompted me to do so at once. When a man like that is on your track, you must be prepared for the worst. Well, I am making my preparations. Day after to-morrow, Wednesday, I shall move. At noon it will be finished. At two o 'clock I shall leave the place, after removing the last trace of our residence there, which will be no small matter. Until then——"

"Well?"

"Until then we must not see each other and no one must see you, Clotilde. Do not go out. I have no fear for myself, but I have for you."

"That Englishman cannot possibly reach me."

"I am not so sure of that. He is a dangerous man. Yesterday I came here to search the cupboard that contains all of Monsieur Destange's old papers and records. There is danger there. There is danger everywhere. I feel that he is watching us—that he is drawing his net around us closer and closer. It is one of those intuitions which never deceive me."

"In that case, Maxime, go, and think no more of my tears. I shall be brave, and wait patiently until the danger is past. Adieu, Maxime."

They held one another for some time in a last fond embrace. And it was she that gently pushed him outside. Sholmes could hear the sound of their voices in the distance.

Emboldened by the necessities of the situation and the urgent need of bringing his investigation to a speedy termination, Sholmes proceeded to make an examination of the house in which he now found himself. He passed through Clotilde's boudoir into a corridor, at the end of which there was a stairway leading to the lower floor; he was about to descend this stairway when he heard voices below, which caused him to change his route. He followed the corridor, which was a circular one, and discovered another stairway, which he descended and found himself amidst surroundings that bore a familiar appearance. He passed through a door that stood partly open and entered a large circular room. It was Monsieur Destange's library.

"Ah! splendid!" he exclaimed. "Now I understand everything. The boudoir of Mademoiselle Clotilde—the blonde Lady—communicates with a room in the adjoining house, and that house does not front on the Place Malesherbes, but upon an adjacent street, the rue Montchanin, if I remember the name correctly.... And I now understand how Clotilde Destange can meet her lover and at the same time create the impression that she never leaves the house; and I understand also how Arsène Lupin was enabled to make his mysterious entrance to the gallery last night. Ah! there must be another connection between the library and the adjoining room. One more house full of ways that are dark! And no doubt Lucien Destange was the architect, as usual!... I should take advantage of this opportunity to examine the contents of the cupboard and perhaps learn the location of other houses with secret passages constructed by Monsieur Destange."

Sholmes ascended to the gallery and concealed himself behind some draperies, where he remained until late in the evening. At last a servant came and turned off the electric lights. An hour later the Englishman, by the light of his lantern, made his way to the cupboard. As he had surmised, it contained the architect's old papers, plans, specifications and books of account. It also contained a series of registers, arranged according to date, and Sholmes, having selected those of the most recent dates, searched in the indexes for the name "Harmingeat." He found it in one of the registers with a reference to page 63. Turning to that page, he read:

"Harmingeat, 40 rue Chalgrin."

This was followed by a detailed account of the work done in and about the installation of a furnace in the house. And in the margin of the book someone had written these words: "See account M.B."

"Ah! I thought so!" said Sholmes; "the account M.B. is the one I want. I shall learn from it the actual residence of Monsieur Lupin."

It was morning before he found that important account. It comprised sixteen pages, one of which was a copy of the page on which was described the work done for Mon. Harmingeat of the rue Chalgrin. Another page described the work performed for Mon. Vatinel as owner of the house at No. 25 rue Clapeyron. Another page was reserved for the Baron d'Hautrec, 134 avenue Henri-Martin; another was devoted to the Château de Crozon, and the eleven other pages to various owners of houses in Paris.

Sholmes made a list of those eleven names and addresses; after which he returned the books to their proper places, opened a window, jumped out onto the deserted street and closed the shutters behind him.

When he reached his room at the hotel he lighted his pipe with all the solemnity with which he was wont to characterize that act, and amidst clouds of smoke he studied the deductions that might be drawn from the account of M.B., or rather, from the account of Maxime Bermond alias Arsène Lupin.

At eight o 'clock he sent the following message to Ganimard:

"I expect to pass through the rue Pergolese this forenoon and will inform you of a person whose arrest is of the highest importance. In any event, be at home to-night and to-morrow until noon and have at least thirty men at your service."

Then he engaged an automobile at the stand on the boulevard, choosing one whose chauffeur looked good-natured but dull-witted, and instructed him to drive to the Place Malesherbes, where he stopped him about one hundred feet from Monsieur Destange's house.

"My boy, close your carriage," he said to the chauffeur; "turn up the collar of your coat, for the wind is cold, and wait patiently. At the end of an hour and a half, crank up your machine. When I return we will go to the rue Pergolese."

As he was ascending the steps leading to the door a doubt entered his mind. Was it not a mistake on his part to be spending his time on the affairs of the blonde Lady, while Arsène Lupin was preparing to move? Would he not be better engaged in trying to find the abode of his adversary amongst the eleven houses on his list?

"Ah!" he exclaimed, "when the blonde Lady becomes my prisoner, I shall be master of the situation."

And he rang the bell.

Monsieur Destange was already in the library. They had been working only a few minutes, when Clotilde entered, bade her father good morning, entered the adjoining parlor and sat down to write. From his place Sholmes could see her leaning over the table and from time to time absorbed in deep meditation. After a short time he picked up a book and said to Monsieur Destange:

"Here is a book that Mademoiselle Destange asked me to bring to her when I found it."

He went into the little parlor, stood before Clotilde in such a manner that her father could not see her, and said:

"I am Monsieur Stickmann, your father's new secretary."

"Ah!" said Clotilde, without moving, "my father has changed his secretary? I didn't know it."

"Yes, mademoiselle, and I desire to speak with you."

"Kindly take a seat, monsieur; I have finished."

She added a few words to her letter, signed it, enclosed it in the envelope, sealed it, pushed her writing material away, rang the telephone, got in communication with her dressmaker, asked the latter to hasten the completion of a traveling dress, as she required it at once, and then, turning to Sholmes, she said:

"I am at your service, monsieur. But do you wish to speak before my father? Would not that be better?"

"No, mademoiselle; and I beg of you, do not raise your voice. It is better that Monsieur Destange should not hear us."

"For whose sake is it better?"

"Yours, mademoiselle."

"I cannot agree to hold any conversation with you that my father may not hear."

"But you must agree to this. It is imperative."

Both of them arose, eye to eye. She said:

"Speak, monsieur."

Still standing, he commenced:

"You will be so good as to pardon me if I am mistaken on certain points of secondary importance. I will guarantee, however, the general accuracy of my statements."

"Can we not dispense with these preliminaries, monsieur? Or are they necessary?"

Sholmes felt the young woman was on her guard, so he replied:

"Very well; I will come to the point. Five years ago your father made the acquaintance of a certain young man called Maxime Bermond, who was introduced as a contractor or an architect, I am not sure which it was; but it was one or the other. Monsieur Destange took a liking to the young man, and as the state of his health compelled him to retire from active business, he entrusted to Monsieur Bermond the execution of certain orders he had received from some of his old customers and which seemed to come within the scope of Monsieur Bermond's ability."

Herlock Sholmes stopped. It seemed to him that the girl's pallor had increased. Yet there was not the slightest tremor in her voice when she said:

"I know nothing about the circumstances to which you refer, monsieur, and I do not see in what way they can interest me."

"In this way, mademoiselle: You know, as well as I, that Maxime Bermond is also known by the name of Arsène Lupin."

She laughed, and said:

"Nonsense! Arsène Lupin? Maxime Bermond is Arsène Lupin? Oh! no! It isn't possible!"

"I have the honor to inform you of that fact, and since you refuse to understand my meaning, I will add that Arsène Lupin has found in this house a friend—more than a friend—and accomplice, blindly and passionately devoted to him."

Without emotion, or at least with so little emotion that Sholmes was astonished at her self-control, she declared:

"I do not understand your object, monsieur, and I do not care to; but I command you to say no more and leave this house."

"I have no intention of forcing my presence on you," replied Sholmes, with equal sang-froid, "but I shall not leave this house alone."

"And who will accompany you, monsieur?"

"You will."

"I?"

"Yes, mademoiselle, we will leave this house together, and you will follow me without one word of protest."

The strange feature of the foregoing interview was the absolute coolness of the two adversaries. It bore no resemblance to an implacable duel between two powerful wills; but, judging solely from their attitude and the tone of their voices, an onlooker would have supposed their conversation to be nothing more serious than a courteous argument over some impersonal subject.

Clotilde resumed her seat without deigning to reply to the last remark of Herlock Sholmes, except by a shrug of her shoulders. Sholmes looked at his watch and said:

"It is half-past ten. We will leave here in five minutes."

"Perhaps."

"If not, I shall go to Monsieur Destange, and tell him——"

"What?"

"The truth. I will tell him of the vicious life of Maxime Bermond, and I will tell him of the double life of his accomplice."

"Of his accomplice?"

"Yes, of the woman known as the blonde Lady, of the woman who was blonde."

"What proofs will you give him?"

"I will take him to the rue Chalgrin, and show him the secret passage made by Arsène Lupin's workmen,—while doing the work of which he had the control—between the houses numbered 40 and 42; the passage which you and he used two nights ago."

"Well?"

"I will then take Monsieur Destange to the house of Monsieur Detinan; we will descend the servant's stairway which was used by you and Arsène Lupin when you escaped from Ganimard, and we will search together the means of communication with the adjoining house, which fronts on the Boulevard des Batignolles, and not upon the rue Clapeyron."

"Well?"

"I will take Monsieur Destange to the château de Crozon, and it will be easy for him, who knows the nature of the work performed by Arsène Lupin in the restoration of the Château, to discover the secret passages constructed there by his workmen. It will thus be established that those passages allowed the blonde Lady to make a nocturnal visit to the Countess' room and take the blue diamond from the mantel; and, two weeks later, by similar means, to enter the room of Herr Bleichen and conceal the blue diamond in his tooth-powder—a strange action, I confess; a woman's revenge, perhaps; but I don't know, and I don't care."

"Well?"

"After that," said Herlock Sholmes, in a more serious tone, "I will take Monsieur Destange to 134 avenue Henri-Martin, and we will learn how the Baron d'Hautrec——"

"No, no, keep quiet," stammered the girl, struck with a sudden terror, "I forbid you!... you dare to say that it was I ... you accuse me?..."

"I accuse you of having killed the Baron d'Hautrec."

"No, no, it is a lie."

"You killed the Baron d'Hautrec, mademoiselle. You entered his service under the name of Antoinette Bréhat, for the purpose of stealing the blue diamond and you killed him."

"Keep quiet, monsieur," she implored him. "Since you know so much, you must know that I did not murder the baron."

"I did not say that you murdered him, mademoiselle. Baron d'Hautrec was subject to fits of insanity that only Sister Auguste could control. She told me so herself. In her absence, he must have attacked you, and in the course of the struggle you struck him in order to save your own life. Frightened at your awful situation, you rang the bell, and fled without even taking the blue diamond from the finger of your victim. A few minutes later you returned with one of Arsène Lupin's accomplices, who was a servant in the adjoining house, you placed the baron on the bed, you put the room in order, but you were afraid to take the blue diamond. Now, I have told you what happened on that night. I repeat, you did not murder the baron, and yet it was your hand that struck the blow."

She had crossed them over her forehead—those long delicate white hands—and kept them thus for a long time. At last, loosening her fingers, she said, in a voice rent by anguish:

"And do you intend to tell all that to my father?"

"Yes; and I will tell him that I have secured as witnesses: Mademoiselle Gerbois, who will recognize the blonde Lady; Sister Auguste, who will recognize Antoinette Bréhat; and the Countess de Crozon, who will recognize Madame de Réal. That is what I shall tell him."

"You will not dare," she said, recovering her self-possession in the face of an immediate peril.

He arose, and made a step toward the library. Clotilde stopped him:

"One moment, monsieur."

She paused, reflected a moment, and then, perfect mistress of herself, said:

"You are Herlock Sholmes?"

"Yes."

"What do you want of me?"

"What do I want? I am fighting a duel with Arsène Lupin, and I must win. The contest is now drawing to a climax, and I have an idea that a hostage as precious as you will give me an important advantage over my adversary. Therefore, you will follow me, mademoiselle; I will entrust you to one of my friends. As soon as the duel is ended, you will be set at liberty."

"Is that all?"

"That is all. I do not belong to the police service of this country, and, consequently, I do not consider that I am under any obligation ... to cause your arrest."

She appeared to have come to a decision ... yet she required a momentary respite. She closed her eyes, the better to concentrate her thoughts. Sholmes looked at her in surprise; she was now so tranquil and, apparently, indifferent to the dangers which threatened her. Sholmes thought: Does she believe that she is in danger? Probably not—since Lupin protects her. She has confidence in him. She believes that Lupin is omnipotent, and infallible.

"Mademoiselle," he said, "I told you that we would leave here in five minutes. That time has almost expired."

"Will you permit me to go to my room, monsieur, to get some necessary articles?"

"Certainly, mademoiselle; and I will wait for you in the rue Montchanin. Jeanniot, the concierge, is a friend of mine."

"Ah! you know...." she said, visibly alarmed.

"I know many things."

"Very well. I will ring for the maid."

The maid brought her hat and jacket. Then Sholmes said:

"You must give Monsieur Destange some reason for our departure, and, if possible, let your excuse serve for an absence of several days."

"That shall not be necessary. I shall be back very soon."

"They exchanged defiant glances and an ironic smile.

"What faith you have in him!" said Sholmes.

"Absolute."

"He does everything well, doesn't he? He succeeds in everything he undertakes. And whatever he does receives your approval and cooperation."

"I love him," she said, with a touch of passion in her voice.

"And you think that he will save you?"

She shrugged her shoulders, and, approaching her father, she said:

"I am going to deprive you of Monsieur Stickmann. We are going to the National Library."

"You will return for luncheon?"

"Perhaps ... no, I think not ... but don't be uneasy."

Then she said to Sholmes, in a firm voice:

"I am at your service, monsieur."

"Absolutely?"

"Quite so."

"I warn you that if you attempt to escape, I shall call the police and have you arrested. Do not forget that the blonde Lady is on parole."

"I give you my word of honor that I shall not attempt to escape."

"I believe you. Now, let us go."

They left the house together, as he had predicted.

The automobile was standing where Sholmes had left it. As they approached it, Sholmes could hear the rumbling of the motor. He opened the door, asked Clotilde to enter, and took a seat beside her. The machine started at once, gained the exterior boulevards, the avenue Hoche and the avenue de la Grande-Armée. Sholmes was considering his plans. He thought:

"Ganimard is at home. I will leave the girl in his care. Shall I tell him who she is? No, he would take her to prison at once, and that would spoil everything. When I am alone, I can consult my list of addresses taken from the 'account M.B.,' and run them down. To-night, or to-morrow morning at the latest, I shall go to Ganimard, as I agreed, and deliver into his hands Arsène Lupin and all his band."

He rubbed his hand, gleefully, at the thought that his duel with Lupin was drawing to a close, and he could not see any serious obstacle in the way of his success. And, yielding to an irrepressible desire to give vent to his feelings—an unusual desire on his part—he exclaimed:

"Excuse me, mademoiselle, if I am unable to conceal my satisfaction and delight. The battle has been a difficult one, and my success is, therefore, more enjoyable."

"A legitimate success, monsieur, of which you have a just right to be proud."

"Thank you. But where are we going? The chauffeur must have misunderstood my directions."

At that moment they were leaving Paris by the gate de Neuilly. That was strange, as the rue Pergolese is not outside the fortifications. Sholmes lowered the glass, and said:

"Chauffeur, you have made a mistake.... Rue Pergolese!"

The man made no reply. Sholmes repeated, in a louder voice:

"I told you to go to the rue Pergolese."

Still the man did not reply.

"Ah! but you are deaf, my friend. Or is he doing it on purpose? We are very much out of our way.... Rue Pergolese!... Turn back at once!... Rue Pergolese!"

The chauffeur made no sign of having heard the order. The Englishman fretted with impatience. He looked at Clotilde; a mysterious smile played upon her lips.

"Why do you laugh?" he said. "It is an awkward mistake, but it won't help you."

"Of course not," she replied.

Then an idea occurred to him. He rose and made a careful scrutiny of the chauffeur. His shoulders were not so broad; his bearing was not so stiff and mechanical. A cold perspiration covered his forehead and his hands clenched with sudden fear, as his mind was seized with the conviction that the chauffeur was Arsène Lupin.

"Well, Monsieur Sholmes, what do you think of our little ride?"

"Delightful, monsieur, really delightful," replied Sholmes.

Never in his life had he experienced so much difficulty in uttering a few simple words without a tremor, or without betraying his feelings in his voice. But quickly, by a sort of reaction, a flood of hatred and rage burst its bounds, overcame his self-control, and, brusquely drawing his revolver, he pointed it at Mademoiselle Destange.

"Lupin, stop, this minute, this second, or I fire at mademoiselle."

"I advise you to aim at the cheek if you wish to hit the temple," replied Lupin, without turning his head.

"Maxime, don't go so fast," said Clotilde, "the pavement is slippery and I am very timid."

She was smiling; her eyes were fixed on the pavement, over which the carriage was traveling at enormous speed.

"Let him stop! Let him stop!" said Sholmes to her, wild with rage, "I warn you that I am desperate."

The barrel of the revolver brushed the waving locks of her hair. She replied, calmly:

"Maxime is so imprudent. He is going so fast, I am really afraid of some accident."

Sholmes returned the weapon to his pocket and seized the handle of the door, as if to alight, despite the absurdity of such an act. Clotilde said to him:

"Be careful, monsieur, there is an automobile behind us."

He leaned over. There was an automobile close behind; a large machine of formidable aspect with its sharp prow and blood-red body, and holding four men clad in fur coats.

"Ah! I am well guarded," thought Sholmes. "I may as well be patient."

He folded his arms across his chest with that proud air of submission so frequently assumed by heroes when fate has turned against them. And while they crossed the river Seine and rushed through Suresnes, Rueil and Chatou, motionless and resigned, controlling his actions and his passions, he tried to explain to his own satisfaction by what miracle Arsène Lupin had substituted himself for the chauffeur. It was quite improbable that the honest-looking fellow he had selected on the boulevard that morning was an accomplice placed there in advance. And yet Arsène Lupin had received a warning in some way, and it must have been after he, Sholmes, had approached Clotilde in the house, because no one could have suspected his project prior to that time. Since then, Sholmes had not allowed Clotilde out of his sight.

Then an idea struck him: the telephone communication desired by Clotilde and her conversation with the dressmaker. Now, it was all quite clear to him. Even before he had spoken to her, simply upon his request to speak to her as the new secretary of Monsieur Destange, she had scented the danger, surmised the name and purpose of the visitor, and, calmly, naturally, as if she were performing a commonplace action of her every-day life, she had called Arsène Lupin to her assistance by some preconcerted signal.

How Arsène Lupin had come and caused himself to be substituted for the chauffeur were matters of trifling importance. That which affected Sholmes, even to the point of appeasing his fury, was the recollection of that incident whereby an ordinary woman, a sweetheart it is true, mastering her nerves, controlling her features, and subjugating the expression of her eyes, had completely deceived the astute detective Herlock Sholmes. How difficult to overcome an adversary who is aided by such confederates, and who, by the mere force of his authority, inspires in a woman so much courage and strength!

They crossed the Seine and climbed the hill at Saint-Germain; but, some five hundred metres beyond that town, the automobile slackened its speed. The other automobile advanced, and the two stopped, side by side. There was no one else in the neighborhood.

"Monsieur Sholmes," said Lupin, "kindly exchange to the other machine. Ours is really a very slow one."

"Indeed!" said Sholmes, calmly, convinced that he had no choice.

"Also, permit me to loan you a fur coat, as we will travel quite fast and the air is cool. And accept a couple of sandwiches, as we cannot tell when we will dine."

The four men alighted from the other automobile. One of them approached, and, as he raised his goggles, Sholmes recognized in him the gentleman in the frock coat that he had seen at the Hungarian restaurant. Lupin said to him:

"You will return this machine to the chauffeur from whom I hired it. He is waiting in the first wine-shop to the right as you go up the rue Legendre. You will give him the balance of the thousand francs I promised him.... Ah! yes, kindly give your goggles to Monsieur Sholmes."

He talked to Mlle. Destange for a moment, then took his place at the wheel and started, with Sholmes at his side and one of his men behind him. Lupin had not exaggerated when he said "we will travel quite fast." From the beginning he set a breakneck pace. The horizon rushed to meet them, as if attracted by some mysterious force, and disappeared instantly as though swallowed up in an abyss, into which many other things, such as trees, houses, fields and forests, were hurled with the tumultuous fury and haste of a torrent as it approached the cataract.

Sholmes and Lupin did not exchange a word. Above their heads the leaves of the poplars made a great noise like the waves of the sea, rhythmically arranged by the regular spacing of the trees. And the towns swept by like spectres: Manteo, Vernon, Gaillon. From one hill to the other, from Bon-Secours to Canteleu, Rouen, its suburbs, its harbor, its miles of wharves, Rouen seemed like the straggling street of a country village. And this was Duclair, Caudebec, the country of Caux which they skimmed over in their terrific flight, and Lillebonne, and Quillebeuf. Then, suddenly, they found themselves on the banks of the Seine, at the extremity of a little wharf, beside which lay a staunch sea-going yacht that emitted great volumes of black smoke from its funnel.

The automobile stopped. In two hours they had traveled over forty leagues.

A man, wearing a blue uniform and a goldlaced cap, came forward and saluted. Lupin said to him:

"All ready, captain? Did you receive my telegram?"

"Yes, I got it."

"Is *The Swallow* ready?"

"Yes, monsieur."

"Come, Monsieur Sholmes."

The Englishman looked around, saw a group of people on the terrace in front of a café, hesitated a moment, then, realizing that before he could secure any assistance he would be seized, carried aboard and placed in the bottom of the hold, he crossed the gang-plank and followed Lupin into the captain's cabin. It was quite a large room, scrupulously clean, and presented a cheerful appearance with its varnished woodwork and polished brass. Lupin closed the door and addressed Sholmes abruptly, and almost rudely, as he said:

"Well, what do you know?"

"Everything."

"Everything? Come, be precise."

His voice contained no longer that polite, if ironical, tone, which he had affected when speaking to the Englishman. Now, his voice had the imperious tone of a master accustomed to command and accustomed to be obeyed— even by a Herlock Sholmes. They measured each other by their looks, enemies now—open and implacable foes. Lupin spoke again, but in a milder tone:

"I have grown weary of your pursuit, and do not intend to waste any more time in avoiding the traps you lay for me. I warn you that my treatment of you will depend on your reply. Now, what do you know?"

"Everything, monsieur."

Arsène Lupin controlled his temper and said, in a jerky manner:

"I will tell you what you know. You know that, under the name of Maxime Bermond, I have ... *improved* fifteen houses that were originally constructed by Monsieur Destange."

"Yes."

"Of those fifteen houses, you have seen four."

"Yes."

"And you have a list of the other eleven."

"Yes."

"You made that list at Monsieur Destange's house on that night, no doubt."

"Yes."

"And you have an idea that, amongst those eleven houses, there is one that I have kept for the use of myself and my friends, and you have intrusted to Ganimard the task of finding my retreat."

"No."

"What does that signify?"

"It signifies that I choose to act alone, and do not want his help."

"Then I have nothing to fear, since you are in my hands."

"You have nothing to fear as long as I remain in your hands."

"You mean that you will not remain?"

"Yes."

Arsène Lupin approached the Englishman and, placing his hand on the latter's shoulder, said:

"Listen, monsieur; I am not in a humor to argue with you, and, unfortunately for you, you are not in a position to choose. So let us finish our business."

"Very well."

"You are going to give me your word of honor that you will not try to escape from this boat until you arrive in English waters."

"I give you my word of honor that I shall escape if I have an opportunity," replied the indomitable Sholmes.

"But, sapristi! you know quite well that at a word from me you would soon be rendered helpless. All these men will obey me blindly. At a sign from me they would place you in irons——"

"Irons can be broken."

"And throw you overboard ten miles from shore."

"I can swim."

"I hadn't thought of that," said Lupin, with a laugh. "Excuse me, master ... and let us finish. You will agree that I must take the measures necessary to protect myself and my friends."

"Certainly; but they will be useless."

"And yet you do not wish me to take them."

"It is your duty."

"Very well, then."

Lupin opened the door and called the captain and two sailors. The latter seized the Englishman, bound him hand and foot, and tied him to the captain's bunk.

"That will do," said Lupin. "It was only on account of your obstinacy and the unusual gravity of the situation, that I ventured to offer you this indignity."

The sailors retired. Lupin said to the captain:

"Let one of the crew remain here to look after Monsieur Sholmes, and you can give him as much of your own company as possible. Treat him with all due respect and consideration. He is not a prisoner, but a guest. What time have you, captain?"

"Five minutes after two."

Lupin consulted his watch, then looked at the clock that was attached to the wall of the cabin.

"Five minutes past two is right. How long will it take you to reach Southampton?"

"Nine hours, easy going."

"Make it eleven. You must not land there until after the departure of the midnight boat, which reaches Havre at eight o'clock in the morning. Do you understand, captain? Let me repeat: As it would be very dangerous for all of us to permit Monsieur to return to France by that boat, you must not reach Southampton before one o'clock in the morning."

"I understand."

"Au revoir, master; next year, in this world or in the next."

"Until to-morrow," replied Sholmes.

A few minutes later Sholmes heard the automobile going away, and at the same time the steam puffed violently in the depths of *The Swallow*. The boat had started for England. About three o'clock the vessel left the mouth of the river and plunged into the open sea. At that moment Sholmes was lying on the captain's bunk, sound asleep.

Next morning—it being the tenth and last day of the duel between Sholmes and Lupin—the *Echo de France* published this interesting bit of news:

"Yesterday a judgment of ejectment was entered in the case of Arsène Lupin against Herlock Sholmes, the English detective. Although signed at noon, the judgment was executed the same day. At one o'clock this morning Sholmes was landed at Southampton."

VI. SECOND ARREST OF ARSÈNE LUPIN.

Since eight o'clock a dozen moving-vans had encumbered the rue Crevaux between the avenue du Bois-de-Boulogne and the avenue Bugeaud. Mon. Felix Davey was leaving the apartment in which he lived on the fourth floor of No. 8; and Mon. Dubreuil, who had united into a single apartment the fifth floor of the same house and the fifth floor of the two adjoining houses, was moving on the same day—a mere coincidence, since the gentlemen were unknown to each other—the vast collection of furniture regarding which so many foreign agents visited him every day.

A circumstance which had been noticed by some of the neighbors, but was not spoken of until later, was this: None of the twelve vans bore the name and address of the owner, and none of the men accompanying them visited the neighboring wine shops. They worked so diligently that the furniture was all out by eleven o'clock. Nothing remained but those scraps of papers and rags that are always left behind in the corners of the empty rooms.

Mon. Felix Davey, an elegant young man, dressed in the latest fashion, carried in his hand a walking-stick, the weight of which indicated that its owner possessed extraordinary biceps—Mon. Felix Davey walked calmly away and took a seat on a bench in the avenue du Bois-de-Boulogne facing the rue Pergolese. Close to him a woman, dressed in a neat but inexpensive costume, was reading a newspaper, whilst a child was playing with a shovel in a heap of sand.

After a few minutes Felix Davey spoke to the woman, without turning his head:

"Ganimard!"

"Went out at nine o'clock this morning."

"Where?"

"To police headquarters."

"Alone?"

"Yes."

"No telegram during the night?"

"No."

"Do they suspect you in the house?"

"No; I do some little things for Madame Ganimard, and she tells me everything her husband does. I have been with her all morning."

"Very well. Until further orders come here every day at eleven o'clock."

He rose and walked away in the direction of the Dauphine gate, stopping at the Chinese pavilion, where he partook of a frugal repast consisting of two eggs, with some fruit and vegetables. Then he returned to the rue Crevaux and said to the concierge:

"I will just glance through the rooms and then give you the keys."

He finished his inspection of the room that he had used as a library; then he seized the end of a gas-pipe, which hung down the side of the chimney. The pipe was bent and a hole made in the elbow. To this hole he fitted a small instrument in the form of an ear-trumpet and blew into it. A slight whistling sound came by way of reply. Placing the trumpet to his mouth, he said:

"Anyone around, Dubreuil?"

"No."

"May I come up!"

"Yes."

He returned the pipe to its place, saying to himself:

"How progressive we are! Our century abounds with little inventions which render life really charming and picturesque. And so amusing!... especially when a person knows how to enjoy life as I do."

He turned one of the marble mouldings of the mantel, and the entire half of the mantel moved, and the mirror above it glided in invisible grooves, disclosing an opening and the lower steps of a stairs built in the very body of the chimney; all very clean and complete—the stairs were constructed of polished metal and the walls of white tiles. He ascended the steps, and at the fifth floor there was the same opening in the chimney. Mon. Dubreuil was waiting for him.

"Have you finished in your rooms?"

"Yes."

"Everything cleared out?"

"Yes."

"And the people?"

"Only the three men on guard."

"Very well; come on."

They ascended to the upper floor by the same means, one after the other, and there found three men, one of whom was looking through the window.

"Anything new?"

"Nothing, governor."

"All quiet in the street?"

"Yes."

"In ten minutes I will be ready to leave. You will go also. But in the meantime if you see the least suspicious movement in the street, warn me."

"I have my finger on the alarm-bell all the time."

"Dubreuil, did you tell the moving men not to touch the wire of that bell?"

"Certainly; it is working all right."

"That is all I want to know."

The two gentlemen then descended to the apartment of Felix Davey and the latter, after adjusting the marble mantel, exclaimed, joyfully:

"Dubreuil, I should like to see the man who is able to discover all the ingenious devices, warning bells, net-works of electric wires and acoustic tubes, invisible passages, moving floors and hidden stairways. A real fairy-land!"

"What fame for Arsène Lupin!"

"Fame I could well dispense with. It's a pity to be compelled to leave a place so well equipped, and commence all over again, Dubreuil ... and on a new model, of course, for it would never do to duplicate this. Curse Herlock Sholmes!"

"Has he returned to Paris?"

"How could he? There has been only one boat come from Southampton and it left there at midnight; only one train from Havre, leaving there at eight o'clock this morning and due in Paris at eleven fifteen. As he could not catch the midnight boat at Southampton—and the instructions to the captain on that point were explicit—he cannot reach France until this evening via Newhaven and Dieppe."

"Do you think he will come back?"

"Yes; he never gives up. He will return to Paris; but it will be too late. We will be far away."

"And Mademoiselle Destange?"

"I am to see her in an hour."

"At her house?"

"Oh! no; she will not return there for several days. But you, Dubreuil, you must hurry. The loading of our goods will take a long time and you should be there to look after them."

"Are you sure that we are not being watched?"

"By whom? I am not afraid of anyone but Sholmes."

Dubreuil retired. Felix Davey made a last tour of the apartment, picked up two or three torn letters, then, noticing a piece of chalk, he took it and, on the dark paper of the drawing-room, drew a large frame and wrote within it the following:

"*Arsène Lupin, gentleman-burglar, lived here for five years at the beginning of the twentieth century.*"

This little pleasantry seemed to please him very much. He looked at it for a moment, whistling a lively air, then said to himself:

"Now that I have placed myself in touch with the historians of future generations, I can go. You must hurry, Herlock Sholmes, as I shall leave my present abode in three minutes, and your defeat will be an accomplished fact.... Two minutes more! you are keeping me waiting, Monsieur Sholmes.... One minute more! Are you not coming? Well, then, I proclaim your downfall and my apotheosis. And now I make my escape. Farewell, kingdom of Arsène Lupin! I shall never see you again. Farewell to the fifty-five rooms of the six apartments over which I reigned! Farewell, my own royal bed chamber!"

His outburst of joy was interrupted by the sharp ringing of a bell, which stopped twice, started again and then ceased. It was the alarm bell.

What was wrong? What unforeseen danger? Ganimard? No; that wasn't possible!

He was on the point of returning to his library and making his escape. But, first, he went to the window. There was no one in the street. Was the enemy already in the house? He listened and thought he could discern certain confused sounds. He hesitated no longer. He ran to his library, and as he crossed the threshold he heard the noise of a key being inserted in the lock of the vestibule door.

"The deuce!" he murmured; "I have no time to lose. The house may be surrounded. The servants' stairway—impossible! Fortunately, there is the chimney."

He pushed the moulding; it did not move. He made a greater effort—still it refused to move. At the same time he had the impression that the door below opened and that he could hear footsteps.

"Good God!" he cried; "I am lost if this cursed mechanism—"

He pushed with all his strength. Nothing moved—nothing! By some incredible accident, by some evil stroke of fortune, the mechanism, which had worked only a few moments ago, would not work now.

He was furious. The block of marble remained immovable. He uttered frightful imprecations on the senseless stone. Was his escape to be prevented by that stupid obstacle? He struck the marble wildly, madly; he hammered it, he cursed it.

"Ah! what's the matter, Monsieur Lupin? You seem to be displeased about something."

Lupin turned around. Herlock Sholmes stood before him!

Herlock Sholmes!... Lupin gazed at him with squinting eyes as if his sight were defective and misleading. Herlock Sholmes in Paris! Herlock Sholmes, whom he had shipped to England only the day before as a dangerous person, now stood before him free and victorious!... Ah! such a thing was nothing less than a miracle; it was contrary to all natural laws; it was the culmination of all that is illogical and abnormal.... Herlock Sholmes here—before his face!

And when the Englishman spoke his words were tinged with that keen sarcasm and mocking politeness with which his adversary had so often lashed him. He said:

"Monsieur Lupin, in, the first place I have the honor to inform you that at this time and place I blot from my memory forever all thoughts of the miserable night that you forced me to endure in the house of Baron d'Hautrec, of the injury done to my friend Wilson, of my abduction in the automobile, and of the voyage I took yesterday under your orders, bound to a very uncomfortable couch. But the joy of this moment effaces all those bitter memories. I forgive everything. I forget everything—I wipe out the debt. I am paid—and royally paid."

Lupin made no reply. So the Englishman continued:

"Don't you think so yourself?"

He appeared to insist as if demanding an acquiescence, as a sort of receipt in regard to the past.

After a moment's reflection, during which the Englishman felt that he was scrutinized to the very depth of his soul, Lupin declared:

"I presume, monsieur, that your conduct is based upon serious motives?"

"Very serious."

"The fact that you have escaped from my captain and his crew is only a secondary incident of our struggle. But the fact that you are here before me alone—understand, alone—face to face with Arsène Lupin, leads me to think that your revenge is as complete as possible."

"As complete as possible."

"This house?"

"Surrounded."

"The two adjoining houses?"

"Surrounded."

"The apartment above this?"

"The *three* apartments on the fifth floor that were formerly occupied by Monsieur Dubreuil are surrounded."

"So that——"

"So that you are captured, Monsieur Lupin—absolutely captured."

The feelings that Sholmes had experienced during his trip in the automobile were now suffered by Lupin, the same concentrated fury, the same revolt, and also, let us admit, the same loyalty of submission to force of circumstances. Equally brave in victory or defeat.

"Our accounts are squared, monsieur," said Lupin, frankly.

The Englishman was pleased with that confession. After a short silence Lupin, now quite self-possessed, said smiling:

"And I am not sorry! It becomes monotonous to win all the time. Yesterday I had only to stretch out my hand to finish you forever. Today I belong to you. The game is yours." Lupin laughed heartily and then continued: "At last the gallery will be entertained! Lupin in prison! How will he get out? In prison!... What an adventure!... Ah! Sholmes, life is just one damn thing after another!"

He pressed his closed hands to his temples as if to suppress the tumultuous joy that surged within him, and his actions indicated that he was moved by an uncontrollable mirth. At last, when he had recovered his self-possession, he approached the detective and said:

"And now what are you waiting for?"

"What am I waiting for?"

"Yes; Ganimard is here with his men—why don't they come in?"

"I asked him not to."

"And he consented?"

"I accepted his services on condition that he would be guided by me. Besides, he thinks that Felix Davey is only an accomplice of Arsène Lupin."

"Then I will repeat my question in another form. Why did you come in alone?"

"Because I wished to speak to you alone."

"Ah! ah! you have something to say to me."

That idea seemed to please Lupin immensely. There are certain circumstances in which words are preferable to deeds.

"Monsieur Sholmes, I am sorry I cannot offer you an easy chair. How would you like that broken box? Or perhaps you would prefer the window ledge? I am sure a glass of beer would be welcome ... light or dark?... But sit down, please."

"Thank you; we can talk as well standing up."

"Very well—proceed."

"I will be brief. The object of my sojourn in France was not to accomplish your arrest. If I have been led to pursue you, it was because I saw no other way to achieve my real object."

"Which was?"

"To recover the blue diamond."

"The blue diamond!"

"Certainly; since the one found in Herr Bleichen's tooth-powder was only an imitation."

"Quite right; the genuine diamond was taken by the blonde Lady. I made an exact duplicate of it and then, as I had designs on other jewels belonging to the Countess and as the Consul Herr Bleichen was already under suspicion, the aforesaid blonde Lady, in order to avert suspicion, slipped the false stone into the aforesaid Consul's luggage."

"While you kept the genuine diamond?"

"Of course."

"That diamond—I want it."

"I am very sorry, but it is impossible."

"I have promised it to the Countess de Crozon. I must have it."

"How will you get it, since it is in my possession?"

"That is precisely the reason—because it is in your possession."

"Oh! I am to give it to you?"

"Yes."

"Voluntarily?"

"I will buy it."

"Ah!" exclaimed Lupin, in an access of mirth, "you are certainly an Englishman. You treat this as a matter of business."

"It is a matter of business."

"Well! what is your offer?"

"The liberty of Mademoiselle Destange."

"Her liberty?... I didn't know she was under arrest."

"I will give Monsieur Ganimard the necessary information. When deprived of your protection, she can readily be taken."

Lupin laughed again, and said:

"My dear monsieur, you are offering me something you do not possess. Mademoiselle Destange is in a place of safety, and has nothing to fear. You must make me another offer."

The Englishman hesitated, visibly embarrassed and vexed. Then, placing his hand on the shoulder of his adversary, he said:

"And if I should propose to you-"

"My liberty?"

"No ... but I can leave the room to consult with Ganimard."

"And leave me alone!"

"Yes."

"Ah! mon dieu, what good would that be? The cursed mechanism will not work," said Lupin, at the same time savagely pushing the moulding of the mantel. He stifled a cry of surprise; this time fortune favored him—the block of marble moved. It was his salvation; his hope of escape. In that event, why submit to the conditions imposed by Sholmes? He paced up and down the room, as if he were considering his reply. Then, in his turn, he placed his hand on the shoulder of his adversary, and said:

"All things considered, Monsieur Sholmes, I prefer to do my own business in my own way."

"But—"

"No, I don't require anyone's assistance."

"When Ganimard gets his hand on you, it will be all over. You can't escape from them."

"Who knows?"

"Come, that is foolish. Every door and window is guarded."

"Except one."

"Which?"

"*The one I will choose.*"

"Mere words! Your arrest is as good as made."

"Oh! no—not at all."

"Well?"

"I shall keep the blue diamond."

Sholmes looked at his watch, and said:

"It is now ten minutes to three. At three o'clock I shall call Ganimard."

"Well, then, we have ten minutes to chat. And to satisfy my curiosity, Monsieur Sholmes, I should like to know how you procured my address and my name of Felix Davey?"

Although his adversary's easy manner caused Sholmes some anxiety, he was willing to give Lupin the desired information since it reflected credit on his professional astuteness; so he replied:

"Your address? I got it from the blonde Lady."

"Clotilde!"

"Herself. Do you remember, yesterday morning, when I wished to take her away in the automobile, she telephoned to her dressmaker."

"Well?"

"Well, I understood, later, that you were the dressmaker. And last night, on the boat, by exercising my memory—and my memory is something I have good reason to be proud of—I was able to recollect the last two figures of your telephone number—73. Then, as I possessed a list of the houses you had 'improved,' it was an easy matter, on my arrival in Paris at eleven o'clock this morning, to search in the telephone directory and find there the name and address of Felix Davey. Having obtained that information, I asked the aid of Monsieur Ganimard."

"Admirable! I congratulate you. But bow did you manage to catch the eight o'clock train at Havre! How did you escape from *The Swallow*?"

"I did not escape."

"But——"

"You ordered the captain not to reach Southampton before one o'clock. He landed me there at midnight. I was able to catch the twelve o'clock boat for Havre."

"Did the captain betray me? I can't believe it."

"No, he did not betray you."

"Well, what then?"

"It was his watch."

"His watch?"

"Yes, I put it ahead one hour."

"How?"

"In the usual way, by turning the hands. We were sitting side by side, talking, and I was telling him some funny stories.... Why! he never saw me do it."

"Bravo! a very clever trick. I shall not forget it. But the clock that was hanging on the wall of the cabin?"

"Ah! the clock was a more difficult matter, as my feet were tied, but the sailor, who guarded me during the captain's absence, was kind enough to turn the hands for me."

"He? Nonsense! He wouldn't do it."

"Oh! but he didn't know the importance of his act. I told him I must catch the first train for London, at any price, and ... he allowed himself to be persuaded——"

"By means of——"

"By means of a slight gift, which the excellent fellow, loyal and true to his master, intends to send to you."

"What was it!"

"A mere trifle."

"But what?"

"The blue diamond."

"The blue diamond!"

"Yes, the false stone that you substituted for the Countess' diamond. She gave it to me."

There was a sudden explosion of violent laughter. Lupin laughed until the tears started in his eyes.

"Mon dieu, but it is funny! My false diamond palmed off on my innocent sailor! And the captain's watch! And the hands of the clock!"

Sholmes felt that the duel between him and Lupin was keener than ever. His marvellous instinct warned him that, behind his adversary's display of mirth, there was a shrewd intellect debating the ways and means to escape. Gradually Lupin approached the Englishman, who recoiled, and, unconsciously, slipped his hand into his watch-pocket.

"It is three o'clock, Monsieur Lupin."

"Three o'clock, already! What a pity! We were enjoying our chat so much."

"I am waiting for your answer."

"My answer? Mon dieu! but you are particular!... And so this is the last move in our little game—and the stake is my liberty!"

"Or the blue diamond."

"Very well. It's your play. What are you going to do!"

"I play the king," said Sholmes, as he fired his revolver.

"And I the ace," replied Lupin, as he struck at Sholmes with his fist.

Sholmes had fired into the air, as a signal to Ganimard, whose assistance he required. But Lupin's fist had caught Sholmes in the stomach, and caused him to double up with pain. Lupin rushed to the fireplace and set the marble slab in motion.... Too late! The door opened.

"Surrender, Lupin, or I fire!"

Ganimard, doubtless stationed closer than Lupin had thought, Ganimard was there, with his revolver turned on Lupin. And behind Ganimard there were twenty men, strong and ruthless fellows, who would beat him like a dog at the least sign of resistance.

"Hands down! I surrender!" said Lupin, calmly; and he folded his arms across his breast.

Everyone was amazed. In the room, divested of its furniture and hangings, Arsène Lupin's words sounded like an echo.... "I surrender!" ... It seemed incredible. No one would have been astonished if he had suddenly vanished through a trap, or if a section of the wall had rolled away and allowed him to escape. But he surrendered!

Ganimard advanced, nervously, and with all the gravity that the importance of the occasion demanded, he placed his hand on the shoulder of his adversary, and had the infinite pleasure of saying:

"I arrest you, Arsène Lupin."

"Brrr!" said Lupin, "you make me shiver, my dear Ganimard. What a lugubrious face! One would imagine you were speaking over the grave of a friend. For Heaven's sake, don't assume such a funereal air."

"I arrest you."

"Don't let that worry you! In the name of the law, of which he is a well-deserving pillar, Ganimard, the celebrated Parisian detective, arrests the wicked Arsène Lupin. An historic event, of which you will appreciate the true importance.... And it is the second time that it has happened. Bravo, Ganimard, you are sure of advancement in your chosen profession!"

And he held out his wrists for the hand-cuffs. Ganimard adjusted them in a most solemn manner. The numerous policemen, despite their customary presumption and the bitterness of their feelings toward Lupin, conducted themselves with becoming modesty, astonished at being permitted to gaze upon that mysterious and intangible creature.

"My poor Lupin," sighed our hero, "what would your aristocratic friends say if they should see you in this humiliating position?"

He pulled his wrists apart with all his strength. The veins in his forehead expanded. The links of the chain cut into his flesh. The chain fell off— broken.

"Another, comrades, that one was useless."

They placed two on him this time.

"Quite right," he said. "You cannot be too careful."

Then, counting the detectives and policemen, he said:

"How many are you, my friends? Twenty-five? Thirty? That's too many. I can't do anything. Ah! if there had been only fifteen!"

There was something fascinating about Lupin; it was the fascination of the great actor who plays his rôle with spirit and understanding, combined with assurance and ease. Sholmes regarded him as one might regard a beautiful painting with a due appreciation of all its perfection in coloring and technique. And he really thought that it was an equal struggle between those thirty men on one side, armed as they were with all the strength and majesty of the law, and, on the other side, that solitary individual, unarmed and handcuffed. Yes, the two sides were well-matched.

"Well, master," said Lupin to the Englishman, "this is your work. Thanks to you, Lupin is going to rot on the damp straw of a dungeon. Confess that your conscience pricks you a little, and that your soul is filled with remorse."

In spite of himself, Sholmes shrugged his shoulders, as if to say: "It's your own fault."

"Never! never!" exclaimed Lupin. "Give you the blue diamond? Oh! no, it has cost me too much trouble. I intend to keep it. On my occasion of my first visit to you in London—which will probably be next month—I will tell you my reasons. But will you be in London next month! Or do you prefer Vienna! Or Saint Petersburg?"

Then Lupin received a surprise. A bell commenced to ring. It was not the alarm-bell, but the bell of the telephone which was located between the two windows of the room and had not yet been removed.

The telephone! Ah! Who could it be? Who was about to fall into this unfortunate trap? Arsène Lupin exhibited an access of rage against the unlucky instrument as if he would like to break it into a thousand pieces and thus stifle the mysterious voice that was calling for him. But it was Ganimard who took down the receiver, and said:

"Hello!... Hello!... number 648.73 ... yes, this is it."

Then Sholmes stepped up, and, with an air of authority, pushed Ganimard aside, took the receiver, and covered the transmitter with his handkerchief in order to obscure the tone of his voice. At that moment he glanced toward Lupin, and the look which they exchanged indicated that the same idea had occurred to each of them, and that they fore-saw the ultimate result of that theory: it was the blonde Lady who was telephoning. She wished to telephone to Felix Davey, or rather to Maxime Bermond, and it was to Sholmes she was about to speak. The Englishman said:

"Hello ... Hello!"

Then, after a silence, he said:

"Yes, it is I, Maxime."

The drama had commenced and was progressing with tragic precision. Lupin, the irrepressible and nonchalant Lupin, did not attempt to conceal his anxiety, and he strained every nerve in a desire to hear or, at least, to divine the purport of the conversation. And Sholmes continued, in reply to the mysterious voice:

"Hello!... Hello!... Yes, everything has been moved, and I am just ready to leave here and meet you as we agreed.... Where?... Where you are now.... Don't believe that he is here yet!..."

Sholmes stopped, seeking for words. It was clear that he was trying to question the girl without betraying himself, and that he was ignorant of her whereabouts. Moreover, Ganimard's presence seemed to embarrass him.... Ah! if some miracle would only interrupt that cursed conversation! Lupin prayed for it with all his strength, with all the intensity of his incited nerves! After a momentary pause, Sholmes continued:

"Hello!... Hello!... Do you hear me?... I can't hear you very well.... Can scarcely make out what you say.... Are you listening? Well, I think you had better return home.... No danger now.... But he is in England! I have received a telegram from Southampton announcing his arrival."

The sarcasm of those words! Sholmes uttered them with an inexpressible comfort. And he added:

"Very well, don't lose any time. I will meet you there."

He hung up the receiver.

"Monsieur Ganimard, can you furnish me with three men?"

"For the blonde Lady, eh?"

"Yes."

"You know who she is, and where she is?"

"Yes."

"Good! That settles Monsieur Lupin.... Folenfant, take two men, and go with Monsieur Sholmes."

The Englishman departed, accompanied by the three men.

The game was ended. The blonde Lady was, also, about to fall into the hands of the Englishman. Thanks to his commendable persistence and to a combination of fortuitous circumstances, the battle had resulted in a victory for the detective, and in irreparable disaster for Lupin.

"Monsieur Sholmes!"

The Englishman stopped.

"Monsieur Lupin?"

Lupin was clearly shattered by this final blow. His forehead was marked by deep wrinkles. He was sullen and dejected. However, he pulled himself together, and, notwithstanding his defeat, he exclaimed, in a cheerful tone:

"You will concede that fate has been against me. A few minutes ago, it prevented my escape through that chimney, and delivered me into your hands. Now, by means of the telephone, it presents you with the blonde Lady. I submit to its decrees."

"What do you mean?"

"I mean that I am ready to re-open our negotiation."

Sholmes took Ganimard aside and asked, in a manner that did not permit a reply, the authority to exchange a few words with the prisoner. Then he approached Lupin, and said, in a sharp, nervous tone:

"What do you want?"

"Mademoiselle Destange's liberty."

"You know the price."

"Yes."

"And you accept?"

"Yes; I accept your terms."

"Ah!" said the Englishman, in surprise, "but ... you refused ... for yourself——"

"Yes, I can look out for myself, Monsieur Sholmes, but now the question concerns a young woman ... and a woman I love. In France, understand, we have very decided ideas about such things. And Lupin has the same feelings as other people."

He spoke with simplicity and candor. Sholmes replied by an almost imperceptible inclination of his head, and murmured:

"Very well, the blue diamond."

"Take my cane, there, at the end of the mantel. Press on the head of the cane with one hand, and, with the other, turn the iron ferrule at the bottom."

Holmes took the cane and followed the directions. As he did so, the head of the cane divided and disclosed a cavity which contained a small ball of wax which, in turn, enclosed a diamond. He examined it. It was the blue diamond.

"Monsieur Lupin, Mademoiselle Destange is free."

"Is her future safety assured? Has she nothing to fear from you?"

"Neither from me, nor anyone else."

"How can you manage it?"

"Quite easily. I have forgotten her name and address."

"Thank you. And au revoir——for I will see you again, sometime, Monsieur Sholmes?"

"I have no doubt of it."

Then followed an animated conversation between Sholmes and Ganimard, which was abruptly terminated by the Englishman, who said:

"I am very sorry, Monsieur Ganimard, that we cannot agree on that point, but I have no time to waste trying to convince you. I leave for England within an hour."

"But ... the blonde Lady?"

"I do not know such a person."

"And yet, a moment ago——"

"You must take the affair as it stands. I have delivered Arsène Lupin into your hands. Here is the blue diamond, which you will have the pleasure of returning to the Countess de Crozon. What more do you want?"

"The blonde Lady."

"Find her."

Sholmes pulled his cap down over his forehead and walked rapidly away, like a man who is accustomed to go as soon as his business is finished.

"Bon voyage, monsieur," cried Lupin, "and, believe me, I shall never forget the friendly way in which our little business affairs have been arranged. My regards to Monsieur Wilson."

Not receiving any reply, Lupin added, sneeringly:

"That is what is called 'taking British leave.' Ah! their insular dignity lacks the flower of courtesy by which we are distinguished. Consider for a moment, Ganimard, what a charming exit a Frenchman would have made under similar circumstances! With what exquisite courtesy he would have masked his triumph!... But, God bless me, Ganimard, what are you doing? Making a search? Come, what's the use? There is nothing left—not even a scrap of paper. I assure you my archives are in a safe place."

"I am not so sure of that," replied Ganimard. "I must search everything."

Lupin submitted to the operation. Held by two detectives and surrounded by the others, he patiently endured the proceedings for twenty minutes, then he said:

"Hurry up, Ganimard, and finish!"

"You are in a hurry."

"Of course I am. An important appointment."

"At the police station?"

"No; in the city."

"Ah! at what time?"

"Two o'clock."

"It is three o'clock now."

"Just so; I will be late. And punctuality is one of my virtues."

"Well, give me five minutes."

"Not a second more," said Lupin.

"I am doing my best to expedite——"

"Oh! don't talk so much.... Still searching that cupboard? It is empty."

"Here are some letters."

"Old invoices, I presume!"

"No; a packet tied with a ribbon."

"A red ribbon? Oh! Ganimard, for God's sake, don't untie it!"

"From a woman?"

"Yes."

"A woman of the world?"

"The best in the world."

"Her name?"

"Madame Ganimard."

"Very funny! very funny!" exclaimed the detective.

At that moment the men, who had been sent to search the other rooms, returned and announced their failure to find anything. Lupin laughed and said:

"Parbleu! Did you expect to find my visiting list, or evidence of my business relations with the Emperor of Germany? But I can tell you what you should investigate, Ganimard: All the little mysteries of this apartment. For instance, that gas-pipe is a speaking tube. That chimney contains a stairway. That wall is hollow. And the marvellous system of bells! Ah! Ganimard, just press that button!"

Ganimard obeyed.

"Did you hear anything?" asked Lupin.

"No."

"Neither did I. And yet you notified my aeronaut to prepare the dirigible balloon which will soon carry us into the clouds.

"Come!" said Ganimard, who had completed his search; "we've had enough nonsense—let's be off."

He started away, followed by his men. Lupin did not move. His guardians pushed him in vain.

"Well," said Ganimard, "do you refuse to go?"

"Not at all. But it depends."

"On what?"

"Where you want to take me."

"To the station-house, of course."

"Then I refuse to go. I have no business there."

"Are you crazy?"

"Did I not tell you that I had an important appointment?"

"Lupin!"

"Why, Ganimard, I have an appointment with the blonde Lady, and do you suppose I would be so discourteous as to cause her a moment's anxiety? That would be very ungentlemanly."

"Listen, Lupin," said the detective, who was becoming annoyed by this persiflage; "I have been very patient with you, but I will endure no more. Follow me."

"Impossible; I have an appointment and I shall keep it."

"For the last time—follow me!"

"Im-pos-sible!"

At a sign from Ganimard two men seized Lupin by the arms; but they released him at once, uttering cries of pain. Lupin had thrust two long needles into them. The other men now rushed at Lupin with cries of rage and hatred, eager to avenge their comrades and to avenge themselves for the many affronts he had heaped upon them; and now they struck and beat him to their heart's desire. A violent blow on the temple felled Lupin to the floor.

"If you hurt him you will answer to me," growled Ganimard, in a rage.

He leaned over Lupin to ascertain his condition. Then, learning that he was breathing freely, Ganimard ordered his men to carry the prisoner by the head and feet, while he himself supported the body.

"Go gently, now!... Don't jolt him. Ah! the brutes would have killed him.... Well, Lupin, how goes it!"

"None too well, Ganimard ... you let them knock me out."

"It was your own fault; you were so obstinate," replied Ganimard. "But I hope they didn't hurt you."

They had left the apartment and were now on the landing. Lupin groaned and stammered:

"Ganimard ... the elevator ... they are breaking my bones."

"A good idea, an excellent idea," replied Ganimard. "Besides, the stairway is too narrow."

He summoned the elevator. They placed Lupin on the seat with the greatest care. Ganimard took his place beside him and said to his men:

"Go down the stairs and wait for me below. Understand?"

Ganimard closed the door of the elevator. Suddenly the elevator shot upward like a balloon released from its cable. Lupin burst into a fit of sardonic laughter.

"Good God!" cried Ganimard, as he made a frantic search in the dark for the button of descent. Having found it, he cried:

"The fifth floor! Watch the door of the fifth floor."

His assistants clambered up the stairs, two and three steps at a time. But this strange circumstance happened: The elevator seemed to break through the ceiling of the last floor, disappeared from the sight of Ganimard's assistants, suddenly made its appearance on the upper floor—the servants' floor—and stopped. Three men were there waiting for it. They opened the door. Two of them seized Ganimard, who, astonished at the sudden attack, scarcely made any defence. The other man carried off Lupin.

"I warned you, Ganimard ... about the dirigible balloon. Another time, don't be so tender-hearted. And, moreover, remember that Arsène Lupin doesn't allow himself to be struck and knocked down without sufficient reason. Adieu."

The door of the elevator was already closed on Ganimard, and the machine began to descend; and it all happened so quickly that the old detective reached the ground floor as soon as his assistants. Without exchanging a word they crossed the court and ascended the servants' stairway, which was the only way to reach the servants' floor through which the escape had been made.

A long corridor with several turns and bordered with little numbered rooms led to a door that was not locked. On the other side of this door and, therefore, in another house there was another corridor with similar turns and similar rooms, and at the end of it a servants' stairway. Ganimard descended it, crossed a court and a vestibule and found himself in the rue Picot. Then he understood the situation: the two houses, built the entire depth of the lots, touched at the rear, while the fronts of the houses faced upon two streets that ran parallel to each other at a distance of more than sixty metres apart.

He found the concierge and, showing his card, enquired:

"Did four men pass here just now?"

"Yes; the two servants from the fourth and fifth floors, with two friends."

"Who lives on the fourth and fifth floors?"

"Two men named Fauvel and their cousins, whose name is Provost. They moved to-day, leaving the two servants, who went away just now."

"Ah!" thought Ganimard; "what a grand opportunity we have missed! The entire band lived in these houses."

And he sank down on a chair in despair.

Forty minutes later two gentlemen were driven up to the station of the Northern Railway and hurried to the Calais express, followed by a porter who carried their valises. One of them had his arm in a sling, and the pallor of his face denoted some illness. The other man was in a jovial mood.

"We must hurry, Wilson, or we will miss the train.... Ah! Wilson, I shall never forget these ten days."

"Neither will I."

"Ah! it was a great struggle!"

"Superb!"

"A few repulses, here and there—"

"Of no consequence."

"And, at last, victory all along the line. Lupin arrested! The blue diamond recovered!"

"My arm broken!"

"What does a broken arm count for in such a victory as that?"

"Especially when it is my arm."

"Ah! yes, don't you remember, Wilson, that it was at the very time you were in the pharmacy, suffering like a hero, that I discovered the clue to the whole mystery!"

"How lucky!"

The doors of the carriages were being closed.

"All aboard. Hurry up, gentlemen!"

The porter climbed into an empty compartment and placed their valises in the rack, whilst Sholmes assisted the unfortunate Wilson.

"What's the matter, Wilson? You're not done up, are you? Come, pull your nerves together."

"My nerves are all right."

"Well, what is it, then?"

"I have only one hand."

"What of it?" exclaimed Sholmes, cheerfully. "You are not the only one who has had a broken arm. Cheer up!"

Sholmes handed the porter a piece of fifty centimes.

"Thank you, Monsieur Sholmes," said the porter.

The Englishman looked at him; it was Arsène Lupin.

"You!... you!" he stammered, absolutely astounded.

And Wilson brandished his sound arm in the manner of a man who demonstrates a fact as he said:

"You! you! but you were arrested! Sholmes told me so. When he left you Ganimard and thirty men had you in charge."

Lupin folded his arms and said, with an air of indignation:

"Did you suppose I would let you go away without bidding you adieu? After the very friendly relations that have always existed between us! That would be discourteous and ungrateful on my part."

The train whistled. Lupin continued:

"I beg your pardon, but have you everything you need? Tobacco and matches ... yes ... and the evening papers? You will find in them an account of my arrest—your last exploit, Monsieur Sholmes. And now, au revoir. Am delighted to have made your acquaintance. And if ever I can be of any service to you, I shall be only too happy...." He leaped to the platform and closed the door.

"Adieu," he repeated, waving his handkerchief. "Adieu.... I shall write to you.... You will write also, eh? And your arm broken, Wilson.... I am truly sorry.... I shall expect to hear from both of you. A postal card, now and then, simply address: Lupin, Paris. That is sufficient.... Adieu.... See you soon."

VII. THE JEWISH LAMP.

Herlock Sholmes and Wilson were sitting in front of the fireplace, in comfortable armchairs, with the feet extended toward the grateful warmth of a glowing coke fire.

Sholmes' pipe, a short brier with a silver band, had gone out. He knocked out the ashes, filled it, lighted it, pulled the skirts of his dressing-gown over his knees, and drew from his pipe great puffs of smoke, which ascended toward the ceiling in scores of shadow rings.

Wilson gazed at him, as a dog lying curled up on a rug before the fire might look at his master, with great round eyes which have no hope other than to obey the least gesture of his owner. Was the master going to break the silence? Would he reveal to Wilson the subject of his reverie and admit his satellite into the charmed realm of his thoughts? When Sholmes had maintained his silent attitude for some time. Wilson ventured to speak:

"Everything seems quiet now. Not the shadow of a case to occupy our leisure moments."

Sholmes did not reply, but the rings of smoke emitted by Sholmes were better formed, and Wilson observed that his companion drew considerable pleasure from that trifling fact—an indication that the great man was not absorbed in any serious meditation. Wilson, discouraged, arose and went to the window.

The lonely street extended between the gloomy façades of grimy houses, unusually gloomy this morning by reason of a heavy downfall of rain. A cab passed; then another. Wilson made an entry of their numbers in his memorandum-book. One never knows!

"Ah!" he exclaimed, "the postman."

The man entered, shown in by the servant.

"Two registered letters, sir ... if you will sign, please?"

Sholmes signed the receipts, accompanied the man to the door, and was opening one of the letters as he returned.

"It seems to please you," remarked Wilson, after a moment's silence.

"This letter contains a very interesting proposition. You are anxious for a case—here's one. Read——"

Wilson read:

"Monsieur,

"I desire the benefit of your services and experience. I have been the victim of a serious theft, and the investigation has as yet been unsuccessful. I am sending to you by this mail a number of newspapers which will inform you of the affair, and if you will undertake the case, I will place my house at your disposal and ask you to fill in the enclosed check, signed by me, for whatever sum you require for your expenses.

"Kindly reply by telegraph, and much oblige,

"Your humble servant,

"Baron Victor d'Imblevalle,

"18 rue Murillo, Paris."

"Ah!" exclaimed Sholmes, "that sounds good ... a little trip to Paris ... and why not, Wilson? Since my famous duel with Arsène Lupin, I have not had an excuse to go there. I should be pleased to visit the capital of the world under less strenuous conditions."

He tore the check into four pieces and, while Wilson, whose arm had not yet regained its former strength, uttered bitter words against Paris and the Parisians, Sholmes opened the second envelope. Immediately, he made a gesture of annoyance, and a wrinkle appeared on his forehead during the reading of the letter; then, crushing the paper into a ball, he threw it, angrily, on the floor.

"Well! What's the matter?" asked Wilson, anxiously.

He picked up the ball of paper, unfolded it, and read, with increasing amazement:

"My Dear Monsieur:

"You know full well the admiration I have for you and the interest I take in your renown. Well, believe me, when I warn you to have nothing whatever to do with the case on which you have just now been called to Paris. Your intervention will cause much harm; your efforts will produce a most lamentable result; and you will be obliged to make a public confession of your defeat.

"Having a sincere desire to spare you such humiliation, I implore you, in the name of the friendship that unites us, to remain peacefully reposing at your own fireside.

"My best wishes to Monsieur Wilson, and, for yourself, the sincere regards of your devoted ARSÈNE LUPIN."

"Arsène Lupin!" repeated Wilson, astounded.

Sholmes struck the table with his fist, and exclaimed:

"Ah! he is pestering me already, the fool! He laughs at me as if I were a schoolboy! The public confession of my defeat! Didn't I force him to disgorge the blue diamond?"

"I tell you—he's afraid," suggested Wilson.

"Nonsense! Arsène Lupin is not afraid, and this taunting letter proves it."

"But how did he know that the Baron d'Imblevalle had written to you?"

"What do I know about it? You do ask some stupid questions, my boy."

"I thought ... I supposed——"

"What? That I am a clairvoyant? Or a sorcerer?"

"No, but I have seen you do some marvellous things."

"No person can perform *marvellous* things. I no more than you. I reflect, I deduct, I conclude—that is all; but I do not divine. Only fools divine."

Wilson assumed the attitude of a whipped cur, and resolved not to make a fool of himself by trying to divine why Sholmes paced the room with quick, nervous strides. But when Sholmes rang for the servant and ordered his valise, Wilson thought that he was in possession of a material fact which gave him the right to reflect, deduct and conclude that his associate was about to take a journey. The same mental operation permitted him to assert, with almost mathematical exactness:

"Sholmes, you are going to Paris."

"Possibly."

"And Lupin's affront impels you to go, rather than the desire to assist the Baron d'Imblevalle."

"Possibly."

"Sholmes, I shall go with you."

"Ah; ah! my old friend," exclaimed Sholmes, interrupting his walking, "you are not afraid that your right arm will meet the same fate as your left?"

"What can happen to me? You will be there."

"That's the way to talk, Wilson. We will show that clever Frenchman that he made a mistake when he threw his glove in our faces. Be quick, Wilson, we must catch the first train."

"Without waiting for the papers the baron has sent you?"

"What good are they?"

"I will send a telegram."

"No; if you do that, Arsène Lupin will know of my arrival. I wish to avoid that. This time, Wilson, we must fight under cover."

That afternoon, the two friends embarked at Dover. The passage was a delightful one. In the train from Calais to Paris, Sholmes had three hours sound sleep, while Wilson guarded the door of the compartment.

Sholmes awoke in good spirits. He was delighted at the idea of another duel with Arsène Lupin, and he rubbed his hands with the satisfied air of a man who looks forward to a pleasant vacation.

"At last!" exclaimed Wilson, "we are getting to work again."

And he rubbed his hands with the same satisfied air.

At the station, Sholmes took the wraps and, followed by Wilson, who carried the valises, he gave up his tickets and started off briskly.

"Fine weather, Wilson.... Blue sky and sunshine! Paris is giving us a royal reception."

"Yes, but what a crowd!"

"So much the better, Wilson, we will pass unnoticed. No one will recognize us in such a crowd."

"Is this Monsieur Sholmes?"

He stopped, somewhat puzzled. Who the deuce could thus address him by his name? A woman stood beside him; a young girl whose simple dress outlined her slender form and whose pretty face had a sad and anxious expression. She repeated her enquiry:

"You are Monsieur Sholmes?"

As he still remained silent, as much from confusion as from a habit of prudence, the girl asked a third time:

"Have I the honor of addressing Monsieur Sholmes?"

"What do you want?" he replied, testily, considering the incident a suspicious one.

"You must listen to me, Monsieur Sholmes, as it is a serious matter. I know that you are going to the rue Murillo."

"What do you say?"

"I know ... I know ... rue Murillo ... number 18. Well, you must not go ... no, you must not. I assure you that you will regret it. Do not think that I have any interest in the matter. I do it because it is right ... because my conscience tells me to do it."

Sholmes tried to get away, but she persisted:

"Oh! I beg of you, don't neglect my advice.... Ah! if I only knew how to convince you! Look at me! Look into my eyes! They are sincere ... they speak the truth."

She gazed at Sholmes, fearlessly but innocently, with those beautiful eyes, serious and clear, in which her very soul seemed to be reflected.

Wilson nodded his head, as he said:

"Mademoiselle looks honest."

"Yes," she implored, "and you must have confidence———"

"I have confidence in you, mademoiselle," replied Wilson.

"Oh, how happy you make me! And so has your friend? I feel it ... I am sure of it! What happiness! Everything will be all right now!... What a good idea of mine!... Ah! yes, there is a train for Calais in twenty minutes. You will take it.... Quick, follow me ... you must come this way ... there is just time."

She tried to drag them along. Sholmes seized her arm, and in as gentle a voice as he could assume, said to her:

"Excuse me, mademoiselle, if I cannot yield to your wishes, but I never abandon a task that I have once undertaken."

"I beseech you ... I implore you.... Ah if you could only understand!"

Sholmes passed outside and walked away at a quick pace. Wilson said to the girl:

"Have no fear ... he will be in at the finish. He never failed yet."

And he ran to overtake Sholmes.

HERLOCK SHOLMES—ARSÈNE LUPIN.

These words, in great black letters, met their gaze as soon as they left the railway station. A number of sandwich-men were parading through the street, one behind the other, carrying heavy canes with iron ferrules with which they struck the pavement in harmony, and, on their backs, they carried large posters, on which one could read the following notice:

THE MATCH BETWEEN HERLOCK SHOLMES
AND ARSÈNE LUPIN. ARRIVAL OF THE ENGLISH
CHAMPION. THE GREAT DETECTIVE ATTACKS
THE MYSTERY OF THE RUE MURILLO. READ THE
DETAILS IN THE "ECHO DE FRANCE".

Wilson shook his head, and said:

"Look at that, Sholmes, and we thought we were traveling incognito! I shouldn't be surprised to find the republican guard waiting for us at the rue Murillo to give us an official reception with toasts and champagne."

"Wilson, when you get funny, you get beastly funny," growled Sholmes.

Then he approached one of the sandwich-men with the obvious intention of seizing him in his powerful grip and crushing him, together with his infernal sign-board. There was quite a crowd gathered about the men, reading the notices, and joking and laughing.

Repressing a furious access of rage, Sholmes said to the man:

"When did they hire you?"

"This morning."

"How long have you been parading?"

"About an hour."

"But the boards were ready before that?"

"Oh, yes, they were ready when we went to the agency this morning."

So then it appears that Arsène Lupin had foreseen that he, Sholmes, would accept the challenge. More than that, the letter written by Lupin showed that he was eager for the fray and that he was prepared to measure swords once more with his formidable rival. Why! What motive could Arsène Lupin have in renewing the struggle!

Sholmes hesitated for a moment. Lupin must be very confident of his success to show so much insolence in advance; and was not he, Sholmes, falling into a trap by rushing into the battle at the first call for help?

However, he called a carriage.

"Come, Wilson!... Driver, 18 rue Murillo!" he exclaimed, with an outburst of his accustomed energy. With distended veins and clenched fists, as if he were about to engage in a boxing bout, he jumped into the carriage.

The rue Murillo is bordered with magnificent private residences, the rear of which overlook the Parc Monceau. One of the most pretentious of these houses is number 18, owned and occupied by the Baron d'Imblevalle and furnished in a luxurious manner consistent with the owner's taste and wealth. There was a courtyard in front of the house, and, in the rear, a garden well filled with trees whose branches mingle with those of the park.

After ringing the bell, the two Englishmen were admitted, crossed the courtyard, and were received at the door by a footman who showed them into a small parlor facing the garden in the rear of the house. They sat down and, glancing about, made a rapid inspection of the many valuable objects with which the room was filled.

"Everything very choice," murmured Wilson, "and in the best of taste. It is a safe deduction to make that those who had the leisure to collect these articles must now be at least fifty years of age."

The door opened, and the Baron d'Imblevalle entered, followed by his wife. Contrary to the deduction made by Wilson, they were both quite young, of elegant appearance, and vivacious in speech and action. They were profuse in their expressions of gratitude.

"So kind of you to come! Sorry to have caused you so much trouble! The theft now seems of little consequence, since it has procured us this pleasure."

"How charming these French people are!" thought Wilson, evolving one of his commonplace deductions.

"But time is money," exclaimed the baron, "especially your time, Monsieur Sholmes. So I will come to the point. Now, what do you think of the affair? Do you think you can succeed in it?"

"Before I can answer that I must know what it is about."

"I thought you knew."

"No; so I must ask you for full particulars, even to the smallest detail. First, what is the nature of the case?"

"A theft."

"When did it take place?"

"Last Saturday," replied the baron, "or, at least, some time during Saturday night or Sunday morning."

"That was six days ago. Now, you can tell me all about it."

"In the first place, monsieur, I must tell you that my wife and I, conforming to the manner of life that our position demands, go out very little. The education of our children, a few receptions, and the care and decoration of our house—such constitutes our life; and nearly all our evenings are spent in this little room, which is my wife's boudoir, and in which we have gathered a few artistic objects. Last Saturday night, about eleven o'clock, I turned off the electric lights, and my wife and I retired, as usual, to our room."

"Where is your room?"

"It adjoins this. That is the door. Next morning, that is to say, Sunday morning, I arose quite early. As Suzanne, my wife, was still asleep, I passed into the boudoir as quietly as possible so as not to wake her. What was my astonishment when I found that window open—as we had left it closed the evening before!"

"A servant——"

"No one enters here in the morning until we ring. Besides, I always take the precaution to bolt the second door which communicates with the ante-chamber. Therefore, the window must have been opened from the outside. Besides, I have some evidence of that: the second pane of glass from the right—close to the fastening—had been cut."

"And what does that window overlook?"

"As you can see for yourself, it opens on a little balcony, surrounded by a stone railing. Here, we are on the first floor, and you can see the garden behind the house and the iron fence which separates it from the Parc Monceau. It is quite certain that the thief came through the park, climbed the fence by the aid of a ladder, and thus reached the terrace below the window."

"That is quite certain, you say!"

"Well, in the soft earth on either side of the fence, they found the two holes made by the bottom of the ladder, and two similar holes can be seen below the window. And the stone railing of the balcony shows two scratches which were doubtless made by the contact of the ladder."

"Is the Parc Monceau closed at night?"

"No; but if it were, there is a house in course of erection at number 14, and a person could enter that way."

Herlock Sholmes reflected for a few minutes, and then said:

"Let us come down to the theft. It must have been committed in this room?"

"Yes; there was here, between that twelfth century Virgin and that tabernacle of chased silver, a small Jewish lamp. It has disappeared."

"And is that all?"

"That is all."

"Ah!... And what is a Jewish lamp!"

"One of those copper lamps used by the ancient Jews, consisting of a standard which supported a bowl containing the oil, and from this bowl projected several burners intended for the wicks."

"Upon the whole, an object of small value."

"No great value, of course. But this one contained a secret hiding-place in which we were accustomed to place a magnificent jewel, a chimera in gold, set with rubies and emeralds, which was of great value."

"Why did you hide it there?"

"Oh! I can't give any reason, monsieur, unless it was an odd fancy to utilize a hiding-place of that kind."

"Did anyone know it?"

"No."

"No one—except the thief," said Sholmes. "Otherwise he would not have taken the trouble to steal the lamp."

"Of course. But how could he know it, as it was only by accident that the secret mechanism of the lamp was revealed to us."

"A similar accident has revealed it to some one else ... a servant ... or an acquaintance. But let us proceed: I suppose the police have been notified?"

"Yes. The examining magistrate has completed his investigation. The reporter-detectives attached to the leading newspapers have also made their investigations. But, as I wrote to you, it seems to me the mystery will never be solved."

Sholmes arose, went to the window, examined the casement, the balcony, the terrace, studied the scratches on the stone railing with his magnifying-glass, and then requested Mon. d'Imblevalle to show him the garden.

Outside, Sholmes sat down in a rattan chair and gazed at the roof of the house in a dreamy way. Then he walked over to the two little wooden boxes with which they had covered the holes made in the ground by the bottom of the ladder with a view of preserving them intact. He raised the boxes, kneeled on the ground, scrutinized the holes and made some measurements. After making a similar examination of the holes near the fence, he and the baron returned to the boudoir where Madame d'Imblevalle was waiting for them. After a short silence Sholmes said:

"At the very outset of your story, baron, I was surprised at the very simple methods employed by the thief. To raise a ladder, cut a window-pane, select a valuable article, and walk out again—no, that is not the way such things are done. All that is too plain, too simple."

"Well, what do you think!"

"That the Jewish lamp was stolen under the direction of Arsène Lupin."

"Arsène Lupin!" exclaimed the baron.

"Yes, but he did not do it himself, as no one came from the outside. Perhaps a servant descended from the upper floor by means of a waterspout that I noticed when I was in the garden."

"What makes you think so!"

"Arsène Lupin would not leave this room empty-handed."

"Empty-handed! But he had the lamp."

"But that would not have prevented his taking that snuff-box, set with diamonds, or that opal necklace. When he leaves anything, it is because he can't carry it away."

"But the marks of the ladder outside!"

"A false scent. Placed there simply to avert suspicion."

"And the scratches on the balustrade?"

"A farce! They were made with a piece of sandpaper. See, here are scraps of the paper that I picked up in the garden."

"And what about the marks made by the bottom of the ladder?"

"Counterfeit! Examine the two rectangular holes below the window, and the two holes near the fence. They are of a similar form, but I find that the two holes near the house are closer to each other than the two holes near the fence. What does that fact suggest? To me, it suggested that the four holes were made by a piece of wood prepared for the purpose."

"The better proof would be the piece of wood itself."

"Here it is," said Sholmes, "I found it in the garden, under the box of a laurel tree."

The baron bowed to Sholmes in recognition of his skill. Only forty minutes had elapsed since the Englishman had entered the house, and he had already exploded all the theories theretofore formed, and which had been based on what appeared to be obvious and undeniable facts. But what now appeared to be the real facts of the case rested upon a more solid foundation, to-wit, the astute reasoning of a Herlock Sholmes.

"The accusation which you make against one of our household is a very serious matter," said the baroness. "Our servants have been with us a long time and none of them would betray our trust."

"If none of them has betrayed you, how can you explain the fact that I received this letter on the same day and by the same mail as the letter you wrote to me?"

He handed to the baroness the letter that he had received from Arsène Lupin. She exclaimed, in amazement:

"Arsène Lupin! How could he know?"

"Did you tell anyone that you had written to me?"

"No one," replied the baron. "The idea occurred to us the other evening at the dinner-table."

"Before the servants?"

"No, only our two children. Oh, no ... Sophie and Henriette had left the table, hadn't they, Suzanne?"

Madame d'Imblevalle, after a moment's reflection, replied:

"Yes, they had gone to Mademoiselle."

"Mademoiselle?" queried Sholmes.

"The governess, Mademoiselle Alice Demun."

"Does she take her meals with you?"

"No. Her meals are served in her room."

Wilson had an idea. He said:

"The letter written to my friend Herlock Sholmes was posted?"

"Of course."

"Who posted it?"

"Dominique, who has been my valet for twenty years," replied the baron. "Any search in that direction would be a waste of time."

"One never wastes his time when engaged in a search," said Wilson, sententiously.

This preliminary investigation now ended, and Sholmes asked permission to retire.

At dinner, an hour later, he saw Sophie and Henriette, the two children of the family, one was six and the other eight years of age. There was very little conversation at the table. Sholmes responded to the friendly advances of his hosts in such a curt manner that they were soon reduced to silence. When the coffee was served, Sholmes swallowed the contents of his cup, and rose to take his leave.

At that moment, a servant entered with a telephone message addressed to Sholmes. He opened it, and read:

"You have my enthusiastic admiration. The results attained by you in so short a time are simply marvellous. I am dismayed.

"ARSÈNE LUPIN."

Sholmes made a gesture of indignation and handed the message to the baron, saying:

"What do you think now, monsieur? Are the walls of your house furnished with eyes and ears?"

"I don't understand it," said the baron, in amazement.

"Nor do I; but I do understand that Lupin has knowledge of everything that occurs in this house. He knows every movement, every word. There is no doubt of it. But how does he get his information? That is the first mystery I have to solve, and when I know that I will know everything."

That night, Wilson retired with the clear conscience of a man who has performed his whole duty and thus acquired an undoubted right to sleep and repose. So he fell asleep very quickly, and was soon enjoying the most delightful dreams in which he pursued Lupin and captured him single-handed; and the sensation was so vivid and exciting that it woke him from his sleep. Someone was standing at his bedside. He seized his revolver, and cried:

"Don't move, Lupin, or I'll fire."

"The deuce! Wilson, what do you mean?"

"Oh! it is you, Sholmes. Do you want me!"

"I want to show you something. Get up."

Sholmes led him to the window, and said:

"Look!... on the other side of the fence...."

"In the park?"

"Yes. What do you see?"

"I don't see anything."

"Yes, you do see something."

"Ah! of course, a shadow ... two of them."

"Yes, close to the fence. See, they are moving. Come, quick!"

Quickly they descended the stairs, and reached a room which opened into the garden. Through the glass door they could see the two shadowy forms in the same place.

"It is very strange," said Sholmes, "but it seems to me I can hear a noise inside the house."

"Inside the house? Impossible! Everybody is asleep."

"Well, listen——"

At that moment a low whistle came from the other side of the fence, and they perceived a dim light which appeared to come from the house.

"The baron must have turned on the light in his room. It is just above us."

"That must have been the noise you heard," said Wilson. "Perhaps they are watching the fence also."

Then there was a second whistle, softer than before.

"I don't understand it; I don't understand," said Sholmes, irritably.

"No more do I," confessed Wilson.

Sholmes turned the key, drew the bolt, and quietly opened the door. A third whistle, louder than before, and modulated to another form. And the noise above their heads became more pronounced. Sholmes said:

"It seems to be on the balcony outside the boudoir window."

He put his head through the half-opened door, but immediately recoiled, with a stifled oath. Then Wilson looked. Quite close to them there was a ladder, the upper end of which was resting on the balcony.

"The deuce!" said Sholmes, "there is someone in the boudoir. That is what we heard. Quick, let us remove the ladder."

But at that instant a man slid down the ladder and ran toward the spot where his accomplices were waiting for him outside the fence. He carried the ladder with him. Sholmes and Wilson pursued the man and overtook him just as he was placing the ladder against the fence. From the other side of the fence two shots were fired.

"Wounded?" cried Sholmes.

"No," replied Wilson.

Wilson seized the man by the body and tried to hold him, but the man turned and plunged a knife into Wilson's breast. He uttered a groan, staggered and fell.

"Damnation!" muttered Sholmes, "if they have killed him I will kill them."

He laid Wilson on the grass and rushed toward the ladder. Too late—the man had climbed the fence and, accompanied by his confederates, had fled through the bushes.

"Wilson, Wilson, it is not serious, hein? Merely a scratch."

The house door opened, and Monsieur d'Imblevalle appeared, followed by the servants, carrying candles.

"What's the matter?" asked the baron. "Is Monsieur Wilson wounded?"

"Oh! it's nothing—a mere scratch," repeated Sholmes, trying to deceive himself.

The blood was flowing profusely, and Wilson's face was livid. Twenty minutes later the doctor ascertained that the point of the knife had penetrated to within an inch and a half of the heart.

"An inch and a half of the heart! Wilson always was lucky!" said Sholmes, in an envious tone.

"Lucky ... lucky...." muttered the doctor.

"Of course! Why, with his robust constitution he will soon be out again."

"Six weeks in bed and two months of convalescence."

"Not more?"

"No, unless complications set in."

"Oh! the devil! what does he want complications for?"

Fully reassured, Sholmes joined the baron in the boudoir. This time the mysterious visitor had not exercised the same restraint. Ruthlessly, he had laid his vicious hand upon the diamond snuff-box, upon the opal necklace, and, in a general way, upon everything that could find a place in the greedy pockets of an enterprising burglar.

The window was still open; one of the window-panes had been neatly cut; and, in the morning, a summary investigation showed that the ladder belonged to the house then in course of construction.

"Now, you can see," said Mon. d'Imblevalle, with a touch of irony, "it is an exact repetition of the affair of the Jewish lamp."

"Yes, if we accept the first theory adopted by the police."

"Haven't you adopted it yet? Doesn't this second theft shatter your theory in regard to the first?"

"It only confirms it, monsieur."

"That is incredible! You have positive evidence that last night's theft was committed by an outsider, and yet you adhere to your theory that the Jewish lamp was stolen by someone in the house."

"Yes, I am sure of it."

"How do you explain it?"

"I do not explain anything, monsieur; I have established two facts which do not appear to have any relation to each other, and yet I am seeking the missing link that connects them."

His conviction seemed to be so earnest and positive that the baron submitted to it, and said:

"Very well, we will notify the police———"

"Not at all!" exclaimed the Englishman, quickly, "not at all! I intend to ask for their assistance when I need it—but not before."

"But the attack on your friend?"

"That's of no consequence. He is only wounded. Secure the license of the doctor. I shall be responsible for the legal side of the affair."

The next two days proved uneventful. Yet Sholmes was investigating the case with a minute care, and with a sense of wounded pride resulting from that audacious theft, committed under his nose, in spite of his presence and beyond his power to prevent it. He made a thorough investigation of the house and garden, interviewed the servants, and paid lengthy visits to the kitchen and stables. And, although his efforts were fruitless, he did not despair.

"I will succeed," he thought, "and the solution must be sought within the walls of this house. This affair is quite different from that of the blonde Lady, where I had to work in the dark, on unknown ground. This time I am on the battlefield itself. The enemy is not the elusive and invisible Lupin, but the accomplice, in flesh and blood, who lives and moves within the confines of this house. Let me secure the slightest clue and the game is mine!"

That clue was furnished to him by accident.

On the afternoon of the third day, when he entered a room located above the boudoir, which served as a study for the children, he found Henriette, the younger of the two sisters. She was looking for her scissors.

"You know," she said to Sholmes, "I make papers like that you received the other evening."

"The other evening?"

"Yes, just as dinner was over, you received a paper with marks on it ... you know, a telegram.... Well, I make them, too."

She left the room. To anyone else these words would seem to be nothing more than the insignificant remark of a child, and Sholmes himself listened to them with a distracted air and continued his investigation. But, suddenly, he ran after the child, and overtook her at the head of the stairs. He said to her:

"So you paste stamps and marks on papers?"

Henriette, very proudly, replied:

"Yes, I cut them out and paste them on."

"Who taught you that little game?"

"Mademoiselle ... my governess ... I have seen her do it often. She takes words out of the newspapers and pastes them——"

"What does she make out of them?"

"Telegrams and letters that she sends away."

Herlock Sholmes returned to the study, greatly puzzled by the information and seeking to draw from it a logical deduction. There was a pile of newspapers on the mantel. He opened them and found that many words and, in some places, entire lines had been cut out. But, after reading a few of the word's which preceded or followed, he decided that the missing words had been cut out at random—probably by the child. It was possible that one of the newspapers had been cut by mademoiselle; but how could he assure himself that such was the case?

Mechanically, Sholmes turned over the school-books on the table; then others which were lying on the shelf of a bookcase. Suddenly he uttered a cry of joy. In a corner of the bookcase, under a pile of old exercise books, he found a child's alphabet-book, in which the letters were ornamented with pictures, and on one of the pages of that book he discovered a place where a word had been removed. He examined it. It was a list of the days of the week. Monday, Tuesday, Wednesday, etc. The word "Saturday" was missing. Now, the theft of the Jewish lamp had occurred on a Saturday night.

Sholmes experienced that slight fluttering of the heart which always announced to him, in the clearest manner, that he had discovered the road which leads to victory. That ray of truth, that feeling of certainty, never deceived him.

With nervous fingers he hastened to examine the balance of the book. Very soon he made another discovery. It was a page composed of capital letters, followed by a line of figures. Nine of those letters and three of those figures had been carefully cut out. Sholmes made a list of the missing letters and figures in his memorandum book, in alphabetical and numerical order, and obtained the following result:

CDEHNOPEZ—237.

"Well! at first sight, it is a rather formidable puzzle," he murmured, "but, by transposing the letters and using all of them, is it possible to form one, two or three complete words?"

Sholmes tried it, in vain.

Only one solution seemed possible; it constantly appeared before him, no matter which way he tried to juggle the letters, until, at length, he was satisfied it was the true solution, since it harmonized with the logic of the facts and the general circumstances of the case.

As that page of the book did not contain any duplicate letters it was probable, in fact quite certain, that the words he could form from those letters would be incomplete, and that the original words had been completed with letters taken from other pages. Under those conditions he obtained the following solution, errors and omissions excepted:

REPOND Z—CH—237.

The first word was quite clear: répondez [reply], a letter E is missing because it occurs twice in the word, and the book furnished only one letter of each kind.

As to the second incomplete word, no doubt it formed, with the aid of the number 237, an address to which the reply was to be sent. They appointed Saturday as the time, and requested a reply to be sent to the address CH. 237.

Or, perhaps, CH. 237 was an address for a letter to be sent to the "general delivery" of some postoffice, or, again, they might form a part of some incomplete word. Sholmes searched the book once more, but did not discover that any other letters had been removed. Therefore, until further orders, he decided to adhere to the foregoing interpretation.

Henriette returned and observed what he was doing.

"Amusing, isn't it?"

"Yes, very amusing," he replied. "But, have you any other papers?... Or, rather, words already cut out that I can paste?"

"Papers?... No.... And Mademoiselle wouldn't like it."

"Mademoiselle?"

"Yes, she has scolded me already."

"Why?"

"Because I have told you some things ... and she says that a person should never tell things about those they love."

"You are quite right."

Henriette was delighted to receive his approbation, in fact so highly pleased that she took from a little silk bag that was pinned to her dress some scraps of cloth, three buttons, two cubes of sugar and, lastly, a piece of paper which she handed to Sholmes.

"See, I give it to you just the same."

It was the number of a cab—8,279.

"Where did this number come from?"

"It fell out of her pocketbook."

"When?"

"Sunday, at mass, when she was taking out some sous for the collection."

"Exactly! And now I shall tell you how to keep from being scolded again. Do not tell Mademoiselle that you saw me."

Sholmes then went to Mon. d'Imblevalle and questioned him in regard to Mademoiselle. The baron replied, indignantly:

"Alice Demun! How can you imagine such a thing? It is utterly impossible!"

"How long has she been in your service?"

"Only a year, but there is no one in the house in whom I have greater confidence."

"Why have I not seen her yet?"

"She has been away for a few days."

"But she is here now."

"Yes; since her return she has been watching at the bedside of your friend. She has all the qualities of a nurse ... gentle ... thoughtful ... Monsieur Wilson seems much pleased...."

"Ah!" said Sholmes, who had completely neglected to inquire about his friend. After a moment's reflection he asked:

"Did she go out on Sunday morning?"

"The day after the theft?"

"Yes."

The baron called his wife and asked her. She replied:

"Mademoiselle went to the eleven o'clock mass with the children, as usual."

"But before that?"

"Before that? No.... Let me see!... I was so upset by the theft ... but I remember now that, on the evening before, she asked permission to go out on Sunday morning ... to see a cousin who was passing through Paris, I think. But, surely, you don't suspect her?"

"Of course not ... but I would like to see her."

He went to Wilson's room. A woman dressed in a gray cloth dress, as in the hospitals, was bending over the invalid, giving him a drink. When she turned her face Sholmes recognized her as the young girl who had accosted him at the railway station.

Alice Demun smiled sweetly; her great serious, innocent eyes showed no sign of embarrassment. The Englishman tried to speak, muttered a few syllables, and stopped. Then she resumed her work, acting quite naturally under Sholmes' astonished gaze, moved the bottles, unrolled and rolled cotton bandages, and again regarded Sholmes with her charming smile of pure innocence.

He turned on his heels, descended the stairs, noticed Mon. d'Imblevalle's automobile in the courtyard, jumped into it, and went to Levallois, to the office of the cab company whose address was printed on the paper he had received from Henriette. The man who had driven carriage number 8,279 on Sunday morning not being there, Sholmes dismissed the automobile and waited for the man's return. He told Sholmes that he had picked up a woman in the vicinity of the Parc Monceau, a young woman dressed in black, wearing a heavy veil, and, apparently, quite nervous.

"Did she have a package?"

"Yes, quite a long package."

"Where did you take her?"

"Avenue des Ternes, corner of the Place Saint-Ferdinand. She remained there about ten minutes, and then returned to the Parc Monceau."

"Could you recognize the house in the avenue des Ternes?"

"Parbleu! Shall I take you there?"

"Presently. First take me to 36 quai des Orfèvres."

At the police office he saw Detective Ganimard.

"Monsieur Ganimard, are you at liberty?"

"If it has anything to do with Lupin—no!"

"It has something to do with Lupin."

"Then I do not go."

"What! you surrender——"

"I bow to the inevitable. I am tired of the unequal struggle, in which we are sure to be defeated. Lupin is stronger than I am—stronger than the two of us; therefore, we must surrender."

"I will not surrender."

"He will make you, as he has all others."

"And you would be pleased to see it—eh, Ganimard?"

"At all events, it is true," said Ganimard, frankly. "And since you are determined to pursue the game, I will go with you."

Together they entered the carriage and were driven to the avenue des Ternes. Upon their order the carriage stopped on the other side of the street, at some distance from the house, in front of a little café, on the terrace of which the two men took seats amongst the shrubbery. It was commencing to grow dark.

"Waiter," said Sholmes, "some writing material."

He wrote a note, recalled the waiter and gave him the letter with instructions to deliver it to the concierge of the house which he pointed out.

In a few minutes the concierge stood before them. Sholmes asked him if, on the Sunday morning, he had seen a young woman dressed in black.

"In black! Yes, about nine o'clock. She went to the second floor."

"Have you seen her often?"

"No, but for some time—well, during the last few weeks, I have seen her almost every day."

"And since Sunday?"

"Only once ... until to-day."

"What! Did she come to-day?"

"She is here now."

"Here now?"

"Yes, she came about ten minutes ago. Her carriage is standing in the Place Saint-Ferdinand, as usual. I met her at the door."

"Who is the occupant of the second floor?"

"There are two: a modiste, Mademoiselle Langeais, and a gentleman who rented two furnished rooms a month ago under the name of Bresson."

"Why do you say 'under the name'?"

"Because I have an idea that it is an assumed name. My wife takes care of his rooms, and ... well, there are not two shirts there with the same initials."

"Is he there much of the time?"

"No; he is nearly always out. He has not been here for three days."

"Was he here on Saturday night?"

"Saturday night?... Let me think.... Yes, Saturday night, he came in and stayed all night."

"What sort of a man is he?"

"Well, I can scarcely answer that. He is so changeable. He is, by turns, big, little, fat, thin ... dark and light. I do not always recognize him."

Ganimard and Sholmes exchanged looks.

"That is he, all right," said Ganimard.

"Ah!" said the concierge, "there is the girl now."

Mademoiselle had just emerged from the house and was walking toward her carriage in the Place Saint-Ferdinand.

"And there is Monsieur Bresson."

"Monsieur Bresson? Which is he?"

"The man with the parcel under his arm."

"But he is not looking after the girl. She is going to her carriage alone."

"Yes, I have never seen them together."

The two detectives had arisen. By the light of the street-lamps they recognized the form of Arsène Lupin, who had started off in a direction opposite to that taken by the girl.

"Which will you follow?" asked Ganimard.

"I will follow him, of course. He's the biggest game."

"Then I will follow the girl," proposed Ganimard.

"No, no," said Sholmes, quickly, who did not wish to disclose the girl's identity to Ganimard, "I know where to find her. Come with me."

They followed Lupin at a safe distance, taking care to conceal themselves as well as possible amongst the moving throng and behind the newspaper kiosks. They found the pursuit an easy one, as he walked steadily forward without turning to the right or left, but with a slight limp in the right leg, so slight as to require the keen eye of a professional observer to detect it. Ganimard observed it, and said:

"He is pretending to be lame. Ah! if we could only collect two or three policemen and pounce on our man! We run a chance to lose him."

But they did not meet any policemen before they reached the Porte des Ternes, and, having passed the fortifications, there was no prospect of receiving any assistance.

"We had better separate," said Sholmes, "as there are so few people on the street."

They were now on the Boulevard Victor-Hugo. They walked one on each side of the street, and kept well in the shadow of the trees. They continued thus for twenty minutes, when Lupin turned to the left and followed the Seine. Very soon they saw him descend to the edge of the river. He remained there only a few seconds, but they could not observe his movements. Then Lupin retraced his steps. His pursuers concealed themselves in the shadow of a gateway. Lupin passed in front of them. His parcel had disappeared. And as he walked away another man emerged from the shelter of a house and glided amongst the trees.

"He seems to be following him also," said Sholmes, in a low voice.

The pursuit continued, but was now embarrassed by the presence of the third man. Lupin returned the same way, passed through the Porte des Ternes, and re-entered the house in the avenue des Ternes.

The concierge was closing the house for the night when Ganimard presented himself.

"Did you see him?"

"Yes," replied the concierge, "I was putting out the gas on the landing when he closed and bolted his door."

"Is there any person with him?"

"No; he has no servant. He never eats here."

"Is there a servants' stairway?"

"No."

Ganimard said to Sholmes:

"I had better stand at the door of his room while you go for the commissary of police in the rue Demours."

"And if he should escape during that time?" said Sholmes.

"While I am here! He can't escape."

"One to one, with Lupin, is not an even chance for you."

"Well, I can't force the door. I have no right to do that, especially at night."

Sholmes shrugged his shoulders and said:

"When you arrest Lupin no one will question the methods by which you made the arrest. However, let us go up and ring, and see what happens then."

They ascended to the second floor. There was a double door at the left of the landing. Ganimard rang the bell. No reply. He rang again. Still no reply.

"Let us go in," said Sholmes.

"All right, come on," replied Ganimard.

Yet, they stood still, irresolute. Like people who hesitate when they ought to accomplish a decisive action they feared to move, and it seemed to them impossible that Arsène Lupin was there, so close to them, on the other side of that fragile door that could be broken down by one blow of the fist. But they knew Lupin too well to suppose that he would allow himself to be trapped in that stupid manner. No, no—a thousand times, no—Lupin was no longer there. Through the adjoining houses, over the roofs, by some conveniently prepared exit, he must have already made his escape, and, once more, it would only be Lupin's shadow that they would seize.

They shuddered as a slight noise, coming from the other side of the door, reached their ears. Then they had the impression, amounting almost to a certainty, that he was there, separated from them by that frail wooden door, and that he was listening to them, that he could hear them.

What was to be done? The situation was a serious one. In spite of their vast experience as detectives, they were so nervous and excited that they thought they could hear the beating of their own hearts. Ganimard questioned Sholmes by a look. Then he struck the door a violent blow with his fist. Immediately they heard the sound of footsteps, concerning which there was no attempt at concealment.

Ganimard shook the door. Then he and Sholmes, uniting their efforts, rushed at the door, and burst it open with their shoulders. Then they stood still, in surprise. A shot had been fired in the adjoining room. Another shot, and the sound of a falling body.

When they entered they saw the man lying on the floor with his face toward the marble mantel. His revolver had fallen from his hand. Ganimard stooped and turned the man's head. The face was covered with blood, which was flowing from two wounds, one in the cheek, the other in the temple.

"You can't recognize him for blood."

"No matter!" said Sholmes. "It is not Lupin."

"How do you know? You haven't even looked at him."

"Do you think that Arsène Lupin is the kind of a man that would kill himself?" asked Sholmes, with a sneer.

"But we thought we recognized him outside."

"We thought so, because the wish was father to the thought. That man has us bewitched."

"Then it must be one of his accomplices."

"The accomplices of Arsène Lupin do not kill themselves."

"Well, then, who is it?"

They searched the corpse. In one pocket Herlock Sholmes found an empty pocketbook; in another Ganimard found several louis. There were no marks of identification on any part of his clothing. In a trunk and two valises they found nothing but wearing apparel. On the mantel there was a pile of newspapers. Ganimard opened them. All of them contained articles referring to the theft of the Jewish lamp.

An hour later, when Ganimard and Sholmes left the house, they had acquired no further knowledge of the strange individual who had been driven to suicide by their untimely visit.

Who was he! Why had he killed himself? What was his connection with the affair of the Jewish lamp? Who had followed him on his return from the river? The situation involved many complex questions—many mysteries—

Herlock Sholmes went to bed in a very bad humor. Early next morning he received the following telephonic message: "Arsène Lupin has the honor to inform you of his tragic death in the person of Monsieur Bresson, and requests the honor of your presence at the funeral service and burial, which will be held at the public expense on Thursday, 25 June."

VII. THE SHIPWRECK.

"That's what I don't like, Wilson," said Herlock Sholmes, after he had read Arsène Lupin's message; "that is what exasperates me in this affair—to feel that the cunning, mocking eye of that fellow follows me everywhere. He sees everything; he knows everything; he reads my inmost thoughts; he even foresees my slightest movement. Ah! he is possessed of a marvellous intuition, far surpassing that of the most instinctive woman, yes, surpassing even that of Herlock Sholmes himself. Nothing escapes him. I resemble an actor whose every step and movement are directed by a stage-manager; who says this and does that in obedience to a superior will. That is my position. Do you understand, Wilson?"

Certainly Wilson would have understood if his faculties had not been deadened by the profound slumber of a man whose temperature varies between one hundred and one hundred and three degrees. But whether he heard or not was a matter of no consequence to Herlock Sholmes, who continued:

"I have to concentrate all my energy and bring all my resources into action in order to make the slightest progress. And, fortunately for me, those petty annoyances are like so many pricks from a needle and serve only to stimulate me. As soon as the heat of the wound is appeased and the shock to my vanity has subsided I say to myself: 'Amuse yourself, my dear fellow, but remember that he who laughs last laughs best. Sooner or later you will betray yourself.' For you know, Wilson, it was Lupin himself, who, by his first dispatch and the observation that it suggested to little Henriette, disclosed to me the secret of his correspondence with Alice Hemun. Have you forgotten that circumstance, dear boy?"

But Wilson was asleep; and Sholmes, pacing to and fro, resumed his speech:

"And, now, things are not in a bad shape; a little obscure, perhaps, but the light is creeping in. In the first place, I must learn all about Monsieur Bresson. Ganimard and I will visit the bank of the river, at the spot where Bresson threw away the package, and the particular rôle of that gentleman will be known to me. After that the game will be played between me and Alice Demun. Rather a light-weight opponent, hein, Wilson? And do you not think that I will soon know the phrase represented by the letters clipped from the alphabet-book, and what the isolated letters—the 'C' and the 'H'—mean? That is all I want to know, Wilson."

Mademoiselle entered at that moment, and, observing Sholmes gesticulating, she said, in her sweetest manner:

"Monsieur Sholmes, I must scold you if you waken my patient. It isn't nice of you to disturb him. The doctor has ordered absolute rest."

He looked at her in silence, astonished, as on their first meeting, at her wonderful self-possession.

"Why do you look at me so, Monsieur Sholmes?... You seem to be trying to read my thoughts.... No?... Then what is it?"

She questioned him with the most innocent expression on her pretty face and in her frank blue eyes. A smile played upon her lips; and she displayed so much unaffected candor that the Englishman almost lost his temper. He approached her and said, in a low voice:

"Bresson killed himself last night."

She affected not to understand him; so he repeated:

"Bresson killed himself yesterday...."

She did not show the slightest emotion; she acted as if the matter did not concern or interest her in any way.

"You have been informed," said Sholmes, displaying his annoyance. "Otherwise, the news would have caused you to start, at least. Ah! you are stronger than I expected. But what's the use of your trying to conceal anything from me?"

He picked up the alphabet-book, which he had placed on a convenient table, and, opening it at the mutilated page, said:

"Will you tell me the order in which the missing letters should be arranged in order to express the exact wording of the message you sent to Bresson four days before the theft of the Jewish lamp?"

"The order?... Bresson?... the theft of the Jewish lamp?"

She repeated the words slowly, as if trying to grasp their meaning. He continued:

"Yes. Here are the letters employed ... on this bit of paper.... What did you say to Bresson?"

"The letters employed ... what did I say...."

Suddenly she burst into laughter:

"Ah! that is it! I understand! I am an accomplice in the crime! There is a Monsieur Bresson who stole the Jewish lamp and who has now committed suicide. And I am the friend of that gentleman. Oh! how absurd you are!"

"Whom did you go to see last night on the second floor of a house in the avenue des Ternes?"

"Who? My modiste, Mademoiselle Langeais. Do you suppose that my modiste and my friend Monsieur Bresson are the same person?"

Despite all he knew, Sholmes was now in doubt. A person can feign terror, joy, anxiety, in fact all emotions; but a person cannot feign absolute indifference or light, careless laughter. Yet he continued to question her:

"Why did you accost me the other evening at the Northern Railway station? And why did you entreat me to leave Paris immediately without investigating this theft?"

"Ah! you are too inquisitive, Monsieur Sholmes," she replied, still laughing in the most natural manner. "To punish you I will tell you nothing, and, besides, you must watch the patient while I go to the pharmacy on an urgent message. Au revoir."

She left the room.

"I am beaten ... by a girl," muttered Sholmes. "Not only did I get nothing out of her but I exposed my hand and put her on her guard."

And he recalled the affair of the blue diamond and his first interview with Clotilde Destange. Had not the blonde Lady met his question with the same unruffled serenity, and was he not once more face to face with one of those creatures who, under the protection and influence of Arsène Lupin, maintain the utmost coolness in the face of a terrible danger?

"Sholmes ... Sholmes...."

It was Wilson who called him. Sholmes approached the bed, and, leaning over, said:

"What's the matter, Wilson? Does your wound pain you?"

Wilson's lips moved, but he could not speak. At last, with a great effort, he stammered:

"No ... Sholmes ... it is not she ... that is impossible——"

"Come, Wilson, what do you know about it? I tell you that it is she! It is only when I meet one of Lupin's creatures, prepared and instructed by him, that I lose my head and make a fool of myself.... I bet you that within an hour Lupin will know all about our interview. Within an hour? What am I saying?... Why, he may know already. The visit to the pharmacy ... urgent message. All nonsense!... She has gone to telephone to Lupin."

Sholmes left the house hurriedly, went down the avenue de Messine, and was just in time to see Mademoiselle enter a pharmacy. Ten minutes later she emerged from the shop carrying some small packages and a bottle wrapped in white paper. But she had not proceeded far, when she was accosted by a man who, with hat in hand and an obsequious air, appeared to be asking for charity. She stopped, gave him something, and proceeded on her way.

"She spoke to him," said the Englishman to himself.

If not a certainty, it was at least an intuition, and quite sufficient to cause him to change his tactics. Leaving the girl to pursue her own course, he followed the suspected mendicant, who walked slowly to the avenue des Ternes and lingered for a long time around the house in which Bresson had lived, sometimes raising his eyes to the windows of the second floor and watching the people who entered the house.

At the end of an hour he climbed to the top of a tramcar going in the direction of Neuilly. Sholmes followed and took a seat behind the man, and beside a gentleman who was concealed behind the pages of a newspaper. At the fortifications the gentleman lowered the paper, and Sholmes recognized Ganimard, who thereupon whispered, as he pointed to the man in front:

"It is the man who followed Bresson last night. He has been watching the house for an hour."

"Anything new in regard to Bresson?" asked Sholmes.

"Yes, a letter came to his address this morning."

"This morning? Then it was posted yesterday before the sender could know of Bresson's death."

"Exactly. It is now in the possession of the examining magistrate. But I read it. It says: *He will not accept any compromise. He wants everything—the first thing as well as those of the second affair. Otherwise he will proceed.*"

"There is no signature," added Ganimard. "It seems to me those few lines won't help us much."

"I don't agree with you, Monsieur Ganimard. To me those few lines are very interesting."

"Why so? I can't see it."

"For reasons that are personal to me," replied Sholmes, with the indifference that he frequently displayed toward his colleague.

The tramcar stopped at the rue de Château, which was the terminus. The man descended and walked away quietly. Sholmes followed at so short a distance that Ganimard protested, saying:

"If he should turn around he will suspect us."

"He will not turn around."

"How do you know?"

"He is an accomplice of Arsène Lupin, and the fact that he walks in that manner, with his hands in his pockets, proves, in the first place, that he knows he is being followed and, in the second place, that he is not afraid."

"But I think we are keeping too close to him."

"Not too close to prevent his slipping through our fingers. He is too sure of himself."

"Ah! Look there! In front of that café there are two of the bicycle police. If I summon them to our assistance, how can the man slip through our fingers?"

"Well, our friend doesn't seem to be worried about it. In fact, he is asking for their assistance himself."

"Mon Dieu!" exclaimed Ganimard, "he has a nerve."

The man approached the two policemen just as they were mounting their bicycles. After a few words with them he leaped on a third bicycle, which was leaning against the wall of the café, and rode away at a fast pace, accompanied by the two policemen.

"Hein! one, two, three and away!" growled Sholmes. "And through, whose agency, Monsieur Ganimard? Two of your colleagues.... Ah! but Arsène Lupin has a wonderful organization! Bicycle policemen in his service!... I told you our man was too calm, too sure of himself."

"Well, then," said Ganimard, quite vexed, "what are we to do now? It is easy enough to laugh! Anyone can do that."

"Come, come, don't lose your temper! We will get our revenge. But, in the meantime, we need reinforcements."

"Folenfant is waiting for me at the end of the avenue de Neuilly."

"Well, go and get him and join me later. I will follow our fugitive."

Sholmes followed the bicycle tracks, which were plainly visible in the dust of the road as two of the machines were furnished with striated tires. Very soon he ascertained that the tracks were leading him to the edge of the Seine, and that the three men had turned in the direction taken by Bresson on the preceding evening. Thus he arrived at the gateway where he and Ganimard had concealed themselves, and, a little farther on, he discovered a mingling of the bicycle tracks which showed that the men had halted at that spot. Directly opposite there was a little point of land which projected into the river and, at the extremity thereof, an old boat was moored.

It was there that Bresson had thrown away the package, or, rather, had dropped it. Sholmes descended the bank and saw that the declivity was not steep and the water quite shallow, so it would be quite easy to recover the package, provided the three men had not forestalled him.

"No, that can't be," he thought, "they have not had time. A quarter of an hour at the most. And yet, why did they come this way?"

A fisherman was seated on the old boat. Sholmes asked him:

"Did you see three men on bicycles a few minutes ago?"

The fisherman made a negative gesture. But Sholmes insisted:

"Three men who stopped on the road just on top of the bank?"

The fisherman rested his pole under his arm, took a memorandum book from his pocket, wrote on one of the pages, tore it out, and handed it to Sholmes. The Englishman gave a start of surprise. In the middle of the paper which he held in his hand he saw the series of letters cut from the alphabet-book:

CDEHNOPRZEO—237.

The man resumed his fishing, sheltered from the sun by a large straw hat, with his coat and vest lying beside him. He was intently watching the cork attached to his line as it floated on the surface of the water.

There was a moment of silence—solemn and terrible.

"Is it he?" conjectured Sholmes, with an anxiety that was almost pitiful. Then the truth burst upon him:

"It is he! It is he! No one else could remain there so calmly, without the slightest display of anxiety, without the least fear of what might happen. And who else would know the story of those mysterious letters? Alice had warned him by means of her messenger."

Suddenly the Englishman felt that his hand—that his own hand had involuntarily seized the handle of his revolver, and that his eyes were fixed on the man's back, a little below the neck. One movement, and the drama would be finished; the life of the strange adventurer would come to a miserable end.

The fisherman did not stir.

Sholmes nervously toyed with his revolver, and experienced a wild desire to fire it and end everything; but the horror of such an act was repugnant to his nature. Death would be certain and would end all.

"Ah!" he thought, "let him get up and defend himself. If he doesn't, so much the worse for him. One second more ... and I fire...."

But a sound of footsteps behind him caused him to turn his head. It was Ganimard coming with some assistants.

Then, quickly changing his plans, Sholmes leaped into the boat, which was broken from its moorings by his sudden action; he pounced upon the man and seized him around the body. They rolled to the bottom of the boat together.

"Well, now!" exclaimed Lupin, struggling to free himself, "what does this mean? When one of us has conquered the other, what good will it do? You will not know what to do with me, nor I with you. We will remain here like two idiots."

The two oars slipped into the water. The boat drifted into the stream.

"Good Lord, what a fuss you make! A man of your age ought to know better! You act like a child."

Lupin succeeded in freeing himself from the grasp of the detective, who, thoroughly exasperated and ready to kill, put his hand in his pocket. He uttered an oath: Lupin had taken his revolver. Then he knelt down and tried to capture one of the lost oars in order to regain the shore, while Lupin was trying to capture the other oar in order to drive the boat down the river.

"It's gone! I can't reach it," said Lupin. "But it's of no consequence. If you get your oar I can prevent your using it. And you could do the same to me. But, you see, that is the way in this world, we act without any purpose or reason, as our efforts are in vain since Fate decides everything. Now, don't you see, Fate is on the side of his friend Lupin. The game is mine! The current favors me!"

The boat was slowly drifting down the river.

"Look out!" cried Lupin, quickly.

Someone on the bank was pointing a revolver. Lupin stooped, a shot was fired; it struck the water beyond the boat. Lupin burst into laughter.

"God bless me! It's my friend Ganimard! But it was very wrong of you to do that, Ganimard. You have no right to shoot except in self-defense. Does poor Lupin worry you so much that you forget yourself?... Now, be good, and don't shoot again!... If you do you will hit our English friend."

He stood behind Sholmes, facing Ganimard, and said:

"Now, Ganimard, I am ready! Aim for his heart!... Higher!... A little to the left.... Ah! you missed that time ... deuced bad shot.... Try again.... Your hand shakes, Ganimard.... Now, once more ... one, two, three, fire!... Missed!... Parbleu! the authorities furnish you with toy-pistols."

Lupin drew a long revolver and fired without taking aim. Ganimard put his hand to his hat: the bullet had passed through it.

"What do you think of that, Ganimard! Ah! that's a real revolver! A genuine English bulldog. It belongs to my friend, Herlock Sholmes."

And, with a laugh, he threw the revolver to the shore, where it landed at Ganimard's feet.

Sholmes could not withhold a smile of admiration. What a torrent of youthful spirits! And how he seemed to enjoy himself! It appeared as if the sensation of peril caused him a physical pleasure; and this extraordinary man had no other purpose in life than to seek for dangers simply for the amusement it afforded him in avoiding them.

Many people had now gathered on the banks of the river, and Ganimard and his men followed the boat as it slowly floated down the stream. Lupin's capture was a mathematical certainty.

"Confess, old fellow," said Lupin, turning to the Englishman, "that you would not exchange your present position for all the gold in the Transvaal! You are now in the first row of the orchestra chairs! But, in the first place, we must have the prologue ... after which we can leap, at one bound, to the fifth act of the drama, which will represent the capture or escape of Arsène Lupin. Therefore, I am going to ask you a plain question, to which I request a plain answer—a simple yes or no. Will you renounce this affair? At present I can repair the damage you have done; later it will be beyond my power. Is it a bargain?"

"No."

Lupin's face showed his disappointment and annoyance. He continued:

"I insist. More for your sake than my own, I insist, because I am certain you will be the first to regret your intervention. For the last time, yes or no?"

"No."

Lupin stooped down, removed one of the boards in the bottom of the boat, and, for some minutes, was engaged in a work the nature of which Sholmes could not discern. Then he arose, seated himself beside the Englishman, and said:

"I believe, monsieur, that we came to the river to-day for the same purpose: to recover the object which Bresson threw away. For my part I had invited a few friends to join me here, and I was on the point of making an examination of the bed of the river when my friends announced your approach. I confess that the news did not surprise me, as I have been notified every hour concerning the progress of your investigation. That was an easy matter. Whenever anything occurred in the rue Murillo that might interest me, simply a ring on the telephone and I was informed."

He stopped. The board that he had displaced in the bottom of the boat was rising and water was working into the boat all around it.

"The deuce! I didn't know how to fix it. I was afraid this old boat would leak. You are not afraid, monsieur?"

Sholmes shrugged his shoulders. Lupin continued:

"You will understand then, in those circumstances, and knowing in advance that you would be more eager to seek a battle than I would be to avoid it, I assure you I was not entirely displeased to enter into a contest of which the issue is quite certain, since I hold all the trump cards in my hand. And I desired that our meeting should be given the widest publicity in order that your defeat may be universally known, so that another Countess de Crozon or another Baron d'Imblevalle may not be tempted to solicit your aid against me. Besides, my dear monsieur—"

He stopped again and, using his half-closed hands as a lorgnette, he scanned the banks of the river.

"Mon Dieu! they have chartered a superb boat, a real war-vessel, and see how they are rowing. In five minutes they will be along-side, and I am lost. Monsieur Sholmes, a word of advice; you seize me, bind me and deliver me to the officers of the law. Does that programme please you?... Unless, in the meantime, we are shipwrecked, in which event we can do nothing but prepare our wills. What do you think?"

They exchanged looks. Sholmes now understood Lupin's scheme: he had scuttled the boat. And the water was rising. It had reached the soles of their boots. Then it covered their feet; but they did not move. It was half-way to their knees. The Englishman took out his tobacco, rolled a cigarette, and lighted it. Lupin continued to talk:

"But do not regard that offer as a confession of my weakness. I surrender to you in a battle in which I can achieve a victory in order to avoid a struggle upon a field not of my own choosing. In so doing I recognize the fact that Sholmes is the only enemy I fear, and announce my anxiety that Sholmes will not be diverted from my track. I take this opportunity to tell you these things since fate has accorded me the honor of a conversation with you. I have only one regret; it is that our conversation should have occurred while we are taking a foot-bath ... a situation that is lacking in dignity, I must confess.... What did I say? A foot-bath? It is worse than that."

The water had reached the board on which they were sitting, and the boat was gradually sinking.

Sholmes, smoking his cigarette, appeared to be calmly admiring the scenery. For nothing in the world, while face to face with that man who, while threatened by dangers, surrounded by a crowd, followed by a posse of police, maintained his equanimity and good humor, for nothing in the world would he, Sholmes, display the slightest sign of nervousness.

Each of them looked as if he might say: Should a person be disturbed by such trifles? Are not people drowned in a river every day? Is it such an unusual event as to deserve special attention? One chatted, whilst the other dreamed; both concealing their wounded pride beneath a mask of indifference.

One minute more and the boat will sink. Lupin continued his chatter:

"The important thing to know is whether we will sink before or after the arrival of the champions of the law. That is the main question. As to our shipwreck, that is a fore-gone conclusion. Now, monsieur, the hour has come in which we must make our wills. I give, devise and bequeath all my property to Herlock Sholmes, a citizen of England, for his own use and benefit. But, mon Dieu, how quickly the champions of the law are approaching! Ah! the brave fellows! It is a pleasure to watch them. Observe the precision of the oars! Ah! is it you, Brigadier Folenfant? Bravo! The idea of a war-vessel is an excellent one. I commend you to your superiors, Brigadier Folenfant.... Do you wish a medal? You shall have it. And your comrade Dieuzy, where is he?... Ah! yes, I think I see him on the left bank of the river at the head of a hundred natives. So that, if I escape shipwreck, I shall be captured on the left by Dieuzy and his natives, or, on the right, by Ganimard and the populace of Neuilly. An embarrassing dilemma!"

The boat entered an eddy; it swung around and Sholmes caught hold of the oarlocks. Lupin said to him:

"Monsieur, you should remove your coat. You will find it easier to swim without a coat. No? You refuse? Then I shall put on my own."

He donned his coat, buttoned it closely, the same as Sholmes, and said:

"What a discourteous man you are! And what a pity that you should be so stubborn in this affair, in which, of course, you display your strength, but, oh! so vainly! really, you mar your genius————"

"Monsieur Lupin," interrupted Sholmes, emerging from his silence, "you talk too much, and you frequently err through excess of confidence and through your frivolity."

"That is a severe reproach."

"Thus, without knowing it, you furnished me, only a moment ago, with the information I required."

"What! you required some information and you didn't tell me?"

"I had no occasion to ask you for it—you volunteered it. Within three hours I can deliver the key of the mystery to Monsieur d'Imblevalle. That is the only reply———"

He did not finish the sentence. The boat suddenly sank, taking both of the men down with it. It emerged immediately, with its keel in the air. Shouts were heard on either bank, succeeded by an anxious moment of silence. Then the shouts were renewed: one of the shipwrecked party had come to the surface.

It was Herlock Sholmes. He was an excellent swimmer, and struck out, with powerful strokes, for Folenfant's boat.

"Courage, Monsieur Sholmes," shouted Folenfant; "we are here. Keep it up ... we will get you ... a little more, Monsieur Sholmes ... catch the rope."

The Englishman seized the rope they had thrown to him. But, while they were hauling him into the boat, he heard a voice behind him, saying:

"The key of the mystery, monsieur, yes, you shall have it. I am astonished that you haven't got it already. What then? What good will it do you? By that time you will have lost the battle...."

Now comfortably installed astride the keel of the boat, Lupin continued his speech with solemn gestures, as if he hoped to convince his adversary.

"You must understand, my dear Sholmes, there is nothing to be done, absolutely nothing. You find yourself in the deplorable position of a gentleman———"

"Surrender, Lupin!" shouted Folenfant.

"You are an ill-bred fellow, Folenfant, to interrupt me in the middle of a sentence. I was saying———"

"Surrender, Lupin!"

"Oh! parbleu! Brigadier Folenfant, a man surrenders only when he is in danger. Surely, you do not pretend to say that I am in any danger."

"For the last time, Lupin, I call on you to surrender."

"Brigadier Folenfant, you have no intention of killing me; you may wish to wound me since you are afraid I may escape. But if by chance the wound prove mortal! Just think of your remorse! It would embitter your old age."

The shot was fired.

Lupin staggered, clutched at the keel of the boat for a moment, then let go and disappeared.

It was exactly three o'clock when the foregoing events transpired. Precisely at six o'clock, as he had foretold, Herlock Sholmes, dressed in trousers that were too short and a coat that was too small, which he had borrowed from an innkeeper at Neuilly, wearing a cap and a flannel shirt, entered the boudoir in the Rue Murillo, after having sent word to Monsieur and Madame d'Imblevalle that he desired an interview.

They found him walking up and down the room. And he looked so ludicrous in his strange costume that they could scarcely suppress their mirth. With pensive air and stooped shoulders, he walked like an automaton from the window to the door and from the door to the window, taking each time the same number of steps, and turning each time in the same manner.

He stopped, picked up a small ornament, examined it mechanically, and resumed his walk. At last, planting himself before them, he asked:

"Is Mademoiselle here?"

"Yes, she is in the garden with the children.'"

"I wish Mademoiselle to be present at this interview."

"Is it necessary——"

"Have a little patience, monsieur. From the facts I am going to present to you, you will see the necessity for her presence here."

"Very well. Suzanne, will you call her?"

Madame d'Imblevalle arose, went out, and returned almost immediately, accompanied by Alice Demun. Mademoiselle, who was a trifle paler than usual, remained standing, leaning against a table, and without even asking why she had been called. Sholmes did not look at her, but, suddenly turning toward Monsieur d'Imblevalle, he said, in a tone which did not admit of a reply:

"After several days' investigation, monsieur, I must repeat what I told you when I first came here: the Jewish lamp was stolen by some one living in the house."

"The name of the guilty party?"

"I know it."

"Your proof?"

"I have sufficient to establish that fact."

"But we require more than that. We desire the restoration of the stolen goods."

"The Jewish lamp? It is in my possession."

"The opal necklace? The snuff-box?"

"The opal necklace, the snuff-box, and all the goods stolen on the second occasion are in my possession."

Sholmes delighted in these dramatic dialogues, and it pleased him to announce his victories in that curt manner. The baron and his wife were amazed, and looked at Sholmes with a silent curiosity, which was the highest praise.

He related to them, very minutely, what he had done during those three days. He told of his discovery of the alphabet book, wrote upon a sheet of paper the sentence formed by the missing letters, then related the journey of Bresson to the bank of the river and the suicide of the adventurer, and, finally, his struggle with Lupin, the shipwreck, and the disappearance of Lupin. When he had finished, the baron said, in a low voice:

"Now, you have told us everything except the name of the guilty party. Whom do you accuse?"

"I accuse the person who cut the letters from the alphabet book, and communicated with Arsène Lupin by means of those letters."

"How do you know that such correspondence was carried on with Arsène Lupin?"

"My information comes from Lupin himself."

He produced a piece of paper that was wet and crumpled. It was the page which Lupin had torn from his memorandum-book, and upon which he had written the phrase.

"And you will notice," said Sholmes, with satisfaction, "that he was not obliged to give me that sheet of paper, and, in that way, disclose his identity. Simple childishness on his part, and yet it gave me exactly the information I desired."

"What was it?" asked the baron. "I don't understand."

Sholmes took a pencil and made a fresh copy of the letters and figures.

"CDEHNOPRZEO—237."

"Well?" said the baron; "it is the formula you showed me yourself."

"No. If you had turned and returned that formula in every way, as I have done, you would have seen at first glance that this formula is not like the first one."

"In what respect do they differ?"

"This one has two more letters—an E and an O."

"Really; I hadn't noticed that."

"Join those two letters to the C and the H which remained after forming the word 'respondez,' and you will agree with me that the only possible word is ECHO."

"What does that mean?"

"It refers to the *Echo de France*, Lupin's newspaper, his official organ, the one in which he publishes his communications. Reply in the *Echo de France*, in the personal advertisements, under number 237. That is the key to the mystery, and Arsène Lupin was kind enough to furnish it to me. I went to the newspaper office."

"What did you find there?"

"I found the entire story of the relations between Arsène Lupin and his accomplice."

Sholmes produced seven newspapers which he opened at the fourth page and pointed to the following lines:

1. Ars. Lup. Lady implores protection. 540.

2. 540. Awaiting particulars. A.L.

3. A.L. Under domin. enemy. Lost.

4. 540. Write address. Will make investigation.

5. A.L. Murillo.

6. 540. Park three o'clock. Violets.

7. 237. Understand. Sat. Will be Sun. morn. park.

"And you call that the whole story!" exclaimed the baron.

"Yes, and if you will listen to me for a few minutes, I think I can convince you. In the first place, a lady who signs herself 540 implores the protection of Arsène Lupin, who replies by asking for particulars. The lady replies that she is under the domination of an enemy—who is Bresson, no doubt—and that she is lost if some one does not come to her assistance. Lupin is suspicious and does not yet venture to appoint an interview with the unknown woman, demands the address and proposes to make an investigation. The lady hesitates for four days—look at the dates—finally, under stress of circumstances and influenced by Bresson's threats, she gives the name of the street—Murillo. Next day, Arsène Lupin announces that he will be in the Park Monceau at three o'clock, and asks his unknown correspondent to wear a bouquet of violets as a means of identification. Then there is a lapse of eight days in the correspondence. Arsène Lupin and the lady do not require to correspond through the newspaper now, as they see each other or write directly. The scheme is arranged in this way: in order to satisfy Bresson's demands, the lady is to carry off the Jewish lamp. The date is not yet fixed. The lady who, as a matter of prudence, corresponds by means of letters cut out of a book, decides on Saturday and adds: *Reply Echo 237.* Lupin replies that it is understood and that he will be in the park on Sunday morning. Sunday morning, the theft takes place."

"Really, that is an excellent chain of circumstantial evidence and every link is complete," said the baron.

"The theft has taken place," continued Sholmes. "The lady goes out on Sunday morning, tells Lupin what she has done, and carries the Jewish lamp to Bresson. Everything occurs then exactly as Lupin had foreseen. The officers of the law, deceived by an open window, four holes in the ground and two scratches on the balcony railing, immediately advance the theory that the theft was committed by a burglar. The lady is safe."

"Yes, I confess the theory was a logical one," said the baron. "But the second theft—"

"The second theft was provoked by the first. The newspapers having related how the Jewish lamp had disappeared, some one conceived the idea of repeating the crime and carrying away what had been left. This time, it was not a simulated theft, but a real one, a genuine burglary, with ladders and other paraphernalia—"

"Lupin, of course—"

"No. Lupin does not act so stupidly. He doesn't fire at people for trifling reasons."

"Then, who was it?"

"Bresson, no doubt, and unknown to the lady whom he had menaced. It was Bresson who entered here; it was Bresson that I pursued; it was Bresson who wounded poor Wilson."

"Are you sure of it?"

"Absolutely. One of Bresson's accomplices wrote to him yesterday, before his suicide, a letter which proves that negotiations were pending between this accomplice and Lupin for the restitution of all the articles stolen from your house. Lupin demanded everything, '*the first thing* (that is, the Jewish lamp) *as well as those of the second affair.*' Moreover, he was watching Bresson. When the latter returned from the river last night, one of Lupin's men followed him as well as we."

"What was Bresson doing at the river?"

"Having been warned of the progress of my investigations———"

"Warned! by whom?"

"By the same lady, who justly feared that the discovery of the Jewish lamp would lead to the discovery of her own adventure. Thereupon, Bresson, having been warned, made into a package all the things that could compromise him and threw them into a place where he thought he could get them again when the danger was past. It was after his return, tracked by Ganimard and myself, having, no doubt, other sins on his conscience, that he lost his head and killed himself."

"But what did the package contain?"

"The Jewish lamp and your other ornaments."

"Then, they are not in your possession?"

"Immediately after Lupin's disappearance, I profited by the bath he had forced upon me, went to the spot selected by Bresson, where I found the stolen articles wrapped in some soiled linen. They are there, on the table."

Without a word, the baron cut the cord, tore open the wet linen, picked out the lamp, turned a screw in the foot, then divided the bowl of the lamp which opened in two equal parts and there he found the golden chimera, set with rubies and emeralds.

It was intact.

There was in that scene, so natural in appearance and which consisted of a simple exposition of facts, something which rendered it frightfully tragic— it was the formal, direct, irrefutable accusation that Sholmes launched in each of his words against Mademoiselle. And it was also the impressive silence of Alice Demun.

During that long, cruel accumulation of accusing circumstances heaped one upon another, not a muscle of her face had moved, not a trace of revolt or fear had marred the serenity of her limpid eyes. What were her thoughts. And, especially, what was she going to say at the solemn moment when it would become necessary for her to speak and defend herself in order to break the chain of evidence that Herlock Sholmes had so cleverly woven around her?

That moment had come, but the girl was silent.

"Speak! Speak!" cried Mon. d'Imblevalle.

She did not speak. So he insisted:

"One word will clear you. One word of denial, and I will believe you."

That word, she would not utter.

The baron paced to and fro in his excitement; then, addressing Sholmes, he said:

"No, monsieur, I cannot believe it, I do not believe it. There are impossible crimes! and this is opposed to all I know and to all that I have seen during the past year. No, I cannot believe it."

He placed his hand on the Englishman's shoulder, and said:

"But you yourself, monsieur, are you absolutely certain that you are right?"

Sholmes hesitated, like a man on whom a sudden demand is made and cannot frame an immediate reply. Then he smiled, and said:

"Only the person whom I accuse, by reason of her situation in your house, could know that the Jewish lamp contained that magnificent jewel."

"I cannot believe it," repeated the baron.

"Ask her."

It was, really, the very thing he would not have done, blinded by the confidence the girl had inspired in him. But he could no longer refrain from doing it. He approached her and, looking into her eyes, said:

"Was it you, mademoiselle? Was it you who took the jewel? Was it you who corresponded with Arsène Lupin and committed the theft?"

"It was I, monsieur," she replied.

She did not drop her head. Her face displayed no sign of shame or fear.

"Is it possible?" murmured Mon. d'Imblevalle. "I would never have believed it.... You are the last person in the world that I would have suspected. How did you do it?"

"I did it exactly as Monsieur Sholmes has told it. On Saturday night I came to the boudoir, took the lamp, and, in the morning I carried it ... to that man."

"No," said the baron; "what you pretend to have done is impossible."

"Impossible—why?"

"Because, in the morning I found the door of the boudoir bolted."

She blushed, and looked at Sholmes as if seeking his counsel. Sholmes was astonished at her embarrassment. Had she nothing to say? Did the confessions, which had corroborated the report that he, Sholmes, had made concerning the theft of the Jewish lamp, merely serve to mask a lie? Was she misleading them by a false confession?

The baron continued:

"That door was locked. I found the door exactly as I had left it the night before. If you entered by that door, as you pretend, some one must have opened it from the interior—that is to say, from the boudoir or from our chamber. Now, there was no one inside these two rooms ... there was no one except my wife and myself."

Sholmes bowed his head and covered his face with his hands in order to conceal his emotion. A sudden light had entered his mind, that startled him and made him exceedingly uncomfortable. Everything was revealed to him, like the sudden lifting of a fog from the morning landscape. He was annoyed as well as ashamed, because his deductions were fallacious and his entire theory was wrong.

Alice Demun was innocent!

Alice Demun was innocent. That proposition explained the embarrassment he had experienced from the beginning in directing the terrible accusation against that young girl. Now, he saw the truth; he knew it. After a few seconds, he raised his head, and looked at Madame d'Imblevalle as naturally as he could. She was pale—with that unusual pallor which invades us in the relentless moments of our lives. Her hands, which she endeavored to conceal, were trembling as if stricken with palsy.

"One minute more," thought Sholmes, "and she will betray herself."

He placed himself between her and her husband in the desire to avert the awful danger which, *through his fault*, now threatened that man and woman. But, at sight of the baron, he was shocked to the very centre of his soul. The same dreadful idea had entered the mind of Monsieur d'Imblevalle. The same thought was at work in the brain of the husband. He understood, also! He saw the truth!

In desperation, Alice Demun hurled herself against the implacable truth, saying:

"You are right, monsieur. I made a mistake. I did not enter by this door. I came through the garden and the vestibule ... by aid of a ladder—"

It was a supreme effort of true devotion. But a useless effort! The words rang false. The voice did not carry conviction, and the poor girl no longer displayed those clear, fearless eyes and that natural air of innocence which had served her so well. Now, she bowed her head—vanquished.

The silence became painful. Madame d'Imblevalle was waiting for her husband's next move, overwhelmed with anxiety and fear. The baron appeared to be struggling against the dreadful suspicion, as if he would not submit to the overthrow of his happiness. Finally, he said to his wife:

"Speak! Explain!"

"I have nothing to tell you," she replied, in a very low voice, and with features drawn by anguish.

"So, then ... Mademoiselle...."

"Mademoiselle saved me ... through devotion ... through affection ... and accused herself...."

"Saved you from what? From whom?"

"From that man."

"Bresson?"

"Yes; it was I whom he held in fear by threats.... I met him at one of my friends'.... and I was foolish enough to listen to him. Oh! there was nothing that you cannot pardon. But I wrote him two letters ... letters which you will see.... I had to buy them back ... you know how.... Oh! have pity on me!... I have suffered so much!"

"You! You! Suzanne!"

He raised his clenched fists, ready to strike her, ready to kill her. But he dropped his arms, and murmured:

"You, Suzanne.... You!... Is it possible?"

By short detached sentences, she related the heartrending story, her dreadful awakening to the infamy of the man, her remorse, her fear, and she also told of Alice's devotion; how the young girl divined the sorrow of her mistress, wormed a confession out of her, wrote to Lupin, and devised the scheme of the theft in order to save her from Bresson.

"You, Suzanne, you," repeated Monsieur d'Imblevalle, bowed with grief and shame.... "How could you?"

On the same evening, the steamer "City of London," which plies between Calais and Dover, was gliding slowly over the smooth sea. The night was dark; the wind was fainter than a zephyr. The majority of the passengers had retired to their cabins; but a few, more intrepid, were promenading on the deck or sleeping in large rocking-chairs, wrapped in their travelling-rugs. One could see, here and there, the light of a cigar, and one could hear, mingled with the soft murmur of the breeze, the faint sound of voices which were carefully subdued to harmonize with the deep silence of the night.

One of the passengers, who had been pacing to and fro upon the deck, stopped before a woman who was lying on a bench, scrutinized her, and, when she moved a little, he said:

"I thought you were asleep, Mademoiselle Alice."

"No, Monsieur Sholmes, I am not sleepy. I was thinking."

"Of what? If I may be so bold as to inquire?"

"I was thinking of Madame d'Imblevalle. She must be very unhappy. Her life is ruined."

"Oh! no, no," he replied quickly. "Her mistake was not a serious one. Monsieur d'Imblevalle will forgive and forget it. Why, even before we left, his manner toward her had softened."

"Perhaps ... but he will remember it for a long time ... and she will suffer a great deal."

"You love her?"

"Very much. It was my love for her that gave me strength to smile when I was trembling from fear, that gave me courage to look in your face when I desired to hide from your sight."

"And you are sorry to leave her?"

"Yes, very sorry. I have no relatives, no friends—but her."

"You will have friends," said the Englishman, who was affected by her sorrow. "I have promised that. I have relatives ... and some influence. I assure you that you will have no cause to regret coming to England."

"That may be, monsieur, but Madame d'Imblevalle will not be there."

Herlock Sholmes resumed his promenade upon the deck. After a few minutes, he took a seat near his travelling companion, filled his pipe, and struck four matches in a vain effort to light it. Then, as he had no more matches, he arose and said to a gentleman who was sitting near him:

"May I trouble you for a match?"

The gentleman opened a box of matches and struck one. The flame lighted up his face. Sholmes recognized him—it was Arsène Lupin.

If the Englishman had not given an almost imperceptible movement of surprise, Lupin would have supposed that his presence on board had been known to Sholmes, so well did he control his feelings and so natural was the easy manner in which he extended his hand to his adversary.

"How's the good health, Monsieur Lupin?"

"Bravo!" exclaimed Lupin, who could not repress a cry of admiration at the Englishman's sang-froid.

"Bravo? and why?"

"Why? Because I appear before you like a ghost, only a few hours after you saw me drowned in the Seine; and through pride—a quality that is essentially English—you evince not the slightest surprise. You greet me as a matter of course. Ah! I repeat: Bravo! Admirable!"

"There is nothing remarkable about it. From the manner in which you fell from the boat, I knew very well that you fell voluntarily, and that the bullet had not touched you."

"And you went away without knowing what had become of me?"

"What had become of you? Why, I knew that. There were at least five hundred people on the two banks of the river within a space of half-a-mile. If you escaped death, your capture was certain."

"And yet I am here."

"Monsieur Lupin, there are two men in the world at whom I am never astonished: in the first place, myself—and then, Arsène Lupin."

The treaty of peace was concluded.

If Sholmes had not been successful in his contests with Arsène Lupin; if Lupin remained the only enemy whose capture he must never hope to accomplish; if, in the course of their struggles, he had not always displayed a superiority, the Englishman had, none the less, by means of his extraordinary intuition and tenacity, succeeded in recovering the Jewish lamp as well as the blue diamond.

This time, perhaps, the finish had not been so brilliant, especially from the stand-point of the public spectators, since Sholmes was obliged to maintain a discreet silence in regard to the circumstances in which the Jewish lamp had been recovered, and to announce that he did not know the name of the thief. But as man to man, Arsène Lupin against Herlock Sholmes, detective against burglar, there was neither victor nor vanquished. Each of them had won corresponding victories.

Therefore they could now converse as courteous adversaries who had lain down their arms and held each other in high regard.

At Sholmes' request, Arsène Lupin related the strange story of his escape.

"If I may dignify it by calling it an escape," he said. "It was so simple! My friends were watching for me, as I had asked them to meet me there to recover the Jewish lamp. So, after remaining a good half-hour under the overturned boat, I took advantage of an occasion when Folenfant and his men were searching for my dead body along the bank of the river, to climb on top of the boat. Then my friends simply picked me up as they passed by in their motor-boat, and we sailed away under the staring eyes of an astonished multitude, including Ganimard and Folenfant."

"Very good," exclaimed Sholmes, "very neatly played. And now you have some business in England?"

"Yes, some accounts to square up.... But I forgot ... what about Monsieur d'Imblevalle?"

"He knows everything."

"Ah! my dear Sholmes, what did I tell you? The wrong is now irreparable. Would it not have been better to have allowed me to carry out the affair in my own way? In a day or two more, I should have recovered the stolen goods from Bresson, restored them to Monsieur d'Imblevalle, and those two honest citizens would have lived together in peace and happiness ever after. Instead of that—"

"Instead of that," said Sholmes, sneeringly, "I have mixed the cards and sown the seeds of discord in the bosom of a family that was under your protection."

"Mon Dieu! of course, I was protecting them. Must a person steal, cheat and wrong all the time?"

"Then you do good, also?"

"When I have the time. Besides, I find it amusing. Now, for instance, in our last adventure, I found it extremely diverting that I should be the good genius seeking to help and save unfortunate mortals, while you were the evil genius who dispensed only despair and tears."

"Tears! Tears!" protested Sholmes.

"Certainly! The d'Imblevalle household is demolished, and Alice Demun weeps."

"She could not remain any longer. Ganimard would have discovered her some day, and, through her, reached Madame d'Imblevalle."

"Quite right, monsieur; but whose fault is it?"

Two men passed by. Sholmes said to Lupin, in a friendly tone:

"Do you know those gentlemen?"

"I thought I recognized one of them as the captain of the steamer."

"And the other?"

"I don't know."

"It is Austin Gilett, who occupies in London a position similar to that of Monsieur Dudouis in Paris."

"Ah! how fortunate! Will you be so kind as to introduce me? Monsieur Dudouis is one of my best friends, and I shall be delighted to say as much of Monsieur Austin Gilett."

The two gentlemen passed again.

"And if I should take you at your word, Monsieur Lupin?" said Sholmes, rising, and seizing Lupin's wrist with a hand of iron.

"Why do you grasp me so tightly, monsieur? I am quite willing to follow you."

In fact, he allowed himself to be dragged along without the least resistance. The two gentlemen were disappearing from sight. Sholmes quickened his pace. His finger-nails even sank into Lupin's flesh.

"Come! Come!" he exclaimed, with a sort of feverish haste, in harmony with his action. "Come! quicker than that."

But he stopped suddenly. Alice Demun was following them.

"What are you doing, Mademoiselle? You need not come. You must not come!"

It was Lupin who replied:

"You will notice, monsieur, that she is not coming of her own free will. I am holding her wrist in the same tight grasp that you have on mine."

"Why!"

"Because I wish to present her also. Her part in the affair of the Jewish lamp is much more important than mine. Accomplice of Arsène Lupin, accomplice of Bresson, she has a right to tell her adventure with the Baroness d'Imblevalle—which will deeply interest Monsieur Gilett as an officer of the law. And by introducing her also, you will have carried your gracious intervention to the very limit, my dear Sholmes."

The Englishman released his hold on his prisoner's wrist. Lupin liberated Mademoiselle.

They stood looking at each other for a few seconds, silently and motionless. Then Sholmes returned to the bench and sat down, followed by Lupin and the girl. After a long silence, Lupin said: "You see, monsieur, whatever we may do, we will never be on the same side. You are on one side of the fence; I am on the other. We can exchange greetings, shake hands, converse a moment, but the fence is always there. You will remain Herlock Sholmes, detective, and I, Arsène Lupin, gentleman-burglar. And Herlock Sholmes will ever obey, more or less spontaneously, with more or less propriety, his instinct as a detective, which is to pursue the burglar and run him down, if possible. And Arsène Lupin, in obedience to his burglarious instinct, will always be occupied in avoiding the reach of the detective, and making sport of the detective, if he can do it. And, this time, he can do it. Ha-ha-ha!"

He burst into a loud laugh, cunning, cruel and odious.

Then, suddenly becoming serious, he addressed Alice Demun:

"You may be sure, mademoiselle, even when reduced to the last extremity, I shall not betray you. Arsène Lupin never betrays anyone—especially those whom he loves and admires. And, may I be permitted to say, I love and admire the brave, dear woman you have proved yourself to be."

He took from his pocket a visiting card, tore it in two, gave one-half of it to the girl, as he said, in a voice shaken with emotion:

"If Monsieur Sholmes' plans for you do not succeed, mademoiselle, go to Lady Strongborough—you can easily find her address—and give her that half of the card, and, at the same time, say to her: *Faithful friend*. Lady Strongborough will show you the true devotion of a sister."

"Thank you," said the girl; "I shall see her to-morrow."

"And now, Monsieur Sholmes," exclaimed Lupin, with the satisfied air of a gentleman who has fulfilled his duty, "I will say good-night. We will not land for an hour yet, so I will get that much rest."

He lay down on the bench, with his hands beneath his head.

In a short time the high cliffs of the English coast loomed up in the increasing light of a new-born day. The passengers emerged from the cabins and crowded the deck, eagerly gazing on the approaching shore. Austin Gilette passed by, accompanied by two men whom Sholmes recognized as sleuths from Scotland Yard.

Lupin was asleep, on his bench.

THE END.

BOOK THREE.
ARSENE LUPIN

I. THE MILLIONAIRE'S DAUGHTER

The rays of the September sun flooded the great halls of the old chateau of the Dukes of Charmerace, lighting up with their mellow glow the spoils of so many ages and many lands, jumbled together with the execrable taste which so often afflicts those whose only standard of value is money. The golden light warmed the panelled walls and old furniture to a dull lustre, and gave back to the fading gilt of the First Empire chairs and couches something of its old brightness. It illumined the long line of pictures on the walls, pictures of dead and gone Charmeraces, the stern or debonair faces of the men, soldiers, statesmen, dandies, the gentle or imperious faces of beautiful women. It flashed back from armour of brightly polished steel, and drew dull gleams from armour of bronze. The hues of rare porcelain, of the rich inlays of Oriental or Renaissance cabinets, mingled with the hues of the pictures, the tapestry, the Persian rugs about the polished floor to fill the hall with a rich glow of colour.

But of all the beautiful and precious things which the sun-rays warmed to a clearer beauty, the face of the girl who sat writing at a table in front of the long windows, which opened on to the centuries-old turf of the broad terrace, was the most beautiful and the most precious.

It was a delicate, almost frail, beauty. Her skin was clear with the transparent lustre of old porcelain, and her pale cheeks were only tinted with the pink of the faintest roses. Her straight nose was delicately cut, her rounded chin admirably moulded. A lover of beauty would have been at a loss whether more to admire her clear, germander eyes, so melting and so adorable, or the sensitive mouth, with its rather full lips, inviting all the kisses. But assuredly he would have been grieved by the perpetual air of sadness which rested on the beautiful face—the wistful melancholy of the Slav, deepened by something of personal misfortune and suffering.

Her face was framed by a mass of soft fair hair, shot with strands of gold where the sunlight fell on it; and little curls, rebellious to the comb, strayed over her white forehead, tiny feathers of gold.

She was addressing envelopes, and a long list of names lay on her left hand. When she had addressed an envelope, she slipped into it a wedding-card. On each was printed:

"M. Gournay-Martin has the honour to inform
you of the marriage of his daughter
Germaine to the Duke of Charmerace."

She wrote steadily on, adding envelope after envelope to the pile ready for the post, which rose in front of her. But now and again, when the flushed and laughing girls who were playing lawn-tennis on the terrace, raised their voices higher than usual as they called the score, and distracted her attention from her work, her gaze strayed through the open window and lingered on them wistfully; and as her eyes came back to her task she sighed with so faint a wistfulness that she hardly knew she sighed. Then a voice from the terrace cried, "Sonia! Sonia!"

"Yes. Mlle. Germaine?" answered the writing girl.

"Tea! Order tea, will you?" cried the voice, a petulant voice, rather harsh to the ear.

"Very well, Mlle. Germaine," said Sonia; and having finished addressing the envelope under her pen, she laid it on the pile ready to be posted, and, crossing the room to the old, wide fireplace, she rang the bell.

She stood by the fireplace a moment, restoring to its place a rose which had fallen from a vase on the mantelpiece; and her attitude, as with arms upraised she arranged the flowers, displayed the delightful line of a slender figure. As she let fall her arms to her side, a footman entered the room.

"Will you please bring the tea, Alfred," she said in a charming voice of that pure, bell-like tone which has been Nature's most precious gift to but a few of the greatest actresses.

"For how many, miss?" said Alfred.

"For four—unless your master has come back."

"Oh, no; he's not back yet, miss. He went in the car to Rennes to lunch; and it's a good many miles away. He won't be back for another hour."

"And the Duke—he's not back from his ride yet, is he?"

"Not yet, miss," said Alfred, turning to go.

"One moment," said Sonia. "Have all of you got your things packed for the journey to Paris? You will have to start soon, you know. Are all the maids ready?"

"Well, all the men are ready, I know, miss. But about the maids, miss, I can't say. They've been bustling about all day; but it takes them longer than it does us."

"Tell them to hurry up; and be as quick as you can with the tea, please," said Sonia.

Alfred went out of the room; Sonia went back to the writing-table. She did not take up her pen; she took up one of the wedding-cards; and her lips moved slowly as she read it in a pondering depression.

The petulant, imperious voice broke in upon her musing.

"Whatever are you doing, Sonia? Aren't you getting on with those letters?" it cried angrily; and Germaine Gournay-Martin came through the long window into the hall.

The heiress to the Gournay-Martin millions carried her tennis racquet in her hand; and her rosy cheeks were flushed redder than ever by the game. She was a pretty girl in a striking, high-coloured, rather obvious way—the very foil to Sonia's delicate beauty. Her lips were a little too thin, her eyes too shallow; and together they gave her a rather hard air, in strongest contrast to the gentle, sympathetic face of Sonia.

The two friends with whom Germaine had been playing tennis followed her into the hall: Jeanne Gautier, tall, sallow, dark, with a somewhat malicious air; Marie Bullier, short, round, commonplace, and sentimental.

They came to the table at which Sonia was at work; and pointing to the pile of envelopes, Marie said, "Are these all wedding-cards?"

"Yes; and we've only got to the letter V," said Germaine, frowning at Sonia.

"Princesse de Vernan—Duchesse de Vauvieuse—Marquess—Marchioness? You've invited the whole Faubourg Saint-Germain," said Marie, shuffling the pile of envelopes with an envious air.

"You'll know very few people at your wedding," said Jeanne, with a spiteful little giggle.

"I beg your pardon, my dear," said Germaine boastfully. "Madame de Relzieres, my fiance's cousin, gave an At Home the other day in my honour. At it she introduced half Paris to me—the Paris I'm destined to know, the Paris you'll see in my drawing-rooms."

"But we shall no longer be fit friends for you when you're the Duchess of Charmerace," said Jeanne.

"Why?" said Germaine; and then she added quickly, "Above everything, Sonia, don't forget Veaulegise, 33, University Street—33, University Street."

"Veaulegise—33, University Street," said Sonia, taking a fresh envelope, and beginning to address it.

"Wait—wait! don't close the envelope. I'm wondering whether Veaulegise ought to have a cross, a double cross, or a triple cross," said Germaine, with an air of extreme importance.

"What's that?" cried Marie and Jeanne together.

"A single cross means an invitation to the church, a double cross an invitation to the marriage and the wedding-breakfast, and the triple cross means an invitation to the marriage, the breakfast, and the signing of the marriage-contract. What do you think the Duchess of Veauleglise ought to have?"

"Don't ask me. I haven't the honour of knowing that great lady," cried Jeanne.

"Nor I," said Marie.

"Nor I," said Germaine. "But I have here the visiting-list of the late Duchess of Charmerace, Jacques' mother. The two duchesses were on excellent terms. Besides the Duchess of Veauleglise is rather worn-out, but greatly admired for her piety. She goes to early service three times a week."

"Then put three crosses," said Jeanne.

"I shouldn't," said Marie quickly. "In your place, my dear, I shouldn't risk a slip. I should ask my fiance's advice. He knows this world."

"Oh, goodness—my fiance! He doesn't care a rap about this kind of thing. He has changed so in the last seven years. Seven years ago he took nothing seriously. Why, he set off on an expedition to the South Pole—just to show off. Oh, in those days he was truly a duke."

"And to-day?" said Jeanne.

"Oh, to-day he's a regular slow-coach. Society gets on his nerves. He's as sober as a judge," said Germaine.

"He's as gay as a lark," said Sonia, in sudden protest.

Germaine pouted at her, and said: "Oh, he's gay enough when he's making fun of people. But apart from that he's as sober as a judge."

"Your father must be delighted with the change," said Jeanne.

"Naturally he's delighted. Why, he's lunching at Rennes to-day with the Minister, with the sole object of getting Jacques decorated."

"Well, the Legion of Honour is a fine thing to have," said Marie.

"My dear! The Legion of Honour is all very well for middle-class people, but it's quite out of place for a duke!" cried Germaine.

Alfred came in, bearing the tea-tray, and set it on a little table near that at which Sonia was sitting.

Germaine, who was feeling too important to sit still, was walking up and down the room. Suddenly she stopped short, and pointing to a silver statuette which stood on the piano, she said, "What's this? Why is this statuette here?"

314

"Why, when we came in, it was on the cabinet, in its usual place," said Sonia in some astonishment.

"Did you come into the hall while we were out in the garden, Alfred?" said Germaine to the footman.

"No, miss," said Alfred.

"But some one must have come into it," Germaine persisted.

"I've not heard any one. I was in my pantry," said Alfred.

"It's very odd," said Germaine.

"It is odd," said Sonia. "Statuettes don't move about of themselves."

All of them stared at the statuette as if they expected it to move again forthwith, under their very eyes. Then Alfred put it back in its usual place on one of the cabinets, and went out of the room.

Sonia poured out the tea; and over it they babbled about the coming marriage, the frocks they would wear at it, and the presents Germaine had already received. That reminded her to ask Sonia if any one had yet telephoned from her father's house in Paris; and Sonia said that no one had.

"That's very annoying," said Germaine. "It shows that nobody has sent me a present to-day."

Pouting, she shrugged her shoulders with an air of a spoiled child, which sat but poorly on a well-developed young woman of twenty-three.

"It's Sunday. The shops don't deliver things on Sunday," said Sonia gently.

But Germaine still pouted like a spoiled child.

"Isn't your beautiful Duke coming to have tea with us?" said Jeanne a little anxiously.

"Oh, yes; I'm expecting him at half-past four. He had to go for a ride with the two Du Buits. They're coming to tea here, too," said Germaine.

"Gone for a ride with the two Du Buits? But when?" cried Marie quickly.

"This afternoon."

"He can't be," said Marie. "My brother went to the Du Buits' house after lunch, to see Andre and Georges. They went for a drive this morning, and won't be back till late to-night."

"Well, but—but why did the Duke tell me so?" said Germaine, knitting her brow with a puzzled air.

"If I were you, I should inquire into this thoroughly. Dukes—well, we know what dukes are—it will be just as well to keep an eye on him," said Jeanne maliciously.

Germaine flushed quickly; and her eyes flashed. "Thank you. I have every confidence in Jacques. I am absolutely sure of him," she said angrily.

"Oh, well—if you're sure, it's all right," said Jeanne.

The ringing of the telephone-bell made a fortunate diversion.

Germaine rushed to it, clapped the receiver to her ear, and cried: "Hello, is that you, Pierre? ... Oh, it's Victoire, is it? ... Ah, some presents have come, have they? ... Well, well, what are they? ... What! a paper-knife—another paper-knife! ... Another Louis XVI. inkstand—oh, bother! ... Who are they from? ... Oh, from the Countess Rudolph and the Baron de Valery." Her voice rose high, thrilling with pride.

Then she turned her face to her friends, with the receiver still at her ear, and cried: "Oh, girls, a pearl necklace too! A large one! The pearls are big ones!"

"How jolly!" said Marie.

"Who sent it?" said Germaine, turning to the telephone again. "Oh, a friend of papa's," she added in a tone of disappointment. "Never mind, after all it's a pearl necklace. You'll be sure and lock the doors carefully, Victoire, won't you? And lock up the necklace in the secret cupboard.... Yes; thanks very much, Victoire. I shall see you to-morrow."

She hung up the receiver, and came away from the telephone frowning.

"It's preposterous!" she said pettishly. "Papa's friends and relations give me marvellous presents, and all the swells send me paper-knives. It's all Jacques' fault. He's above all this kind of thing. The Faubourg Saint-Germain hardly knows that we're engaged."

"He doesn't go about advertising it," said Jeanne, smiling.

"You're joking, but all the same what you say is true," said Germaine. "That's exactly what his cousin Madame de Relzieres said to me the other day at the At Home she gave in my honour—wasn't it, Sonia?" And she walked to the window, and, turning her back on them, stared out of it.

"She HAS got her mouth full of that At Home," said Jeanne to Marie in a low voice.

There was an awkward silence. Marie broke it:

"Speaking of Madame de Relzieres, do you know that she is on pins and needles with anxiety? Her son is fighting a duel to-day," she said.

"With whom?" said Sonia.

"No one knows. She got hold of a letter from the seconds," said Marie.

"My mind is quite at rest about Relzieres," said Germaine. "He's a first-class swordsman. No one could beat him."

Sonia did not seem to share her freedom from anxiety. Her forehead was puckered in little lines of perplexity, as if she were puzzling out some problem; and there was a look of something very like fear in her gentle eyes.

"Wasn't Relzieres a great friend of your fiance at one time?" said Jeanne.

"A great friend? I should think he was," said Germaine. "Why, it was through Relzieres that we got to know Jacques."

"Where was that?" said Marie.

"Here—in this very chateau," said Germaine.

"Actually in his own house?" said Marie, in some surprise.

"Yes; actually here. Isn't life funny?" said Germaine. "If, a few months after his father's death, Jacques had not found himself hard-up, and obliged to dispose of this chateau, to raise the money for his expedition to the South Pole; and if papa and I had not wanted an historic chateau; and lastly, if papa had not suffered from rheumatism, I should not be calling myself in a month from now the Duchess of Charmerace."

"Now what on earth has your father's rheumatism got to do with your being Duchess of Charmerace?" cried Jeanne.

"Everything," said Germaine. "Papa was afraid that this chateau was damp. To prove to papa that he had nothing to fear, Jacques, en grand seigneur, offered him his hospitality, here, at Charmerace, for three weeks."

"That was truly ducal," said Marie.

"But he is always like that," said Sonia.

"Oh, he's all right in that way, little as he cares about society," said Germaine. "Well, by a miracle my father got cured of his rheumatism here. Jacques fell in love with me; papa made up his mind to buy the chateau; and I demanded the hand of Jacques in marriage."

"You did? But you were only sixteen then," said Marie, with some surprise.

"Yes; but even at sixteen a girl ought to know that a duke is a duke. I did," said Germaine. "Then since Jacques was setting out for the South Pole, and papa considered me much too young to get married, I promised Jacques to wait for his return."

"Why, it was everything that's romantic!" cried Marie.

"Romantic? Oh, yes," said Germaine; and she pouted. "But between ourselves, if I'd known that he was going to stay all that time at the South Pole—"

"That's true," broke in Marie. "To go away for three years and stay away seven—at the end of the world."

"All Germaine's beautiful youth," said Jeanne, with her malicious smile.

"Thanks!" said Germaine tartly.

"Well, you ARE twenty-three. It's the flower of one's age," said Jeanne.

"Not quite twenty-three," said Germaine hastily. "And look at the wretched luck I've had. The Duke falls ill and is treated at Montevideo. As soon as he recovers, since he's the most obstinate person in the world, he resolves to go on with the expedition. He sets out; and for an age, without a word of warning, there's no more news of him—no news of any kind. For six months, you know, we believed him dead."

"Dead? Oh, how unhappy you must have been!" said Sonia.

"Oh, don't speak of it! For six months I daren't put on a light frock," said Germaine, turning to her.

"A lot she must have cared for him," whispered Jeanne to Marie.

"Fortunately, one fine day, the letters began again. Three months ago a telegram informed us that he was coming back; and at last the Duke returned," said Germaine, with a theatrical air.

"The Duke returned," cried Jeanne, mimicking her.

"Never mind. Fancy waiting nearly seven years for one's fiance. That was constancy," said Sonia.

"Oh, you're a sentimentalist, Mlle. Kritchnoff," said Jeanne, in a tone of mockery. "It was the influence of the castle."

"What do you mean?" said Germaine.

"Oh, to own the castle of Charmerace and call oneself Mlle. Gournay-Martin—it's not worth doing. One MUST become a duchess," said Jeanne.

"Yes, yes; and for all this wonderful constancy, seven years of it, Germaine was on the point of becoming engaged to another man," said Marie, smiling.

"And he a mere baron," said Jeanne, laughing.

"What? Is that true?" said Sonia.

"Didn't you know, Mlle. Kritchnoff? She nearly became engaged to the Duke's cousin, the Baron de Relzieres. It was not nearly so grand."

"Oh, it's all very well to laugh at me; but being the cousin and heir of the Duke, Relzieres would have assumed the title, and I should have been Duchess just the same," said Germaine triumphantly.

"Evidently that was all that mattered," said Jeanne. "Well, dear, I must be off. We've promised to run in to see the Comtesse de Grosjean. You know the Comtesse de Grosjean?"

She spoke with an air of careless pride, and rose to go.

"Only by name. Papa used to know her husband on the Stock Exchange when he was still called simply M. Grosjean. For his part, papa preferred to keep his name intact," said Germaine, with quiet pride.

"Intact? That's one way of looking at it. Well, then, I'll see you in Paris. You still intend to start to-morrow?" said Jeanne.

"Yes; to-morrow morning," said Germaine.

Jeanne and Marie slipped on their dust-coats to the accompaniment of chattering and kissing, and went out of the room.

As she closed the door on them, Germaine turned to Sonia, and said: "I do hate those two girls! They're such horrible snobs."

"Oh, they're good-natured enough," said Sonia.

"Good-natured? Why, you idiot, they're just bursting with envy of me— bursting!" said Germaine. "Well, they've every reason to be," she added confidently, surveying herself in a Venetian mirror with a petted child's self-content.

II. THE COMING OF THE CHAROLAIS

Sonia went back to her table, and once more began putting wedding-cards in their envelopes and addressing them. Germaine moved restlessly about the room, fidgeting with the bric-a-brac on the cabinets, shifting the pieces about, interrupting Sonia to ask whether she preferred this arrangement or that, throwing herself into a chair to read a magazine, getting up in a couple of minutes to straighten a picture on the wall, throwing out all the while idle questions not worth answering. Ninety-nine human beings would have been irritated to exasperation by her fidgeting; Sonia endured it with a perfect patience. Five times Germaine asked her whether she should wear her heliotrope or her pink gown at a forthcoming dinner at Madame de Relzieres'. Five times Sonia said, without the slightest variation in her tone, "I think you look better in the pink." And all the while the pile of addressed envelopes rose steadily.

Presently the door opened, and Alfred stood on the threshold.

"Two gentlemen have called to see you, miss," he said.

"Ah, the two Du Buits," cried Germaine.

"They didn't give their names, miss."

"A gentleman in the prime of life and a younger one?" said Germaine.

"Yes, miss."

"I thought so. Show them in."

"Yes, miss. And have you any orders for me to give Victoire when we get to Paris?" said Alfred.

"No. Are you starting soon?"

"Yes, miss. We're all going by the seven o'clock train. It's a long way from here to Paris; we shall only reach it at nine in the morning. That will give us just time to get the house ready for you by the time you get there to-morrow evening," said Alfred.

"Is everything packed?"

"Yes, miss—everything. The cart has already taken the heavy luggage to the station. All you'll have to do is to see after your bags."

"That's all right. Show M. du Buit and his brother in," said Germaine.

She moved to a chair near the window, and disposed herself in an attitude of studied, and obviously studied, grace.

As she leant her head at a charming angle back against the tall back of the chair, her eyes fell on the window, and they opened wide.

"Why, whatever's this?" she cried, pointing to it.

"Whatever's what?" said Sonia, without raising her eyes from the envelope she was addressing.

"Why, the window. Look! one of the panes has been taken out. It looks as if it had been cut."

"So it has—just at the level of the fastening," said Sonia. And the two girls stared at the gap.

"Haven't you noticed it before?" said Germaine.

"No; the broken glass must have fallen outside," said Sonia.

The noise of the opening of the door drew their attention from the window. Two figures were advancing towards them—a short, round, tubby man of fifty-five, red-faced, bald, with bright grey eyes, which seemed to be continually dancing away from meeting the eyes of any other human being. Behind him came a slim young man, dark and grave. For all the difference in their colouring, it was clear that they were father and son: their eyes were set so close together. The son seemed to have inherited, along with her black

320

eyes, his mother's nose, thin and aquiline; the nose of the father started thin from the brow, but ended in a scarlet bulb eloquent of an exhaustive acquaintance with the vintages of the world.

Germaine rose, looking at them with an air of some surprise and uncertainty: these were not her friends, the Du Buits.

The elder man, advancing with a smiling bonhomie, bowed, and said in an adenoid voice, ingratiating of tone: "I'm M. Charolais, young ladies—M. Charolais—retired brewer—chevalier of the Legion of Honour—landowner at Rennes. Let me introduce my son." The young man bowed awkwardly. "We came from Rennes this morning, and we lunched at Kerlor's farm."

"Shall I order tea for them?" whispered Sonia.

"Gracious, no!" said Germaine sharply under her breath; then, louder, she said to M. Charolais, "And what is your object in calling?"

"We asked to see your father," said M. Charolais, smiling with broad amiability, while his eyes danced across her face, avoiding any meeting with hers. "The footman told us that M. Gournay-Martin was out, but that his daughter was at home. And we were unable, quite unable, to deny ourselves the pleasure of meeting you." With that he sat down; and his son followed his example.

Sonia and Germaine, taken aback, looked at one another in some perplexity.

"What a fine chateau, papa!" said the young man.

"Yes, my boy; it's a very fine chateau," said M. Charolais, looking round the hall with appreciative but greedy eyes.

There was a pause.

"It's a very fine chateau, young ladies," said M. Charolais.

"Yes; but excuse me, what is it you have called about?" said Germaine.

M. Charolais crossed his legs, leant back in his chair, thrust his thumbs into the arm-holes of his waistcoat, and said: "Well, we've come about the advertisement we saw in the RENNES ADVERTISER, that M. Gournay-Martin wanted to get rid of a motor-car; and my son is always saying to me, 'I should like a motor-car which rushes the hills, papa.' He means a sixty horse-power."

"We've got a sixty horse-power; but it's not for sale. My father is even using it himself to-day," said Germaine.

"Perhaps it's the car we saw in the stable-yard," said M. Charolais.

"No; that's a thirty to forty horse-power. It belongs to me. But if your son really loves rushing hills, as you say, we have a hundred horse-power car which my father wants to get rid of. Wait; where's the photograph of it, Sonia? It ought to be here somewhere."

The two girls rose, went to a table set against the wall beyond the window, and began turning over the papers with which it was loaded in the search for the photograph. They had barely turned their backs, when the hand of young Charolais shot out as swiftly as the tongue of a lizard catching a fly, closed round the silver statuette on the top of the cabinet beside him, and flashed it into his jacket pocket.

Charolais was watching the two girls; one would have said that he had eyes for nothing else, yet, without moving a muscle of his face, set in its perpetual beaming smile, he hissed in an angry whisper, "Drop it, you idiot! Put it back!"

The young man scowled askance at him.

"Curse you! Put it back!" hissed Charolais.

The young man's arm shot out with the same quickness, and the statuette stood in its place.

There was just the faintest sigh of relief from Charolais, as Germaine turned and came to him with the photograph in her hand. She gave it to him.

"Ah, here we are," he said, putting on a pair of gold-rimmed pince-nez. "A hundred horse-power car. Well, well, this is something to talk over. What's the least you'll take for it?"

"I have nothing to do with this kind of thing," cried Germaine. "You must see my father. He will be back from Rennes soon. Then you can settle the matter with him."

M. Charolais rose, and said: "Very good. We will go now, and come back presently. I'm sorry to have intruded on you, young ladies—taking up your time like this—"

"Not at all—not at all," murmured Germaine politely.

"Good-bye—good-bye," said M. Charolais; and he and his son went to the door, and bowed themselves out.

"What creatures!" said Germaine, going to the window, as the door closed behind the two visitors. "All the same, if they do buy the hundred horse-power, papa will be awfully pleased. It is odd about that pane. I wonder how it happened. It's odd too that Jacques hasn't come back yet. He told me that he would be here between half-past four and five."

"And the Du Buits have not come either," said Sonia. "But it's hardly five yet."

"Yes; that's so. The Du Buits have not come either. What on earth are you wasting your time for?" she added sharply, raising her voice. "Just finish addressing those letters while you're waiting."

"They're nearly finished," said Sonia.

"Nearly isn't quite. Get on with them, can't you!" snapped Germaine.

Sonia went back to the writing-table; just the slightest deepening of the faint pink roses in her cheeks marked her sense of Germaine's rudeness. After three years as companion to Germaine Gournay-Martin, she was well inured to millionaire manners; they had almost lost the power to move her.

Germaine dropped into a chair for twenty seconds; then flung out of it.

"Ten minutes to five!" she cried. "Jacques is late. It's the first time I've ever known him late."

She went to the window, and looked across the wide stretch of meadow-land and woodland on which the chateau, set on the very crown of the ridge, looked down. The road, running with the irritating straightness of so many of the roads of France, was visible for a full three miles. It was empty.

"Perhaps the Duke went to the Chateau de Relzieres to see his cousin—though I fancy that at bottom the Duke does not care very much for the Baron de Relzieres. They always look as though they detested one another," said Sonia, without raising her eyes from the letter she was addressing.

"You've noticed that, have you?" said Germaine. "Now, as far as Jacques is concerned—he's—he's so indifferent. None the less, when we were at the Relzieres on Thursday, I caught him quarrelling with Paul de Relzieres."

"Quarrelling?" said Sonia sharply, with a sudden uneasiness in air and eyes and voice.

"Yes; quarrelling. And they said good-bye to one another in the oddest way."

"But surely they shook hands?" said Sonia.

"Not a bit of it. They bowed as if each of them had swallowed a poker."

"Why—then—then—" said Sonia, starting up with a frightened air; and her voice stuck in her throat.

"Then what?" said Germaine, a little startled by her panic-stricken face.

"The duel! Monsieur de Relzieres' duel!" cried Sonia.

"What? You don't think it was with Jacques?"

"I don't know—but this quarrel—the Duke's manner this morning—the Du Buits' drive—" said Sonia.

"Of course—of course! It's quite possible—in fact it's certain!" cried Germaine.

"It's horrible!" gasped Sonia. "Consider—just consider! Suppose something happened to him. Suppose the Duke—"

"It's me the Duke's fighting about!" cried Germaine proudly, with a little skipping jump of triumphant joy.

Sonia stared through her without seeing her. Her face was a dead white—fear had chilled the lustre from her skin; her breath panted through her parted lips; and her dilated eyes seemed to look on some dreadful picture.

Germaine pirouetted about the hall at the very height of triumph. To have a Duke fighting a duel about her was far beyond the wildest dreams of snobbishness. She chuckled again and again, and once she clapped her hands and laughed aloud.

"He's fighting a swordsman of the first class—an invincible swordsman—you said so yourself," Sonia muttered in a tone of anguish. "And there's nothing to be done—nothing."

She pressed her hands to her eyes as if to shut out a hideous vision.

Germaine did not hear her; she was staring at herself in a mirror, and bridling to her own image.

Sonia tottered to the window and stared down at the road along which must come the tidings of weal or irremediable woe. She kept passing her hand over her eyes as if to clear their vision.

Suddenly she started, and bent forward, rigid, all her being concentrated in the effort to see.

Then she cried: "Mademoiselle Germaine! Look! Look!"

"What is it?" said Germaine, coming to her side.

"A horseman! Look! There!" said Sonia, waving a hand towards the road.

"Yes; and isn't he galloping!" said Germaine.

"It's he! It's the Duke!" cried Sonia.

"Do you think so?" said Germaine doubtfully.

"I'm sure of it—sure!"

"Well, he gets here just in time for tea," said Germaine in a tone of extreme satisfaction. "He knows that I hate to be kept waiting. He said to me, 'I shall be back by five at the latest.' And here he is."

"It's impossible," said Sonia. "He has to go all the way round the park. There's no direct road; the brook is between us."

"All the same, he's coming in a straight line," said Germaine.

It was true. The horseman had left the road and was galloping across the meadows straight for the brook. In twenty seconds he reached its treacherous bank, and as he set his horse at it, Sonia covered her eyes.

"He's over!" said Germaine. "My father gave three hundred guineas for that horse."

III. LUPIN'S WAY

Sonia, in a sudden revulsion of feeling, in a reaction from her fears, slipped back and sat down at the tea-table, panting quickly, struggling to keep back the tears of relief. She did not see the Duke gallop up the slope, dismount, and hand over his horse to the groom who came running to him. There was still a mist in her eyes to blur his figure as he came through the window.

"If it's for me, plenty of tea, very little cream, and three lumps of sugar," he cried in a gay, ringing voice, and pulled out his watch. "Five to the minute—that's all right." And he bent down, took Germaine's hand, and kissed it with an air of gallant devotion.

If he had indeed just fought a duel, there were no signs of it in his bearing. His air, his voice, were entirely careless. He was a man whose whole thought at the moment was fixed on his tea and his punctuality.

He drew a chair near the tea-table for Germaine; sat down himself; and Sonia handed him a cup of tea with so shaky a hand that the spoon clinked in the saucer.

"You've been fighting a duel?" said Germaine.

"What! You've heard already?" said the Duke in some surprise.

"I've heard," said Germaine. "Why did you fight it?"

"You're not wounded, your Grace?" said Sonia anxiously.

"Not a scratch," said the Duke, smiling at her.

"Will you be so good as to get on with those wedding-cards, Sonia," said Germaine sharply; and Sonia went back to the writing-table.

Turning to the Duke, Germaine said, "Did you fight on my account?"

"Would you be pleased to know that I had fought on your account?" said the Duke; and there was a faint mocking light in his eyes, far too faint for the self-satisfied Germaine to perceive.

"Yes. But it isn't true. You've been fighting about some woman," said Germaine petulantly.

"If I had been fighting about a woman, it could only be you," said the Duke.

"Yes, that is so. Of course. It could hardly be about Sonia, or my maid," said Germaine. "But what was the reason of the duel?"

"Oh, the reason of it was entirely childish," said the Duke. "I was in a bad temper; and De Relzieres said something that annoyed me."

"Then it wasn't about me; and if it wasn't about me, it wasn't really worth while fighting," said Germaine in a tone of acute disappointment.

The mocking light deepened a little in the Duke's eyes.

"Yes. But if I had been killed, everybody would have said, 'The Duke of Charmerace has been killed in a duel about Mademoiselle Gournay-Martin.' That would have sounded very fine indeed," said the Duke; and a touch of mockery had crept into his voice.

"Now, don't begin trying to annoy me again," said Germaine pettishly.

"The last thing I should dream of, my dear girl," said the Duke, smiling.

"And De Relzieres? Is he wounded?" said Germaine.

"Poor dear De Relzieres: he won't be out of bed for the next six months," said the Duke; and he laughed lightly and gaily.

"Good gracious!" cried Germaine.

"It will do poor dear De Relzieres a world of good. He has a touch of enteritis; and for enteritis there is nothing like rest," said the Duke.

Sonia was not getting on very quickly with the wedding-cards. Germaine was sitting with her back to her; and over her shoulder Sonia could watch the face of the Duke—an extraordinarily mobile face, changing with every passing mood. Sometimes his eyes met hers; and heis fell before them. But as soon as they turned away from her she was watching him again, almost greedily, as if she could not see enough of his face in which strength of will and purpose was mingled with a faint, ironic scepticism, and tempered by a fine air of race.

He finished his tea; then he took a morocco case from his pocket, and said to Germaine, "It must be quite three days since I gave you anything."

He opened the case, disclosed a pearl pendant, and handed it to her.

"Oh, how nice!" she cried, taking it.

She took it from the case, saying that it was a beauty. She showed it to Sonia; then she put it on and stood before a mirror admiring the effect. To tell the truth, the effect was not entirely desirable. The pearls did not improve the look of her rather coarse brown skin; and her skin added nothing to the beauty of the pearls. Sonia saw this, and so did the Duke. He looked at Sonia's white throat. She met his eyes and blushed. She knew that the same thought was in both their minds; the pearls would have looked infinitely better there.

Germaine finished admiring herself; she was incapable even of suspecting that so expensive a pendant could not suit her perfectly.

The Duke said idly: "Goodness! Are all those invitations to the wedding?"

"That's only down to the letter V," said Germaine proudly.

"And there are twenty-five letters in the alphabet! You must be inviting the whole world. You'll have to have the Madeleine enlarged. It won't hold them all. There isn't a church in Paris that will," said the Duke.

"Won't it be a splendid marriage!" said Germaine. "There'll be something like a crush. There are sure to be accidents."

"If I were you, I should have careful arrangements made," said the Duke.

"Oh, let people look after themselves. They'll remember it better if they're crushed a little," said Germaine.

There was a flicker of contemptuous wonder in the Duke's eyes. But he only shrugged his shoulders, and turning to Sonia, said, "Will you be an angel and play me a little Grieg, Mademoiselle Kritchnoff? I heard you playing yesterday. No one plays Grieg like you."

"Excuse me, Jacques, but Mademoiselle Kritchnoff has her work to do," said Germaine tartly.

"Five minutes' interval—just a morsel of Grieg, I beg," said the Duke, with an irresistible smile.

"All right," said Germaine grudgingly. "But I've something important to talk to you about."

"By Jove! So have I. I was forgetting. I've the last photograph I took of you and Mademoiselle Sonia." Germaine frowned and shrugged her shoulders. "With your light frocks in the open air, you look like two big flowers," said the Duke.

"You call that important!" cried Germaine.

"It's very important—like all trifles," said the Duke, smiling. "Look! isn't it nice?" And he took a photograph from his pocket, and held it out to her.

"Nice? It's shocking! We're making the most appalling faces," said Germaine, looking at the photograph in his hand.

"Well, perhaps you ARE making faces," said the Duke seriously, considering the photograph with grave earnestness. "But they're not appalling faces—not by any means. You shall be judge, Mademoiselle Sonia. The faces—well, we won't talk about the faces—but the outlines. Look at the movement of your scarf." And he handed the photograph to Sonia.

"Jacques!" said Germaine impatiently.

"Oh, yes, you've something important to tell me. What is it?" said the Duke, with an air of resignation; and he took the photograph from Sonia and put it carefully back in his pocket.

"Victoire has telephoned from Paris to say that we've had a paper-knife and a Louis Seize inkstand given us," said Germaine.

"Hurrah!" cried the Duke in a sudden shout that made them both jump.

"And a pearl necklace," said Germaine.

"Hurrah!" cried the Duke.

"You're perfectly childish," said Germaine pettishly. "I tell you we've been given a paper-knife, and you shout 'hurrah!' I say we've been given a pearl necklace, and you shout 'hurrah!' You can't have the slightest sense of values."

"I beg your pardon. This pearl necklace is from one of your father's friends, isn't it?" said the Duke.

"Yes; why?" said Germaine.

"But the inkstand and the paper-knife must be from the Faubourg Saint-Germain, and well on the shabby side?" said the Duke.

"Yes; well?"

"Well then, my dear girl, what are you complaining about? They balance; the equilibrium is restored. You can't have everything," said the Duke; and he laughed mischievously.

Germaine flushed, and bit her lip; her eyes sparkled.

"You don't care a rap about me," she said stormily.

"But I find you adorable," said the Duke.

"You keep annoying me," said Germaine pettishly. "And you do it on purpose. I think it's in very bad taste. I shall end by taking a dislike to you— I know I shall."

"Wait till we're married for that, my dear girl," said the Duke; and he laughed again, with a blithe, boyish cheerfulness, which deepened the angry flush in Germaine's cheeks.

"Can't you be serious about anything?" she cried.

"I am the most serious man in Europe," said the Duke.

Germaine went to the window and stared out of it sulkily.

The Duke walked up and down the hall, looking at the pictures of some of his ancestors—somewhat grotesque persons—with humorous appreciation. Between addressing the envelopes Sonia kept glancing at him. Once he caught her eye, and smiled at her. Germaine's back was eloquent of her displeasure. The Duke stopped at a gap in the line of pictures in which there hung a strip of old tapestry.

"I can never understand why you have left all these ancestors of mine staring from the walls and have taken away the quite admirable and interesting portrait of myself," he said carelessly.

Germaine turned sharply from the window; Sonia stopped in the middle of addressing an envelope; and both the girls stared at him in astonishment.

"There certainly was a portrait of me where that tapestry hangs. What have you done with it?" said the Duke.

"You're making fun of us again," said Germaine.

"Surely your Grace knows what happened," said Sonia.

"We wrote all the details to you and sent you all the papers three years ago. Didn't you get them?" said Germaine.

"Not a detail or a newspaper. Three years ago I was in the neighbourhood of the South Pole, and lost at that," said the Duke.

"But it was most dramatic, my dear Jacques. All Paris was talking of it," said Germaine. "Your portrait was stolen."

"Stolen? Who stole it?" said the Duke.

Germaine crossed the hall quickly to the gap in the line of pictures.

"I'll show you," she said.

She drew aside the piece of tapestry, and in the middle of the panel over which the portrait of the Duke had hung he saw written in chalk the words:
ARSENE LUPIN

"What do you think of that autograph?" said Germaine.

"'Arsene Lupin?'" said the Duke in a tone of some bewilderment.

"He left his signature. It seems that he always does so," said Sonia in an explanatory tone.

"But who is he?" said the Duke.

"Arsene Lupin? Surely you know who Arsene Lupin is?" said Germaine impatiently.

"I haven't the slightest notion," said the Duke.

"Oh, come! No one is as South-Pole as all that!" cried Germaine. "You don't know who Lupin is? The most whimsical, the most audacious, and the most genial thief in France. For the last ten years he has kept the police at bay. He has baffled Ganimard, Holmlock Shears, the great English detective, and even Guerchard, whom everybody says is the greatest detective we've had in France since Vidocq. In fact, he's our national robber. Do you mean to say you don't know him?"

"Not even enough to ask him to lunch at a restaurant," said the Duke flippantly. "What's he like?"

"Like? Nobody has the slightest idea. He has a thousand disguises. He has dined two evenings running at the English Embassy."

"But if nobody knows him, how did they learn that?" said the Duke, with a puzzled air.

"Because the second evening, about ten o'clock, they noticed that one of the guests had disappeared, and with him all the jewels of the ambassadress."

"All of them?" said the Duke.

"Yes; and Lupin left his card behind him with these words scribbled on it:"

"'This is not a robbery; it is a restitution. You took the Wallace collection from us.'"

"But it was a hoax, wasn't it?" said the Duke.

"No, your Grace; and he has done better than that. You remember the affair of the Daray Bank—the savings bank for poor people?" said Sonia, her gentle face glowing with a sudden enthusiastic animation.

"Let's see," said the Duke. "Wasn't that the financier who doubled his fortune at the expense of a heap of poor wretches and ruined two thousand people?"

"Yes; that's the man," said Sonia. "And Lupin stripped Daray's house and took from him everything he had in his strong-box. He didn't leave him a sou of the money. And then, when he'd taken it from him, he distributed it among all the poor wretches whom Daray had ruined."

"But this isn't a thief you're talking about—it's a philanthropist," said the Duke.

"A fine sort of philanthropist!" broke in Germaine in a peevish tone. "There was a lot of philanthropy about his robbing papa, wasn't there?"

"Well," said the Duke, with an air of profound reflection, "if you come to think of it, that robbery was not worthy of this national hero. My portrait, if you except the charm and beauty of the face itself, is not worth much."

"If you think he was satisfied with your portrait, you're very much mistaken. All my father's collections were robbed," said Germaine.

"Your father's collections?" said the Duke. "But they're better guarded than the Bank of France. Your father is as careful of them as the apple of his eye."

"That's exactly it—he was too careful of them. That's why Lupin succeeded."

"This is very interesting," said the Duke; and he sat down on a couch before the gap in the pictures, to go into the matter more at his ease. "I suppose he had accomplices in the house itself?"

"Yes, one accomplice," said Germaine.

"Who was that?" asked the Duke.

"Papa!" said Germaine.

"Oh, come! what on earth do you mean?" said the Duke. "You're getting quite incomprehensible, my dear girl."

"Well, I'll make it clear to you. One morning papa received a letter—but wait. Sonia, get me the Lupin papers out of the bureau."

Sonia rose from the writing-table, and went to a bureau, an admirable example of the work of the great English maker, Chippendale. It stood on the other side of the hall between an Oriental cabinet and a sixteenth-century Italian cabinet—for all the world as if it were standing in a crowded curiosity shop—with the natural effect that the three pieces, by their mere incongruity, took something each from the beauty of the other. Sonia raised the flap of the bureau, and taking from one of the drawers a small portfolio, turned over the papers in it and handed a letter to the Duke.

"This is the envelope," she said. "It's addressed to M. Gournay-Martin, Collector, at the Chateau de Charmerace, Ile-et-Vilaine."

The Duke opened the envelope and took out a letter.

"It's an odd handwriting," he said.

"Read it—carefully," said Germaine.

It was an uncommon handwriting. The letters of it were small, but perfectly formed. It looked the handwriting of a man who knew exactly what he wanted to say, and liked to say it with extreme precision. The letter ran:

"DEAR SIR,"

"Please forgive my writing to you without our having been introduced to one another; but I flatter myself that you know me, at any rate, by name."

"There is in the drawing-room next your hall a Gainsborough of admirable quality which affords me infinite pleasure. Your Goyas in the same drawing-room are also to my liking, as well as your Van Dyck. In the further drawing-room I note the Renaissance cabinets—a marvellous pair—the Flemish tapestry, the Fragonard, the clock signed Boulle, and various other objects of less importance. But above all I have set my heart on that coronet which you bought at the sale of the Marquise de Ferronaye, and which was formerly worn by the unfortunate Princesse de Lamballe. I take the greatest interest in this coronet: in the first place, on account of the charming and tragic memories which it calls up in the mind of a poet passionately fond of history, and in the second place—though it is hardly worth while talking about that kind of thing—on account of its intrinsic value. I reckon indeed that the stones in your coronet are, at the very lowest, worth half a million francs."

"I beg you, my dear sir, to have these different objects properly packed up, and to forward them, addressed to me, carriage paid, to the Batignolles Station. Failing this, I shall Proceed to remove them myself on the night of Thursday, August 7th."

"Please pardon the slight trouble to which I am putting you, and believe me,"

"Yours very sincerely,"

"ARSENE LUPIN."

"P.S.—It occurs to me that the pictures have not glass before them. It would be as well to repair this omission before forwarding them to me, and I am sure that you will take this extra trouble cheerfully. I am aware, of course, that some of the best judges declare that a picture loses some of its quality when seen through glass. But it preserves them, and we should always be ready and willing to sacrifice a portion of our own pleasure for the benefit of posterity. France demands it of us.—A. L."

The Duke laughed, and said, "Really, this is extraordinarily funny. It must have made your father laugh."

"Laugh?" said Germaine. "You should have seen his face. He took it seriously enough, I can tell you."

"Not to the point of forwarding the things to Batignolles, I hope," said the Duke.

332

"No, but to the point of being driven wild," said Germaine. "And since the police had always been baffled by Lupin, he had the brilliant idea of trying what soldiers could do. The Commandant at Rennes is a great friend of papa's; and papa went to him, and told him about Lupin's letter and what he feared. The colonel laughed at him; but he offered him a corporal and six soldiers to guard his collection, on the night of the seventh. It was arranged that they should come from Rennes by the last train so that the burglars should have no warning of their coming. Well, they came, seven picked men—men who had seen service in Tonquin. We gave them supper; and then the corporal posted them in the hall and the two drawing-rooms where the pictures and things were. At eleven we all went to bed, after promising the corporal that, in the event of any fight with the burglars, we would not stir from our rooms. I can tell you I felt awfully nervous. I couldn't get to sleep for ages and ages. Then, when I did, I did not wake till morning. The night had passed absolutely quietly. Nothing out of the common had happened. There had not been the slightest noise. I awoke Sonia and my father. We dressed as quickly as we could, and rushed down to the drawing-room."

She paused dramatically.

"Well?" said the Duke.

"Well, it was done."

"What was done?" said the Duke.

"Everything," said Germaine. "Pictures had gone, tapestries had gone, cabinets had gone, and the clock had gone."

"And the coronet too?" said the Duke.

"Oh, no. That was at the Bank of France. And it was doubtless to make up for not getting it that Lupin stole your portrait. At any rate he didn't say that he was going to steal it in his letter."

"But, come! this is incredible. Had he hypnotized the corporal and the six soldiers? Or had he murdered them all?" said the Duke.

"Corporal? There wasn't any corporal, and there weren't any soldiers. The corporal was Lupin, and the soldiers were part of his gang," said Germaine.

"I don't understand," said the Duke. "The colonel promised your father a corporal and six men. Didn't they come?"

"They came to the railway station all right," said Germaine. "But you know the little inn half-way between the railway station and the chateau? They stopped to drink there, and at eleven o'clock next morning one of the villagers found all seven of them, along with the footman who was guiding them to the chateau, sleeping like logs in the little wood half a mile from the inn. Of course the innkeeper could not explain when their wine was drugged. He could only tell us that a motorist, who had stopped at the inn to get some supper, had called the soldiers in and insisted on standing them drinks. They had seemed a little fuddled before they left the inn, and the motorist had insisted on driving them to the chateau in his car. When the drug took effect he simply carried them out of it one by one, and laid them in the wood to sleep it off."

"Lupin seems to have made a thorough job of it, anyhow," said the Duke.

"I should think so," said Germaine. "Guerchard was sent down from Paris; but he could not find a single clue. It was not for want of trying, for he hates Lupin. It's a regular fight between them, and so far Lupin has scored every point."

"He must be as clever as they make 'em," said the Duke.

"He is," said Germaine. "And do you know, I shouldn't be at all surprised if he's in the neighbourhood now."

"What on earth do you mean?" said the Duke.

"I'm not joking," said Germaine. "Odd things are happening. Some one has been changing the place of things. That silver statuette now—it was on the cabinet, and we found it moved to the piano. Yet nobody had touched it. And look at this window. Some one has broken a pane in it just at the height of the fastening."

"The deuce they have!" said the Duke.

IV. THE DUKE INTERVENES

The Duke rose, came to the window, and looked at the broken pane. He stepped out on to the terrace and looked at the turf; then he came back into the room.

"This looks serious," he said. "That pane has not been broken at all. If it had been broken, the pieces of glass would be lying on the turf. It has been cut out. We must warn your father to look to his treasures."

"I told you so," said Germaine. "I said that Arsene Lupin was in the neighbourhood."

"Arsene Lupin is a very capable man," said the Duke, smiling. "But there's no reason to suppose that he's the only burglar in France or even in Ile-et-Vilaine."

"I'm sure that he's in the neighbourhood. I have a feeling that he is," said Germaine stubbornly.

The Duke shrugged his shoulders, and said a smile: "Far be it from me to contradict you. A woman's intuition is always—well, it's always a woman's intuition."

He came back into the hall, and as he did so the door opened and a shock-headed man in the dress of a gamekeeper stood on the threshold.

"There are visitors to see you, Mademoiselle Germaine," he said, in a very deep bass voice.

"What! Are you answering the door, Firmin?" said Germaine.

"Yes, Mademoiselle Germaine: there's only me to do it. All the servants have started for the station, and my wife and I are going to see after the family to-night and to-morrow morning. Shall I show these gentlemen in?"

"Who are they?" said Germaine.

"Two gentlemen who say they have an appointment."

"What are their names?" said Germaine.

"They are two gentlemen. I don't know what their names are. I've no memory for names."

"That's an advantage to any one who answers doors," said the Duke, smiling at the stolid Firmin.

"Well, it can't be the two Charolais again. It's not time for them to come back. I told them papa would not be back yet," said Germaine.

"No, it can't be them, Mademoiselle Germaine," said Firmin, with decision.

"Very well; show them in," she said.

Firmin went out, leaving the door open behind him; and they heard his hob-nailed boots clatter and squeak on the stone floor of the outer hall.

"Charolais?" said the Duke idly. "I don't know the name. Who are they?"

"A little while ago Alfred announced two gentlemen. I thought they were Georges and Andre du Buit, for they promised to come to tea. I told Alfred to show them in, and to my surprise there appeared two horrible provincials. I never—Oh!"

She stopped short, for there, coming through the door, were the two Charolais, father and son.

M. Charolais pressed his motor-cap to his bosom, and bowed low. "Once more I salute you, mademoiselle," he said.

His son bowed, and revealed behind him another young man.

"My second son. He has a chemist's shop," said M. Charolais, waving a large red hand at the young man.

The young man, also blessed with the family eyes, set close together, entered the hall and bowed to the two girls. The Duke raised his eyebrows ever so slightly.

"I'm very sorry, gentlemen," said Germaine, "but my father has not yet returned."

"Please don't apologize. There is not the slightest need," said M. Charolais; and he and his two sons settled themselves down on three chairs, with the air of people who had come to make a considerable stay.

For a moment, Germaine, taken aback by their coolness, was speechless; then she said hastily: "Very likely he won't be back for another hour. I shouldn't like you to waste your time."

"Oh, it doesn't matter," said M. Charolais, with an indulgent air; and turning to the Duke, he added, "However, while we're waiting, if you're a member of the family, sir, we might perhaps discuss the least you will take for the motor-car."

"I'm sorry," said the Duke, "but I have nothing to do with it."

Before M. Charolais could reply the door opened, and Firmin's deep voice said:

"Will you please come in here, sir?"

A third young man came into the hall.

"What, you here, Bernard?" said M. Charolais. "I told you to wait at the park gates."

"I wanted to see the car too," said Bernard.

"My third son. He is destined for the Bar," said M. Charolais, with a great air of paternal pride.

"But how many are there?" said Germaine faintly.

Before M. Charolais could answer, Firmin once more appeared on the threshold.

"The master's just come back, miss," he said.

"Thank goodness for that!" said Germaine; and turning to M. Charolais, she added, "If you will come with me, gentlemen, I will take you to my father, and you can discuss the price of the car at once."

As she spoke she moved towards the door. M. Charolais and his sons rose and made way for her. The father and the two eldest sons made haste to follow her out of the room. But Bernard lingered behind, apparently to admire the bric-a-brac on the cabinets. With infinite quickness he grabbed two objects off the nearest, and followed his brothers. The Duke sprang across the hall in three strides, caught him by the arm on the very threshold, jerked him back into the hall, and shut the door.

"No you don't, my young friend," he said sharply.

"Don't what?" said Bernard, trying to shake off his grip.

"You've taken a cigarette-case," said the Duke.

"No, no, I haven't—nothing of the kind!" stammered Bernard.

The Duke grasped the young man's left wrist, plunged his hand into the motor-cap which he was carrying, drew out of it a silver cigarette-case, and held it before his eyes.

Bernard turned pale to the lips. His frightened eyes seemed about to leap from their sockets.

"It—it—was a m-m-m-mistake," he stammered.

The Duke shifted his grip to his collar, and thrust his hand into the breast-pocket of his coat. Bernard, helpless in his grip, and utterly taken aback by his quickness, made no resistance.

The Duke drew out a morocco case, and said: "Is this a mistake too?"

"Heavens! The pendant!" cried Sonia, who was watching the scene with parted lips and amazed eyes.

Bernard dropped on his knees and clasped his hands.

"Forgive me!" he cried, in a choking voice. "Forgive me! Don't tell any one! For God's sake, don't tell any one!"

And the tears came streaming from his eyes.

"You young rogue!" said the Duke quietly.

"I'll never do it again—never! Oh, have pity on me! If my father knew! Oh, let me off!" cried Bernard.

The Duke hesitated, and looked down on him, frowning and pulling at his moustache. Then, more quickly than one would have expected from so careless a trifler, his mind was made up.

"All right," he said slowly. "Just for this once ... be off with you." And he jerked him to his feet and almost threw him into the outer hall.

"Thanks! ... oh, thanks!" said Bernard.

The Duke shut the door and looked at Sonia, breathing quickly.

"Well? Did you ever see anything like that? That young fellow will go a long way. The cheek of the thing! Right under our very eyes! And this pendant, too: it would have been a pity to lose it. Upon my word, I ought to have handed him over to the police."

"No, no!" cried Sonia. "You did quite right to let him off—quite right."

The Duke set the pendant on the ledge of the bureau, and came down the hall to Sonia.

"What's the matter?" he said gently. "You're quite pale."

"It has upset me ... that unfortunate boy," said Sonia; and her eyes were swimming with tears.

"Do you pity the young rogue?" said the Duke.

"Yes; it's dreadful. His eyes were so terrified, and so boyish. And, to be caught like that ... stealing ... in the act. Oh, it's hateful!"

"Come, come, how sensitive you are!" said the Duke, in a soothing, almost caressing tone. His eyes, resting on her charming, troubled face, were glowing with a warm admiration.

"Yes; it's silly," said Sonia; "but you noticed his eyes—the hunted look in them? You pitied him, didn't you? For you are kind at bottom."

"Why at bottom?" said the Duke.

"Oh, I said at bottom because you look sarcastic, and at first sight you're so cold. But often that's only the mask of those who have suffered the most.... They are the most indulgent," said Sonia slowly, hesitating, picking her words.

"Yes, I suppose they are," said the Duke thoughtfully.

"It's because when one has suffered one understands.... Yes: one understands," said Sonia.

There was a pause. The Duke's eyes still rested on her face. The admiration in them was mingled with compassion.

"You're very unhappy here, aren't you?" he said gently.

"Me? Why?" said Sonia quickly.

"Your smile is so sad, and your eyes so timid," said the Duke slowly. "You're just like a little child one longs to protect. Are you quite alone in the world?"

His eyes and tones were full of pity; and a faint flush mantled Sonia's cheeks.

"Yes, I'm alone," she said.

"But have you no relations—no friends?" said the Duke.

"No," said Sonia.

"I don't mean here in France, but in your own country.... Surely you have some in Russia?"

"No, not a soul. You see, my father was a Revolutionist. He died in Siberia when I was a baby. And my mother, she died too—in Paris. She had fled from Russia. I was two years old when she died."

"It must be hard to be alone like that," said the Duke.

"No," said Sonia, with a faint smile, "I don't mind having no relations. I grew used to that so young ... so very young. But what is hard—but you'll laugh at me—"

"Heaven forbid!" said the Duke gravely.

"Well, what is hard is, never to get a letter ... an envelope that one opens ... from some one who thinks about one—"

She paused, and then added gravely: "But I tell myself that it's nonsense. I have a certain amount of philosophy."

She smiled at him—an adorable child's smile.

The Duke smiled too. "A certain amount of philosophy," he said softly. "You look like a philosopher!"

As they stood looking at one another with serious eyes, almost with eyes that probed one another's souls, the drawing-room door flung open, and Germaine's harsh voice broke on their ears.

"You're getting quite impossible, Sonia!" she cried. "It's absolutely useless telling you anything. I told you particularly to pack my leather writing-case in my bag with your own hand. I happen to open a drawer, and what do I see? My leather writing-case."

"I'm sorry," said Sonia. "I was going—"

"Oh, there's no need to bother about it. I'll see after it myself," said Germaine. "But upon my word, you might be one of our guests, seeing how easily you take things. You're negligence personified."

"Come, Germaine ... a mere oversight," said the Duke, in a coaxing tone.

"Now, excuse me, Jacques; but you've got an unfortunate habit of interfering in household matters. You did it only the other day. I can no longer say a word to a servant—"

"Germaine!" said the Duke, in sharp protest.

Germaine turned from him to Sonia, and pointed to a packet of envelopes and some letters, which Bernard Charolais had knocked off the table, and said, "Pick up those envelopes and letters, and bring everything to my room, and be quick about it!"

She flung out of the room, and slammed the door behind her.

Sonia seemed entirely unmoved by the outburst: no flush of mortification stained her cheeks, her lips did not quiver. She stooped to pick up the fallen papers.

"No, no; let me, I beg you," said the Duke, in a tone of distress. And dropping on one knee, he began to gather together the fallen papers. He set them on the table, and then he said: "You mustn't mind what Germaine says. She's—she's—she's all right at heart. It's her manner. She's always been happy, and had everything she wanted. She's been spoiled, don't you know. Those kind of people never have any consideration for any one else. You mustn't let her outburst hurt you."

"Oh, but I don't. I don't really," protested Sonia.

"I'm glad of that," said the Duke. "It isn't really worth noticing."

He drew the envelopes and unused cards into a packet, and handed them to her.

"There!" he said, with a smile. "That won't be too heavy for you."

"Thank you," said Sonia, taking it from him.

"Shall I carry them for you?" said the Duke.

"No, thank you, your Grace," said Sonia.

With a quick, careless, almost irresponsible movement, he caught her hand, bent down, and kissed it. A great wave of rosy colour flowed over her face, flooding its whiteness to her hair and throat. She stood for a moment turned to stone; she put her hand to her heart. Then on hasty, faltering feet she went to the door, opened it, paused on the threshold, turned and looked back at him, and vanished.

V. A LETTER FROM LUPIN

The Duke stood for a while staring thoughtfully at the door through which Sonia had passed, a faint smile playing round his lips. He crossed the hall to the Chippendale bureau, took a cigarette from a box which stood on the ledge of it, beside the morocco case which held the pendant, lighted it, and went slowly out on to the terrace. He crossed it slowly, paused for a moment on the edge of it, and looked across the stretch of country with musing eyes, which saw nothing of its beauty. Then he turned to the right, went down a flight of steps to the lower terrace, crossed the lawn, and took a narrow path which led into the heart of a shrubbery of tall deodoras. In the middle of it he came to one of those old stone benches, moss-covered and weather-stained, which adorn the gardens of so many French chateaux. It faced a marble basin from which rose the slender column of a pattering fountain. The figure of a Cupid danced joyously on a tall pedestal to the right of the basin. The Duke sat down on the bench, and was still, with that rare stillness which only comes of nerves in perfect harmony, his brow knitted in careful thought. Now and again the frown cleared from his face, and his intent features relaxed into a faint smile, a smile of pleasant memory. Once he rose, walked round the fountains frowning, came back to the bench, and sat down again. The early September dusk was upon him when at last he rose and with quick steps took his way through the shrubbery, with the air of a man whose mind, for good or ill, was at last made up.

When he came on to the upper terrace his eyes fell on a group which stood at the further corner, near the entrance of the chateau, and he sauntered slowly up to it.

In the middle of it stood M. Gournay-Martin, a big, round, flabby hulk of a man. He was nearly as red in the face as M. Charolais; and he looked a great deal redder owing to the extreme whiteness of the whiskers which stuck out on either side of his vast expanse of cheek. As he came up, it struck the Duke as rather odd that he should have the Charolais eyes, set close together; any one who did not know that they were strangers to one another might have thought it a family likeness.

The millionaire was waving his hands and roaring after the manner of a man who has cultivated the art of brow-beating those with whom he does business; and as the Duke neared the group, he caught the words:

"No; that's the lowest I'll take. Take it or leave it. You can say Yes, or you can say Good-bye; and I don't care a hang which."

"It's very dear," said M. Charolais, in a mournful tone.

"Dear!" roared M. Gournay-Martin. "I should like to see any one else sell a hundred horse-power car for eight hundred pounds. Why, my good sir, you're having me!"

"No, no," protested M. Charolais feebly.

"I tell you you're having me," roared M. Gournay-Martin. "I'm letting you have a magnificent car for which I paid thirteen hundred pounds for eight hundred! It's scandalous the way you've beaten me down!"

"No, no," protested M. Charolais.

He seemed frightened out of his life by the vehemence of the big man.

"You wait till you've seen how it goes," said M. Gournay-Martin.

"Eight hundred is very dear," said M. Charolais.

"Come, come! You're too sharp, that's what you are. But don't say any more till you've tried the car."

He turned to his chauffeur, who stood by watching the struggle with an appreciative grin on his brown face, and said: "Now, Jean, take these gentlemen to the garage, and run them down to the station. Show them what the car can do. Do whatever they ask you—everything."

He winked at Jean, turned again to M. Charolais, and said: "You know, M. Charolais, you're too good a man of business for me. You're hot stuff, that's what you are—hot stuff. You go along and try the car. Good-bye—good-bye."

The four Charolais murmured good-bye in deep depression, and went off with Jean, wearing something of the air of whipped dogs. When they had gone round the corner the millionaire turned to the Duke and said, with a chuckle: "He'll buy the car all right—had him fine!"

"No business success of yours could surprise me," said the Duke blandly, with a faint, ironical smile.

M. Gournay-Martin's little pig's eyes danced and sparkled; and the smiles flowed over the distended skin of his face like little ripples over a stagnant pool, reluctantly. It seemed to be too tightly stretched for smiles.

"The car's four years old," he said joyfully. "He'll give me eight hundred for it, and it's not worth a pipe of tobacco. And eight hundred pounds is just the price of a little Watteau I've had my eye on for some time—a first-class investment."

They strolled down the terrace, and through one of the windows into the hall. Firmin had lighted the lamps, two of them. They made but a small oasis of light in a desert of dim hall. The millionaire let himself down very gingerly into an Empire chair, as if he feared, with excellent reason, that it might collapse under his weight.

"Well, my dear Duke," he said, "you don't ask me the result of my official lunch or what the minister said."

"Is there any news?" said the Duke carelessly.

"Yes. The decree will be signed to-morrow. You can consider yourself decorated. I hope you feel a happy man," said the millionaire, rubbing his fat hands together with prodigious satisfaction.

"Oh, charmed—charmed," said the Duke, with entire indifference.

"As for me, I'm delighted—delighted," said the millionaire. "I was extremely keen on your being decorated. After that, and after a volume or two of travels, and after you've published your grandfather's letters with a good introduction, you can begin to think of the Academy."

"The Academy!" said the Duke, startled from his usual coolness. "But I've no title to become an Academician."

"How, no title?" said the millionaire solemnly; and his little eyes opened wide. "You're a duke."

"There's no doubt about that," said the Duke, watching him with admiring curiosity.

"I mean to marry my daughter to a worker—a worker, my dear Duke," said the millionaire, slapping his big left hand with his bigger right. "I've no prejudices—not I. I wish to have for son-in-law a duke who wears the Order of the Legion of Honour, and belongs to the Academie Francaise, because that is personal merit. I'm no snob."

A gentle, irrepressible laugh broke from the Duke.

"What are you laughing at?" said the millionaire, and a sudden lowering gloom overspread his beaming face.

"Nothing—nothing," said the Duke quietly. "Only you're so full of surprises."

"I've startled you, have I? I thought I should. It's true that I'm full of surprises. It's my knowledge. I understand so much. I understand business, and I love art, pictures, a good bargain, bric-a-brac, fine tapestry. They're first-class investments. Yes, certainly I do love the beautiful. And I don't want to boast, but I understand it. I have taste, and I've something better than taste; I have a flair, the dealer's flair."

"Yes, your collections, especially your collection in Paris, prove it," said the Duke, stifling a yawn.

"And yet you haven't seen the finest thing I have—the coronet of the Princesse de Lamballe. It's worth half a million francs."

"So I've heard," said the Duke, a little wearily. "I don't wonder that Arsene Lupin envied you it."

The Empire chair creaked as the millionaire jumped.

"Don't speak of the swine!" he roared. "Don't mention his name before me."

"Germaine showed me his letter," said the Duke. "It is amusing."

"His letter! The blackguard! I just missed a fit of apoplexy from it," roared the millionaire. "I was in this very hall where we are now, chatting quietly, when all at once in comes Firmin, and hands me a letter."

He was interrupted by the opening of the door. Firmin came clumping down the room, and said in his deep voice, "A letter for you, sir."

"Thank you," said the millionaire, taking the letter, and, as he fitted his eye-glass into his eye, he went on, "Yes, Firmin brought me a letter of which the handwriting,"—he raised the envelope he was holding to his eyes, and bellowed, "Good heavens!"

"What's the matter?" said the Duke, jumping in his chair at the sudden, startling burst of sound.

"The handwriting!—the handwriting!—it's THE SAME HANDWRITING!" gasped the millionaire. And he let himself fall heavily backwards against the back of his chair.

There was a crash. The Duke had a vision of huge arms and legs waving in the air as the chair-back gave. There was another crash. The chair collapsed. The huge bulk banged to the floor.

The laughter of the Duke rang out uncontrollably. He caught one of the waving arms, and jerked the flabby giant to his feet with an ease which seemed to show that his muscles were of steel.

"Come," he said, laughing still. "This is nonsense! What do you mean by the same handwriting? It can't be."

"It is the same handwriting. Am I likely to make a mistake about it?" spluttered the millionaire. And he tore open the envelope with an air of frenzy.

He ran his eyes over it, and they grew larger and larger—they grew almost of an average size.

"Listen," he said "listen:"

"DEAR SIR,"

"My collection of pictures, which I had the pleasure of starting three years ago with some of your own, only contains, as far as Old Masters go, one Velasquez, one Rembrandt, and three paltry Rubens. You have a great many more. Since it is a shame such masterpieces should be in your hands, I propose to appropriate them; and I shall set about a respectful acquisition of them in your Paris house tomorrow morning."

"Yours very sincerely,"

"ARSENE LUPIN."

"He's humbugging," said the Duke.

"Wait! wait!" gasped the millionaire. "There's a postscript. Listen:"

"P.S.—You must understand that since you have been keeping the coronet of the Princesse de Lamballe during these three years, I shall avail myself of the same occasion to compel you to restore that piece of jewellery to me.—A. L."

"The thief! The scoundrel! I'm choking!" gasped the millionaire, clutching at his collar.

To judge from the blackness of his face, and the way he staggered and dropped on to a couch, which was fortunately stronger than the chair, he was speaking the truth.

"Firmin! Firmin!" shouted the Duke. "A glass of water! Quick! Your master's ill."

He rushed to the side of the millionaire, who gasped· "Telephone! Telephone to the Prefecture of Police! Be quick!"

The Duke loosened his collar with deft fingers; tore a Van Loo fan from its case hanging on the wall, and fanned him furiously. Firmin came clumping into the room with a glass of water in his hand.

The drawing-room door opened, and Germaine and Sonia, alarmed by the Duke's shout, hurried in.

"Quick! Your smelling-salts!" said the Duke.

Sonia ran across the hall, opened one of the drawers in the Oriental cabinet, and ran to the millionaire with a large bottle of smelling-salts in her hand. The Duke took it from her, and applied it to the millionaire's nose. The millionaire sneezed thrice with terrific violence. The Duke snatched the glass from Firmin and dashed the water into his host's purple face. The millionaire gasped and spluttered.

Germaine stood staring helplessly at her gasping sire.

"Whatever's the matter?" she said.

"It's this letter," said the Duke. "A letter from Lupin."

"I told you so—I said that Lupin was in the neighbourhood," cried Germaine triumphantly.

"Firmin—where's Firmin?" said the millionaire, dragging himself upright. He seemed to have recovered a great deal of his voice. "Oh, there you are!"

He jumped up, caught the gamekeeper by the shoulder, and shook him furiously.

"This letter. Where did it come from? Who brought it?" he roared.

"It was in the letter-box—the letter-box of the lodge at the bottom of the park. My wife found it there," said Firmin, and he twisted out of the millionaire's grasp.

"Just as it was three years ago," roared the millionaire, with an air of desperation. "It's exactly the same coup. Oh, what a catastrophe! What a catastrophe!"

He made as if to tear out his hair; then, remembering its scantiness, refrained.

"Now, come, it's no use losing your head," said the Duke, with quiet firmness. "If this letter isn't a hoax——"

"Hoax?" bellowed the millionaire. "Was it a hoax three years ago?"

"Very good," said the Duke. "But if this robbery with which you're threatened is genuine, it's just childish."

"How?" said the millionaire.

"Look at the date of the letter—Sunday, September the third. This letter was written to-day."

"Yes. Well, what of it?" said the millionaire.

"Look at the letter: 'I shall set about a respectful acquisition of them in your Paris house to-morrow morning'—to-morrow morning."

"Yes, yes; 'to-morrow morning'—what of it?" said the millionaire.

"One of two things," said the Duke. "Either it's a hoax, and we needn't bother about it; or the threat is genuine, and we have the time to stop the robbery."

"Of course we have. Whatever was I thinking of?" said the millionaire. And his anguish cleared from his face.

"For once in a way our dear Lupin's fondness for warning people will have given him a painful jar," said the Duke.

"Come on! let me get at the telephone," cried the millionaire.

"But the telephone's no good," said Sonia quickly.

"No good! Why?" roared the millionaire, dashing heavily across the room to it.

"Look at the time," said Sonia; "the telephone doesn't work as late as this. It's Sunday."

The millionaire stopped dead.

"It's true. It's appalling," he groaned.

"But that doesn't matter. You can always telegraph," said Germaine.

"But you can't. It's impossible," said Sonia. "You can't get a message through. It's Sunday; and the telegraph offices shut at twelve o'clock."

"Oh, what a Government!" groaned the millionaire. And he sank down gently on a chair beside the telephone, and mopped the beads of anguish from his brow. They looked at him, and they looked at one another, cudgelling their brains for yet another way of communicating with the Paris police.

"Hang it all!" said the Duke. "There must be some way out of the difficulty."

"What way?" said the millionaire.

The Duke did not answer. He put his hands in his pockets and walked impatiently up and down the hall. Germaine sat down on a chair. Sonia put her hands on the back of a couch, and leaned forward, watching him. Firmin stood by the door, whither he had retired to be out of the reach of his excited master, with a look of perplexity on his stolid face. They all watched the Duke with the air of people waiting for an oracle to deliver its message. The millionaire kept mopping the beads of anguish from his brow. The more he thought of his impending loss, the more freely he perspired. Germaine's maid, Irma, came to the door leading into the outer hall, which Firmin, according to his usual custom, had left open, and peered in wonder at the silent group.

"I have it!" cried the Duke at last. "There is a way out."

"What is it?" said the millionaire, rising and coming to the middle of the hall.

"What time is it?" said the Duke, pulling out his watch.

The millionaire pulled out his watch. Germaine pulled out hers. Firmin, after a struggle, produced from some pocket difficult of access an object not unlike a silver turnip. There was a brisk dispute between Germaine and the millionaire about which of their watches was right. Firmin, whose watch apparently did not agree with the watch of either of them, made his deep voice heard above theirs. The Duke came to the conclusion that it must be a few minutes past seven.

"It's seven or a few minutes past," he said sharply. "Well, I'm going to take a car and hurry off to Paris. I ought to get there, bar accidents, between two and three in the morning, just in time to inform the police and catch the burglars in the very midst of their burglary. I'll just get a few things together."

So saying, he rushed out of the hall.

"Excellent! excellent!" said the millionaire. "Your young man is a man of resource, Germaine. It seems almost a pity that he's a duke. He'd do wonders in the building trade. But I'm going to Paris too, and you're coming with me. I couldn't wait idly here, to save my life. And I can't leave you here, either. This scoundrel may be going to make a simultaneous attempt on the chateau—not that there's much here that I really value. There's that statuette that moved, and the pane cut out of the window. I can't leave you two girls with burglars in the house. After all, there's the sixty horse-power and the thirty horse-power car—there'll be lots of room for all of us."

"Oh, but it's nonsense, papa; we shall get there before the servants," said Germaine pettishly. "Think of arriving at an empty house in the dead of night."

"Nonsense!" said the millionaire. "Hurry off and get ready. Your bag ought to be packed. Where are my keys? Sonia, where are my keys—the keys of the Paris house?"

"They're in the bureau," said Sonia.

"Well, see that I don't go without them. Now hurry up. Firmin, go and tell Jean that we shall want both cars. I will drive one, the Duke the other. Jean must stay with you and help guard the chateau."

So saying he bustled out of the hall, driving the two girls before him.

VI. AGAIN THE CHAROLAIS

Hardly had the door closed behind the millionaire when the head of M. Charolais appeared at one of the windows opening on to the terrace. He looked round the empty hall, whistled softly, and stepped inside. Inside of ten seconds his three sons came in through the windows, and with them came Jean, the millionaire's chauffeur.

"Take the door into the outer hall, Jean," said M. Charolais, in a low voice. "Bernard, take that door into the drawing-room. Pierre and Louis, help me go through the drawers. The whole family is going to Paris, and if we're not quick we shan't get the cars."

"That comes of this silly fondness for warning people of a coup," growled Jean, as he hurried to the door of the outer hall. "It would have been so simple to rob the Paris house without sending that infernal letter. It was sure to knock them all silly."

"What harm can the letter do, you fool?" said M. Charolais. "It's Sunday. We want them knocked silly for to-morrow, to get hold of the coronet. Oh, to get hold of that coronet! It must be in Paris. I've been ransacking this chateau for hours."

Jean opened the door of the outer hall half an inch, and glued his eyes to it. Bernard had done the same with the door opening into the drawing-room. M. Charolais, Pierre, and Louis were opening drawers, ransacking them, and shutting them with infinite quickness and noiselessly.

"Bureau! Which is the bureau? The place is stuffed with bureaux!" growled M. Charolais. "I must have those keys."

"That plain thing with the brass handles in the middle on the left—that's a bureau," said Bernard softly.

"Why didn't you say so?" growled M. Charolais.

He dashed to it, and tried it. It was locked.

"Locked, of course! Just my luck! Come and get it open, Pierre. Be smart!"

The son he had described as an engineer came quickly to the bureau, fitting together as he came the two halves of a small jemmy. He fitted it into the top of the flap. There was a crunch, and the old lock gave. He opened the flap, and he and M. Charolais pulled open drawer after drawer.

"Quick! Here's that fat old fool!" said Jean, in a hoarse, hissing whisper.

He moved down the hall, blowing out one of the lamps as he passed it. In the seventh drawer lay a bunch of keys. M. Charolais snatched it up, glanced at it, took a bunch of keys from his own pocket, put it in the drawer, closed it, closed the flap, and rushed to the window. Jean and his sons were already out on the terrace.

M. Charolais was still a yard from the window when the door into the outer hall opened and in came M. Gournay-Martin.

He caught a glimpse of a back vanishing through the window, and bellowed: "Hi! A man! A burglar! Firmin! Firmin!"

He ran blundering down the hall, tangled his feet in the fragments of the broken chair, and came sprawling a thundering cropper, which knocked every breath of wind out of his capacious body. He lay flat on his face for a couple of minutes, his broad back wriggling convulsively—a pathetic sight!—in the painful effort to get his breath back. Then he sat up, and with perfect frankness burst into tears. He sobbed and blubbered, like a small child that has hurt itself, for three or four minutes. Then, having recovered his magnificent voice, he bellowed furiously: "Firmin! Firmin! Charmerace! Charmerace!"

Then he rose painfully to his feet, and stood staring at the open windows.

Presently he roared again: "Firmin! Firmin! Charmerace! Charmerace!"

He kept looking at the window with terrified eyes, as though he expected somebody to step in and cut his throat from ear to ear.

"Firmin! Firmin! Charmerace! Charmerace!" he bellowed again.

The Duke came quietly into the hall, dressed in a heavy motor-coat, his motor-cap on his head, and carrying a kit-bag in his hand.

"Did I hear you call?" he said.

"Call?" said the millionaire. "I shouted. The burglars are here already. I've just seen one of them. He was bolting through the middle window."

The Duke raised his eyebrows.

"Nerves," he said gently—"nerves."

"Nerves be hanged!" said the millionaire. "I tell you I saw him as plainly as I see you."

"Well, you can't see me at all, seeing that you're lighting an acre and a half of hall with a single lamp," said the Duke, still in a tone of utter incredulity.

"It's that fool Firmin! He ought to have lighted six. Firmin! Firmin!" bellowed the millionaire.

They listened for the sonorous clumping of the promoted gamekeeper's boots, but they did not hear it. Evidently Firmin was still giving his master's instructions about the cars to Jean.

"Well, we may as well shut the windows, anyhow," said the Duke, proceeding to do so. "If you think Firmin would be any good, you might post him in this hall with a gun to-night. There could be no harm in putting a charge of small shot into the legs of these ruffians. He has only to get one of them, and the others will go for their lives. Yet I don't like leaving you and Germaine in this big house with only Firmin to look after you."

"I shouldn't like it myself, and I'm not going to chance it," growled the millionaire. "We're going to motor to Paris along with you, and leave Jean to help Firmin fight these burglars. Firmin's all right—he's an old soldier. He fought in '70. Not that I've much belief in soldiers against this cursed Lupin, after the way he dealt with that corporal and his men three years ago."

"I'm glad you're coming to Paris," said the Duke. "It'll be a weight off my mind. I'd better drive the limousine, and you take the landaulet."

"That won't do," said the millionaire. "Germaine won't go in the limousine. You know she has taken a dislike to it."

"Nevertheless, I'd better bucket on to Paris, and let you follow slowly with Germaine. The sooner I get to Paris the better for your collection. I'll take Mademoiselle Kritchnoff with me, and, if you like, Irma, though the lighter I travel the sooner I shall get there."

"No, I'll take Irma and Germaine," said the millionaire. "Germaine would prefer to have Irma with her, in case you had an accident. She wouldn't like to get to Paris and have to find a fresh maid."

The drawing-room door opened, and in came Germaine, followed by Sonia and Irma. They wore motor-cloaks and hoods and veils. Sonia and Irma were carrying hand-bags.

"I think it's extremely tiresome your dragging us off to Paris like this in the middle of the night," said Germaine pettishly.

"Do you?" said the millionaire. "Well, then, you'll be interested to hear that I've just seen a burglar here in this very room. I frightened him, and he bolted through the window on to the terrace."

"He was greenish-pink, slightly tinged with yellow," said the Duke softly.

"Greenish-pink? Oh, do stop your jesting, Jacques! Is this a time for idiocy?" cried Germaine, in a tone of acute exasperation.

"It was the dim light which made your father see him in those colours. In a bright light, I think he would have been an Alsatian blue," said the Duke suavely.

"You'll have to break yourself of this silly habit of trifling, my dear Duke, if ever you expect to be a member of the Academie Francaise," said the millionaire with some acrimony. "I tell you I did see a burglar."

"Yes, yes. I admitted it frankly. It was his colour I was talking about," said the Duke, with an ironical smile.

"Oh, stop your idiotic jokes! We're all sick to death of them!" said Germaine, with something of the fine fury which so often distinguished her father.

"There are times for all things," said the millionaire solemnly. "And I must say that, with the fate of my collection and of the coronet trembling in the balance, this does not seem to me a season for idle jests."

"I stand reproved," said the Duke; and he smiled at Sonia.

"My keys, Sonia—the keys of the Paris house," said the millionaire.

Sonia took her own keys from her pocket and went to the bureau. She slipped a key into the lock and tried to turn it. It would not turn; and she bent down to look at it.

"Why—why, some one's been tampering with the lock! It's broken!" she cried.

"I told you I'd seen a burglar!" cried the millionaire triumphantly. "He was after the keys."

Sonia drew back the flap of the bureau and hastily pulled open the drawer in which the keys had been.

"They're here!" she cried, taking them out of the drawer and holding them up.

"Then I was just in time," said the millionaire. "I startled him in the very act of stealing the keys."

"I withdraw! I withdraw!" said the Duke. "You did see a burglar, evidently. But still I believe he was greenish-pink. They often are. However, you'd better give me those keys, Mademoiselle Sonia, since I'm to get to Paris first. I should look rather silly if, when I got there, I had to break into the house to catch the burglars."

Sonia handed the keys to the Duke. He contrived to take her little hand, keys and all, into his own, as he received them, and squeezed it. The light was too dim for the others to see the flush which flamed in her face. She went back and stood beside the bureau.

"Now, papa, are you going to motor to Paris in a thin coat and linen waistcoat? If we're going, we'd better go. You always do keep us waiting half an hour whenever we start to go anywhere," said Germaine firmly.

The millionaire bustled out of the room. With a gesture of impatience Germaine dropped into a chair. Irma stood waiting by the drawing-room door. Sonia sat down by the bureau.

There came a sharp patter of rain against the windows.

"Rain! It only wanted that! It's going to be perfectly beastly!" cried Germaine.

"Oh, well, you must make the best of it. At any rate you're well wrapped up, and the night is warm enough, though it is raining," said the Duke. "Still, I could have wished that Lupin confined his operations to fine weather." He paused, and added cheerfully, "But, after all, it will lay the dust."

They sat for three or four minutes in a dull silence, listening to the pattering of the rain against the panes. The Duke took his cigarette-case from his pocket and lighted a cigarette.

Suddenly he lost his bored air; his face lighted up; and he said joyfully: "Of course, why didn't I think of it? Why should we start from a pit of gloom like this? Let us have the proper illumination which our enterprise deserves."

With that he set about lighting all the lamps in the hall. There were lamps on stands, lamps on brackets, lamps on tables, and lamps which hung from the roof—old-fashioned lamps with new reservoirs, new lamps of what is called chaste design, brass lamps, silver lamps, and lamps in porcelain. The Duke lighted them one after another, patiently, missing none, with a cold perseverance. The operation was punctuated by exclamations from Germaine. They were all to the effect that she could not understand how he could be such a fool. The Duke paid no attention whatever to her. His face illumined with boyish glee, he lighted lamp after lamp.

Sonia watched him with a smiling admiration of the childlike enthusiasm with which he performed the task. Even the stolid face of the ox-eyed Irma relaxed into grins, which she smoothed quickly out with a respectful hand.

The Duke had just lighted the twenty-second lamp when in bustled the millionaire.

"What's this? What's this?" he cried, stopping short, blinking.

"Just some more of Jacques' foolery!" cried Germaine in tones of the last exasperation.

"But, my dear Duke!—my dear Duke! The oil!—the oil!" cried the millionaire, in a tone of bitter distress. "Do you think it's my object in life to swell the Rockefeller millions? We never have more than six lamps burning unless we are holding a reception."

"I think it looks so cheerful," said the Duke, looking round on his handiwork with a beaming smile of satisfaction. "But where are the cars? Jean seems a deuce of a time bringing them round. Does he expect us to go to the garage through this rain? We'd better hurry him up. Come on; you've got a good carrying voice."

He caught the millionaire by the arm, hurried him through the outer hall, opened the big door of the chateau, and said: "Now shout!"

The millionaire looked at him, shrugged his shoulders, and said: "You don't beat about the bush when you want anything."

"Why should I?" said the Duke simply. "Shout, my good chap—shout!"

The millionaire raised his voice in a terrific bellow of "Jean! Jean! Firmin! Firmin!"

There was no answer.

VII. THE THEFT OF THE MOTOR-CARS

The night was very black; the rain pattered in their faces.

Again the millionaire bellowed: "Jean! Firmin! Firmin! Jean!"

No answer came out of the darkness, though his bellow echoed and re-echoed among the out-buildings and stables away on the left.

He turned and looked at the Duke and said uneasily, "What on earth can they be doing?"

"I can't conceive," said the Duke. "I suppose we must go and hunt them out."

"What! in this darkness, with these burglars about?" said the millionaire, starting back.

"If we don't, nobody else will," said the Duke. "And all the time that rascal Lupin is stealing nearer and nearer your pictures. So buck up, and come along!"

He seized the reluctant millionaire by the arm and drew him down the steps. They took their way to the stables. A dim light shone from the open door of the motor-house. The Duke went into it first, and stopped short.

"Well, I'll be hanged!" he cried,

Instead of three cars the motor-house held but one—the hundred horse-power Mercrac. It was a racing car, with only two seats. On them sat two figures, Jean and Firmin.

"What are you sitting there for? You idle dogs!" bellowed the millionaire.

Neither of the men answered, nor did they stir. The light from the lamp gleamed on their fixed eyes, which stared at their infuriated master.

"What on earth is this?" said the Duke; and seizing the lamp which stood beside the car, he raised it so that its light fell on the two figures. Then it was clear what had happened: they were trussed like two fowls, and gagged.

The Duke pulled a penknife from his pocket, opened the blade, stepped into the car and set Firmin free. Firmin coughed and spat and swore. The Duke cut the bonds of Jean.

"Well," said the Duke, in a tone of cutting irony, "what new game is this? What have you been playing at?"

"It was those Charolais—those cursed Charolais!" growled Firmin.

"They came on us unawares from behind," said Jean.

"They tied us up, and gagged us—the swine!" said Firmin.

"And then—they went off in the two cars," said Jean.

"Went off in the two cars?" cried the millionaire, in blank stupefaction.

The Duke burst into a shout of laughter.

"Well, your dear friend Lupin doesn't do things by halves," he cried. "This is the funniest thing I ever heard of."

"Funny!" howled the millionaire. "Funny! Where does the fun come in? What about my pictures and the coronet?"

The Duke laughed his laugh out; then changed on the instant to a man of action.

"Well, this means a change in our plans," he said. "I must get to Paris in this car here."

"It's such a rotten old thing," said the millionaire. "You'll never do it."

"Never mind," said the Duke. "I've got to do it somehow. I daresay it's better than you think. And after all, it's only a matter of two hundred miles." He paused, and then said in an anxious tone: "All the same I don't like leaving you and Germaine in the chateau. These rogues have probably only taken the cars out of reach just to prevent your getting to Paris. They'll leave them in some field and come back."

"You're not going to leave us behind. I wouldn't spend the night in the chateau for a million francs. There's always the train," said the millionaire.

"The train! Twelve hours in the train—with all those changes! You don't mean that you will actually go to Paris by train?" said the Duke.

"I do," said the millionaire. "Come along—I must go and tell Germaine; there's no time to waste," and he hurried off to the chateau.

"Get the lamps lighted, Jean, and make sure that the tank's full. As for the engine, I must humour it and trust to luck. I'll get her to Paris somehow," said the Duke.

He went back to the chateau, and Firmin followed him.

When the Duke came into the great hall he found Germaine and her father indulging in recriminations. She was declaring that nothing would induce her to make the journey by train; her father was declaring that she should. He bore down her opposition by the mere force of his magnificent voice.

When at last there came a silence, Sonia said quietly: "But is there a train? I know there's a train at midnight; but is there one before?"

"A time-table—where's a time-table?" said the millionaire.

"Now, where did I see a time-table?" said the Duke. "Oh, I know; there's one in the drawer of that Oriental cabinet." Crossing to the cabinet, he opened the drawer, took out the time-table, and handed it to M. Gournay-Martin.

The millionaire took it and turned over the leaves quickly, ran his eye down a page, and said, "Yes, thank goodness, there is a train. There's one at a quarter to nine."

"And what good is it to us? How are we to get to the station?" said Germaine.

They looked at one another blankly. Firmin, who had followed the Duke into the hall, came to the rescue.

"There's the luggage-cart," he said.

"The luggage-cart!" cried Germaine contemptuously.

"The very thing!" said the millionaire. "I'll drive it myself. Off you go, Firmin; harness a horse to it."

Firmin went clumping out of the hall.

It was perhaps as well that he went, for the Duke asked what time it was; and since the watches of Germaine and her father differed still, there ensued an altercation in which, had Firmin been there, he would doubtless have taken part.

The Duke cut it short by saying: "Well, I don't think I'll wait to see you start for the station. It won't take you more than half an hour. The cart is light. You needn't start yet. I'd better get off as soon as the car is ready. It isn't as though I could trust it."

"One moment," said Germaine. "Is there a dining-car on the train? I'm not going to be starved as well as have my night's rest cut to pieces."

"Of course there isn't a dining-car," snapped her father. "We must eat something now, and take something with us."

"Sonia, Irma, quick! Be off to the larder and see what you can find. Tell Mother Firmin to make an omelette. Be quick!"

Sonia went towards the door of the hall, followed by Irma.

"Good-night, and bon voyage, Mademoiselle Sonia," said the Duke.

"Good-night, and bon voyage, your Grace," said Sonia.

The Duke opened the door of the hall for her; and as she went out, she said anxiously, in a low voice: "Oh, do—do be careful. I hate to think of your hurrying to Paris on a night like this. Please be careful."

"I will be careful," said the Duke.

The honk of the motor-horn told him that Jean had brought the car to the door of the chateau. He came down the room, kissed Germaine's hands, shook hands with the millionaire, and bade them good-night. Then he went out to the car. They heard it start; the rattle of it grew fainter and fainter down the long avenue and died away.

M. Gournay-Martin arose, and began putting out lamps. As he did so, he kept casting fearful glances at the window, as if he feared lest, now that the Duke had gone, the burglars should dash in upon him.

There came a knock at the door, and Jean appeared on the threshold.

"His Grace told me that I was to come into the house, and help Firmin look after it," he said.

The millionaire gave him instructions about the guarding of the house. Firmin, since he was an old soldier, was to occupy the post of honour, and guard the hall, armed with his gun. Jean was to guard the two drawing-rooms, as being less likely points of attack. He also was to have a gun; and the millionaire went with him to the gun-room and gave him one and a dozen cartridges. When they came back to the hall, Sonia called them into the dining-room; and there, to the accompaniment of an unsubdued grumbling from Germaine at having to eat cold food at eight at night, they made a hasty but excellent meal, since the chef had left an elaborate cold supper ready to be served.

They had nearly finished it when Jean came in, his gun on his arm, to say that Firmin had harnessed the horse to the luggage-cart, and it was awaiting them at the door of the chateau.

"Send him in to me, and stand by the horse till we come out," said the millionaire.

Firmin came clumping in.

The millionaire gazed at him solemnly, and said: "Firmin, I am relying on you. I am leaving you in a position of honour and danger—a position which an old soldier of France loves."

Firmin did his best to look like an old soldier of France. He pulled himself up out of the slouch which long years of loafing through woods with a gun on his arm had given him. He lacked also the old soldier of France's fiery gaze. His eyes were lack-lustre.

"I look for anything, Firmin—burglary, violence, an armed assault," said the millionaire.

"Don't be afraid, sir. I saw the war of '70," said Firmin boldly, rising to the occasion.

"Good!" said the millionaire. "I confide the chateau to you. I trust you with my treasures."

He rose, and saying "Come along, we must be getting to the station," he led the way to the door of the chateau.

The luggage-cart stood rather high, and they had to bring a chair out of the hall to enable the girls to climb into it. Germaine did not forget to give her real opinion of the advantages of a seat formed by a plank resting on the sides of the cart. The millionaire climbed heavily up in front, and took the reins.

"Never again will I trust only to motor-cars. The first thing I'll do after I've made sure that my collections are safe will be to buy carriages— something roomy," he said gloomily, as he realized the discomfort of his seat.

He turned to Jean and Firmin, who stood on the steps of the chateau watching the departure of their master, and said: "Sons of France, be brave—be brave!"

The cart bumped off into the damp, dark night.

Jean and Firmin watched it disappear into the darkness. Then they came into the chateau and shut the door.

Firmin looked at Jean, and said gloomily: "I don't like this. These burglars stick at nothing. They'd as soon cut your throat as look at you."

"It can't be helped," said Jean. "Besides, you've got the post of honour. You guard the hall. I'm to look after the drawing-rooms. They're not likely to break in through the drawing-rooms. And I shall lock the door between them and the hall."

"No, no; you won't lock that door!" cried Firmin.

"But I certainly will," said Jean. "You'd better come and get a gun."

They went to the gun-room, Firmin still protesting against the locking of the door between the drawing-rooms and the hall. He chose his gun; and they went into the kitchen. Jean took two bottles of wine, a rich-looking pie, a sweet, and carried them to the drawing-room. He came back into the hall, gathered together an armful of papers and magazines, and went back to the drawing-room. Firmin kept trotting after him, like a little dog with a somewhat heavy footfall.

On the threshold of the drawing-room Jean paused and said: "The important thing with burglars is to fire first, old cock. Good-night. Pleasant dreams."

He shut the door and turned the key. Firmin stared at the decorated panels blankly. The beauty of the scheme of decoration did not, at the moment, move him to admiration.

He looked fearfully round the empty hall and at the windows, black against the night. Under the patter of the rain he heard footsteps—distinctly. He went hastily clumping down the hall, and along the passage to the kitchen.

His wife was setting his supper on the table.

"My God!" he said. "I haven't been so frightened since '70." And he mopped his glistening forehead with a dish-cloth. It was not a clean dish-cloth; but he did not care.

"Frightened? What of?" said his wife.

"Burglars! Cut-throats!" said Firmin.

He told her of the fears of M. Gournay-Martin, and of his own appointment to the honourable and dangerous post of guard of the chateau.

"God save us!" said his wife. "You lock the door of that beastly hall, and come into the kitchen. Burglars won't bother about the kitchen."

"But the master's treasures!" protested Firmin. "He confided them to me. He said so distinctly."

"Let the master look after his treasures himself," said Madame Firmin, with decision. "You've only one throat; and I'm not going to have it cut. You sit down and eat your supper. Go and lock that door first, though."

Firmin locked the door of the hall; then he locked the door of the kitchen; then he sat down, and began to eat his supper. His appetite was hearty, but none the less he derived little pleasure from the meal. He kept stopping with the food poised on his fork, midway between the plate and his mouth, for several seconds at a time, while he listened with straining ears for the sound of burglars breaking in the windows of the hall. He was much too far from those windows to hear anything that happened to them, but that did not prevent him from straining his ears. Madame Firmin ate her supper with an air of perfect ease. She felt sure that burglars would not bother with the kitchen.

Firmin's anxiety made him terribly thirsty. Tumbler after tumbler of wine flowed down the throat for which he feared. When he had finished his supper he went on satisfying his thirst. Madame Firmin lighted his pipe for him, and went and washed up the supper-dishes in the scullery. Then she came back, and sat down on the other side of the hearth, facing him. About the middle of his third bottle of wine, Firmin's cold, relentless courage was suddenly restored to him. He began to talk firmly about his duty to his master, his resolve to die, if need were, in defence of his interests, of his utter contempt for burglars—probably Parisians. But he did not go into the hall. Doubtless the pleasant warmth of the kitchen fire held him in his chair.

He had described to his wife, with some ferocity, the cruel manner in which he would annihilate the first three burglars who entered the hall, and was proceeding to describe his method of dealing with the fourth, when there came a loud knocking on the front door of the chateau.

Stricken silent, turned to stone, Firmin sat with his mouth open, in the midst of an unfinished word. Madame Firmin scuttled to the kitchen door she had left unlocked on her return from the scullery, and locked it. She turned, and they stared at one another.

The heavy knocker fell again and again and again. Between the knocking there was a sound like the roaring of lions. Husband and wife stared at one another with white faces. Firmin picked up his gun with trembling hands, and the movement seemed to set his teeth chattering. They chattered like castanets.

The knocking still went on, and so did the roaring.

It had gone on at least for five minutes, when a slow gleam of comprehension lightened Madame Firmin's face.

"I believe it's the master's voice," she said.

"The master's voice!" said Firmin, in a hoarse, terrified whisper.

"Yes," said Madame Firmin. And she unlocked the thick door and opened it a few inches.

The barrier removed, the well-known bellow of the millionaire came distinctly to their ears. Firmin's courage rushed upon him in full flood. He clumped across the room, brushed his wife aside, and trotted to the door of the chateau. He unlocked it, drew the bolts, and threw it open. On the steps stood the millionaire, Germaine, and Sonia. Irma stood at the horse's head.

"What the devil have you been doing?" bellowed the millionaire. "What do you keep me standing in the rain for? Why didn't you let me in?"

"B-b-b-burglars—I thought you were b-b-b-burglars," stammered Firmin.

"Burglars!" howled the millionaire. "Do I sound like a burglar?"

At the moment he did not; he sounded more like a bull of Bashan. He bustled past Firmin to the door of the hall.

"Here! What's this locked for?" he bellowed.

"I—I—locked it in case burglars should get in while I was opening the front door," stammered Firmin.

The millionaire turned the key, opened the door, and went into the hall. Germaine followed him. She threw off her dripping coat, and said with some heat: "I can't conceive why you didn't make sure that there was a train at a quarter to nine. I will not go to Paris to-night. Nothing shall induce me to take that midnight train!"

"Nonsense!" said the millionaire. "Nonsense—you'll have to go! Where's that infernal time-table?" He rushed to the table on to which he had thrown the time-table after looking up the train, snatched it up, and looked at the cover. "Why, hang it!" he cried. "It's for June—June, 1903!"

"Oh!" cried Germaine, almost in a scream. "It's incredible! It's one of Jacques' jokes!"

VIII. THE DUKE ARRIVES

The morning was gloomy, and the police-station with its bare, white-washed walls—their white expanse was only broken by notice-boards to which were pinned portraits of criminals with details of their appearance, their crime, and the reward offered for their apprehension—with its shabby furniture, and its dingy fireplace, presented a dismal and sordid appearance entirely in keeping with the September grey. The inspector sat at his desk, yawning after a night which had passed without an arrest. He was waiting to be relieved. The policeman at the door and the two policemen sitting on a bench by the wall yawned in sympathy.

The silence of the street was broken by the rattle of an uncommonly noisy motor-car. It stopped before the door of the police-station, and the eyes of the inspector and his men turned, idly expectant, to the door of the office.

It opened, and a young man in motor-coat and cap stood on the threshold.

He looked round the office with alert eyes, which took in everything, and said, in a brisk, incisive voice: "I am the Duke of Charmerace. I am here on behalf of M. Gournay-Martin. Last evening he received a letter from Arsene Lupin saying he was going to break into his Paris house this very morning."

At the name of Arsene Lupin the inspector sprang from his chair, the policemen from their bench. On the instant they were wide awake, attentive, full of zeal.

"The letter, your Grace!" said the inspector briskly.

The Duke pulled off his glove, drew the letter from the breast-pocket of his under-coat, and handed it to the inspector.

The inspector glanced through it, and said. "Yes, I know the handwriting well." Then he read it carefully, and added, "Yes, yes: it's his usual letter."

"There's no time to be lost," said the Duke quickly. "I ought to have been here hours ago—hours. I had a break-down. I'm afraid I'm too late as it is."

"Come along, your Grace—come along, you," said the inspector briskly.

The four of them hurried out of the office and down the steps of the police-station. In the roadway stood a long grey racing-car, caked with muds—grey mud, brown mud, red mud—from end to end. It looked as if it had brought samples of the soil of France from many districts.

"Come along; I'll take you in the car. Your men can trot along beside us," said the Duke to the inspector.

He slipped into the car, the inspector jumped in and took the seat beside him, and they started. They went slowly, to allow the two policemen to keep up with them. Indeed, the car could not have made any great pace, for the tyre of the off hind-wheel was punctured and deflated.

In three minutes they came to the Gournay-Martin house, a wide-fronted mass of undistinguished masonry, in an undistinguished row of exactly the same pattern. There were no signs that any one was living in it. Blinds were drawn, shutters were up over all the windows, upper and lower. No smoke came from any of its chimneys, though indeed it was full early for that.

Pulling a bunch of keys from his pocket, the Duke ran up the steps. The inspector followed him. The Duke looked at the bunch, picked out the latch-key, and fitted it into the lock. It did not open it. He drew it out and tried another key and another. The door remained locked.

"Let me, your Grace," said the inspector. "I'm more used to it. I shall be quicker."

The Duke handed the keys to him, and, one after another, the inspector fitted them into the lock. It was useless. None of them opened the door.

"They've given me the wrong keys," said the Duke, with some vexation. "Or no—stay—I see what's happened. The keys have been changed."

"Changed?" said the inspector. "When? Where?"

"Last night at Charmerace," said the Duke. "M. Gournay-Martin declared that he saw a burglar slip out of one of the windows of the hall of the chateau, and we found the lock of the bureau in which the keys were kept broken."

The inspector seized the knocker, and hammered on the door.

"Try that door there," he cried to his men, pointing to a side-door on the right, the tradesmen's entrance, giving access to the back of the house. It was locked. There came no sound of movement in the house in answer to the inspector's knocking.

"Where's the concierge?" he said.

The Duke shrugged his shoulders. "There's a housekeeper, too—a woman named Victoire," he said. "Let's hope we don't find them with their throats cut."

"That isn't Lupin's way," said the inspector. "They won't have come to much harm."

"It's not very likely that they'll be in a position to open doors," said the Duke drily.

"Hadn't we better have it broken open and be done with it?"

The inspector hesitated.

"People don't like their doors broken open," he said. "And M. Gournay-Martin—"

"Oh, I'll take the responsibility of that," said the Duke.

"Oh, if you say so, your Grace," said the inspector, with a brisk relief. "Henri, go to Ragoneau, the locksmith in the Rue Theobald. Bring him here as quickly as ever you can get him."

"Tell him it's a couple of louis if he's here inside of ten minutes," said the Duke.

The policeman hurried off. The inspector bent down and searched the steps carefully. He searched the roadway. The Duke lighted a cigarette and watched him. The house of the millionaire stood next but one to the corner of a street which ran at right angles to the one in which it stood, and the corner house was empty. The inspector searched the road, then he went round the corner. The other policeman went along the road, searching in the opposite direction. The Duke leant against the door and smoked on patiently. He showed none of the weariness of a man who has spent the night in a long and anxious drive in a rickety motor-car. His eyes were bright and clear; he looked as fresh as if he had come from his bed after a long night's rest. If he had not found the South Pole, he had at any rate brought back fine powers of endurance from his expedition in search of it.

The inspector came back, wearing a disappointed air.

"Have you found anything?" said the Duke.

"Nothing," said the inspector.

He came up the steps and hammered again on the door. No one answered his knock. There was a clatter of footsteps, and Henri and the locksmith, a burly, bearded man, his bag of tools slung over his shoulder, came hurrying up. He was not long getting to work, but it was not an easy job. The lock was strong. At the end of five minutes he said that he might spend an hour struggling with the lock itself; should he cut away a piece of the door round it?

"Cut away," said the Duke.

The locksmith changed his tools, and in less than three minutes he had cut away a square piece from the door, a square in which the lock was fixed, and taken it bodily away.

The door opened. The inspector drew his revolver, and entered the house. The Duke followed him. The policemen drew their revolvers, and followed the Duke. The big hall was but dimly lighted. One of the policemen quickly threw back the shutters of the windows and let in the light. The hall was empty, the furniture in perfect order; there were no signs of burglary there.

"The concierge?" said the inspector, and his men hurried through the little door on the right which opened into the concierge's rooms. In half a minute one of them came out and said: "Gagged and bound, and his wife too."

"But the rooms which were to be plundered are upstairs," said the Duke—"the big drawing-rooms on the first floor. Come on; we may be just in time. The scoundrels may not yet have got away."

He ran quickly up the stairs, followed by the inspector, and hurried along the corridor to the door of the big drawing-room. He threw it open, and stopped dead on the threshold. He had arrived too late.

The room was in disorder. Chairs were overturned, there were empty spaces on the wall where the finest pictures of the millionaire had been hung. The window facing the door was wide open. The shutters were broken; one of them was hanging crookedly from only its bottom hinge. The top of a ladder rose above the window-sill, and beside it, astraddle the sill, was an Empire card-table, half inside the room, half out. On the hearth-rug, before a large tapestry fire-screen, which masked the wide fireplace, built in imitation of the big, wide fireplaces of our ancestors, and rose to the level of the chimney-piece—a magnificent chimney-piece in carved oak—were some chairs tied together ready to be removed.

The Duke and the inspector ran to the window, and looked down into the garden. It was empty. At the further end of it, on the other side of its wall, rose the scaffolding of a house a-building. The burglars had found every convenience to their hand—a strong ladder, an egress through the door in the garden wall, and then through the gap formed by the house in process of erection, which had rendered them independent of the narrow passage between the walls of the gardens, which debouched into a side-street on the right.

The Duke turned from the window, glanced at the wall opposite, then, as if something had caught his eye, went quickly to it.

"Look here," he said, and he pointed to the middle of one of the empty spaces in which a picture had hung.

There, written neatly in blue chalk, were the words:

ARSENE LUPIN

"This is a job for Guerchard," said the inspector. "But I had better get an examining magistrate to take the matter in hand first." And he ran to the telephone.

The Duke opened the folding doors which led into the second drawing-room. The shutters of the windows were open, and it was plain that Arsene Lupin had plundered it also of everything that had struck his fancy. In the gaps between the pictures on the walls was again the signature "Arsene Lupin."

The inspector was shouting impatiently into the telephone, bidding a servant wake her master instantly. He did not leave the telephone till he was sure that she had done so, that her master was actually awake, and had been informed of the crime. The Duke sat down in an easy chair and waited for him.

When he had finished telephoning, the inspector began to search the two rooms for traces of the burglars. He found nothing, not even a finger-mark.

When he had gone through the two rooms he said, "The next thing to do is to find the house-keeper. She may be sleeping still—she may not even have heard the noise of the burglars."

"I find all this extremely interesting," said the Duke; and he followed the inspector out of the room.

The inspector called up the two policemen, who had been freeing the concierge and going through the rooms on the ground-floor. They did not then examine any more of the rooms on the first floor to discover if they also had been plundered. They went straight up to the top of the house, the servants' quarters.

The inspector called, "Victoire! Victoire!" two or three times; but there was no answer.

They opened the door of room after room and looked in, the inspector taking the rooms on the right, the policemen the rooms on the left.

"Here we are," said one of the policemen. "This room's been recently occupied." They looked in, and saw that the bed was unmade. Plainly Victoire had slept in it.

"Where can she be?" said the Duke.

"Be?" said the inspector. "I expect she's with the burglars—an accomplice."

"I gather that M. Gournay-Martin had the greatest confidence in her," said the Duke.

"He'll have less now," said the inspector drily. "It's generally the confidential ones who let their masters down."

The inspector and his men set about a thorough search of the house. They found the other rooms undisturbed. In half an hour they had established the fact that the burglars had confined their attention to the two drawing-rooms. They found no traces of them; and they did not find Victoire. The concierge could throw no light on her disappearance. He and his wife had been taken by surprise in their sleep and in the dark.

They had been gagged and bound, they declared, without so much as having set eyes on their assailants. The Duke and the inspector came back to the plundered drawing-room.

The inspector looked at his watch and went to the telephone.

"I must let the Prefecture know," he said.

"Be sure you ask them to send Guerchard," said the Duke.

"Guerchard?" said the inspector doubtfully.

"M. Formery, the examining magistrate, does not get on very well with Guerchard."

"What sort of a man is M. Formery? Is he capable?" said the Duke.

"Oh, yes—yes. He's very capable," said the inspector quickly. "But he doesn't have very good luck."

"M. Gournay-Martin particularly asked me to send for Guerchard if I arrived too late, and found the burglary already committed," said the Duke. "It seems that there is war to the knife between Guerchard and this Arsene Lupin. In that case Guerchard will leave no stone unturned to catch the rascal and recover the stolen treasures. M. Gournay-Martin felt that Guerchard was the man for this piece of work very strongly indeed."

"Very good, your Grace," said the inspector. And he rang up the Prefecture of Police.

The Duke heard him report the crime and ask that Guerchard should be sent. The official in charge at the moment seemed to make some demur.

The Duke sprang to his feet, and said in an anxious tone, "Perhaps I'd better speak to him myself."

He took his place at the telephone and said, "I am the Duke of Charmerace. M. Gournay-Martin begged me to secure the services of M. Guerchard. He laid the greatest stress on my securing them, if on reaching Paris I found that the crime had already been committed."

The official at the other end of the line hesitated. He did not refuse on the instant as he had refused the inspector. It may be that he reflected that M. Gournay-Martin was a millionaire and a man of influence; that the Duke of Charmerace was a Duke; that he, at any rate, had nothing whatever to gain by running counter to their wishes. He said that Chief-Inspector Guerchard was not at the Prefecture, that he was off duty; that he would send down two detectives, who were on duty, at once, and summon Chief-Inspector Guerchard with all speed. The Duke thanked him and rang off.

"That's all right," he said cheerfully, turning to the inspector. "What time will M. Formery be here?"

"Well, I don't expect him for another hour," said the inspector. "He won't come till he's had his breakfast. He always makes a good breakfast before setting out to start an inquiry, lest he shouldn't find time to make one after he's begun it."

"Breakfast—breakfast—that's a great idea," said the Duke. "Now you come to remind me, I'm absolutely famished. I got some supper on my way late last night; but I've had nothing since. I suppose nothing interesting will happen till M. Formery comes; and I may as well get some food. But I don't want to leave the house. I think I'll see what the concierge can do for me."

So saying, he went downstairs and interviewed the concierge. The concierge seemed to be still doubtful whether he was standing on his head or his heels, but he undertook to supply the needs of the Duke. The Duke gave him a louis, and he hurried off to get food from a restaurant.

The Duke went upstairs to the bathroom and refreshed himself with a cold bath. By the time he had bathed and dressed the concierge had a meal ready for him in the dining-room. He ate it with the heartiest appetite. Then he sent out for a barber and was shaved.

He then repaired to the pillaged drawing-room, disposed himself in the most restful attitude on a sofa, and lighted an excellent cigar. In the middle of it the inspector came to him. He was not wearing a very cheerful air; and he told the Duke that he had found no clue to the perpetrators of the crime, though M. Dieusy and M. Bonavent, the detectives from the Prefecture of Police, had joined him in the search.

The Duke was condoling with him on this failure when they heard a knocking at the front door, and then voices on the stairs.

"Ah! Here is M. Formery!" said the inspector cheerfully. "Now we can get on."

IX. M. FORMERY OPENS THE INQUIRY

The examining magistrate came into the room. He was a plump and pink little man, with very bright eyes. His bristly hair stood up straight all over his head, giving it the appearance of a broad, dapple-grey clothes-brush. He appeared to be of the opinion that Nature had given the world the toothbrush as a model of what a moustache should be; and his own was clipped to that pattern.

"The Duke of Charmerace, M. Formery," said the inspector.

The little man bowed and said, "Charmed, charmed to make your acquaintance, your Grace—though the occasion—the occasion is somewhat painful. The treasures of M. Gournay-Martin are known to all the world. France will deplore his losses." He paused, and added hastily, "But we shall recover them—we shall recover them."

The Duke rose, bowed, and protested his pleasure at making the acquaintance of M. Formery.

"Is this the scene of the robbery, inspector?" said M. Formery; and he rubbed his hands together with a very cheerful air.

"Yes, sir," said the inspector. "These two rooms seem to be the only ones touched, though of course we can't tell till M. Gournay-Martin arrives. Jewels may have been stolen from the bedrooms."

"I fear that M. Gournay-Martin won't be of much help for some days," said the Duke. "When I left him he was nearly distracted; and he won't be any better after a night journey to Paris from Charmerace. But probably these are the only two rooms touched, for in them M. Gournay-Martin had gathered together the gems of his collection. Over the doors hung some pieces of Flemish tapestry—marvels—the composition admirable—the colouring delightful."

"It is easy to see that your Grace was very fond of them," said M. Formery.

"I should think so," said the Duke. "I looked on them as already belonging to me, for my father-in-law was going to give them to me as a wedding present."

"A great loss—a great loss. But we will recover them, sooner or later, you can rest assured of it. I hope you have touched nothing in this room. If anything has been moved it may put me off the scent altogether. Let me have the details, inspector."

The inspector reported the arrival of the Duke at the police-station with Arsene Lupin's letter to M. Gournay-Martin; the discovery that the keys had been changed and would not open the door of the house; the opening of it by the locksmith; the discovery of the concierge and his wife gagged and bound.

"Probably accomplices," said M. Formery.

"Does Lupin always work with accomplices?" said the Duke. "Pardon my ignorance—but I've been out of France for so long—before he attained to this height of notoriety."

"Lupin—why Lupin?" said M. Formery sharply.

"Why, there is the letter from Lupin which my future father-in-law received last night; its arrival was followed by the theft of his two swiftest motor-cars; and then, these signatures on the wall here," said the Duke in some surprise at the question.

"Lupin! Lupin! Everybody has Lupin on the brain!" said M. Formery impatiently. "I'm sick of hearing his name. This letter and these signatures are just as likely to be forgeries as not."

"I wonder if Guerchard will take that view," said the Duke.

"Guerchard? Surely we're not going to be cluttered up with Guerchard. He has Lupin on the brain worse than any one else."

"But M. Gournay-Martin particularly asked me to send for Guerchard if I arrived too late to prevent the burglary. He would never forgive me if I had neglected his request: so I telephoned for him—to the Prefecture of Police," said the Duke.

"Oh, well, if you've already telephoned for him. But it was unnecessary—absolutely unnecessary," said M. Formery sharply.

"I didn't know," said the Duke politely.

"Oh, there was no harm in it—it doesn't matter," said M. Formery in a discontented tone with a discontented air.

He walked slowly round the room, paused by the windows, looked at the ladder, and scanned the garden:

"Arsene Lupin," he said scornfully. "Arsene Lupin doesn't leave traces all over the place. There's nothing but traces. Are we going to have that silly Lupin joke all over again?"

"I think, sir, that this time joke is the word, for this is a burglary pure and simple," said the inspector.

"Yes, it's plain as daylight," said M. Formery "The burglars came in by this window, and they went out by it."

He crossed the room to a tall safe which stood before the unused door. The safe was covered with velvet, and velvet curtains hung before its door. He drew the curtains, and tried the handle of the door of the safe. It did not turn; the safe was locked.

"As far as I can see, they haven't touched this," said M. Formery.

"Thank goodness for that," said the Duke. "I believe, or at least my fiancee does, that M. Gournay-Martin keeps the most precious thing in his collection in that safe—the coronet."

"What! the famous coronet of the Princesse de Lamballe?" said M. Formery.

"Yes," said the Duke.

"But according to your report, inspector, the letter signed 'Lupin' announced that he was going to steal the coronet also."

"It did—in so many words," said the Duke.

"Well, here is a further proof that we're not dealing with Lupin. That rascal would certainly have put his threat into execution, M. Formery," said the inspector.

"Who's in charge of the house?" said M. Formery.

"The concierge, his wife, and a housekeeper—a woman named Victoire," said the inspector.

"I'll see to the concierge and his wife presently. I've sent one of your men round for their dossier. When I get it I'll question them. You found them gagged and bound in their bedroom?"

"Yes, M. Formery; and always this imitation of Lupin—a yellow gag, blue cords, and the motto, 'I take, therefore I am,' on a scrap of cardboard—his usual bag of tricks."

"Then once again they're going to touch us up in the papers. It's any odds on it," said M. Formery gloomily. "Where's the housekeeper? I should like to see her."

"The fact is, we don't know where she is," said the inspector.

"You don't know where she is?" said M. Formery.

"We can't find her anywhere," said the inspector.

"That's excellent, excellent. We've found the accomplice," said M. Formery with lively delight; and he rubbed his hands together. "At least, we haven't found her, but we know her."

"I don't think that's the case," said the Duke. "At least, my future father-in-law and my fiancee had both of them the greatest confidence in her.

Yesterday she telephoned to us at the Chateau de Charmerace. All the jewels were left in her charge, and the wedding presents as they were sent in."

"And these jewels and wedding presents—have they been stolen too?" said M. Formery.

"They don't seem to have been touched," said the Duke, "though of course we can't tell till M. Gournay-Martin arrives. As far as I can see, the burglars have only touched these two drawing-rooms."

"That's very annoying," said M. Formery.

"I don't find it so," said the Duke, smiling.

"I was looking at it from the professional point of view," said M. Formery. He turned to the inspector and added, "You can't have searched thoroughly. This housekeeper must be somewhere about—if she's really trustworthy. Have you looked in every room in the house?"

"In every room—under every bed—in every corner and every cupboard," said the inspector.

"Bother!" said M. Formery. "Are there no scraps of torn clothes, no blood-stains, no traces of murder, nothing of interest?"

"Nothing!" said the inspector.

"But this is very regrettable," said M. Formery. "Where did she sleep? Was her bed unmade?"

"Her room is at the top of the house," said the inspector. "The bed had been slept in, but she does not appear to have taken away any of her clothes."

"Extraordinary! This is beginning to look a very complicated business," said M. Formery gravely.

"Perhaps Guerchard will be able to throw a little more light on it," said the Duke.

M. Formery frowned and said, "Yes, yes. Guerchard is a good assistant in a business like this. A little visionary, a little fanciful—wrong-headed, in fact; but, after all, he IS Guerchard. Only, since Lupin is his bugbear, he's bound to find some means of muddling us up with that wretched animal. You're going to see Lupin mixed up with all this to a dead certainty, your Grace."

The Duke looked at the signatures on the wall. "It seems to me that he is pretty well mixed up with it already," he said quietly.

"Believe me, your Grace, in a criminal affair it is, above all things, necessary to distrust appearances. I am growing more and more confident that some ordinary burglars have committed this crime and are trying to put us off the scent by diverting our attention to Lupin."

The Duke stooped down carelessly and picked up a book which had fallen from a table.

"Excuse me, but please—please—do not touch anything," said M. Formery quickly.

"Why, this is odd," said the Duke, staring at the floor.

"What is odd?" said M. Formery.

"Well, this book looks as if it had been knocked off the table by one of the burglars. And look here; here's a footprint under it—a footprint on the carpet," said the Duke.

M. Formery and the inspector came quickly to the spot. There, where the book had fallen, plainly imprinted on the carpet, was a white footprint. M. Formery and the inspector stared at it.

"It looks like plaster. How did plaster get here?" said M. Formery, frowning at it.

"Well, suppose the robbers came from the garden," said the Duke.

"Of course they came from the garden, your Grace. Where else should they come from?" said M. Formery, with a touch of impatience in his tone.

"Well, at the end of the garden they're building a house," said the Duke.

"Of course, of course," said M. Formery, taking him up quickly. "The burglars came here with their boots covered with plaster. They've swept away all the other marks of their feet from the carpet; but whoever did the sweeping was too slack to lift up that book and sweep under it. This footprint, however, is not of great importance, though it is corroborative of all the other evidence we have that they came and went by the garden. There's the ladder, and that table half out of the window. Still, this footprint may turn out useful, after all. You had better take the measurements of it, inspector. Here's a foot-rule for you. I make a point of carrying this foot-rule about with me, your Grace. You would be surprised to learn how often it has come in useful."

He took a little ivory foot-rule from his waist-coat pocket, and gave it to the inspector, who fell on his knees and measured the footprint with the greatest care.

"I must take a careful look at that house they're building. I shall find a good many traces there, to a dead certainty," said M. Formery.

The inspector entered the measurements of the footprint in his note-book. There came the sound of a knocking at the front door.

"I shall find footprints of exactly the same dimensions as this one at the foot of some heap of plaster beside that house," said M. Formery; with an air of profound conviction, pointing through the window to the house building beyond the garden.

A policeman opened the door of the drawing-room and saluted.

"If you please, sir, the servants have arrived from Charmerace," he said.

"Let them wait in the kitchen and the servants' offices," said M. Formery. He stood silent, buried in profound meditation, for a couple of minutes. Then he turned to the Duke and said, "What was that you said about a theft of motor-cars at Charmerace?"

"When he received the letter from Arsene Lupin, M. Gournay-Martin decided to start for Paris at once," said the Duke. "But when we sent for the cars we found that they had just been stolen. M. Gournay-Martin's chauffeur and another servant were in the garage gagged and bound. Only an old car, a hundred horse-power Mercrac, was left. I drove it to Paris, leaving M. Gournay-Martin and his family to come on by train."

"Very important—very important indeed," said M. Formery. He thought for a moment, and then added. "Were the motor-cars the only things stolen? Were there no other thefts?"

"Well, as a matter of fact, there was another theft, or rather an attempt at theft," said the Duke with some hesitation. "The rogues who stole the motor-cars presented themselves at the chateau under the name of Charolais—a father and three sons—on the pretext of buying the hundred-horse-power Mercrac. M. Gournay-Martin had advertised it for sale in the Rennes Advertiser. They were waiting in the big hall of the chateau, which the family uses as the chief living-room, for the return of M. Gournay-Martin. He came; and as they left the hall one of them attempted to steal a pendant set with pearls which I had given to Mademoiselle Gournay-Martin half an hour before. I caught him in the act and saved the pendant."

"Good! good! Wait—we have one of the gang—wait till I question him," said M. Formery, rubbing his hands; and his eyes sparkled with joy.

"Well, no; I'm afraid we haven't," said the Duke in an apologetic tone.

"What! We haven't? Has he escaped from the police? Oh, those country police!" cried M. Formery.

"No; I didn't charge him with the theft," said the Duke.

"You didn't charge him with the theft?" cried M. Formery, astounded.

"No; he was very young and he begged so hard. I had the pendant. I let him go," said the Duke.

"Oh, your Grace, your Grace! Your duty to society!" cried M. Formery.

"Yes, it does seem to have been rather weak," said the Duke; "but there you are. It's no good crying over spilt milk."

M. Formery folded his arms and walked, frowning, backwards and forwards across the room.

He stopped, raised his hand with a gesture commanding attention, and said, "I have no hesitation in saying that there is a connection—an intimate connection—between the thefts at Charmerace and this burglary!"

The Duke and the inspector gazed at him with respectful eyes—at least, the eyes of the inspector were respectful; the Duke's eyes twinkled.

"I am gathering up the threads," said M. Formery. "Inspector, bring up the concierge and his wife. I will question them on the scene of the crime. Their dossier should be here. If it is, bring it up with them; if not, no matter; bring them up without it."

The inspector left the drawing-room. M. Formery plunged at once into frowning meditation.

"I find all this extremely interesting," said the Duke.

"Charmed! Charmed!" said M. Formery, waving his hand with an absent-minded air.

The inspector entered the drawing-room followed by the concierge and his wife. He handed a paper to M. Formery. The concierge, a bearded man of about sixty, and his wife, a somewhat bearded woman of about fifty-five, stared at M. Formery with fascinated, terrified eyes. He sat down in a chair, crossed his legs, read the paper through, and then scrutinized them keenly.

"Well, have you recovered from your adventure?" he said.

"Oh, yes, sir," said the concierge. "They hustled us a bit, but they did not really hurt us."

"Nothing to speak of, that is," said his wife. "But all the same, it's a disgraceful thing that an honest woman can't sleep in peace in her bed of a night without being disturbed by rascals like that. And if the police did their duty things like this wouldn't happen. And I don't care who hears me say it."

"You say that you were taken by surprise in your sleep?" said M. Formery. "You say you saw nothing, and heard nothing?"

"There was no time to see anything or hear anything. They trussed us up like greased lightning," said the concierge.

"But the gag was the worst," said the wife. "To lie there and not be able to tell the rascals what I thought about them!"

"Didn't you hear the noise of footsteps in the garden?" said M. Formery.

"One can't hear anything that happens in the garden from our bedroom," said the concierge.

"Even the night when Mlle. Germaine's great Dane barked from twelve o'clock till seven in the morning, all the household was kept awake except us; but bless you, sir, we slept like tops," said his wife proudly.

"If they sleep like that it seems rather a waste of time to have gagged them," whispered the Duke to the inspector.

The inspector grinned, and whispered scornfully, "Oh, them common folks; they do sleep like that, your Grace."

"Didn't you hear any noise at the front door?" said M. Formery.

"No, we heard no noise at the door," said the concierge.

"Then you heard no noise at all the whole night?" said M. Formery.

"Oh, yes, sir, we heard noise enough after we'd been gagged," said the concierge.

"Now, this is important," said M. Formery. "What kind of a noise was it?"

"Well, it was a bumping kind of noise," said the concierge. "And there was a noise of footsteps, walking about the room."

"What room? Where did these noises come from?" said M. Formery.

"From the room over our heads—the big drawing-room," said the concierge.

"Didn't you hear any noise of a struggle, as if somebody was being dragged about—no screaming or crying?" said M. Formery.

The concierge and his wife looked at one another with inquiring eyes.

"No, I didn't," said the concierge.

"Neither did I," said his wife.

M. Formery paused. Then he said, "How long have you been in the service of M. Gournay-Martin?"

"A little more than a year," said the concierge.

M. Formery looked at the paper in his hand, frowned, and said severely, "I see you've been convicted twice, my man."

"Yes, sir, but—"

"My husband's an honest man, sir—perfectly honest," broke in his wife. "You've only to ask M. Gournay-Martin; he'll—"

"Be so good as to keep quiet, my good woman," said M. Formery; and, turning to her husband, he went on: "At your first conviction you were sentenced to a day's imprisonment with costs; at your second conviction you got three days' imprisonment."

"I'm not going to deny it, sir," said the concierge; "but it was an honourable imprisonment."

"Honourable?" said M. Formery.

"The first time, I was a gentleman's servant, and I got a day's imprisonment for crying, 'Hurrah for the General Strike!'—on the first of May."

"You were a valet? In whose service?" said M. Formery.

"In the service of M. Genlis, the Socialist leader."

"And your second conviction?" said M. Formery.

"It was for having cried in the porch of Ste. Clotilde, 'Down with the cows!'—meaning the police, sir," said the concierge.

"And were you in the service of M. Genlis then?" said M. Formery.

"No, sir; I was in the service of M. Bussy-Rabutin, the Royalist deputy."

"You don't seem to have very well-defined political convictions," said M. Formery.

"Oh, yes, sir, I have," the concierge protested. "I'm always devoted to my masters; and I have the same opinions that they have—always."

"Very good; you can go," said M. Formery.

The concierge and his wife left the room, looking as if they did not quite know whether to feel relieved or not.

"Those two fools are telling the exact truth, unless I'm very much mistaken," said M. Formery.

"They look honest enough people," said the Duke.

"Well, now to examine the rest of the house," said M. Formery.

"I'll come with you, if I may," said the Duke.

"By all means, by all means," said M. Formery.

"I find it all so interesting," said the Duke,

X. GUERCHARD ASSISTS

Leaving a policeman on guard at the door of the drawing-room M. Formery, the Duke, and the inspector set out on their tour of inspection. It was a long business, for M. Formery examined every room with the most scrupulous care—with more care, indeed, than he had displayed in his examination of the drawing-rooms. In particular he lingered long in the bedroom of Victoire, discussing the possibilities of her having been murdered and carried away by the burglars along with their booty. He seemed, if anything, disappointed at finding no blood-stains, but to find real consolation in the thought that she might have been strangled. He found the inspector in entire agreement with every theory he enunciated, and he grew more and more disposed to regard him as a zealous and trustworthy officer. Also he was not at all displeased at enjoying this opportunity of impressing the Duke with his powers of analysis and synthesis. He was unaware that, as a rule, the Duke's eyes did not usually twinkle as they twinkled during this solemn and deliberate progress through the house of M. Gournay-Martin. M. Formery had so exactly the air of a sleuthhound; and he was even noisier.

Having made this thorough examination of the house, M. Formery went out into the garden and set about examining that. There were footprints on the turf about the foot of the ladder, for the grass was close-clipped, and the rain had penetrated and softened the soil; but there were hardly as many footprints as might have been expected, seeing that the burglars must have made many journeys in the course of robbing the drawing-rooms of so many objects of art, some of them of considerable weight. The footprints led to a path of hard gravel; and M. Formery led the way down it, out of the door in the wall at the bottom of the garden, and into the space round the house which was being built.

As M. Formery had divined, there was a heap, or, to be exact, there were several heaps of plaster about the bottom of the scaffolding. Unfortunately, there were also hundreds of footprints. M. Formery looked at them with longing eyes; but he did not suggest that the inspector should hunt about for a set of footprints of the size of the one he had so carefully measured on the drawing-room carpet.

While they were examining the ground round the half-built house a man came briskly down the stairs from the second floor of the house of M. Gournay-Martin. He was an ordinary-looking man, almost insignificant, of between forty and fifty, and of rather more than middle height. He had an ordinary, rather shapeless mouth, an ordinary nose, an ordinary chin, an ordinary forehead, rather low, and ordinary ears. He was wearing an ordinary top-hat, by no means new. His clothes were the ordinary clothes of a fairly well-to-do citizen; and his boots had been chosen less to set off any slenderness his feet might possess than for their comfortable roominess. Only his eyes relieved his face from insignificance. They were extraordinarily alert eyes, producing in those on whom they rested the somewhat uncomfortable impression that the depths of their souls were being penetrated. He was the famous Chief-Inspector Guerchard, head of the Detective Department of the Prefecture of Police, and sworn foe of Arsene Lupin.

The policeman at the door of the drawing-room saluted him briskly. He was a fine, upstanding, red-faced young fellow, adorned by a rich black moustache of extraordinary fierceness.

"Shall I go and inform M. Formery that you have come, M. Guerchard?" he said.

"No, no; there's no need to take the trouble," said Guerchard in a gentle, rather husky voice. "Don't bother any one about me—I'm of no importance."

"Oh, come, M. Guerchard," protested the policeman.

"Of no importance," said M. Guerchard decisively. "For the present, M. Formery is everything. I'm only an assistant."

He stepped into the drawing-room and stood looking about it, curiously still. It was almost as if the whole of his being was concentrated in the act of seeing—as if all the other functions of his mind and body were in suspension.

"M. Formery and the inspector have just been up to examine the housekeeper's room. It's right at the top of the house—on the second floor. You take the servants' staircase. Then it's right at the end of the passage on the left. Would you like me to take you up to it, sir?" said the policeman eagerly. His heart was in his work.

"Thank you, I know where it is—I've just come from it," said Guerchard gently.

A grin of admiration widened the already wide mouth of the policeman, and showed a row of very white, able-looking teeth.

"Ah, M. Guerchard!" he said, "you're cleverer than all the examining magistrates in Paris put together!"

"You ought not to say that, my good fellow. I can't prevent you thinking it, of course; but you ought not to say it," said Guerchard with husky gentleness; and the faintest smile played round the corners of his mouth.

He walked slowly to the window, and the policeman walked with him.

"Have you noticed this, sir?" said the policeman, taking hold of the top of the ladder with a powerful hand. "It's probable that the burglars came in and went away by this ladder."

"Thank you," said Guerchard.

"They have even left this card-table on the window-sill," said the policeman; and he patted the card-table with his other powerful hand.

"Thank you, thank you," said Guerchard.

"They don't think it's Lupin's work at all," said the policeman. "They think that Lupin's letter announcing the burglary and these signatures on the walls are only a ruse."

"Is that so?" said Guerchard.

"Is there any way I can help you, sir?" said policeman.

"Yes," said Guerchard. "Take up your post outside that door and admit no one but M. Formery, the inspector, Bonavent, or Dieusy, without consulting me." And he pointed to the drawing-room door.

"Shan't I admit the Duke of Charmerace? He's taking a great interest in this affair," said the policeman.

"The Duke of Charmerace? Oh, yes—admit the Duke of Charmerace," said Guerchard.

The policeman went to his post of responsibility, a proud man.

Hardly had the door closed behind him when Guerchard was all activity—activity and eyes. He examined the ladder, the gaps on the wall from which the pictures had been taken, the signatures of Arsene Lupin. The very next thing he did was to pick up the book which the Duke had set on the top of the footprint again, to preserve it; and he measured, pacing it, the distance between the footprint and the window.

The result of this measuring did not appear to cause him any satisfaction, for he frowned, measured the distance again, and then stared out of the window with a perplexed air, thinking hard. It was curious that, when he concentrated himself on a process of reasoning, his eyes seemed to lose something of their sharp brightness and grew a little dim.

At last he seemed to come to some conclusion. He turned away from the window, drew a small magnifying-glass from his pocket, dropped on his hands and knees, and began to examine the surface of the carpet with the most minute care.

He examined a space of it nearly six feet square, stopped, and gazed round the room. His eyes rested on the fireplace, which he could see under the bottom of the big tapestried fire-screen which was raised on legs about a foot high, fitted with big casters. His eyes filled with interest; without rising, he crawled quickly across the room, peeped round the edge of the screen and rose, smiling.

He went on to the further drawing-room and made the same careful examination of it, again examining a part of the surface of the carpet with his magnifying-glass. He came back to the window to which the ladder had been raised and examined very carefully the broken shutter. He whistled softly to himself, lighted a cigarette, and leant against the side of the window. He looked out of it, with dull eyes which saw nothing, the while his mind worked upon the facts he had discovered.

He had stood there plunged in reflection for perhaps ten minutes, when there came a sound of voices and footsteps on the stairs. He awoke from his absorption, seemed to prick his ears, then slipped a leg over the window-ledge, and disappeared from sight down the ladder.

The door opened, and in came M. Formery, the Duke, and the inspector. M. Formery looked round the room with eyes which seemed to expect to meet a familiar sight, then walked to the other drawing-room and looked round that. He turned to the policeman, who had stepped inside the drawing-room, and said sharply, "M. Guerchard is not here."

"I left him here," said the policeman. "He must have disappeared. He's a wonder."

"Of course," said M. Formery. "He has gone down the ladder to examine that house they're building. He's just following in our tracks and doing all over again the work we've already done. He might have saved himself the trouble. We could have told him all he wants to know. But there! He very likely would not be satisfied till he had seen everything for himself."

"He may see something which we have missed," said the Duke.

M. Formery frowned, and said sharply "That's hardly likely. I don't think that your Grace realizes to what a perfection constant practice brings one's power of observation. The inspector and I will cheerfully eat anything we've missed—won't we, inspector?" And he laughed heartily at his joke.

"It might always prove a large mouthful," said the Duke with an ironical smile.

M. Formery assumed his air of profound reflection, and walked a few steps up and down the room, frowning:

"The more I think about it," he said, "the clearer it grows that we have disposed of the Lupin theory. This is the work of far less expert rogues than Lupin. What do you think, inspector?"

"Yes; I think you have disposed of that theory, sir," said the inspector with ready acquiescence.

"All the same, I'd wager anything that we haven't disposed of it to the satisfaction of Guerchard," said M. Formery.

"Then he must be very hard to satisfy," said the Duke.

"Oh, in any other matter he's open to reason," said M. Formery; "but Lupin is his fixed idea; it's an obsession—almost a mania."

"But yet he never catches him," said the Duke.

"No; and he never will. His very obsession by Lupin hampers him. It cramps his mind and hinders its working," said M. Formery.

He resumed his meditative pacing, stopped again, and said:

"But considering everything, especially the absence of any traces of violence, combined with her entire disappearance, I have come to another conclusion. Victoire is the key to the mystery. She is the accomplice. She never slept in her bed. She unmade it to put us off the scent. That, at any rate, is something gained, to have found the accomplice. We shall have this good news, at least, to tell M, Gournay-Martin on his arrival."

"Do you really think that she's the accomplice?" said the Duke.

"I'm dead sure of it," said M. Formery. "We will go up to her room and make another thorough examination of it."

Guerchard's head popped up above the window-sill:

"My dear M. Formery," he said, "I beg that you will not take the trouble."

M. Formery's mouth opened: "What! You, Guerchard?" he stammered.

"Myself," said Guerchard; and he came to the top of the ladder and slipped lightly over the window-sill into the room.

He shook hands with M. Formery and nodded to the inspector. Then he looked at the Duke with an air of inquiry.

"Let me introduce you," said M. Formery. "Chief-Inspector Guerchard, head of the Detective Department—the Duke of Charmerace."

The Duke shook hands with Guerchard, saying, "I'm delighted to make your acquaintance, M. Guerchard. I've been expecting your coming with the greatest interest. Indeed it was I who begged the officials at the Prefecture of Police to put this case in your hands. I insisted on it."

"What were you doing on that ladder?" said M. Formery, giving Guerchard no time to reply to the Duke.

"I was listening," said Guerchard simply—"listening. I like to hear people talk when I'm engaged on a case. It's a distraction—and it helps. I really must congratulate you, my dear M. Formery, on the admirable manner in which you have conducted this inquiry."

M. Formery bowed, and regarded him with a touch of suspicion.

"There are one or two minor points on which we do not agree, but on the whole your method has been admirable," said Guerchard.

"Well, about Victoire," said M. Formery. "You're quite sure that an examination, a more thorough examination, of her room, is unnecessary?"

"Yes, I think so," said Guerchard. "I have just looked at it myself."

The door opened, and in came Bonavent, one of the detectives who had come earlier from the Prefecture. In his hand he carried a scrap of cloth.

He saluted Guerchard, and said to M. Formery, "I have just found this scrap of cloth on the edge of the well at the bottom of the garden. The concierge's wife tells me that it has been torn from Victoire's dress."

"I feared it," said M. Formery, taking the scrap of cloth from him. "I feared foul play. We must go to the well at once, send some one down it, or have it dragged."

He was moving hastily to the door, when Guerchard said, in his husky, gentle voice, "I don't think there is any need to look for Victoire in the well."

"But this scrap of cloth," said M. Formery, holding it out to him.

"Yes, yes, that scrap of cloth," said Guerchard. And, turning to the Duke, he added, "Do you know if there's a dog or cat in the house, your Grace? I suppose that, as the fiance of Mademoiselle Gournay-Martin, you are familiar with the house?"

"What on earth—" said M. Formery.

"Excuse me," interrupted Guerchard. "But this is important—very important."

"Yes, there is a cat," said the Duke. "I've seen a cat at the door of the concierge's rooms."

"It must have been that cat which took this scrap of cloth to the edge of the well," said Guerchard gravely.

"This is ridiculous—preposterous!" cried M. Formery, beginning to flush. "Here we're dealing with a most serious crime—a murder—the murder of Victoire—and you talk about cats!"

"Victoire has not been murdered," said Guerchard; and his husky voice was gentler than ever, only just audible.

"But we don't know that—we know nothing of the kind," said M. Formery.

"I do," said Guerchard.

"You?" said M. Formery.

"Yes," said Guerchard.

"Then how do you explain her disappearance?"

"If she had disappeared I shouldn't explain it," said Guerchard.

"But since she has disappeared?" cried M. Formery, in a tone of exasperation.

"She hasn't," said Guerchard.

"You know nothing about it!" cried M. Formery, losing his temper.

"Yes, I do," said Guerchard, with the same gentleness.

"Come, do you mean to say that you know where she is?" cried M. Formery.

"Certainly," said Guerchard.

"Do you mean to tell us straight out that you've seen her?" cried M. Formery.

"Oh, yes; I've seen her," said Guerchard.

"You've seen her—when?" cried M. Formery.

Guerchard paused to consider. Then he said gently:

"It must have been between four and five minutes ago."

"But hang it all, you haven't been out of this room!" cried M. Formery.

"No, I haven't," said Guerchard.

"And you've seen her?" cried M. Formery.

"Yes," said Guerchard, raising his voice a little.

"Well, why the devil don't you tell us where she is? Tell us!" cried M. Formery, purple with exasperation.

"But you won't let me get a word out of my mouth," protested Guerchard with aggravating gentleness.

"Well, speak!" cried M. Formery; and he sank gasping on to a chair.

"Ah, well, she's here," said Guerchard.

"Here! How did she GET here?" said M. Formery.

"On a mattress," said Guerchard.

M. Formery sat upright, almost beside himself, glaring furiously at Guerchard:

"What do you stand there pulling all our legs for?" he almost howled.

"Look here," said Guerchard.

He walked across the room to the fireplace, pushed the chairs which stood bound together on the hearth-rug to one side of the fireplace, and ran the heavy fire-screen on its casters to the other side of it, revealing to their gaze the wide, old-fashioned fireplace itself. The iron brazier which held the coals had been moved into the corner, and a mattress lay on the floor of the fireplace. On the mattress lay the figure of a big, middle-aged woman, half-dressed. There was a yellow gag in her mouth; and her hands and feet were bound together with blue cords.

"She is sleeping soundly," said Guerchard. He stooped and picked up a handkerchief, and smelt it. "There's the handkerchief they chloroformed her with. It still smells of chloroform."

They stared at him and the sleeping woman.

"Lend a hand, inspector," he said. "And you too, Bonavent. She looks a good weight."

The three of them raised the mattress, and carried it and the sleeping woman to a broad couch, and laid them on it. They staggered under their burden, for truly Victoire was a good weight.

M. Formery rose, with recovered breath, but with his face an even richer purple. His eyes were rolling in his head, as if they were not under proper control.

He turned on the inspector and cried savagely, "You never examined the fireplace, inspector!"

"No, sir," said the downcast inspector.

"It was unpardonable—absolutely unpardonable!" cried M. Formery. "How is one to work with subordinates like this?"

"It was an oversight," said Guerchard.

M. Formery turned to him and said, "You must admit that it was materially impossible for me to see her."

"It was possible if you went down on all fours," said Guerchard.

"On all fours?" said M. Formery.

"Yes; on all fours you could see her heels sticking out beyond the mattress," said Guerchard simply.

M. Formery shrugged his shoulders: "That screen looked as if it had stood there since the beginning of the summer," he said.

"The first thing, when you're dealing with Lupin, is to distrust appearances," said Guerchard.

"Lupin!" cried M. Formery hotly. Then he bit his lip and was silent.

He walked to the side of the couch and looked down on the sleeping Victoire, frowning: "This upsets everything," he said. "With these new conditions, I've got to begin all over again, to find a new explanation of the affair. For the moment—for the moment, I'm thrown completely off the track. And you, Guerchard?"

"Oh, well," said Guerchard, "I have an idea or two about the matter still."

"Do you really mean to say that it hasn't thrown you off the track too?" said M. Formery, with a touch of incredulity in his tone.

"Well, no—not exactly," said Guerchard. "I wasn't on that track, you see."

"No, of course not—of course not. You were on the track of Lupin," said M. Formery; and his contemptuous smile was tinged with malice.

The Duke looked from one to the other of them with curious, searching eyes: "I find all this so interesting," he said.

"We do not take much notice of these checks; they do not depress us for a moment," said M. Formery, with some return of his old grandiloquence. "We pause hardly for an instant; then we begin to reconstruct—to reconstruct."

"It's perfectly splendid of you," said the Duke, and his limpid eyes rested on M. Formery's self-satisfied face in a really affectionate gaze; they might almost be said to caress it.

Guerchard looked out of the window at a man who was carrying a hod-full of bricks up one of the ladders set against the scaffolding of the building house. Something in this honest workman's simple task seemed to amuse him, for he smiled.

Only the inspector, thinking of the unexamined fireplace, looked really depressed.

"We shan't get anything out of this woman till she wakes," said M. Formery, "When she does, I shall question her closely and fully. In the meantime, she may as well be carried up to her bedroom to sleep off the effects of the chloroform."

Guerchard turned quickly: "Not her own bedroom, I think," he said gently.

"Certainly not—of course, not her own bedroom," said M. Formery quickly.

"And I think an officer at the door of whatever bedroom she does sleep in," said Guerchard.

"Undoubtedly—most necessary," said M. Formery gravely. "See to it, inspector. You can take her away."

The inspector called in a couple of policemen, and with their aid he and Bonavent raised the sleeping woman, a man at each corner of the mattress, and bore her from the room.

"And now to reconstruct," said M. Formery; and he folded his arms and plunged into profound reflection.

The Duke and Guerchard watched him in silence.

XI. THE FAMILY ARRIVES

In carrying out Victoire, the inspector had left the door of the drawing-room open. After he had watched M. Formery reflect for two minutes, Guerchard faded—to use an expressive Americanism—through it. The Duke felt in the breast-pocket of his coat, murmured softly, "My cigarettes," and followed him.

He caught up Guerchard on the stairs and said, "I will come with you, if I may, M. Guerchard. I find all these investigations extraordinarily interesting. I have been observing M. Formery's methods—I should like to watch yours, for a change."

"By all means," said Guerchard. "And there are several things I want to hear about from your Grace. Of course it might be an advantage to discuss them together with M. Formery, but—" and he hesitated.

"It would be a pity to disturb M. Formery in the middle of the process of reconstruction," said the Duke; and a faint, ironical smile played round the corners of his sensitive lips.

Guerchard looked at him quickly: "Perhaps it would," he said.

They went through the house, out of the back door, and into the garden. Guerchard moved about twenty yards from the house, then he stopped and questioned the Duke at great length. He questioned him first about the Charolais, their appearance, their actions, especially about Bernard's attempt to steal the pendant, and the theft of the motor-cars.

"I have been wondering whether M. Charolais might not have been Arsene Lupin himself," said the Duke.

"It's quite possible," said Guerchard. "There seem to be no limits whatever to Lupin's powers of disguising himself. My colleague, Ganimard, has come across him at least three times that he knows of, as a different person. And no single time could he be sure that it was the same man. Of course, he had a feeling that he was in contact with some one he had met before, but that was all. He had no certainty. He may have met him half a dozen times besides without knowing him. And the photographs of him—they're all different. Ganimard declares that Lupin is so extraordinarily successful in his disguises because he is a great actor. He actually becomes for the time being the person he pretends to be. He thinks and feels absolutely like that person. Do you follow me?"

"Oh, yes; but he must be rather fluid, this Lupin," said the Duke; and then he added thoughtfully, "It must be awfully risky to come so often into actual contact with men like Ganimard and you."

"Lupin has never let any consideration of danger prevent him doing anything that caught his fancy. He has odd fancies, too. He's a humourist of the most varied kind—grim, ironic, farcical, as the mood takes him. He must be awfully trying to live with," said Guerchard.

"Do you think humourists are trying to live with?" said the Duke, in a meditative tone. "I think they brighten life a good deal; but of course there are people who do not like them—the middle-classes."

"Yes, yes, they're all very well in their place; but to live with they must be trying," said Guerchard quickly.

He went on to question the Duke closely and at length about the household of M. Gournay-Martin, saying that Arsene Lupin worked with the largest gang a burglar had ever captained, and it was any odds that he had introduced one, if not more, of that gang into it. Moreover, in the case of a big affair like this, Lupin himself often played two or three parts under as many disguises.

"If he was Charolais, I don't see how he could be one of M. Gournay-Martin's household, too," said the Duke in some perplexity.

"I don't say that he WAS Charolais," said Guerchard. "It is quite a moot point. On the whole, I'm inclined to think that he was not. The theft of the motor-cars was a job for a subordinate. He would hardly bother himself with it."

The Duke told him all that he could remember about the millionaire's servants—and, under the clever questioning of the detective, he was surprised to find how much he did remember—all kinds of odd details about them which he had scarcely been aware of observing.

The two of them, as they talked, afforded an interesting contrast: the Duke, with his air of distinction and race, his ironic expression, his mobile features, his clear enunciation and well-modulated voice, his easy carriage of an accomplished fencer—a fencer with muscles of steel—seemed to be a man of another kind from the slow-moving detective, with his husky voice, his common, slurring enunciation, his clumsily moulded features, so ill adapted to the expression of emotion and intelligence. It was a contrast almost between the hawk and the mole, the warrior and the workman. Only in their eyes were they alike; both of them had the keen, alert eyes of observers. Perhaps the most curious thing of all was that, in spite of the fact that he had for so much of his life been an idler, trifling away his time in the pursuit of pleasure, except when he had made his expedition to the South Pole, the Duke gave one the impression of being a cleverer man, of a far finer brain, than the detective who had spent so much of his life sharpening his wits on the more intricate problems of crime.

When Guerchard came to the end of his questions, the Duke said: "You have given me a very strong feeling that it is going to be a deuce of a job to catch Lupin. I don't wonder that, so far, you have none of you laid hands on him."

"But we have!" cried Guerchard quickly. "Twice Ganimard has caught him. Once he had him in prison, and actually brought him to trial. Lupin became another man, and was let go from the very dock."

"Really? It sounds absolutely amazing," said the Duke.

"And then, in the affair of the Blue Diamond, Ganimard caught him again. He has his weakness, Lupin—it's women. It's a very common weakness in these masters of crime. Ganimard and Holmlock Shears, in that affair, got the better of him by using his love for a woman—'the fair-haired lady,' she was called—to nab him."

"A shabby trick," said the Duke.

"Shabby?" said Guerchard in a tone of utter wonder. "How can anything be shabby in the case of a rogue like this?"

"Perhaps not—perhaps not—still—" said the Duke, and stopped.

The expression of wonder faded from Guerchard's face, and he went on, "Well, Holmlock Shears recovered the Blue Diamond, and Ganimard nabbed Lupin. He held him for ten minutes, then Lupin escaped."

"What became of the fair-haired lady?" said the Duke.

"I don't know. I have heard that she is dead," said Guerchard. "Now I come to think of it, I heard quite definitely that she died."

"It must be awful for a woman to love a man like Lupin—the constant, wearing anxiety," said the Duke thoughtfully.

"I dare say. Yet he can have his pick of sweethearts. I've been offered thousands of francs by women—women of your Grace's world and wealthy Viennese—to make them acquainted with Lupin," said Guerchard.

"You don't surprise me," said the Duke with his ironic smile. "Women never do stop to think—where one of their heroes is concerned. And did you do it?"

"How could I? If I only could! If I could find Lupin entangled with a woman like Ganimard did—well—" said Guerchard between his teeth.

"He'd never get out of YOUR clutches," said the Duke with conviction.

"I think not—I think not," said Guerchard grimly. "But come, I may as well get on."

He walked across the turf to the foot of the ladder and looked at the footprints round it. He made but a cursory examination of them, and took his way down the garden-path, out of the door in the wall into the space about the house that was building. He was not long examining it, and he went right through it out into the street on which the house would face when it was finished. He looked up and down it, and began to retrace his footsteps.

"I've seen all I want to see out here. We may as well go back to the house," he said to the Duke.

"I hope you've seen what you expected to see," said the Duke.

"Exactly what I expected to see—exactly," said Guerchard.

"That's as it should be," said the Duke.

They went back to the house and found M. Formery in the drawing-room, still engaged in the process of reconstruction.

"The thing to do now is to hunt the neighbourhood for witnesses of the departure of the burglars with their booty. Loaded as they were with such bulky objects, they must have had a big conveyance. Somebody must have noticed it. They must have wondered why it was standing in front of a half-built house. Somebody may have actually seen the burglars loading it, though it was so early in the morning. Bonavent had better inquire at every house in the street on which that half-built house faces. Did you happen to notice the name of it?" said M. Formery.

"It's Sureau Street," said Guerchard. "But Dieusy has been hunting the neighbourhood for some one who saw the burglars loading their conveyance, or saw it waiting to be loaded, for the last hour."

"Good," said M. Formery. "We are getting on."

M. Formery was silent. Guerchard and the Duke sat down and lighted cigarettes.

"You found plenty of traces," said M. Formery, waving his hand towards the window.

"Yes; I've found plenty of traces," said Guerchard.

"Of Lupin?" said M. Formery, with a faint sneer.

"No; not of Lupin," said Guerchard.

A smile of warm satisfaction illumined M. Formery's face:

"What did I tell you?" he said. "I'm glad that you've changed your mind about that."

"I have hardly changed my mind," said Guerchard, in his husky, gentle voice.

There came a loud knocking on the front door, the sound of excited voices on the stairs. The door opened, and in burst M. Gournay-Martin. He took one glance round the devastated room, raised his clenched hands towards the ceiling, and bellowed, "The scoundrels! the dirty scoundrels!" And his voice stuck in his throat. He tottered across the room to a couch, dropped heavily to it, gazed round the scene of desolation, and burst into tears.

Germaine and Sonia came into the room. The Duke stepped forward to greet them.

"Do stop crying, papa. You're as hoarse as a crow as it is," said Germaine impatiently. Then, turning on the Duke with a frown, she said: "I think that joke of yours about the train was simply disgraceful, Jacques. A joke's a joke, but to send us out to the station on a night like last night, through all that heavy rain, when you knew all the time that there was no quarter-to-nine train—it was simply disgraceful."

"I really don't know what you're talking about," said the Duke quietly. "Wasn't there a quarter-to-nine train?"

"Of course there wasn't," said Germaine. "The time-table was years old. I think it was the most senseless attempt at a joke I ever heard of."

"It doesn't seem to me to be a joke at all," said the Duke quietly. "At any rate, it isn't the kind of a joke I make—it would be detestable. I never thought to look at the date of the time-table. I keep a box of cigarettes in that drawer, and I have noticed the time-table there. Of course, it may have been lying there for years. It was stupid of me not to look at the date."

"I said it was a mistake. I was sure that his Grace would not do anything so unkind as that," said Sonia.

The Duke smiled at her.

"Well, all I can say is, it was very stupid of you not to look at the date," said Germaine.

M. Gournay-Martin rose to his feet and wailed, in the most heartrending fashion: "My pictures! My wonderful pictures! Such investments! And my cabinets! My Renaissance cabinets! They can't be replaced! They were unique! They were worth a hundred and fifty thousand francs."

M. Formery stepped forward with an air and said, "I am distressed, M. Gournay-Martin—truly distressed by your loss. I am M. Formery, examining magistrate."

"It is a tragedy, M. Formery—a tragedy!" groaned the millionaire.

"Do not let it upset you too much. We shall find your masterpieces—we shall find them. Only give us time," said M. Formery in a tone of warm encouragement.

The face of the millionaire brightened a little.

"And, after all, you have the consolation, that the burglars did not get hold of the gem of your collection. They have not stolen the coronet of the Princesse de Lamballe," said M. Formery.

"No," said the Duke. "They have not touched this safe. It is unopened."

"What has that got to do with it?" growled the millionaire quickly. "That safe is empty."

"Empty ... but your coronet?" cried the Duke.

"Good heavens! Then they HAVE stolen it," cried the millionaire hoarsely, in a panic-stricken voice.

"But they can't have—this safe hasn't been touched," said the Duke.

"But the coronet never was in that safe. It was—have they entered my bedroom?" said the millionaire.

"No," said M. Formery.

"They don't seem to have gone through any of the rooms except these two," said the Duke.

"Ah, then my mind is at rest about that. The safe in my bedroom has only two keys. Here is one." He took a key from his waistcoat pocket and held it out to them. "And the other is in this safe."

The face of M. Formery was lighted up with a splendid satisfaction. He might have rescued the coronet with his own hands. He cried triumphantly, "There, you see!"

"See? See?" cried the millionaire in a sudden bellow. "I see that they have robbed me—plundered me. Oh, my pictures! My wonderful pictures! Such investments!"

XII. THE THEFT OF THE PENDANT

They stood round the millionaire observing his anguish, with eyes in which shone various degrees of sympathy. As if no longer able to bear the sight of such woe, Sonia slipped out of the room.

The millionaire lamented his loss and abused the thieves by turns, but always at the top of his magnificent voice.

Suddenly a fresh idea struck him. He clapped his hand to his brow and cried: "That eight hundred pounds! Charolais will never buy the Mercrac now! He was not a bona fide purchaser!"

The Duke's lips parted slightly and his eyes opened a trifle wider than their wont. He turned sharply on his heel, and almost sprang into the other drawing-room. There he laughed at his ease.

M. Formery kept saying to the millionaire: "Be calm, M. Gournay-Martin. Be calm! We shall recover your masterpieces. I pledge you my word. All we need is time. Have patience. Be calm!"

His soothing remonstrances at last had their effect. The millionaire grew calm:

"Guerchard?" he said. "Where is Guerchard?"

M. Formery presented Guerchard to him.

"Are you on their track? Have you a clue?" said the millionaire.

"I think," said M. Formery in an impressive tone, "that we may now proceed with the inquiry in the ordinary way."

He was a little piqued by the millionaire's so readily turning from him to the detective. He went to a writing-table, set some sheets of paper before him, and prepared to make notes on the answers to his questions. The Duke came back into the drawing-room; the inspector was summoned. M. Gournay-Martin sat down on a couch with his hands on his knees and gazed gloomily at M. Formery. Germaine, who was sitting on a couch near the door, waiting with an air of resignation for her father to cease his lamentations, rose and moved to a chair nearer the writing-table. Guerchard kept moving restlessly about the room, but noiselessly. At last he came to a standstill, leaning against the wall behind M. Formery.

M. Formery went over all the matters about which he had already questioned the Duke. He questioned the millionaire and his daughter about the Charolais, the theft of the motor-cars, and the attempted theft of the pendant. He questioned them at less length about the composition of their household—the servants and their characters. He elicited no new fact.

He paused, and then he said, carelessly as a mere matter of routine: "I should like to know, M. Gournay-Martin, if there has ever been any other robbery committed at your house?"

"Three years ago this scoundrel Lupin—" the millionaire began violently.

"Yes, yes; I know all about that earlier burglary. But have you been robbed since?" said M. Formery, interrupting him.

"No, I haven't been robbed since that burglary; but my daughter has," said the millionaire.

"Your daughter?" said M. Formery.

"Yes; I have been robbed two or three times during the last three years," said Germaine.

"Dear me! But you ought to have told us about this before. This is extremely interesting, and most important," said M. Formery, rubbing his hands, "I suppose you suspect Victoire?"

"No, I don't," said Germaine quickly. "It couldn't have been Victoire. The last two thefts were committed at the chateau when Victoire was in Paris in charge of this house."

M. Formery seemed taken aback, and he hesitated, consulting his notes. Then he said: "Good—good. That confirms my hypothesis."

"What hypothesis?" said M. Gournay-Martin quickly.

"Never mind—never mind," said M. Formery solemnly. And, turning to Germaine, he went on: "You say, Mademoiselle, that these thefts began about three years ago?"

"Yes, I think they began about three years ago in August."

"Let me see. It was in the month of August, three years ago, that your father, after receiving a threatening letter like the one he received last night, was the victim of a burglary?" said M. Formery.

"Yes, it was—the scoundrels!" cried the millionaire fiercely.

"Well, it would be interesting to know which of your servants entered your service three years ago," said M. Formery.

"Victoire has only been with us a year at the outside," said Germaine.

"Only a year?" said M. Formery quickly, with an air of some vexation. He paused and added, "Exactly—exactly. And what was the nature of the last theft of which you were the victim?"

"It was a pearl brooch—not unlike the pendant which his Grace gave me yesterday," said Germaine.

"Would you mind showing me that pendant? I should like to see it," said M. Formery.

"Certainly—show it to him, Jacques. You have it, haven't you?" said Germaine, turning to the Duke.

"Me? No. How should I have it?" said the Duke in some surprise. "Haven't you got it?"

"I've only got the case—the empty case," said Germaine, with a startled air.

"The empty case?" said the Duke, with growing surprise.

"Yes," said Germaine. "It was after we came back from our useless journey to the station. I remembered suddenly that I had started without the pendant. I went to the bureau and picked up the case; and it was empty."

"One moment—one moment," said M. Formery. "Didn't you catch this young Bernard Charolais with this case in his hands, your Grace?"

"Yes," said the Duke. "I caught him with it in his pocket."

"Then you may depend upon it that the young rascal had slipped the pendant out of its case and you only recovered the empty case from him," said M. Formery triumphantly.

"No," said the Duke. "That is not so. Nor could the thief have been the burglar who broke open the bureau to get at the keys. For long after both of them were out of the house I took a cigarette from the box which stood on the bureau beside the case which held the pendant. And it occurred to me that the young rascal might have played that very trick on me. I opened the case and the pendant was there."

"It has been stolen!" cried the millionaire; "of course it has been stolen."

"Oh, no, no," said the Duke. "It hasn't been stolen. Irma, or perhaps Mademoiselle Kritchnoff, has brought it to Paris for Germaine."

"Sonia certainly hasn't brought it. It was she who suggested to me that you had seen it lying on the bureau, and slipped it into your pocket," said Germaine quickly.

"Then it must be Irma," said the Duke.

"We had better send for her and make sure," said M. Formery. "Inspector, go and fetch her."

The inspector went out of the room and the Duke questioned Germaine and her father about the journey, whether it had been very uncomfortable, and if they were very tired by it. He learned that they had been so fortunate as to find sleeping compartments on the train, so that they had suffered as little as might be from their night of travel.

M. Formery looked through his notes; Guerchard seemed to be going to sleep where he stood against the wall.

The inspector came back with Irma. She wore the frightened, half-defensive, half-defiant air which people of her class wear when confronted by the authorities. Her big, cow's eyes rolled uneasily.

"Oh, Irma—" Germaine began.

M. Formery cut her short, somewhat brusquely. "Excuse me, excuse me. I am conducting this inquiry," he said. And then, turning to Irma, he added, "Now, don't be frightened, Mademoiselle Irma; I want to ask you a question or two. Have you brought up to Paris the pendant which the Duke of Charmerace gave your mistress yesterday?"

"Me, sir? No, sir. I haven't brought the pendant," said Irma.

"You're quite sure?" said M. Formery.

"Yes, sir; I haven't seen the pendant. Didn't Mademoiselle Germaine leave it on the bureau?" said Irma.

"How do you know that?" said M. Formery.

"I heard Mademoiselle Germaine say that it had been on the bureau. I thought that perhaps Mademoiselle Kritchnoff had put it in her bag."

"Why should Mademoiselle Kritchnoff put it in her bag?" said the Duke quickly.

"To bring it up to Paris for Mademoiselle Germaine," said Irma.

"But what made you think that?" said Guerchard, suddenly intervening.

"Oh, I thought Mademoiselle Kritchnoff might have put it in her bag because I saw her standing by the bureau," said Irma.

"Ah, and the pendant was on the bureau?" said M. Formery.

"Yes, sir," said Irma.

There was a silence. Suddenly the atmosphere of the room seemed to have become charged with an oppression—a vague menace. Guerchard seemed to have become wide awake again. Germaine and the Duke looked at one another uneasily.

"Have you been long in the service of Mademoiselle Gournay-Martin?" said M. Formery.

"Six months, sir," said Irma.

"Very good, thank you. You can go," said M. Formery. "I may want you again presently."

Irma went quickly out of the room with an air of relief.

M. Formery scribbled a few words on the paper before him and then said: "Well, I will proceed to question Mademoiselle Kritchnoff."

"Mademoiselle Kritchnoff is quite above suspicion," said the Duke quickly.

"Oh, yes, quite," said Germaine.

"How long has Mademoiselle Kritchnoff been in your service, Mademoiselle?" said Guerchard.

"Let me think," said Germaine, knitting her brow.

"Can't you remember?" said M. Formery.

"Just about three years," said Germaine.

"That's exactly the time at which the thefts began," said M. Formery.

"Yes," said Germaine, reluctantly.

"Ask Mademoiselle Kritchnoff to come here, inspector," said M. Formery.

"Yes, sir," said the inspector.

"I'll go and fetch her—I know where to find her," said the Duke quickly, moving toward the door.

"Please, please, your Grace," protested Guerchard. "The inspector will fetch her."

The Duke turned sharply and looked at him: "I beg your pardon, but do you—" he said.

"Please don't be annoyed, your Grace," Guerchard interrupted. "But M. Formery agrees with me—it would be quite irregular."

"Yes, yes, your Grace," said M. Formery. "We have our method of procedure. It is best to adhere to it—much the best. It is the result of years of experience of the best way of getting the truth."

"Just as you please," said the Duke, shrugging his shoulders.

The inspector came into the room: "Mademoiselle Kritchnoff will be here in a moment. She was just going out."

"She was going out?" said M. Formery. "You don't mean to say you're letting members of the household go out?"

"No, sir," said the inspector. "I mean that she was just asking if she might go out."

M. Formery beckoned the inspector to him, and said to him in a voice too low for the others to hear:

"Just slip up to her room and search her trunks."

"There is no need to take the trouble," said Guerchard, in the same low voice, but with sufficient emphasis.

"No, of course not. There's no need to take the trouble," M. Formery repeated after him.

The door opened, and Sonia came in. She was still wearing her travelling costume, and she carried her cloak on her arm. She stood looking round her with an air of some surprise; perhaps there was even a touch of fear in it. The long journey of the night before did not seem to have dimmed at all her delicate beauty. The Duke's eyes rested on her in an inquiring, wondering, even searching gaze. She looked at him, and her own eyes fell.

"Will you come a little nearer, Mademoiselle?" said M. Formery. "There are one or two questions—"

"Will you allow me?" said Guerchard, in a tone of such deference that it left M. Formery no grounds for refusal.

M. Formery flushed and ground his teeth. "Have it your own way!" he said ungraciously.

"Mademoiselle Kritchnoff," said Guerchard, in a tone of the most good-natured courtesy, "there is a matter on which M. Formery needs some information. The pendant which the Duke of Charmerace gave Mademoiselle Gournay-Martin yesterday has been stolen."

"Stolen? Are you sure?" said Sonia in a tone of mingled surprise and anxiety.

"Quite sure," said Guerchard. "We have exactly determined the conditions under which the theft was committed. But we have every reason to believe that the culprit, to avoid detection, has hidden the pendant in the travelling-bag or trunk of somebody else in order to—"

"My bag is upstairs in my bedroom, sir," Sonia interrupted quickly. "Here is the key of it."

In order to free her hands to take the key from her wrist-bag, she set her cloak on the back of a couch. It slipped off it, and fell to the ground at the feet of the Duke, who had not returned to his place beside Germaine. While she was groping in her bag for the key, and all eyes were on her, the Duke, who had watched her with a curious intentness ever since her entry into the room, stooped quietly down and picked up the cloak. His hand slipped into the pocket of it; his fingers touched a hard object wrapped in tissue-paper. They closed round it, drew it from the pocket, and, sheltered by the cloak, transferred it to his own. He set the cloak on the back of the sofa, and very softly moved back to his place by Germaine's side. No one in the room observed the movement, not even Guerchard: he was watching Sonia too intently.

Sonia found the key, and held it out to Guerchard.

He shook his head and said: "There is no reason to search your bag— none whatever. Have you any other luggage?"

She shrank back a little from his piercing eyes, almost as if their gaze scared her.

"Yes, my trunk ... it's upstairs in my bedroom too ... open."

She spoke in a faltering voice, and her troubled eyes could not meet those of the detective.

"You were going out, I think," said Guerchard gently.

"I was asking leave to go out. There is some shopping that must be done," said Sonia.

"You do not see any reason why Mademoiselle Kritchnoff should not go out, M. Formery, do you?" said Guerchard.

"Oh, no, none whatever; of course she can go out," said M. Formery.

Sonia turned round to go.

"One moment," said Guerchard, coming forward. "You've only got that wrist-bag with you?"

"Yes," said Sonia. "I have my money and my handkerchief in it." And she held it out to him.

Guerchard's keen eyes darted into it; and he muttered, "No point in looking in that. I don't suppose any one would have had the audacity—" and he stopped.

Sonia made a couple of steps toward the door, turned, hesitated, came back to the couch, and picked up her cloak.

There was a sudden gleam in Guerchard's eyes—a gleam of understanding, expectation, and triumph. He stepped forward, and holding out his hands, said: "Allow me."

"No, thank you," said Sonia. "I'm not going to put it on."

"No ... but it's possible ... some one may have ... have you felt in the pockets of it? That one, now? It seems as if that one—"

He pointed to the pocket which had held the packet.

Sonia started back with an air of utter dismay; her eyes glanced wildly round the room as if seeking an avenue of escape; her fingers closed convulsively on the pocket.

"But this is abominable!" she cried. "You look as if—"

"I beg you, mademoiselle," interrupted Guerchard. "We are sometimes obliged—"

"Really, Mademoiselle Sonia," broke in the Duke, in a singularly clear and piercing tone, "I cannot see why you should object to this mere formality."

"Oh, but—but—" gasped Sonia, raising her terror-stricken eyes to his.

The Duke seemed to hold them with his own; and he said in the same clear, piercing voice, "There isn't the slightest reason for you to be frightened."

Sonia let go of the cloak, and Guerchard, his face all alight with triumph, plunged his hand into the pocket. He drew it out empty, and stared at it, while his face fell to an utter, amazed blankness.

"Nothing? nothing?" he muttered under his breath. And he stared at his empty hand as if he could not believe his eyes.

By a violent effort he forced an apologetic smile on his face, and said to Sonia: "A thousand apologies, mademoiselle."

He handed the cloak to her. Sonia took it and turned to go. She took a step towards the door, and tottered.

The Duke sprang forward and caught her as she was falling.

"Do you feel faint?" he said in an anxious voice.

"Thank you, you just saved me in time," muttered Sonia.

"I'm really very sorry," said Guerchard.

"Thank you, it was nothing. I'm all right now," said Sonia, releasing herself from the Duke's supporting arm.

She drew herself up, and walked quietly out of the room.

Guerchard went back to M. Formery at the writing-table.

"You made a clumsy mistake there, Guerchard," said M. Formery, with a touch of gratified malice in his tone.

Guerchard took no notice of it: "I want you to give orders that nobody leaves the house without my permission," he said, in a low voice.

"No one except Mademoiselle Kritchnoff, I suppose," said M. Formery, smiling.

"She less than any one," said Guerchard quickly.

"I don't understand what you're driving at a bit," said M. Formery. "Unless you suppose that Mademoiselle Kritchnoff is Lupin in disguise."

Guerchard laughed softly: "You will have your joke, M. Formery," he said.

"Well, well, I'll give the order," said M. Formery, somewhat mollified by the tribute to his humour.

He called the inspector to him and whispered a word in his ear. Then he rose and said: "I think, gentlemen, we ought to go and examine the bedrooms, and, above all, make sure that the safe in M. Gournay-Martin's bedroom has not been tampered with."

"I was wondering how much longer we were going to waste time here talking about that stupid pendant," grumbled the millionaire; and he rose and led the way.

"There may also be some jewel-cases in the bedrooms," said M. Formery. "There are all the wedding presents. They were in charge of Victoire." said Germaine quickly. "It would be dreadful if they had been stolen. Some of them are from the first families in France."

"They would replace them ... those paper-knives," said the Duke, smiling.

Germaine and her father led the way. M. Formery, Guerchard, and the inspector followed them. At the door the Duke paused, stopped, closed it on them softly. He came back to the window, put his hand in his pocket, and drew out the packet wrapped in tissue-paper.

He unfolded the paper with slow, reluctant fingers, and revealed the pendant.

XIII. LUPIN WIRES

The Duke stared at the pendant, his eyes full of wonder and pity.

"Poor little girl!" he said softly under his breath.

He put the pendant carefully away in his waistcoat-pocket and stood staring thoughtfully out of the window.

The door opened softly, and Sonia came quickly into the room, closed the door, and leaned back against it. Her face was a dead white; her skin had lost its lustre of fine porcelain, and she stared at him with eyes dim with anguish.

In a hoarse, broken voice, she muttered: "Forgive me! Oh, forgive me!"

"A thief—you?" said the Duke, in a tone of pitying wonder.

Sonia groaned.

"You mustn't stop here," said the Duke in an uneasy tone, and he looked uneasily at the door.

"Ah, you don't want to speak to me any more," said Sonia, in a heartrending tone, wringing her hands.

"Guerchard is suspicious of everything. It is dangerous for us to be talking here. I assure you that it's dangerous," said the Duke.

"What an opinion must you have of me! It's dreadful—cruel!" wailed Sonia.

"For goodness' sake don't speak so loud," said the Duke, with even greater uneasiness. "You MUST think of Guerchard."

"What do I care?" cried Sonia. "I've lost the liking of the only creature whose liking I wanted. What does anything else matter? What DOES it matter?"

"We'll talk somewhere else presently. That'll be far safer," said the Duke.

"No, no, we must talk now!" cried Sonia. "You must know.... I must tell ... Oh, dear! ... Oh, dear! ... I don't know how to tell you.... And then it is so unfair.... she ... Germaine ... she has everything," she panted. "Yesterday, before me, you gave her that pendant, ... she smiled ... she was proud of it.... I saw her pleasure.... Then I took it—I took it—I took it! And if I could, I'd take her fortune, too.... I hate her! Oh, how I hate her!"

"What!" said the Duke.

"Yes, I do ... I hate her!" said Sonia; and her eyes, no longer gentle, glowed with the sombre resentment, the dull rage of the weak who turn on Fortune. Her gentle voice was harsh with rebellious wrath.

"You hate her?" said the Duke quickly.

"I should never have told you that.... But now I dare.... I dare speak out.... It's you! ... It's you—" The avowal died on her lips. A burning flush crimsoned her cheeks and faded as quickly as it came: "I hate her!" she muttered.

"Sonia—" said the Duke gently.

"Oh! I know that it's no excuse.... I know that you're thinking 'This is a very pretty story, but it's not her first theft'; ... and it's true—it's the tenth, ... perhaps it's the twentieth.... It's true—I am a thief." She paused, and the glow deepened in her eyes. "But there's one thing you must believe—you shall believe; since you came, since I've known you, since the first day you set eyes on me, I have stolen no more ... till yesterday when you gave her the pendant before me. I could not bear it ... I could not." She paused and looked at him with eyes that demanded an assent.

"I believe you," said the Duke gravely.

She heaved a deep sigh of relief, and went on more quietly—some of its golden tone had returned to her voice: "And then, if you knew how it began ... the horror of it," she said.

"Poor child!" said the Duke softly.

"Yes, you pity me, but you despise me—you despise me beyond words. You shall not! I will not have it!" she cried fiercely.

"Believe me, no," said the Duke, in a soothing tone.

"Listen," said Sonia. "Have you ever been alone—alone in the world? ... Have you ever been hungry? Think of it ... in this big city where I was starving in sight of bread ... bread in the shops .... One only had to stretch out one's hand to touch it ... a penny loaf. Oh, it's commonplace!" she broke off: "quite commonplace!"

"Go on: tell me," said the Duke curtly.

"There was one way I could make money and I would not do it: no, I would not," she went on. "But that day I was dying ... understand, I was dying ....I went to the rooms of a man I knew a little. It was my last resource. At first I was glad ... he gave me food and wine ... and then, he talked to me ... he offered me money."

"What!" cried the Duke; and a sudden flame of anger flared up in his eyes.

"No; I could not ... and then I robbed him.... I preferred to ... it was more decent. Ah, I had excuses then. I began to steal to remain an honest woman ... and I've gone on stealing to keep up appearances. You see ... I joke about it." And she laughed, the faint, dreadful, mocking laugh of a damned soul.

"Oh, dear! Oh, dear!" she cried; and, burying her face in her hands, she burst into a storm of weeping.

"Poor child," said the Duke softly. And he stared gloomily on the ground, overcome by this revelation of the tortures of the feeble in the underworld beneath the Paris he knew.

"Oh, you do pity me ... you do understand ... and feel," said Sonia, between her sobs.

The Duke raised his head and gazed at her with eyes full of an infinite sympathy and compassion.

"Poor little Sonia," he said gently. "I understand."

She gazed at him with incredulous eyes, in which joy and despair mingled, struggling.

He came slowly towards her, and stopped short. His quick ear had caught the sound of a footstep outside the door.

"Quick! Dry your eyes! You must look composed. The other room!" he cried, in an imperative tone.

He caught her hand and drew her swiftly into the further drawing-room.

With the quickness which came of long practice in hiding her feelings Sonia composed her face to something of its usual gentle calm. There was even a faint tinge of colour in her cheeks; they had lost their dead whiteness. A faint light shone in her eyes; the anguish had cleared from them. They rested on the Duke with a look of ineffable gratitude. She sat down on a couch. The Duke went to the window and lighted a cigarette. They heard the door of the outer drawing-room open, and there was a pause. Quick footsteps crossed the room, and Guerchard stood in the doorway. He looked from one to the other with keen and eager eyes. Sonia sat staring rather listlessly at the carpet. The Duke turned, and smiled at him.

"Well, M. Guerchard," he said. "I hope the burglars have not stolen the coronet."

"The coronet is safe, your Grace," said Guerchard.

"And the paper-knives?" said the Duke.

"The paper-knives?" said Guerchard with an inquiring air.

"The wedding presents," said the Duke.

"Yes, your Grace, the wedding presents are safe," said Guerchard.

"I breathe again," said the Duke languidly.

Guerchard turned to Sonia and said, "I was looking for you, Mademoiselle, to tell you that M. Formery has changed his mind. It is impossible for you to go out. No one will be allowed to go out."

"Yes?" said Sonia, in an indifferent tone.

"We should be very much obliged if you would go to your room," said Guerchard. "Your meals will be sent up to you."

"What?" said Sonia, rising quickly; and she looked from Guerchard to the Duke. The Duke gave her the faintest nod.

"Very well, I will go to my room," she said coldly.

They accompanied her to the door of the outer drawing-room. Guerchard opened it for her and closed it after her.

"Really, M. Guerchard," said the Duke, shrugging his shoulders. "This last measure—a child like that!"

"Really, I'm very sorry, your Grace; but it's my trade, or, if you prefer it, my duty. As long as things are taking place here which I am still the only one to perceive, and which are not yet clear to me, I must neglect no precaution."

"Of course, you know best," said the Duke. "But still, a child like that—you're frightening her out of her life."

Guerchard shrugged his shoulders, and went quietly out of the room.

The Duke sat down in an easy chair, frowning and thoughtful. Suddenly there struck on his ears the sound of a loud roaring and heavy bumping on the stairs, the door flew open, and M. Gournay-Martin stood on the threshold waving a telegram in his hand.

M. Formery and the inspector came hurrying down the stairs behind him, and watched his emotion with astonished and wondering eyes.

"Here!" bellowed the millionaire. "A telegram! A telegram from the scoundrel himself! Listen! Just listen:"

"A thousand apologies for not having been able to keep my promise about the coronet. Had an appointment at the Acacias. Please have coronet ready in your room to-night. Will come without fail to fetch it, between a quarter to twelve and twelve o'clock."

"Yours affectionately,"

"ARSENE LUPIN."

"There! What do you think of that?"

"If you ask me, I think he's humbug," said the Duke with conviction.

"Humbug! You always think it's humbug! You thought the letter was humbug; and look what has happened!" cried the millionaire.

"Give me the telegram, please," said M. Formery quickly.

The millionaire gave it to him; and he read it through.

"Find out who brought it, inspector," he said.

The inspector hurried to the top of the staircase and called to the policeman in charge of the front door. He came back to the drawing-room and said: "It was brought by an ordinary post-office messenger, sir."

"Where is he?" said M. Formery. "Why did you let him go?"

"Shall I send for him, sir?" said the inspector.

"No, no, it doesn't matter," said M. Formery; and, turning to M. Gournay-Martin and the Duke, he said, "Now we're really going to have trouble with Guerchard. He is going to muddle up everything. This telegram will be the last straw. Nothing will persuade him now that this is not Lupin's work. And just consider, gentlemen: if Lupin had come last night, and if he had really set his heart on the coronet, he would have stolen it then, or at any rate he would have tried to open the safe in M. Gournay-Martin's bedroom, in which the coronet actually is, or this safe here"—he went to the safe and rapped on the door of it—"in which is the second key."

"That's quite clear," said the inspector.

"If, then, he did not make the attempt last night, when he had a clear field—when the house was empty—he certainly will not make the attempt now when we are warned, when the police are on the spot, and the house is surrounded. The idea is childish, gentlemen"—he leaned against the door of the safe—"absolutely childish, but Guerchard is mad on this point; and I foresee that his madness is going to hamper us in the most idiotic way."

He suddenly pitched forward into the middle of the room, as the door of the safe opened with a jerk, and Guerchard shot out of it.

"What the devil!" cried M. Formery, gaping at him.

"You'd be surprised how clearly you hear everything in these safes—you'd think they were too thick," said Guerchard, in his gentle, husky voice.

"How on earth did you get into it?" cried M. Formery.

"Getting in was easy enough. It's the getting out that was awkward. These jokers had fixed up some kind of a spring so that I nearly shot out with the door," said Guerchard, rubbing his elbow.

"But how did you get into it? How the deuce DID you get into it?" cried M. Formery.

"Through the little cabinet into which that door behind the safe opens. There's no longer any back to the safe; they've cut it clean out of it—a very neat piece of work. Safes like this should always be fixed against a wall, not stuck in front of a door. The backs of them are always the weak point."

"And the key? The key of the safe upstairs, in my bedroom, where the coronet is—is the key there?" cried M. Gournay-Martin.

Guerchard went back into the empty safe, and groped about in it. He came out smiling.

"Well, have you found the key?" cried the millionaire.

"No. I haven't; but I've found something better," said Guerchard.

"What is it?" said M. Formery sharply.

"I'll give you a hundred guesses," said Guerchard with a tantalizing smile.

"What is it?" said M. Formery.

"A little present for you," said Guerchard.

"What do you mean?" cried M. Formery angrily.

Guerchard held up a card between his thumb and forefinger and said quietly:

"The card of Arsene Lupin."

XIV. GUERCHARD PICKS UP THE TRUE SCENT

The millionaire gazed at the card with stupefied eyes, the inspector gazed at it with extreme intelligence, the Duke gazed at it with interest, and M. Formery gazed at it with extreme disgust.

"It's part of the same ruse—it was put there to throw us off the scent. It proves nothing—absolutely nothing," he said scornfully.

"No; it proves nothing at all," said Guerchard quietly.

"The telegram is the important thing—this telegram," said M. Gournay-Martin feverishly. "It concerns the coronet. Is it going to be disregarded?"

"Oh, no, no," said M. Formery in a soothing tone. "It will be taken into account. It will certainly be taken into account."

M. Gournay-Martin's butler appeared in the doorway of the drawing-room: "If you please, sir, lunch is served," he said.

At the tidings some of his weight of woe appeared to be lifted from the head of the millionaire. "Good!" he said, "good! Gentlemen, you will lunch with me, I hope."

"Thank you," said M. Formery. "There is nothing else for us to do, at any rate at present, and in the house. I am not quite satisfied about Mademoiselle Kritchnoff—at least Guerchard is not. I propose to question her again—about those earlier thefts."

"I'm sure there's nothing in that," said the Duke quickly.

"No, no; I don't think there is," said M. Formery. "But still one never knows from what quarter light may come in an affair like this. Accident often gives us our best clues."

"It seems rather a shame to frighten her—she's such a child," said the Duke.

"Oh, I shall be gentle, your Grace—as gentle as possible, that is. But I look to get more from the examination of Victoire. She was on the scene. She has actually seen the rogues at work; but till she recovers there is nothing more to be done, except to wait the discoveries of the detectives who are working outside; and they will report here. So in the meantime we shall be charmed to lunch with you, M. Gournay-Martin."

They went downstairs to the dining-room and found an elaborate and luxurious lunch, worthy of the hospitality of a millionaire, awaiting them. The skill of the cook seemed to have been quite unaffected by the losses of his master. M. Formery, an ardent lover of good things, enjoyed himself immensely. He was in the highest spirits. Germaine, a little upset by the night-journey, was rather querulous. Her father was plunged in a gloom which lifted for but a brief space at the appearance of a fresh delicacy. Guerchard ate and drank seriously, answering the questions of the Duke in a somewhat absent-minded fashion. The Duke himself seemed to have lost his usual flow of good spirits, and at times his brow was knitted in an anxious frown. His questions to Guerchard showed a far less keen interest in the affair.

To him the lunch seemed very long and very tedious; but at last it came to an end. M. Gournay-Martin seemed to have been much cheered by the wine he had drunk. He was almost hopeful. M. Formery, who had not by any means trifled with the champagne, was raised to the very height of sanguine certainty. Their coffee and liqueurs were served in the smoking-room. Guerchard lighted a cigar, refused a liqueur, drank his coffee quickly, and slipped out of the room.

The Duke followed him, and in the hall said: "I will continue to watch you unravel the threads of this mystery, if I may, M. Guerchard."

Good Republican as Guerchard was, he could not help feeling flattered by the interest of a Duke; and the excellent lunch he had eaten disposed him to feel the honour even more deeply.

"I shall be charmed," he said. "To tell the truth, I find the company of your Grace really quite stimulating."

"It must be because I find it all so extremely interesting," said the Duke.

They went up to the drawing-room and found the red-faced young policeman seated on a chair by the door eating a lunch, which had been sent up to him from the millionaire's kitchen, with a very hearty appetite.

They went into the drawing-room. Guerchard shut the door and turned the key: "Now," he said, "I think that M. Formery will give me half an hour to myself. His cigar ought to last him at least half an hour. In that time I shall know what the burglars really did with their plunder—at least I shall know for certain how they got it out of the house."

"Please explain," said the Duke. "I thought we knew how they got it out of the house." And he waved his hand towards the window.

"Oh, that!—that's childish," said Guerchard contemptuously. "Those are traces for an examining magistrate. The ladder, the table on the window-sill, they lead nowhere. The only people who came up that ladder were the two men who brought it from the scaffolding. You can see their footsteps. Nobody went down it at all. It was mere waste of time to bother with those traces."

"But the footprint under the book?" said the Duke.

"Oh, that," said Guerchard. "One of the burglars sat on the couch there, rubbed plaster on the sole of his boot, and set his foot down on the carpet. Then he dusted the rest of the plaster off his boot and put the book on the top of the footprint."

"Now, how do you know that?" said the astonished Duke.

"It's as plain as a pike-staff," said Guerchard. "There must have been several burglars to move such pieces of furniture. If the soles of all of them had been covered with plaster, all the sweeping in the world would not have cleared the carpet of the tiny fragments of it. I've been over the carpet between the footprint and the window with a magnifying glass. There are no fragments of plaster on it. We dismiss the footprint. It is a mere blind, and a very fair blind too—for an examining magistrate."

"I understand," said the Duke.

"That narrows the problem, the quite simple problem, how was the furniture taken out of the room. It did not go through that window down the ladder. Again, it was not taken down the stairs, and out of the front door, or the back. If it had been, the concierge and his wife would have heard the noise. Besides that, it would have been carried down into a main street, in which there are people at all hours. Somebody would have been sure to tell a policeman that this house was being emptied. Moreover, the police were continually patrolling the main streets, and, quickly as a man like Lupin would do the job, he could not do it so quickly that a policeman would not have seen it. No; the furniture was not taken down the stairs or out of the front door. That narrows the problem still more. In fact, there is only one mode of egress left."

"The chimney!" cried the Duke.

"You've hit it," said Guerchard, with a husky laugh. "By that well-known logical process, the process of elimination, we've excluded all methods of egress except the chimney."

He paused, frowning, in some perplexity; and then he said uneasily: "What I don't like about it is that Victoire was set in the fireplace. I asked myself at once what was she doing there. It was unnecessary that she should be drugged and set in the fireplace—quite unnecessary."

"It might have been to put off an examining magistrate," said the Duke. "Having found Victoire in the fireplace, M. Formery did not look for anything else."

"Yes, it might have been that," said Guerchard slowly. "On the other hand, she might have been put there to make sure that I did not miss the road the burglars took. That's the worst of having to do with Lupin. He knows me to the bottom of my mind. He has something up his sleeve—some surprise for me. Even now, I'm nowhere near the bottom of the mystery. But come along, we'll take the road the burglars took. The inspector has put my lantern ready for me."

As he spoke he went to the fireplace, picked up a lantern which had been set on the top of the iron fire-basket, and lighted it. The Duke stepped into the great fireplace beside him. It was four feet deep, and between eight and nine feet broad. Guerchard threw the light from the lantern on to the back wall of it. Six feet from the floor the soot from the fire stopped abruptly, and there was a dappled patch of bricks, half of them clean and red, half of them blackened by soot, five feet broad, and four feet high.

"The opening is higher up than I thought," said Guerchard. "I must get a pair of steps."

He went to the door of the drawing-room and bade the young policeman fetch him a pair of steps. They were brought quickly. He took them from the policeman, shut the door, and locked it again. He set the steps in the fireplace and mounted them.

"Be careful," he said to the Duke, who had followed him into the fireplace, and stood at the foot of the steps. "Some of these bricks may drop inside, and they'll sting you up if they fall on your toes."

The Duke stepped back out of reach of any bricks that might fall.

Guerchard set his left hand against the wall of the chimney-piece between him and the drawing-room, and pressed hard with his right against the top of the dappled patch of bricks. At the first push, half a dozen of them fell with a bang on to the floor of the next house. The light came flooding in through the hole, and shone on Guerchard's face and its smile of satisfaction. Quickly he pushed row after row of bricks into the next house until he had cleared an opening four feet square.

"Come along," he said to the Duke, and disappeared feet foremost through the opening.

The Duke mounted the steps, and found himself looking into a large empty room of the exact size and shape of the drawing-room of M. Gournay-Martin, save that it had an ordinary modern fireplace instead of one of the antique pattern of that in which he stood. Its chimney-piece was a few inches below the opening. He stepped out on to the chimney-piece and dropped lightly to the floor.

"Well," he said, looking back at the opening through which he had come. "That's an ingenious dodge."

"Oh, it's common enough," said Guerchard. "Robberies at the big jewellers' are sometimes worked by these means. But what is uncommon about it, and what at first sight put me off the track, is that these burglars had the cheek to pierce the wall with an opening large enough to enable them to remove the furniture of a house."

"It's true," said the Duke. "The opening's as large as a good-sized window. Those burglars seem capable of everything—even of a first-class piece of mason's work."

"Oh, this has all been prepared a long while ago. But now I'm really on their track. And after all, I haven't really lost any time. Dieusy wasted no time in making inquiries in Sureau Street; he's been working all this side of the house."

Guerchard drew up the blinds, opened the shutters, and let the daylight flood the dim room. He came back to the fireplace and looked down at the heap of bricks, frowning:

"I made a mistake there," he said. "I ought to have taken those bricks down carefully, one by one."

Quickly he took brick after brick from the pile, and began to range them neatly against the wall on the left. The Duke watched him for two or three minutes, then began to help him. It did not take them long, and under one of the last few bricks Guerchard found a fragment of a gilded picture-frame.

"Here's where they ought to have done their sweeping," he said, holding it up to the Duke.

"I tell you what," said the Duke, "I shouldn't wonder if we found the furniture in this house still."

"Oh, no, no!" said Guerchard. "I tell you that Lupin would allow for myself or Ganimard being put in charge of the case; and he would know that we should find the opening in the chimney. The furniture was taken straight out into the side-street on to which this house opens." He led the way out of the room on to the landing and went down the dark staircase into the hall. He opened the shutters of the hall windows, and let in the light. Then he examined the hall. The dust lay thick on the tiled floor. Down the middle of it was a lane formed by many feet. The footprints were faint, but still plain in the layer of dust. Guerchard came back to the stairs and began to examine them. Half-way up the flight he stooped, and picked up a little spray of flowers: "Fresh!" he said. "These have not been long plucked."

"Salvias," said the Duke.

"Salvias they are," said Guerchard. "Pink salvias; and there is only one gardener in France who has ever succeeded in getting this shade—M. Gournay-Martin's gardener at Charmerace. I'm a gardener myself."

"Well, then, last night's burglars came from Charmerace. They must have," said the Duke.

"It looks like it," said Guerchard.

"The Charolais," said the Duke.

"It looks like it," said Guerchard.

"It must be," said the Duke. "This IS interesting—if only we could get an absolute proof."

"We shall get one presently," said Guerchard confidently.

"It is interesting," said the Duke in a tone of lively enthusiasm. "These clues—these tracks which cross one another—each fact by degrees falling into its proper place—extraordinarily interesting." He paused and took out his cigarette-case: "Will you have a cigarette?" he said.

"Are they caporal?" said Guerchard.

"No, Egyptians—Mercedes."

"Thank you," said Guerchard; and he took one.

The Duke struck a match, lighted Guerchard's cigarette, and then his own:

"Yes, it's very interesting," he said. "In the last quarter of an hour you've practically discovered that the burglars came from Charmerace—that they were the Charolais—that they came in by the front door of this house, and carried the furniture out of it."

"I don't know about their coming in by it," said Guerchard. "Unless I'm very much mistaken, they came in by the front door of M. Gournay-Martin's house."

"Of course," said the Duke. "I was forgetting. They brought the keys from Charmerace."

"Yes, but who drew the bolts for them?" said Guerchard. "The concierge bolted them before he went to bed. He told me so. He was telling the truth— I know when that kind of man is telling the truth."

"By Jove!" said the Duke softly. "You mean that they had an accomplice?"

"I think we shall find that they had an accomplice. But your Grace is beginning to draw inferences with uncommon quickness. I believe that you would make a first-class detective yourself—with practice, of course—with practice."

"Can I have missed my true career?" said the Duke, smiling. "It's certainly a very interesting game."

"Well, I'm not going to search this barracks myself," said Guerchard. "I'll send in a couple of men to do it; but I'll just take a look at the steps myself."

So saying, he opened the front door and went out and examined the steps carefully.

"We shall have to go back the way we came," he said, when he had finished his examination. "The drawing-room door is locked. We ought to find M. Formery hammering on it." And he smiled as if he found the thought pleasing.

They went back up the stairs, through the opening, into the drawing-room of M. Gournay-Martin's house. Sure enough, from the other side of the locked door came the excited voice of M. Formery, crying:

"Guerchard! Guerchard! What are you doing? Let me in! Why don't you let me in?"

Guerchard unlocked the door; and in bounced M. Formery, very excited, very red in the face.

"Hang it all, Guerchard! What on earth have you been doing?" he cried. "Why didn't you open the door when I knocked?"

"I didn't hear you," said Guerchard. "I wasn't in the room."

"Then where on earth have you been?" cried M. Formery.

Guerchard looked at him with a faint, ironical smile, and said in his gentle voice, "I was following the real track of the burglars."

XV. THE EXAMINATION OF SONIA

M. Formery gasped: "The real track?" he muttered.

"Let me show you," said Guerchard. And he led him to the fireplace, and showed him the opening between the two houses.

"I must go into this myself!" cried M. Formery in wild excitement.

Without more ado he began to mount the steps. Guerchard followed him. The Duke saw their heels disappear up the steps. Then he came out of the drawing-room and inquired for M. Gournay-Martin. He was told that the millionaire was up in his bedroom; and he went upstairs, and knocked at the door of it.

M. Gournay-Martin bade him enter in a very faint voice, and the Duke found him lying on the bed. He was looking depressed, even exhausted, the shadow of the blusterous Gournay-Martin of the day before. The rich rosiness of his cheeks had faded to a moderate rose-pink.

"That telegram," moaned the millionaire. "It was the last straw. It has overwhelmed me. The coronet is lost."

"What, already?" said the Duke, in a tone of the liveliest surprise.

"No, no; it's still in the safe," said the millionaire. "But it's as good as lost—before midnight it will be lost. That fiend will get it."

"If it's in this safe now, it won't be lost before midnight," said the Duke. "But are you sure it's there now?"

"Look for yourself," said the millionaire, taking the key of the safe from his waistcoat pocket, and handing it to the Duke.

The Duke opened the safe. The morocco case which held the coronet lay on the middle shell in front of him. He glanced at the millionaire, and saw that he had closed his eyes in the exhaustion of despair. Whistling softly, the Duke opened the case, took out the diadem, and examined it carefully, admiring its admirable workmanship. He put it back in the case, turned to the millionaire, and said thoughtfully:

"I can never make up my mind, in the case of one of these old diadems, whether one ought not to take out the stones and have them re-cut. Look at this emerald now. It's a very fine stone, but this old-fashioned cutting does not really do it justice."

"Oh, no, no: you should never interfere with an antique, historic piece of jewellery. Any alteration decreases its value—its value as an historic relic," cried the millionaire, in a shocked tone.

"I know that," said the Duke, "but the question for me is, whether one ought not to sacrifice some of its value to increasing its beauty."

"You do have such mad ideas," said the millionaire, in a tone of peevish exasperation.

"Ah, well, it's a nice question," said the Duke.

He snapped the case briskly, put it back on the shelf, locked the safe, and handed the key to the millionaire. Then he strolled across the room and looked down into the street, whistling softly.

"I think—I think—I'll go home and get out of these motoring clothes. And I should like to have on a pair of boots that were a trifle less muddy," he said slowly.

M. Gournay-Martin sat up with a jerk and cried, "For Heaven's sake, don't you go and desert me, my dear chap! You don't know what my nerves are like!"

"Oh, you've got that sleuth-hound, Guerchard, and the splendid Formery, and four other detectives, and half a dozen ordinary policemen guarding you. You can do without my feeble arm. Besides, I shan't be gone more than half an hour—three-quarters at the outside. I'll bring back my evening clothes with me, and dress for dinner here. I don't suppose that anything fresh will happen between now and midnight; but I want to be on the spot, and hear the information as it comes in fresh. Besides, there's Guerchard. I positively cling to Guerchard. It's an education, though perhaps not a liberal education, to go about with him," said the Duke; and there was a sub-acid irony in his voice.

"Well, if you must, you must," said M. Gournay-Martin grumpily.

"Good-bye for the present, then," said the Duke. And he went out of the room and down the stairs. He took his motor-cap from the hall-table, and had his hand on the latch of the door, when the policeman in charge of it said, "I beg your pardon, sir, but have you M. Guerchard's permission to leave the house?"

"M. Guerchard's permission?" said the Duke haughtily. "What has M. Guerchard to do with me? I am the Duke of Charmerace." And he opened the door.

"It was M. Formery's orders, your Grace," stammered the policeman doubtfully.

"M. Formery's orders?" said the Duke, standing on the top step. "Call me a taxi-cab, please."

The concierge, who stood beside the policeman, ran down the steps and blew his whistle. The policeman gazed uneasily at the Duke, shifting his weight from one foot to the other; but he said no more.

A taxi-cab came up to the door, the Duke went down the steps, stepped into it, and drove away.

Three-quarters of an hour later he came back, having changed into clothes more suited to a Paris drawing-room. He went up to the drawing-room, and there he found Guerchard, M. Formery, and the inspector, who had just completed their tour of inspection of the house next door and had satisfied themselves that the stolen treasures were not in it. The inspector and his men had searched it thoroughly just to make sure; but, as Guerchard had foretold, the burglars had not taken the chance of the failure of the police to discover the opening between the two houses. M. Formery told the Duke about their tour of inspection at length. Guerchard went to the telephone and told the exchange to put him through to Charmerace. He was informed that the trunk line was very busy and that he might have to wait half an hour.

The Duke inquired if any trace of the burglars, after they had left with their booty, had yet been found. M. Formery told him that, so far, the detectives had failed to find a single trace. Guerchard said that he had three men at work on the search, and that he was hopeful of getting some news before long.

"The layman is impatient in these matters," said M. Formery, with an indulgent smile. "But we have learnt to be patient, after long experience."

He proceeded to discuss with Guerchard the new theories with which the discovery of the afternoon had filled his mind. None of them struck the Duke as being of great value, and he listened to them with a somewhat absent-minded air. The coming examination of Sonia weighed heavily on his spirit. Guerchard answered only in monosyllables to the questions and suggestions thrown out by M. Formery. It seemed to the Duke that he paid very little attention to him, that his mind was still working hard on the solution of the mystery, seeking the missing facts which would bring him to the bottom of it. In the middle of one of M. Formery's more elaborate dissertations the telephone bell rang.

Guerchard rose hastily and went to it. They heard him say: "Is that Charmerace? ... I want the gardener.... Out? When will he be back? ... Tell him to ring me up at M. Gournay-Martin's house in Paris the moment he gets back.... Detective-Inspector Guerchard ... Guerchard ... Detective-Inspector."

He turned to them with a frown, and said, "Of course, since I want him, the confounded gardener has gone out for the day. Still, it's of very little importance—a mere corroboration I wanted." And he went back to his seat and lighted another cigarette.

M. Formery continued his dissertation. Presently Guerchard said, "You might go and see how Victoire is, inspector—whether she shows any signs of waking. What did the doctor say?"

"The doctor said that she would not really be sensible and have her full wits about her much before ten o'clock to-night," said the inspector; but he went to examine her present condition.

M. Formery proceeded to discuss the effects of different anesthetics. The others heard him with very little attention.

The inspector came back and reported that Victoire showed no signs of awaking.

"Well, then, M. Formery, I think we might get on with the examination of Mademoiselle Kritchnoff," said Guerchard. "Will you go and fetch her, inspector?"

"Really, I cannot conceive why you should worry that poor child," the Duke protested, in a tone of some indignation.

"It seems to me hardly necessary," said M. Formery.

"Excuse me," said Guerchard suavely, "but I attach considerable importance to it. It seems to me to be our bounden duty to question her fully. One never knows from what quarter light may come."

"Oh, well, since you make such a point of it," said M. Formery. "Inspector, ask Mademoiselle Kritchnoff to come here. Fetch her."

The inspector left the room.

Guerchard looked at the Duke with a faint air of uneasiness: "I think that we had better question Mademoiselle Kritchnoff by ourselves," he said.

M. Formery looked at him and hesitated. Then he said: "Oh, yes, of course, by ourselves."

"Certainly," said the Duke, a trifle haughtily. And he rose and opened the door. He was just going through it when Guerchard said sharply:

"Your Grace—"

The Duke paid no attention to him. He shut the door quickly behind him and sprang swiftly up the stairs. He met the inspector coming down with Sonia. Barring their way for a moment he said, in his kindliest voice: "Now you mustn't be frightened, Mademoiselle Sonia. All you have to do is to try to remember as clearly as you can the circumstances of the earlier thefts at Charmerace. You mustn't let them confuse you."

"Thank you, your Grace, I will try and be as clear as I can," said Sonia; and she gave him an eloquent glance, full of gratitude for the warning; and went down the stairs with firm steps.

The Duke went on up the stairs, and knocked softly at the door of M. Gournay-Martin's bedroom. There was no answer to his knock, and he quietly opened the door and looked in. Overcome by his misfortunes, the millionaire had sunk into a profound sleep and was snoring softly. The Duke stepped inside the room, left the door open a couple of inches, drew a chair to it, and sat down watching the staircase through the opening of the door.

He sat frowning, with a look of profound pity on his face. Once the suspense grew too much for him. He rose and walked up and down the room. His well-bred calm seemed to have deserted him. He muttered curses on Guerchard, M. Formery, and the whole French criminal system, very softly, under his breath. His face was distorted to a mask of fury; and once he wiped the little beads of sweat from his forehead with his handkerchief. Then he recovered himself, sat down in the chair, and resumed his watch on the stairs.

At last, at the end of half an hour, which had seemed to him months long, he heard voices. The drawing-room door shut, and there were footsteps on the stairs. The inspector and Sonia came into view.

He waited till they were at the top of the stairs: then he came out of the room, with his most careless air, and said: "Well, Mademoiselle Sonia, I hope you did not find it so very dreadful, after all."

She was very pale, and there were undried tears on her cheeks. "It was horrible," she said faintly. "Horrible. M. Formery was all right—he believed me; but that horrible detective would not believe a word I said. He confused me. I hardly knew what I was saying."

The Duke ground his teeth softly. "Never mind, it's over now. You had better lie down and rest. I will tell one of the servants to bring you up a glass of wine."

He walked with her to the door of her room, and said: "Try to sleep—sleep away the unpleasant memory."

She went into her room, and the Duke went downstairs and told the butler to take a glass of champagne up to her. Then he went upstairs to the drawing-room. M. Formery was at the table writing. Guerchard stood beside him. He handed what he had written to Guerchard, and, with a smile of satisfaction, Guerchard folded the paper and put it in his pocket.

"Well, M. Formery, did Mademoiselle Kritchnoff throw any fresh light on this mystery?" said the Duke, in a tone of faint contempt.

"No—in fact she convinced ME that she knew nothing whatever about it. M. Guerchard seems to entertain a different opinion. But I think that even he is convinced that Mademoiselle Kritchnoff is not a friend of Arsene Lupin."

"Oh, well, perhaps she isn't. But there's no telling," said Guerchard slowly.

"Arsene Lupin?" cried the Duke. "Surely you never thought that Mademoiselle Kritchnoff had anything to do with Arsene Lupin?"

"I never thought so," said M. Formery. "But when one has a fixed idea ... well, one has a fixed idea." He shrugged his shoulders, and looked at Guerchard with contemptuous eyes.

The Duke laughed, an unaffected ringing laugh, but not a pleasant one: "It's absurd!" he cried.

"There are always those thefts," said Guerchard, with a nettled air.

"You have nothing to go upon," said M. Formery. "What if she did enter the service of Mademoiselle Gournay-Martin just before the thefts began? Besides, after this lapse of time, if she had committed the thefts, you'd find it a job to bring them home to her. It's not a job worth your doing, anyhow— it's a job for an ordinary detective, Guerchard."

"There's always the pendant," said Guerchard. "I am convinced that that pendant is in the house."

"Oh, that stupid pendant! I wish I'd never given it to Mademoiselle Gournay-Martin," said the Duke lightly.

"I have a feeling that if I could lay my hand on that pendant—if I could find who has it, I should have the key to this mystery."

"The devil you would!" said the Duke softly. "That is odd. It is the oddest thing about this business I've heard yet."

"I have that feeling—I have that feeling," said Guerchard quietly.

The Duke smiled.

XVI. VICTOIRE'S SLIP

They were silent. The Duke walked to the fireplace, stepped into it, and studied the opening. He came out again and said: "Oh, by the way, M. Formery, the policeman at the front door wanted to stop me going out of the house when I went home to change. I take it that M. Guerchard's prohibition does not apply to me?"

"Of course not—of course not, your Grace," said M. Formery quickly.

"I saw that you had changed your clothes, your Grace," said Guerchard. "I thought that you had done it here."

"No," said the Duke, "I went home. The policeman protested; but he went no further, so I did not throw him into the middle of the street."

"Whatever our station, we should respect the law," said M. Formery solemnly.

"The Republican Law, M. Formery? I am a Royalist," said the Duke, smiling at him.

M. Formery shook his head sadly.

"I was wondering," said the Duke, "about M. Guerchard's theory that the burglars were let in the front door of this house by an accomplice. Why, when they had this beautiful large opening, did they want a front door, too?"

"I did not know that that was Guerchard's theory?" said M. Formery, a trifle contemptuously. "Of course they had no need to use the front door."

"Perhaps they had no need to use the front door," said Guerchard; "but, after all, the front door was unbolted, and they did not draw the bolts to put us off the scent. Their false scent was already prepared"—he waved his hand towards the window—"moreover, you must bear in mind that that opening might not have been made when they entered the house. Suppose that, while they were on the other side of the wall, a brick had fallen on to the hearth, and alarmed the concierge. We don't know how skilful they are; they might not have cared to risk it. I'm inclined to think, on the whole, that they did come in through the front door."

M. Formery sniffed contemptuously.

"Perhaps you're right," said the Duke. "But the accomplice?"

"I think we shall know more about the accomplice when Victoire awakes," said Guerchard.

"The family have such confidence in Victoire," said the Duke.

"Perhaps Lupin has, too," said Guerchard grimly.

"Always Lupin!" said M. Formery contemptuously.

There came a knock at the door, and a footman appeared on the threshold. He informed the Duke that Germaine had returned from her shopping expedition, and was awaiting him in her boudoir. He went to her, and tried to persuade her to put in a word for Sonia, and endeavour to soften Guerchard's rigour.

She refused to do anything of the kind, declaring that, in view of the value of the stolen property, no stone must be left unturned to recover it. The police knew what they were doing; they must have a free hand. The Duke did not press her with any great vigour; he realized the futility of an appeal to a nature so shallow, so self-centred, and so lacking in sympathy. He took his revenge by teasing her about the wedding presents which were still flowing in. Her father's business friends were still striving to outdo one another in the costliness of the jewelry they were giving her. The great houses of the Faubourg Saint-Germain were still refraining firmly from anything that savoured of extravagance or ostentation. While he was with her the eleventh paper-knife came—from his mother's friend, the Duchess of Veauleglise. The Duke was overwhelmed with joy at the sight of it, and his delighted comments drove Germaine to the last extremity of exasperation. The result was that she begged him, with petulant asperity, to get out of her sight.

He complied with her request, almost with alacrity, and returned to M. Formery and Guerchard. He found them at a standstill, waiting for reports from the detectives who were hunting outside the house for information about the movements of the burglars with the stolen booty, and apparently finding none. The police were also hunting for the stolen motor-cars, not only in Paris and its environs, but also all along the road between Paris and Charmerace.

At about five o'clock Guerchard grew tired of the inaction, and went out himself to assist his subordinates, leaving M. Formery in charge of the house itself. He promised to be back by half-past seven, to let the examining magistrate, who had an engagement for the evening, get away. The Duke spent his time between the drawing-room, where M. Formery entertained him with anecdotes of his professional skill, and the boudoir, where Germaine was entertaining envious young friends who came to see her wedding presents. The friends of Germaine were always a little ill at ease in the society of the Duke, belonging as they did to that wealthy middle class which has made France what she is. His indifference to the doings of the old friends of his family saddened them; and they were unable to understand his airy and persistent trifling. It seemed to them a discord in the cosmic tune.

The afternoon wore away, and at half-past seven Guerchard had not returned. M. Formery waited for him, fuming, for ten minutes, then left the house in charge of the inspector, and went off to his engagement. M. Gournay-Martin was entertaining two financiers and their wives, two of their daughters, and two friends of the Duke, the Baron de Vernan and the Comte de Vauvineuse, at dinner that night. Thanks to the Duke, the party was of a liveliness to which the gorgeous dining-room had been very little used since it had been so fortunate as to become the property of M. Gournay-Martin.

The millionaire had been looking forward to an evening of luxurious woe, deploring the loss of his treasures—giving their prices—to his sympathetic friends. The Duke had other views; and they prevailed. After dinner the guests went to the smoking-room, since the drawing-rooms were in possession of Guerchard. Soon after ten the Duke slipped away from them, and went to the detective. Guerchard's was not a face at any time full of expression, and all that the Duke saw on it was a subdued dulness.

"Well, M. Guerchard," he said cheerfully, "what luck? Have any of your men come across any traces of the passage of the burglars with their booty?"

"No, your Grace; so far, all the luck has been with the burglars. For all that any one seems to have seen them, they might have vanished into the bowels of the earth through the floor of the cellars in the empty house next door. That means that they were very quick loading whatever vehicle they used with their plunder. I should think, myself, that they first carried everything from this house down into the hall of the house next door; and then, of course, they could be very quick getting them from hall to their van, or whatever it was. But still, some one saw that van—saw it drive up to the house, or waiting at the house, or driving away from it."

"Is M. Formery coming back?" said the Duke.

"Not to-night," said Guerchard. "The affair is in my hands now; and I have my own men on it—men of some intelligence, or, at any rate, men who know my ways, and how I want things done."

"It must be a relief," said the Duke.

"Oh, no, I'm used to M. Formery—to all the examining magistrates in Paris, and in most of the big provincial towns. They do not really hamper me; and often I get an idea from them; for some of them are men of real intelligence."

"And others are not: I understand," said the Duke.

The door opened and Bonavent, the detective, came in.

"The housekeeper's awake, M. Guerchard," he said.

"Good, bring her down here," said Guerchard.

"Perhaps you'd like me to go," said the Duke.

"Oh, no," said Guerchard. "If it would interest you to hear me question her, please stay."

Bonavent left the room. The Duke sat down in an easy chair, and Guerchard stood before the fireplace.

"M. Formery told me, when you were out this afternoon, that he believed this housekeeper to be quite innocent," said the Duke idly.

"There is certainly one innocent in this affair," said Guerchard, grinning.

"Who is that?" said the Duke.

"The examining magistrate," said Guerchard.

The door opened, and Bonavent brought Victoire in. She was a big, middle-aged woman, with a pleasant, cheerful, ruddy face, black-haired, with sparkling brown eyes, which did not seem to have been at all dimmed by her long, drugged sleep. She looked like a well-to-do farmer's wife, a buxom, good-natured, managing woman.

As soon as she came into the room, she said quickly:

"I wish, Mr. Inspector, your man would have given me time to put on a decent dress. I must have been sleeping in this one ever since those rascals tied me up and put that smelly handkerchief over my face. I never saw such a nasty-looking crew as they were in my life."

"How many were there, Madame Victoire?" said Guerchard.

"Dozens! The house was just swarming with them. I heard the noise; I came downstairs; and on the landing outside the door here, one of them jumped on me from behind and nearly choked me—to prevent me from screaming, I suppose."

"And they were a nasty-looking crew, were they?" said Guerchard. "Did you see their faces?"

"No, I wish I had! I should know them again if I had; but they were all masked," said Victoire.

"Sit down, Madame Victoire. There's no need to tire you," said Guerchard. And she sat down on a chair facing him.

"Let's see, you sleep in one of the top rooms, Madame Victoire. It has a dormer window, set in the roof, hasn't it?" said Guerchard, in the same polite, pleasant voice.

"Yes; yes. But what has that got to do with it?" said Victoire.

"Please answer my questions," said Guerchard sharply. "You went to sleep in your room. Did you hear any noise on the roof?"

"On the roof? How should I hear it on the roof? There wouldn't be any noise on the roof," said Victoire.

"You heard nothing on the roof?" said Guerchard.

"No; the noise I heard was down here," said Victoire.

"Yes, and you came down to see what was making it. And you were seized from behind on the landing, and brought in here," said Guerchard.

"Yes, that's right," said Madame Victoire.

"And were you tied up and gagged on the landing, or in here?" said Guerchard.

"Oh, I was caught on the landing, and pushed in here, and then tied up," said Victoire.

"I'm sure that wasn't one man's job," said Guerchard, looking at her vigorous figure with admiring eyes.

"You may be sure of that," said Victoire. "It took four of them; and at least two of them have some nice bruises on their shins to show for it."

"I'm sure they have. And it serves them jolly well right," said Guerchard, in a tone of warm approval. "And, I suppose, while those four were tying you up the others stood round and looked on."

"Oh, no, they were far too busy for that," said Victoire.

"What were they doing?" said Guerchard.

"They were taking the pictures off the walls and carrying them out of the window down the ladder," said Victoire.

Guerchard's eyes flickered towards the Duke, but the expression of earnest inquiry on his face never changed.

"Now, tell me, did the man who took a picture from the walls carry it down the ladder himself, or did he hand it through the window to a man who was standing on the top of a ladder ready to receive it?" he said.

Victoire paused as if to recall their action; then she said, "Oh, he got through the window, and carried it down the ladder himself."

"You're sure of that?" said Guerchard.

"Oh, yes, I am quite sure of it—why should I deceive you, Mr. Inspector?" said Victoire quickly; and the Duke saw the first shadow of uneasiness on her face.

"Of course not," said Guerchard. "And where were you?"

"Oh, they put me behind the screen."

"No, no, where were you when you came into the room?"

"I was against the door," said Victoire.

"And where was the screen?" said Guerchard. "Was it before the fireplace?"

"No; it was on one side—the left-hand side," said Victoire.

"Oh, will you show me exactly where it stood?" said Guerchard.

Victoire rose, and, Guerchard aiding her, set the screen on the left-hand side of the fireplace.

Guerchard stepped back and looked at it.

"Now, this is very important," he said. "I must have the exact position of the four feet of that screen. Let's see ... some chalk ... of course.... You do some dressmaking, don't you, Madame Victoire?"

"Oh, yes, I sometimes make a dress for one of the maids in my spare time," said Victoire.

"Then you've got a piece of chalk on you," said Guerchard.

"Oh, yes," said Victoire, putting her hand to the pocket of her dress.

She paused, took a step backwards, and looked wildly round the room, while the colour slowly faded in her ruddy cheeks.

"What am I talking about?" she said in an uncertain, shaky voice. "I haven't any chalk—I—ran out of chalk the day before yesterday."

"I think you have, Madame Victoire. Feel in your pocket and see," said Guerchard sternly. His voice had lost its suavity; his face its smile: his eyes had grown dangerous.

"No, no; I have no chalk," cried Victoire.

With a sudden leap Guerchard sprang upon her, caught her in a firm grip with his right arm, and his left hand plunged into her pocket.

"Let me go! Let me go! You're hurting," she cried.

Guerchard loosed her and stepped back.

"What's this?" he said; and he held up between his thumb and forefinger a piece of blue chalk.

Victoire drew herself up and faced him gallantly: "Well, what of it?—it is chalk. Mayn't an honest woman carry chalk in her pockets without being insulted and pulled about by every policeman she comes across?" she cried.

"That will be for the examining magistrate to decide," said Guerchard; and he went to the door and called Bonavent. Bonavent came in, and Guerchard said: "When the prison van comes, put this woman in it; and send her down to the station."

"But what have I done?" cried Victoire. "I'm innocent! I declare I'm innocent. I've done nothing at all. It's not a crime to carry a piece of chalk in one's pocket."

"Now, that's a matter for the examining magistrate. You can explain it to him," said Guerchard. "I've got nothing to do with it: so it's no good making a fuss now. Do go quietly, there's a good woman."

He spoke in a quiet, business-like tone. Victoire looked him in the eyes, then drew herself up, and went quietly out of the room.

XVII. SONIA'S ESCAPE

"One of M. Formery's innocents," said Guerchard, turning to the Duke.

"The chalk?" said the Duke. "Is it the same chalk?"

"It's blue," said Guerchard, holding it out. "The same as that of the signatures on the walls. Add that fact to the woman's sudden realization of what she was doing, and you'll see that they were written with it."

"It is rather a surprise," said the Duke. "To look at her you would think that she was the most honest woman in the world."

"Ah, you don't know Lupin, your Grace," said Guerchard. "He can do anything with women; and they'll do anything for him. And, what's more, as far as I can see, it doesn't make a scrap of difference whether they're honest or not. The fair-haired lady I was telling you about was probably an honest woman; Ganimard is sure of it. We should have found out long ago who she was if she had been a wrong 'un. And Ganimard also swears that when he arrested Lupin on board the Provence some woman, some ordinary, honest woman among the passengers, carried away Lady Garland's jewels, which he had stolen and was bringing to America, and along with them a matter of eight hundred pounds which he had stolen from a fellow-passenger on the voyage."

"That power of fascination which some men exercise on women is one of those mysteries which science should investigate before it does anything else," said the Duke, in a reflective tone. "Now I come to think of it, I had much better have spent my time on that investigation than on that tedious journey to the South Pole. All the same, I'm deucedly sorry for that woman, Victoire. She looks such a good soul."

Guerchard shrugged his shoulders: "The prisons are full of good souls," he said, with cynical wisdom born of experience. "They get caught so much more often than the bad."

"It seems rather mean of Lupin to make use of women like this, and get them into trouble," said the Duke.

"But he doesn't," said Guerchard quickly. "At least he hasn't up to now. This Victoire is the first we've caught. I look on it as a good omen."

He walked across the room, picked up his cloak, and took a card-case from the inner pocket of it. "If you don't mind, your Grace, I want you to show this permit to my men who are keeping the door, whenever you go out of the house. It's just a formality; but I attach considerable importance to it, for I really ought not to make exceptions in favour of any one. I have two men at the door, and they have orders to let nobody out without my written permission. Of course M. Gournay-Martin's guests are different. Bonavent has orders to pass them out. And, if your Grace doesn't mind, it will help me. If you carry a permit, no one else will dream of complaining of having to do so."

"Oh, I don't mind, if it's of any help to you," said the Duke cheerfully.

"Thank you," said Guerchard. And he wrote on his card and handed it to the Duke.

The Duke took it and looked at it. On it was written:

"Pass the Duke of Charmerace."

"J. GUERCHARD."

"It's quite military," said the Duke, putting the card into his waistcoat pocket.

There came a knock at the door, and a tall, thin, bearded man came into the room.

"Ah, Dieusy! At last! What news?" cried Guerchard.

Dieusy saluted: "I've learnt that a motor-van was waiting outside the next house—in the side street," he said.

"At what time?" said Guerchard.

"Between four and five in the morning," said Dieusy.

"Who saw it?" said Guerchard.

"A scavenger. He thinks that it was nearly five o'clock when the van drove off."

"Between four and five—nearly five. Then they filled up the opening before they loaded the van. I thought they would," said Guerchard, thoughtfully. "Anything else?"

"A few minutes after the van had gone a man in motoring dress came out of the house," said Dieusy.

"In motoring dress?" said Guerchard quickly.

"Yes. And a little way from the house he threw away his cigarette. The scavenger thought the whole business a little queer, and he picked up the cigarette and kept it. Here it is."

He handed it to Guerchard, whose eyes scanned it carelessly and then glued themselves to it.

"A gold-tipped cigarette ... marked Mercedes ... Why, your Grace, this is one of your cigarettes!"

"But this is incredible!" cried the Duke.

426

"Not at all," said Guerchard. "It's merely another link in the chain. I've no doubt you have some of these cigarettes at Charmerace."

"Oh, yes, I've had a box on most of the tables," said the Duke.

"Well, there you are," said Guerchard.

"Oh, I see what you're driving at," said the Duke. "You mean that one of the Charolais must have taken a box."

"Well, we know that they'd hardly stick at a box of cigarettes," said Guerchard.

"Yes ... but I thought ..." said the Duke; and he paused.

"You thought what?" said Guerchard.

"Then Lupin ... since it was Lupin who managed the business last night—since you found those salvias in the house next door ... then Lupin came from Charmerace."

"Evidently," said Guerchard.

"And Lupin is one of the Charolais."

"Oh, that's another matter," said Guerchard.

"But it's certain, absolutely certain," said the Duke. "We have the connecting links ... the salvias ... this cigarette."

"It looks very like it. You're pretty quick on a scent, I must say," said Guerchard. "What a detective you would have made! Only ... nothing is certain."

"But it IS. Whatever more do you want? Was he at Charmerace yesterday, or was he not? Did he, or did he not, arrange the theft of the motor-cars?"

"Certainly he did. But he himself might have remained in the background all the while," said Guerchard.

"In what shape? ... Under what mask? ... By Jove, I should like to see this fellow!" said the Duke.

"We shall see him to-night," said Guerchard.

"To-night?" said the Duke.

"Of course we shall; for he will come to steal the coronet between a quarter to twelve and midnight," said Guerchard.

"Never!" said the Duke. "You don't really believe that he'll have the cheek to attempt such a mad act?"

"Ah, you don't know this man, your Grace ... his extraordinary mixture of coolness and audacity. It's the danger that attracts him. He throws himself into the fire, and he doesn't get burnt. For the last ten years I've been saying to myself, 'Here we are: this time I've got him! ... At last I'm going to nab him.' But I've said that day after day," said Guerchard; and he paused.

"Well?" said the Duke.

"Well, the days pass; and I never nab him. Oh, he is thick, I tell you.... He's a joker, he is ... a regular artist"—he ground his teeth—"The damned thief!"

The Duke looked at him, and said slowly, "Then you think that to-night Lupin—"

"You've followed the scent with me, your Grace," Guerchard interrupted quickly and vehemently. "We've picked up each clue together. You've almost seen this man at work.... You've understood him. Isn't a man like this, I ask you, capable of anything?"

"He is," said the Duke, with conviction.

"Well, then," said Guerchard.

"Perhaps you're right," said the Duke.

Guerchard turned to Dieusy and said, in a quieter voice, "And when the scavenger had picked up the cigarette, did he follow the motorist?"

"Yes, he followed him for about a hundred yards. He went down into Sureau Street, and turned westwards. Then a motor-car came along; he got into it, and went off."

"What kind of a motor-car?" said Guerchard.

"A big car, and dark red in colour," said Dieusy.

"The Limousine!" cried the Duke.

"That's all I've got so far, sir," said Dieusy.

"Well, off you go," said Guerchard. "Now that you've got started, you'll probably get something else before very long."

Dieusy saluted and went.

"Things are beginning to move," said Guerchard cheerfully. "First Victoire, and now this motor-van."

"They are indeed," said the Duke.

"After all, it ought not to be very difficult to trace that motor-van," said Guerchard, in a musing tone. "At any rate, its movements ought to be easy enough to follow up till about six. Then, of course, there would be a good many others about, delivering goods."

"You seem to have all the possible information you can want at your finger-ends," said the Duke, in an admiring tone.

"I suppose I know the life of Paris as well as anybody," said Guerchard.

428

They were silent for a while. Then Germaine's maid, Irma, came into the room and said:

"If you please, your Grace, Mademoiselle Kritchnoff would like to speak to you for a moment."

"Oh? Where is she?" said the Duke.

"She's in her room, your Grace."

"Oh, very well, I'll go up to her," said the Duke. "I can speak to her in the library."

He rose and was going towards the door when Guerchard stepped forward, barring his way, and said, "No, your Grace."

"No? Why?" said the Duke haughtily.

"I beg you will wait a minute or two till I've had a word with you," said Guerchard; and he drew a folded sheet of paper from his pocket and held it up.

The Duke looked at Guerchard's face, and he looked at the paper in his hand; then he said: "Oh, very well." And, turning to Irma, he added quietly, "Tell Mademoiselle Kritchnoff that I'm in the drawing-room."

"Yes, your Grace, in the drawing-room," said Irma; and she turned to go.

"Yes; and say that I shall be engaged for the next five minutes—the next five minutes, do you understand?" said the Duke.

"Yes, your Grace," said Irma; and she went out of the door.

"Ask Mademoiselle Kritchnoff to put on her hat and cloak," said Guerchard.

"Yes, sir," said Irma; and she went.

The Duke turned sharply on Guerchard, and said: "Now, why on earth? ... I don't understand."

"I got this from M. Formery," said Guerchard, holding up the paper.

"Well," said the Duke. "What is it?"

"It's a warrant, your Grace," said Guerchard.

"What! ... A warrant! ... Not for the arrest of Mademoiselle Kritchnoff?"

"Yes," said Guerchard.

"Oh, come, it's impossible," said the Duke. "You're never going to arrest that child?"

"I am, indeed," said Guerchard. "Her examination this afternoon was in the highest degree unsatisfactory. Her answers were embarrassed, contradictory, and in every way suspicious."

"And you've made up your mind to arrest her?" said the Duke slowly, knitting his brow in anxious thought.

"I have, indeed," said Guerchard. "And I'm going to do it now. The prison van ought to be waiting at the door." He looked at his watch. "She and Victoire can go together."

"So ... you're going to arrest her ... you're going to arrest her?" said the Duke thoughtfully: and he took a step or two up and down the room, still thinking hard.

"Well, you understand the position, don't you, your Grace?" said Guerchard, in a tone of apology. "Believe me that, personally, I've no animosity against Mademoiselle Kritchnoff. In fact, the child attracts me."

"Yes," said the Duke softly, in a musing tone. "She has the air of a child who has lost its way ... lost its way in life.... And that poor little hiding-place she found ... that rolled-up handkerchief ... thrown down in the corner of the little room in the house next door ... it was absolutely absurd."

"What! A handkerchief!" cried Guerchard, with an air of sudden, utter surprise.

"The child's clumsiness is positively pitiful," said the Duke.

"What was in the handkerchief? ... The pearls of the pendant?" cried Guerchard.

"Yes: I supposed you knew all about it. Of course M. Formery left word for you," said the Duke, with an air of surprise at the ignorance of the detective.

"No: I've heard nothing about it," cried Guerchard.

"He didn't leave word for you?" said the Duke, in a tone of greater surprise. "Oh, well, I dare say that he thought to-morrow would do. Of course you were out of the house when he found it. She must have slipped out of her room soon after you went."

"He found a handkerchief belonging to Mademoiselle Kritchnoff. Where is it?" cried Guerchard.

"M. Formery took the pearls, but he left the handkerchief. I suppose it's in the corner where he found it," said the Duke.

"He left the handkerchief?" cried Guerchard. "If that isn't just like the fool! He ought to keep hens; it's all he's fit for!"

He ran to the fireplace, seized the lantern, and began lighting it: "Where is the handkerchief?" he cried.

"In the left-hand corner of the little room on the right on the second floor. But if you're going to arrest Mademoiselle Kritchnoff, why are you bothering about the handkerchief? It can't be of any importance," said the Duke.

"I beg your pardon," said Guerchard. "But it is."

"But why?" said the Duke.

"I was arresting Mademoiselle Kritchnoff all right because I had a very strong presumption of her guilt. But I hadn't the slightest proof of it," said Guerchard.

"What?" cried the Duke, in a horrified tone.

"No, you've just given me the proof; and since she was able to hide the pearls in the house next door, she knew the road which led to it. Therefore she's an accomplice," said Guerchard, in a triumphant tone.

"What? Do you think that, too?" cried the Duke. "Good Heavens! And it's me! ... It's my senselessness! ... It's my fault that you've got your proof!" He spoke in a tone of acute distress.

"It was your duty to give it me," said Guerchard sternly; and he began to mount the steps.

"Shall I come with you? I know where the handkerchief is," said the Duke quickly.

"No, thank you, your Grace," said Guerchard. "I prefer to go alone."

"You'd better let me help you," said the Duke.

"No, your Grace," said Guerchard firmly.

"I must really insist," said the Duke.

"No—no—no," said Guerchard vehemently, with stern decision. "It's no use your insisting, your Grace; I prefer to go alone. I shall only be gone a minute or two."

"Just as you like," said the Duke stiffly.

The legs of Guerchard disappeared up the steps. The Duke stood listening with all his ears. Directly he heard the sound of Guerchard's heels on the floor, when he dropped from the chimney-piece of the next room, he went swiftly to the door, opened it, and went out. Bonavent was sitting on the chair on which the young policeman had sat during the afternoon. Sonia, in her hat and cloak, was half-way down the stairs.

The Duke put his head inside the drawing-room door, and said to the empty room: "Here is Mademoiselle Kritchnoff, M. Guerchard." He held open the door, Sonia came down the stairs, and went through it. The Duke followed her into the drawing-room, and shut the door.

"There's not a moment to lose," he said in a low voice.

"Oh, what is it, your Grace?" said Sonia anxiously.

"Guerchard has a warrant for your arrest."

"Then I'm lost!" cried Sonia, in a panic-stricken voice.

"No, you're not. You must go—at once," said the Duke.

"But how can I go? No one can get out of the house. M. Guerchard won't let them," cried Sonia, panic-stricken.

"We can get over that," said the Duke.

He ran to Guerchard's cloak, took the card-case from the inner pocket, went to the writing-table, and sat down. He took from his waist-coat pocket the permit which Guerchard had given him, and a pencil. Then he took a card from the card-case, set the permit on the table before him, and began to imitate Guerchard's handwriting with an amazing exactness. He wrote on the card:

"Pass Mademoiselle Kritchnoff."

"J. GUERCHARD."

Sonia stood by his side, panting quickly with fear, and watched him do it. He had scarcely finished the last stroke, when they heard a noise on the other side of the opening into the empty house. The Duke looked at the fireplace, and his teeth bared in an expression of cold ferocity. He rose with clenched fists, and took a step towards the fireplace.

"Your Grace? Your Grace?" called the voice of Guerchard.

"What is it?" answered the Duke quietly.

"I can't see any handkerchief," said Guerchard. "Didn't you say it was in the left-hand corner of the little room on the right?"

"I told you you'd better let me come with you, and find it," said the Duke, in a tone of triumph. "It's in the right-hand corner of the little room on the left."

"I could have sworn you said the little room on the right," said Guerchard.

They heard his footfalls die away.

"Now, you must get out of the house quickly." said the Duke. "Show this card to the detectives at the door, and they'll pass you without a word."

He pressed the card into her hand.

"But—but—this card?" stammered Sonia.

"There's no time to lose," said the Duke.

"But this is madness," said Sonia. "When Guerchard finds out about this card—that you—you—"

"There's no need to bother about that," interrupted the Duke quickly. "Where are you going to?"

"A little hotel near the Star. I've forgotten the name of it," said Sonia. "But this card—"

"Has it a telephone?" said the Duke.

"Yes—No. 555, Central," said Sonia.

"If I haven't telephoned to you before half-past eight to-morrow morning, come straight to my house," said the Duke, scribbling the telephone number on his shirt-cuff.

"Yes, yes," said Sonia. "But this card.... When Guerchard knows ... when he discovers.... Oh, I can't let you get into trouble for me."

"I shan't. But go—go," said the Duke, and he slipped his right arm round her and drew her to the door.

"Oh, how good you are to me," said Sonia softly.

The Duke's other arm went round her; he drew her to him, and their lips met.

He loosed her, and opened the door, saying loudly: "You're sure you won't have a cab, Mademoiselle Kritchnoff?"

"No; no, thank you, your Grace. Goodnight," said Sonia. And she went through the door with a transfigured face.

XVIII. THE DUKE STAYS

The Duke shut the door and leant against it, listening anxiously, breathing quickly. There came the bang of the front door. With a deep sigh of relief he left the door, came briskly, smiling, across the room, and put the card-case back into the pocket of Guerchard's cloak. He lighted a cigarette, dropped into an easy chair, and sat waiting with an entirely careless air for the detective's return. Presently he heard quick footsteps on the bare boards of the empty room beyond the opening. Then Guerchard came down the steps and out of the fireplace.

His face wore an expression of extreme perplexity:

"I can't understand it," he said. "I found nothing."

"Nothing?" said the Duke.

"No. Are you sure you saw the handkerchief in one of those little rooms on the second floor—quite sure?" said Guerchard.

"Of course I did," said the Duke. "Isn't it there?"

"No," said Guerchard.

"You can't have looked properly," said the Duke, with a touch of irony in his voice. "If I were you, I should go back and look again."

"No. If I've looked for a thing, I've looked for it. There's no need for me to look a second time. But, all the same, it's rather funny. Doesn't it strike you as being rather funny, your Grace?" said Guerchard, with a worried air.

"It strikes me as being uncommonly funny," said the Duke, with an ambiguous smile.

Guerchard looked at him with a sudden uneasiness; then he rang the bell.

Bonavent came into the room.

"Mademoiselle Kritchnoff, Bonavent. It's quite time," said Guerchard.

"Mademoiselle Kritchnoff?" said Bonavent, with an air of surprise.

"Yes, it's time that she was taken to the police-station."

"Mademoiselle Kritchnoff has gone, sir," said Bonavent, in a tone of quiet remonstrance.

"Gone? What do you mean by gone?" said Guerchard.

"Gone, sir, gone!" said Bonavent patiently.

"But you're mad.... Mad!" cried Guerchard.

"No, I'm not mad," said Bonavent. "Gone! But who let her go?" cried Guerchard.

"The men at the door," said Bonavent.

"The men at the door," said Guerchard, in a tone of stupefaction. "But she had to have my permit ... my permit on my card! Send the fools up to me!"

Bonavent went to the top of the staircase, and called down it. Guerchard followed him. Two detectives came hurrying up the stairs and into the drawing-room.

"What the devil do you mean by letting Mademoiselle Kritchnoff leave the house without my permit, written on my card?" cried Guerchard violently.

"But she had your permit, sir, and it WAS written on your card," stammered one of the detectives.

"It was? ... it was?" said Guerchard. "Then, by Jove, it was a forgery!"

He stood thoughtful for a moment. Then quietly he told his two men to go back to their post. He did not stir for a minute or two, puzzling it out, seeking light.

Then he came back slowly into the drawing-room and looked uneasily at the Duke. The Duke was sitting in his easy chair, smoking a cigarette with a listless air. Guerchard looked at him, and looked at him, almost as if he now saw him for the first time.

"Well?" said the Duke, "have you sent that poor child off to prison? If I'd done a thing like that I don't think I should sleep very well, M. Guerchard."

"That poor child has just escaped, by means of a forged permit," said Guerchard very glumly.

"By Jove, I AM glad to hear that!" cried the Duke. "You'll forgive my lack of sympathy, M. Guerchard; but she was such a child."

"Not too young to be Lupin's accomplice," said Guerchard drily.

"You really think she is?" said the Duke, in a tone of doubt.

"I'm sure of it," said Guerchard, with decision; then he added slowly, with a perplexed air:

"But how—how—could she get that forged permit?"

The Duke shook his head, and looked as solemn as an owl. Guerchard looked at him uneasily, went out of the drawing-room, and shut the door.

"How long has Mademoiselle Kritchnoff been gone?" he said to Bonavent.

"Not much more than five minutes," said Bonavent. "She came out from talking to you in the drawing-room—"

"Talking to me in the drawing-room!" exclaimed Guerchard.

"Yes," said Bonavent. "She came out and went straight down the stairs and out of the house."

A faint, sighing gasp came from Guerchard's lips. He dashed into the drawing-room, crossed the room quickly to his cloak, picked it up, took the card-case out of the pocket, and counted the cards in it. Then he looked at the Duke.

The Duke smiled at him, a charming smile, almost caressing.

There seemed to be a lump in Guerchard's throat; he swallowed it loudly.

He put the card-case into the breast-pocket of the coat he was wearing. Then he cried sharply, "Bonavent! Bonavent!"

Bonavent opened the door, and stood in the doorway.

"You sent off Victoire in the prison-van, I suppose," said Guerchard.

"Oh, a long while ago, sir," said Bonavent.

"The van had been waiting at the door since half-past nine."

"Since half-past nine? ... But I told them I shouldn't want it till a quarter to eleven. I suppose they were making an effort to be in time for once. Well, it doesn't matter," said Guerchard.

"Then I suppose I'd better send the other prison-van away?" said Bonavent.

"What other van?" said Guerchard.

"The van which has just arrived," said Bonavent.

"What! What on earth are you talking about?" cried Guerchard, with a sudden anxiety in his voice and on his face.

"Didn't you order two prison-vans?" said Bonavent.

Guerchard jumped; and his face went purple with fury and dismay. "You don't mean to tell me that two prison-vans have been here?" he cried.

"Yes, sir," said Bonavent.

"Damnation!" cried Guerchard. "In which of them did you put Victoire? In which of them?"

"Why, in the first, sir," said Bonavent.

"Did you see the police in charge of it? The coachman?"

"Yes, sir," said Bonavent.

"Did you recognize them?" said Guerchard.

"No," said Bonavent; "they must have been new men. They told me they came from the Sante."

"You silly fool!" said Guerchard through his teeth. "A fine lot of sense you've got."

"Why, what's the matter?" said Bonavent.

"We're done, done in the eye!" roared Guerchard. "It's a stroke—a stroke—"

"Of Lupin's!" interposed the Duke softly.

"But I don't understand," said Bonavent.

"You don't understand, you idiot!" cried Guerchard. "You've sent Victoire away in a sham prison-van—a prison-van belonging to Lupin. Oh, that scoundrel! He always has something up his sleeve."

"He certainly shows foresight," said the Duke. "It was very clever of him to foresee the arrest of Victoire and provide against it."

"Yes, but where is the leakage? Where is the leakage?" cried Guerchard, fuming. "How did he learn that the doctor said that she would recover her wits at ten o'clock? Here I've had a guard at the door all day; I've imprisoned the household; all the provisions have been received directly by a man of mine; and here he is, ready to pick up Victoire the very moment she gives herself away! Where is the leakage?"

He turned on Bonavent, and went on: "It's no use your standing there with your mouth open, looking like a fool. Go upstairs to the servants' quarters and search Victoire's room again. That fool of an inspector may have missed something, just as he missed Victoire herself. Get on! Be smart!"

Bonavent went off briskly. Guerchard paced up and down the room, scowling.

"Really, I'm beginning to agree with you, M. Guerchard, that this Lupin is a remarkable man," said the Duke. "That prison-van is extraordinarily neat."

"I'll prison-van him!" cried Guerchard. "But what fools I have to work with. If I could get hold of people of ordinary intelligence it would be impossible to play such a trick as that."

"I don't know about that," said the Duke thoughtfully. "I think it would have required an uncommon fool to discover that trick."

"What on earth do you mean? Why?" said Guerchard.

"Because it's so wonderfully simple," said the Duke. "And at the same time it's such infernal cheek."

"There's something in that," said Guerchard grumpily. "But then, I'm always saying to my men, 'Suspect everything; suspect everybody; suspect,

437

suspect, suspect.' I tell you, your Grace, that there is only one motto for the successful detective, and that is that one word, 'suspect.'"

"It can't be a very comfortable business, then," said the Duke. "But I suppose it has its charms."

"Oh, one gets used to the disagreeable part," said Guerchard.

The telephone bell rang; and he rose and went to it. He put the receiver to his ear and said, "Yes; it's I—Chief-Inspector Guerchard."

He turned and said to the Duke, "It's the gardener at Charmerace, your Grace."

"Is it?" said the Duke indifferently.

Guerchard turned to the telephone. "Are you there?" he said. "Can you hear me clearly? ... I want to know who was in your hot-house yesterday ... who could have gathered some of your pink salvias?"

"I told you that it was I," said the Duke.

"Yes, yes, I know," said Guerchard. And he turned again to the telephone. "Yes, yesterday," he said. "Nobody else? ... No one but the Duke of Charmerace? ... Are you sure?... quite sure?... absolutely sure? ... Yes, that's all I wanted to know ... thank you."

He turned to the Duke and said, "Did you hear that, your Grace? The gardener says that you were the only person in his hot-houses yesterday, the only person who could have plucked any pink salvias."

"Does he?" said the Duke carelessly.

Guerchard looked at him, his brow knitted in a faint, pondering frown. Then the door opened, and Bonavent came in: "I've been through Victoire's room," he said, "and all I could find that might be of any use is this—a prayer-book. It was on her dressing-table just as she left it. The inspector hadn't touched it."

"What about it?" said Guerchard, taking the prayer-book.

"There's a photograph in it," said Bonavent. "It may come in useful when we circulate her description; for I suppose we shall try to get hold of Victoire."

Guerchard took the photograph from the prayer-book and looked at it: "It looks about ten years old," he said. "It's a good deal faded for reproduction. Hullo! What have we here?"

The photograph showed Victoire in her Sunday best, and with her a boy of seventeen or eighteen. Guerchard's eyes glued themselves to the face of the boy. He stared at it, holding the portrait now nearer, now further off. His eyes kept stealing covertly from the photograph to the face of the Duke.

The Duke caught one of those covert glances, and a vague uneasiness flickered in his eyes. Guerchard saw it. He came nearer to the Duke and looked at him earnestly, as if he couldn't believe his eyes.

"What's the matter?" said the Duke. "What are you looking at so curiously? Isn't my tie straight?" And he put up his hand and felt it.

"Oh, nothing, nothing," said Guerchard. And he studied the photograph again with a frowning face.

There was a noise of voices and laughter in the hall.

"Those people are going," said the Duke. "I must go down and say good-bye to them." And he rose and went out of the room.

Guerchard stood staring, staring at the photograph.

The Duke ran down the stairs, and said goodbye to the millionaire's guests. After they had gone, M. Gournay-Martin went quickly up the stairs; Germaine and the Duke followed more slowly.

"My father is going to the Ritz to sleep," said Germaine, "and I'm going with him. He doesn't like the idea of my sleeping in this house to-night. I suppose he's afraid that Lupin will make an attack in force with all his gang. Still, if he did, I think that Guerchard could give a good account of himself—he's got men enough in the house, at any rate. Irma tells me it's swarming with them. It would never do for me to be in the house if there were a fight."

"Oh, come, you don't really believe that Lupin is coming to-night?" said the Duke, with a sceptical laugh. "The whole thing is sheer bluff—he has no more intention of coming tonight to steal that coronet than—than I have."

"Oh, well, there's no harm in being on the safe side," said Germaine. "Everybody's agreed that he's a very terrible person. I'll just run up to my room and get a wrap; Irma has my things all packed. She can come round tomorrow morning to the Ritz and dress me."

She ran up the stairs, and the Duke went into the drawing-room. He found Guerchard standing where he had left him, still frowning, still thinking hard.

"The family are off to the Ritz. It's rather a reflection on your powers of protecting them, isn't it?" said the Duke.

"Oh, well, I expect they'd be happier out of the house," said Guerchard. He looked at the Duke again with inquiring, searching eyes.

"What's the matter?" said the Duke. "IS my tie crooked?"

"Oh, no, no; it's quite straight, your Grace," said Guerchard, but he did not take his eyes from the Duke's face.

The door opened, and in came M. Gournay-Martin, holding a bag in his hand. "It seems to be settled that I'm never to sleep in my own house again," he said in a grumbling tone.

"There's no reason to go," said the Duke. "Why ARE you going?"

"Danger," said M. Gournay-Martin. "You read Lupin's telegram: 'I shall come to-night between a quarter to twelve and midnight to take the coronet.' He knows that it was in my bedroom. Do you think I'm going to sleep in that room with the chance of that scoundrel turning up and cutting my throat?"

"Oh, you can have a dozen policemen in the room if you like," said the Duke. "Can't he, M. Guerchard?"

"Certainly," said Guerchard. "I can answer for it that you will be in no danger, M. Gournay-Martin."

"Thank you," said the millionaire. "But all the same, outside is good enough for me."

Germaine came into the room, cloaked and ready to start.

"For once in a way you are ready first, papa," she said. "Are you coming, Jacques?"

"No; I think I'll stay here, on the chance that Lupin is not bluffing," said the Duke. "I don't think, myself, that I'm going to be gladdened by the sight of him—in fact, I'm ready to bet against it. But you're all so certain about it that I really must stay on the chance. And, after all, there's no doubt that he's a man of immense audacity and ready to take any risk."

"Well, at any rate, if he does come he won't find the diadem," said M. Gournay-Martin, in a tone of triumph. "I'm taking it with me—I've got it here." And he held up his bag.

"You are?" said the Duke.

"Yes, I am," said M. Gournay-Martin firmly.

"Do you think it's wise?" said the Duke.

"Why not?" said M. Gournay-Martin.

"If Lupin's really made up his mind to collar that coronet, and if you're so sure that, in spite of all these safeguards, he's going to make the attempt, it seems to me that you're taking a considerable risk. He asked you to have it ready for him in your bedroom. He didn't say which bedroom."

"Good Lord! I never thought of that!" said M. Gournay-Martin, with an air of sudden and very lively alarm.

"His Grace is right," said Guerchard. "It would be exactly like Lupin to send that telegram to drive you out of the house with the coronet to some place where you would be less protected. That is exactly one of his tricks."

"Good Heavens!" said the millionaire, pulling out his keys and unlocking the bag. He opened it, paused hesitatingly, and snapped it to again.

"Half a minute," he said. "I want a word with you, Duke."

He led the way out of the drawing-room door and the Duke followed him. He shut the door and said in a whisper:

"In a case like this, I suspect everybody."

"Everybody suspects everybody, apparently," said the Duke. "Are you sure you don't suspect me?"

"Now, now, this is no time for joking," said the millionaire impatiently. "What do you think about Guerchard?"

"About Guerchard?" said the Duke. "What do you mean?"

"Do you think I can put full confidence in Guerchard?" said M. Gournay-Martin.

"Oh, I think so," said the Duke. "Besides, I shall be here to look after Guerchard. And, though I wouldn't undertake to answer for Lupin, I think I can answer for Guerchard. If he tries to escape with the coronet, I will wring his neck for you with pleasure. It would do me good. And it would do Guerchard good, too."

The millionaire stood reflecting for a minute or two. Then he said, "Very good; I'll trust him."

Hardly had the door closed behind the millionaire and the Duke, when Guerchard crossed the room quickly to Germaine and drew from his pocket the photograph of Victoire and the young man.

"Do you know this photograph of his Grace, mademoiselle?" he said quickly.

Germaine took the photograph and looked at it.

"It's rather faded," she said.

"Yes; it's about ten years old," said Guerchard.

"I seem to know the face of the woman," said Germaine. "But if it's ten years old it certainly isn't the photograph of the Duke."

"But it's like him?" said Guerchard.

"Oh, yes, it's like the Duke as he is now—at least, it's a little like him. But it's not like the Duke as he was ten years ago. He has changed so," said Germaine.

"Oh, has he?" said Guerchard.

"Yes; there was that exhausting journey of his—and then his illness. The doctors gave up all hope of him, you know."

"Oh, did they?" said Guerchard.

"Yes; at Montevideo. But his health is quite restored now."

The door opened and the millionaire and the Duke came into the room. M. Gournay-Martin set his bag upon the table, unlocked it, and with a solemn air took out the case which held the coronet. He opened it; and they looked at it.

"Isn't it beautiful?" he said with a sigh.

"Marvellous!" said the Duke.

M. Gournay-Martin closed the case, and said solemnly:

"There is danger, M. Guerchard, so I am going to trust the coronet to you. You are the defender of my hearth and home—you are the proper person to guard the coronet. I take it that you have no objection?"

"Not the slightest, M. Gournay-Martin," said Guerchard. "It's exactly what I wanted you to ask me to do."

M. Gournay-Martin hesitated. Then he handed the coronet to Guerchard, saying with a frank and noble air, "I have every confidence in you, M. Guerchard."

"Thank you," said Guerchard.

"Good-night," said M. Gournay-Martin.

"Good-night, M. Guerchard," said Germaine.

"I think, after all, I'll change my mind and go with you. I'm very short of sleep," said the Duke. "Good-night, M. Guerchard."

"You're never going too, your Grace!" cried Guerchard.

"Why, you don't want me to stay, do you?" said the Duke.

"Yes," said Guerchard slowly.

"I think I would rather go to bed," said the Duke gaily.

"Are you afraid?" said Guerchard, and there was challenge, almost an insolent challenge, in his tone.

There was a pause. The Duke frowned slightly with a reflective air. Then he drew himself up; and said a little haughtily:

"You've certainly found the way to make me stay, M. Guerchard."

"Yes, yes; stay, stay," said M. Gournay-Martin hastily. "It's an excellent idea, excellent. You're the very man to help M. Guerchard, Duke. You're an intrepid explorer, used to danger and resourceful, absolutely fearless."

"Do you really mean to say you're not going home to bed, Jacques?" said Germaine, disregarding her father's wish with her usual frankness.

"No; I'm going to stay with M. Guerchard," said the Duke slowly.

"Well, you will be fresh to go to the Princess's to-morrow night." said Germaine petulantly. "You didn't get any sleep at all last night, you couldn't have. You left Charmerace at eight o'clock; you were motoring all the night, and only got to Paris at six o'clock this morning."

"Motoring all night, from eight o'clock to six!" muttered Guerchard under his breath.

"Oh, that will be all right," said the Duke carelessly. "This interesting affair is to be over by midnight, isn't it?"

"Well, I warn you that, tired or fresh, you will have to come with me to the Princess's to-morrow night. All Paris will be there—all Paris, that is, who are in Paris."

"Oh, I shall be fresh enough," said the Duke.

They went out of the drawing-room and down the stairs, all four of them. There was an alert readiness about Guerchard, as if he were ready to spring. He kept within a foot of the Duke right to the front door. The detective in charge opened it; and they went down the steps to the taxi-cab which was awaiting them. The Duke kissed Germaine's fingers and handed her into the taxi-cab.

M. Gournay-Martin paused at the cab-door, and turned and said, with a pathetic air, "Am I never to sleep in my own house again?" He got into the cab and drove off.

The Duke turned and came up the steps, followed by Guerchard. In the hall he took his opera-hat and coat from the stand, and went upstairs. Half-way up the flight he paused and said:

"Where shall we wait for Lupin, M. Guerchard? In the drawing-room, or in M. Gournay-Martin's bedroom?"

"Oh, the drawing-room," said Guerchard. "I think it very unlikely that Lupin will look for the coronet in M. Gournay-Martin's bedroom. He would know very well that that is the last place to find it now."

The Duke went on into the drawing-room. At the door Guerchard stopped and said: "I will just go and post my men, your Grace."

"Very good," said the Duke; and he went into the drawing-room.

He sat down, lighted a cigarette, and yawned. Then he took out his watch and looked at it.

"Another twenty minutes," he said.

XIX. THE DUKE GOES

When Guerchard joined the Duke in the drawing-room, he had lost his calm air and was looking more than a little nervous. He moved about the room uneasily, fingering the bric-a-brac, glancing at the Duke and looking quickly away from him again. Then he came to a standstill on the hearth-rug with his back to the fireplace.

"Do you think it's quite safe to stand there, at least with your back to the hearth? If Lupin dropped through that opening suddenly, he'd catch you from behind before you could wink twice," said the Duke, in a tone of remonstrance.

"There would always be your Grace to come to my rescue," said Guerchard; and there was an ambiguous note in his voice, while his piercing eyes now rested fixed on the Duke's face. They seemed never to leave it; they explored, and explored it.

"It's only a suggestion," said the Duke.

"This is rather nervous work, don't you know."

"Yes; and of course you're hardly fit for it," said Guerchard. "If I'd known about your break-down in your car last night, I should have hesitated about asking you—"

"A break-down?" interrupted the Duke.

"Yes, you left Charmerace at eight o'clock last night. And you only reached Paris at six this morning. You couldn't have had a very high-power car?" said Guerchard.

"I had a 100 h.-p. car," said the Duke.

"Then you must have had a devil of a break-down," said Guerchard.

"Yes, it was pretty bad, but I've known worse," said the Duke carelessly. "It lost me about three hours: oh, at least three hours. I'm not a first class repairer, though I know as much about an engine as most motorists."

"And there was nobody there to help you repair it?" said Guerchard.

"No; M. Gournay-Martin could not let me have his chauffeur to drive me to Paris, because he was keeping him to help guard the chateau. And of course there was nobody on the road, because it was two o'clock in the morning."

"Yes, there was no one," said Guerchard slowly.

"Not a soul," said the Duke.

"It was unfortunate," said Guerchard; and there was a note of incredulity in his voice.

"My having to repair the car myself?" said the Duke.

"Yes, of course," said Guerchard, hesitating a little over the assent.

The Duke dropped the end of his cigarette into a tray, and took out his case. He held it out towards Guerchard, and said, "A cigarette? or perhaps you prefer your caporal?"

"Yes, I do, but all the same I'll have one," said Guerchard, coming quickly across the room. And he took a cigarette from the case, and looked at it.

"All the same, all this is very curious," he said in a new tone, a challenging, menacing, accusing tone.

"What?" said the Duke, looking at him curiously.

"Everything: your cigarettes ... the salvias ... the photograph that Bonavent found in Victoire's prayer-book ... that man in motoring dress ... and finally, your break-down," said Guerchard; and the accusation and the threat rang clearer.

The Duke rose from his chair quickly and said haughtily, in icy tones: "M. Guerchard, you've been drinking!"

He went to the chair on which he had set his overcoat and his hat, and picked them up. Guerchard sprang in front of him, barring his way, and cried in a shaky voice: "No; don't go! You mustn't go!"

"What do you mean?" said the Duke, and paused. "What DO you mean?"

Guerchard stepped back, and ran his hand over his forehead. He was very pale, and his forehead was clammy to his touch:

"No ... I beg your pardon ... I beg your pardon, your Grace ... I must be going mad," he stammered.

"It looks very like it," said the Duke coldly.

"What I mean to say is," said Guerchard in a halting, uncertain voice, "what I mean to say is: help me ... I want you to stay here, to help me against Lupin, you understand. Will you, your Grace?"

"Yes, certainly; of course I will, if you want me to," said the Duke, in a more gentle voice. "But you seem awfully upset, and you're upsetting me too. We shan't have a nerve between us soon, if you don't pull yourself together."

"Yes, yes, please excuse me," muttered Guerchard.

"Very good," said the Duke. "But what is it we're going to do?"

Guerchard hesitated. He pulled out his handkerchief, and mopped his forehead: "Well ... the coronet ... is it in this case?" he said in a shaky voice, and set the case on the table.

"Of course it is," said the Duke impatiently.

Guerchard opened the case, and the coronet sparkled and gleamed brightly in the electric light: "Yes, it is there; you see it?" said Guerchard.

"Yes, I see it; well?" said the Duke, looking at him in some bewilderment, so unlike himself did he seem.

"We're going to wait," said Guerchard.

"What for?" said the Duke.

"Lupin," said Guerchard.

"Lupin? And you actually do believe that, just as in a fairy tale, when that clock strikes twelve, Lupin will enter and take the coronet?"

"Yes, I do; I do," said Guerchard with stubborn conviction. And he snapped the case to.

"This is most exciting," said the Duke.

"You're sure it doesn't bore you?" said Guerchard huskily.

"Not a bit of it," said the Duke, with cheerful derision. "To make the acquaintance of this scoundrel who has fooled you for ten years is as charming a way of spending the evening as I can think of."

"You say that to me?" said Guerchard with a touch of temper.

"Yes," said the Duke, with a challenging smile. "To you."

He sat down in an easy chair by the table. Guerchard sat down in a chair on the other side of it, and set his elbows on it. They were silent.

Suddenly the Duke said, "Somebody's coming."

Guerchard started, and said: "No, I don't hear any one."

Then there came distinctly the sound of a footstep and a knock at the door.

"You've got keener ears than I," said Guerchard grudgingly. "In all this business you've shown the qualities of a very promising detective." He rose, went to the door, and unlocked it.

Bonavent came in: "I've brought you the handcuffs, sir," he said, holding them out. "Shall I stay with you?"

"No," said Guerchard. "You've two men at the back door, and two at the front, and a man in every room on the ground-floor?"

"Yes, and I've got three men on every other floor," said Bonavent, in a tone of satisfaction.

"And the house next door?" said Guerchard.

"There are a dozen men in it," said Bonavent. "No communication between the two houses is possible any longer."

446

Guerchard watched the Duke's face with intent eyes. Not a shadow flickered its careless serenity.

"If any one tries to enter the house, collar him. If need be, fire on him," said Guerchard firmly. "That is my order; go and tell the others."

"Very good, sir," said Bonavent; and he went out of the room.

"By Jove, we are in a regular fortress," said the Duke.

"It's even more of a fortress than you think, your Grace. I've four men on that landing," said Guerchard, nodding towards the door.

"Oh, have you?" said the Duke, with a sudden air of annoyance.

"You don't like that?" said Guerchard quickly.

"I should jolly well think not," said the Duke. "With these precautions, Lupin will never be able to get into this room at all."

"He'll find it a pretty hard job," said Guerchard, smiling. "Unless he falls from the ceiling, or unless—"

"Unless you're Arsene Lupin," interrupted the Duke.

"In that case, you'd be another, your Grace," said Guerchard.

They both laughed. The Duke rose, yawned, picked up his coat and hat, and said, "Ah, well, I'm off to bed."

"What?" said Guerchard.

"Well," said the Duke, yawning again, "I was staying to see Lupin. As there's no longer any chance of seeing him—"

"But there is ... there is ... so stay," cried Guerchard.

"Do you still cling to that notion?" said the Duke wearily.

"We SHALL see him," said Guerchard.

"Nonsense!" said the Duke.

Guerchard lowered his voice and said with an air of the deepest secrecy: "He's already here, your Grace."

"Lupin? Here?" cried the Duke.

"Yes; Lupin," said Guerchard.

"Where?" cried the astonished Duke.

"He is," said Guerchard.

"As one of your men?" said the Duke eagerly.

"I don't think so," said Guerchard, watching him closely.

"Well, but, well, but—if he's here we've got him.... He is going to turn up," said the Duke triumphantly; and he set down his hat on the table beside the coronet.

"I hope so," said Guerchard. "But will he dare to?"

"How do you mean?" said the Duke, with a puzzled air.

"Well, you have said yourself that this is a fortress. An hour ago, perhaps, Lupin was resolved to enter this room, but is he now?"

"I see what you mean," said the Duke, in a tone of disappointment.

"Yes; you see that now it needs the devil's own courage. He must risk everything to gain everything, and throw off the mask. Is Lupin going to throw himself into the wolf's jaws? I dare not think it. What do you think about it?"

Guerchard's husky voice had hardened to a rough harshness; there was a ring of acute anxiety in it, and under the anxiety a faint note of challenge, of a challenge that dare not make itself too distinct. His anxious, challenging eyes burned on the face of the Duke, as if they strove with all intensity to pierce a mask.

The Duke looked at him curiously, as if he were trying to divine what he would be at, but with a careless curiosity, as if it were a matter of indifference to him what the detective's object was; then he said carelessly: "Well, you ought to know better than I. You have known him for ten years ...." He paused, and added with just the faintest stress in his tone, "At least, by reputation."

The anxiety in the detective's face grew plainer, it almost gave him the air of being unnerved; and he said quickly, in a jerky voice: "Yes, and I know his way of acting too. During the last ten years I have learnt to unravel his intrigues—to understand and anticipate his manoeuvres.... Oh, his is a clever system! ... Instead of lying low, as you'd expect, he attacks his opponent ... openly.... He confuses him—at least, he tries to." He smiled a half-confident, a half-doubtful smile, "It is a mass of entangled, mysterious combinations. I've been caught in them myself again and again. You smile?"

"It interests me so," said the Duke, in a tone of apology.

"Oh, it interests me," said Guerchard, with a snarl. "But this time I see my way clearly. No more tricks—no more secret paths ... We're fighting in the light of day." He paused, and said in a clear, sneering voice, "Lupin has pluck, perhaps, but it's only thief's pluck."

"Oh, is it?" said the Duke sharply, and there was a sudden faint glitter in his eyes.

"Yes; rogues have very poor qualities," sneered Guerchard.

"One can't have everything," said the Duke quietly; but his languid air had fallen from him.

"Their ambushes, their attacks, their fine tactics aren't up to much," said Guerchard, smiling contemptuously.

"You go a trifle too far, I think," said the Duke, smiling with equal contempt.

They looked one another in the eyes with a long, lingering look. They had suddenly the air of fencers who have lost their tempers, and are twisting the buttons off their foils.

"Not a bit of it, your Grace," said Guerchard; and his voice lingered on the words "your Grace" with a contemptuous stress. "This famous Lupin is immensely overrated."

"However, he has done some things which aren't half bad," said the Duke, with his old charming smile.

He had the air of a duelist drawing his blade lovingly through his fingers before he falls to.

"Oh, has he?" said Guerchard scornfully.

"Yes; one must be fair. Last night's burglary, for instance: it is not unheard of, but it wasn't half bad. And that theft of the motorcars: it was a neat piece of work," said the Duke in a gentle, insolent voice, infinitely aggravating.

Guerchard snorted scornfully.

"And a robbery at the British Embassy, another at the Treasury, and a third at M. Lepine's—all in the same week—it wasn't half bad, don't you know?" said the Duke, in the same gentle, irritating voice.

"Oh, no, it wasn't. But—"

"And the time when he contrived to pass as Guerchard—the Great Guerchard—do you remember that?" the Duke interrupted. "Come, come— to give the devil his due—between ourselves—it wasn't half bad."

"No," snarled Guerchard. "But he has done better than that lately.... Why don't you speak of that?"

"Of what?" said the Duke.

"Of the time when he passed as the Duke of Charmerace," snapped Guerchard.

"What! Did he do that?" cried the Duke; and then he added slowly, "But, you know, I'm like you—I'm so easy to imitate."

"What would have been amusing, your Grace, would have been to get as far as actual marriage," said Guerchard more calmly.

"Oh, if he had wanted to," said the Duke; and he threw out his hands. "But you know—married life—for Lupin."

"A large fortune ... a pretty girl," said Guerchard, in a mocking tone.

"He must be in love with some one else," said the Duke.

"A thief, perhaps," sneered Guerchard.

"Like himself.... And then, if you wish to know what I think, he must have found his fiancee rather trying," said the Duke, with his charming smile.

"After all, it's pitiful—heartrending, you must admit it, that, on the very eve of his marriage, he was such a fool as to throw off the mask. And yet at bottom it's quite logical; it's Lupin coming out through Charmerace. He had to grab at the dowry at the risk of losing the girl," said Guerchard, in a reflective tone; but his eyes were intent on the face of the Duke.

"Perhaps that's what one should call a marriage of reason," said the Duke, with a faint smile.

"What a fall!" said Guerchard, in a taunting voice. "To be expected, eagerly, at the Princess's to-morrow evening, and to pass the evening in a police-station ... to have intended in a month's time, as the Duke of Charmerace, to mount the steps of the Madeleine with all pomp and to fall down the father-in-law's staircase this evening—this very evening"—his voice rose suddenly on a note of savage triumph—"with the handcuffs on! What? Is that a good enough revenge for Guerchard—for that poor old idiot, Guerchard? The rogues' Brummel in a convict's cap! The gentleman-burglar in a gaol! For Lupin it's only a trifling annoyance, but for a duke it's a disaster! Come, in your turn, be frank: don't you find that amusing?"

The Duke rose quietly, and said coldly, "Have you finished?"

"DO you?" cried Guerchard; and he rose and faced him.

"Oh, yes; I find it quite amusing," said the Duke lightly.

"And so do I," cried Guerchard.

"No; you're frightened," said the Duke calmly.

"Frightened!" cried Guerchard, with a savage laugh.

"Yes, you're frightened," said the Duke. "And don't think, policeman, that because I'm familiar with you, I throw off a mask. I don't wear one. I've none to throw off. I AM the Duke of Charmerace."

"You lie! You escaped from the Sante four years ago. You are Lupin! I recognize you now."

"Prove it," said the Duke scornfully.

"I will!" cried Guerchard.

"You won't. I AM the Duke of Charmerace."

Guerchard laughed wildly.

"Don't laugh. You know nothing—nothing, dear boy," said the Duke tauntingly.

"Dear boy?" cried Guerchard triumphantly, as if the word had been a confession.

"What do I risk?" said the Duke, with scathing contempt. "Can you arrest me? ... You can arrest Lupin ... but arrest the Duke of Charmerace, an honourable gentleman, member of the Jockey Club, and of the Union, residing at his house, 34 B, University Street ... arrest the Duke of Charmerace, the fiance of Mademoiselle Gournay-Martin?"

"Scoundrel!" cried Guerchard, pale with sudden, helpless fury.

"Well, do it," taunted the Duke. "Be an ass.... Make yourself the laughing-stock of Paris ... call your coppers in. Have you a proof—one single proof? Not one."

"Oh, I shall get them," howled Guerchard, beside himself.

"I think you may," said the Duke coolly. "And you might be able to arrest me next week ... the day after to-morrow perhaps ... perhaps never ... but not to-night, that's certain."

"Oh, if only somebody could hear you!" gasped Guerchard.

"Now, don't excite yourself," said the Duke. "That won't produce any proofs for you.... The fact is, M. Formery told you the truth when he said that, when it is a case of Lupin, you lose your head. Ah, that Formery—there is an intelligent man if you like."

"At all events, the coronet is safe ... to-night—"

"Wait, my good chap ... wait," said the Duke slowly; and then he snapped out: "Do you know what's behind that door?" and he flung out his hand towards the door of the inner drawing-room, with a mysterious, sinister air.

"What?" cried Guerchard; and he whipped round and faced the door, with his eyes starting out of his head.

"Get out, you funk!" said the Duke, with a great laugh.

"Hang you!" said Guerchard shrilly.

"I said that you were going to be absolutely pitiable," said the Duke, and he laughed again cruelly.

"Oh, go on talking, do!" cried Guerchard, mopping his forehead.

"Absolutely pitiable," said the Duke, with a cold, disquieting certainty. "As the hand of that clock moves nearer and nearer midnight, you will grow more and more terrified." He paused, and then shouted violently, "Attention!"

Guerchard jumped; and then he swore.

"Your nerves are on edge," said the Duke, laughing.

"Joker!" snarled Guerchard.

"Oh, you're as brave as the next man. But who can stand the anguish of the unknown thing which is bound to happen? ... I'm right. You feel it, you're sure of it. At the end of these few fixed minutes an inevitable, fated event must happen. Don't shrug your shoulders, man; you're green with fear."

The Duke was no longer a smiling, cynical dandy. There emanated from him an impression of vivid, terrible force. His voice had deepened. It thrilled with a consciousness of irresistible power; it was overwhelming, paralyzing. His eyes were terrible.

"My men are outside ... I'm armed," stammered Guerchard.

"Child! Bear in mind ... bear in mind that it is always when you have foreseen everything, arranged everything, made every combination ... bear in mind that it is always then that some accident dashes your whole structure to the ground," said the Duke, in the same deep, thrilling voice. "Remember that it is always at the very moment at which you are going to triumph that he beats you, that he only lets you reach the top of the ladder to throw you more easily to the ground."

"Confess, then, that you are Lupin," muttered Guerchard.

"I thought you were sure of it," said the Duke in a jeering tone.

Guerchard dragged the handcuffs out of his pocket, and said between his teeth, "I don't know what prevents me, my boy."

The Duke drew himself up, and said haughtily, "That's enough."

"What?" cried Guerchard.

"I say that that's enough," said the Duke sternly. "It's all very well for me to play at being familiar with you, but don't you call me 'my boy.'"

"Oh, you won't impose on me much longer," muttered Guerchard; and his bloodshot, haggard eyes scanned the Duke's face in an agony, an anguish of doubting impotence.

"If I'm Lupin, arrest me," said the Duke.

"I'll arrest you in three minutes from now, or the coronet will be untouched," cried Guerchard in a firmer tone.

"In three minutes from now the coronet will have been stolen; and you will not arrest me," said the Duke, in a tone of chilling certainty.

"But I will! I swear I will!" cried Guerchard.

"Don't swear any foolish oaths! ... THERE ARE ONLY TWO MINUTES LEFT," said the Duke; and he drew a revolver from his pocket.

"No, you don't!" cried Guerchard, drawing a revolver in his turn.

"What's the matter?" said the Duke, with an air of surprise. "You haven't forbidden me to shoot Lupin. I have my revolver ready, since he's going to come.... THERE'S ONLY A MINUTE LEFT."

"There are plenty of us," said Guerchard; and he went towards the door.

"Funk!" said the Duke scornfully.

Guerchard turned sharply. "Very well," he said, "I'll stick it out alone."

"How rash!" sneered the Duke.

Guerchard ground his teeth. He was panting; his bloodshot eyes rolled in their sockets; the beads of cold sweat stood out on his forehead. He came back towards the table on unsteady feet, trembling from head to foot in the last excitation of the nerves. He kept jerking his head to shake away the mist which kept dimming his eyes.

"At your slightest gesture, at your slightest movement, I'll fire," he said jerkily, and covered the Duke with his revolver.

"I call myself the Duke of Charmerace. You will be arrested to-morrow!" said the Duke, in a compelling, thrilling voice.

"I don't care a curse!" cried Guerchard.

"Only FIFTY SECONDS!" said the Duke.

"Yes, yes," muttered Guerchard huskily. And his eyes shot from the coronet to the Duke, from the Duke to the coronet.

"In fifty seconds the coronet will be stolen," said the Duke.

"No!" cried Guerchard furiously.

"Yes," said the Duke coldly.

"No! no! no!" cried Guerchard.

Their eyes turned to the clock.

To Guerchard the hands seemed to be standing still. He could have sworn at them for their slowness.

Then the first stroke rang out; and the eyes of the two men met like crossing blades. Twice the Duke made the slightest movement. Twice Guerchard started forward to meet it.

At the last stroke both their hands shot out. Guerchard's fell heavily on the case which held the coronet. The Duke's fell on the brim of his hat; and he picked it up.

Guerchard gasped and choked. Then he cried triumphantly:

"I HAVE it; now then, have I won? Have I been fooled this time? Has Lupin got the coronet?"

"It doesn't look like it. But are you quite sure?" said the Duke gaily.

"Sure?" cried Guerchard.

"It's only the weight of it," said the Duke, repressing a laugh. "Doesn't it strike you that it's just a trifle light?"

"What?" cried Guerchard.

"This is merely an imitation." said the Duke, with a gentle laugh.

"Hell and damnation!" howled Guerchard. "Bonavent! Dieusy!"

The door flew open, and half a dozen detectives rushed in.

Guerchard sank into a chair, stupefied, paralyzed; this blow, on the top of the strain of the struggle with the Duke, had broken him.

"Gentlemen," said the Duke sadly, "the coronet has been stolen."

They broke into cries of surprise and bewilderment, surrounding the gasping Guerchard with excited questions.

The Duke walked quietly out of the room.

Guerchard sobbed twice; his eyes opened, and in a dazed fashion wandered from face to face; he said faintly: "Where is he?"

"Where's who?" said Bonavent.

"The Duke—the Duke!" gasped Guerchard.

"Why, he's gone!" said Bonavent.

Guerchard staggered to his feet and cried hoarsely, frantically: "Stop him from leaving the house! Follow him! Arrest him! Catch him before he gets home!"

XX. LUPIN COMES HOME

The cold light of the early September morning illumined but dimly the charming smoking-room of the Duke of Charmerace in his house at 34 B, University Street, though it stole in through two large windows. The smoking-room was on the first floor; and the Duke's bedroom opened into it. It was furnished in the most luxurious fashion, but with a taste which nowadays infrequently accompanies luxury. The chairs were of the most comfortable, but their lines were excellent; the couch against the wall, between the two windows, was the last word in the matter of comfort. The colour scheme, of a light greyish-blue, was almost too bright for a man's room; it would have better suited a boudoir. It suggested that the owner of the room enjoyed an uncommon lightness and cheerfulness of temperament. On the walls, with wide gaps between them so that they did not clash, hung three or four excellent pictures. Two ballet-girls by Degas, a group of shepherdesses and shepherds, in pink and blue and white beribboned silk, by Fragonard, a portrait of a woman by Bastien-Lepage, a charming Corot, and two Conder fans showed that the taste of their fortunate owner was at any rate eclectic. At the end of the room was, of all curious things, the opening into the well of a lift. The doors of it were open, though the lift itself was on some other floor. To the left of the opening stood a book-case, its shelves loaded with books of a kind rather suited to a cultivated, thoughtful man than to an idle dandy.

Beside the window, half-hidden, and peering through the side of the curtain into the street, stood M. Charolais. But it was hardly the M. Charolais who had paid M. Gournay-Martin that visit at the Chateau de Charmerace, and departed so firmly in the millionaire's favourite motor-car. This was a paler M. Charolais; he lacked altogether the rich, ruddy complexion of the millionaire's visitor. His nose, too, was thinner, and showed none of the ripe acquaintance with the vintages of the world which had been so plainly displayed on it during its owner's visit to the country. Again, hair and eyebrows were no longer black, but fair; and his hair was no longer curly and luxuriant, but thin and lank. His moustache had vanished, and along with it the dress of a well-to-do provincial man of business. He wore a livery of the Charmeraces, and at that early morning hour had not yet assumed the blue waistcoat which is an integral part of it. Indeed it would have required an acute and experienced observer to recognize in him the bogus purchaser of the Mercrac. Only his eyes, his close-set eyes, were unchanged.

Walking restlessly up and down the middle of the room, keeping out of sight of the windows, was Victoire. She wore a very anxious air, as did Charolais too. By the door stood Bernard Charolais; and his natural, boyish timidity, to judge from his frightened eyes, had assumed an acute phase.

"By the Lord, we're done!" cried Charolais, starting back from the window. "That was the front-door bell."

"No, it was only the hall clock," said Bernard.

"That's seven o'clock! Oh, where can he be?" said Victoire, wringing her hands. "The coup was fixed for midnight.... Where can he be?"

"They must be after him," said Charolais. "And he daren't come home." Gingerly he drew back the curtain and resumed his watch.

"I've sent down the lift to the bottom, in case he should come back by the secret entrance," said Victoire; and she went to the opening into the well of the lift and stood looking down it, listening with all her ears.

"Then why, in the devil's name, have you left the doors open?" cried Charolais irritably. "How do you expect the lift to come up if the doors are open?"

"I must be off my head!" cried Victoire.

She stepped to the side of the lift and pressed a button. The doors closed, and there was a grunting click of heavy machinery settling into a new position.

"Suppose we telephone to Justin at the Passy house?" said Victoire.

"What on earth's the good of that?" said Charolais impatiently. "Justin knows no more than we do. How can he know any more?"

"The best thing we can do is to get out," said Bernard, in a shaky voice.

"No, no; he will come. I haven't given up hope," Victoire protested. "He's sure to come; and he may need us."

"But, hang it all! Suppose the police come! Suppose they ransack his papers.... He hasn't told us what to do ... we are not ready for them.... What are we to do?" cried Charolais, in a tone of despair.

"Well, I'm worse off than you are; and I'm not making a fuss. If the police come they'll arrest me," said Victoire.

"Perhaps they've arrested him," said Bernard, in his shaky voice.

"Don't talk like that," said Victoire fretfully. "Isn't it bad enough to wait and wait, without your croaking like a scared crow?"

She started again her pacing up and down the room, twisting her hands, and now and again moistening her dry lips with the tip of her tongue.

Presently she said: "Are those two plain-clothes men still there watching?" And in her anxiety she came a step nearer the window.

"Keep away from the window!" snapped Charolais. "Do you want to be recognized, you great idiot?" Then he added, more quietly, "They're still there all right, curse them, in front of the cafe.... Hullo!"

"What is it, now?" cried Victoire, starting.

"A copper and a detective running," said Charolais. "They are running for all they're worth."

"Are they coming this way?" said Victoire; and she ran to the door and caught hold of the handle.

"No," said Charolais.

"Thank goodness!" said Victoire.

"They're running to the two men watching the house ... they're telling them something. Oh, hang it, they're all running down the street."

"This way? ... Are they coming this way?" cried Victoire faintly; and she pressed her hand to her side.

"They are!" cried Charolais. "They are!" And he dropped the curtain with an oath.

"And he isn't here! Suppose they come.... Suppose he comes to the front door! They'll catch him!" cried Victoire.

There came a startling peal at the front-door bell. They stood frozen to stone, their eyes fixed on one another, staring.

The bell had hardly stopped ringing, when there was a slow, whirring noise. The doors of the lift flew open, and the Duke stepped out of it. But what a changed figure from the admirably dressed dandy who had walked through the startled detectives and out of the house of M. Gournay-Martin at midnight! He was pale, exhausted, almost fainting. His eyes were dim in a livid face; his lips were grey. He was panting heavily. He was splashed with mud from head to foot: one sleeve of his coat was torn along half its length. The sole of his left-hand pump was half off; and his cut foot showed white and red through the torn sock.

"The master! The master!" cried Charolais in a tone of extravagant relief; and he danced round the room snapping his fingers.

"You're wounded?" cried Victoire.

"No," said Arsene Lupin.

The front-door bell rang out again, startling, threatening, terrifying.

The note of danger seemed to brace Lupin, to spur him to a last effort.

He pulled himself together, and said in a hoarse but steady voice: "Your waistcoat, Charolais.... Go and open the door ... not too quickly ... fumble the bolts.... Bernard, shut the book-case. Victoire, get out of sight, do you want to ruin us all? Be smart now, all of you. Be smart!"

He staggered past them into his bedroom, and slammed the door. Victoire and Charolais hurried out of the room, through the anteroom, on to the landing. Victoire ran upstairs, Charolais went slowly down. Bernard pressed the button. The doors of the lift shut and there was a slow whirring as it went down. He pressed another button, and the book-case slid slowly across and hid the opening into the lift-well. Bernard ran out of the room and up the stairs.

Charolais went to the front door and fumbled with the bolts. He bawled through the door to the visitors not to be in such a hurry at that hour in the morning; and they bawled furiously at him to be quick, and knocked and rang again and again. He was fully three minutes fumbling with the bolts, which were already drawn. At last he opened the door an inch or two, and looked out.

On the instant the door was dashed open, flinging him back against the wall; and Bonavent and Dieusy rushed past him, up the stairs, as hard as they could pelt. A brown-faced, nervous, active policeman followed them in and stopped to guard the door.

On the landing the detectives paused, and looked at one another, hesitating.

"Which way did he go?" said Bonavent. "We were on his very heels."

"I don't know; but we've jolly well stopped his getting into his own house; and that's the main thing," said Dieusy triumphantly.

"But are you sure it was him?" said Bonavent, stepping into the anteroom.

"I can swear to it," said Dieusy confidently; and he followed him.

Charolais came rushing up the stairs and caught them up as they were entering the smoking-room:

"Here! What's all this?" he cried. "You mustn't come in here! His Grace isn't awake yet."

"Awake? Awake? Your precious Duke has been galloping all night," cried Dieusy. "And he runs devilish well, too."

The door of the bedroom opened; and Lupin stood on the threshold in slippers and pyjamas.

"What's all this?" he snapped, with the irritation of a man whose sleep has been disturbed; and his tousled hair and eyes dim with exhaustion gave him every appearance of being still heavy with sleep.

The eyes and mouths of Bonavent and Dieusy opened wide; and they stared at him blankly, in utter bewilderment and wonder.

"Is it you who are making all this noise?" said Lupin, frowning at them. "Why, I know you two; you're in the service of M. Guerchard."

"Yes, your Grace," stammered Bonavent.

"Well, what are you doing here? What is it you want?" said Lupin.

"Oh, nothing, your Grace ... nothing ... there's been a mistake," stammered Bonavent.

"A mistake?" said Lupin haughtily. "I should think there had been a mistake. But I take it that this is Guerchard's doing. I'd better deal with him directly. You two can go." He turned to Charolais and added curtly, "Show them out."

Charolais opened the door, and the two detectives went out of the room with the slinking air of whipped dogs. They went down the stairs in silence, slowly, reflectively; and Charolais let them out of the front door.

As they went down the steps Dieusy said: "What a howler! Guerchard risks getting the sack for this!"

"I told you so," said Bonavent. "A duke's a duke."

When the door closed behind the two detectives Lupin tottered across the room, dropped on to the couch with a groan of exhaustion, and closed his eyes. Presently the door opened, Victoire came in, saw his attitude of exhaustion, and with a startled cry ran to his side.

"Oh, dearie! dearie!" she cried. "Pull yourself together! Oh, do try to pull yourself together." She caught his cold hands and began to rub them, murmuring words of endearment like a mother over a young child. Lupin did not open his eyes; Charolais came in.

"Some breakfast!" she cried. "Bring his breakfast ... he's faint ... he's had nothing to eat this morning. Can you eat some breakfast, dearie?"

"Yes," said Lupin faintly.

"Hurry up with it," said Victoire in urgent, imperative tones; and Charolais left the room at a run.

"Oh, what a life you lead!" said Victoire, or, to be exact, she wailed it. "Are you never going to change? You're as white as a sheet.... Can't you speak, dearie?"

She stooped and lifted his legs on to the couch.

He stretched himself, and, without opening his eyes, said in a faint voice: "Oh, Victoire, what a fright I've had!"

"You? You've been frightened?" cried Victoire, amazed.

"Yes. You needn't tell the others, though. But I've had a night of it ... I did play the fool so ... I must have been absolutely mad. Once I had changed the coronet under that fat old fool Gournay-Martin's very eyes ... once you and Sonia were out of their clutches, all I had to do was to slip away. Did I? Not a bit of it! I stayed there out of sheer bravado, just to score off Guerchard.... And then I ... I, who pride myself on being as cool as a cucumber ... I did the one thing I ought not to have done.... Instead of going quietly away as the Duke of Charmerace ... what do you think I did? ... I bolted ... I started running ... running like a thief.... In about two seconds I saw the slip I had made. It did not take me longer; but that was too long—Guerchard's men were on my track ... I was done for."

"Then Guerchard understood—he recognized you?" said Victoire anxiously.

"As soon as the first paralysis had passed, Guerchard dared to see clearly ... to see the truth," said Lupin. "And then it was a chase. There were ten—fifteen of them on my heels. Out of breath—grunting, furious—a mob—a regular mob. I had passed the night before in a motor-car. I was dead beat. In fact, I was done for before I started ... and they were gaining ground all the time."

"Why didn't you hide?" said Victoire.

"For a long while they were too close. They must have been within five feet of me. I was done. Then I was crossing one of the bridges. ... There was the Seine ... handy ... I made up my mind that, rather than be taken, I'd make an end of it ... I'd throw myself over."

"Good Lord!—and then?" cried Victoire.

"Then I had a revulsion of feeling. At any rate, I'd stick it out to the end. I gave myself another minute... one more minute—the last, and I had my revolver on me... but during that minute I put forth every ounce of strength I had left ... I began to gain ground ... I had them pretty well strung out already ... they were blown too. The knowledge gave me back my courage, and I plugged on ... my feet did not feel so much as though they were made of lead. I began to run away from them ... they were dropping behind ... all of them but one ... he stuck to me. We went at a jog-trot, a slow jog-trot, for I don't know how long. Then we dropped to a walk—we could run no more; and on we went. My strength and wind began to come back. I suppose my pursuer's did too; for exactly what I expected happened. He gave a yell and dashed for me. I was ready for him. I pretended to start running, and when he was within three yards of me I dropped on one knee, caught his ankles, and chucked him over my head. I don't know whether he broke his neck or not. I hope he did."

"Splendid!" said Victoire. "Splendid!"

"Well, there I was, outside Paris, and I'm hanged if I know where. I went on half a mile, and then I rested. Oh, how sleepy I was! I would have given a hundred thousand francs for an hour's sleep—cheerfully. But I dared not let myself sleep. I had to get back here unseen. There were you and Sonia."

"Sonia? Another woman?" cried Victoire. "Oh, it's then that I'm frightened ... when you get a woman mixed up in your game. Always, when you come to grief ... when you really get into danger, there's a woman in it."

"Oh, but she's charming!" protested Lupin.

"They always are," said Victoire drily. "But go on. Tell me how you got here."

460

"Well, I knew it was going to be a tough job, so I took a good rest—an hour, I should think. And then I started to walk back. I found that I had come a devil of a way—I must have gone at Marathon pace. I walked and walked, and at last I got into Paris, and found myself with still a couple of miles to go. It was all right now; I should soon find a cab. But the luck was dead against me. I heard a man come round the corner of a side-street into a long street I was walking down. He gave a yell, and came bucketing after me. It was that hound Dieusy. He had recognized my figure. Off I went; and the chase began again. I led him a dance, but I couldn't shake him off. All the while I was working my way towards home. Then, just at last, I spurted for all I was worth, got out of his sight, bolted round the corner of the street into the secret entrance, and here I am." He smiled weakly, and added, "Oh, my dear Victoire, what a profession it is!"

XXI. THE CUTTING OF THE TELEPHONE WIRES

The door opened, and in came Charolais, bearing a tray.

"Here's your breakfast, master," he said.

"Don't call me master—that's how his men address Guerchard. It's a disgusting practice," said Lupin severely.

Victoire and Charolais were quick laying the table. Charolais kept up a running fire of questions as he did it; but Lupin did not trouble to answer them. He lay back, relaxed, drawing deep breaths. Already his lips had lost their greyness, and were pink; there was a suggestion of blood under the skin of his pale face. They soon had the table laid; and he walked to it on fairly steady feet. He sat down; Charolais whipped off a cover, and said:

"Anyhow, you've got out of the mess neatly. It was a jolly smart escape."

"Oh, yes. So far it's all right," said Lupin. "But there's going to be trouble presently—lots of it. I shall want all my wits. We all shall."

He fell upon his breakfast with the appetite but not the manners of a wolf. Charolais went out of the room. Victoire hovered about him, pouring out his coffee and putting sugar into it.

"By Jove, how good these eggs are!" he said. "I think that, of all the thousand ways of cooking eggs, en cocotte is the best."

"Heavens! how empty I was!" he said presently. "What a meal I'm making! It's really a very healthy life, this of mine, Victoire. I feel much better already."

"Oh, yes; it's all very well to talk," said Victoire, in a scolding tone; for since he was better, she felt, as a good woman should, that the time had come to put in a word out of season. "But, all the same, you're trying to kill yourself—that's what you're doing. Just because you're young you abuse your youth. It won't last for ever; and you'll be sorry you used it up before it's time. And this life of lies and thefts and of all kinds of improper things—I suppose it's going to begin all over again. It's no good your getting a lesson. It's just thrown away upon you."

"What I want next is a bath," said Lupin.

"It's all very well your pretending not to listen to me, when you know very well that I'm speaking for your good," she went on, raising her voice a little. "But I tell you that all this is going to end badly. To be a thief gives you no position in the world—no position at all—and when I think of what you made me do the night before last, I'm just horrified at myself."

"We'd better not talk about that—the mess you made of it! It was positively excruciating!" said Lupin.

"And what did you expect? I'm an honest woman, I am!" said Victoire sharply. "I wasn't brought up to do things like that, thank goodness! And to begin at my time of life!"

"It's true, and I often ask myself how you bring yourself to stick to me," said Lupin, in a reflective, quite impersonal tone. "Please pour me out another cup of coffee."

"That's what I'm always asking myself," said Victoire, pouring out the coffee. "I don't know—I give it up. I suppose it is because I'm fond of you."

"Yes, and I'm very fond of you, my dear Victoire," said Lupin, in a coaxing tone.

"And then, look you, there are things that there's no understanding. I often talked to your poor mother about them. Oh, your poor mother! Whatever would she have said to these goings-on?"

Lupin helped himself to another cutlet; his eyes twinkled and he said, "I'm not sure that she would have been very much surprised. I always told her that I was going to punish society for the way it had treated her. Do you think she would have been surprised?"

"Oh, nothing you did would have surprised her," said Victoire. "When you were quite a little boy you were always making us wonder. You gave yourself such airs, and you had such nice manners of your own—altogether different from the other boys. And you were already a bad boy, when you were only seven years old, full of all kinds of tricks; and already you had begun to steal."

"Oh, only sugar," protested Lupin.

"Yes, you began by stealing sugar," said Victoire, in the severe tones of a moralist. "And then it was jam, and then it was pennies. Oh, it was all very well at that age—a little thief is pretty enough. But now—when you're twenty-eight years old."

"Really, Victoire, you're absolutely depressing," said Lupin, yawning; and he helped himself to jam.

"I know very well that you're all right at heart," said Victoire. "Of course you only rob the rich, and you've always been kind to the poor.... Yes; there's no doubt about it: you have a good heart."

"I can't help it—what about it?" said Lupin, smiling.

"Well, you ought to have different ideas in your head. Why are you a burglar?"

"You ought to try it yourself, my dear Victoire," said Lupin gently; and he watched her with a humorous eye.

"Goodness, what a thing to say!" cried Victoire.

"I assure you, you ought," said Lupin, in a tone of thoughtful conviction. "I've tried everything. I've taken my degree in medicine and in law. I have been an actor, and a professor of Jiu-jitsu. I have even been a member of the detective force, like that wretched Guerchard. Oh, what a dirty world that is! Then I launched out into society. I have been a duke. Well, I give you my word that not one of these professions equals that of burglar—not even the profession of Duke. There is so much of the unexpected in it, Victoire—the splendid unexpected.... And then, it's full of variety, so terrible, so fascinating." His voice sank a little, and he added, "And what fun it is!"

"Fun!" cried Victoire.

"Yes ... these rich men, these swells in their luxury—when one relieves them of a bank-note, how they do howl! ... You should have seen that fat old Gournay-Martin when I relieved him of his treasures—what an agony! You almost heard the death-rattle in his throat. And then the coronet! In the derangement of their minds—and it was sheer derangement, mind you—already prepared at Charmerace, in the derangement of Guerchard, I had only to put out my hand and pluck the coronet. And the joy, the ineffable joy of enraging the police! To see Guerchard's furious eyes when I downed him.... And look round you!" He waved his hand round the luxurious room. "Duke of Charmerace! This trade leads to everything ... to everything on condition that one sticks to it ....I tell you, Victoire, that when one cannot be a great artist or a great soldier, the only thing to be is a great thief!"

"Oh, be quiet!" cried Victoire. "Don't talk like that. You're working yourself up; you're intoxicating yourself! And all that, it is not Catholic. Come, at your age, you ought to have one idea in your head which should drive out all these others, which should make you forget all these thefts.... Love ... that would change you, I'm sure of it. That would make another man of you. You ought to marry."

"Yes ... perhaps ... that would make another man of me. That's what I've been thinking. I believe you're right," said Lupin thoughtfully.

"Is that true? Have you really been thinking of it?" cried Victoire joyfully.

"Yes," said Lupin, smiling at her eagerness. "I have been thinking about it—seriously."

"No more messing about—no more intrigues. But a real woman ... a woman for life?" cried Victoire.

"Yes," said Lupin softly; and his eyes were shining in a very grave face.

"Is it serious—is it real love, dearie?" said Victoire. "What's she like?"

"She's beautiful," said Lupin.

"Oh, trust you for that. Is she a blonde or a brunette?"

"She's very fair and delicate—like a princess in a fairy tale," said Lupin softly.

"What is she? What does she do?" said Victoire.

"Well, since you ask me, she's a thief," said Lupin with a mischievous smile.

"Good Heavens!" cried Victoire.

"But she's a very charming thief," said Lupin; and he rose smiling.

He lighted a cigar, stretched himself and yawned: "She had ever so much more reason for stealing than ever I had," he said. "And she has always hated it like poison."

"Well, that's something," said Victoire; and her blank and fallen face brightened a little.

Lupin walked up and down the room, breathing out long luxurious puffs of smoke from his excellent cigar, and watching Victoire with a humorous eye. He walked across to his book-shelf, and scanned the titles of his books with an appreciative, almost affectionate smile.

"This is a very pleasant interlude," he said languidly. "But I don't suppose it's going to last very long. As soon as Guerchard recovers from the shock of learning that I spent a quiet night in my ducal bed as an honest duke should, he'll be getting to work with positively furious energy, confound him! I could do with a whole day's sleep—twenty-four solid hours of it."

"I'm sure you could, dearie," said Victoire sympathetically.

"The girl I'm going to marry is Sonia Kritchnoff," he said.

"Sonia? That dear child! But I love her already!" cried Victoire. "Sonia, but why did you say she was a thief? That was a silly thing to say."

"It's my extraordinary sense of humour," said Lupin.

The door opened and Charolais bustled in: "Shall I clear away the breakfast?" he said.

Lupin nodded; and then the telephone bell rang. He put his finger on his lips and went to it.

"Are you there?" he said. "Oh, it's you, Germaine.... Good morning.... Oh, yes, I had a good night—excellent, thank you.... You want to speak to me presently? ... You're waiting for me at the Ritz?"

"Don't go—don't go—it isn't safe," said Victoire, in a whisper.

"All right, I'll be with you in about half an hour, or perhaps three-quarters. I'm not dressed yet ... but I'm ever so much more impatient than you ... good-bye for the present." He put the receiver on the stand.

"It's a trap," said Charolais.

"Never mind, what if it is? Is it so very serious?" said Lupin. "There'll be nothing but traps now; and if I can find the time I shall certainly go and take a look at that one."

"And if she knows everything? If she's taking her revenge ... if she's getting you there to have you arrested?" said Victoire.

"Yes, M. Formery is probably at the Ritz with Gournay-Martin. They're probably all of them there, weighing the coronet," said Lupin, with a chuckle.

He hesitated a moment, reflecting; then he said, "How silly you are! If they wanted to arrest me, if they had the material proof which they haven't got, Guerchard would be here already!"

"Then why did they chase you last night?" said Charolais.

"The coronet," said Lupin. "Wasn't that reason enough? But, as it turned out, they didn't catch me: and when the detectives did come here, they disturbed me in my sleep. And that me was ever so much more me than the man they followed. And then the proofs ... they must have proofs. There aren't any—or rather, what there are, I've got!" He pointed to a small safe let into the wall. "In that safe are the coronet, and, above all, the death certificate of the Duke of Charmerace ... everything that Guerchard must have to induce

M. Formery to proceed. But still, there is a risk—I think I'd better have those things handy in case I have to bolt."

He went into his bedroom and came back with the key of the safe and a kit-bag. He opened the safe and took out the coronet, the real coronet of the Princesse de Lamballe, and along with it a pocket-book with a few papers in it. He set the pocket-book on the table, ready to put in his coat-pocket when he should have dressed, and dropped the coronet into the kit-bag.

"I'm glad I have that death certificate; it makes it much safer," he said. "If ever they do nab me, I don't wish that rascal Guerchard to accuse me of having murdered the Duke. It might prejudice me badly. I've not murdered anybody yet."

"That comes of having a good heart," said Victoire proudly.

"Not even the Duke of Charmerace," said Charolais sadly. "And it would have been so easy when he was ill—just one little draught. And he was in such a perfect place—so out of the way—no doctors."

"You do have such disgusting ideas, Charolais," said Lupin, in a tone of severe reproof.

"Instead of which you went and saved his life," said Charolais, in a tone of deep discontent; and he went on clearing the table.

"I did, I did: I had grown quite fond of him," said Lupin, with a meditative air. "For one thing, he was so very like one. I'm not sure that he wasn't even better-looking."

"No; he was just like you," said Victoire, with decision. "Any one would have said you were twin brothers."

"It gave me quite a shock the first time I saw his portrait," said Lupin. "You remember, Charolais? It was three years ago, the day, or rather the night, of the first Gournay-Martin burglary at Charmerace. Do you remember?"

"Do I remember?" said Charolais. "It was I who pointed out the likeness to you. I said, 'He's the very spit of you, master.' And you said, 'There's something to be done with that, Charolais.' And then off you started for the ice and snow and found the Duke, and became his friend; and then he went and died, not that you'd have helped him to, if he hadn't."

"Poor Charmerace. He was indeed grand seigneur. With him a great name was about to be extinguished.... Did I hesitate? ... No.... I continued it," said Lupin.

He paused and looked at the clock. "A quarter to eight," he said, hesitating. "Shall I telephone to Sonia, or shall I not? Oh, there's no hurry; let the poor child sleep on. She must be worn out after that night-journey and that cursed Guerchard's persecution yesterday. I'll dress first, and telephone to her afterwards. I'd better be getting dressed, by the way. The work I've got to do can't be done in pyjamas. I wish it could; for bed's the place for me. My wits aren't quite as clear as I could wish them to deal with an awkward business like this. Well, I must do the best I can with them."

He yawned and went to the bedroom, leaving the pocket-book on the table.

"Bring my shaving-water, Charolais, and shave me," he said, pausing; and he went into the bedroom and shut the door.

"Ah," said Victoire sadly, "what a pity it is! A few years ago he would have gone to the Crusades; and to-day he steals coronets. What a pity it is!"

"I think myself that the best thing we can do is to pack up our belongings," said Charolais. "And I don't think we've much time to do it either. This particular game is at an end, you may take it from me."

"I hope to goodness it is: I want to get back to the country," said Victoire.

He took up the tray; and they went out of the room. On the landing they separated; she went upstairs and he went down. Presently he came up with the shaving water and shaved his master; for in the house in University Street he discharged the double functions of valet and butler. He had just finished his task when there came a ring at the front-door bell.

"You'd better go and see who it is," said Lupin.

"Bernard is answering the door," said Charolais. "But perhaps I'd better keep an eye on it myself; one never knows."

He put away the razor leisurely, and went. On the stairs he found Bonavent, mounting—Bonavent, disguised in the livery and fierce moustache of a porter from the Ritz.

"Why didn't you come to the servants' entrance?" said Charolais, with the truculent air of the servant of a duke and a stickler for his master's dignity.

"I didn't know that there was one," said Bonavent humbly. "Well, you ought to have known that there was; and it's plain enough to see. What is it you want?" said Charolais.

"I've brought a letter—a letter for the Duke of Charmerace," said Bonavent.

"Give it to me," said Charolais. "I'll take it to him."

"No, no; I'm to give it into the hands of the Duke himself and to nobody else," said Bonavent.

"Well, in that case, you'll have to wait till he's finished dressing," said Charolais.

They went on up to the stairs into the ante-room. Bonavent was walking straight into the smoking-room.

"Here! where are you going to? Wait here," said Charolais quickly. "Take a chair; sit down."

Bonavent sat down with a very stolid air, and Charolais looked at him doubtfully, in two minds whether to leave him there alone or not. Before he had decided there came a thundering knock on the front door, not only loud but protracted. Charolais looked round with a scared air; and then ran out of the room and down the stairs.

On the instant Bonavent was on his feet, and very far from stolid. He opened the door of the smoking-room very gently and peered in. It was empty. He slipped noiselessly across the room, a pair of clippers ready in his hand, and cut the wires of the telephone. His quick eye glanced round the room and fell on the pocket-book on the table. He snatched it up, and slipped it into the breast of his tunic. He had scarcely done it—one button of his tunic was still to fasten—when the bedroom door opened, and Lupin came out:

"What do you want?" he said sharply; and his keen eyes scanned the porter with a disquieting penetration.

"I've brought a letter to the Duke of Charmerace, to be given into his own hands," said Bonavent, in a disguised voice.

"Give it to me," said Lupin, holding out his hand.

"But the Duke?" said Bonavent, hesitating.

"I am the Duke," said Lupin.

Bonavent gave him the letter, and turned to go.

"Don't go," said Lupin quietly. "Wait, there may be an answer."

There was a faint glitter in his eyes; but Bonavent missed it.

Charolais came into the room, and said, in a grumbling tone, "A run-away knock. I wish I could catch the brats; I'd warm them. They wouldn't go fetching me away from my work again, in a hurry, I can tell you."

Lupin opened the letter, and read it. As he read it, at first he frowned; then he smiled; and then he laughed joyously. It ran:

"SIR,"

"M. Guerchard has told me everything. With regard to Sonia I have judged you: a man who loves a thief can be nothing but a rogue. I have two

468

pieces of news to announce to you: the death of the Duke of Charmerace, who died three years ago, and my intention of becoming engaged to his cousin and heir, M. de Relzieres, who will assume the title and the arms."

"For Mademoiselle Gournay-Martin,"

"Her maid, IRMA."

"She does write in shocking bad taste," said Lupin, shaking his head sadly. "Charolais, sit down and write a letter for me."

"Me?" said Charolais.

"Yes; you. It seems to be the fashion in financial circles; and I am bound to follow it when a lady sets it. Write me a letter," said Lupin.

Charolais went to the writing-table reluctantly, sat down, set a sheet of paper on the blotter, took a pen in his hand, and sighed painfully.

"Ready?" said Lupin; and he dictated:

"MADEMOISELLE,"

"I have a very robust constitution, and my indisposition will very soon be over. I shall have the honour of sending, this afternoon, my humble wedding present to the future Madame de Relzieres."

"For Jacques de Bartut, Marquis de Relzieres, Prince of Virieux, Duke of Charmerace."

"His butler, ARSENE."

"Shall I write Arsene?" said Charolais, in a horrified tone.

"Why not?" said Lupin. "It's your charming name, isn't it?"

Bonavent pricked up his ears, and looked at Charolais with a new interest.

Charolais shrugged his shoulders, finished the letter, blotted it, put it in an envelope, addressed it, and handed it to Lupin.

"Take this to Mademoiselle Gournay-Martin," said Lupin, handing it to Bonavent.

Bonavent took the letter, turned, and had taken one step towards the door when Lupin sprang. His arm went round the detective's neck; he jerked him backwards off his feet, scragging him.

"Stir, and I'll break your neck!" he cried in a terrible voice; and then he said quietly to Charolais, "Just take my pocket-book out of this fellow's tunic."

Charolais, with deft fingers, ripped open the detective's tunic, and took out the pocket-book.

"This is what they call Jiu-jitsu, old chap! You'll be able to teach it to your colleagues," said Lupin. He loosed his grip on Bonavent, and knocked him straight with a thump in the back, and sent him flying across the room. Then he took the pocket-book from Charolais and made sure that its contents were untouched.

"Tell your master from me that if he wants to bring me down he'd better fire the gun himself," said Lupin contemptuously. "Show the gentleman out, Charolais."

Bonavent staggered to the door, paused, and turned on Lupin a face livid with fury.

"He will be here himself in ten minutes," he said.

"Many thanks for the information," said Lupin quietly.

XXII. THE BARGAIN

Charolais conducted the detective down the stairs and let him out of the front door, cursing and threatening vengeance as he went. Charolais took no notice of his words—he was the well-trained servant. He came back upstairs, and on the landing called to Victoire and Bernard. They came hurrying down; and the three of them went into the smoking-room.

"Now we know where we are," said Lupin, with cheerful briskness. "Guerchard will be here in ten minutes with a warrant for my arrest. All of you clear out."

"It won't be so precious easy. The house is watched," said Charolais. "And I'll bet it's watched back and front."

"Well, slip out by the secret entrance. They haven't found that yet," said Lupin. "And meet me at the house at Passy."

Charolais and Bernard wanted no more telling; they ran to the book-case and pressed the buttons; the book-case slid aside; the doors opened and disclosed the lift. They stepped into it. Victoire had followed them. She paused and said: "And you? Are you coming?"

"In an instant I shall slip out the same way," he said.

"I'll wait for him. You go on," said Victoire; and the lift went down.

Lupin went to the telephone, rang the bell, and put the receiver to his ear.

"You've no time to waste telephoning. They may be here at any moment!" cried Victoire anxiously.

"I must. If I don't telephone Sonia will come here. She will run right into Guerchard's arms. Why the devil don't they answer? They must be deaf!" And he rang the bell again.

"Let's go to her! Let's get out of here!" cried Victoire, more anxiously. "There really isn't any time to waste."

"Go to her? But I don't know where she is. I lost my head last night," cried Lupin, suddenly anxious himself. "Are you there?" he shouted into the telephone. "She's at a little hotel near the Star. ... Are you there? ... But there are twenty hotels near the Star.... Are you there? ... Oh, I did lose my head last night. ... Are you there? Oh, hang this telephone! Here I'm fighting with a piece of furniture. And every second is important!"

He picked up the machine, shook it, saw that the wires were cut, and cried furiously: "Ha! They've played the telephone trick on me! That's Guerchard.... The swine!"

"And now you can come along!" cried Victoire.

"But that's just what I can't do!" he cried.

"But there's nothing more for you to do here, since you can no longer telephone," said Victoire, bewildered.

Lupin caught her arm and shook her, staring into her face with panic-stricken eyes. "But don't you understand that, since I haven't telephoned, she'll come here?" he cried hoarsely. "Five-and-twenty minutes past eight! At half-past eight she will start—start to come here."

His face had suddenly grown haggard; this new fear had brought back all the exhaustion of the night; his eyes were panic-stricken.

"But what about you?" said Victoire, wringing her hands.

"What about her?" said Lupin; and his voice thrilled with anguished dread.

"But you'll gain nothing by destroying both of you—nothing at all."

"I prefer it," said Lupin slowly, with a suddenly stubborn air.

"But they're coming to take you," cried Victoire, gripping his arm.

"Take me?" cried Lupin, freeing himself quietly from her grip. And he stood frowning, plunged in deep thought, weighing the chances, the risks, seeking a plan, saving devices.

He crossed the room to the writing-table, opened a drawer, and took out a cardboard box about eight inches square and set it on the table.

"They shall never take me alive," he said gloomily.

"Oh, hush, hush!" said Victoire. "I know very well that you're capable of anything ... and they too—they'll destroy you. No, look you, you must go. They won't do anything to her—a child like that—so frail. She'll get off quite easily. You're coming, aren't you?"

"No, I'm not," said Lupin stubbornly.

"Oh, well, if you won't," said Victoire; and with an air of resolution she went to the side of the lift-well, and pressed the buttons. The doors closed; the book-case slid across. She sat down and folded her arms.

"What, you're not going to stop here?" cried Lupin.

"Make me stir if you can. I'm as fond of you as she is—you know I am," said Victoire, and her face set stonily obstinate.

Lupin begged her to go; ordered her to go; he seized her by the shoulder, shook her, and abused her like a pickpocket. She would not stir. He abandoned the effort, sat down, and knitted his brow again in profound and painful thought, working out his plan. Now and again his eyes flashed, once or twice they twinkled. Victoire watched his face with just the faintest hope on her own.

It was past five-and-twenty minutes to nine when the front-door bell rang. They gazed at one another with an unspoken question on their lips. The eyes of Victoire were scared, but in the eyes of Lupin the light of battle was gathering.

"It's her," said Victoire under her breath.

"No," said Lupin. "It's Guerchard."

He sprang to his feet with shining eyes. His lips were curved in a fighting smile. "The game isn't lost yet," he said in a tense, quiet voice. "I'm going to play it to the end. I've a card or two left still—good cards. I'm still the Duke of Charmerace." He turned to her.

"Now listen to me," he said. "Go down and open the door for him."

"What, you want me to?" said Victoire, in a shaky voice.

"Yes, I do. Listen to me carefully. When you have opened the door, slip out of it and watch the house. Don't go too far from it. Look out for Sonia. You'll see her coming. Stop her from entering, Victoire—stop her from entering." He spoke coolly, but his voice shook on the last words.

"But if Guerchard arrests me?" said Victoire.

"He won't. When he comes in, stand behind the door. He will be too eager to get to me to stop for you. Besides, for him you don't count in the game. Once you're out of the house, I'll hold him here for—for half an hour. That will leave a margin. Sonia will hurry here. She should be here in twelve minutes. Get her away to the house at Passy. If I don't come keep her there; she's to live with you. But I shall come."

As he spoke he was pushing her towards the door.

The bell rang again. They were at the top of the stairs.

"And suppose he does arrest me?" said Victoire breathlessly.

"Never mind, you must go all the same," said Lupin. "Don't give up hope—trust to me. Go—go—for my sake."

"I'm going, dearie," said Victoire; and she went down the stairs steadily, with a brave air.

He watched her half-way down the flight; then he muttered:

"If only she gets to Sonia in time."

He turned, went into the smoking-room, and shut the door. He sat quietly down in an easy chair, lighted a cigarette, and took up a paper. He heard the noise of the traffic in the street grow louder as the front door was opened. There was a pause; then he heard the door bang. There was the sound of a hasty footstep on the stairs; the door flew open, and Guerchard bounced into the room.

He stopped short in front of the door at the sight of Lupin, quietly reading, smoking at his ease. He had expected to find the bird flown. He stood still, hesitating, shuffling his feet—all his doubts had returned; and Lupin smiled at him over the lowered paper.

Guerchard pulled himself together by a violent effort, and said jerkily, "Good-morning, Lupin."

"Good-morning, M. Guerchard," said Lupin, with an ambiguous smile and all the air of the Duke of Charmerace.

"You were expecting me? ... I hope I haven't kept you waiting," said Guerchard, with an air of bravado.

"No, thank you: the time has passed quite quickly. I have so much to do in the morning always," said Lupin. "I hope you had a good night after that unfortunate business of the coronet. That was a disaster; and so unexpected too."

Guerchard came a few steps into the room, still hesitating:

"You've a very charming house here," he said, with a sneer.

"It's central," said Lupin carelessly. "You must please excuse me, if I cannot receive you as I should like; but all my servants have bolted. Those confounded detectives of yours have frightened them away."

"You needn't bother about that. I shall catch them," said Guerchard.

"If you do, I'm sure I wish you joy of them. Do, please, keep your hat on," said Lupin with ironic politeness.

Guerchard came slowly to the middle of the room, raising his hand to his hat, letting it fall again without taking it off. He sat down slowly facing him, and they gazed at one another with the wary eyes of duellists crossing swords at the beginning of a duel.

"Did you get M. Formery to sign a little warrant?" said Lupin, in a caressing tone full of quiet mockery.

"I did," said Guerchard through his teeth.

"And have you got it on you?" said Lupin.

"I have," said Guerchard.

"Against Lupin, or against the Duke of Charmerace?" said Lupin.

"Against Lupin, called Charmerace," said Guerchard.

"Well, that ought to cover me pretty well. Why don't you arrest me? What are you waiting for?" said Lupin. His face was entirely serene, his eyes were careless, his tone indifferent.

"I'm not waiting for anything," said Guerchard thickly; "but it gives me such pleasure that I wish to enjoy this minute to the utmost, Lupin," said Guerchard; and his eyes gloated on him.

"Lupin, himself," said Lupin, smiling.

"I hardly dare believe it," said Guerchard.

"You're quite right not to," said Lupin.

"Yes, I hardly dare believe it. You alive, here at my mercy?"

"Oh, dear no, not yet," said Lupin.

"Yes," said Guerchard, in a decisive tone. "And ever so much more than you think." He bent forwards towards him, with his hands on his knees, and said, "Do you know where Sonia Kritchnoff is at this moment?"

"What?" said Lupin sharply.

"I ask if you know where Sonia Kritchnoff is?" said Guerchard slowly, lingering over the words.

"Do you?" said Lupin.

"I do," said Guerchard triumphantly.

"Where is she?" said Lupin, in a tone of utter incredulity.

"In a small hotel near the Star. The hotel has a telephone; and you can make sure," said Guerchard.

"Indeed? That's very interesting. What's the number of it?" said Lupin, in a mocking tone.

"555 Central: would you like to telephone to her?" said Guerchard; and he smiled triumphantly at the disabled instrument.

Lupin shock his head with a careless smile, and said, "Why should I telephone to her? What are you driving at?"

"Nothing ... that's all," said Guerchard. And he leant back in his chair with an ugly smile on his face.

"Evidently nothing. For, after all, what has that child got to do with you? You're not interested in her, plainly. She's not big enough game for you. It's me you are hunting ... it's me you hate ... it's me you want. I've played you tricks enough for that, you old scoundrel. So you're going to leave that child in peace? ... You're not going to revenge yourself on her? ... It's all very well for you to be a policeman; it's all very well for you to hate me; but there are things one does not do." There was a ring of menace and appeal in the deep, ringing tones of his voice. "You're not going to do that, Guerchard.... You will not do it.... Me—yes—anything you like. But her—her you must not touch." He gazed at the detective with fierce, appealing eyes.

"That depends on you," said Guerchard curtly.

"On me?" cried Lupin, in genuine surprise.

"Yes, I've a little bargain to propose to you," said Guerchard.

"Have you?" said Lupin; and his watchful face was serene again, his smile almost pleasant.

"Yes," said Guerchard. And he paused, hesitating.

"Well, what is it you want?" said Lupin. "Out with it! Don't be shy about it."

"I offer you—"

"You offer me?" cried Lupin. "Then it isn't true. You're fooling me."

"Reassure yourself," said Guerchard coldly. "To you personally I offer nothing."

"Then you are sincere," said Lupin. "And putting me out of the question?"

"I offer you liberty."

"Who for? For my concierge?" said Lupin.

"Don't play the fool. You care only for a single person in the world. I hold you through her: Sonia Kritchnoff."

Lupin burst into a ringing, irrepressible laugh:

"Why, you're trying to blackmail me, you old sweep!" he cried.

"If you like to call it so," said Guerchard coldly.

Lupin rose and walked backwards and forwards across the room, frowning, calculating, glancing keenly at Guerchard, weighing him. Twice he looked at the clock.

He stopped and said coldly: "So be it. For the moment you're the stronger.... That won't last.... But you offer me this child's liberty."

"That's my offer," said Guerchard; and his eyes brightened at the prospect of success.

"Her complete liberty? ... on your word of honour?" said Lupin; and he had something of the air of a cat playing with a mouse.

"On my word of honour," said Guerchard.

"Can you do it?" said Lupin, with a sudden air of doubt; and he looked sharply from Guerchard to the clock.

"I undertake to do it," said Guerchard confidently.

"But how?" said Lupin, looking at him with an expression of the gravest doubt.

"Oh, I'll put the thefts on your shoulders. That will let her out all right," said Guerchard.

"I've certainly good broad shoulders," said Lupin, with a bitter smile. He walked slowly up and down with an air that grew more and more depressed: it was almost the air of a beaten man. Then he stopped and faced Guerchard, and said: "And what is it you want in exchange?"

"Everything," said Guerchard, with the air of a man who is winning. "You must give me back the pictures, tapestry, Renaissance cabinets, the coronet, and all the information about the death of the Duke of Charmerace. Did you kill him?"

"If ever I commit suicide, you'll know all about it, my good Guerchard. You'll be there. You may even join me," said Lupin grimly; he resumed his pacing up and down the room.

"Done for, yes; I shall be done for," he said presently. "The fact is, you want my skin."

"Yes, I want your skin," said Guerchard, in a low, savage, vindictive tone.

"My skin," said Lupin thoughtfully.

"Are you going to do it? Think of that girl," said Guerchard, in a fresh access of uneasy anxiety.

Lupin laughed: "I can give you a glass of port," he said, "but I'm afraid that's all I can do for you."

"I'll throw Victoire in," said Guerchard.

"What?" cried Lupin. "You've arrested Victoire?" There was a ring of utter dismay, almost despair, in his tone.

"Yes; and I'll throw her in. She shall go scot-free. I won't bother with her," said Guerchard eagerly.

The front-door bell rang.

"Wait, wait. Let me think," said Lupin hoarsely; and he strove to adjust his jostling ideas, to meet with a fresh plan this fresh disaster.

He stood listening with all his ears. There were footsteps on the stairs, and the door opened. Dieusy stood on the threshold.

"Who is it?" said Guerchard.

"I accept—I accept everything," cried Lupin in a frantic tone.

"It's a tradesman; am I to detain him?" said Dieusy. "You told me to let you know who came and take instructions."

"A tradesman? Then I refuse!" cried Lupin, in an ecstasy of relief.

"No, you needn't keep him," said Guerchard, to Dieusy.

Dieusy went out and shut the door.

"You refuse?" said Guerchard.

"I refuse," said Lupin.

"I'm going to gaol that girl," said Guerchard savagely; and he took a step towards the door.

"Not for long," said Lupin quietly. "You have no proof."

"She'll furnish the proof all right herself—plenty of proofs," said Guerchard brutally. "What chance has a silly child like that got, when we really start questioning her? A delicate creature like that will crumple up before the end of the third day's cross-examination."

"You swine!" said Lupin. "You know well enough that I can do it—on my head—with a feeble child like that; and you know your Code; five years is the minimum," said Guerchard, in a tone of relentless brutality, watching him carefully, sticking to his hope.

"By Jove, I could wring your neck!" said Lupin, trembling with fury. By a violent effort he controlled himself, and said thoughtfully, "After all, if I give up everything to you, I shall be free to take it back one of these days."

"Oh, no doubt, when you come out of prison," said Guerchard ironically; and he laughed a grim, jeering laugh.

"I've got to go to prison first," said Lupin quietly.

"Pardon me—if you accept, I mean to arrest you," said Guerchard.

"Manifestly you'll arrest me if you can," said Lupin.

"Do you accept?" said Guerchard. And again his voice quivered with anxiety.

"Well," said Lupin. And he paused as if finally weighing the matter.

"Well?" said Guerchard, and his voice shook.

"Well—no!" said Lupin; and he laughed a mocking laugh.

"You won't?" said Guerchard between his teeth.

"No; you wish to catch me. This is just a ruse," said Lupin, in quiet, measured tones. "At bottom you don't care a hang about Sonia, Mademoiselle Kritchnoff. You will not arrest her. And then, if you did you have no proofs. There ARE no proofs. As for the pendant, you'd have to prove it. You can't prove it. You can't prove that it was in her possession one moment. Where is the pendant?" He paused, and then went on in the same quiet tone: "No, Guerchard; after having kept out of your clutches for the last ten years, I'm not going to be caught to save this child, who is not even in danger. She has a very useful friend in the Duke of Charmerace. I refuse."

Guerchard stared at him, scowling, biting his lips, seeking a fresh point of attack. For the moment he knew himself baffled, but he still clung tenaciously to the struggle in which victory would be so precious.

The front-door bell rang again.

"There's a lot of ringing at your bell this morning," said Guerchard, under his breath; and hope sprang afresh in him.

Again they stood silent, waiting.

Dieusy opened the door, put in his head, and said, "It's Mademoiselle Kritchnoff."

"Collar her! ... Here's the warrant! ... collar her!" shouted Guerchard, with savage, triumphant joy.

"Never! You shan't touch her! By Heaven, you shan't touch her!" cried Lupin frantically; and he sprang like a tiger at Guerchard.

Guerchard jumped to the other side of the table. "Will you accept, then?" he cried.

Lupin gripped the edge of the table with both hands, and stood panting, grinding his teeth, pale with fury. He stood silent and motionless for perhaps half a minute, gazing at Guerchard with burning, murderous eyes. Then he nodded his head.

"Let Mademoiselle Kritchnoff wait," said Guerchard, with a sigh of deep relief. Dieusy went out of the room.

"Now let us settle exactly how we stand," said Lupin, in a clear, incisive voice. "The bargain is this: If I give you the pictures, the tapestry, the cabinets, the coronet, and the death-certificate of the Duke of Charmerace, you give me your word of honour that Mademoiselle Kritchnoff shall not be touched."

"That's it!" said Guerchard eagerly.

"Once I deliver these things to you, Mademoiselle Kritchnoff passes out of the game."

"Yes," said Guerchard.

"Whatever happens afterwards. If I get back anything—if I escape—she goes scot-free," said Lupin.

"Yes," said Guerchard; and his eyes were shining.

"On your word of honour?" said Lupin.

"On my word of honour," said Guerchard.

"Very well," said Lupin, in a quiet, businesslike voice. "To begin with, here in this pocket-book you'll find all the documents relating to the death of the Duke of Charmerace. In it you will also find the receipt of the Plantin furniture repository at Batignolles for the objects of art which I collected at Gournay-Martin's. I sent them to Batignolles because, in my letters asking the owners of valuables to forward them to me, I always make Batignolles the place to which they are to be sent; therefore I knew that you would never look there. They are all in cases; for, while you were making those valuable inquiries yesterday, my men were putting them into cases. You'll not find the receipt in the name of either the Duke of Charmerace or my own. It is in the name of a respected proprietor of Batignolles, a M. Pierre Servien. But he has lately left that charming suburb, and I do not think he will return to it."

Guerchard almost snatched the pocket-book out of his hand. He verified the documents in it with greedy eyes; and then he put them back in it, and stuffed it into the breast-pocket of his coat.

"And where's the coronet?" he said, in an excited voice.

"You're nearly standing on it," said Lupin.

"It's in that kit-bag at your feet, on the top of the change of clothes in it."

Guerchard snatched up the kit-bag, opened it, and took out the coronet.

"I'm afraid I haven't the case," said Lupin, in a tone of regret. "If you remember, I left it at Gournay-Martin's—in your charge."

Guerchard examined the coronet carefully. He looked at the stones in it; he weighed it in his right hand, and he weighed it in his left.

"Are you sure it's the real one?" said Lupin, in a tone of acute but affected anxiety. "Do not—oh, do not let us have any more of these painful mistakes about it. They are so wearing."

"Yes—yes—this is the real one," said Guerchard, with another deep sigh of relief.

"Well, have you done bleeding me?" said Lupin contemptuously.

"Your arms," said Guerchard quickly.

"They weren't in the bond," said Lupin. "But here you are." And he threw his revolver on the table.

Guerchard picked it up and put it into his pocket. He looked at Lupin as if he could not believe his eyes, gloating over him. Then he said in a deep, triumphant tone:

"And now for the handcuffs!"

XXIII. THE END OF THE DUEL

"The handcuffs?" said Lupin; and his face fell. Then it cleared; and he added lightly, "After all, there's nothing like being careful; and, by Jove, with me you need to be. I might get away yet. What luck it is for you that I'm so soft, so little of a Charmerace, so human! Truly, I can't be much of a man of the world, to be in love like this!"

"Come, come, hold out your hands!" said Guerchard, jingling the handcuffs impatiently.

"I should like to see that child for the last time," said Lupin gently.

"All right," said Guerchard.

"Arsene Lupin—and nabbed by you! If you aren't in luck! Here you are!" said Lupin bitterly; and he held out his wrists.

Guerchard snapped the handcuffs on them with a grunt of satisfaction.

Lupin gazed down at them with a bitter face, and said: "Oh, you are in luck! You're not married by any chance?"

"Yes, yes; I am," said Guerchard hastily; and he went quickly to the door and opened it: "Dieusy!" he called. "Dieusy! Mademoiselle Kritchnoff is at liberty. Tell her so, and bring her in here."

Lupin started back, flushed and scowling; he cried: "With these things on my hands! ... No! ... I can't see her!"

Guerchard stood still, looking at him. Lupin's scowl slowly softened, and he said, half to himself, "But I should have liked to see her ... very much ... for if she goes like that ... I shall not know when or where—" He stopped short, raised his eyes, and said in a decided tone: "Ah, well, yes; I should like to see her."

"If you've quite made up your mind," said Guerchard impatiently, and he went into the anteroom.

Lupin stood very still, frowning thoughtfully. He heard footsteps on the stairs, and then the voice of Guerchard in the anteroom, saying, in a jeering tone, "You're free, mademoiselle; and you can thank the Duke for it. You owe your liberty to him."

"Free! And I owe it to him?" cried the voice of Sonia, ringing and golden with extravagant joy.

"Yes, mademoiselle," said Guerchard. "You owe it to him."

She came through the open door, flushed deliciously and smiling, her eyes brimming with tears of joy. Lupin had never seen her look half so adorable.

"Is it to you I owe it? Then I shall owe everything to you. Oh, thank you—thank you!" she cried, holding out her hands to him.

Lupin half turned away from her to hide his handcuffs.

She misunderstood the movement. Her face fell suddenly like that of a child rebuked: "Oh, I was wrong. I was wrong to come here!" she cried quickly, in changed, dolorous tones. "I thought yesterday ... I made a mistake ... pardon me. I'm going. I'm going."

Lupin was looking at her over his shoulder, standing sideways to hide the handcuffs. He said sadly. "Sonia—"

"No, no, I understand! It was impossible!" she cried quickly, cutting him short. "And yet if you only knew—if you knew how I have changed—with what a changed spirit I came here.... Ah, I swear that now I hate all my past. I loathe it. I swear that now the mere presence of a thief would overwhelm me with disgust."

"Hush!" said Lupin, flushing deeply, and wincing. "Hush!"

"But, after all, you're right," she said, in a gentler voice. "One can't wipe out what one has done. If I were to give back everything I've taken—if I were to spend years in remorse and repentance, it would be no use. In your eyes I should always be Sonia Kritchnoff, the thief!" The great tears welled slowly out of her eyes and rolled down her cheeks; she let them stream unheeded.

"Sonia!" cried Lupin, protesting.

But she would not hear him. She broke out with fresh vehemence, a feverish passion: "And yet, if I'd been a thief, like so many others... but you know why I stole. I'm not trying to defend myself, but, after all, I did it to keep honest; and when I loved you it was not the heart of a thief that thrilled, it was the heart of a poor girl who loved...that's all...who loved."

"You don't know what you're doing! You're torturing me! Be quiet!" cried Lupin hoarsely, beside himself.

"Never mind...I'm going...we shall never see one another any more," she sobbed. "But will you...will you shake hands just for the last time?"

"No!" cried Lupin.

"You won't?" wailed Sonia in a heartrending tone.

"I can't!" cried Lupin.

"You ought not to be like this.... Last night ... if you were going to let me go like this ... last night ... it was wrong," she wailed, and turned to go.

"Wait, Sonia! Wait!" cried Lupin hoarsely. "A moment ago you said something.... You said that the mere presence of a thief would overwhelm you with disgust. Is that true?"

"Yes, I swear it is," cried Sonia.

Guerchard appeared in the doorway.

"And if I were not the man you believe?" said Lupin sombrely.

"What?" said Sonia; and a faint bewilderment mingled with her grief. "If I were not the Duke of Charmerace?"

"Not the Duke?"

"If I were not an honest man?" said Lupin.

"You?" cried Sonia.

"If I were a thief? If I were—"

"Arsene Lupin," jeered Guerchard from the door.

Lupin turned and held out his manacled wrists for her to see.

"Arsene Lupin! ... it's ... it's true!" stammered Sonia. "But then, but then ... it must be for my sake that you've given yourself up. And it's for me you're going to prison. Oh, Heavens! How happy I am!"

She sprang to him, threw her arms round his neck, and pressed her lips to his.

"And that's what women call repenting," said Guerchard.

He shrugged his shoulders, went out on to the landing, and called to the policeman in the hall to bid the driver of the prison-van, which was waiting, bring it up to the door.

"Oh, this is incredible!" cried Lupin, in a trembling voice; and he kissed Sonia's lips and eyes and hair. "To think that you love me enough to go on loving me in spite of this—in spite of the fact that I'm Arsene Lupin. Oh, after this, I'll become an honest man! It's the least I can do. I'll retire."

"You will?" cried Sonia.

"Upon my soul, I will!" cried Lupin; and he kissed her again and again.

Guerchard came back into the room. He looked at them with a cynical grin, and said, "Time's up."

"Oh, Guerchard, after so many others, I owe you the best minute of my life!" cried Lupin.

Bonavent, still in his porter's livery, came hurrying through the anteroom: "Master," he cried, "I've found it."

"Found what?" said Guerchard.

"The secret entrance. It opens into that little side street. We haven't got the door open yet; but we soon shall."

"The last link in the chain," said Guerchard, with warm satisfaction. "Come along, Lupin."

"But he's going to take you away! We're going to be separated!" cried Sonia, in a sudden anguish of realization.

"It's all the same to me now!" cried Lupin, in the voice of a conqueror.

"Yes, but not to me!" cried Sonia, wringing her hands.

"Now you must keep calm and go. I'm not going to prison," said Lupin, in a low voice. "Wait in the hall, if you can. Stop and talk to Victoire; condole with her. If they turn you out of the house, wait close to the front door."

"Come, mademoiselle," said Guerchard. "You must go."

"Go, Sonia, go—good-bye—good-bye," said Lupin; and he kissed her.

She went quietly out of the room, her handkerchief to her eyes. Guerchard held open the door for her, and kept it open, with his hand still on the handle; he said to Lupin: "Come along."

Lupin yawned, stretched himself, and said coolly, "My dear Guerchard, what I want after the last two nights is rest—rest." He walked quickly across the room and stretched himself comfortably at full length on the couch.

"Come, get up," said Guerchard roughly. "The prison-van is waiting for you. That ought to fetch you out of your dream."

"Really, you do say the most unlucky things," said Lupin gaily.

He had resumed his flippant, light-hearted air; his voice rang as lightly and pleasantly as if he had not a care in the world.

"Do you mean that you refuse to come?" cried Guerchard in a rough, threatening tone.

"Oh, no," said Lupin quickly: and he rose.

"Then come along!" said Guerchard.

"No," said Lupin, "after all, it's too early." Once more he stretched himself out on the couch, and added languidly, "I'm lunching at the English Embassy."

"Now, you be careful!" cried Guerchard angrily. "Our parts are changed. If you're snatching at a last straw, it's waste of time. All your tricks—I know them. Understand, you rogue, I know them."

"You know them?" said Lupin with a smile, rising. "It's fatality!"

He stood before Guerchard, twisting his hands and wrists curiously. Half a dozen swift movements; and he held out his handcuffs in one hand and threw them on the floor.

"Did you know that trick, Guerchard? One of these days I shall teach you to invite me to lunch," he said slowly, in a mocking tone; and he gazed at the detective with menacing, dangerous eyes.

"Come, come, we've had enough of this!" cried Guerchard, in mingled astonishment, anger, and alarm. "Bonavent! Boursin! Dieusy! Here! Help! Help!" he shouted.

"Now listen, Guerchard, and understand that I'm not humbugging," said Lupin quickly, in clear, compelling tones. "If Sonia, just now, had had one word, one gesture of contempt for me, I'd have given way—yielded ... half-yielded, at any rate; for, rather than fall into your triumphant clutches, I'd have blown my brains out. I've now to choose between happiness, life with Sonia, or prison. Well, I've chosen. I will live happy with her, or else, my dear Guerchard, I'll die with you. Now let your men come—I'm ready for them."

Guerchard ran to the door and shouted again.

"I think the fat's in the fire now," said Lupin, laughing.

He sprang to the table, opened the cardboard box, whipped off the top layer of cotton-wool, and took out a shining bomb.

He sprang to the wall, pressed the button, the bookshelf glided slowly to one side, the lift rose to the level of the floor and its doors flew open just as the detectives rushed in.

"Collar him!" yelled Guerchard.

"Stand back—hands up!" cried Lupin, in a terrible voice, raising his right hand high above his head. "You know what this is ... a bomb.... Come and collar me now, you swine! ... Hands up, you ... Guerchard!"

"You silly funks!" roared Guerchard. "Do you think he'd dare?"

"Come and see!" cried Lupin.

"I will!" cried Guerchard. And he took a step forward.

As one man his detectives threw themselves upon him. Three of them gripped his arms, a fourth gripped him round the waist; and they all shouted at him together, not to be a madman! ... To look at Lupin's eyes! ... That Lupin was off his head!

"What miserable swine you are!" cried Lupin scornfully. He sprang forward, caught up the kit-bag in his left hand, and tossed it behind him into the lift. "You dirty crew!" he cried again. "Oh, why isn't there a photographer here? And now, Guerchard, you thief, give me back my pocket-book."

"Never!" screamed Guerchard, struggling with his men, purple with fury.

"Oh, Lord, master! Do be careful! Don't rile him!" cried Bonavent in an agony.

"What? Do you want me to smash up the whole lot?" roared Lupin, in a furious, terrible voice. "Do I look as if I were bluffing, you fools?"

"Let him have his way, master!" cried Dieusy.

"Yes, yes!" cried Bonavent.

"Let him have his way!" cried another.

"Give him his pocket-book!" cried a third.

"Never!" howled Guerchard.

"It's in his pocket—his breast-pocket! Be smart!" roared Lupin.

"Come, come, it's got to be given to him," cried Bonavent. "Hold the master tight!" And he thrust his hand into the breast of Guerchard's coat, and tore out the pocket-book.

"Throw it on the table!" cried Lupin.

Bonavent threw it on to the table; and it slid along it right to Lupin. He caught it in his left hand, and slipped it into his pocket. "Good!" he said. And then he yelled ferociously, "Look out for the bomb!" and made a feint of throwing it.

The whole group fell back with an odd, unanimous, sighing groan.

Lupin sprang into the lift, and the doors closed over the opening. There was a great sigh of relief from the frightened detectives, and then the chunking of machinery as the lift sank.

Their grip on Guerchard loosened. He shook himself free, and shouted, "After him! You've got to make up for this! Down into the cellars, some of you! Others go to the secret entrance! Others to the servants' entrance! Get into the street! Be smart! Dieusy, take the lift with me!"

The others ran out of the room and down the stairs, but with no great heartiness, since their minds were still quite full of the bomb, and Lupin still had it with him. Guerchard and Dieusy dashed at the doors of the opening of the lift-well, pulling and wrenching at them. Suddenly there was a click; and they heard the grunting of the machinery. There was a little bump and a jerk, the doors flew open of themselves; and there was the lift, empty, ready for them. They jumped into it; Guerchard's quick eye caught the button, and he pressed it. The doors banged to, and, to his horror, the lift shot upwards about eight feet, and stuck between the floors.

As the lift stuck, a second compartment, exactly like the one Guerchard and Dieusy were in, came up to the level of the floor of the smoking-room; the doors opened, and there was Lupin. But again how changed! The clothes of the Duke of Charmerace littered the floor; the kit-bag was open; and he was wearing the very clothes of Chief-Inspector Guerchard, his seedy top-hat, his cloak. He wore also Guerchard's sparse, lank, black hair, his little, bristling, black moustache. His figure, hidden by the cloak, seemed to have shrunk to the size of Guerchard's.

He sat before a mirror in the wall of the lift, a make-up box on the seat beside him. He darkened his eyebrows, and put a line or two about his eyes. That done he looked at himself earnestly for two or three minutes; and, as he looked, a truly marvellous transformation took place: the features of Arsene Lupin, of the Duke of Charmerace, decomposed, actually decomposed, into the features of Jean Guerchard. He looked at himself and laughed, the gentle, husky laugh of Guerchard.

He rose, transferred the pocket-book to the coat he was wearing, picked up the bomb, came out into the smoking-room, and listened. A muffled roaring thumping came from the well of the lift. It almost sounded as if, in their exasperation, Guerchard and Dieusy were engaged in a struggle to the death. Smiling pleasantly, he stole to the window and looked out. His eyes brightened at the sight of the motor-car, Guerchard's car, waiting just before the front door and in charge of a policeman. He stole to the head of the stairs, and looked down into the hall. Victoire was sitting huddled together on a chair; Sonia stood beside her, talking to her in a low voice; and, keeping guard on Victoire, stood a brown-faced, active, nervous policeman, all alertness, briskness, keenness.

"Hi! officer! come up here! Be smart," cried Lupin over the bannisters, in the husky, gentle voice of Chief-Inspector Guerchard.

The policeman looked up, recognized the great detective, and came bounding zealously up the stairs.

Lupin led the way through the anteroom into the sitting-room. Then he said sharply: "You have your revolver?"

"Yes," said the young policeman. And he drew it with a flourish.

"Put it away! Put it away at once!" said Lupin very smartly. "You're not to use it. You're not to use it on any account! You understand?"

"Yes," said the policeman firmly; and with a slightly bewildered air he put the revolver away.

"Here! Stand here!" cried Lupin, raising his voice. And he caught the policeman's arm, and hustled him roughly to the front of the doors of the lift-well. "Do you see these doors? Do you see them?" he snapped.

"Yes, yes," said the policeman, glaring at them.

"They're the doors of a lift," said Lupin. "In that lift are Dieusy and Lupin. You know Dieusy?"

"Yes, yes," said the policeman.

"There are only Dieusy and Lupin in the lift. They are struggling together. You can hear them," shouted Lupin in the policeman's ear. "Lupin is disguised. You understand—Dieusy and a disguised man are in the lift. The disguised man is Lupin. Directly the lift descends and the doors open, throw yourself on him! Hold him! Shout for assistance!" He almost bellowed the last words into the policeman's ear.

"Yes, yes," said the policeman. And he braced himself before the doors of the lift-well, gazing at them with harried eyes, as if he expected them to bite him.

"Be brave! Be ready to die in the discharge of your duty!" bellowed Lupin; and he walked out of the room, shut the door, and turned the key.

The policeman stood listening to the noise of the struggle in the lift, himself strung up to fighting point; he was panting. Lupin's instructions were whirling and dancing in his head.

Lupin went quietly down the stairs. Victoire and Sonia saw him coming. Victoire rose; and as he came to the bottom of the stairs Sonia stepped forward and said in an anxious, pleading voice:

"Oh, M. Guerchard, where is he?"

"He's here," said Lupin, in his natural voice.

Sonia sprang to him with outstretched arms.

"It's you! It IS you!" she cried.

"Just look how like him I am!" said Lupin, laughing triumphantly. "But do I look quite ruffian enough?"

"Oh, NO! You couldn't!" cried Sonia.

"Isn't he a wonder?" said Victoire.

"This time the Duke of Charmerace is dead, for good and all," said Lupin.

"No; it's Lupin that's dead," said Sonia softly.

"Lupin?" he said, surprised.

"Yes," said Sonia firmly.

"It would be a terrible loss, you know—a loss for France," said Lupin gravely.

"Never mind," said Sonia.

"Oh, I must be in love with you!" said Lupin, in a wondering tone; and he put his arm round her and kissed her violently.

"And you won't steal any more?" said Sonia, holding him back with both hands on his shoulders, looking into his eyes.

"I shouldn't dream of such a thing," said Lupin. "You are here. Guerchard is in the lift. What more could I possibly desire?" His voice softened and grew infinitely caressing as he went on: "Yet when you are at my side I shall always have the soul of a lover and the soul of a thief. I long to steal your kisses, your thoughts, the whole of your heart. Ah, Sonia, if you want me to steal nothing else, you have only to stay by my side."

Their lips met in a long kiss.

Sonia drew herself out of his arms and cried, "But we're wasting time! We must make haste! We must fly!"

"Fly?" said Lupin sharply. "No, thank you; never again. I did flying enough last night to last me a lifetime. For the rest of my life I'm going to crawl—crawl like a snail. But come along, you two, I must take you to the police-station."

He opened the front door, and they came out on the steps. The policeman in charge of the car saluted.

Lupin paused and said softly: "Hark! I hear the sound of wedding bells."

They went down the steps.

Even as they were getting into the car some chance blow of Guerchard or Dieusy struck a hidden spring and released the lift. It sank to the level of Lupin's smoking-room and stopped. The doors flew open, Dieusy and Guerchard sprang out of it; and on the instant the brown-faced, nervous policeman sprang actively on Guerchard and pinned him. Taken by surprise, Guerchard yelled loudly, "You stupid idiot!" somehow entangled his legs in those of his captor, and they rolled on the floor. Dieusy surveyed them for a moment with blank astonishment. Then, with swift intelligence, grasped the fact that the policeman was Lupin in disguise. He sprang upon them, tore them asunder, fell heavily on the policeman, and pinned him to the floor with a strangling hand on his throat.

Guerchard dashed to the door, tried it, and found it locked, dashed for the window, threw it open, and thrust out his head. Forty yards down the street a motor-car was rolling smoothly away—rolling to a honeymoon.

"Oh, hang it!" he screamed. "He's doing a bunk in my motor-car!"

The end

Printed in Great Britain
by Amazon